Adonis Awakens

Doug Young

Published by Doug Young

ISBN: 9781791347789

#AdonisAwakens

@AdonisAwakens

Dedicated to my Wife Betty

About the Author

It is not uncommon to hear the elderly complain about being old. For the authors of this saga we find it a distinct advantage to be octogenarians. It has given us a world view that can only be had by *Living It,* a far different perspective than having *Learned It.*

We were born into the early years of the so-called *Great Depression and* listened to the radio to hear the declaration of *The Second World War.* Thereafter, we lived through minor wars and *rumours of war* until the nineteen-seventies. We witnessed disasters in our home-state and around the world, some natural, like floods, and fire, and others as a result of human greed and corruption: like, stock market crashes, inflation and health disasters like the Polio Epidemic of 1937, the Thalidomide Tragedy of 1960, and Tuberculosis, endemic in Australia since 1850 and on the rise again today

But today, everyone has joined us to witnesses history being made in the Financial Services Royal Commission. We ask our readers to remember this low point in the mismanagement of some of our greatest institutions.

In publishing, it is not uncommon to have husband and wife as joint-authors. Perhaps in this case it is a little unusual, as my wife of sixty-three years passed away on the fourteenth of May 2018. If you ask me whether Betty still participates in this work, I can answer *YES!* Not only through the history we shared, but through the communications we have shared since the day she passed from this life.

About the Book

Throughout the book you will find links that will take you places. These links are aimed at enhancing your experience as you read.

Some links take you to further information and details on things in the book. Other links will take you to music and videos.

Some links take you to entries in the diary of characters in the book. Giving you another perspective than that in the book.

Enjoy the pages of the book, but the author also encourages you to further experience the book outside its pages.

See what you think. We hope you enjoy this unique reading experience.

Table of Contents

Chapter 1

Adonis Awakens

Saturday 17 November 2012 – 0210 hrs

Introduction http://www.futuristic.guru/welcome

I glared at the bedside clock. Two-ten: it seemed an hour had passed since it showed two-five and still sleep did not come. What with my thoughts of loss and the sobs of grief coming from my mother's room it was going to be a long night.

Saturday 17 November 2012 – 0400 hrs

"Hold me please Brad," Mum sobbed. I suddenly realised I wasn't dreaming. I turned and wrapped my right arm around her shoulders and with my left hand in the small of her back pulled her closer to me.

"I miss him terribly Brad," Mum said.

"I do too Mum, it's happened so quickly. Last week we were laughing and joking and planning what to do this weekend and now he's gone."

"We still have each other, Brad, you're man of the house now," she sobbed.

Her distress had caused a tear to fall from my eye to her forehead. She sat up and wiped the tears from my cheek with the very damp hankie she held in her hand. Her sobs quietened as she diverted her thoughts from her own loss to mine. She put her head down on my shoulder and I tried to comfort her: holding her firmly and stroking her honey-blonde hair. Feeling so close to her took me back to those times, as a three or four-year-old, I would go running and sobbing to her for comfort. 'It was only a dream, darling,' she would say as I wrapped my arms around her neck and she would stroke my hair. I started whispering the words of Brahms' Lullaby, as she had done for me:

Lullaby and goodnight, with roses bedight

With lilies o'er spread is baby's wee bed

Lay thee down now and rest, may thy slumber be blessed

Lay thee down now and rest, may thy slumber be blessed

Lullaby and goodnight, thy mother's delight

Bright angels beside my darling abide

They will guard thee at rest, thou shall wake on my breast

They will guard thee at rest, thou shall wake on my breast

At last she drifted into sleep and I resolved to watch over her for the rest of the night. But this was no bad dream: it was cold, hard fact of the worst kind: **my family http://www.futuristic.guru/bruce-clifford** has been shattered. For the last four days since Dad's death Mum had dressed automatically in what she called her work clothes; although she had immediately gone on leave from the moment the news reached her. Her dress had been the same, but her radiant smile had gone: her eyes were dimmed, tearful and red from wiping. To me they had seemed to say, 'Please help me.' I had felt totally out of my depth: at a loss, impotent. All I could do was drive her to the hospital and wait with her. I saw to it that she had coffee and ate at least something at each meal. We had talked little: not knowing what to say that would not cause more tears. Mum had gone to her room early each night, but the walls did not hide the fact that she cried herself to sleep.

She had been by Dad's side all the time he had been lying in the ICU on life-support. As a scientist, she knew there was no hope for any sort of recovery. Dad was already gone from this body: its lungs kept breathing and its heart kept pumping by machines with the sole purpose of fulfilling Dad's wishes: to have every useful organ and tissue harvested to help others in need. Mum needed no counsel from priests or advisers: she gave her assent for the surgeons to proceed. She told our extended family when and how the memorial service Dad had specified in his will would be held and at the same time cancelled the eighteenth birthday celebration for me that was to have been held tonight.

On Thursday, she stoically donned a surgical gown and mask to attend the harvesting of Dad's organs. She sent each package forward to the recipient with her blessing knowing that she was fulfilling Dad's instructions. Nothing was to remain for burial or cremation, anything not immediately sought by patients was to be packaged and sent to the ANU for analysis, dissection or storage for future use. The harvesting had taken over twelve hours. I had sat with her in the operating theatre and once an hour took her out to walk about or have something to eat or drink. The surgeons came, retrieved their organs or body parts and then departed to allow others to take over. The long row of refrigerated containers lining the wall of the theatre slowly dwindled. The whole process had been planned to the minute to ensure organs were retrieved in the best possible sequence to ensure their chances for successful transplanting. Now all she heard was the sound of the heart-lung machine keeping the organs alive until they were taken and packed for transport. Even Dad's hands were required. Then there was the sound of the bone saw. Mum shuddered and clung to my arm. She knew the surgeon was performing a craniotomy to remove Dad's brain from his skull. When the last surgical team left the theatre, she faced a bare operating table with every trace of Dad's physical existence gone. All his parts had been given to others except for the tiniest parts of all: there was to be no harvesting of the build-up of mature semen. Mum had agreed to be present and with her scientific knowledge confirm that Dad's testicles were destroyed. Neither could bear to think of Dad's sperm being used indiscriminately. Mum never thought the day would arrive when she would be required to honour this promise.

When we stood to leave the operating theatre, tears were streaming down her cheeks. I held her to me and wiped away her tears with a fresh soft handkerchief from my pocket. I had carried a ready supply for the past few days. She had held grimly to my arm as I escorted her back to the car and drove home. Yesterday, she clung to my arm at the memorial held for Dad at the ANU. She held herself together as family, friends and university colleagues called at our house to extend their condolences. Some passed through in a few minutes while close family members hung around having a Scotch, beer or wine and a snack from the finger food Mum's mother, and her cousin, Jan, had arranged on the terrace. I had played drink waiter to keep myself busy and avoid some of the reminiscences that might quickly bring me to tears. The last thing I wanted to do was to break down in front of Mum and have her coming to comfort me. The last family members took their leave around eight-thirty. Jan had cleared away the remains of the buffet and washed the dishes. After saying goodnight to Nan and Jan, Mum had turned to me and said, "You don't mind if I leave you Brad; I feel I must lie down and sleep at last."

I could only agree with her as she gave me a kiss on the cheek and went to her room. I would have loved her to stay but I knew that would be terribly selfish of me. She needed to be alone — I was a bit afraid to be. I would have liked Jan to stay a while, but she was driving Nan and I would not ask. I had danced with **Jan http://www.futuristic.guru/jan-franklin** her twenty-first birthday only two months ago and it was then I realised how alike she was to Mum. They had the same wavy hair except Jan was a striking brunette while Mum was a natural honey-blonde. Her smile lit up her face and they had the same trim figures; they could easily wear each other's dresses, I had thought. Jan was the only relative around my own age with whom I felt comfortable. I don't know why I didn't pursue her after her birthday party. I was certainly excited by her but feared she might think me too young and laugh at me. Then there was the matter of us being cousins and she was leaving the next day to go to Genoa to compete in the Paganini Competition, and I was studying for my final exams. At midnight, after sitting alone in the lounge trying to watch a re-run movie, I threw down a double Scotch, thinking that it might help me sleep, and went to bed.

Mum was right though: I am now the man of the house and my first duty is to protect her. As I drifted into sleep, I felt Mum's right hand stretch out through the hairs on my chest and I gently tightened my hold on her with my right arm around her shoulders and felt the comfort of her head against my cheek. She told me later the feel of her right hand running through my chest hair, was the same as the feelings she had experienced so many times with my father. To Mum, she was drifting off to sleep in her dead husband's arms. In our sleep, Mum's hand had slowly slid from my chest until it came to rest in my groin. This caused her no concern as her hand frequently arrived there around sunrise much to Dad's delight. Her hand discerned no difference: to it, my dimensions of girth and length at this time of the day were the same as Dad's.

Saturday 17 November 2012 – 0630 hrs

I woke from my highly erotic dream of sucking her titties with a start and a moan. Mum woke beside me to find her hand on my dick. Mum's nightdress, my pyjama pants and the sheets were getting a massive burst of my semen. I was left squirming: trying to halt the flow as it squirted again and again. Mum kept pumping and threw herself onto my chest pressing me down with her breasts while kissing me long and full on the lips — a lover's kiss: not a mother's kiss! My arms circled her and held her tight returning her kisses while my involuntary spasms faded.

"Please bring me too, Adonis?" Mum asked unashamedly.

I brought my left hand up between her thighs, pushing my now soft cock out of the way while getting a dribble of semen on my fingers to smooth the opening of Mum's crack. Two fingers went straight to work extracting sweet vengeance for the rude awakening I had received. Raising herself a little, she slipped her right breast from her nightdress and pushed its nipple between my open lips. I took suck immediately, as if still in my dream, but soon realised I wasn't there for milk but to give my mother relief and quickly changed my action from sucking to licking, squeezing and stimulating. Mum spread her legs wide and my fingers did the rest. My cock hung down in a sulk: having shot its bolt in my wet dream it took no part in the action. Mum collapsed in a spasm of delight and relief, squeezing my fingers inside her. She turned her face up to be kissed and I kissed and fondled her tenderly for the next half-hour. Neither Mum nor I offered any excuse or explanation for what had just happened.

When we roused from our half-awake state, we realised that we were lying in a tangle of nighties, pyjamas, and sheets: all stained and sticky with my pent-up discharge of semen and a little dribble from Mum.

"If you would like to run the spa bath, I'll throw all of this into the washing machine and come and wash your back," Mum said.

"You can wash me all over if you like, just like you used to?"

"I'd like," she quickly replied.

I did as I was told, kicked off my sticky pyjama pants and went to my bathroom. I turned on the water in the spa and lathered my face for my regular morning shave. By the time Mum entered the bathroom I had finished shaving and now lay back in the bath with the bubbles forming around me. I had splashed a liberal amount of perfume into the water and the room was softly lit from the high window on the eastern wall. In the mirror, I saw her pause at the door. She looked gorgeous. She had washed all signs of tears away, brushed her hair and now wore a smile, and a sheer sarong reaching down to her knees and tied with a bow above her breasts.

“Are you asleep?” Mum asked quietly.

Aphrodite’s Diary http://www.futuristic.guru/copy-of-aphrodite-1-1 “No, just resting my eyes and day-dreaming. I was wondering whether I had dreamt it all and any moment Dad would walk in and say, ‘Come on mate, remember what day this is’,” I replied.

“Oh, I’m so sorry,” Mum said. “In my grief and self-pity, I forgot your birthday. Happy birthday darling,” she said as she knelt beside the spa and reaching over gave me a congratulatory kiss. “And you’re eighteen today,” Mum added almost in a tone of disbelief that those eighteen years had passed so quickly. She had a faraway look in her eyes as her thoughts started to drift back to those early days: meeting and marrying Dad when she was only seventeen. Such a brilliant man: he had accomplished so much in the past eighteen years and had promise of greater things to come. Now, cut down at only forty-two by some drunken idiot trying to outrun the police.

“At least now they won’t be able to get you for child abuse,” I laughed. Mum snapped out of her reverie and laughed too.

“No, only something far worse that could wreck everything including your father’s plans for the future.”

“I think the Clinton defence would suffice for what happened this morning,” I replied, knowing that I would rather give up any contact with her body if it meant losing her respect for me.

“Let’s not talk about it now. Remember, I came to bath my baby so roll over.”

Mum soaped the sponge and started on my back. Shoulders, arms and armpits were thoroughly washed. I felt her part my cheeks, sponge my anus, and wash the backs of my legs. She indicated to me to turn over.

"You weren't this hairy last time I bathed you," Mum quipped as she soaped my chest and abdomen, reaching all the way down to my lower belly but not quite to my groin. I was lying back in the spa with bubbles coming up around me, my eyes were almost shut and waiting for the feel of her fingers on my hard again cock. The touch did not come. Mum had now turned her attention to my feet and after taking my left foot in her hand and scrubbing the heel, sole and instep she played, 'This little piggy went to market' with my toes, as she had done many times before in those early years of motherhood. When the last little piggy went wee wee all the way home her index and middle fingers trotted up my thigh and although I had slipped down the bath towards her, spreading my knees further apart, her fingers failed to reach all the way. Mum acted as if she didn't notice my not too subtle suggestion.

"Now for your eyes and ears," I heard her say. "I know you don't like it so shut your eyes to keep out the soap and Mummy will have it done soon." She got the job done and I said, "You missed a bit, Mummy," and pointed between my legs.

"Just like your father," Mum scolded me, "at least it is easier to wash when it's big and hard."

She soaped her hands and with just a little pressure ran her right hand up and down the shaft of my dick and gently around its head. Her left hand had gone around my scrotum, ever so gently washing the hairs clean and ensuring I felt no hurt to those ever so sensitive balls, veins and tendons. She finished her washing of these most precious possessions with a final rinse to the glans of my hard horn. She followed that up with a kiss; for an instant she parted her lips over its head and delivered a little tickle with her tongue. I whispered a thank-you for this first-time experience and feared that I might come then and there. Throughout the bathing, Mum's breasts moved about under the soft silk of her sarong and her firm nipples were obvious. I had silently watched in delight her movements and on the occasions, when she stood from her kneeling position, I would see her thigh become uncovered and glimpse the soft curls of blonde hair on her pussy. This time as she stood, I caught the end of the bow where she had tied it above her breasts. As she rose, the sarong fell to the floor and I moved over to make room for her. She kicked off her slippers and stepped in beside me. At that moment, I could only see Mum as a girl my own age: a beautifully sculptured young body, blemish free skin, a smiling sensitive face, bright intelligent blue eyes and wavy honey-blonde hair — a vision to delight in.

"Your turn now," she said, as she gave me the sponge.

"Would you like your hair washed too Mum?" I asked.

"Yes please. I put the shampoo on the ledge behind you," Mum replied. "There's a jar of my special balm there too, don't get them mixed up."

"I'll start with your hair," I said as I relaxed my grip on her shoulders and reached for the shampoo. Mum arched her back and while I supported her with my left arm she immersed her head to her forehead. I lifted her head from the water and squirted a little shampoo on her hair with my right hand. After putting the shampoo down and washing her hair I couldn't resist the urge to give a little squeeze to her breasts and kiss her. How strange it felt, but natural, to be taking such liberties. I was thrilled that Mum had snapped out of her grief since we woke and happy to be giving her some pleasure. I pulled down the flexible hose from behind the spa and while I continued to support her with my left arm I directed the spray to her hair while Mum rinsed out the remains of the shampoo with her hands. I returned the spray to its holder and gently rolled her, still in my left arm, and gave her back from top to bottom the same wash as she had given me. Rolling her back to face me I thought it proper to take a little time out for another cuddle and kisses before I soaped down her chest and belly, I too stopped just short of the curly mound at the top of her thighs. Unlike when Mum washed my feet and legs Mum was now in the spa with me so in one smooth movement, I raised her back and turned her to face me. At the same time, I slid back a little so that her feet now rested in my lap. Mum gripped my proud horn with her toes and squeezed. Not to be deterred, I took her right foot in my hand to wash and knead its sole, not to tickle but to send messages of expectation through her body. I devoted my attention to one toe at a time. I didn't repeat the 'Little pigs' routine that she had done so expertly, instead, I departed each toe with a kiss and slid my tongue into the gap between toes causing a little thrill to follow up her legs. With her feet thoroughly cleansed, I slid slightly forward. I raised, soaped and rinsed her right calf and then her left. A further slide forward brought her thighs to me for the same treatment. I could see she had some concern as to how I was going to deal with her lady bits. I slid forward again, elevating her groin into my lap, my legs went under her for support and Mum's legs went around me. She relaxed, supporting herself on her elbows and leant her head back to show she had no fear of putting herself in my hands. With nothing more to depend on than my high school biology diagrams I firstly soaped and rinsed her curly mound. I gently parted her crack; one by one I sponged Mum's outer and inner lips and ever so gently around her clitoris which was offering its own claim for attention. Feeling that I had now fulfilled my task I rinsed her vulva with a luke-warm spray of water from the flexible shower.

"Now the other jar darling," Mum began, "take a little on your fingers and smooth it around my pussy; then slide two fingers inside and smooth it on the walls of my vagina."

I did as she asked, concentrating, so as not to let my hand shake betraying my nervousness. Mum showed she enjoyed my attention. She was flushed with excitement and turned around to be alongside me again. She kissed me passionately.

“Thank you darling. It’s a special balm Doc had prepared for me long ago and I’ve used it ever since. It keeps my pussy strong but soft and flexible,” Mum told me. “If you had got them mixed-up, I would have been blowing bubbles when I peed,” she added and giggled at the thought.

“It’s time Adonis,” Mum said as I wrapped my arms around her and we kissed.

“Why did you call me Adonis?” I asked.

“I’ll explain later darling,” Mum replied.

“Yes Aphrodite, it’s time,” I replied as my cock, pressing against her belly, gained a full hard-on. Mum lifted her left leg over me and lowered her foot to hold me to her as her freshly invigorated pussy sought to invite her new master in.

Suddenly, as our passion mounted, the beautiful moment was broken by the shrill ringing of the phone extension. I jumped at the surprise and Mum paused our embrace to whisper, “Forget it Adonis, they’ll ring back if it’s important.” The phone rang out but instead of silence returning the caller rang back immediately.

“Sounds as though it may be important,” Mum accepted.

I untangled myself from her arms and leg and dripped my way to the phone on the bathroom wall.

“Hello,” I said, trying to get my mind, manner and demeanour back into the persona of a grieving son.

"Hello Nan," Mum heard me reply. "Yes, I'm fine thank you. I am sorry that I didn't get to the phone on your first call, I was in the shower. Mum? I haven't seen her this morning. Just wait a moment and I'll give her a call. She'll answer from her bedroom if she's not out in the kitchen. 'Mum, Nan is on the phone'. I'll see you later Nan," I ended my conversation as I heard Mum lift the handset in her bedroom. The spell was broken when Mum heard me say 'Nan' and she quickly left the spa and went to her bedroom to dry herself and dress. I replaced the handset and leant back against the wall. The proud horn that I had when I reached for the phone had gone and my floppy old fella now stared dejectedly at the floor: cheated again, but not next time I promised.

So, the subterfuge has begun. I now realised I had two personalities to maintain: a dutiful son to a widowed mother when in public, and an ardent lover to a beautiful and desirable woman in private. Surely, we would be permitted many hours of privacy away from prying eyes; even if I must lie to those I love. I dried myself, wrapped my towel around my waist and went to find Mum.

Saturday 17 November 2012 – 0900 hrs

I paused at her open bedroom door.

Mum was holding her hairdryer high in her left hand while she brushed her hair with her right. The back view of her naked body revealed her perfectly proportioned figure while the reflection in the mirror highlighted her trim breasts as they rose higher with the action of drying and brushing her hair. She had an enigmatic smile on her face and her eyes appeared only half-open as she brushed her hair dreamily. Then she caught sight of me in the mirror. She put down her hairdryer and brush, turned, and ran into my arms.

"Oh, Adonis, I feared you might not have come."

Our lips met and there was no need for me to answer. My left hand went around her waist and my right to fondle her left breast. Our kisses became urgent and Mum fumbled to free the towel from around me. I took her down onto the crisp white sheets of her freshly made bed. While I kissed her fervently, she guided my horn into her crack and wrapped her legs around my thighs I was trembling with desire and didn't dare speak. I hardly knew what to do: how hard to press against her or how deep to thrust. I soon felt the control Mum could exercise on the walls of her vagina as she seemed to suck me in with every lunge of mine and urge me forward with her heels behind my thighs.

"Oh Adonis, Adonis, Adonis," she cried out.

Our lips came together again in long tongue kisses until she broke away gasping for air and moaning, "Yes! Yes! Yes!"

I was panting along with Mum and lost control as my ejaculation spurted deep inside. She writhed and throbbed underneath me as her orgasm took hold. My horn throbbed too, and I collapsed on her, crushing her into the bed. Fearful of hurting her I tried to pull back, but she tightened her legs around me trying to pull me even further in. I wrapped her in my arms and rolled her with me onto our sides. She kept hold of my dick in her vagina and I felt the fading spasms of her orgasm as we entered that first period of afterglow together. We didn't talk but shared long kisses and with my right arm holding her to me my left hand was free to caress her.

I smoothed her hair out over the pillow, kissed her brow, eyes and neck and back to her lips. Her eyes were bright and smiling and our love was profound.

"Why did you call me Adonis?" I asked at last.

"Darling, in my dream I was being lifted out of my despair in the arms of Adonis, the Greek god of masculine beauty and desire who no woman can resist. He brought me back to life by ravishing me," Mum explained.

"You were raped in your dream?"

"No darling, I was ravished, enraptured, powerless to resist, but a willing partner being brought back to life. It was you Brad who was my Adonis," Mum explained. "And you called me Aphrodite?"

"For me to be Adonis you must be Aphrodite," I explained. "I can't call you Mum when we are alone like this," I said with some concern.

"No, please call me Mary. You must think of me as the scared, lost girl who crept into your bed this morning and you were kind enough to give me your shoulder to cry on. I know you love me as a mother and always will. Now I want you to love me as a lover too. I am only thirty-six and everyone would expect me to find a lover and perhaps even marry again, but nobody but you can make up for the loss of Bruce. He was exceptional and so are you."

"When you're in my arms you will be Adonis's lover, Aphrodite, when we are alone you will be Mary and when we are in public you will still be Mum, and I will be your dutiful son."

"I could ask for no more Adonis," Mary closed the subject with a passionate kiss.

"There is much more for me to tell you Adonis, but it can wait until we have more time," Mary said.

We kissed and cuddled for a while longer.

"Is there somebody else darling?" Mary asked with a hint of fear in her voice.

“No,” I answered quickly and sincerely. “I have been rather busy what with school, sport and flying. I haven’t had much time to be mixed up in silly situations that aren’t going anywhere. I have never wanted to get into a relationship where the girl could reasonably expect me to be offering marriage and I’ve never met a girl like you Mary.”

“After this morning it is hard to believe you have never had sex darling,” Mary said enquiringly.

“Only by masturbating with you in my imagination Mary; the walls are rather thin between our bedrooms,” I answered.

“That’s sweet darling. You can give your hand a rest from now on.”

We enjoyed another fifteen minutes of caressing and fondling and realised that the time was approaching midday. The phone rang again but this time Mary only had to reach over me to the handset at the bedside to answer.

“Yes Gran, thank you. I’m feeling much better today,” Mary said. “Yes Gran, what you and Mum have arranged will be fine for us. We’ll be to your place around one o’clock.”

Mary reached across me to replace the handset and I cuddled her to me for what I knew was going to be a parting kiss for now.

“We are expected by your Clifford Grands and Greats at one o’clock and my mob about three. None of your uncles, aunts or cousins will be there as they have agreed to wait until your party in two weeks’ time. We should be home by five,” Mary began. “I’d like to organise a birthday party for you at home tonight Brad, just for the two of us.”

“I’d like that very much Mary,” I replied.

"When we get home from visiting you can go to the drome to prepare Bravo Mike Charlie for tomorrow while I get our dinner ready," Mary said.

"You remember then; you do still want to do it?" I asked.

"Even more so darling, it will give us a chance to talk without any distraction. There is a lot for us to discuss. Now we had better have a quick snack and visit your Grands and Greats."

I left Mary to dress and quickly put on grey slacks, casual shirt and shoes. By the time Mary joined me in the kitchen I had coffee brewed and waiting on the table and was cutting the first toasted sandwiches.

"I'll make it up to you at dinner tonight darling," Mary said and came into my arms for a quick kiss and cuddle.

"To mark the occasion darling I'd like us to dress for dinner. I'll lay out your dinner suit in your old bedroom. If you call for me at eight o'clock, I will be ready to dance and dine. Will you choose the music you like to dance to?"

We ate in silence for a few minutes.

"It must be exceptional for an eighteen-year-old to be able to visit four grandparents and eight great-grandparents on his birthday," I remarked.

"Yes, it is exceptional, particularly so as only one is over ninety," Mary said. "If I had my work clothes on, I could quote you the probabilities."

"I can clearly remember my great-great-grandfather Clifford too, Mary. I was six years old when he died at one-hundred and four and half my other great-greats lived past one-hundred as well. We must come from very good stock," I said.

"We certainly do and one of these days, in the not too distant future, we will have some pretty serious discussions on that subject," Mary said. "On the way to the Grands I'll do lists of what we'll need for the trip," May said. "If you drop them into the butcher and supermarket on the way to the drome, they'll have them ready for us as we pass in the morning."

As we left the kitchen Mary picked up the keys to Bruce's XK Jag and threw them to me.

"These are yours now lover, think you can handle her?" I instantly caught the tease and the innuendo in her voice.

"You made me man of the house lover. I'll handle everything that comes with that responsibility."

Mary went to her bedroom to make her final preparations to leave and I turned my attention to some preparations for tonight. I selected a bottle of Bruce's special occasion Dom Perignon from his wine cupboard and slid it into the bottom of the fridge to cool for dinner. I was certain that one bottle will be sufficient, as I neither wanted to impair Mary's or my faculties in any way for this evening or for our flight away tomorrow morning.

I visualised the lounge room with its concealed lighting dimmed to just the right level and I selected a playlist of background music which I arranged in sequence to what I guessed would be the times that we ate our meal, made small talk between courses or danced on the polished board section of the lounge. With these plans tucked away, I went to the garage and fired up the Jag. It sprung to life instantly, so I rolled out and lined up the passenger side at the front door. I went inside to find Mary just as she was coming out of her room, now more appropriately clad in a dark blue slack suit, medium-heeled shoes and wearing dark glasses. I held the door of the Jag open and saw her comfortably into the passenger seat. As soon as we were out the gate, Mary produced her notebook and started making her two lists.

Saturday 17 November 2012 – 1300 hrs

Right on one o'clock we pulled up at **Bruce's parents'** home. **http://www.futuristic.guru/clifford-grands-greats** Gran Clifford was quick to open the door.

"How are you my Dear?" Gran said with sincere sympathy. "Better than yesterday I hope?"

"Yes Gran," Mary replied. "After everyone left the realisation hit me rather hard. I had been too busy during the week to be able to let go but I'm feeling much better now."

"How are you Brad?" Gran asked with obvious concern.

"I'm OK thanks Gran," I quickly reassured her.

"Make sure you look out for your mother now," she admonished.

"I will Gran," I confirmed without moving my eyes from her gaze, "I will."

"Come in, come in, what am I thinking keeping you out here," Gran was now a little flustered.

I followed Mary as she led us into the lounge room to be greeted by my paternal grandfather and great-grandparents. There were hugs all around with Great-Grandfather Clifford being first to speak.

"You're man of the house now young fellow, I know you will cope," he said as he pumped my hand while holding a firm grasp above my wrist with his left.

"I will Pops," I managed to say. There was no need to act or play the innocent.

"What's on now Mary?" Bruce's father asked.

"I'm on indefinite leave from the Uni for the moment," Mary replied. "Bruce had arranged a circumnavigation flight around Australia for Brad's birthday this weekend, so we have decided to go ahead with that. As you know Brad's birthday party will now be family only in two weeks' time but after that there are no plans at all."

"What about the Chair at the Uni?" Pops asked.

"I don't know Pops," Mary answered softly. "Everything is on hold until we can discuss the future for both of us. Bruce and Brad had planned an introductory trip to Clifford Engineering overseas companies during the coming year, so we have a lot to discuss."

"I'm sure you two will make the best decisions possible," Gran stopped the questioning. "What with the youngest professor in Australia and the highest ever Uni entrance score how can any of us advise you?"

"You've got every right Gran," I was quick to reassure her. "But we will be OK. We just need a little time to work it out. The new academic year doesn't start for three months."

The conversation transferred smoothly to less emotive subjects and by two-thirty it was time to take our leave.

"Oh Brad, you came so we could wish you happy birthday and all we have dwelt on is the untimely loss of Bruce," Gran exclaimed.

"That's OK Gran, I haven't thought a great deal about it either to tell you the truth," I replied as the Grans gathered around to kiss me and the Granddads shook my hand, man-to-man. The Grans walked us back to the Jag and we sedately glided away. A little way down the road wet eyes met wet eyes as we conveyed the emotional strain, we had both been under.

Saturday 17 November 2012 – 1430 hrs

At **Mary's mother's home http://www.futuristic.guru/franklin-grands-greats** the vibes were a little different. While the loss of Bruce was a shock to all of them, for they had accepted him as a son from the day they had met him, Nan Franklin's daughter was still here with them unlike Gran Clifford's son who was gone forever. With another cup of coffee in hand and Nan spreading hot scones from the oven the atmosphere was a little lighter. The only time any real concern was raised was when Mary spoke of the circumnavigation of Australia we were to start in the morning. After all Bruce already had his commercial pilot's licence when they met and had kept well on top of the art ever since.

"Will you be safe without Bruce on board?" Nan asked.

"Yes Mum," Mary was quick to reply, "Brad and I are both fully licensed for the Pilatus and besides it is a sight-seeing trip. We plan to fly below ten thousand feet and only in daylight. We will be flying VFR and won't be going near bad weather. I promise to phone you every time we land and tell you where we are," Mary reassured her mother.

"I know you are both capable," Nan replied, "but after the last week you can understand our concern."

"Nan, we are far safer up there than down here on the road where Dad was killed while doing nothing wrong," I tried to console my grandmother. "Pilots rarely drink and fly and if caught they lose their licence. We'll be fine."

"Sure Brad, just look after my little girl," Nan replied. "I will Nan, she's most important to me too," I answered.

Inevitably, the conversation turned to our plans for the future and Mary dealt with these in the same way as she had done at Gran's. In the meantime, I pondered on the fact that as an eighteen-year-old I was visiting four grandparents and eight great-grandparents in a single afternoon. The only gap in the four generations was my father, plucked from us by a cruel trick of fate. I began to understand how Mary became engrossed and expert in the study of genetics and realised how exceptional she must be to be offered a Chair at the ANU at her young age of thirty-six years. Out of my reveries, I suddenly realised another insight from this afternoon's visits: everyone one present, husband and wife, had married in their late teens or very early twenties, a tendency which was no longer common as the mode was now for both partners to work on into their late twenties or early thirties before commencing a family. Remarkable too was that none had ever divorced.

I returned my attention to the Grands to hear Mary making our departures and was happy to tag along as the somewhat shy and grieving son. We promised to take care during our flight and to see them all again at the delayed family gathering for my birthday.

When we got home, I pulled up at the front door to let Mary out. I opened Mary's door and offered my hand to help her out of the low-slung Jag. I knew full well that she was quite active and agile enough to do that for herself, particularly as she drove a sporty 'J Type' of her own, but it felt nice to observe the old-fashion courtesies I had learnt as a child from the people we had visited today. I saw Mary inside and after a kiss and hug she gave me her shopping list.

"Call for me at eight?" she asked. "Don't spend too much time with Bravo Mike Charlie," she called after me as I turned for the door.

Saturday 17 November 2012 – 1600 hrs

Driving out the gate my thoughts turned to Bravo Mike Charlie: a beautifully fitted out Pilatus PC-12 Turboprop. Bruce had upgraded to the latest model only twelve months ago and carried on the Bravo Mike Charlie call sign that he had obtained when he registered his first plane shortly after he married Mary. B for Bruce, M for Mary and C for Clifford, without any disrespect for Bruce I now saw it as B for Brad and I knew Mary would see it that way too. I delivered Mary's shopping lists, went on to the airport, and was soon rolling back the hangar door to walk around the bird on a minute inspection. I let my hand run along her smooth skin and it brought back recollections of my hand on Mary's ever so much smoother and silkier skin, particularly her breasts and inner thighs. I brought my attention back to the job at hand and set about loading our camping gear. I moved each item from its well-ordered shelf in the hangar into its allotted space in the luggage compartment. The fuel truck I had ordered arrived and the driver called out, "How much?"

"To the top," I replied. "We're travelling light."

I filled the fresh-water tank, checked the batteries and checked everything else. Returning to the front of the aircraft just as the driver was winding in his hose, I checked the tanks, secured the caps and examined the fuel samples. I signed the driver's delivery docket and started locking up as the fuel truck drove off. Tomorrow I would only have to do a brisk walk around and a re-examination of the fuel for quantity and quality and we would be away. When it comes to fuel, I knew that you can never be too careful, even when it has been locked up in a secure hangar overnight.

On the way home, I stopped at the shopping centre and purchased a very nice orchid corsage for Mary. Returning from the florist something in the window of the jeweller's store caught my eye. I went over to the window to see that it was the glint from a pair of Lalique flutes. I felt stunned. Having decided to be bold enough to use Bruce and Mary's special occasion flutes this evening I was now confronted with this equally beautiful pair of flutes. I didn't even look at the price or think of asking for a discount but simply handed over my credit card and watched as the assistant carefully wrapped the flutes in crepe paper and inserted them in their own pre-formed box. These will now be Adonis and Aphrodite's special occasion flutes.

Holding the flutes carefully in one hand and the orchid corsage in the other I returned to the Jag and drove sedately home; fighting the instincts from within that would have me yell 'Yahoo' and press the pedal to the metal. I had no intention of being picked up by the cops and having to have my mother come and bail me out: not with a hot date with Aphrodite coming up in less than one hour's time.

On entering the house, I heard the first tune from my playlist begin. **What a Difference a Day Made http://www.futuristic.guru/copy-of-goddess-kate**

"I'm home Mary," I called.

"Great, I've laid out your clothes. I'll be ready at eight," Mary confirmed.

"I entered the lounge to find that in my absence Mary had laid the small table more suitable for intimate dinners rather that the large table in the dining room which we used for family and larger gatherings. I was quick to notice that she had used the best sterling silver and Wedgewood china that only ever made an appearance on special occasions. I was also quick to see that she had graced the table with hers and Bruce's Lalique crystal flutes. Her generosity went straight to my heart, but I picked them up and returned them to their home in the crystal cabinet. I placed the orchid bouquet on the table near her chair and went to the kitchen to quickly unpack, wash and dry the new flutes and buff them to a spotless shine before I carefully placed them on the table.

I went to my bathroom, stripped off my clothes, shaved, showered and went to my bedroom to dress. I judged the time as being seven-forty-five: not from the bedside clock, that had been such trouble last night, but from the music drifting through the house from my automatic playlist. I found my clothes for the evening laid out on my bed as promised. I quickly pulled on the ironed and folded Jockey shorts, wondering whether Mary had selected these in preference to the boxer shorts as they would exercise some restraint on man's organ which, having a mind of its own, could quickly stick out, spoiling the line of the best cut suit trousers and make dancing and even walking uncomfortable. On with the socks, dress shirt, studs and trousers. This was the first time that I had dressed for dinner at home. On one other occasion, I dressed for a formal dinner at the university with my parents. I folded my shirt cuffs and picked up the first cuff link. In gold lettering in a black onyx setting shone BMC. Mary had provided my father's special occasion cufflinks. I knew Mary had given them to Dad on their wedding day. BMC on the cufflinks was the same as Bravo Mike Charlie on the Pilatus. I pulled on my polished black dancing pumps, stood up, clipped on my black bow tie and donned my dinner jacket. I checked myself in the wall mirror and adjusted my tie. I was satisfied that I had done all I could to come up to Mary's high standards. I stood straight, braced my shoulders, turned out the lights and closed my bedroom door. I was shutting the door on my childhood and tonight I will move in with my lover.

Saturday 17 November 2012 – 2000 hrs

I tapped on Mary's door just as the sound of Henry Mancini's Orchestra playing *That Old Black Magic,* my eight o'clock timeslot, started playing.

Mary opened her door; took one step out into the hall and did a spin around holding her hands out to the sides at waist level.

“Will I do, Brad?” Mary asked.

“Mary, darling, you look stunning.”

Mary was wearing an evening gown that I had never seen before. Perhaps it was one that she had selected for some upcoming formal event with Bruce. It was full length, red but deepening into magenta when the light fell upon it as she moved. She was fully covered from the waist down except for her toes that peeped out beneath in gold shoes as she walked. The neckline plunged to her waist revealing a little evenly tanned skin all the way through. While still modest and without any hint of cheapness it was what it didn’t reveal that made it so attractive. When she spun around the back was also divided showing a wider expanse of skin as it too tapered to the waist.

The dress was trimmed with a golden chain at the waist and her only other jewellery was a simple gold chain at her neck and equally simple gold clip-on earrings. In her left hand she carried a small, but also very smart, evening purse.

Her hands and forearms were modestly covered with formal white evening gloves that reached to just below her elbows. Her hair was done in a more grown-up, chic sort of way than usual and the most delicate feminine perfume accompanied her — she was a vision of loveliness. For the moment, I was lost for words, so I took her outstretched hands and moving closer to her gave her a very gentle, chaste kiss on the forehead. Mary had obviously taken great care with her make-up, for although it was very light and subtle, she was also aware of the effect that a little shadow here or a little highlight there can have on us mere males.

Still holding Mary’s left hand just above waist level, we walked along the hall to the lounge. When we reached the polished section of the lounge room the playlist obligingly changed to Bing Crosby crooning *Too Romantic.* I smoothly turned Mary into my arms and moved into a slow foxtrot around the room. With Mary wearing high heels she was more able to dance cheek-to-cheek with me and with the demands of ballroom dancing requiring body contact at the waist Mary was well aware that her choice of underwear for me was the correct one. I could feel the growing pressure, but it was restrained from getting in the way of our steps as we glided around the room. We didn't speak until the music moved on and I guided Mary to her chair.

"I think it's time for a drink," I said.

"Brad, the orchids are lovely," Mary exclaimed. "When did you get them?"

"On the way back from the drome, I'm glad you like them," I replied. I lifted the champagne from the ice bucket and popped the cork. I lifted Mary's glass and poured.

"I put out our flutes Brad, these are different," Mary said with some surprise.

"I know, but they were yours and Dad's. Nobody else had ever drunk from them. I have taken so much of his already; even these BMC cuff links. I had planned to use your flutes until after collecting the orchids something caught my eye from the jewellery store and it was these. I thought that we would start tonight, and our new life, with new special occasion flutes of our own."

"That's sweet of you Brad. They're lovely, classical Lalique, it never fails," Mary said. "Were they very expensive? Sorry, I shouldn't have asked that," Mary quickly corrected her slip in manners.

"I honestly don't know," I replied. "I rushed into the shop, asked them to wrap them, swiped my card, put in my PIN and walked out with a big grin on my face."

Mary had removed her left glove to take the champagne and I quickly noticed that her beautifully manicured hands carried no other jewellery than her wedding ring.

“Please never remove you wedding ring Mary; let it be a link for us with Bruce,” I asked.

“I won’t, I promise,” Mary replied and smiled at me. “You are very special Brad.”

“Thanks Mary,” was all that I could say.

“Before we get onto brighter subjects let me reassure you about your father’s wishes,” Mary began. “He knew that he could take nothing from this world other than his own personal spirit. You saw how he wanted his body disposed. As far as his personal possessions are concerned, he has formally bequeathed them all to you except for any that I may wish to retain. Financially, he has left us very well provided for and there will never be any concern for either of us about the future. That brings us to the one remaining big question for you. Remember, you are fifty per cent Bruce and his ancestors and fifty per cent me and mine. If Bruce no longer has a body to hold me would he want me to be in the arms of a stranger or would he want me to be in the arms of the man he helped make, with his one and only love?”

I put the bottle down, having now filled my own glass, and reached down for Mary’s hands to raise her to her feet. Taking her into my arms I said:

“That is a very simple question to answer Mary. He would want you in my arms. I love you Mary Clifford and to see you in another’s arms I would be devastated.”

“I love you too Brad Clifford, I am here for you for as long as you might want or need me,” Mary declared looking me squarely in the eye all the time.

We kissed a long and passionate kiss. Mary was the first to recover.

“I’ll serve the entrée,” Mary said, and added with a seductive glance. “Before our appetite for food is overtaken by an appetite that can’t be satisfied in evening dress.”

Mary went to the serving fridge that was built into the dining room buffet and produced two plates of Oysters Natural. She had shopped for and prepared our dinner while I was at the drome. Mary placed the plate with the dozen oysters in front of my chair and the plate six in front of hers. I was waiting at the back of her chair to push it into position as she sat. Now seated, we turned to each other, raised our glasses and drank to the toast of a long and happy life for us that I proposed. We became conscious of the music again as the intensity of our last conversation faded away. We were the happy young boy and girlfriend out on a special date.

Our conversation returned to our trip around Australia; for many it would be a lifetime highlight. For us it was to be the beginning of an adventurous life. We only had to guard ourselves against the taboo that could at any instant rob us of our happiness.

“We have lots to talk about during our flight,” Mary offered. We had finished our oysters and noticed that the music had now advanced to a quickstep.

“Shall we dance?” I offered and rose to take Mary’s hand. This time we kept our heads further apart and looked into each other’s eyes as we took faster steps around the room. I delighted in doing a pivot at each end of the room: placing my foot between Mary’s feet and still holding her pressed to my waist as I had seen it done on the dancing shows. When the music changed again I guided Mary back to her seat with my hand still resting on the bare skin of her back. I collected the entrée plates stacked them on the buffet and returned to top-up our glasses. We raised them again in another toast to each other, each sensing a growing satisfaction within and knowing by our smiles that the other was enjoying the same sensation.

I picked-up Mary's free hand and asked, "Such as?"

"Such as what?" Mary asked in return.

"Things to talk about on our trip," I explained.

"Oh that, I thought you had forgotten, or ignored me," Mary replied.

"No, I would never ignore you but when we got into the dance, I was too busy ensuring that I didn't tread on your dainty little toes and cripple you for the night," I said, "but now you have my full attention."

"There are many things we need to talk about," Mary began. "There's your career and the courses you wish to take, and your gap year. There's my work and the chair I have been offered and I want to fully make known to you the importance of the two sets of genes you have inherited from Bruce and me and back through the Grands and Greats and beyond."

"I thought these things were cut and dried, signed, sealed and delivered as it were," I said.

"Until last week they were. Bruce's untimely death changes everything. There are no certainties now."

"It's a brave new world?" I suggested.

"It could well be, and to avoid this taboo we might just be called upon to play a very significant role in it," Mary answered.

"How?" I answered naively.

"As I said, we have a lot to talk about during our trip. There is far too much to tell you tonight unless you want to talk into the early hours of the morning," Mary replied and raised her eyebrows suggestively.

"I'm sure it can wait until tomorrow darling," I replied.

"Will you collect our main course from the warming oven please Adonis?" Mary asked.

The Adonis in me quickly responded to Mary's request. Anything that needed to be talked about could wait if it meant that it would keep Aphrodite from coming into my arms tonight.

The Lobster Mornays I placed before us were done to perfection with tinges of rich brown on the melted cheese. They tasted as good as they looked, and I complimented Mary on their preparation. She had certainly been busy while I had been at the drome. After our main course the music went into a slow foxtrot and Mary snuggled into my neck with her head on my shoulder, whispered the words, while I held her close to me, and guided her around the room.

Before the next number began, we paused where we stopped. She brought her arms up around my neck, raised her lips to mine, and we kissed so tenderly.

"Do you really want desert Adonis?" Mary asked.

"No Aphrodite, there is only one thing I want to complete my birthday."

I picked her up in my arms and she clung to my lips while I carried her back to her room. This time there was not the urgency that had preceded our first coupling. We still undressed quickly, but carefully, and hung Mary's evening gown and my dinner suit on their hangers. I held her around the waist and she pushed her mound against me as she leaned back to undo the studs on my shirt and take my cufflinks from my sleeves. I slipped her panties from her hips and she pushed my underpants down to let my old fella free, at last, to push up between her thighs.

"I must go to the bathroom first, Adonis," Mary said as she broke our kiss. I went to my bathroom in the adjoining bedroom to take a leek and clean any trace of the Lobster Mornay from my teeth. I remembered that we had not emptied the bottle of Dom Perignon and returned to the lounge room and topped-up our glasses. When Mary returned, I presented her with her glass and we paused for a moment at the glass doors to the patio to let the moonlight fall on us.

"To you Adonis for lifting me out of the worst day of my life and wanting to make me live again," Mary said and lifted her glass to me.

"To you Aphrodite for making a man of me," I toasted her in return.

We drained our glasses. Aphrodite turned into my arms and we held our kiss while we sunk onto the bed. I took the time now to explore her body as she relaxed in the moonlight. It was a new and different experience than soaping and sponging her all over in the spa. My hands were dry now and Aphrodite's skin was soft, pliant and silky. I held her gaze while I brought my hands up from her slender waist to encompass her breasts and tease her nipples with thumbs and forefingers. She sighed approvingly. I felt her back arch slightly as she lifted her lips to meet mine.

"Ravish me again, Adonis," she said as her breathing became pronounced.

This time I found myself more able to control my ejaculation. As I felt it rising within me, I slowed my movements and concentrated on stimulating Mary more with my hands, lips and tongue. Aphrodite though was sending ripples along the walls of her vagina to thrill me even more. She broke off her kisses and cried, "Oh Adonis, Adonis, I'm coming Adonis".

I rode her harder still, reached my hand down over her curly mound, and tickled her clitoris. Aphrodite's orgasm burst upon her and I gave up any further attempt to hold it back and shot my bolt.

"It felt like I was trying to go back to where I came from," I managed to say at last.

"You would not have found it darling. My womb went when you were born. We both nearly died that day eighteen years ago," Mary said softly, and I saw tears glisten in her eyes.

"Please tell me about it?" I asked and kissed the tears that escaped. There was no sobbing or distress, only the pain of recollection.

"The delivery had been going well but then you stopped moving. The nurse was calling 'Push', 'Push,' I remember pushing with all my strength and your head came out, but you were going blue and they rushed you away to revive you. Much of my uterus and vagina had torn away too leaving me in danger of bleeding to death. Doc rushed me into an operating theatre and acted quickly: first to save my life and then to assess the damage that had been done. He managed a temporary repair and insisted on convalescence and a full recovery before he subjected me to the reconstruction, he was sure would give me a full life, with one exception: I would never have another child; there would be no place where a fertilized egg could embed. I would no longer menstruate, and he refashioned my vagina to accept a penis any man would be proud of. Just as well darling as Bruce and you are both well endowed. We were shattered that we could have no more children: we wanted a family of three or four. Bruce was by my side every possible moment and after two years we were permitted to 'get it together again' which we did with ever increasing confidence and pleasure. You pretty well know the rest darling. The three of us had a great life together until last week."

From the time we climaxed Mary had held me inside her with her legs still around my thighs and my head on her chest. Every little while she exerted a squeeze on my old fella stopping it from slipping away.

"I'm sorry I caused you so much pain Aphrodite," I whispered.

"It wasn't your fault darling. It was an event that nobody could see coming, not even Doc. He saved our lives and has looked after me with the greatest of care ever since."

When we did come apart, I wrapped her in my arms as I had done in the early hours of yesterday morning. She wasn't sobbing now but I again stroked her hair and softly whispered:

Bright angels beside my darling abide
They will guard thee at rest, thou shalt wake on my breast

I felt her hand run through the hair on my chest and this time my hand did move from her hair to her breast. Mary roused sufficiently to display a serene smile on her face and kiss me goodnight before falling to sleep in my arms.

'What a perfect day,' I thought to myself, and drifted into sleep.

Aphrodite's Diary http://www.futuristic.guru/aphrodite-3

Chapter 2

Around Australia

Sunday 18 November 2012 – 0700 hrs

We woke at seven. There was no wet dream this morning. It was well into the early hours before we went to sleep, and we woke with Aphrodite still wrapped in my arms. We lingered in bed for the next hour, showered and had a light breakfast. We planned to leave Canberra at eleven o'clock local time and take a leisurely flight to Cairns with an ETA of five in the afternoon.

Sunday 18 November 2012 – 1100 hrs

"Toss you to see who takes the left seat first Mary."

"OK, you call," she said, taking a twenty-cent piece from the pocket of her shorts.

"Heads," I called.

"Heads it is," Mary said. "You're on first," she added with mock disappointment knowing that we would swap places half way to Cairns.

"I'd like you to wear this Brad?" Mary asked as she produced a crisp white shirt with four gold captain's bars on the epaulettes. "Might as well look the part," she said. I peeled-off the shirt I had worn to the drome and Mary handed me the new one. She did-up the buttons and handed me my Ray-Bans.

"That's much better," she complimented me. I watched in admiration as Mary slipped off her blouse and donned her own white shirt with the two gold bars of a first officer. Mary was making it quite plain the role she was happy to take on this flight. After doing my final walk-around we went up the steps and closed the door. Any observer watching us would see no difference in our manner or professionalism as they would see in any other pilot and co-pilot as we ran our pre-flight and start-up checklists.

“Canberra Ground this is Pilatus Bravo Mike Charlie request taxi clearance to zero six with Delta,” I spoke confidently into the mike of my headset.

“Bravo Mike Charlie good morning, cleared to taxi to zero six and hold, report when ready.” **Glossary http://www.futuristic.guru/glossary**

“Bravo Mike Charlie,” I acknowledged. At the holding point I ran my final checklist.

“Bravo Mike Charlie Ready.”

“Bravo Mike Charlie Line Up, Clear for Take Off, Remain under fifteen hundred until clear of the zone. Call Flight Service on two two zero decimal fife,” the controller replied crisply.

“Bravo Mike Charlie, fifteen hundred,” I replied. I glanced at Mary as her hand joined mine on the throttle, as if we were pushing the throttles forward on a jumbo jet. Mary had a flush of excitement on her face. She blew me a kiss and I quickly turned my attention to the centreline in front of me to ensure our mini-airliner made a flawless departure from the country’s capital.

“V1 - Rotate,” I heard my co-pilot call. I eased back on the control column and the bird lifted gracefully into her true environment, eager to get to cleaner air. I maintained the runway centreline even though my view was now skyward. Passing the end of the runway a gentle tilt to the right brought Bravo Mike Charlie on line for Kiama where we will cross the coast and then fly coastal to Cairns. I eased back on the throttle and engaged the autopilot. We passed the outer limit of the Canberra Control Zone, so I switched to the Flight Service frequency.

“Flight Service this is Bravo Mike Charlie Departed Canberra at zero one zero zero (airways universal time) on climb to five thousand at Kiama then coastal to Cairns.”

"Good morning Bravo Mike Charlie area QNH is 1013 decimal 2 winds are fifteen knots at five thousand from 180 degrees twenty-two knots at ten thousand from 190 degrees CAVOK."

"Thanks sir I'll be tracking the GA lane through Sydney terminal zone, Bravo Mike Charlie."

"Bravo Mike Charlie call again on entering the lane. Will you be requiring the harbour circuit?"

"Bravo Mike Charlie affirmative," I replied.

"Bravo Mike Charlie enter the prescribed route by North Head, I say again North carry out one left hand orbit of the harbour and re-join the GA lane from South Head maintain listening watch for other traffic in the lane. Have a nice flight."

"Bravo Mike Charlie," my exchanges with Flight Centre came to an end for now. While all of this had been going on Bravo Mike Charlie had reached five thousand feet. I set our cruising speed and trimmed the craft to maintain altitude and heading. When I turned to Mary, she noticed the little beads of perspiration that had broken out on my forehead, which was to be expected with this fairly heavy workload for an inexperienced turbine pilot. She could also read the satisfaction that I felt for having come through without a hitch. Nobody on the other end would detect that I had only turned eighteen yesterday and been under severe emotional stress for the past week. Last night, from the time I collected Mary for dinner until the time she went to sleep in my arms, I felt that I was undertaking an examination far more difficult and searching than any I had done at school or flying. This morning when she said, "You thrilled me darling," it was as if my 'Licence for Living' had just been endorsed 'Qualified to Thrill Discerning Women'. I let the autopilot do the work and relaxed back into my chair.

"I made notes of the important bits," Mary said as she lifted her kneepad into the air. "Nice work by the way. Why Sydney Harbour?"

"I thought you would like to see it from this aspect," I added. "We're tourists for this weekend remember?"

"Why North Head?' Mary asked, "seeing that we are coming from the South."

"There are northbound and southbound tracks in the lane but only one track around the harbour otherwise head-ons would be frequent with pilots and passengers alike taking in the view," I replied.

In twenty minutes we were over Kiama and banking to turn north. I didn't need to be fussy about the track until we got to the GA lane under the Sydney International glidepath. Mary had said to me before leaving, "Just keep Australia on your left, OK?"

Mary busied herself getting two cameras ready for the photo-shoot she intended to do as we swept around Sydney Harbour. She mounted a video recorder on top of the control panel and was going to use the standard camera for views from the cabin windows.

"Flight Centre this is Bravo Mike Charlie."

"Bravo Mike Charlie," Flight Centre acknowledged they had my attention.

"Bravo Mike Charlie entering Sydney Northbound Lane at one thousand," I rattled off.

"Bravo Mike Charlie confirm that you will be orbiting the harbour."

"Bravo Mike Charlie affirmative North Head at one thousand five hundred."

"Bravo Mike Charlie report rounding North Head."

"Bravo Mike Charlie," I completed the report.

As soon as I started lifting Bravo Mike Charlie's nose to round North Head at fifteen hundred Mary got up and moved into the cabin to get her shots as we passed South Head and rounded North.

"Bravo Mike Charlie rounding North Head at fifteen hundred," Right on the money I thought to myself. Chasing an assigned level was a sure sign of an amateur and I knew that not only was I in voice contact, but I would be monitored by one or more people maintaining radar watch of the Sydney Control Zone.

"Bravo Mike Charlie," I acknowledged.

I could hear Mary's comments as she snapped away happily. She moved from the left side to the right after we rounded North Head and levelled out over Manly. She fired away at anything and everything; we could easily edit out the rubbish later. I held the wings level for the run up the harbour with Mary snapping away at the north-shore suburbs, ferries, and anything else that caught her eye. She came forward and straddled her seat to take head-on shots of the Sydney Harbour Bridge knowing that it might be difficult to get good shots of the 'Coat-Hanger' once I had to bank to turn.

"There's a bonus," I said, pointing out to the left where Queen Mary 2 was tied up at the International Terminal. "You'll be able to get some shots of her from the right-hand side after we turn."

I judged my turn with minimum bank while sticking like glue to the assigned fifteen hundred feet. Mary had gone back to the cabin where she could get shots of the Bridge, Circular Quay and her namesake without her view being blocked by the wings. I levelled out for the run back down the harbour. As my excitement subsided, I set the glide to reach South Head at one thousand feet, scanned the southern approach to the GA lane for other traffic and knowing we were clear and safe I called Flight Centre.

"Bravo Mike Charlie, South Head joining northbound lane at one thousand," I said knowing that my voice sounded more confident that what I really felt.

"Bravo Mike Charlie hope you enjoyed your visit come back again sometime." Mary and I smiled as we appreciated the controller's little extra levity, also understanding that my performance had no blemishes.

"Bravo Mike Charlie until next time," I replied.

We continued our run up the northbound lane. Mary was sitting in a left-hand cabin seat clicking away at the sights of the northern beach suburbs. I was content to have these few moments of solitude knowing that Mary was right there the moment I spoke. At the end of the lane I gave an all stations report to let other pilots on the frequency know what I was doing.

"All stations this is Pilatus PC-12 Bravo Mike Charlie leaving northbound lane on climb to five thousand," I announced.

Two other pilots responded: a Beechcraft A36 declared he was crossing above at six thousand and had us visual, and a Cessna 182 entering the southbound lane at fifteen hundred also acknowledging that he had the Pilatus in sight. As we passed Barrenjoey Heads and the entrance to the Hawkesbury River Mary came forward to her seat.

"I think I'll have a rest from that for a while," she began. "Do you feel like breakfast yet?"

"Good Lord, I'd forgotten all about that," I replied. "No wonder I'm feeling a bit drained."

"Won't be long, don't go away," she said giving me a kiss on the forehead as she left. Mary was soon back with a good-sized mug of coffee and a ham and tomato sandwich.

"I've got another sandwich toasting for you in our little battery run oven; I've wanted to see how it worked," Mary left again to monitor the oven and before I had finished my first sandwich, she was back with a toasted sandwich for each of us.

When we finished our late breakfast, Mary cleared away the plates and mugs and returned to relax in her seat.

"Would you like to stretch your legs, take a pee or something," she said.

"That's a good idea," I said. "We're near enough to half way so will you take over now and I'll catch up on some sleep."

"I'd love to darling," Mary replied. "You've certainly lost some sleep lately, looking after me."

I went to the rear of the cabin and lowered the divan into its double bed position. I pulled out a soft pillow and a small rug to cover my feet and after kicking off my shoes fell back on the bed. Mary gave the trim wheel an ever so slight adjustment to compensate for my moving from the front of the plane to the rear and ever sensitive to the slightest variation in my spatial positioning I murmured, 'Thanks Mary, that's nice,' and was sound asleep.

I slept soundly for three hours before reappearing at the cockpit entrance.

"Hello lover," Mary greeted me. "I was just about to send a search party out for you. You've missed about fifteen hundred kilometres of coast line while you slept."

"I really needed that," I explained. "Feel great now though. I'll catch up on the scenery next time."

"You have been carrying a big load, besides, I've enjoyed a little time for solitary thinking," Mary replied.

"We've two hours' fuel on board with forty minutes to go; the tail wind has stayed with us and the weather is still CAVOK. God's in his heaven and all's well with the world," she added the last non-aeronautical phrase for my amusement.

"Did any inspirations come from your solitary thinking?" I asked.

"Of course," she replied cheerfully, "and more are in the pipeline."

"Do you wish to share them, I'm a willing listener," I said.

"After darling," Mary replied. "Let's get this bird safely back on the ground first."

"That makes a lot of sense," I agreed. "Do you want to do a dummy run of the landing checklist Mary?"

"Good idea," Mary agreed, "it's a little while since I've landed this darling and the last thing I would want to do is miss the slightest detail."

We ran the checklist, simulating the movements of changing heading, lowering flaps and wheels, cabin pressure, seat belts and all the other items including getting the ATIS and Mary reciting aloud the radio calls.

Nearing the approach point Mary called for her clearance to enter Cairns controlled airspace and joined the circuit for a smoothly executed approach to runway one eight. On final, she received her 'clear to land' and with gear down and locked she held Bravo Mike Charlie off for those critical seconds, allowing her to settle on her mains at the five hundred feet markers, and still holding her let her nose wheel settle gently on the centreline. At the first taxiway she received taxiing instructions to the GA parking area. Mary swung into her allotted space, ever mindful of the wide wingspan of the Pilatus. We ran the shutdown checklist and heard the big turbine wind-down.

We sat back in our chairs and congratulated each other on a fine day's flying. Any fears or nervousness that we had held before the flight had now evaporated and we looked forward to the coming days together with Bravo Mike Charlie. I called the fuel truck saying that we were ready for the delivery we had pre-ordered and waited for its arrival. We squared away our belongings and moved the divan to its upright position.

The truck arrived and after giving instructions to fill the tanks to the brim we changed out of our pilot's shirts and looked over tomorrow's route and weather forecasts. That done we locked up and hand-in-hand strolled over to the Pilots' Club to see if we might eat there rather than preparing our own. We fronted the bar and thought a nice cold beer was well earned. We planned to sit on the veranda and watch the sun go down.

"You're the couple who just came in with Bravo Mike Charlie aren't you?" the bartender greeted us.

"Yes," I answered in all innocence.

"Are you alone?" the barman persisted.

"Yes," again I replied. "What's up?"

"Well, haven't that lot got it wrong," the barman replied pointing to the TV on the wall.

"Why?" It was me now doing the questioning.

"Well, they think it was some top-notch pilot on a publicity shoot for Pilatus at the controls, you see," he continued in the typical Aussie style. "There was a news chopper following you around and when you rolled out with the old Coat Hanger behind you and Queen Mary under your right wing, a news photographer, who just happened to be on the viewing deck of Centrepoint Tower, got a beautiful still and the chopper filmed the whole sequence, you're famous mate. They think you work for Pilatus Publicity, but truth will out. You're bound to be on the cover of FLYING next month; wouldn't be surprised if you get offers from Pilatus either," he said as he turned away to serve other thirsty pilots after their day in the air, and no doubt telling them that he had just served Bravo Mike Charlie's crew.

Mary reached up and whispered in my ear, "Don't pick up the glasses, don't wait for your change, let's quietly walk out of here."

As we neared the door, we couldn't miss seeing an enlarged glossy of the still that the barman had talked about. It was indeed beautiful, but we didn't wait to admire it.

"I know a place," Mary said and took the controls.

She got her taxi clearance and within five minutes we were climbing out of the Cairns control area.

"Where are we going?" I asked.

"Bruce and I visited a client forty kilometres from here when I was doing my training," Mary answered. "I'm sure I can find it before it gets too dark."

"That's it," Mary said five minutes later as the low light of the setting sun caught the windsock on the dirt strip.

Mary pulled a steep turn to line up the runway and glided in to her second perfect landing of the day. We rolled out onto a grassy verge at the end of the strip. Mary picked up her smartphone and, after a quick search, found the owner's number and dialled.

Sunday 18 November 2012 – 1800 hrs

"Good evening Jack, it's Mary Clifford speaking. We have dropped in on your strip; would you mind if we camped for the night?" Mary asked.

"Of course not Mary. Barbara and I have just been watching the news and saw where Bravo Mike Charlie made a quick getaway from Cairns. We're out at a friend's place tonight but come for breakfast in the morning; I'll call for you at seven."

"How is Barbara, Jack," Mary asked.

"Barbara is fine thanks Mary. We'll have a good chat in the morning before you fly off again."

We sat back and relaxed.

"Thanks for that darling," I offered, knowing that it was scant praise for the way Mary got us out of Cairns.

"That was a close one lover," Mary rose from her seat, dropped herself into my lap and threw her arms around my neck. I responded by pressing my lips to hers and holding one of our ever-lengthening kisses.

"Look," Mary said as she hit YouTube on her smartphone, "lots of people have posted clips of our orbit of the harbour."

"That will teach a bloke for trying to impress his best girl," I said sadly.

"Never mind lover," Mary replied. "It certainly impressed me, and the notoriety will soon fade as it is directed at Bravo Mike Charlie and some unknown corporate jock, not two crazy lovebirds."

"Let's go for a look around outside before it gets too dark," I said.

Aphrodite's Diary http://www.futuristic.guru/copy-of-aphrodite-3

We made a meal from the Esky and afterwards it was time for May and I to have the conversation that would have kept us up late last night.

"What does all this mean Mary?"

"Have I shocked you Brad?" I asked, forcing myself to think of him as my son.

"When we woke in my wet-dream Mary you were no longer my mother but the beautiful Aphrodite, the goddess of love. I was no longer your son but your lover Adonis. I fell in love with you instantly. I was filled with desire and now nothing else in the world matters to me. It was as if you and I stepped out of this world into another where the rules and laws we know don't exist."

"That was the way it was for me too. I'm not being unfaithful to your father darling Adonis. He would want us to cling together and fuck. He's probably right here in this same world with Adonis and Aphrodite."

"I know he would expect me to care for you and protect you but where do we go from here?"

"While you slept this afternoon, I had time to get my thoughts in order. I think I can explain what has happened now.

"It all began when my collaborators on the Human Genome Project determined that the male line in human genetic inheritance was in a very bad way and getting worse. As a theoretical exercise we determined what the ideal genome of a new male progenitor of the human race would be. A new Most Recent Common Ancestor

(MRCA), darling. We were looking for the one man who would have abundant health and strength with immunity to the ills that plague our world. But most importantly there would be no inheritance of greed or injustice. He would be the man who will father a new race of healthy, ethical people. People who will be able to manage the world we live on, in the twenty-second century. We named our ideal genome Adonis and referred to this study as Project Adonis. Over the next few years we matched every male DNA swab that came to our members with Adonis's genome. Four years ago, we found a match. Can you see where I am going Brad?"

"You called me Adonis darling."

"Yes Brad. You are Adonis. The inheritance that came down to you from Bruce and me and those who had gone before us has made you what you are. The world is waiting for you darling."

"But I'm only one-man Mary," I protested.

"The gene map that we constructed showed us that no one woman could hold Adonis's attention for long. There would need to be three women to satisfy Adonis's needs both physically and mentally. We identified the genetic make-up of these women who we call Adonis's Goddesses. Adonis's interests span the whole gamut of human activity: music, literature, theatre, science, feats of physical endurance, everything. He has power over men without exercising his obvious strength and power over women without knowing that he is exerting any power at all. He has a devotion to justice as distinct from a blind obedience to law and a similar devotion to seeking economic justice. He has an abhorrence of any type of rage or violence against anyone, but particularly against women and children. In short, Adonis and his progeny will reinvigorate HOMO SAPIENS. The fourteen team leaders from the universities collaborating on the genome project accepted two years ago that no other male DNA had come anywhere near challenging their choice. We then began our search for Adonis's three goddesses.

"But, even if I have children with three desirable women such a family will still take a very long time to have any impact on the human race, no matter how many children they each have."

"The three goddesses and their children will be Adonis's family Brad and their children will grow up to be world leaders."

"But that is going to take years to have any effect."

"No, they will be contributing valuable information on parent matching to produce healthy, happy and socially responsible people almost from the time of their conception. Adonis's children with his goddesses will possess the best genes possible by scientifically matched parents. However, there is more darling. The Faculty has identified many young women around the world who, while not being of the calibre of his goddesses, would produce outstanding children. They will help the goddesses' children succeed. They will all be half-siblings."

"You're not talking AI or IVF are you Mary?" I asked.

"No darling, Adonis would only donate his sperm the old-fashioned way."

"So, Adonis will just be a stud, a gigolo?"

"Not at all Brad, he will find the mothers of all his children irresistible and his life will be very rich and rewarding — he will be changing the world in his own lifetime."

"How many of these other girls are there Mary?" I asked.

"In our present population there are millions of girls who would qualify," Mary began. The female line is not the problem: while the male line has degenerated with its lust for war and domination, the female line has become stronger, as mothers have nurtured and protected their children from sometimes brutal fathers and a society that undervalues their efforts. One of the first publications the new Faculty will be making will prove the falling sperm count in men and the state of fitness of people in their child bearing years. We are at risk of raising a generation of sickly kids with a life expectancy less than their parents.

"But I'm still only one-man Mary, how many others would I need to impregnate?"

"I have suggested Adonis could easily impregnate one hundred a year Brad," Mary said quite calmly, as some of the dread she had felt having to make this confession seemed to be lifting.

"It's still a small number when you consider the world's population has exceeded seven billion and will become fourteen billion by twenty-sixty," I said.

"I know darling, but the Faculty will be working very hard to stop people with poor genetic inheritance from breeding and when your children grow up, they will have the best possible partners matched with them. While your daughters will only have few children, your sons and their sons, like you, could be impregnating one hundred or more girls a year, each.

I've done the numbers darling. With the old genetic lines dying out and your line taking over every person of childbearing age by twenty-seventy will be one of your descendants: all unique individuals combining all the so-called races, but all imbued with your sense of truth and justice.

"What about us Mary?" I asked.

"When I woke in your arms, I was your lover Aphrodite. I wasn't faking. You know the state I was in following Bruce's death. What has happened to us since shows the irresistible power you have over women. I wasn't being unfaithful to Bruce. I just wanted to bind you to me and never let you go. When we fuck it has been sublime, completely different to what Bruce and I enjoyed. I've been struggling with myself ever since. How could I tell you this? After this afternoon I felt it only fair to tell you as soon as possible, and now I have."

I turned Aphrodite to me and let her know with my kisses and fondling that I had understood what she had told me and thanked her for doing so.

"What do we do now Aphrodite?"

"Everyone knows you were going to take a gap year to visit the Clifford interests overseas. I'm entitled to take a year's sabbatical and visit my overseas collaborators. Can we go together Adonis?"

"I'd love to do that. I don't need three goddesses and one hundred girls a year to impregnate so long as I have you Aphrodite."

"Darling, you broke out as Adonis to save me. You made me Aphrodite and that is my reward. When the time comes, I must declare to the other universities that you are Adonis. If I don't, they will find you through their genetic scanning anyway. Besides, if I don't release you to fulfil your inheritance it will eventually drive us apart. The only way for us to have any future together is for us both to do what we were born to do. The inheritance of the Clifford and Franklin lines that came together through Bruce and me must be continued. I can't give you children darling."

"How far back does our genetic inheritance go Mary?" I asked as we ate.

"All the way Brad, at least to Mitochondrial Eve who is estimated to have lived 200,000 years ago," Mary replied. "Y-chromosomal Adam, it is thought, may have lived sometime later but there is much debate and conjecture about these events and how they have been ascertained. The most recent common ancestor by the male line of all people living today might be as recent as one thousand years; however, he would have all earlier generations as his ancestors."

"So we are all related Mary, all seven billion of us?"

"Yes, darling, we are all cousins to some degree and all one-hundred billion who have lived before us. What we now call incest runs through all generations, as does polygamy, polyandry and every other expression of human sexuality," Mary replied.

"And any one of us might demonstrate or shall I say reincarnate behaviours of ancestors from thousands of years ago?"

"Yes, darling, while we receive half our chromosomes from each parent, they could have deeply recessive genes which find a new expression in the child, both good and bad," Mary said.

"I think it is time for bed darling," Mary said and cleaned away the remains of our meal. We were both tired from our long day. The two nights that we had slept together hadn't provided much sleep. Exhausted, I held Aphrodite in my arms and we kissed and drifted into sleep.

Monday 19 November 2012 – 0530 hrs

Just as it gets dark early in the evening in the tropics it gets light and bright early in the morning too. I woke to find Mary still in my arms. I didn't move so I could enjoy the intimacy a little longer. I had plenty to think about. First was the realisation that, no matter how much we were in love, ours was not going to be a long-term relationship. I could understand that Mary wanted grandchildren for her and Bruce and the two lines of genetic forebears that have come together in me. I believed what she told me about Project Adonis. She had no reason to make it up and the rest of her collaborators were all involved. Most importantly was the change that came over her in the instant I woke from my wet dream, she was a new woman.

The grieving mother I loved and respected had gone, never to return. I had changed too; I was a man in love with a beautiful woman for the first time. I tried to visualise sharing my life with three beautiful women and impregnating another one hundred girls each year — it was too difficult. I decided to put all thoughts of the future aside and only dwell on what was in front of us now. The thought of going off on a twelve-months' gap year with Mary was most appealing. I could still visit the Clifford company operations overseas and Mary could visit the other universities. We would have lots of time together to see the world and consider how to handle the future that seems to have been pre-ordained for us. My thoughts turned to the practicalities. I thought that Mary, like me, would want to leave as soon as possible and the soonest would be in three weeks' time. My delayed birthday party was in two weeks and we would need the time to arrange our affairs.

To me the obvious way for us to travel would be in Bravo Mike Charlie. We were both IFR rated and Bravo Mike Charlie was equally at home at thirty-thousand feet in controlled airspace and landing at international airports as she was on a scenic flight at low level around Sydney Harbour and landing on this rough farm strip. We would stay at many fine hotels in our travels but travelling in Bravo Mike Charlie we always had our own accommodation with us.

I pictured in my mind the modifications I will have made to Bravo Mike Charlie. The first thing that came to mind was the need for more fuel. The Pilatus already had a generous range of nearly 3,500 kilometres under standard conditions; however, I could see us wanting to fly from Los Angeles to Honolulu during our travels. With only the two of us on board we could easily give up some of the cargo carrying capacity, and space, to accommodate an auxiliary fuel tank adding 1000 kilometres to our range and do some other modifications that will make our travels more enjoyable. I caught a glimpse of the clock to see it was six-fifteen. In my reverie, forty-five minutes had flown by and with Jack picking us up at seven o'clock the opportunity to start the day with a bang had gone. I woke Mary slowly by stroking her hair and planting little kisses on her lips. She opened her eyes to give me a glorious smile and turned to me to join me in full kisses.

"Have we got time Adonis?" Aphrodite asked as she rubbed her right leg up my thigh.

"Regrettably not, Aphrodite, Jack will be here in thirty minutes."

"Until later darling," Aphrodite replied. We enjoyed a long kiss and cuddle and Aphrodite giggled as my old fella still came to attention.

We got up and gave ourselves, and each other, a sponge bath as we stood on a towel at the highest point in the cabin. I made a mental note to include a shower for Mary in the modifications that I planned. I could see that by rearranging the seating it would fit neatly alongside the existing toilet. When Jack arrived Mary was looking relaxed and charming in pale blue slacks with a darker blue top. I wore clean grey trousers and shirt to start the day and with casual shoes and my old Akubra I thought I looked presentable. The last thing I wanted to do was to try to impress a Far-North-Queenslander by looking too flash: I would offend the farmer and Bruce too.

"How do you do Mary; I'm pleased to meet you Brad," Jack said as he gripped my right hand. "Please accept our condolences for the loss of Bruce."

"Thanks Jack," Mary began, "It came as a terrible shock, but we are facing the reality of it. We know Bruce would want it that way."

"Hop in folks," Jack held the door of his ute open for Mary to slide in first, "Barbara will have breakfast on the table for you by the time we get there; it's only a few minutes," he added as an afterthought.

Barbara was at the door waiting to greet us as soon as she heard the Landcruiser drive up.

"Come in, come in. We don't often get celebrities out here," she said.

"Celebrities?" Mary quickly responded. "We saw the news last night in Cairns where the Pilatus was the celebrity and that's when I remembered visiting you with Bruce."

"It seems that the shirts you were wearing, white with shoulder bars, and your Ray-Bans gave them the impression that you were professional pilots," Jack explained.

"It was just a bit of a family joke to boost our confidence," Mary explained.

"Not just that," Barbara was quick to explain, "but while Jack was picking you up, I watched the morning news. A reporter checked the registration of the Pilatus, found that it was registered to Bruce Clifford and knowing that he had so recently met a sudden death went hotfooted after what must be something of a human-interest story. He was told that Bruce's distraught widow had left that morning honouring a plan she had made with Bruce to take their eighteen-year-old son off on a circumnavigation of Australia on his birthday.

"Apparently, as soon as this hit the news every TV Channel, talk show and magazine is looking for the surviving, but missing, Cliffords. Your right by the way. In the late news last night, there was a cross to a reporter at the Pilots' Club in Cairns saying that the Cliffords refuelled there and quickly departed. Social media is abuzz with all sorts of speculation," Barbara stopped at last to draw breath and Jack, seeing the distress building in their guests' faces moved in, pulled out two chairs from the dining table and said with some urgency:

"Forgive our manners, please sit down."

"Oh My God," Mary said looking directly into my eyes. "They must have spoken to Mum or Dad," Mary explained. "In our rush out of Cairns last night I forgot to phone Mum as I'd promised. Please excuse me a moment while I call her now."

Mary got up and went out onto the veranda to call her mother.

"What were your plans for today," Jack asked.

"We were going largely coastal to Darwin, refuelling and then on to Broome for this evening," I said.

"My advice to you is that if you really want to complete this trip, and I don't doubt that you do, you are going to need a new strategy. You can't go near the major dromes, nor controlled airspace," Jack began.

"Where will we refuel?" I asked.

"I have friends and contacts all over the country where you can land, refuel, rest a while if you wish and no one would ever breathe a word that you had passed their way," Jack continued.

Having spoken to her mother, and calmed her fears, Mary returned to the table and caught up on Jack's advice.

"I'll arrange the airstrips and fuel for you as you phone-in or email me your plans. Keep off the airwaves as much as possible, listen and keep a good look out but talk little. You'll be all right," he concluded.

Barbara was dishing up bacon and eggs, with sausages and tomato. Slices of toast appeared, and the table was well supplied with marmalades and other spreads. There were cereals to satisfy any taste and a good array of tropical fruits.

"Dig in," Barbara demanded, "You'll feel much better on a full stomach."

"Who flew the orbit in Sydney Harbour?" Jack asked, displaying real interest in the exploit that could have brought us undone.

"Brad did," Mary was quick to respond with obvious pride in my achievement.

"A fine bit of flying that," Jack explained mainly to his wife. "Well done young fellow, your father would have been very proud. Couldn't have done better myself I'm sure," Jack said and added with sincerity. "I know I couldn't, and I've lost count of the hours I've got in my log book."

Jack went on to explain to Barbara that the harbour orbit was usually flown in little Cessnas, Pipers, floatplanes and light twins. The Pilatus was nothing short of being a small airliner. "Even a Qantas captain would be very cautious pulling that turn near the Harbour Bridge," he explained.

"Careful Jack," Mary said, her spirits coming flooding back. "Wouldn't want him getting a swollen head would we," she added with a laugh. I nearly blushed at her innuendo but held myself together to laugh along with the others.

"Well now, let's get down to brass tacks," Jack took over. "You still want to go mainly coastal, so I suggest you refuel at a mate of mine's property a little south of Darwin at Adelaide River. I'll ring him as you're leaving to make sure he has plenty of fuel on hand for you. You can decide when you are there whether you want to stop overnight or push on to Broome. I'll alert Bill, he's 10 Ks east of Broome, that you will be wanting fuel in the next couple of days. We won't get too far ahead of ourselves, so you can go or stay as the fancy takes you. No good rushing around this country in a couple of days just to say you've circumnavigated the place. And don't bother about the media or anyone. They don't care about you. They only want to use you to sell their newspapers and magazines. When they can't find you in a couple of days, they'll quickly stop outlaying their cash in chasing you around, something easier will come up to take their attention. When do you have to be back in Canberra by the way?"

"Our only confirmed date is for Brad's delayed birthday party on Saturday-week," Mary obliged.

"Good," Jack replied. "You've got ten or eleven days up your sleeves, slow down and enjoy it," he admonished us.

Before we left, I gave Jack our mobile and on-board satellite phone numbers. I also gave him our email addresses and Gran and Nan's home phone numbers in case any emergency arises. Jack was to be our SARTIME service for the remainder of our trip. We will report our departures and arrivals to him. Jack gave me the coordinates for his Adelaide River and Broome mates and Barbara appeared with a basket for Mary.

"Just some nibbles to get you through the day," she said. I collected the thermoses that I had brought with us that were now filled with boiling water and Jack took us back to the airstrip. Barbara came along to see the bird that had started this confusion and to watch us take our leave and fly away.

"Will you fly first today Mary?" I asked. "I want to get a chance to land this bird."

Monday 19 November 2012 – 0900 hrs

"Love to Captain. Let's go and have some fun like Jack demands," Mary said as she strode off to do her pre-flight walk around of the plane. We both knew what Mary meant by having fun. With checklists completed we waved goodbye.

Mary released the brakes and gently pushed the throttle home. Bravo Mike Charlie burst down the bush strip keen to be airborne.

"V1 - Rotate," I called, and she rose gracefully into the air.

Mary established her track along the far north-east coast with the view of making our first mark Thursday Island off the tip of Cape York. Established in calm and level flight with the Daintree Rainforest to our left I got up to get some more photos from the left side cabin windows. When I returned to the cockpit, I took mugs of coffee and the first of Barbara's homemade goodies.

"Good grub," I said as I placed Mary's coffee in the cup holder and offered her first choice of the cookies.

"How are you feeling Mary," I asked after planting my customary kiss on her forehead.

"Great now," she replied, "how about you?"

"Couldn't be better," I said. "How did you get into genetics Mary?" I asked. I was eager to know every little detail of Mary's life, needs, feelings and emotions.

"It all started after you were born. I told you how we both nearly died that day and it was only through Doc's presence that we were saved. As part of my reconstruction he asked me to provide regular specimens of my vaginal secretions for pathology to monitor my progress. To cut a long story short, Bruce was wonderful to me. During the no sex period that Doc imposed on us he never as much glanced at another woman and never tried to hurry the healing process. I managed to keep him excited with my breasts, kisses and hands. I learnt to masturbate him expertly, bringing him to the point time after time and backing off until he couldn't hold it back any longer. He would come all over us, so it was into the shower, into the washing machine with the linen and face a new day.

"You see why you waking from your wet dream the other morning didn't faze me or let you feel any shame. There was no shame there. As much as it released you of many pent-up feelings you lifted my grief as if turning on a light and showing us a new path to take. We doted on our baby Brad of course and the Grands and Greats were marvellous in helping look after you when we both had lectures," Mary paused for a moment as if giving me an opportunity to speak. I was speechless, taking in and processing what I was now hearing. She recounted her early married life with such calm clarity that obviously she was at peace with herself, the world, and her role in it. I just marvelled.

"Although it started out as a requirement in my recovery by the end of the two years when Bruce and I could join together again I had become engrossed in my studies in reproduction and genetics. I had already joined in the world-wide genome project and we were developing a small prac lab at the ANU doing some of our own pathology tests. I started testing my own secretions mainly detecting my ovulations and ensuring that the egg didn't become impregnated with Bruce's sperm and try to attach somewhere else as I now had no womb to host it.

I became fascinated at what was revealed under the large microscope in the lab. I soon had Bruce using a condom occasionally so that I could monitor his semen's volume, and motility: motility darling is a measure of how active the sperm is in seeking the egg to fertilise. I carefully documented all our results and tried to include any known life factors such as overwork, stress and travelling — matching these to the specimens.

"All the girls in the lab provided their swabs and soon they were bringing in knotted condoms containing samples of their husband's or boyfriend's semen. As the word got around their friends, classmates and sometimes families joined our ranks. Each donor was provided with a unique identifier and I was the sole guardian of the record linking names and personal details with the identifiers. I even kept this record encrypted so that if it was read by others it would be meaningless. The place always had an air of excitement. Everyone was keen to get to work each day. By the time you were ten years old I had earned my PhD with my thesis based on my parent-matching research. Since the completion of the Genome Map, we have been encouraging couples to submit swabs of vaginal secretions and semen strength for genome matching. We have had some success in encouraging some couples to reproduce and others not to.

"These warnings are not just restricted to possible physical and medical conditions but go right to the heart of the progeny's makeup including the tendency to anger, violence, rage and even the capacity to rape and murder if their inner demands aren't met. It is a fascinating study and we have only just started. It is beginning to show us that treatments for all medical conditions can only be truly effective if they are prepared specifically to match the demands of that person's genome and mass medication and mass immunisation, for instance, can have drastic results for many individuals. There is little chance that there will ever be a magic cure-all pill no matter how hard the pharmaceutical companies push for it. The fact is we are all unique, all seven billion of us and all the one-hundred billion who have ever lived."

"Like cough mixtures?" I asked.

"Cough mixtures, vitamin supplements, body builders and shapers, even most prescription drugs," Mary continued with enthusiasm. "If they had any confidence in these products, they wouldn't need that folded up page in fine type describing possible side effects, 'This product may cause ....'

"I'll get you a fresh coffee," I interrupted. Mary raised the right wing slightly to make a wide arc around Cape York and sweep over Thursday Island before levelling for the run down the coast past Weipa. I hurried back, replaced Mary's mug in the cup holder and took my seat anxious to hear more.

"Sorry I took so long," I said. "I got a couple of shots of Cape York and the islands. We're climbing?"

"Yes, I thought a little higher view might be better. Easier to see when the northern shore comes into view again," Mary told a little white lie not wanting to reveal her plans just yet. I was keen for the discussion to continue.

"What now?" I asked.

"The work is only just beginning," Mary quickly took up her subject, delighted that I was showing such interest. "The concept of natural selection in the animal kingdom has worked fairly well but, in HOMO SAPIENS it has been an utter disaster. Sure, we've had our Plato, Aristotle, Shakespeare, Beethoven, Mozart, Da Vinci, Einstein and many others of genius over the centuries but these have largely been flukes, long shots of the one random sperm, out of an ejaculation of millions, carrying specific chromosomes. This sperm being the one to penetrate the recently ovulated egg, before any of the other millions of competitors in this massive marathon of sperm get there.

Not only that, but the one egg which was developed for release by one of the ovaries, on this day, in this month from the possibly thousands of potential eggs the girl was born with, just happened to be the only egg in the universe that could have produced that genius," Mary finished her discourse. "Sorry to sound like a professor darling."

"That's OK, you are one, and a beautiful one at that," I added.

"That's my three hours' captain. Time for a toilet break," Mary said, rising from the left seat, "I won't be long."

I left the plane on autopilot and pushed my chair fully back. I started thinking about Mary's words. The mind boggled. What fantastic odds are involved in anyone being who they were. I came out of these thoughts as I heard the music coming through my headset. At first, I thought I was dreaming but then I saw this beautiful creature bend forward and start to undo my belt buckle.

"Get them off, darling. I've come to deliver the rest of your birthday present," she whispered in my ear.

I hastily pushed down my trousers and boxers and opened my shirt. I helped her across the centre console so that she could mount me face to face; with her knees squeezing my hips so she didn't slip from my chair. Mary undid the two buttons that were holding her little white bolero closed and gave her titties a provocative shake.

"Look, it's gift wrapped," Mary added with a giggle. She was wearing what appeared to be a tiny bikini, tied with a bow. "Aren't you going to undo your present Adonis?" Mary asked.

I quickly undid the bow and gently pulled the ribbon until it unwrapped from around her bottom and from between her legs. She pulled my head forward to suck on her left breast and my right hand went down between her legs. I guided my knob up and down between her lips and onto her clit. Mary captured my swollen head.

"I'm fucking you this time Adonis," Mary whispered and proceeded to make all the motion. I laid back and enjoyed it. The sound of my playlist brought thoughts and visions from two nights ago when I received the first half of Mary's two-part gift. I released her nipple to kiss her passionately and let my hands roam all over her. It drove her wild when I matched her movements with my fingers stroking her thighs.

I shot my bolt with a vengeance and Mary gave a cry of delight. She collapsed on my chest. Her movements slowed but now impaled on my still hard cock she was unable to dismount. And so we remained until my old fella, which obviously had a mind of its own, decided to shrink away and slip out. While waiting for that to happen Mary picked up the pin she had placed on the centre console so that it would be in reach for this moment. She pulled her bolero a little closer to reveal her own membership pin.

"I now confirm Adonis to be a fully paid, upright member of the Mile-High-Club," she announced with gravity. "Very upright, I might add."

"Thank you ever so much Aphrodite. What wonderful presents you've given me," I managed to say.

"I must admit it's hard to know what to give a man who has everything," Mary now spoke in her customary honest way.

"Now I do have everything," I said.

"We have held six thousand, haven't we?" Mary said worried that her movements might have reset the trim and let our magic carpet drift down from the magic mile. "I wouldn't want to have to retest you, at least not right now," she smiled.

"No, we're safe," I said. "You didn't bump the transmit button, did you?" I now asked remembering that Mary had operated the sound system to play my music.

"No," Mary replied.

"That's good," I said. "Anyone listening on our frequency would have a laugh, wouldn't they?" It was now I realised that Mary was wearing her Mile-High-Club badge.

"I see that you are a member too," I remarked casually.

"Of course," Mary said. "I thought it strange that you missed it earlier," she added, "You're usually so observant of every little detail."

"Darling, I was totally immersed in you. I wasn't looking anywhere but in your eyes."

"How long ago? Or shouldn't I ask such personal questions," I asked.

"Remember when Bruce bought his first Pilatus?" Mary said. "It was about ten years ago. We took her up and christened her over the ocean between Sydney and Norfolk Island."

We laughed together and as my cock finally softened and slipped out, we clung together for a few more minutes before I helped Mary back onto her feet.

"You go first darling," I suggested, and Mary left the cockpit to clean up and dress.

WHAT A DIFFERENCE A DAY MADE came drifting from the cabin speaker and Mary turned and gave me a big parting kiss.

When she returned, I made a quick trip to the bathroom. Now back in our seats a picture of normality returned to the cockpit. During all our excitement and talks we had crossed the Gulf of Carpentaria, crossed Groote Island and were commencing the swing around Arnhem Land clear of Darwin's controlled airspace. We planned to be on the ground at Jack's mate's strip close to four o'clock local time. In our talking we had decided to take Jack's advice and take it slower. Forget the media and take a little time out for ourselves. We were already having a ball.

"Brad here Jack," I began. "We're fifteen minutes out from your mate's place."

"Have a good trip?" Jack asked.

"Really good Jack thanks again. We're not pushing on today and we might even stick around tomorrow and go into Darwin. We'll wait until we have a chat with our host first. I'll ring him as soon as we hang up."

"Great Brad, he will be expecting you about now."

"I'll give you a call in the morning Jack; thanks again for everything."

"Least I could do mate. Regards to Mary."

"Please tell Barbara her cookies were great," I finished the call.

Monday 19 November 2012 – 1700 hrs

My next call was to Jack's mate. I felt embarrassed now that I hadn't pressed Jack for his name and Jack had no worry about not providing it. To him, if he gave a fellow pilot a mate's coordinates then he knew that the pilot would be welcomed as an honoured guest. My education was moving ahead in leaps and bounds. In the meantime, Mary was having a long heart-to-heart with her mother and then with her father.

"Hello Jack's mate," I began. "Jack only gave me your coordinates and didn't tell me your name. I apologise for not pressing him for it. We're ten minutes out on descent to your strip."

"That's OK young Clifford, we know all about you and that's all that matters. The name is Robert, but everyone calls me Bob. That was just Jack's little joke, perverse bugger isn't he. How are you placed? Jack's call caught me on the hop a bit. I'm away from home and can't get out to pick you up until the morning. Is that OK?"

"Sure Bob, we're self-contained for a few days if necessary."

"Great mate, y'sound just like your old man. Hear you're on the run, hope you can stick around for a day or two, we appreciate good company. Seven in the morning be OK?" Bob rattled all of this off without giving me a chance.

"Seven's great thanks Bob see you in the morning," and I heard Bob click off.

I turned to find Mary who had also just rung off.

"You look a little bemused," Mary said.

"A little daunted perhaps, Bob, for that's Jack's mate's name, rattled off a great welcome, he obviously knew Bruce quite well, knows we're on the run, wants us to stick around for a couple of days but can't collect us until the morning. How did your call go?"

"Well," Mary started and paused to catch her breath, "they were delighted to hear from us and to know that all was well, and we have had no problems with the media. Some of the news reports, seeing that they haven't found us, are suggesting that we may have crashed and burned or gone down over the water. Thankfully, the authorities are saying no reports have been received, no alarms have been triggered from the well-equipped Pilatus and that we have done nothing to scare them into mounting a search effort. A possible search area from where we filled up in Cairns and the range of the Pilatus is so great that they couldn't muster enough aircraft to mount a reasonable search anyway. I told Mum that we won't be back until later next week as we plan to let the media cool down and hopefully forget about us. She thinks that they will still be keen, particularly as the pictures being splashed around are so good. She thought the close-up through the windscreen showing a couple of sharp professional pilots with bars on their shoulders was particularly good.

"I asked Mum to ring around our families: tell them that we are fine and just visiting some friends in Queensland at the moment. I didn't mention we were sitting on the ground in the Northern Territory and heading west in case she gave another honest answer to some reporter."

I realised that Mary's one call was far more pressured and rapid fire than my calls to two of Bruce's mates and followed her report in detail.

"I confirmed that the party was still on for Saturday-week and begged her not to say a word about the party and to ask the others to do likewise. I told her we loved them dearly, were quite safe and happy but wouldn't see them until we arrived at the party. I then spoke to Dad. He is going to call Flight Centre immediately. Tell them that we are safe, on the ground in Queensland visiting friends and ask them to leave us in peace so as not to alert the media any further. Tell them that the next time they will hear Bravo Mike Charlie is when we request clearance to enter Canberra airspace. Dad is going to clear our letterbox tomorrow and keep an eye on the house. That's about it darling," Mary concluded.

"Well, you've got everyone organised. I had better concentrate on putting us down safely on Bob's strip."

I managed a landing to match Mary's of last night and conceded hers was better as it was under the stress of escaping from Cairns and finding Jack's strip in failing light.

"We're dining out tonight, just the two of us, under the stars," I announced.

I set to work, erecting a three-sided tent from the camping gear, camp table and two chairs came out and a portable gas barbecue. I selected two nice prime filet steaks and a bottle of claret which had been chilling in the Esky. Mary appeared carrying plates, cutlery and wine glasses. She had selected another playlist and left the cabin and freight doors of the Pilatus open to let the cooler air into the cabin and for the music to waft over us.

After putting her plates down on the table, she took my hand and passed it around her back so that I must hold her and we held a passionate kiss. The last of her motherly kisses to me now seemed so long ago. With very few words spoken I cooked the steak while Mary prepared a salad. I poured the claret and as we ate we discussed our plans.

"Mary, while I was waiting for you to wake up this morning I considered when and how we can leave for my gap year. The earliest would be in three weeks. We can't go before my party and it will take at least a week to finalise our arrangements at home. As for the how, I want to take Bravo Mike Charlie. It will solve all our transport arrangements and provide us with accommodation anytime we choose to sleep on-board. However, Mary, I wasn't thinking about you. What about the Chair: wouldn't going now cost you the professorship?"

"If we don't go now, we may never go darling. Your goddesses will be found, and I'll lose you. I want you all to myself until then. I am the one being selfish Adonis, you have only to smile at a woman, young or old, and she will fall into your arms. The professorship is no longer important to me."

"Then there will be no regrets darling Aphrodite?"

"None whatsoever Adonis: I can't promise you that we will have a year together. One goddess has already been confirmed, another is being studied and your third goddess could be found at any time. Please let us spend every possible minute together until then."

"I've said I only wanted you in my life Aphrodite. Like your professorship, I am happy to pass up three goddesses and impregnating one hundred beautiful women a year. I only agreed to be Adonis to please you. Let's leave as soon as we can Aphrodite."

Mary rose from her chair, threw her arms around my neck and jumped into my lap. I could hold her light weight with ease, but the poor old camp chair gave up and we were left rolling on the warm grass, laughing, crying and utterly spent by the intense emotions we had just experienced. We lay there looking at the stars shining with the brightness never seen in the city. Only country lovers get to enjoy this vista. We held our kiss while we undressed and sunk onto the blanket.

"Aphrodite would have died of a broken heart if you went without her Adonis," Mary said once she had me safely held with her bare legs and feet.

Now that the decision to go had been taken and confirmed, I set my mind to designing the refit of Bravo Mike Charlie. I was going to make her into a magic carpet to convey Aphrodite into wonderland. Having been blessed with a photographic memory and instant recall of every event and emotion I had experienced since childhood I was able to work on my design anytime I was not engaged personally with anyone else. Every fact about Bravo Mike Charlie's dimensions, weight, balance, performance and even wiring circuits were imprinted on my mind and I could rearrange articles in the cabin with certainty knowing that I would not be breaching her Airworthiness Certificate.

When it was new, the Pilatus had come with an executive fit-out of seven big chairs and a large luggage bay that was accessible from inside the cabin. I decided to have the cabin stripped back to the all-cargo version of the Pilatus and start again. All that would be retained from the original was the flushing toilet. I had read a FLYING magazine article showing the modifications done by Pilatus for an oil sheik. My funds were nothing like those available to an oil sheik, but I didn't want gold plated taps for a start. It was to be a surprise on the grand scale, a gift from the man of the house to his esteemed lady.

The fit-out I designed had an auxiliary fuel tank to give us a minimum range of four thousand five hundred kilometres plus reserves. I knew where the extra tank and the cabling and pipes for its operation needed to be fitted. I placed a shower alongside the existing flushing toilet to simplify the plumbing and electrical installation. I positioned a four-place dining setting on the left side of the cabin. The table could be retracted into the sidewall and it would be a comfortable place to sit and talk. The innermost seating could be converted into a double bed with the seats moving forward and the backs folding down. This would appear to be my sleeping quarters when we slept on-board. Next, proceeding along the cabin were small, but adequate, workstations either side of the central aisle where Mary and I could work at out laptop computers or talk to friends, family or associates on the Pilatus's world-wide communications system. The workstations tended to divide the cabin and a privacy screen at this point separated Mary's boudoir. The divan was mounted against the left wall of the cabin and with a press of a button it extended to a comfortable double bed. Opposite the divan, the existing large cargo door will be hidden behind an array of cupboards that included a floor to ceiling wardrobe.

When Mary opens the door, it will display a full-length mirror to allow her to check her appearance when stepping out. Either side of the bed were bedside cabinets with reading lamps. We would be sleeping apart at times as we would be flying legs of up to eight hours between refuelling stops: sometimes in the daylight and sometimes at night. We will usually be flying as a crew of two: chatting our heads off like any pair of lovebirds but often one could have a sleep for several hours while the other flew alone. The wardrobe, cupboards and drawers would be adequate to hold not only Mary's casual wear but with Mary's position and reputation there were bound to be many occasions where formal dress was required. I was not going to require Mary to turn up looking anything less than her elegant best and clothes dragged out of travelling suitcases just would not do.

Our present arrangements for eating on-board were not very practical with only basic tucker available from the Esky and camp-style cooking done in the open air. Now I was going to take over the unnecessarily large luggage compartment and build in a mini international-airline kitchen. It would not be in the gourmet class, but we would be able to have good meals at any time we wanted to eat on board: in the air or on the ground. We would be able to restock the fridge, freezer and larder with food we personally selected and to cook it to our standards. I planned to take as few risks as possible of picking up any nasty gastric complaints.

Under the workbench, I found space to have a small washing machine for while it wouldn't do a big load, or need a lot of water, it would keep us in fresh shirts, tops and undies if we are away from a laundry for long periods. The remainder of the former luggage bay was going to be my masterpiece. Opening this door Mary will see a mini-lab. It will be small but with the careful arrangement of shelves and drawers I was able to include a sink, a centrifuge, a warming oven for growing cultures and a sophisticated microscope. With my upbringing, I was quite at ease ordering these things and the required accessories and necessaries needed to make the mini-lab not a novelty but a real working laboratory. It included a notebook computer networked of course with Mary's desk in the main cabin, but more importantly to the world. Mary could access any Internet site she might want to reference, contact any of her worldwide colleagues, access her own login at the ANU, have voice calls with any of her department's personnel, or hold teleconferences with many. She would be able to have a chat if she wished with the Vice-Chancellor to keep abreast of campus politics.

To complete the lab was a lab chair that pulled out from under the bench and was adjustable so that the user could adjust to the microscope's eyepiece. My final touch was going to be a new white lab coat hanging behind the door and swinging out when she pulled the door open. I was rightly proud of my design. I would be releasing Mary from any fear that she was being restricted by me: that I was trying to take her out of the world in which she had played a brilliant role to date for her to be my own selfish and private plaything. I didn't realise, that by putting these things at her disposal, I was drawing her more desperately to me.

Tuesday 20 November 2012 – 0700 hrs

We were sitting on the entry steps chatting when Bob drove up in his Landcruiser.

"Glad to meet you Mary, Brad," Bob said grasping one hand from each of us. "No need to lock her up if you want to get some air through her. There's no one around for miles."

He helped pull us up from our seats on the step and ushered us into his car.

"That's my bird over there," he pointed out a tarp-covered crop-duster parked near a substantial stock of 200 litre barrels of aviation fuel. I noticed the typical turboprop nose and blades and realised that she too was a Pilatus.

"Plenty of fuel folks; she drinks the same stuff as yours. Yours looks beaut, comes up well on the TV as well," he said. Mary was sitting in the back with me in the front with Bob. Bob gave Mary a little knowing wink in the rear vision mirror signifying he was well versed in our recent history.

"So sorry to hear about Bruce," Bob rattled on removing any need for us to talk about our unwanted publicity. "I thought it was all a mistake as I was driving up. You're the spitting image of your father Brad. He used to wait on the step like that when he called in, easy to recognise you too Mary from Bruce's description," Bob spoke it as he saw it.

"Thanks mate," I said, relieving Mary of any need to reply. I had dropped into the use of the Aussie 'mate' in the natural manner of two old friends even though we were meeting for the first time. Unless the men have unconsciously established an instant mental connection the word crashes to the ground sounding like a thunderclap in the ears of the party to whom it was addressed. There was no such fear here. There was an instant bond established as it had been with Jack; had there not been Jack would have given Bob's name to me and filled me in on Bob's nature, likes, dislikes and idiosyncrasies. He would not have sent Mary and me off with just the coordinates to his mate's place. Had he done so it would have been a shocking denial of his claim to be saddened by the loss of his mate Bruce. Having sent us off, and later receiving my call that we had landed at his mate's place, he knew that he had made the right call and that he and his other mates that we would meet in the next week would treat us in the same trusting country manner. “We'll soon be there,” Bob said. “Only another half-mile,” he added. Bob went on to explain that his strip was the remains of a Second World War airbase that was hastily thrown together, mainly by the Yanks, following the bombing of Darwin in February 1942. Japan's, ‘Day of Infamy’ at Pearl Harbour was just two months earlier. The Yanks rushed down here to save our bacon and start the fight-back. The space between the homestead and the strip in those days was filled with parking bays for the quickly growing fleet of fighters and bombers, and ground forces were rolling in to mount a counter-attack on Darwin if the Japanese fleet got ground forces ashore. Administration blocks and stores were quickly built and a tent city established. “As you no doubt know the Battle of the Coral Sea was the turning point in the Pacific where the Jap navy was first turned back. It must have been pretty hectic around here in those days,” Bob concluded.

“How long have you been here Bob?” Mary asked with growing interest in our host's history.”

“The folks moved back after the property was returned to them in '48. It had been in Dad's family for fifty years before the war,” Bob explained, “I was born here in '58.”

Mary thought Bob looked younger than his fifty-four years.

“The wife, Kay, was born in Darwin,” Bob continued. Mary smiled at the use of the ‘The’ as many people of his era whose families had been in the outback for many years often did.

“Met her when I went to high school in Darwin. I was home schooled for my primary years with the help of the Classroom of the Air and when I went to high school I was billeted by her parents. They were friends of my folks; didn't have any sons of their own and took me in as one of theirs. I was twelve and Kay was nine. She was the prettiest thing you ever saw, still is. Well I fell in love with her straight away. I'd walk her to her primary school, hand-in-hand, and go on to my high school. Pick her up again on the way home. We were inseparable.

"Of course I was called a cradle snatcher by the kids at school but that didn't matter, nobody else was going to get near my Kay. By the time Kay got to high school I was in the senior years and had an old '49 Ford. We drove to school and could usually manage a little kiss and cuddle on the way home. In those days cars only had bench seats in the front so she could sit right close to me. Naturally, I finished high school three years earlier than Kay, so I learned to fly Dad's old Piper Cub. I could fly over and see her anytime I could get away from the farm. Marvellous how quickly you can get a night rating when you need one desperately, even in a Piper Cub. Well, to cut a long story short, as they say, we rushed to the altar with our parents blessing as soon as I was old enough and Kay was big enough," Bob finished with a sly wink to me.

Bob's history had ended as we pulled up at the typical outback veranda steps. The woman who greeted us as we got out of the car was indeed everything Bob had claimed for her.

"There you see," Bob said proudly, "Did I lie?"

"Not a word Bob," I was the first to agree, as Mary received a big hug from the beautiful Kay.

"What's he on about Mary?" Kay asked.

"He was just telling us about the lovely little girl he used to walk to school, hand-in-hand."

"Oh he's always trying to embarrass me with that," Kay chided him. Mary and I noticed the slight pinking of her cheeks denying any pretence of annoyance and happy that her husband of thirty-five years was so proud of her.

Our breakfast was waiting for us on the kitchen table. The hot food and coffee had just been served as the car pulled up.

"Eat up before it goes cold," Kay spoke that common request. We did as she asked with little conversation until Kay rose to replenish our coffee.

"Long time since we've entertained celebrities Kay," Bob made the declaration now back to his best conversational form.

"Tell us about it Mary. You two young things are famous," Kay was delighted at having our company.

"We shouldn't be called celebrities," I protested.

"What, that orbit around the harbour in a PC-12 would draw anyone's attention. Particularly the way you had Queen Mary 2 under your wing," Bob said. "You weren't just showing off to impress this Mary were you mate?" he added.

Now it was my turn to show a little colour. We all laughed, and I was the loudest. I knew I'd been sprung.

"What's on the agenda for today Brad?" Kay asked, changing the conversation and silencing Bob's quips at the same time.

"We were supposed to go on to Broome yesterday but decided to call it a day; I suppose we'll make tracks soon after breakfast," I told her calmly, happy that Kay had saved me from stumbling into any dangerous territory. I knew now that Bob could read me with ease and mustn't let the slightest signal escape. Don't let my eyes dwell on Mary too long. Don't give her that 'Help me out here Mary look.' Tough it out no matter what Bob throws at me.

"Can't you stay a day longer?" Bob asked Mary. "My mate Jack said that you were extending your trip so that you won't get back to face the music in Canberra until Saturday-week. Seeing you've now missed visiting Darwin we could take a run in there in the 182 after breakfast. I've got a meeting with the accountant at noon. You three can do some shopping and we could have a quick bite and take-off for the sightseeing and get the travel pics you missed because Jack sent you here."

"Sounds great by me Bob," Mary quickly responded. "What do you say Brad?" she asked.

"I've always wanted to see Darwin," I replied.

"Come on Brad," Bob said, rising to his feet. "Well go and pre-flight the Cessna while the girls get ready."

"Right behind you Bob," I said as we headed for the door.

Tuesday 20 November 2012 – 1200 hrs

Bob's Cessna was housed in a small farm shed at one end of a very short backyard strip. I helped Bob roll her out.

"She's a C182R, Brad. The last model Cessna made before the insurance debacle nearly bankrupted Cessna, Piper and Beechcraft. I bought her new in 1982. She only had her flight-testing and ferry hours on the clock. I thought if a ferry pilot was prepared to fly her here from Wichita in the US she must be a pretty reliable ship. I haven't been disappointed. She's on her second engine now of course."

Bob's Cessna was in immaculate condition and had been refurbished inside and repainted outside only eighteen months earlier.

"I didn't get the electronic instrument panel. I don't want to change my way of flying from what I do in the crop duster," he added.

Mary and Kay joined us just as Bob finished his pre-flight inspection.

“Like to take the left seat, Captain?” Bob asked, just as we were about to board.

“No-way mate,” I was quick to answer. “I’d need some practice on this bird before I was game enough to lift her off this little strip,” I was quick to acknowledge that I didn’t possess the skill needed to do what Bob did frequently.

“We trust you implicitly,” I added for good measure.

Mary and I instantly recognised the situation. Bob had obviously spotted those gold bars on our shoulders in the Sydney Harbour windscreen photo. Had I taken up the implicit challenge I would have indeed shown myself to be a fool and Bob would have had to step in and say he was only joking: lest I continued and most likely killed all of us. Such were the unwritten, unspoken rules of this fraternity of men. Nothing more would have been said to or by any in the know. However, the heavens would have moved, and nothing would have been the same again. I would never have known what I had unwittingly lost.

We boarded the Cessna for the short hop into Darwin. Bob was at the left-hand door holding his seat-back forward so that Kay could climb into the rear seat and I was doing the same at the opposite side for Mary. Shielded by the cabin of the plane I managed to apply a little extra assistance to Mary with a gentle squeeze to her bottom as she reached for the step and a soft ‘I love you’ in her ear as she passed by.

Bob and I took the front seats. Bob fired up the engine, gave a quick all stations call for the benefit of any pilot in the vicinity and while holding the Cessna on the brakes eased the throttle fully home, building maximum revs for this critical take-off. He released the brakes and the little bird went flying down the short strip, with no line markers or anything else to guide him, and at the very end of the bitumen pulled the nose up steeply only to level out smoothly at fifty feet to regain power for his standard climb to two thousand for the trip into Darwin. Mary and I had each done a number of short-field take-offs and landings during our initial training and proficiency testing. However, none as smoothly and professionally as this, ours had been performed on city runways, this one was performed on a small strip of narrow bitumen with possibly dire consequences if a wheel had dropped over the side or we had failed to lift off before using up the meagre bit of bitumen available.

"Nice one Bob," I was quick to say as we reached the easy part of the climb.

I was now looking forward to seeing how he'd handle the more difficult task of bringing the little bird back to its nest when we returned home. 'Let's hope there's no crosswind,' I thought.

During the flight, Bob delivered his plans for the rest of the day and the evening. He suggested that after his meeting with the accountant we take a taxi directly to the airport, have a quick snack at the Pilots' Club and then take off for an hour's cruise of the area to gather our pics. Next, we would head home stopping by the Pilatus on the way to refuel her ready for our early departure tomorrow: 'First light if you like?' Bob added. Tonight a few of his special mates and their wives were coming for a barbie on the veranda and then a good old-fashioned sing-along around the old 'Goanna'. They all loved that. Not many people of course: Bruce had met them all and they would never forgive him if he let us go without meeting them. We must be home well before last light because I wouldn't subject you to a night landing on that strip."

"That sounds lovely Bob," Mary was quick to confirm Bob's arrangements. "All of Bruce's friends have been marvellous to us and if there are more in the offing, I would love to meet them."

"Great," Kay added her support.

"Let's make that unanimous," I said.

"Good, after I leave the accountants, I'll do a quick ring around and issue the invites. I won't tell them too much in case anyone let's slip your cover. Wouldn't want the flash lights popping out-there would we?"

"Surely, they're not still that keen, are they?" Mary asked.

"Don't bet on it," Bob replied. His answer didn't suggest that we were out of this yet.

Everything ran to plan. After the long taxi down Darwin's runway and equally long taxiway to the GA parking area we tied-down and headed for the Pilots' Club. As soon as we entered the door, we faced directly the Club's notice board and saw that picture of Bravo Mike Charlie and QM2, together with the close-up of the pilots with their gold bars and Ray-Bans. The club was even running a competition on Bravo Mike Charlie. Blazoned above the photos the sign read, 'Where's Bravo Mike Charlie?'

Below the photo, another announced 'A Slab of the beer of your choice for the first pilot who spots her. Entry ONE DOLLAR'.

"Walk confidently to that table over there without looking at anyone," Bob said as he placed his hand on my shoulder and Kay slipped her hand under Mary's arm at the elbow. We moved casually as a four-person group of pals. We pulled out our chairs and sat. Mary and I were looking out with our backs to the bar with Bob and Kay taking the chairs facing the customers in the bar or eating at the tables.

“Now we’ll have a little chat as if deciding what we want to eat and drink,” Bob began. “I’ll then go to the counter and order.”

Beer, beer, beer the three of us said.

“I’ll get a soft drink for me as the pilot and they will just think of you as joyriders. “I’ll get some pre-packaged sandwiches so that nothing has to be delivered to us and pay. We can eat our sandwiches, quench our thirst then casually slip away.”

Kay reached over to pat the back of Mary’s hand, “We’ll make it up to you tonight dear. Our barbies and sing-alongs are good fun. Best save your appetite until then.”

After making our escape we left Bob at the accountants. I moved between the two ladies and in the manner of years gone by, but remembered by Kay, offered each an arm that they took with a hand grasping me above the elbow and they both gave me a big smile. Each time we passed a newsagency we saw those pictures that were fast gaining icon status. Newspaper headlines asked, ‘Where’s Bravo Mike Charlie?’

Magazines were beginning to appear with photos of Mary and or Bruce on their covers and sensation seeking headlines. Mary recognised some of these as having appeared in Uni publications in other far less newsworthy content and others from my high school yearbooks and some from my underage sporting successes. We were waiting patiently for Bob at the accountant’s office well within the hour. As soon as he appeared, we hailed a cab and went directly to the airport. We left everything to Bob, climbed aboard, and relaxed in our seats. Bob entered, got his clearances and we heard him call ‘Clear Prop’ and taxi out.

“Let’s skip the sightseeing Bob,” I began. “OK with that Mary?”

“Sure, let’s get out of here,” Mary agreed. “No more cities for us on this trip.”

I had slipped into saying ‘Mary’ instead of ‘Mum’ but nobody had noticed. Conversation was relaxed but simple on our return flight. We landed on Bob’s main strip and taxied up to where Bravo Mike Charlie was parked. Bob went to the fuel stock and I taxied Bravo Mike Charlie over to be filled. While Bob and I did the refuelling Mary showed Kay over the cabin. When Mary entered the cockpit, she spotted the two Mile-High-Club badges resting in the console where we had left them after landing. To reach for them now would only draw Kay’s attention to them so Mary tried to keep herself positioned between Kay and the badges. Kay too might well have been a member and probably was. This club however was not one that you bragged about your membership. It didn’t hold annual meetings; it didn’t have a newsletter or even a mailing list. Participants just enjoyed the special moment as Mary and I had done only yesterday. Good clean fun really Mary thought. Her scientific mind suddenly flipped to, ‘Why do the wowsers brand loving sex as unclean?’

She was happy to put that question aside for another day and continued showing Kay the plane’s features. They relaxed in two of the armchairs until Bob and I joined them.

“It’s a bit more comfy than the Cessna, Kay,” Bob said.

“But you couldn’t put this one down in the backyard Bob,” Kay replied.

“Not even with a fifty-knot headwind Kay,” Bob agreed.

“Come on Bob,” I began, “Show us how it’s done mate. We’re eager students.”

The 182, although a very stable craft, was much lighter and therefore more susceptible to any sudden shifts in wind direction and/or speed than the Pilatus. After Bob lined up his approach with her nose to the non-existent centreline of this, from this height, miniscule runway and with a slight crab to offset the dying crosswind approached down final with full flaps and nose high, barely below the stall. Correcting his crab, he placed her main wheels onto the ground on the identical patch of tarmac that he had used to launch her into the air earlier in the day. He had fully closed the power a few feet off the ground and she touched down with the stall warning screaming. With nose still high he applied gentle brake pressure until the nose settled and he was able to apply full brakes and bring her to a halt at the same spot she had occupied at the start. He could have spun her around and done it all again. I looked at Bob and when Bob turned to me his face was calm and showed no stress or strain. My mouth was open and dry.

“Nice one mate,” I managed to say. Bob knew that he had delivered on my request for a master-class in short field landings and I had learned from the experience. Not only for techniques that I might use in the future but also in my own judgement to refuse the offer for me to show off in front of the ladies earlier in the day. Bob had now confirmed to himself that my flawless orbit of Sydney Harbour was not a show-off, or bravado in flying an aircraft that could be judged by some to be above my capabilities, but the proper performance of a procedure published for all pilots wishing to simply do what I simply did. Everyone was happy.

Bob and I pushed the Cessna back into her hangar and joined the ladies in the house. The girls were busy preparing food and setting up to receive their guests. As Bob and I could contribute little we went out onto the veranda and after getting two beers from the bar fridge settled into comfortable chairs and talked of many things as good friends do.

"One of the chaps coming tonight drives right past the airstrip on his way home so when you're ready to go he will take you back. I've got to head off early in the other direction in the Cessna tomorrow, so we'll say our goodbyes tonight."

"I'd better give Jack a report," I said, pulling out my phone.

"Not bad reception from here actually," Bob told me. "Use the land line if you have any problem. Tell him I'm handing you over to Bill tomorrow. I've already told Bill you'll be leaving in the morning and that I will give him an ETA when you are airborne. Just call my bird with the message, 'The bird flew at oh six hundred,' for instance, and an ETA for Bill."

Tuesday 20 November 2012 – 1700 hrs

"I suppose you'll be going to Uni next year?" Bob asked when I finished my talk with Jack.

"I had planned with Dad to take a gap year and visit the Clifford Engineering companies overseas," I replied.

"I was talking with Bruce a week before he died; he told me how you had topped every subject you took. He was very proud of you Brad. I think he was hoping you would do engineering and go into the business with him," Bob said.

"I know, Bob, but over the last three years I've done maths, physics, chemistry, biology, economics, history, literature and done a lot of other reading on the side. My marks mean that I can enter a number of great universities and choose any faculty on the campus."

"Spoilt for choice Brad, that's a problem most people would love to have," Bob added.

"I don't want to waste my time going down the wrong path for a year or two, so a gap year might help me find a path where I can make a worthwhile contribution: not just pass exams and become a teacher. Dad made many worthwhile contributions in engineering and I know Mum is doing so in her field; I don't want to just follow along behind though."

"Do you feel a calling to any of the professions Brad: law, medicine, aviation, accounting, the church?" Bob asked.

"Not one, Bob; I love flying but I wouldn't even want to be flying for Qantas. The only topic that gets my attention is economics and that's for the opposite reason: I'm sure they've got it all wrong."

"In what way, Brad?"

"The present economic systems around the world are stuck in the Boom-and-Bust cycle that has persisted for two-thousand-years, and it's only getting worse.

"For a start, everything is measured by how much greater this year's profit is over last years. Shareholders want to see an increase in their dividends and see the stock market valuation of their shares increase. Directors want to see greater fees. Management want increased salaries, bonuses and commissions. Lower levels of the workforce want more pay and better conditions. Governments too are looking for increased tax revenues from businesses and their workers and don't hesitate to spend public money to lure successful businesses to their area. The only mantra of the board room is 'Maximize Profits'. Everyone believes that if you don't make more money next year you are going backwards, and bigger is always better."

"But isn't that the way it's supposed to be?"

"Everyone believes so Bob, but no. Life has become a feeding frenzy for everyone, and if you can't increase your income or reduce your expenses you quickly fall backwards: as you borrow more or sell up your assets. The incessant inflation that our system produces quickly generates a downturn which is then followed by a slump or depression. No matter what names they are given and no matter what schools of economic thought have propounded over the centuries, we haven't broken free of the cycle. It's a bit like trying to do a vertical climb in a Cessna. Gravity soon pulls you back to earth and that goes for orbiting satellites too unless they are shot free of the earth's gravity.

"Sadly, even our top companies and banks get involved in shady practices that some might consider were criminal."

"Joan and Frank Adams can tell you about that Brad. Their mortgage was with Landmark and now that the ANZ Bank has bought Landmark's loans ledger they want them to enter a new contract on far worse terms than the one they had. They'll be here tonight. I'm sure they would be happy to tell you about it." Bob replied.

"Then you'll be going into politics Brad. Have you settled on a Party?"

"No Bob. I don't believe the present forms of government will solve this problem. It is going to take a radically new approach and even to write about it too soon or push new ideas and concepts on social media: seeking followers and supporters, would be counter-productive."

"Can you do anything about it Brad, alone?"

"I believe I can. It will take a while as there is quite bit of research to do. *Bucky* believed that we should all be living as multi-billionaires, so I will be following up this line of thinking when I get to the USA."

"Who, or what is Bucky, Brad?" Bob asked.

"It's R Buckminster Fuller: ***Bucky* *http://www.futuristic.guru/copy-of-one-aldwych*** to his friends. He was one of the greatest minds of the twentieth century.
https://en.wikipedia.org/wiki/Buckminster_Fuller
https://www.bfi.org/

"I'm sure you'll get it right Brad. With your genes, you'll make a worthwhile contribution whatever you decide to do. Can you leave Mary so soon Brad?"

"Fortunately, Mum wants to take a year's sabbatical and come too. She'll take it up with the Vice-Chancellor as soon as we return to Canberra."

"I can understand her wanting to get away from Canberra for a while," Bob replied.

Tuesday 20 November 2012 – 1800 hrs

"Here are the first guests Kay," Bob called from the veranda as the first of the Landcruisers and Utes came up the kilometre-long entry drive.

A few of Bruce's mates turned into forty. The food and drinks rolled out as some of the new arrivals joined in the preparation. The barbie was lit for steaks and a porker was turning on a spit roast. There would obviously be plenty for all and a bit more in case somebody else just happened to drop by. Conversation was bright and breezy as similar comments, admirations and questions that we faced already on our trip were repeated. Everybody had seen the photos and the speculations. We accepted the commiserations of Bruce's friends, answered questions and remained quietly composed. When passing a group unseen, I would hear 'Isn't he like Bruce,' or, 'A chip off the old block,' or, 'How sad,' or, 'Isn't she beautiful,' or, 'She won't be left on the shelf long'. There was no animosity, only admiration. The guests felt privileged to have been invited and accepted into our trust and confidence. The media would have paid for this privilege. When most had completed their meal, it wasn't long before the tables were pushed back against the wall. The remains of the meal were assembled and covered with fine white mesh to keep flying insects off but left on the table in case anyone happened to feel peckish during the evening. Nobody was pressed to drink; guests simply helped themselves to whatever they fancied from the fridge, the bar or Eskys that some guests had brought with them. Nobody ever over-consumed at these events for all but the hosts had to face drives of forty or more kilometres to get home and all had demanding daytime occupations.

We sung with gusto once Kay sat at the piano and started playing one old song after another from the bundle of sheet music, she had loaded on the music holder. She rarely followed the music for she knew them so well. The music was mainly for the benefit of those who crowded around Kay, reading the words under the notes as she played. Someone nearby would turn the pages at the right time to save Kay the bother. Sometimes, someone would select a tune from down the stack and as one tune finished put it on the music stand and say, "Play this one please Kay?" One could be excused for thinking most of us were well under the influence of drink by the way we laughed and carried on. If something like KNEES UP MOTHER BROWN rose to the top of the stack you could be sure that several would be taking high steps around the central coffee table. They would link arms at the other end of the room to execute a turn, singing with all their might. At the end of the song someone would call, 'One more time,' and Kay would dutifully oblige. When Kay tired and went out onto the veranda for a breath of fresh air there was always someone to take her place.

Mary and I realised that when these people were growing up in the outback the piano, pianola, 78 rpm gramophone and the Saturday night country dances were the main sources of entertainment. Everybody loved it. After some time at the piano Mary and I joined the larger group gathering on the wide veranda to dance. The random playing of tunes meant that dancers would have to change to different steps at a moment's notice, but no one cared. Nobody asked that all the waltzes be gathered together or all the quicksteps: we were even quite adept at forming a ring for a progressive barn dance and even hokey-pokey produced lots of laughter. The fairy lights festooning the veranda produced a soft rainbow of colours. The evening was cooling to a mild twenty-two degrees and the humidity had fallen to manageable levels. The men had long shed the sports coats or jackets that they had arrived in and the ladies mostly wore bright prints with straps for bare shoulders and arms. Their dress, both men and women, had tones more representative of the 80s and 90s than this bold new century. Mary and I were now becoming less of a curiosity as people realised that we had been caught up in a situation not of our own making and had done a runner to the nearest friend who was most happy to help us. As the music slowed for a foxtrot, I found the courage to take Mary in my arms and move out onto the floor. We tried desperately to restrain our emotions and the sensuality of our nearness. We hadn't been this close since Bob collected us at seven in the morning, other than for the little squeeze I had applied to Mary's bottom as I helped her board the Cessna. The night was coming to a close and it was nearing the time when our designated driver was to take us back to the Pilatus. Suddenly the other singers faded away as we heard Bob start singing the song that all who knew him had heard him sing before. In a voice so tender and moving, nothing like the voice and idiom he used in his run of the mill conversation, came the words:

What a difference a day made, twenty-four little hours
Brought the sun and the flowers where there used to be rain
My yesterday was blue dear
Today I'm a part of you dear

My lonely nights are through dear
Since you said you were mine
Oh, what a difference a day made

As the first strains floated across the veranda, I felt Mary go weak at the knees and would have fallen had I not immediately changed my more chaste dancing hold to a full-body hug. Although anyone seeing us would think that we were still dancing, I carried, rather than danced, Mary to the darker end of the veranda.

Alone in the dark I held her until I heard her say, "I'm OK now darling, I think we had better start saying our goodbyes before I spoil it for us."

We quietly danced back into the dimmed fairy-lights and sought out Kay to thank her for our wonderful day and to be able to meet their friends. I had very few adult friends, outside of family, as friends of my childhood were now fading away. Tonight, I had received a score of new friends to add to Jack, Barbara, Bob and Kay. I knew that by the time I got home again I would have a score or two more new friends, mates of the real kind. Despite the stress of the last few minutes I was elated. Kay wheeled us over to Bob and we expressed our thanks again. To save us tracking around all the guests Bob did the spoon on the nearest glass trick to capture their attention and everybody turned to him and did what was expected of the them: shut up for a moment.

"Mary and Brad must leave us folks," Bob began, "They're off at first light so had better call it a day. I'm sure I'm speaking for all of you when I say thank you so very much for calling and trusting yourselves to us. Do come back again and safe skies for the rest of your trip. Oh, and by the way I hope my singing isn't driving you away."

The guests all clapped and cheered. I had remained standing with Mary alongside Bob and Kay and had kept my arm around her as you often see dancers do as they wait for the next song to start or the record to be turned on the gramophone. Nobody thought it strange and I continued to support her.

"Thank you, Bob," I began. "We could listen to you all night mate: never thought you could have a voice like that in you. And thank you all again from Mary and me. We have loved your company and love to sing and laugh. Kay told us at lunchtime the sing-alongs were great nights and now we can vouch for that. The city slickers have lost so much good fun."

We shook hands as we left Bob and kissed Kay and continued through the guests. Shaking hands, receiving kisses and getting pats on the back.

"Good luck mate, keep it up mate," and remarks like that took us to the veranda steps where Joan and Frank Adams were waiting to take us back to the Pilatus. The music faded as we drove down the drive, but Bob's voice came through faintly as he broke into another love song. I was sitting close to Mary in the dark of the back seat and holding her hand. I realised that my silence could be misconstrued, and Mary had hardly spoken a word since the song began. I started up a lively conversation with our hosts. It was revealed, like so many others in the Territory, that they were both well experienced pilots and willing to hear all about the Pilatus's specs and performance and would love to see its fit-out before driving off.

"We've got her photo on the wall at home of course," Frank said," nodding at Bravo Mike Charlie.

"I didn't like to mention it at the party Frank, but Bob said you were having trouble with the ANZ Bank over your mortgage with Landmark?" I asked.

"Are you interested in that sort of thing Brad?" Frank queried me.

"I studied the Wheat Board Scandal in Political Economics last year and got interested in the flow-on of the sale of Landmark's loan book to ANZ." I replied.

"Yes Brad, Joan and I have had a mortgage with Landmark for twenty-years. There are thousands of farmers who are being pressured to sign up to ANZ's new contracts that devalue our properties, demand we reduce our mortgage by thousands of dollars and have higher yearly repayments. Some farmers have already been forced-off their land. **.ANZ - Landmark AWB sells Landmark loans business to ANZ (SMH)** https://www.smh.com.au/business/awb-sells-landmark-loans-business-to-anz-20091208-kgak.html

"Everywhere you go in the outback Brad, somebody is being screwed by the money people. If it's not the banks, it's the Insurance companies and superannuation funds. Everything we need is dearer because of freight but we've grown up with that, along with the floods and droughts."

"And the isolation," Joan added.

"But this AWB and the ANZ Bank thing is a different matter: it's immoral.

"I think we will find it is criminal, Frank," I said. "It is going to change, but it will take some time yet. I thought the Global Financial Crisis was going to be the big one to finally collapse the boom-and bust-economy for the last time, but the big-money governments, and families, bailed out the banks. The banks and major companies that survived are doing everything they can now to make big profits to quickly write off their exposure to GFC's, so called, securities. We can look forward to a few years of corporate and stock-exchange growth, high taxes and a shrinking standard of living for the work-force before the big-one hits.

“I hope we can hang on Brad. But what happens then if it is anything like the Great Depression?” Frank asked.

“No, the next one will be the last. Our present systems of government can no longer support a boom-and-bust economy. We can only hope that the new economy can be got in place before the final collapse. It must be a soft-landing Frank. No wars, no bloodshed.”

“Would you like to see Bravo Mike Charlie from the inside?” Mary asked.

After Joan and Frank inspected the executive layout and sampled the comfortable seats, they were at last on their way. Mary now turned to me and we wrapped our arms around each other. She couldn’t help letting go with several long deep sobs while I held her to me in silence. Not speaking or expecting her to speak to me as the stresses of the day came out and rolled away. We had had a most enjoyable day. However, to see our photos on cheap magazines and seeing our baby being made a game of for a slab of beer didn’t sit well with either of us. Being with such nice people and having to guard one’s words and actions felt just a little demeaning, and to be so nearly brought undone by a love song sung by a man we had only met that day was alarming. But why that love song, with its strong connection to Bruce, and its performance coming upon us so unexpectedly. Was it Bruce with us now, protecting us as he passed us around his mates: gaining their support and that mystical force to help us on our way.

“Get the bed down please Adonis,” she pleaded as she quickly stripped.

I responded immediately, pulling down the divan and tossing aside the few things that were on it. Off went my clothes: shirt, trousers, shoes, socks and those accursed restraining jocks and then I took her down onto the bed with me. I let Mary set the pace, having not seen this urgency in her before. I didn't want to do anything which she did not require at this moment. I felt my cock straighten and stiffen between her thighs.

"Fuck me Adonis, Fuck me, Fuck me, Please, Please, Please," she gasped as she quickly gathered in my swollen head and shaft.

Finally, our pounding and panting subsided. Mary was now lying fully on top of me, impaled as she was in the sky above the Gulf of Carpentaria; and only now realising that in our ardour we hadn't closed the large cargo door or turned a light on but lay naked in the gentle breeze coming through the door. I could see the moonlight gently bathing Mary's sensuous back and her very cute backside.

"I love you Aphrodite, let's get out of Australia just as soon as we can. Let's give the media a year to forget us. A week is obviously not enough."

"I'd really love that Adonis," Mary said as we realised that we were starting to drift into sleep. I gently moved Mary into a sleeping position. I pulled a rug over us and gave up any idea of a first light getaway.

"Any time tomorrow is fine by me as long as Aphrodite is in the other seat," I said softly and felt Mary's gentle squeeze to my hand.

We made no effort to rush away. We woke when the sun came onto our bed to our mutual greetings of 'Hello lover'. Although I woke with a regular hard-on and we were still naked from last night's passion we were content with Mary lying in my right arm as I gently kissed her and stroked her hair. It was a winding-down from last night and foreplay for what we knew must eventuate before we slept again. Mary felt relieved and exhilarated. We took time for a good breakfast, listened to the latest news, got the winds, pressures and forecasts from the aviation website and while Mary dressed and attended to her appearance, I readied Bravo Mike Charlie for the skies. I returned to the cabin to see Mary looking more poised, confident, and glamorous. With her shoulders back and head a little higher, those two soft mounds were higher too; she looked more beautiful than ever.

Wednesday 21 November 2012

"Let's go Captain," Mary smiled at me.

"Your chair ma'am," I replied recalling that I had landed here when we arrived.

Mary eagerly slid into the left seat and began running the checklist with me. After that she did a rolling turn into the wind and smoothly upped the power. I assisted to the extent of calling 'V1 - Rotate' and then keyed the mike to make my cryptic call to Bob.

"Got that folks, have fun," Bob's usual rustic voice came through.

"Was I dreaming his beautiful tenor voice from last night, Brad?"

"No darling, he really can sing," I replied.

It was only a two-hour leg to Bill's and Mary flew all the way. I made coffee and it wasn't long before Mary made a call to Bill's discrete radio telling him of our approach. She flew a standard circuit, turned into the wind and gently eased Bravo Mike Charlie back to earth. We could see the dust from Bill's Ute well before we made out the vehicle. Now with the three of us sitting in the front seat it was permissible for me to have my right arm around Mary's shoulders, ostensibly to steady us and to stop Mary from bumping the driver as we swung around bends on the dirt road.

"How're you going mate, Mary," had been Bill's first words indicating the existence of an already established mateship though we were meeting for the first time. We moved into days of gathering more mates, great experiences and camaraderie. We didn't bother visiting any more towns and were content to be passed from one welcoming bush strip to the next. For the rest of our trip we continued to camp out although there were offers for us to sleep in some of the homesteads we visited.

Friday 23 November 2012 - 0900

I had managed to find time during my flight planning at my notebook to commit the mental picture of my design onto a template of Bravo Mike Charlie's floorplan and 3D structure. This morning I completed my design and list of requirements and sent them to Greg Howard, my LAME in Canberra. I also printed a bill of materials of all equipment and fittings needed for the conversion. Everything new was already aircraft approved and available from Pilatus's Australian agent. I placed my order with them advising that our LAME will collect everything on Tuesday 27 November. I asked for a costing ASAP so that I can pay beforehand. The microscope and lab equipment I ordered from a laboratory supply company and paid for them on line. I arranged for them to be delivered on Friday 7 December. By this time the cabinet work will be complete, and I will install the delicate and expensive equipment for Mary's lab myself. I did another template for the cabinetmaker giving all the measurements and specifying the panelling and finishes that I required. I told him to be in touch with the LAME as he was in total charge of the project and to work with him before any of the new work was covered. I also told him that all work must be finished by three o'clock on Friday 7 December. I sent him a $20,000 deposit and asked that his account be made up for me to settle the balance on the seventh. I attached a copy of what I had sent the cabinet maker to the LAME and told him that we will arrive home before midday on Wednesday 28 November and after we leave the hangar his team can move in and commence work. I asked him to liaise with CASA to verify my design and choice of fittings were approved and that I had done nothing outside Bravo Mike Charlie's airworthiness approval. In addition to the new work in the cabin I asked for a thorough inspection of BMC's power plant, control services and hull and to have his avionics expert test all of Bravo Mike Charlie's extensive electronic and communications systems. I let him know that we were planning to commence an overseas trip of a year on Sunday 9 December. Finally, I stressed that privacy was of the utmost importance and no cameras or phones with cameras were to be taken into BMC's hangar. I asked him to use whatever labour he required in order to make our deadline. I transferred a deposit of $50,000 to his account and asked him to have his account ready for me to pay the balance on 7 December. Finally, I said that I would call on the morning of Thursday 29 November to confirm our arrangements in person. When I pressed the SEND button, I felt a warm glow of satisfaction. I could relax now knowing that I had given the LAME five days' notice for him to organise his team and plan his work to have BMC's refit completed on time. Now I could simply enjoy myself with Mary and our new fiends.

Mary had kept in touch with her mother and father, they had kept the rest of the Grands, and Greats informed. Everything on the home front was under control and all were looking forward to my party night and welcoming us home. Her father told me he had spoken with Flight Service and they were going to make our arrival as smooth as possible. We revelled in the freedom of these days and forgot about media, celebrities, school, Uni, studies, research, professorships and the future. We gave our scientific minds a holiday and relaxed into new knowledge that can only be gained by living it. There was no better place in the world to absorb this knowledge than in the Australian Outback. If you are a mate, that is.

Wednesday 28 November 2012 – 0530 hrs

I woke with a start. Mary was sleeping soundly: her head was resting on my shoulder with my right arm wrapped around her, a position she often chose for sleeping. She looked so peaceful and calm. But I wasn't! Often, I'd roll a little more towards her and my left hand would come up to her right breast. She would open her eyes and give me her welcoming smile and say, 'Good Morning lover'. Then, I would feel her right leg moving up my left thigh. We'd join in our first kiss for the day as my old-fella sprung to attention. But not today!

"Roll over darling," I whispered gently, and began to ease my right arm from around her and adjust the pillow under her head.

Mary gave a little sigh and rolled onto her right side. In a few moments she was sleeping soundly again. I gathered my jeans, joggers and jumper and went outside to dress.

After my talk with Frank Adams it seemed everyone we visited, or their friends and families, had bad experiences with the finance industry.

I knew it was the plight of some of our new friends, their neighbours, friends or families, why I had woken so suddenly. I had known about the Landmark – ANZ Bank deal and studied the Wheat Board scandal, but that was in the classroom. Now, I had seen the effect of those peoples' actions on the faces of the people I had been visiting. They were hurting, if not for themselves then for those around them. There had been family breakups, divorces, depressions and even suicides; many long-term farming families had been forced off their land and left for a life on welfare in the cities.

I set out at a fast walk along Airport Road as other thoughts pressed in for my attention. Newspaper articles, TV news and current affairs programs that I had seen or heard, that had made little impression then, now came flooding back to me as I realised these stories were like what I had been seeing. I quickly realised that the Landmark – ANZ deal was not an isolated case. Company directors, government members, bishops and bureaucrats were being interviewed over the performance of their organization. In most cases *'grilled'* would have been more appropriate than interviewed as the person in the hot-seat tried to justify theirs or their organization's decisions or actions. At the mercy of a skilled interviewer the 'guest' would become very ill-at-ease and possibly make some damaging admissions.

I broke into a jog as I felt the anger rising in me against big business and their methods. As I ran, I realised that there were plenty of small businesses too who used dubious methods to screw the last dollar out of their customers or talk them into buying things they don't really want and certainly didn't need. Was our business doing the same, I asked myself. Am I being *'holier than thou.'* My business: seeing that I am ultimately responsible having inherited Bruce's controlling shares. My jog became a trot as I examined my memory. For the past three-years Bruce had taken me into his full confidence regarding Clifford Holding's and all their subsidiaries and investment activities. Nothing came to mind that could be considered at all questionable. Bruce had been preparing me, from an early age, to go into the family business. I had devoured all the financial reports and studied the business from its formation, by my great-grandfather Clifford, down to the present. Starting with very little Pop Clifford was forced to be frugal. He remained debt free and reinvested as much as possible each year into the business. My father and grandfather followed his example. My stride lengthened. Was I letting Bruce and the family down by not going into the family business immediately and enrolling in an engineering degree at the ANU. My talk with Bob, before the party at his place eight nights ago, came to mind. I couldn't tell him what career I had chosen as I didn't know. I had claimed then that the *'boom-and bust'* economies around the world must soon reach a point of ultimate failure. I told Bob that *Bucky* had claimed that it would only take a new accounting for all people to be living as multi-billionaires and I wanted to spend some time to understand what he meant.

"I know Bruce was keen for you to go into the business with him, Brad," Bob had said.

I told Bob I understood. However, Bruce had been a strong supporter and admirer of *Bucky's* work in engineering and design, particularly his work in Synergistics, tensegrity and ephermeralization. Bruce had always been impressed with *Bucky's* work ethic and his life being devoted to doing what was best for all mankind. He would understand me wanting to bring about *Bucky's* new accounting as I would be doing so with the same motive — for the good of all mankind.

I'd had a sudden flash of inspiration. The banks' own greed was going to bring them down and trigger the final collapse of the banking system, not only in Australia but world-wide. Their own little book of small type known as their Product Disclosure Statement (PDS) will condemn them when their clients want the billions of dollars, the banking system has taken from their accounts returned.

I was running now, not a 4-minute mile pace, but a comfortable marathon rate. I was surprised that I had travelled 4 kilometres along Airport Road since I left Aphrodite sleeping. I stopped at the 4 K marker and did some breathing and stretching exercises to prepare for the run back to Aphrodite. Suddenly, what Aphrodite had planned for me became clear. It too was for the good of all mankind; at the same time, I'll be passing on the inheritance of the Clifford/Franklin line and all those who had gone before.

The thought of Aphrodite quickened my pace. I made it back in fifteen minutes. Aphrodite was still sleeping so I collected my clean clothes and went out to the bush shower I had rigged to shave and shower. I won't be able to do this on the international airports I will be visiting, I thought.

"Move over darling," I heard Mary say.

"I'll get you some warm water; I didn't think I woke you," I said.

"Cold is fine darling; I woke up hot. It's going to be a very hot day this side of the mountain," Mary replied. "I left the bed down and unmade in case you would like to start this last day of our journey with a bang?"

We finished our shower, dried ourselves briskly, and hurried back into Bravo Mike Charlie. I shut the door behind me and decided to risk leaving the cabin air-conditioning on trusting that there will be enough power in the batteries to get us started.

We went down onto the bed together and were immediately at the ready.

"Why so early darling?" Mary asked.

"Thoughts of the plight of some of our friends woke me. I went for a run to see if I could understand what is happening in the world and what, if anything, I could do about it," I answered.

"Did you find any answers to your problem?" Mary asked.

"Yes, Aphrodite darling," I said. "There will be plenty of time to talk about these things when we make our escape."

"Then *bang-me*, darling Adonis and then let's go. home.

I felt strong and refreshed after my run and shower and now the blood pulsed strongly in my veins. I was looking forward to getting home too so we could make our plans and do the many things that must be done before we could leave Australia for twelve months.

Chapter 3

Arriving Home

Wednesday 28 November 2012 – 1100 hrs

It was mid-morning as had been suggested by Flight Service and as our call-sign was now well publicised I made sure that I had the left seat for this arrival.

I couldn't let Mary take the blame for anything that might happen. I knew that this landing had to be what is known in the trade as a 'greaser'; there would be more than one set of binoculars in the tower and elsewhere watching my performance and many more people could be listening on the tower frequency.

"Canberra Tower this is Bravo Mike Charlie request clearance for runway zero six with Oscar," I said following standard procedures.

"Bravo Mike Charlie Good Morning make direct approach for zero six."

"Bravo Mike Charlie," I acknowledged.

I had my approach established early on a long final. The altimeter was unwinding smoothly as we descended through five hundred feet.

"Bravo Mike Charlie Clear to Land, take intersection Alpha cleared to taxi direct to hangar limit 5 minutes."

"Bravo Mike Charlie clear to land and taxi 5 minutes," I thought would be my best acknowledgment of this unusual clearance. Not only did it give me landing rights but also included the taxi clearance usually provided to the pilot by the Canberra Ground operator after the pilot had departed the runway by whatever intersection the pilot managed to take. I was to have right-of-way over all other aircraft. Effectively, Canberra Tower had just given me ownership of the airport for five minutes. Knowing that I had been extended a very rare privilege I was the more determined not to let the side down. Not just for myself: but for Mary, Bruce, the Grands, the Greats, my newly found mates in the bush, the extended family that I must face with Mary on Saturday night, all those who had followed my orbit of Sydney Harbour and were waiting to learn where we had been, even past school friends. If I make an idiot of myself in these next five minutes all our grand plans will go out the window I knew I was on 'a hiding to nothing' my mates would say; perform a perfect procedure and only those few people who are in the know would understand and appreciate the situation. Now the flip side: if I stuff this up in any way all hell will break loose. The media would have a field day. Pub talk would include 'Cocky young bugger, brings 'em all down in the end, don't it!', and of course it would go viral on YouTube.

I forced these rapid-fire thoughts from my mind by commanding myself to concentrate. Passing short final every dial was on the numbers and with the balls of my feet on the rudders and my toes ready to apply the brakes, my left hand on the yoke ready to respond to any wind gusts and my right hand on the throttle I had become a human computer. I was flying the plane but not thinking about it. I had been programmed in my training, and every hour flying since, for my left hand to keep the wings level and know when to pull back to lift the nose for the main wheels to touch first and then ease forward again to gently lower the nose-wheel, my right hand to increase or decrease the power to ensure I landed on the chosen spot, my feet to ensure that we touched down square with the centreline and then my toes to apply increasing pressure on the brakes. All I had to do was keep my eyes on my target and hold my nerve.

We touched down smoothly, slowed to taxiing speed and turned into intersection Alpha. I placed full confidence in the Tower's combined clearance and proceeded to our hangar. We passed one taxiway intersection where three inter-city Boeing 737s were lined up waiting for us to pass and another intersection where an Airbus A380 was waiting to commence its flight to London; their captains must have been wondering who was on board the Pilatus requiring them to wait. There were no bars on our shoulders this time, our private little game which had been set up by Bruce had caused a big enough flap to last us a very long time.

“Canberra Tower, Bravo Mike Charlie hangar door and winding down: thank you for that courtesy,” I reported.

“Bravo Mike Charlie,” Tower began his acknowledgement and added. “Nice job by the way mate, Bruce would be proud of you, pity he wasn’t here.”

“Thank you very much,” I closed communications now relaxing the formality of stating my call sign again. The controller would have known Bruce for many years as he had flown in and out regularly. Bruce would have added the controller’s name to his response or at least called him mate. On this occasion the controller didn’t expect to be acknowledged as we had never met except in this metaphysical world of airwaves. I knew we would meet soon.

I had opened the hangar doors with the remote on our approach and now with her last stored energy Bravo Mike Charlie rolled into her parking position as the big turbine came to a stop.

“Nice one Captain,” I heard Mary say, bringing me back to the present. I turned to see a radiant Mary, bursting with pride and admiration.

“He was here Mary,” I whispered. We rose from our seats and came together in an embrace before moving into the cabin proper.

“Would you like it here Adonis?” Mary whispered. “Or can you wait till we get home?”

“Let’s go home Aphrodite, my turbine is still winding down,” I replied. “It would be safer if you drove; I’m still up there and might try to use my wings to turn a corner. I haven't felt this way since I passed my first solo."

We took the things we might need immediately and drove off with Mary at the wheel.

"I'm not very proficient in this beast Brad," Mary said after a few hundred metres flashed past. "It has far more kick than my little J Type."

We were soon home with the beast safely tucked away in the garage it shared with the little 'J'. We peeled off our clothes, to be picked up later, as we walked to the bathroom. I turned on the jets and the boost heater in the spa, added fresh perfume to the already sparkling water and stepped in. It only took a minute or two for the temperature to come up before we sunk into the water and into the positions we last held when we were so unexpectedly halted by Nan on the phone.

"We have unfinished business here Adonis," Aphrodite said.

Mary's thigh again reached up over mine, my horn again moved up to her Gates to Paradise seeking admission and this time the phone did not ring. We hadn't waited to start a playlist on the sound system but as we lay in the warm water, totally spent of energy and the recent profound emotions we started whispering to each other:

'And the Angels Sing' http://www.futuristic.guru/and-the-angels-sing

We were sublimely happy so why shouldn't the angels sing. For about an hour we laughed and cried and clung together in our afterglow.

"I'll make us lunch," Mary said at last.

We were a little surprised that there had been no attempt by the media to contact us. Obviously, Flight Centre had protected us as requested but I knew there would have been other pilots on the Control Tower frequency who could have used their smartphones to give a friend in the media a quick tip-off. Besides, there are always camera freaks and plane-spotters hanging around major airports and there had been more than enough pictures of Bravo Mike Charlie around to have them flicking their shots to a news service.

"To keep the press away for a while let's get in first with a media release," I suggested. "We put our heads together and came up with the following:

Having not heard from Bravo Mike Charlie since it departed Cairns two weeks ago, we are happy to advise readers/viewers/listeners that the bird has returned home. The sightseeing visit into Sydney Harbour was planned by its owner, the late Bruce Clifford, as part of his son Brad's eighteenth birthday celebration and not some publicity shoot designed by Pilatus and Cunard Line. Following Bruce Clifford's death, in a road tragedy only a week earlier, Bruce's wife, Associate Professor Mary Clifford of the ANU, pressed on to fulfil Bruce's planned circumnavigation of Australia. They landed in Cairns to refuel only to find that fanciful stories were being broadcast by TV channels and radio news services. Certain journalists had been notified that they had landed so they decided to take off, abandon their trip and simply visit some family friends. Unable to complete their planned itinerary they have returned home due to family commitments. They ask the media to grant them their privacy at this time which is so soon after the untimely loss of a loved husband and father. They will not be giving any media interviews and have never consented to the use of their pictures or contributed to any magazine article and have no intention of doing so in the future. Professor Clifford stressed that she would pursue any breach of their rights or the publishing of unauthorised articles in the courts if necessary.

We had composed our document with me at the keyboard and Mary contributing and with one click of the mouse it was off to the main news service's fax machine.

"I suggest we now prepare a checklist of all the things we must do before we can leave. We've only got ten days if we are going to fly out next Sunday," I added.

We sat together at my computer and I opened a blank spreadsheet. I headed the first column 'Date' the second 'Aphrodite', the third 'Adonis' and the fourth 'Together'. Mary smiled and gave my leg a squeeze at the use of our love names. It was obvious that we would need to handle many of the tasks alone.

"If we make our first base London, we will be within easy reach of most of Europe in the Pilatus," Mary began. "As we plan to leave on the ninth, we could easily be in London by the 23rd for a white Christmas. Besides, my most important collaborator has been Rod Senden at Cambridge University and one of the important Clifford managers is Bevis Williams who is also in Cambridge."

"Agreed," I said, "one of my first tasks will be to plot a route for us. Darwin will be our first refuelling stop and we will get our customs departure there. Singapore could be one stop. I'd like to spend a night at Raffles and have a beer with the ghosts of Somerset Maugham and Hemingway. Is there any special place you would like to see on our way to London, Mary?"

"The Taj Mahal and the Trevi Fountain come instantly to mind darling," Mary said and gave my leg another squeeze.

"OK, now that we know where we are going, we can leave our plans beyond Christmas open. Now let's get started on what we must do from today until we leave."

We listed all the things we could think of: Mary's sabbatical, medicals, visas, people to see; transmission of

Bruce's estate including accountants, lawyers, banking and insurance matters. There would be company meetings and arrangements to be made: seeing that I had inherited Bruce's controlling interest. We would need to arrange for the care of our house and garden in our absence and other minor matters. We apportioned the tasks between us and set dates and times for their completion. The first tasks on our lists were for Mary to meet the Vice-Chancellor and apply for her sabbatical and me to go to the airport to finish unpacking Bravo Mike Charlie and to see our LAME about any work that needed to be done to ensure Bravo Mike Charlie was ready to fly away. I switched on the radio seeking a little mood music but instead caught the beginning of the latest news bulletin:

"The mystery of the disappearing Bravo Mike Charlie is solved tonight. The bird and the missing Cliffords arrived back in Canberra this morning and Associate-Professor Clifford immediately forwarded the following press release to all media outlets. In fairness to the Cliffords and as some form of apology for any part this station may have played in their recent distress, I will read the professor's news release in full."

"That's a relief," Mary turned to me. "Click it off, darling, we know the rest."

With a departure date set, and a destination for the first leg of our journey settled, my gap-year and Mary's sabbatical now seemed confirmed. We knew we would be adding to and modifying our departure checklist during the next ten days, but we had begun. Before dinner we phoned around the Grands and Greats and were brought up-to-date on who would be coming to my birthday party on Saturday night. I also prepared a record of the places we visited and photos of Bruce's **Outback Friends** who we met. **http://www.futuristic.guru/outback**

By six-thirty, we had done all we could for now.

"We have the rest of the evening to ourselves Aphrodite," I said. I took her by the hand and she walked with me into the lounge room.

"What would you like to do tonight Adonis?" Mary asked after I sat in one of the large lounge chairs and she came down onto my lap to be kissed and cuddled.

"I'd like to relax and unwind, Aphrodite. We are going to be very busy until we fly out of Darwin."

"It will be wonderful darling Adonis. But right now I'd better make you a nice dinner to keep your strength up. After that a moonlight swim would be good."

"And then I'd like to become better aquatinted with your bedroom, Aphrodite."

"It's your bedroom too, Adonis."

"I know, but I've only slept there once nearly two-weeks' ago."

"Then you will become better acquainted with my bed and what's in it tonight Adonis. Will you lay the table while I get the steak cooking?"

"We'll use the little table again Mary, but not dress for dinner this time,"

"Does that mean we will undress for dinner darling?"

"The skimpy little wrap you have on now will be fine, Aphrodite."

I laid the table using the fine china and cutlery as Mary had done before and placed our special occasion flutes. I put a bottle of Bruce's Dom Perignon in the wine cooler, set the sound system playing and was satisfied. There were no orchids this time, but I quietly gathered a bunch of six roses from the garden and placed them in a vase on the table. I wasn't trying to repeat the night of my birthday but just capture a little bit of its magic for a welcome home party. I joined Mary in the kitchen as she was serving the steak. The eye-fillet looked tender and the salad was fresh.

"Frank and Alison have replenished the fridge for us darling," Mary said.

I carried the plates to the table and Mary joined me. I popped the cork and poured the champagne. Mary accepted hers and her smile was radiant.

"Welcome home darling Aphrodite," I said and raised my glass to her.

"Welcome home darling Adonis," Aphrodite replied.

We didn't talk much as we ate. I complimented Mary on cooking it just the way I liked it. Aphrodite was still Mary in the kitchen, but she did appear in the rest of the house when passions were aroused.

The sun was setting as we ate, and we reviewed some of the events of the last eleven days. When we finished our meal, the soundtrack had moved on to *What a Difference a Day Made.* I hadn't asked but Aphrodite rose from her chair at the same time as I did and came into my arms. We danced quietly around the lounge and this time there was no shock or stumble as there was at Bob and Kay's but only a happy smile as she lifted her face to mine to be kissed.

We pulled the blankets down off the bed, leaving only a sheet to be pulled up if we got too cool.

"It's your bed darling Adonis. I come with it like the sheets and blankets. I want this to be a place of solace for you."

"That's a sweet thought Aphrodite, but we will be leaving it behind in eleven days."

"Yes, but you will be taking that part of the bed that gives you solace with you darling Adonis. While I live, it will always be there for you to claim."

"Then I'm claiming it now, Aphrodite."

Thursday 29 November 2012 – 0700 hrs

We were up early eager to get it over with. I barely recognised Mary as she came out of our bedroom, once more in her work clothes. I knew that it would only be a few more days before we would be away, and she could leave these work clothes in her wardrobe for twelve months. **Aphrodite's Diary http://www.futuristic.guru/copy-of-aphrodite-3-1**

We drove out the gate, Mary in her snappy red J-Type looking the part of the most desirable young professional woman in the National Capital and me following behind, boldly declaring I appreciated beautiful cars and beautiful ladies. At the roundabout Mary took the first exit to drive to the ANU and I took the second exit to go to the airport. Greg Howard was already at work with a team of tradesmen. They had stripped the interior yesterday afternoon and were now working on removing any internal panels where new plumbing, wiring and communications were to be installed. Greg greeted me enthusiastically.

"Your measurements and materials lists worked out perfectly Brad. Pilatus had all your requirements ready when I called on Tuesday morning and Ron Johnstone from CASA came and inspected them on Tuesday afternoon. He checked everything against BMC's original documentation and told me he saw nothing to upset her existing certification. He's coming back this morning at eleven o'clock to confirm this with you. He will return to inspect the finished work before we replace the panels and I will have a demonstration of fuel being transferred from the auxiliary tank to the main tanks for him to see.

"I take it that you can complete the work by Friday the seventh Greg?" I asked.

"Yes Brad; thank you for the deposit. I hadn't budgeted for a wage bill this week for this many engineer. It certainly saved me wasting time going to the bank."

"I'd like you to have your account ready for Friday afternoon. I don't want to leave the country with any debts behind me. There is one thing I must ask of you: I don't want any talk about what we are doing with Bravo Mike Charlie or where and when we are going."

Greg was only too happy to oblige. His association with the Clifford clan went back many years and knowing how most of them were acknowledged as superior aviators he was not going to blot his copybook, particular as the hangar talk around the airport had been all in support of my flying and castigating the media for hounding such a highly regarded family and ruining our trip. As much as he would love to see the fit-out being featured in FLYING, particularly after the head-on of her arrival home, the engineer was happy to agree. My last demand was that nobody working on this project was to bring a camera or even mobile phone into Bravo Mike Charlie's hangar. They were to check them in when arriving at the engineering shop and one of his staff working there would be the runner to bring messages to anyone who was being called. I knew that emphasising my words with a string of epithets such as: 'and I'll have his guts for garters if any fuckin' bastard stuffs this up.' wasn't my style at all and coming from a relative whippersnapper I would only insult the people whose support I needed. I said instead, as if reading the engineer's mind:

"And when we get back, I'll publish a picture book of our travels including plenty of shots of the inside."

"Don't worry mate, I'll have his guts for garters if any fuckin' bastard stuffs this up," the LAME said.

“Thanks mate,” I replied.

Ron Johnstone arrived punctually at eleven o’clock. He confirmed everything he had told Greg and we discussed how the work was to proceed. Greg had planned to work through the weekend and have the new fittings installed by midday Tuesday. Ron will join him then to inspect the work before any panels are replaced and do a test of the workings and gauges of the auxiliary fuel tank on the ground. They would then do a test flight to verify its operation in flight. Once this was done Greg will have his men replace the panelling to allow Mike Smith and his joinery team to move in on Wednesday morning and install the new fittings. Mike needed two days to complete the fit-out. Everything needed will be pre-cut and assembled in the joinery shop and then knocked down and brought flat to the hangar for reassembly. Greg’s work in the cabin will now be complete, all but one engineer, supervising the fixing of the joinery, will move on to giving Bravo Mike Charlie’s power plant, undercarriage and control surfaces a thorough 100-hour inspection to ensure that every component is performing to specification. She will be jacked up off her wheels to test her landing gear extension and retraction. Every joint and bearing will be examined, and greased and new tyres fitted. Every external sensor will be tested, and every control surface examined and verified against the readings on the instrument panel. Every circuit breaker will be shorted and reset and the smoke detectors set-off. Finally, on Friday morning any blemish in her paintwork will be rubbed down and restored and Bravo Mike Charlie will be washed and polished and look like new.

“So, it will be all right if I bring a few beers over for the crew at three o’clock on Friday afternoon?” I asked, looking at Greg.

“I’m sure that will be most appreciated Brad.”

“Make sure you have your account ready Greg. I don’t want to take possession until all this work is paid for,” I added.

“I wish they were all like you Brad.”

“I’ll get out of your way now Greg and go and have a word with Mike.”

“Thanks for your help Ron; you’ll join us for a beer on Thursday?”

“Thanks Brad, I’ll bring an update of your Airworthiness Certificate showing the approval of this unique cabin fit-out,” Ron confirmed.

“Professor, how did it go,” I asked as I recognised Mary’s ring tone. Once when I had a few moments while we were away, I had installed a few bars on my phone of *We meet and the Angels Sing*. I answered it quickly, as I recognised the very first note, in case Greg and Ron thought it a funny old song for a young man. I addressed her as professor instead of darling as most would expect I was talking to a man. I waved to Greg and Ron and went outside to talk.

“Marvellous darling, Don was so protective. He immediately agreed to my leave application, fully understood my desire to get away for a while, asked whether you would be commencing this year and again was supportive when I told him you were taking a gap year to chaperone your mother overseas. Don suggested that I would be doing more of the chaperoning to ensure those little French chicks didn’t get their hooks into you. I’m afraid that in my opening I let it all flow out suggesting that if my lab was to be scaled down and my research diminished, I may as well resign now and seek tenure overseas while I am there. He was shocked and put it down to my stress ensuring me that there would be no such thoughts anywhere in the administration. He said the

Board was meeting tonight to see how they could help us and asked me to call again tomorrow to hear their recommendations from him personally. Once he saw I was no longer upset he smiled and said he was most impressed with our performances in the air, I almost blushed at that one, and was worried that the media was so inconsiderate. I told him that we felt it will soon blow over with our press release but getting away for a while will help. That's my lot lover, how's your day?"

"Nothing as dramatic as that of course. I cleaned up the bird inside and put the luggage we left behind into the car. I've taxied her over to the workshop and am now discussing my work order with the engineer, that's all."

Thursday 29 November 2012 – 1400 hrs

"I've got my big medical with Doc shortly," Mary continued. "Would you like me to make an appointment for you, he hasn't seen you for a while and I am sure he would like to see you."

"I thought he was a women's specialist," I flinched a little.

"Oh no," Mary was quick to reassure me. "He is one of the enlightened ones who know in takes two to tango and it was no good being expert in one set of parts without the other. Bruce kept in touch with him too. He was most helpful to Bruce and me. His discrete little clinic does colonoscopies and prostate tests to look after the entire lower end. I think he would be a good investment in your future darling," Mary stopped, afraid she might scare me off or feel that she hadn't moved from being mother to being lover after all.

"Please do Mary, he should be able to help me with my little problem," I sounded pleased with her suggestion.

"Not so little a problem darling it looks a pretty big one to me. I shouldn't be too late about four-thirty I think," Mary began to close our talk,

"I can keep busy until then," I replied. "Love you darling."

Aphrodite's Diary http://www.futuristic.guru/copy-of-aphrodite-5

Now to the joinery and then home to Mary, I thought. The joinery visit didn't take very long. I handed over my final drawings and the photos of the sheik's plane to Mike Smith, the shop foreman, and said I was happy to pay for the interior that would at least match that and hopefully exceed it. I handed the foreman the careful measurements that I had taken to ensure that all my requirements would fit into the inner skin of Bravo Mike Charlie and explained why the LAME, Greg Howard, was in total control of everything that happened on board. Not only was the engineer's reputation on-the-line every time there was an incident relating to anything that he had signed-off, Mary's and my lives were at risk too. The foreman's look implied to me that he was taking the words of this young bloke with a grain of salt until I carefully explained the intricacies of the electronics on board and a few examples of major airline crashes that were caused by careless workmanship on the ground. What impressed the joiner was my recalling of the Crash Investigation Report that proved that a great modern airliner, with an experienced captain and crew, and with full seats, was brought down with total fatalities because some clumsy bastard fired a staple from the inner lining into strap cabling carrying critical information to the elevator control mechanism. 'That got to him' I thought: this time feeling that 'bastard' was quite appropriate to the example.

"I'll be careful mate," the foreman replied, "I went to the hangar yesterday and checked your measurements against Greg Howards charts of your plane. They matched perfectly."

"There is little I can touch on this bird other than the controls, switches, levers and the mike and I can assure you that's quite enough for me. I trust others properly qualified to do the rest."

"I'm getting the picture mate," the joiner said, and I sensed he was now taking me seriously. This was his first venture into the aviation industry and news of good work always travels fast.

"Call me if you have the slightest problem mate, you've got my number. I don't keep office hours: I'm on my gap-year," I called back as I started back to the Jag.

I jumped into the car thinking' 'back to Mary, never contrary.'

Thursday 29 November 2012 – 1630 hrs

"Tell me all about it darling," I said to Mary as soon as she came in from parking her car.

"Can I get out of these work clothes first please," I'm feeling a little sticky and yucky from the lubricant Doc has to use on the cameras and things that have examined all my pipes and tubes," Mary stated without any embarrassment; she was so accustomed having borne years of similar and worse attacks on her lady bits.

"How about we jump in the spa and I'll tell you all about it as you bathe me?" Mary asked. I quickly showed that I was wrapped in the idea as I started peeling my clothes off without speaking and then turned to Mary and did the same for her. I had no difficulty in picking her up. She wrapped her arms around my neck and cuddled into me.

"That didn't take long darling. I now know how a little swallow feels sitting on a branch," Mary hugged me tight and whispered in my ear, "You might need to be gentle with that big thing this afternoon; I could be a little sore and tender, but I feel hot, sticky and randy as hell so giddy up."

Without speaking I lowered Mary gently into the bubbles and remained outside the spa for a little while having decided to give her a good massage and tend to the less erogenous areas before I got in beside her to give her pussy a bath she might never forget. Mary now laid her head on the floating pillow and I released her honey-blonde hair from its working day setting to float out from the pillow. I thought that would be the best place to start; for many minutes I gently teased it out, shampooed it and rinsed the strands over and over again. I had spread her locks out in an arc around her; they reached down to her shoulders and around to the edges of the spa. I had clicked on a playlist on the way to the spa and it now seemed that I was permitted to stay here and marvel until the beat and mood of the music moved me on.

It was as if Mary's needs, my hands and the music were outside my control. As the music continued, I slowly gathered the arc of hair back and restrained it in a pony-tail so that her neck would remain exposed and available to my hands. Under my fingers and a little massaging lotion, I could feel the strain in her neck muscles slowly relax.

"Do you want to tell me about today now Mary?"' I asked.

"Soon lover, soon, please don't stop," Mary replied as she relaxed even deeper and hardly a sound was heard from her except her quiet breathing, seemingly in time with the music and occasionally emphasised by a deep sigh. As the music changed my hands were working into her shoulders, right side first as that was nearer to me.

I massaged her upper arm, her elbow, her forearm, wrist, hand and fingers. I delivered a little tongue tickle to the centre of her palm. Her fingers, in addition to receiving their massage, each had a turn between my lips, showing them that I considered her digits as important as her clit and would protect and value them just the same. I now concentrated on the rest of her back. I felt the anxiety that had risen today in her shoulder blades and applied a motion without any knowledge where it came from. I was delighted when her muscles relaxed. Working down her spine I felt all its tensions pass away. Her ribcage was damage free but when I came to her kidney's it was as if they were saying to me, 'Oh, that's better, a little to the right, a little to the left. I know Doc had my best interests at heart, but it was distressing.' By the time I left these vital organs I was somehow feeling their thanks. Was I dreaming or was Mary quietly saying these things? I didn't know or understand. What I did know was Mary's breathing was entering into a period of calm, peacefulness. Liver, spleen, gall bladder, ovaries, fallopian tubes where they came near her back and had felt Doc's probing fingers; all praised my gently hands. With one hand I gently parted Mary's buttocks and bathed away the little hurt the colonoscopy inflicted on her. With care I rubbed a little of the salve into her anus without waking her. As the music moved on so did my hands and finally her back was done from her neck to her toes. With extreme care I moved Mary around to be facing the other way and give the same due to her left side from shoulder to fingertips as I had just done for her right. I rolled Mary onto her back.

Mary didn't wake. Her eyes flickered, her lips parted into a smile but still she lay there. She looked supremely happy; it was as if we were in some fantastic intercourse where sexual organs were not required; it was some consummation by our souls which we did not and could not understand. I gently smoothed away the bruising to her breasts that Docs fingers, although soft and tender, could not avoid incurring. Her still erect nipples released their tension and retracted to my soothing touch. 'We won't need these tonight darling,' I thought, and they relaxed for the first time today. Mary's kidneys and ovaries now felt my hands on their forward face to what had been Docs finger probes. There wasn't much time needed at Mary's waist line as it was so trim, Mary was not big boned nor big busted. However, she was so beautifully proportioned that her trim waist contributed to the perfect hourglass figure. How blest I am I thought. I had left the most important part of the job until last. Mary was in a deep sleep or some other dream state. Mary had taken all of Docs, tubes, cameras, instruments and probing fingers without any narcotic to dull her discomfort or pain. Throughout the procedures she would have made no complaint; partly because she wanted to see and know what was happening to her and never handing the total control of her body to anyone, not even Doc. In her dream she was now handing that control to me and was happily abandoning herself to my care. Once I had washed her pubic hair and outer groin I could feel the welcoming opening of her thighs and looking at her face realised that she was still asleep or in a deep trance like state. Had I hypnotised her I wondered? Carefully I slipped two balm-carrying fingers into her vulva, gently massaged her lips and her clitoris and feeling it at last relax from its long day of excitation and quietly sink back behind its hood. Not tonight darling I repeated. Finally, with fresh balm on my fingers I returned to the opening of Mary's vagina. To my first gentle touch it opened completely to invite me in. I inserted my fingers ever so carefully and the muscles in the walls started exerting, drawing my fingers in to deliver their balm. Mary unconsciously imparted a string of contract, relax, contract, relax, motions to her vagina as if thanking me for her treatment, and then gently reversed her efforts to return my fingers to her groin. I suddenly realised that even under this most erotic experience of my young life my most troublesome organ had given up its hold over me and drooped down to stare at the floor; in future, it will submit to my desires and commands.

I had experienced an epiphany: I had passed from lust to almost indescribable love. I was responding to Mary's great desire for an instant and urgent coupling when I carried her to the spa. Mary did not get what she had asked for but I felt that I had given her something more. Neither of us had experienced any form of orgasm.

I felt in the last hour I had grown in stature and wondered what I might see when I look at myself in a mirror. I had not got into the spa with Mary when it was obvious that she was sinking into sleep at my caressing. I was now starting to strain from my position, but I decided to give her a few minutes more of the joy and peace that was evident on her face. I was happy to watch until finally, while still holding my left arm under her shoulders and with my right hand cupping her breast, I began planting ever so gentle baby kisses on her lips. Mary's smile started to flow across her face, and her eyes opened slowly.

"Did we come together darling? I didn't go to sleep on you did I. I had the most beautiful dream. I must try and tell you about it before it escapes me."

"It will never leave you darling and nor will I," I said. "Let me get you up and dry before you catch a chill."

"The old fella looks slack and tired," Mary giggled.

"Yes darling, I've got him under control now," I replied. I selected a full-length bathrobe with long sleeves and fold-up collar and wrapped Mary in it. I thought those sexy, skimpy wraps I loved her to wear could wait another day.

"What time is it Brad," Mary asked.

"I don't know Mary, it was four-thirty when we got home, and we came in here almost immediately," I replied.

"Come on let's go and see. I'm starting to feel a little peckish," Mary replied. She took my hand and almost pulled me towards the kitchen.

"It's eight-thirty," Mary exclaimed.

"Time flies, when you're having fun," was all I could muster. I was equally confused as I had been awake the whole time.

"What happened? I felt pretty yucky when I got home, I remember saying to you," Mary began.

"That's right," I replied, "Do you remember us stripping, me picking you up to cart you off to the tub. Me getting a hard-on and you said something about feeling like a canary sitting on a branch."

"I remember you stripping me, and I can remember saying that, but then it starts to fade away,"

"OK," I began, "Just start from there some time, it will all come back and then you can tell me about it. But now, I'm hungry too."

"I'll knock us up something, lover," Mary began. "We can talk while I do, did I tell you that I've got to see the Vice-Chancellor again tomorrow?"

"Yes," I replied, "and he approved your leave. He is sure your lab will be OK while you're away and be waiting for you when you return, and the Board is meeting tonight to see what they can do for us."

"Pretty good," Mary replied. "Did I tell you that I told him you wouldn't be starting next semester and that you were going to chaperone me around the world."

"No, that's a good one darling,"

"I know, he thought that I'll be chaperoning you to protect you from all those Parisian chicks."

"How little they know," I said.

"Doc said that I'm good for another fifty years at least, so long as you don't ride me too hard."

"I don't believe you said that or him either."

"Oh yes, but he's quite happy with once a day and perhaps another on special occasions," Mary exclaimed. "Well if we didn't do it in there, we could eat our meal quickly and hop off to bed. I'm feeling much better now darling," Mary replied.

"Not tonight darling, if you mean that I have the strength to turn down a good fuck with you then something must have happened to me too," I said so very gently. "You have had enough prodding and poking for one day for me to enjoy inflicting any more on you. I could do some damage and ruin what we have planned. We'd end up stuck here and not be able fly away like that little swallow you mentioned."

"Oh Brad, thank you. I wasn't trying to push you for my sake, truly. I just felt that the way your old fella was behaving before you must have been aching for it by now."

"Let's finish our dinner and we can get our plans together for the rest of the week," Mary smiled back to me. She released her grip and returned to where she had left off serving our dinner.

"What did you do to my hair, it feels great. I remember you shampooing it and teasing it out rinsing it several times. I remember you gathering it back and banding it. I remember you starting to massage my neck; after that I seemed to just drift off. Mind if I leave it all hanging out for a while. It feels so refreshed," Mary said.

"Not in the least," I replied. "The light is reflecting off the waves in your hair as they did in the spa. You had your head on the pillow and it seemed then that you weren't really listening, I asked you whether you wanted to talk about the rest of your day and you replied, 'Soon, lover, soon,' after that we didn't talk anymore."

"I didn't ask you about your day?" Mary seemed to be sorry for her neglect. "It's been all about me since the moment we got home."

"Oh, my day was nothing special," I lied. I knew that what I had arranged was the most special undertaking of my life. I dearly hoped that it would be so for Mary when she sees the finished product. I was confident the finished product would far outshine anything I could show her now on the plans or the interior of the Sheik's plane in the magazine from where my ideas had sprung. She would just have to wait.

"I delivered our bird to the shop for her hundred hourly," I continued. "Bit of a parallel there to you don't you think? My two special birds being pried and poked and examined, stripped of their usual dignity. The engineer will test fly her tomorrow and I've arranged for a couple of jobs to be done after that to make our next trip a bit more comfortable."

"Such as?" Mary asked.

"Things like that food oven," I continued, "It appears she needs the Pilatus generator upgrade to handle these extra appliances. I also collected the new WAC charts I had ordered from the Flight Store."

"When can we go?"

"Sunday seems to be the best day to me," I began. "It will give us enough time to get these things done, packed up, arrangements made for the house while we are away, load the plane and be able to make a clean get away on Sunday morning."

"Provided the Board doesn't throw any spanners in the works tonight," Mary sighed.

"Positive side only Mary," I said and realised that I hadn't heard whether Doc could see me before we left. "Did you make an appointment for me with Doc?"

"Sorry, clean forgot. He's got a full book this week but will be happy to see you at eight o'clock tomorrow before any other patients arrive," Mary said with an apology wrapped up in a smile.

"Come on then we had better hit the cot?" I lifted her into my arms to kiss and carry her to bed.

"Careful lover, we don't want you going there in the morning with a hernia and Doc putting you in hospital, that would be terribly unfair," Mary laughed.

We were soon in bed where Mary had immediately settled on my arm again as she was in the spa, with her head on my shoulder she drifted back into a deep sleep. Perhaps she is looking for what really happened in those hours, I thought. I couldn't remember either where all the time had gone. I couldn't remember how much time I spent on her hair, each knotted muscle or tender organ. All I knew was that I felt changed too.

Friday 30 November 2012 – 0700 hrs

"Friday and counting darling," I greeted Mary for our first kiss and cuddle of the day. We left separately as my appointment with Doc was an hour earlier than Mary's with the Vice-Chancellor.

"I hear you're off on the grand tour Brad," Doc began, "Lucky you, chaperoning a beautiful young lady around the world certainly can't be any hardship."

I offered a big smile as I paused to control my voice and the colour, I felt could soon show in my cheeks at what I felt was a little challenging opening gambit.

"No hardship at all Doc," I replied. I hoped my voice was displaying a calm confident nature that at the present I wasn't feeling inside.

"Now what's your real reason for calling?" Doc continued. "You certainly don't look sick, quite the opposite really, you look like the healthiest and fittest young man in

Canberra to me. I've seen your stats from the GP by the way. Your bloods are all within range, your vision, and hearing, everything else all spot on. It can't be just this going overseas business; you don't need me for that."

"No Doc," I began, feeling what the hell. "I've become a bit unpredictable in the groin, a lot unpredictable really," I managed to get out with what I felt was growing confidence.

"Not unusual mate, particularly at your most blessed stage in life," Doc said. He was deliberately showing me more empathy, man-to-man, building my confidence and willingness to unburden.

"No need for all the usual examination protocols," Doc continued, 'I'll just pull on a pair of gloves, while you drop your daks and we'll see what we can find. I'm sure it's nothing serious but we must check for anything anatomical. There are heaps of nerves down there or it would be a pretty dull experience all together."

I took off my shoes so that I could remove my trousers fully rather than standing in that laughable position often depicted of a bloke with his trousers down around his ankles when his lover's husband comes home. I stood and faced Doc.

"That's fine Brad," Doc said," Don't forget that it was me who gave you that very neat circumcision," Doc now noticed my jocks over the back of the chair. "They've got to go for a start, irrespective of whatever else we find, you'll end up with an erection with a ninety-degree bend in it and I can assure you I've never seen a vagina of that shape, and I've seen quite a few as you can imagine. You will also fry your balls in those things. Man was meant to have his balls hanging down in the airflow for cooling, not pushed up into his hot body. That's why they descended in the first place. The testicles in a loose scrotum will always rise-up closer to the body if cold. They have their own thermostat that second by second knows their state of comfort and adjusts accordingly. Jocks and tight jeans interrupt all of this natural design and are probably one of the main reasons for the recorded fall in sperm count in breeding aged males," he added. "Have you been wearing them for long?"

"Not long," I said. "Only when I'm out and only since it has become noticeable to me. It's really for constraint. When I get home, I change back into boxers straight away."

"You'll need to get it up for the inspection, Brad," Doc began in his best impersonal, professional manner. "Can you manage that, perhaps a girlie magazine would help, or I've got a couple of tapes here that others have found helpful in your position."

"No Doc that's more likely to have the opposite effect," I said, growing in confidence that I was in very good hands. "It only takes a little drifting of my thoughts," I said.

It wasn't long before a full erection was presenting itself for Doc's inspection. He carried out a careful examination. He pointed out the damage that could be done by forcing it to resist its natural urges when it was in a bent position, "Like bending a hose while the tap is on," he said.

"Who were you thinking of when you so easily erected Brad?" Doc asked in all simple sincerity.

"Mary of course," I found myself saying, no thought of saying mum or mother but a very personal Mary. It came out with as little chance of stopping it as I was of controlling that ejaculation in the wet dream with my mother in my arms, and who since that time had become Aphrodite.

"Man to man Brad can I ask you a question?" Doc said.

"Of course, Doc," I replied instantly.

“Are you fucking her Brad?” Doc said. A simple question without any hint of accusation, surprise or judgment of any kind, as innocently as if he had said ‘Are you dancing with her Brad?’ or ‘Are you eating with her Brad?’ He did not say ‘Are you sleeping with her Brad’ or ‘Are you having sex with her Brad.’ ‘No euphemism or beating about the bush would do. No possible claim later that I would think he meant something else or plead the ‘Clinton-defence’ or prevaricate in any way. His question was plain and simple and between men where the one knew that the other would not have asked the question if he didn’t already know the answer my only answer could be ‘Yes,’ anything else would be a lie damning me in Doc’s eyes forever and damaging Mary’s relationship with him.

“Yes Doc,” I said. I was looking directly into Doc’s eyes and held his gaze. “I’m desperately in love with her. And I believe that my love is returned many times over.”

“Brad, please stop for a moment,” Doc began. “Don’t go running off thinking that I expect any sort of explanation from either you or Mary. At my age and in my business, I see many desperate situations where governments and churches have no right to interfere. Of course, for those facing the same challenge as you, under these extreme situations, the one impediment is the possibility of bringing forth a child. The known laws of our genetics make it unacceptable. In Mary’s and your case no such impediment exists. No doubt Mary has told you her medical history by now,” Doc said.

“Yes Doc, my heart bled for Mary and Bruce when I heard the details,” I replied. “To think that I was the cause of such damage and pain made it hard to fight down the nausea I was feeling.”

“You can’t blame yourself Brad,” Doc said, “There were no indications, or I would have interceded earlier in the labour without hesitation. I studied every aspect of the later stages of her pregnancy up to the point of delivery. Your head was out before the event occurred which probably saved your life. Nobody can carry any fault least of all yourself. You were a victim too Brad; in depriving your parents of any more children you were deprived the privilege of brothers and sisters."

I nodded in agreement and went on to tell Doc of the manner in which Mary came to my bed in the early hours of the morning after the memorial. She was in a pathetic state and sought an arm about her and a shoulder to cry on. A wry smile crossed his face as I related the manner in which we woke up. I'm sure I felt Bruce trying to shake us out of grief and saying, 'Now come on you two, get to it. Life is for living'.

"Brad, just accept it was inevitable. Whether it happened in one hour, one day, one or ten years it was inevitable and the very best of all possible outcomes for the three of you. The fact that it happened so soon is actually far, far better still. There has been little chance for depression, Mary must have a close and loving male companionship, and emotional damage to her is equally harmful as physical damage. Bruce and Mary went to their marriage bed as virgins; neither had any sexual contact with any other nor did they before Bruce died. You know how close they were. Do you think Bruce would want Mary in another man's arms? Do you think Mary could find a lover to replace him or even consider marriage in the future?

"Do you think you could bear to see that happening or see Mary go into premature aging by denying her very nature. No Brad forget every other consideration. You are the only man she will love in this way. Only the words have changed she always loved you dearly as did Bruce. You are so much like your father that her love for him can easily be passed on to you without in any way diminishing her love for Bruce."

"Thanks Doc," I said, "You have been a great help."

"Oh, there's one other thing Doc," I now remembered as I was about to get dressed. "I came upon the shoe box where Bruce is stored, that's what she called the dildo you had fashioned for her. Could you have one made of me for when I have to travel?"

"Would you like me to take an impression of you now?" Doc asked.

"You have the gear here?" I asked with some surprise.

"Of course, it's not just you Cliffords that have need for this sort of thing and don't want to be seen anywhere near a sex shop. Besides, this way it can be made to fit the purpose. Can you get it up again while I gather my gear?" Doc said as he went to collect his equipment.

"I barely need speak her name," I said.

When Doc came back with his equipment, I had a roaring horn proudly standing out in front of me making it easy for him to take a good impression first up.

"Mary won't need it for a year Doc," I said. "I'll make sure she does her exercises on the real thing in the meantime."

"Remember, once a day will be good for you with a second on special occasions."

"Mary told me that was your prescription for Bruce and her after she had recovered from her reconstruction," I said.

"Now don't use Jocks again, put them in your pocket now but don't let my secretary see it wobble around as you're leaving, or she might leave her boyfriend and coming running after you and I don't want to lose her," Doc said.

I realised Doc's banter was to ensure the consultation ended on a high note and the morning's discussions and lessons would be observed forever. We gripped hands firmly.

“Give my love to Mary and I hope you both have a wonderful year. Do you know where you will be going?”

“No Doc, we’re hoping to be leaving on the 9th and make about four fuelling stops before we reach London. By then we may have expanded our plans in more detail. Mary will be visiting various Unis, labs and her peers on our journey but she’s determined not to make work the purpose of our trip. I can afford to allow her a little time to delve into things that I don’t really understand,” I finished.

“About that other not so little matter, Mary will help you with that far more than I ever could; she read up on all the ancient and modern methods for gaining mental and muscular control over the Beast when Bruce was having the same problem early in their marriage. You’ll be in very good hands.”

“Thanks Doc, I must be encroaching on other patient’s time, so I will get out of here.”

“Good luck Brad,” Doc had the last word aware that luck played no part in this equation.

My spirits soared as my erection collapsed and I managed to walk past the secretary, acknowledge her smile and continue without a glance. Back in the car I ticked off my visit to Doc on my departure checklist and phoned the Clifford Holding’s company secretary to see if he was available. He was free in half an hour, so I went to his office and had a cup of coffee in the restaurant on the ground level while I waited. I realised that Mary’s meeting with Don or as it amused me to say ‘The Vice’ would be well underway and I might expect a call from her anytime now.

I saw Max Johnstone, the company secretary, at ten-fifteen and after he expressed his condolences again, I asked him to call a meeting of the board for next Thursday, 6th December. I told him that I was still going to take the gap year my father had planned which was going to include visits to our overseas companies and that my mother was taking a year's sabbatical and going too. By Thursday we will have attended to the finalisation of my father's estate and the main item on the agenda for the meeting will be the formalising of the transfer of my father's shares to me and my appointment to the board in his place. Max, of course, knew my father's intentions and he had seen his will. He had already anticipated that this meeting needed to be held as soon as possible and said he would notify the rest of the board today. We discussed my plans for the year ahead and I left him at eleven o'clock.

There still hadn't been a call from Mary; surely her meeting with Doc would have concluded by now. I had another stop to make to collect my WAC, and IFR charts covering the territory we will fly over on our way to London and now I was becoming concerned. It was now midday and still no call from Mary. Silly thoughts were coming into my mind as I drove. Had something gone wrong at her meeting and she didn't want to tell me over the phone? I had to tell myself to keep calm, don't rush, remember what happened to Bruce. What would happen to Mary if anything happened to me on the road. What if anything had happened to Mary while we had been apart these four hours: it seemed we had been apart for much longer than that. Finally, I pulled into the drive to see the garage door open and the little red Jag waiting for her bigger and stronger XK mate to come gliding back to her.

I locked up and hurried to the house not quite running, certainly not gliding, but still showing signs of concern. I opened the door quickly to find Mary trying to open it from the other side. She was a picture of beauty framed in the architrave of the doorway. My mouth sagged a little as I took in her wavy honey-blonde hair now slightly swaying around her shoulders in the gentle breeze; she had shed all the clothes she had worn that morning. She was now clad or was it lightly wrapped in one of her sarongs; as before, this was only tied by two of its corners above her breasts. It was so light and sheer the slightest breeze blew the sides apart to reveal her delicate breasts and protruding nipples. It also revealed her tiny waist, flat stomach and gently raised Mount of Venus displaying those glorious little honey-blonde curls declaring to those very few people in this world who had ever been granted such a view that she was indeed legally blonde. Now she was entrusted to me.

"Come on darling, don't stare, you're frightening me," Mary spoke gently but with concern.

I stepped forward and took her in my arms ever so gently.

"I'm sorry darling, I was transfixed. I hadn't heard from you and I was becoming worried that something had happened. I'd much rather be up there where I can protect you than down here with idiots driving in every direction," I finally got out.

Friday 30 November 2012 – 1345 hrs

"I didn't realise you'd be waiting so desperately on my call, I thought that I would hold the news until I could give it to you personally. It seems so cold over the phone. Come on, you need to cool down, come and have a swim. The water's fine I've already had one swim while I was waiting, I got out because I heard the XK coming down the road. I thought you should have been here by now," Mary said.

"No, I'm early, I called out as I was leaving that I would be home about two."

"I'm sorry, I didn't hear that, come on the swim will do you good," Mary replied so brightly. Mary took me by the hand and led the way onto the patio and directly to the poolside table. She took my keys from my hand and put them on the table, she took my wallet out of my pocket and before I knew it had my watch off my wrist and placed alongside the others. She caught me by surprise and tipped me over into the pool. It was done smoothly and, still in a bit of a stupor, I was caught.

"You little vixen," I said shaking my head to remove some water from my ears. It was the nearest thing that I had said that could be considered as any sort of rebuke.

"You little vixen," I said again as I lunged out to grab her.

"But a cute little vixen don't you think?" Mary quickly teased me. "You were examining me pretty closely out there; did I hypnotise you?" Mary added and dived in beside me. She wrapped her arms around me and kissed me furiously and then unbuttoned my shirt, unclipped my belt, unzipped my trousers only to find that there were no more layers to remove.

"What have you been up to big boy while Mary was at work?" Mary started teasing again, knowing full well that she had arrived home without her panties on several occasions after Doc's examinations.

"Mmmm," Mary said. "No hanky-panky I hope,"

Any possible thought that any such thing could occur would have been quickly allayed by the swelling she felt in her hand.

"No hanky-panky," She taunted again in a charming lilt.

I was at last starting to get in the game by pulling off my shoes and socks and tossing them out of the pool, my trousers went next, followed by my shirt. Seeing that I was now stark naked and getting ready to lunge after her again she lithely jumped out of the pool, preening and posing and shaking her little titties started a slow teasing chant.

"Catch me you can fuck me."

"Catch me you can fuck me."

"Catch me you can fuck me."

Everything about Mary shouted gay abandon as I hurried to chase after her. She was skipping along happily around the other end of the pool still chanting her tease.

"Catch me you can fuck me."

I was struggling on behind, having to hold my now erect cock with one hand and thinking that this could bring on a severe case of lover's nuts — quite a painful condition I had heard around the change rooms.

Seeing that I was at last catching up she propped, I propped, and she started feinting side to side, her unfettered breasts wobbling with her movements, making me wonder in which direction she would go next and totally distracted by the vision in front of me. Mary of course didn't want to go anywhere; she had let me chase her to the place she intended for me to catch her: next to a little table with a bottle of Dom Perignon in an ice bucket and our Lalique flutes. Reaching out she gently took my arm, drawing me to her and at the same time sinking onto the rugs she had so carefully positioned. She wrapped her arms about me and pressed her bare breasts against my chest to hold me in a long embrace of kisses. This time, I felt that time was being distorted. Finally, pulling herself higher so that she could whisper in my ear:

"Shall we talk about this morning Adonis? Shall we drink that sparkling champagne in those beautiful flutes Adonis? Or shall we fuck?" There was no question to be answered.

"I caught you Aphrodite, didn't I (which was a moot point that Mary had no intention of debating) and I claim my prize," I said as I gently slid a hand between her thighs to open the Gates to Paradise. I felt no resistance but only surrender at every step of the way. The anxiety each of us had built up during our morning's separation demanded a quick release and we rose to a resounding climax in a very few minutes.

"I hadn't really looked at this garden until I walked around here while I was waiting for you to come home," Mary began as we drifted in our afterglow. "I felt sorry that I had ignored it for so many years. Happy to take its many gifts as Bruce's mates had kept our fridges and larder stocked and there were always flowers in the house reflecting the changing seasons. I had no idea that I was being so mean. I thought with so little time available that if I could show our appreciation of this beautiful and freely giving place by letting it witness our free and abandoned love it would welcome us back again in twelve months, with a smile, rather than feeling any gloom at our return."

"Beautifully said my darling," I began. "But is this the science professor I hear saying such things, careful, they might run you out as a heretic, stone you, defrock you or something like that."

"Adonis, you know you are the only person who can defrock me and stone me with your stones; you are welcome to do that anytime."

"Once a day and another for special occasions Doc told me," I said bringing a little lightness to our talk.

"Truly Brad, unfortunately you are also the only person who can hurt me or do me any harm at all. I'm not putting any pressure on you but simply acknowledging a simple truth. Nothing else matters to me at all. I wasn't concerned about a professorship; it usually only means a pay rise and a little more kudos. I don't need the money or the kudos. I'm just glad you were prepared to take me with you. For a moment back there, wherever it was, I thought that you had found yourself in over your depth and about to do a runner. Nobody would have blamed you. In fact, that would have looked quite normal and expected by most folks; particularly so coming from a fairly well-to-do-family and under no pressure to get a job or need to hurry through a degree as soon as possible. Taking a gap year and going to see the world, sowing your wild oats, breaking a few hearts and then coming home to live the normal, respectable, unaspiring life in the comfort of his inheritance — that's normal. Taking his mother along isn't so normal though."

"I think we have dealt with that with the chaperone story," I began. "They don't realise that it's just like putting the fox in charge of the chook-house, do they?" I chuckled. "Like the illusionist's ability to hide things in plain sight. Nobody sees what they don't want to see."

Mary hugged me closer.

"Thank you, thank you, and thank you," Mary almost sobbed out the words, punctuated with deep and strong kisses to my lips.

"Why thank me when I should be thanking you for this so unexpected invitation to the garden party of the year. I'm glad nobody else accepted though; I must've looked a fool running around with my hard-on in my hand. Anyone would have thought I was about to rape you."

"Why do you think I let you catch me lover?" We laughed again and kissed again.

"Did it go badly today?" I asked. I thought there may have been a little more to her teasing than just offering her apologies to the garden she had neglected.

"Oh no," Mary began quite casually. "Quite well I suppose really," Mary was still trying to hold back the excitement that was the root cause of her water nymph performance for me. She gathered herself up so that her breasts were resting on my chest and our faces only inches apart. Without stopping to let me say a word she rattled off:

"They are just insisting that I accept the Chair now instead of April next year and take my sabbatical. Professor Jack has agreed to stay on another year as Professor Emeritus (making it perfectly clear that he is in a caretaker role) until I return. I will be kept fully informed of all Professorial Board matters and meetings and be welcome to join in by teleconferencing at any time the facilities are available. Not that they want to make any unnecessary calls on our time, it was purely up to me as they had no intention of doing anything that encroached on my domain without my full knowledge. Professor Jack will deal with anything where he knows from our long association that his actions will not be out of line, he will always annotate those matters and drop them in my dropbox to keep me informed. Not that they expected me to be lugging my notebook everywhere we go but also knowing that I would never go away for twelve months without it. They are proud to have me visiting some of the highest colleges of learning and the grandest laboratories in the world as a full professor and dean of a department rather than a mere associate, they would be devastated if some fat-walleted lab or Uni lured me away from them.

"They consider me the brightest star in the academic firmament, and you had better keep close to protect me from the academic Lotharios bound to be casting eyes at me. As an afterthought, Don added that I had better keep a watch on you. They want you back next year as they wouldn't dare let your inheritance of breeding be snatched up by a foreign Uni either. There's a scholarship on the table for you into any faculty on the campus that you may wish to choose, that's about all darling," Mary said struggling terribly hard to hold back her joy before letting it burst out all over me.

"Just another day at the office," Mary prolonged the tension but at the same time brought her thigh higher towards my chest to make room for my old fella she could feel coming back to attention in honour of her news. Mary lent down on me to give me a deep and challenging French kiss, slipping her tongue erotically in and out between my lips. Mary's water nymph little escapade had relieved the early pressures that we had been holding back and now Mary was about to deliver to me her first real lesson in prolonged and controlled penetration.

"No need to rush darling," Mary whispered. "What we had earlier was our entree while it was nice and hot. Now we can leisurely enjoy our main course. I can control you to make it last. You've felt what I can do with those precious muscles, besides I'm feeling remarkably strong there today. It often takes me several days to feel good again after Doc's annual inspection."

While Mary's calming words were welcome it was difficult for me to hold back but Mary was quick to divert my attention by wanting me to talk.

"How was your day darling?" Mary began, slowing my rhythm as she did. "Please fondle my breasts darling you do it so well; how did you go with Doc by the way? I meant to ask you as soon as you got home but seeing your concern at not hearing from me all I could think of was to drag you out here and relieve you."

"Marvellously actually, he gave me the best advice. He loves you dearly Mary and looked after me as if he had been appointed in LOCO PARENTIS," I was happy to tell her. By this time the urgency in my groin had subsided and my old fella might have escaped had it not responded to the timely and gentle contractions Mary was able to produce, to and fro, with sufficient pressure to ensure that my erection wasn't lost. Now with her breasts getting the gentle handling she desired she laid her cheek on mine leaving us free to talk.

"Does he suspect darling?" She asked quietly.

"Suspect! He knows," I replied.

"Are you sure?" Mary asked with some little concern felt right down the muscles that were doing all the work now.

"Oh yes," I replied.

"How can you be so sure?" Mary asked, becoming more concerned. Any knowledge he may have gained would never be repeated. Her only concern was for the Clifford family's status in Doc's eyes.

"Because I told him darling, how could I lie to him? I knew he wouldn't ask me whether I was fucking Mary if he didn't already know," Mary's contractions stopped for a moment only to return gradually as I comforted her breasts with more fondling and my fingers finally reaching her nipples to tease them out a little more. I gave Mary a blow-by-blow description of the consultation. I could feel her smile as I explained how I had blurted out when asked who I was thinking of to gain my erection and had said 'Mary Doc'. She accepted then that he already knew before that and his interrogation of me was as professional as any investigator could apply to a suspect.

"He must have guessed from how happy and excited I was yesterday, darling. He didn't expect me to be as aroused as I was."

After hearing how Doc supported our actions and would have worried for us both if I had found her in any other man's arms, she was convinced her Doc was happy for us and would support us to the end. She lifted her head from my cheek and met my lips again. I stimulated her nipples and my horn gained full strength.

We'd done with talking and now Aphrodite was calling for More Adonis, More, Oh Yes Adonis. Our climax came with great force and Mary shuddered in my arms as she drained me dry. We rolled onto our sides still joined and while still breathless, I realised that I had, with Mary's help, held my erection for more than forty minutes and every second of that had been exquisite. Finally, having recovered our breathing we looked at each other and burst out laughing in delight as Mary slowly released my old fella from her control. Later we realised we hadn't eaten since our early breakfast. We enjoyed a final long kiss.

"Will you come to dinner with me tonight dear lady?" I asked after we had finally lunched and were now gathering up the rugs, retrieving our unused flutes and unopened Champagne.

"Of course, kind sir, where do you wish to take me?" Mary said, staying in the period chosen by me.

"To the moon dear lady, but for this evening I think a hotel with an orchestra and dance floor or at least a piano bar and a few square metres of polished boards would do. I'd like to dance cheek to cheek with you as part of my training in control procedures. Doc has frightened me off Jockey shorts for ever," I replied.

"Do you think you can manage that while dancing with me in public?" Mary asked.

"If you cooperate and not play the vamp with me I think I can: besides you've drained me pretty well today. Do we count today as a special occasion?" I asked coming back to normal.

"Today is special but I would think that would be a bit hard on us seeing you were only claiming your reward. Let's call it a double header that sounds nice even if we might be trying to stretch Docs prescription a little," Mary replied.

"I think one of the hotels that cater largely for tourists and travelling business people might be a smart move," I said. "We wouldn't need to watch the door for people we might know."

"Good thinking Captain," Mary said. "I'd love to have dinner to celebrate my elevation," Mary continued claiming her new high status. "Oh Oh," Mary started to speak.

"What's the matter darling," I said and was quickly back to her side.

"There is one small matter I forgot from this morning. They insist upon holding a formal bash on Saturday night to honour me and wish us Bon Voyage."

"Don't worry, I won't let you down," I said with clear determination.

"It wasn't you I was worrying about lover," Mary replied. "Yes, dinner tonight is a very good idea. We should be practising our act from now on and this will be a good place to start."

The evening began with us dining in a little in-house restaurant on an upper floor of the Canberra Marriot. Although it was hiding in the open it was also a restaurant aiming to cater for house guests and not the public. There were few diners as we entered, and we were ushered to a quiet corner. The waiter seemed to materialise from nowhere and we ordered light meals as we were now excited with the thought of our escape date approaching so soon. The drink waiter appeared with our one and only bottle of Chardonnay for the night. As soon as he had poured the wine he vanished, and I raised my glass to Mary.

"To the most beautiful, most charming, most gracious, most intelligent Professor in the world; soon to grace the halls of academia on the arm of her ever present, ever attentive, ever guarding escort whose demeanour will clearly announce to all they were free to look but be warned never to touch."

"Brad that was lovely," Mary replied very quietly. "But are you sure that I am worthy of such high praise. To overpraise one can be damaging if it cannot be forever seen to be true. Please don't put me on too high a pedestal, a fall from such a height might not just damage me but prove fatal."

"Should that ever occur, and believe me it won't, I will be right there to catch you in my arms, so easily that you would feel no pain let alone fatality," I replied just as the waiter appeared with our entrée to break the spell.

Our meal was to our liking and between entrée and our main course we danced. This rather intimate restaurant for houseguests had a baby grand in one corner with a small but adequate highly polished dance floor between it and the tables. The pianist played soft background music while the diners ate, sometimes adding a vocal in his fine tenor voice. If couples moved onto the floor he would smoothly move into a dance beat, always trying to select a tune from his vast mental store that would match their body language. There was no sheet music to be seen, he was playing from the heart and always enjoyed his work as much as the patrons enjoyed his music.

When Mary and I went onto the floor he must have pictured me as Gene Kelly and Mary as Debbie Reynolds as Kelly whirled Reynolds around the floor with quick steps, pivots and lifts and all the time singing to her and Debbie's eyes holding Gene's. He could see that I was singing to Mary so held his own voice almost inaudible fearing that he might break the magic that was in the air. It was as if he was the unseen prompter in the theatre in the days before teleprompters, silently mouthing the words to keep his players on their lines and in synch. He was back in time, at the movies, watching this scene being acted out in SINGING IN THE RAIN. It was one of his favourites. He loved the young Debbie Reynolds, she had a beauty that was markedly her own, she was nothing like the normal run of Hollywood starlets. What he was seeing here in Mary reminded him so clearly of his idol. I on the other hand was taller and appeared stronger; perhaps he had been jealous of Kelly for so long that he could now be privy to the same scene being played out by true lovers rather than professional actors. He was enthralled as his hands automatically played the music in the same way as it had been played in the film. He could see me quietly singing to Mary.

You were meant for me
http://www.futuristic.guru/you-were-meant-for-me
And I was meant for you
Nature patterned you
And when she was done
You were all the sweet things
Rolled up in one

As this tune ended the master at the piano took his dancers smoothly through part of his repertoire of love songs. No other couples had joined us on the floor; it was as if he was the puppeteer, Mary and I his marionettes. He had us gliding around the little floor to quiet foxtrots and new-waltz beats, he delighted at the way I held Mary close to me. Here at last he thought was a couple that loved to dance and had a pretty good idea of how it should be done. He had always believed that dancing was an expression of love and could not understand how the fad of raging could ever be thought to be so; perhaps, he conceded that rock and roll and raging might be a prelude to lust but never come close to be a prelude to love. At one point he felt mischievous and his next number began with him singing: ANY TIME YOUR LAMBETH WAY ANY EVENING, ANY DAY, he nearly lost his own way as he saw his marionettes easily transitioning into a 'Lambeth Walk'. They didn't only perform the steps flawlessly but happily sung along with him even down to a big 'Oi' at the end of each chorus. The puppeteer finished his little bracket with FOR ME AND MY GAL. The beat now returned to a foxtrot. He saw his girl puppet whispering something in his boy puppet's ear. He was seeing Mary, on her toes, reaching up to me and whisper in my ear, “That was lovely thank you Brad; you’re doing so well, keep it up, OOPS shouldn’t have said that should I?” My old fella had tried to regain some of the turf that it had relinquished last night, instantly sending a message to the Gates to Paradise. A close observer might have noticed the slight reddening of our faces as, after a little struggle, I brought the unruliest of my body parts under control. The pressure Mary had felt now faded away. Finally, the bracket came to its end. He watched this special couple walk back to their table. My arm was still around Mary as it had been for the final number, Mary’s head was tilted to and resting against my shoulder, the pianist thought them just as in tune walking as they had been dancing. Slowly they faded into the corner and the puppet master gently replaced his dolls in their box.

During our meal we had been talking quietly about Mary’s lost few hours in the spa last night. It was only now that we had found time to discuss it. Mary could recollect the time from when she arrived home until I massaged her neck in the spa, as we had confirmed last night, but after that she had just drifted away. I could only tell her how I had massaged her all over and even how I applied Doc’s balm to her vagina. Mary recalled that in her daze she had happily spread her legs, but when she felt able to use her hands to hug me, I wasn’t there and when she brought her legs together, she couldn’t grip me.

She had woken this morning feeling so refreshed and it had gone on through the day becoming more relaxed and confident, “I’ve tried to come to grips with it, but nothing more comes back,” Mary said.

I explained everything that I did but couldn’t understand why it had taken so long or how I had managed to stay on my knees beside the spa for nearly four hours.

“Brad darling, something happened that we have no explanation for. It could be an aspect of Adonis and

Aphrodite that we have yet to learn about," Mary began. "The Adonis Project found the man with the genome to become the next y-Chromosomal Adam. We expect wonderful, enlightened children will be produced by the girls we select for him to impregnate. Maybe something strange is happening to us when Adonis and Aphrodite fuck. We must not totally ignore that they are also mother and son."

"I know the word aura doesn't hold much standing in the scientific world darling, but I feel that our auras merge and we are communicating on a little understood level," I replied.

"Do you believe in aura Adonis?"

"Yes, I do. When I want to, I can see another person's aura. I don't know how to read it except happy people seem to have bright pastel tints in their auras while unhappy and morose people have shades of brown, green and grey."

"Can you see my aura, darling?"

I sat back in my chair and raised my line of sight a little to put the physical Mary slightly out of focus.

"There are light tints of lemon, blue, peach and apricot shimmering out from your head and shoulders. As I expand my gaze the whole area above the table forms a cocoon of gently pulsing light. It is really beautiful darling."

"You're not just saying this to make me happy Adonis?"

"No Aphrodite, I'm sure you are happy already. When we get home, I will show you."

Mary squeezed my hand across the table and I knew her scientific mind was getting in the way. The pianist was playing a slow foxtrot and I rose and took Mary onto the floor again. As we danced Mary nestled her head on my shoulder and relaxed. We dreamily drifted around the floor and I whispered the words of the songs. Our bodies were pressed together but my old fella behaved himself and hung softly. At eleven o'clock we left for home. We considered we had passed the test we had set for tonight and could safely dance together at my birthday party and the function that was proposed for next Saturday night. When we arrived home, I took Mary straight into our bedroom and undressed. I took her hand and led her to stand in front of the sliding glass door panels of the wardrobe. I had lowered the room lighting until it was now softly diffused around the room without any shadows. We could see ourselves clearly in the mirrors and I directed Mary to look a few inches above her head.

"Let your face go out of focus. At first you will see a faint glow around your head."

"I don't see anything darling except the opposite wall."

"Relax darling, forget the wall, your aura is there, and it will appear to be just behind you at first."

I took her left hand in my right and looked at Mary in the mirror. I didn't bother looking at my aura but simply let my eyes wander over Mary's beautiful body. I could feel my horn rising and expected to hear a giggle from Mary.

"I can see it Brad," Mary spoke excitedly.

"Slowly lift your focus higher and your aura will expand out around you," I said.

"I'm seeing your aura Brad. I am looking above your head and these soft rays of light are all around you. It's beautiful darling."

"Bring your gaze back over your own head and my aura should stay within the range of your peripheral vision."

"I have, and it does. I can see my own aura now and our two auras overlap."

Mary swung around to embrace me and join in a passionate kiss. I looked over her shoulder to the mirror and saw our two auras overlapped and pulsing faintly with our heartbeats. I took her down onto our bed and we fucked.

"What does it mean darling?" Mary asked after we calmed down.

"I don't know. Maybe it's our genes talking to each other and it was something like this that happened to us last night."

"Do you see people's auras as you go about your day Adonis?" Mary asked.

"Only if I consciously look for them as we just did. At other times, the auras are still there but they don't come into the range of our normal vision. However, we all become conscious of domineering people or threatening people without knowing why. I think that our own aura is becoming aware of the fiery reds and depressing browns in the other's aura and is warning us to be cautious."

"Let's sleep on it darling," Mary said as we kissed goodnight.

Saturday 1 December 2012 – 0630 hrs

I woke at my normal time and although it was now two weeks since I moved into Mary's bed, I was still surprised to find her sleeping peacefully in my arms. The items to be ticked off our departure checklist had been done. Now the one commitment to my family, my delayed birthday party, will be ticked off tonight and we will commence our seven-day countdown. We had no need to rush today as there was little we could do before tonight's party. I let

Mary sleep on and reviewed our progress since arriving home.

"Good morning, Adonis," Mary said as her eyes popped open and the smile that greets each new day lit up her face.

"Good morning, Aphrodite," I replied and held her closer to kiss and cuddle.

"What time is it," she asked.

"Seven-thirty, darling," I replied.

"I've slept-in," Mary said with a start.

"You looked so peaceful I wouldn't wake you. We don't need to hurry. The only thing on our to-do list today is my birthday party."

"Then I think I should do my exercises this morning Adonis in case we are too late or too tired tonight."

"I think that is a very good idea Aphrodite. Let's take the morning off from all our planning and organising and just enjoy ourselves. It's already very warm, how about a swim?"

Mary got out of bed and went to the bathroom for towels. For the first day of summer it was unseasonably hot and humid and when we dived into the pool it was invigorating. We swam some lazy laps together and then I brought her to me at the deep end to hold. I was standing on the bottom, but Mary couldn't reach it and clung to me instead.

"I won't let the university take up too much of our time darling and you might find it interesting to meet some of the people I have been collaborating with. I know Rod Senden at Cambridge has a daughter about your age and so does Izumi Sato in Tokyo."

"I know you have told me what awaits Adonis, but I don't want to think about other girls Aphrodite. If it happens, it happens, but it's you who I want to spend my time with."

"Oh Adonis," Aphrodite said as we broke from our kiss. I knew she was responding to the pressure of my old fella as he pressed against her thighs and she parted them to make us comfortable. She had her hands clasped behind my head and wrapped her legs around my waist. I carried her to the steps and out of the pool. I selected a spot that was sheltered from the direct rays of the sun and lowered her feet to the ground. I spread my towel and we went down onto the towel together. For a while we lay side-by-side as we dried. I had my right arm around her shoulders supporting her head and we stretched out. Mary giggled when she saw my old fella rise and point to the heavens. She rolled over to face away from me and I followed to cuddle into her back. She lifted her left leg to let my horn rest between her thighs and I brought my left hand around to fondle her breasts. We were sharing a very comfortable intimacy. In a little while I felt Mary's hand parting her outer lips and pressing my knob against her clitoris. Instinctively I added some backwards and forward motions making my head run up and down her inner lips and then to meet her clitoris again.

"Do you like that Adonis, I do," Mary said.

"I like it too Aphrodite," I said and increased the frequency on my movements.

Mary arched her back to give me a fuller angle of attack and guided my knob into her vagina. I came up onto my knees and lifted her by her hips into my groin. She spread her legs apart and we were now in the full doggy-style position. I ran my hands up to her breasts and fondled them and brought them down to hold her hips to me as I plunged in and out.

"Oh Yes Adonis," Aphrodite cried and sent ripples along my shaft to add to my own motion. I took my hands back to her breasts and then moved them up and down her body in sync with my thrusting. My hands went down into her groin to excite her clit and up over her mound, belly and ribcage to squeeze her breasts and tease her nipples.

"If I could only kiss you now Aphrodite," I gasped.

"Soon darling," Aphrodite gasped too. She caught my right hand on my next pass and held it to her lips to kiss and tongue tickle my palm. She sucked my index and middle fingers into her mouth and gave them oral sex and nibbles. She sent ripples up and down my shaft and I could hold it back no longer.

"Oh darling, darling, I'm coming," Aphrodite cried, and I felt her vagina throb beneath me. I brought my hands back to her hips to support her and only made gentle movements as she sucked out the last of my cum.

"Lean back a little Adonis," Aphrodite said.

I did as she asked, and she performed a very neat 180-degree turn bringing her right leg up and over for me to now face her and claim her lips. I rolled her with me until I was underneath, and she was lying on top of me. I held her tight as her orgasm faded away with little aftershocks.

It was another twenty minutes before I went slack, and Aphrodite released me.

"We'd better get cleaned up and have some breakfast darling," Mary said as last.

We picked up our towels and went to the bathroom to shower together. We put on light wraps and after breakfast we did the housework that needed to be done: made our bed with fresh linen, set the washing machine going and cleaned our bathroom.

We continued to make our house ready for whoever we find to housesit for us while we are away: another one of the items on our checklist.

"I can pack my work clothes away in a storage cupboard and start packing the clothes I will be taking with me; that will free up a lot of space in my wardrobe and drawers," Mary said.

"I have a lot of clothes in my wardrobe that I have outgrown. I'll pack them in boxes and find a charity for them. While we are about it, we may as well pack the clothes we want to take with us. The more we do today the less pressure will be on us during the week," I said.

"It really feels we are on our way darling. Nothing will stop us now," Mary said and came into my arms to be kissed.

I collected suitcases and cartons from the storeroom and by lunchtime we had a considerable collection of cases and cartons stacked in the front hall: some to go to a charity, some to go into store and the remainder to go into the luggage bay of Bravo Mike Charlie — or so Mary thought.

Mary prepared a light salad for lunch and we ate it in the shade of the patio.

"We needn't be concerned about the contents of the refrigerator, freezer or pantry. Whoever minds the house for us will be welcome to their contents and to use anything we leave behind," Mary said.

"We must make finding our house sitters a top priority Mary. We can't just lock the doors and fly away," I said.

"We could start with the Grands and Greats tonight. Now that my sabbatical is approved. We must tell them we are going and that my professorship will be awarded on Saturday night. They might know someone suitable,"

Mary replied, and I agreed it would be a good place to start.

“What I suggest now, seeing that we have a few hours at our disposal is to prepare a slide show from our cameras that we can run at the party. It will show the family that we are prepared to share with them, show them that we are not bound in doom and gloom and at the same time save us repeating our lines over and over again as different ones question us.”

I went to work with a purpose. We had our own shots and downloads from the cameras of mates. We only selected those frames where there was no hint of our love. Those where I was not holding Mary too tight or too close, where we were not exchanging those glances that anyone with half a brain, or any love in their hearts, might instantly recognize our feelings. It was not easy; it was hard.

“I’ll leave you to finish the presentation Brad and begin to get ready,” Mary said.

Now, with the frames selected I only had to arrange them in the sequences I wanted them shown. It only took me half-an-hour to do so and at the same time made a second slideshow containing all the photos we had accumulated but didn’t want anyone else to see: particularly the sequence captured by Mary’s camera when she delivered the second part of my birthday present over the Gulf of Capricorn. I took our private memory stick to give to Mary for safekeeping and put tonight’s slideshow aside for me to take to my party. When I entered our bedroom, Mary was dozing on the bed. Her head was supported on pillows and she appeared asleep. Her right knee was raised, and her left leg lay casually to the side. The loose wrap she was wearing had fallen away from her right knee and breast. It was a glorious sight and I pictured her as the subject of a painting in oils by one of the old masters. I bent over her and gave her a gentle kiss on her lips. Her eyes remained closed, but a faint smile spread across her cheeks. I planted another small kiss on her neck and then on her exposed right breast. My next gentle kiss was given to her curly mound.

"Yes, Adonis," I heard Aphrodite say softly and felt her fingers running through my hair and pressing me deeper into her groin as her legs came apart. I got up onto the bed and Aphrodite opened her outer lips with her fingers while looking at me with a welcoming smile.

"We will probably be late getting home tonight Adonis," Aphrodite said as her excitement increased.

"It was delightful darling Adonis. Next time I want to suck you off. I want to taste you as you have now tasted me."

We lay together under the fan for another forty minutes.

"We have a party to go to Adonis," Aphrodite said at last.

"It's been a wonderful day already Aphrodite, but we did promise," I replied.

We showered together and dressed. Mary had selected for me a dark blue blazer, pale blue shirt, a complementary tie, light grey trousers and dark blue slip on shoes.

"Would you put this in a safe place for us, Mary? It's the unabridged version of what we'll show them tonight."

"I'd love to see it," Mary said. Taking the stick and burying it deep in her bedside cabinet.

Chapter 4

The Party

Saturday 1 December 2012 – 1900 hrs

Now ready to leave we made a splendid looking modern couple. Mary was stunning in her chic, dark blue cocktail dress, suitably demure to match her age, complexion, position and her present marital status of a recently widowed young professional. Nobody at the party had ever seen Mary turned out in anything unsuitable or inappropriate and they would not be disappointed tonight. Although it was my birthday more eyes would be on Mary than anyone else. Her own generation admired her without envy or jealousy, the Grands and Greats absolutely adored her, particularly as they were more aware of her early problems bringing me into the world for them to dote on. The younger generation looked up to her as the epitome of style and strove to emulate her as they matured. Their mothers, having realised that Mary's work must have validity seeing her involvement in the Genome Project and one of their number having heard a briefing of her female swab and male sperm monitoring project encouraged their daughters, on entering puberty, to contact Mary's department and enrol. If Mary was doing this, it must be of importance and might even save their own or daughter's life someday. I tried to present myself as a dutiful son entering adulthood and tragically losing his father just when he needed him most.

"Let's face the music," Mary said, turning to the door. In the car we had planned our strategy. We were not to spend too much time together. I was assigned to mingle with people my own age while Mary would look out for the Grands and Greats and gossip with her generation. All expected stuff. No doubt that the boys and young husbands would gather at times at one end of the hall, telling tall stories and swapping yarns, considered typical Aussie manners.

The girls would often be seen tripping off to the bathroom in twos and threes to powder their nose or touch up their lipstick, a task no young Aussie female can perform alone. There wouldn't be many young monsters running about playing chasings as most parents had opted for babysitters to guard their young children and babies. However, there would still be about sixty-to-seventy guests by Mary's reckoning. We stopped at the foyer of the hotel. The concierge was dutifully at the passenger side door, opening it and holding it back to allow this lady to emerge from the cocoon of the XK like some brilliant butterfly.

I, of course, was soon at Mary's side offering my hand to allow her to emerge elegantly from the low-slung car. As I passed the garage attendant I pressed the keys to the Jag into his hands without the hint of bravado or patronage as if I were a squire of about forty, long accustomed to driving high powered sports cars and escorting beautiful ladies. The attendant was agog that I so readily trusted him with this beautiful machine. He finally dragged his eyes away from the XK to take in Mary, a more splendid vision than the XK, rising from the car to take my arm and with eyes only for me glide away as smoothly as any Jag made. He snapped back to reality as the concierge called, 'Get to it, more are coming'.

The attendant slipped behind the wheel and with infinite care gently glided away. This little beauty would have pride of place in the garage tonight. In the widest bay to ensure that no clumsy bugger would scratch her sides. We walked to the small ballroom and just as we turned into the room the six-piece dance band swung into the first bars of HAPPY BIRTHDAY. Everyone in the room burst into song. As we moved forward to the centre of the room, with Mary holding my arm, I smiled at all the relatives. We were greeted at the mini stage by the most effusive of the Grand's generation playing MC for the evening.

"Happy Birthday Brad, Welcome Home Mary," Bruce's Uncle Bertie almost shouted into the mike. He grasped my hand and pumped it while he turned to Mary and planted a big kiss on her cheek. The guests cheered loudly, determined to keep any doom and gloom away from marring this delayed celebration. "We didn't know whether to walk you in to HAIL TO THE CHIEF," Uncle Bertie continued, knowing that everybody knew it was reserved for the incumbent US President's entrance, "or the GRAND MARCH from Aida; so, we settled for something where everybody knew the words." Laughs and claps greeted Uncle Bertie's overstatement. "Now come on Brad: wheel your mother around the room so we can all get into the action and get this room jumping."

The band responded with a foxtrot and I took Mary into my arms to circle the floor to claps, cheers and smiles from the guests. The whole family loved to dance. They moved onto the floor as Mary and I finished our solo circuit. Grands, uncles, aunts, cousins, nephews and nieces were on the move.

Taking our opportunity Mary and I quietly left the dance to go and greet the Greats who were alone now, tapping their toes and admiring several generations of their descendants. The Greats were sitting together at a top round table. The men rose as they saw us approach, kissed Mary and pumped my hand in succession. Mary and I then followed each other around the table receiving hugs and kisses from the matriarchs of this growing clan. Chairs were pulled up for Mary on one side of the table and me on the other and while the Greats concentrated on Mary, I slipped away to the now open bar and collected each Great's favourite tipple before the dancers tired and would surely head for the bar. Returning to the table I quietly walked behind the chairs and served each with their special drink, without anyone needing to ask for anything. In front of Mary I placed a champagne cocktail and I had brought a schooner of beer for myself, thinking one of these would save me making extra trips to a crowded bar.

"Neat bit of footwork out at the drome on Wednesday Brad," Great-Grandfather Clifford spoke first. "Any old pilot like me would tumble to what was going on."

"What do you mean Pops?" I asked. "Well you wouldn't pull a stunt like that without permission from the tower. You'd soon be without a licence," Pops continued. "Funny to see the big jets queued-up waiting for the Pilatus to pass by."

Already knowing all about the event Mary slipped away, picked up a tray and made a selection for the Greats as the hotel staff was lining the buffet arranged at the side and away from the dance floor.

"The tower offered me both clearances together on short final with a limit of five minutes; I accepted the offer knowing that it gave me protection, all the way home to bed and it worked," I spoke up.

"It wouldn't have meant much if you bounced down the runway though son," Pops sounded a word of warning.

"Oh, I pondered it a little, knowing that I was on a hiding to nothing if I failed, but I had the bird well established before the offer, three greens, the turbine purring and ready for some reverse thrust as we touched-down, it seemed the logical thing to do after being hounded by the press."

"When I thanked the controller as I shut down, he remarked that it was the least he could do as he had known Dad for a long time," I said, remembering to speak of their grandson as my father rather than the now more familiar Bruce.

"Well we were most impressed. The Pilatus looks stunning head on with that big prop spinning," Mary's side of the family spoke up in support.

"I'm glad we found you together," I said changing the subject completely. "We have some important news to tell you and we want you to be first to know." My eight great-grandparents immediately stopped talking and were attentive. "Dad wanted me to take a gap year and amongst other things visit the Clifford interests overseas. Mum wanted to take a year's sabbatical and come too, but that would have meant passing up the professorship she was expecting in April. The ANU Board met on Thursday night and granted Mum her sabbatical and to allay her fears that her work might be diminished in the hands of some other appointment brought her appointment to the Chair forward to next week. Professor Jack is to remain in a caretaker role as Professor Emeritus until her return."

"That's wonderful news Brad and Mary," Great-Gran Clifford said. "We'll miss you both terribly, but it will be a marvellous experience.

"We will tell my grandparents when they come off the floor, but we won't tell anyone else until after we are gone. It seems the media has lost interest in us now and we don't want to stir them up again."

Bruce's parents, Jean and Robert Clifford and Mary's parents, Francine and William Franklin returned to our table. I rose to kiss my grandmothers and shake my grandfathers' hand.

"Brad's got some exciting news for you," Great-Gran Clifford spoke up.

"I'm going on the gap year that Dad had planned, and Mum is taking her sabbatical and coming too," I announced.

"What about the Chair, Mary. Will it go to someone else now?"

“No, the Board has brought it forward to next Saturday night. Professor Jack is to remain in a caretaker role until I return,” Mary explained.

“When will you leave?” Nan Franklin asked.

“Next Sunday, we hope. One of the most important things we have to do is to find someone suitable as house-sitters while we are away. We thought we’d ask you tonight if you can recommend anyone,” I said.

“Chris and Jo are looking for a place to rent while they have their house renovated,” Gran Clifford was quick to reply, “You could have a talk to them.”

“If they are interested, they would be perfect. We know they would look after it as their own,” Mary replied.

Mary and I did another round of the table for more kisses and handshakes; well wishes for our trip and congratulations for Mary on her appointment.

“So that’s what the email I received from Don this morning was all about,” Pops Clifford spoke up. “It simply said, ‘Please be available for a function at ANU on Saturday night 8 December — Details to follow’.”

“I got one of them too,” each of the other men confirmed.

With the dancers leaving the floor on seeing the table ready for service they began serving themselves, it was mostly a case of the women and girls getting two serves from the table and the men and boys collecting two drinks from the bar. A waiter came to the Grands and Greats table and took their orders. Mary and I excused ourselves.

“If you don’t mind, we’ll find Chris and Jo and see if they have found anything yet, and we had better mingle with the other guests,” Mary said.

“Happy birthday Brad,” Jo said and kissed me on the cheek.

“Thank you, Aunty Jo,” I replied as Uncle Chris took my hand in a firm grip.

“Please drop the ‘Aunty’ business Brad. You’re too grown up and handsome for that,” Jo added.

“That goes for me too Brad,” Chris began. “You realise you are my boss now of course.”

“Rest assured there will be no change of direction now Dad’s gone. I want to earn for myself the trust that everyone placed in Dad. Particularly the Grands and Greats,” I replied.

“They look pretty happy tonight Brad,” Chris continued.

“We have just told them I am going to take the gap year Dad had planned and Mum is going to take a year’s sabbatical and come too,” I explained.

“Gran Clifford said you were looking for a place to rent while your renovations are done, Chris,” Mary said. “What about our place?”

“It would be perfect Mary. What’s the rent?”

“Don’t bring me to tears Chris; how could I charge Bruce’s brother rent. Brad and I can’t use it for a year why shouldn’t you, there’s no mortgage Bruce has left us debt free, please do us a favour and say ‘Yes’. We could then go away without any concern knowing home will still be home on our return.”

Chris happily accepted Mary’s offer.

“Will you come and collect the keys and see the workings of the place on Friday at noon?” I asked.

"We will be leaving on Sunday. Finding the right people to look after our home was the most important thing for us to do before we leave," I said. "We're not telling anyone else our plans as we don't want any more attention from the media."

"We won't say a word Brad," Jo confirmed, and Chris nodded his head.

Mary and I went to mingle as we had planned. As expected, the younger aunts and cousins paid me some attention as I chatted along with them while slipping in a few bush yarns for the young men. Dancers were coming back onto the floor and I worked my way around one side of the floor while Mary went around the other. After about an hour Uncle Bertie was back on the mike asking them to pause for the birthday cake ritual. The cake was delivered, lights were dimmed and with the usual banter as I cut the cake there was a second rendition of HAPPY BIRTHDAY followed with the, as usual, rough attempt at FOR HE'S A JOLLY GOOD FELLOW and ending with loud calls of speech, speech. For the first time in many minutes Mary and I came together again for Mary to deliver the expected chaste kiss to her son's cheek and so did many of the girls. Uncle Bertie came forward with the mike for me and after I made the usual brief speech thanking them for their attendance and support for my mother and myself. I then introduced my slideshow:

"Instead of trying to tell you where we have been these last two weeks, I put together a short video of some of the places we visited and friends of Dad's who we were privileged to meet for the first time," I paused briefly. A member of the staff moved in front of me on my pre-arranged cue, placing the projector near me and the screen in a position where all could see. I inserted the memory stick; the staff adjusted the lights and I switched on the projector and continued.

"As most of you know Dad designed and supervised many major engineering works around Australia with quite a few in the outback. In doing so he met and kept in touch with many fine people and I believe that is why he chose this gift for me for my birthday." During this period, our departure from Canberra, run up the coast and entry to Sydney Harbour was running.

"You are now seeing what we saw from inside the cabin with what the media has shown you from the outside," I continued. There were some gasps of surprise at the head on to the bridge and the pull away to the next views showing Queen Mary 2.

"The next section is our run up the east coast to Cairns. Once we realised that the barman had placed us with the Pilatus that had just landed, we hotfooted it out of there and headed to the one place near Cairns where Mum had once travelled with Dad." Getting the expected words indicating relationships out was now coming to me more confidently.

"They were only too happy to take in Bruce Clifford's family; all were distressed by his death. They were most solicitous of us and continued to pass us on to one old mate after another until we arrived back here on Wednesday morning." The segments showing our arrival at Jack's and our time with them, our rounding of Cape York and the run down as far as Weipa where Mary left the cockpit followed. The next slides were from Bob's place and included evidence of Bob's most remarkable short-field take-off and landing that one can expect to see in a Cessna 182.

There were quite a few pilots in the room, particularly on the Cliffords' side and expressions of 'wow' and 'my God' were heard as Bob demonstrated his calm and faultless operation, caught on camera by me from the front seat.

“Bob offered me the left seat for the take-off and you can see, and would agree, that I did the only sane thing by refusing.

I explained that the views we expected to take of Darwin and its approaches were abandoned when we entered the Pilots’ Club on Darwin airport only to find that they too had got in on the act by offering any pilot who spotted Bravo Mike Charlie a slab of beer in return for a dollar entry fee. We slipped out quickly and didn’t approach any major airport again nor visit any towns. The show was coming to a conclusion and I finished by saying, “I cannot imagine any better present parents could give a son than putting him in command of Bravo Mike Charlie. (I lied, and Mary knew I did.) At first, we thought that the media had wrecked our trip. However, as we progressed, we were sure that this was where Dad intended to take us. This trip was for him to introduce me as his, now adult, son to people around the country with whom he enjoyed a long-standing mateship.” The show came to a finish with a round of applause and a few quite audible ‘Thanks Brad’ and ‘Great shots’.

The band came to life again and couples soon moved back to the floor. Mary had slipped away, and I noticed my first drink was still half-full and no doubt too warm to be palatable. I left it for the cleaners, accepted a cold stubby from the bar and continued to mingle.

“Ladies and Gentlemen,” Uncle Bertie began when the bracket finished. “I prevailed upon Jan to bring her violin along tonight and give us a tune.”

There was polite applause as Jan walked onto the bandstand. Everyone started drifting off the floor expecting to hear Jan perform a classical piece. Jan started with a very lively rendition of **I’ve been everywhere. https://www.youtube.com/watch?v=-UAh7ogwAYQ**

"In consideration of where Mary and Brad have been these past ten days, I've put together a little Bush Music – Please take your partners for a barn dance."

Jan started immediately with **Waltzing Matilda https://www.youtube.com/watch?v=CwvazMc5EfE** and when most of the guests were on the floor Uncle Bertie was on the mike, "Make a circle everyone and let's go progressive," he called firmly and the dancers complied. Jan followed with **The Pub with no Beer, https://www.youtube.com/watch?v=8E0aZ387M_I Road to Gundagai ,_Home among the Gumtrees**, **https://www.youtube.com/watch?v=MLWzPQmd5sc UpThereCazaly https://www.youtube.com/watch?v=2IAa0bsjGZI** and **Where the dog sits on the Tucker Box**. **https://www.youtube.com/watch?v=XxYSegLL3Fk** Everyone was singing and smiling to their partners as the ladies progressed around the circle. Uncle Bertie was back on the mike again as Jan finished the last number.

"Squares of four, ladies and gentlemen," he called.

Jan lowered her violin from her shoulder to her chest and like a Hill-Billy Fiddler broke into a vigorous TURKEY IN THE STRAW. Once the squares had formed, she began playing PRETTY LADY and Uncle Bertie started the call, "Bow to your corner," I never realised Uncle Bertie had it in him. Just like Bob singing WHAT A DIFFERENCE A DAY MADE his call was complete and professional as he took us through Allemandes left, Circle right, Acey Deucey, Do Sa Do, Drive thru and Boys and Girls trades. He kept us, and Jan, going with Swings and Promenades for fifteen minutes before he ended it with Bow to Your Partner and Promenade Home. Everyone stood where they finished and turned to clap Jan and Uncle Bertie before leaving the floor.

"I can see you want more," Uncle Bertie began again. "If you form six rows down the hall I'm sure Jan will play

Achy Breaky Heart https://www.youtube.com/watch?v=byQIPdHMpjc for a little boot-scooting line dancing."

The lines formed quickly as Jan played the introduction. Uncle Bertie began to sing.

You can tell the world you never was my girl
You can burn my clothes up when I'm gone

From the first line it was clear he had a beautiful singing voice. Not only was it different from his normal voice but also to his voice calling the square dance. Everyone was happily dancing and adding claps of their hands, nobody was thinking about the words they were singing, but I was. When Uncle Bertie sang the chorus for the first time the last line hit me, 'HE MIGHT BLOW UP AND KILL THIS MAN'. It was only yesterday I voiced similar feelings if I found Mary in another man's arms. I nearly lost the step but recovered in time. 'Would I?' I asked myself. The dance came to an end. Carol was dancing next to me in the line.

"I hope you will like living in our house for a while Carol," I said.

"What do you mean Brad?"

"Mum and I are going away for a year and your mother and father have agreed to housesit for us while your house is being renovated."

"I didn't know, but that will be nice. I've always liked your place," Carol replied.

"Mum and I only arranged it with your folks this evening Carol. I've jumped the gun I'm afraid."

"That's all right Brad. I'll act surprised when they tell me."

Carol stopped to talk to her brother and I went off in the opposite direction.

Jan was putting her violin away, so I thanked her for her impromptu performance.

"I love playing dance music Brad. It's a break from the classics and fun when people don't expect it."

"Like tonight Jan?

"Yes, people usually expect to be bored and I get a kick out of them getting a surprise."

"Happy birthday Brad," Jan said and gave me the expected kiss on the cheek.

"Thanks Jan, would you like to dance?" I asked.

"I'd love to Brad," Jan replied and put her left hand on my shoulder and raised her right hand to meet my left. My right hand went to the small of her back to hold her to me. Jan wanted to be held and to dance in the old way, and I was keen to oblige. We danced well together but hadn't had much opportunity to do so lately.

The band was playing Rock and Roll music, but I led her in a fast quickstep around the outside of the main bunch of dancers in the middle of the floor. I incorporated spins and pivots and Jan's dress flared out as she turned and when I twirled her back from a spin our bodies came together firmly as my hand went to her back again pulling her close to me.

When the music stopped everyone clapped for more and then Jan replaced her left hand on my shoulder. I hadn't clapped but left it to Jan and my right hand remained in the middle of her back ready to move off again. The band took a break and we smiled at each other and walked off the floor without breaking our hold.

"Congratulations on winning the Paganini Competition, Jan," I said. "How's the orchestra going?"

"Really great Brad. I've taken over from Mum as first violin. She graciously announced that after ten years as leader the orchestra needed a younger person in the role and nominated me. It's quite a promotion."

"That's marvellous Jan, you're very young to be the leader of a national orchestra."

"I know Brad, it's a big honour and a big responsibility. I think I was elected to the job because I won the Paganini. It was the first time for an Australian. Some years they don't even award a first prize. I didn't think I'd even be considered as I've never had a celebrated European teacher."

"If your parents weren't recognised before they certainly will be now, and you have brought them this respect. "You are so much like Mum Jan," I said remembering to use the right name.

"That's a very big compliment Brad, Mary is beautiful and has always been my idol. "You're so much like your father Brad."

"That's a very big compliment too Jan," I replied.

"It must have been a wonderful trip you had. They seemed such a nice lot of friends you met."

"They are Jan; there are no false airs and graces in the outback. Would you like to come for a spin in the Pilatus one day?" I offered.

"I'd love to Brad," Jan was quick to reply.

"I'm sorry Jan," I said after a short pause, "I shouldn't have said that. I would like to take you for a flight, but it won't be for a while. Please don't tell anyone but we're planning to go overseas for a year. I'm having a gap year and Mum's taking a year's sabbatical."

"Oh, that would be wonderful Brad, I'm sure you'll have a great time," Jan said with a smile while trying to keep her voice cheerful. The band started again with a slow foxtrot and Jan and I moved off together again. Jan kept a smile on her face but didn't look into my eyes again. The bandleader gave a fair rendition of Ray Charles singing **Half as Much** and when he sang the last two lines:

I know that I would never be this blue
If you only loved me half as much as I love you

Jan said, "Have a nice trip Brad; I must go, Mum's waiting for me," She gave me a quick kiss on the cheek and hurried away.

The music was heating up along with the noise and the Greats decided it was time to go. Mary and I reached the door having each mingled along the opposite sides of the room. We arrived along with the Greats to thank them again and to say goodnight. We crossed over, passing with a quick wink and a squeeze to Mary's hand as we brushed together. We continued on, each now working the opposite side. We knew that while we were expected to be the last to arrive, we were also expected to be the last to leave.

The music was really starting to thump now, and I peeled off my jacket to join the others. I got to dance with my aunties, grandmothers and Jan's mother. They were all good dancers and while most were dancing disco in the middle of the floor my partners and I preferred to dance quicksteps and foxtrots around the outside. The band started packing up due to a midnight noise embargo on the hotel. Fortunately, the guests had got the message from Mary's mum that I would be happier not to receive presents. I had enjoyed my **Birthday Party**

http://www.futuristic.guru/birthday-party more than I had expected.

After retrieving my memory stick, I took all my presents by the arm and walked out the door. I passed the concierge five bucks as he held the door open for me to lower Mary neatly into the XK. I gave the garage attendant the same as I was handed my keys and slid in behind the wheel and glided away.

“Proud of you Captain,” Mary spoke softly as she turned to watch me.

“I love you too darling,” I replied, not diverting my eyes from the road. Like my approach on Wednesday morning I was not going to risk my precious cargo on a brief glimpse when I knew there was so much more waiting for me when we got home. The loss of Bruce was enough to make me a very wary driver for evermore. We completed our drive in silence. It was to become an acceptable part of our life that we were happy to chat away merrily on our headsets in the air, and even play little games. We knew we had all sorts of protection around us and could include up and down in our heading if needed. We also had the aid of the latest autopilot and many alarms to alert us to any possible malfunction. We also knew that for much of our time in the air some radar operator would be seeing our blip on his screen and that there were operators on a number of frequencies waiting in case they heard the call ‘Bravo Mike Charlie’. Up there I was happy to sit back and let my eyes feast on Mary but never down here amongst the road-ragers. I exerted every ounce of my powers to keep harm away.

Sunday 2 December 2012 – 0100 hrs

Home again we sat on the two-piece lounge for a last cup of coffee that we could drink to the end.

“What did you say to Jan, darling?” Mary asked.

"We talked of several things. I congratulated her on being appointed first violin of the national orchestra and her winning the Paganini Competition. I remarked how alike she was to you and that I'd take her for a flight in Bravo Mike Charlie. Then I apologised because we'd be away for twelve months. I asked her not to tell anybody else though. Why?"

"When she left you, she went hurrying into the ladies' room dabbing her eyes with a hankie. Do you remember what the band was playing Brad?"

"HALF AS MUCH, I believe."

"If you only loved me half as much as I love you," Mary crooned to me. "Jan's in love with you darling."

"I like Jan a lot, more than anyone else in the family other than you, but I've never said anything to her suggesting that we get closer. I was always shy of our age difference for one thing and we are cousins," I replied. "I'd never say anything to upset her."

"What about our age difference darling? Jan is only three years older than you, not eighteen."

"It may as well be Mary, when you're fifteen," I replied. "That's when I first really noticed her and how alike she was to you."

"I'm sure she will get over it darling. She won't be lonely long."

I leant over and kissed her, "Time for bed," I said. I stood, bent over and Mary placed her arms around my neck. She instinctively held one wrist with her other hand, as children do when they have to be moved without being disturbed, she rested her head on my shoulder and I easily lifted her and carried her off to bed. By the time we got to the bedroom Mary was asleep. I threw the bedclothes back with one hand and managed to undo the long zipper at her back and unclip her bra, before I lowered her so gently to the bed. The chic cocktail dress I eased from under her bottom and carefully hung it on a rack. I slipped off her little bra with ease but then I had to contend with a suspender belt which was new territory for me, I felt a little out of my depth. The front suspenders came away but then I had to lift one leg at a time to manipulate the one at the rear. With each leg I rolled the stocking down from Mary's thigh so that I didn't have to raise her legs again. This could really be fun, I thought if she was awake. For a moment, I thought she might have been foxing; teasing me and that she would at some time pull me down on top of her and smother me with kisses. But it was not so. After easing her skimpy panties from under her bottom and sliding them off her legs. I straightened my back and then gazed down at Mary's curly mound. I resisted the urge to plant a goodnight kiss on it before I carefully replaced the bedcovers. I undressed, made a quick trip to the bathroom and on my return found that Mary had rolled onto her side and was fast asleep. I slipped in behind her and carefully placed my left hand on her hip. A few minutes passed while I relaxed alongside her. Almost stealthily, I felt my hand being pulled up to cup her left breast and heard Mary whisper, "Thank-you".

Chapter 5

Preparations

Sunday 2 December 2012 – 0700 hrs

"Good morning Adonis," Mary said as she woke in my arms.

"Good morning Aphrodite," I replied and welcomed the new day with a kiss.

With only a week to go and our last major item accounted for we lingered over breakfast to coordinate our movements and to make sure we had covered all bases before leaving.

From the moment we made our decision to go we had been compiling our departure checklist for the Pilatus and ourselves. There was to be no chance of our being in Customs in Darwin and presenting to do our departures only to find that one of our passports was missing or out of date. We were both too well organised to let any such thing happen, but we knew there would be many things to do. As we were ticking one item off this pre-flight list we would often be adding two or more. Like the day Don told Mary of her appointment having to add the dinner in her honour for Saturday and a whole new sub-list for that: dress, shoes, accessories, hair appointment, how we would get there, whether she would need an acceptance speech and all manner of things.

Today, Mary was shopping for a new dress and as this could involve looking for shoes and perhaps some other accessory it could take quite a while; then there was a meeting in town for coffee with a few of her non-working girl friends.

Thursday was earmarked for her to take her last visit to the ANU campus, for quite a while, and for me to attend the Clifford Holdings meeting. Mary had to say goodbye to many of her own department: assuring them that she would keep in touch via Skype, email and phone and the year would go only too quickly. Mary planned to borrow a golf cart to tour the other faculties where she and Bruce had accumulated personal and professional friends over the past two decades. She received many congratulations on being appointed to the Chair, as news like this always gets about, even though it was only set for publication at the dinner. She left each with good wishes and blessings.

Finally, Mary collected a big bundle of introductions from the Vice-Chancellor to his opposite number at many famous institutions. Mary of course had her own list of contacts in most places. She was well known internationally already and although she had met few of these people face-to-face, the internet had proved its worth.

The Vice-Chancellor's introductions were a professional courtesy by one respected institution to another. It was a security blanket thrown over us insuring our safe conduct; a touring professor already held in high regard would be well protected wherever that person went and one so elegantly beautiful even more so. Mary didn't really understand or properly see the effect she made or brought out in other people.

Mary had selected her dress and accessories, done the rounds of the Uni, gathered her bundle of introductions and said her goodbyes to the ANU with only her reception to go. When I asked to see her dress she declined and said, "Wait until it's fully loaded darling, only fools and school children see a job half-done remember?" I couldn't resist thinking of the job I had half-done and the surprise that it was sure to create when Mary saw Bravo Mike Charlie fully loaded.

Friday 7 December 2012 – 1000 hrs

The main item on the on the list was to bring Bruce's younger brother and his family to the house to get to know where everything was: how it worked and what matters needed to be taken care of over the period of the year. I had asked Frank and Alison Swann to come to meet Chris and his family on Friday at 10 am. Frank was the current, youngish, retiree looking after the Clifford-house garden. Frank and his wife Alison were in their early fifties. He had been made redundant from his position as a gardener with the Canberra government in their latest cost-cutting drive. The Swann's lived in the original house my great-grandfather had built on the adjacent corner of our large block. Frank had tended the garden and kept us supplied with eggs, poultry, fresh fruit, vegetables and flowers. The garden always produced more than our needs and Bruce's arrangement with Frank was for him to take whatever he required for him and Alison and then give the rest to anyone who might be in need. Alison was always available to help with the housework: preserve or freeze seasonal surpluses and help with the cooking if Mary and Bruce entertained.

Chris and Jo arrived bringing with them their son Rick and daughter Carol. Rick was very close to my age, had finished high school this year, and was continuing directly into a computer-technology degree course. Carol had just finished year eleven and had her eye on a nursing career following her mother's example.

Frank and Alison arrived through the rear door having walked across the garden from their home. Mary made the introductions and with Frank and Alison showed them around the house and its workings.

During our walk around the garden Rick and I ended up in the garage. It was the right time to spring my surprise on Rick. I handed him the keys to my two-year-old Ford Focus and said, "We hope you will accept this as your birthday present from Mum, Dad and me. She's all paid-up for rego and insurance for the year ahead, still under warranty with free service, you'll only have to put petrol in her and she's not very thirsty."

Rick was amazed, "Brad are you sure?'" he felt obliged to ask.

"Of course, mate, Dad would be horrified if I clung to this after taking over his XK. It was a simple choice. Give you the Ford or give you the Jag. I'm no saint mate."

I felt the wonderful warm glow of giving a good present and seeing it joyfully received. We walked back to our parents; Rick was tossing up and catching his car keys.

"Why so happy Rick?" Jo asked having spotted the expression on his face.

"I've just received my first birthday present."

"But your birthday isn't until next month," Jo continued.

"I know but they won't be here next month," Rick replied and turned to Mary. "How can I thank you Auntie Mary but thank you. I wish Uncle Bruce was here."

Mary gave Rick a hug and planted a kiss on his cheek.

"We do too Rick, but don't be too sure that he isn't," Mary turned to Jo, "Which reminds me Jo, would you mind driving my little red terror, I'd hate to think of her becoming stuck to the floor from lack of use. It wouldn't be the same car when we come back if her cogs were left stuck in the one place. Don't worry about a thing: rego and insurances are all on auto-payment I'll leave a note about where to take her for a service, she's still under warranty. I'll need her until Saturday afternoon Jo, but I'll leave the keys on the hook over there. We've only told the Grands and Greats so far, but we'll be gone from here by eight on Sunday morning, don't tell anyone else though."

“Who are you flying with Mary?” Jo asked innocently.

Mary looked at her with a somewhat puzzled look on her face, “Brad of course.”

Chris quickly picked this up, “In the Pilatus?”

“Of course,” Mary replied, her voice indicating an unspoken ‘Why not?’

“But?” Chris attempted to justify the surprise on the faces of his family.

“Don’t worry Chris that last two weeks was just a shakedown trip. I had been planning this with Bruce for some months. With the Chair in sight I had to make a study tour, Bruce was going to join us as much as possible and catch up on a few year’s untaken annual leave, let alone his accrued long service. Now I’m sure he’ll be with us all the way. As we walked Chris’s family back to the car Mary realised that Carol was leaving without any apparent benefit from the day, although she would be thrilled with her room and the facilities of this house.

“We’ll have a car for you too Carol for your eighteenth, but I’ll be looking out for something nice for you in Paris,” Mary said.

“Thanks Auntie Mary that would be nice,” Carol replied.

As soon as our house sitters were out the gate Mary tuned to me, “Quick lover, we’ve got our checklists to complete. I plan to get a sandwich and coffee for lunch somewhere, will you do the same? If we get going now, I can be home by seven to get you a nice tea, nothing fancy mind you but you can debrief me then if you would like.”

“Brazen hussy,” I replied. “Putting thoughts about how I’m going to do that in my mind for the afternoon while I’ve got so much work to do.”

We closed the house and came close together in the garage to share a parting kiss before we mounted our own steeds and rode away. Mary was heading to the bank to complete the financial arrangements that I had initiated earlier in the week. We were ensuring that all financial commitments would be met by due date while we were away. Mary also had appointments with our accountant to complete her tax matters for last year and with the solicitors to ensure that Bruce’s estate could be closed out in our absence. She expected no glitches as Bruce had carefully planned for this event. Being an astute engineer and a pilot, he was always mindful of the damage loose ends or sloppy planning could cause. His will of course was a classic in ensuring clarity and precision: the disposal of his body being the most obvious example. After several other minor stops, Mary would make it home by seven.

I was now free to attend to what I considered my prime task. I hadn’t seen Bravo Mike Charlie since I handed the job over to Greg Howard on the 28th of November. I had kept out of the way of the engineer and joinery foreman during the week and I was confident that I was not about to be disappointed. I chose to do all my off-airport calls first and that would have me arriving at the airport around three o’clock.

I asked them to hold their employees who had worked on the refit so that I could get some good photos for the book I would publish on our return. I asked the engineer what brand his crew drank and how many would be there. I was told that twenty-four people had been involved and that half preferred Fosters Draught and half XXXX Gold. I picked up four cold slabs on the way, calculating that four beers each during two hours of hangar talk, after a very busy and strenuous week, was to be all that I was going to allow to be held against my conscience. I thought Bravo Mike Charlie would be quite satisfied with that degree of head wetting after her refit. I consciously refrained from calling it a re-christening for I would never change her call sign no matter how recognisable it became.

I delivered the beer to the hangar and went with the engineer and the joinery foreman to the engineer's office to receive their invoices.

"Checked these haven't you?" I asked.

"Of course, Brad," their answers came in unison.

"You're sure there are no errors in my favour?" I asked.

They were obviously stunned that my having walked in ten days ago with a grand plan for a design that would equal any corporate jet in the air, and after putting the job in their hands along with a healthy deposit and didn't interfere, I was now concerned that they might have made a mistake in my favour. They recovered their composure and again began almost in unison. "No mate, everyone has been paid over the rate, everyone gets their holidays, their super, and every rule in the book has been observed. It only remains for that bloke from the CAA to deliver her upgraded Airworthy with her modifications and additions approved and you can fly her around the world,"

"That's just what I intend do fellas, can I borrow that PC? I'll do the bank transfers and then we can go and have a look at this little lady."

The engineer and foreman again looked at each other while I transferred the six- figure sums without the slightest blink. One gave a slight lift to his shoulders as if saying 'This bloke is doing this all back to front.' Every customer they had every had at this level had been looking over their shoulder or had some flunky or bean-counter doing it. They would have examined the finished job in detail: hoping to be able to demand a more than comparable discount for any blemish. They would have examined their invoice looking for any slight variation from the initial order on which they could do the same. Grudgingly, after several months they would pay up, sometimes even at what is known in the debt-trade as 'on-the-courthouse-steps'. This didn't only apply to rich individuals but some very high-ranking companies who always thought they could hold back the due claims of their creditors to make that money work a little longer for them. I had no such qualms. The golden rule was a fundamental in the houses of my Grands and Greats and I had spent many pleasurable hours with them in my formative years. Here I had absorbed, not learnt, that the only way to be trusted was to trust. Along with this strength came the love of fine music, the love songs of the forties where so many lovers were parted through war, including some of the Greats that helped raise me, and the impeccable manners so easily delivered that I had no idea that it made me stand out in this modern crowd.

We mounted the cabin steps to the sound of the tradesmen opening their first stubbies and toasting each other on a job well done. Their money was in the bank, they would not now be at ease until they saw my acceptance of their labours displayed in my eyes, words no longer mattered. I entered the cabin and sat in the first chair facing to the rear, where the lab was located. They could see I was visibly moved. I knew at once that Mary would be thrilled: this was a palace in the air suitable for any queen, a golden chariot, a magic carpet. I looked up at the men who had brought my plans to life and said:

"This is all I could have asked for and a bit more than I expected. If you would just help me position the lab equipment we can go and crack a stubby fellas."

The engineer and joiner started down the steps and no sooner than the engineer had pulled three stubbies from the giant ice bucket, in the form of half a 200-litre fuel tank filled with several bags of ice, then I was at their side and the engineer made his first toast.

"Listen up you blokes," he easily rose above the hangar talk. "Our client is delighted with your efforts and Mike, indicating the joiner, and I have agreed there will be a tax free extra hundred in your pay envelopes next week."

This brought cheers as one would expect and trips to the ice bucket for the next beer. Only one more item to tick on my checklist., I was thinking with just a little bit of anxiety rising within; that little bit of paper, the updated Airworthiness Certificate with the approval of the extra tank, shower and appliances was all that was holding Bravo Mike Charlie, with Mary and me on board, from taking to the skies. My fears soon vanished. Ron Johnstone from the CAA pulled up outside and came in with the treasured piece of paper in his hand. I thanked him, invited him to join us for a beer and once settled with a stubby in hand I politely asked the examiner whether any photos of the refit had been taken for their office files.

"No mate, we got your message from Greg, we know the press gave you a bit of a hiding and this little beauty would have them running off with all that fuckin silver spoon, spoilt rich boy nonsense, no-way mate, it's all in the files as drawings and specs but nobody's interested in that stuff. Naturally we'd love to have a good set of your pics when you're ready to release them, all in your own good time."

I thanked him sincerely.

"She must be the best Pilatus in the air now," the CAA bloke continued, "'what have you got, about four thousand kilometres or eight hours?"

"Yes, that will be quite comfortable," I confirmed. "She will always be flying well under maximum weight. With all tanks full, a good wind and an economical cruise setting she will probably make five thousand with reserves,"

"You don't mind staying aloft that long?" the CAA bloke asked.

"Not in the least," I was quick to reply. 'We're both fully licensed, she's single pilot as you know, one can go for a walk, take a leak, get food, do some other work or have a sleep while the other flies."

"You don't mind if I say my goodbyes and beat a quick retreat. Now that I've got this bit of paper in my pocket I'd better get home and do some packing."

"Not at all mate, I'd have been gone in a flash. Give my regards to Dr Clifford, you're lucky to have such a co-pilot. Gawd your old man would have loved to see what you have achieved here."

I thanked the CAA examiner again and moved through the crew thanking everyone personally.

I met the engineer and joiner near the exit door. Greg had BMC's service manual with him and sat down to sign-off on the work done, putting his reputation on the line in doing so and then signed **Bravo Mike Charlie's http://www.futuristic.guru/bmc-refit** daily maintenance log that rides along on-board.

"She's all yours Captain," Greg said and shook my hand again. There were more handshakes and wishes for 'CAVOK – all the way', and then I was able to leave. I too would be home by seven but with the new burden of keeping this now certified project quiet until Sunday morning.

We arrived home together.

As soon as we had closed the front door behind us Mary grabbed my hand, "Come on lover were going to strip off and get into the spa together. This little bird isn't going to sit on that branch tonight or let your fingers put her to sleep as you did last time."

"Wait, wait a second," I said and dropped her hand to get the Airworthy out of my pocket. "Look what I've got. Were up, up and away,"

"Well come on then darling, time to get up. We haven't even taken our medicine once today and this is a special occasion if I ever I saw one," Mary giggled with delight at her ability to turn every situation into a teasing horn-provoker, as she had once called it.

"I'm right behind you baby," I said. "I'm just making a slight detour through the lounge," I gathered our flutes holding them carefully in the one hand, "I'm coming through the kitchen," I opened the fridge and grabbed Tuesday's unopened bottle of Dom Perignon. Mary had stopped by our bedroom to step out of her clothes and lay them neatly on our bed; she wasn't much into ripping good things off and throwing them crumpled to what would soon be a damp bathroom floor. I arrived in the bathroom before her and quickly shaved. By the time Mary arrived I had shed my clothes and shoes to the floor; I didn't consider what I was wearing to be so highly prized that they would deprive me of a minute in Mary's arms.

"Ooh," Mary exclaimed arriving stark naked to see me standing in all my glory with my old fella stiff at attention.

"Ooh" Mary cried again as the cork flew out of the champagne, flew over her head and bounced off two walls. I pressed the first glass into Mary's hand, quickly filled my own, put the bottle close by the spa so that I could reach it and then joined hands with Mary, so we could step into the spa together.

"To Bravo Mike Charlie," I proposed.

“To Bravo Mike Charlie,” Mary joyously agreed, “happy skies to all who her fly in her.”

We paused, still holding hands, and with our free hands we sipped champagne and confirmed that each other’s checklist was complete except for the packing we must do tonight and the few remaining things that we had earlier listed for tomorrow. We sunk into the spa and talked about our day’s doings. I told Mary of the few beers I had shouted Greg’s crew (for that was what our engineer’s name really was). Among ourselves we would often say the ‘LayMe said this or the LayMe said that’ in a rough but funny way of talking about our LAME which everyone in our circle knew was a Licensed Aircraft Maintenance Engineer. The LAME in fact held more power over an aircraft than its pilots or owners; the bird just did not fly without his signature. I slipped the piece of paper into a drawer to ensure it stayed dry. I saw that Mary had accepted my enthusiasm over the paper as being the sign off for Bravo Mike Charlie’s latest hundred hourly and the little ritual of a few beers was to wish us well as we were going off for the year. I took Mary’s now empty flute and placed it alongside mine on the floor where I knew they would come to no harm. I didn’t even offer Mary a refill as I could feel her excitement growing along with my own and the last thing, we needed was alcohol. As I settled back into the spa Mary rolled over onto me.

“No funny business tonight lover,” Mary began. “You won’t put me to sleep again or hypnotise me.”

Even after my explanation to Mary at dinner on Tuesday night we couldn’t understand what I had done to her physically because I would never forget the messages my fingers gave or received. However, neither of us could account for the time and that was a little scary for both of us. Heaven’s above if we became so entranced while flying. Mary had found my demonstration of the aura exciting and interesting but not something she could use as a matter of course.

"It's my turn now to weave a bit of magic Adonis," Mary said.

"What are you going to do?" I asked with a little bit of apprehension following Tuesday night's occurrence.

"Nothing much," Mary answered quite innocently, "I'll bet you that I can have you inside me without you even knowing it?"

"That's silly, Aphrodite, of course I would know. I can feel the old fella now throbbing and trying to push open the Gates to Paradise. Can't you feel that too."

"Of course, I can darling," Mary spoke quietly now, beginning to weave her brand of magic as she pushed our pubes together and immediately noticing the little shift in my attention from my hard-on as I now enjoyed the pressure being applied to my pubic bone.

"What's the bet Aphrodite?" I asked cheerfully.

"Double or nothing," Mary replied casually.

"What do you mean Aphrodite, double or nothing of what?" I asked.

"Is that what you meant darling by two millionaires getting together?" Mary asked feigning innocence as she pressed harder against my pubes.

"Wouldn't you agree," I asked. Mary now knew that she had me. Like a chess master, she knew that from this opening gambit Bruce had never won, even after their many years together. She was now diverting my attention away from my horn and the only trick now was to keep me hard and weave a little more magic. Once she had me talking I had no chance.

"But what about the bet, double of what?" I persisted.

“Oh, If I win, you must thrill me again before midnight and we will have had our special occasion day,” Mary explained.

“But if I win?” I was starting to get a little concerned.

“Oh, you can still try again, Adonis,” Mary said very cheerfully. “You know I could never hold you out.”

Mary’s voice and words were providing all the stimulus to keeping my old fella hard and even that act was working to Mary’s advantage dimming the sensation of any little movement she might make. She was deliberately causing some movement as she provided some varying pressure through our millionaires. She had my old fella so perfectly aligned with the entry to her vagina that when she had totally relaxed, she would have no trouble in allowing it to slide in without sensation until she flexed her vaginal wall, cried ‘Gotcha’ and win her bet. But there was just a little more to do while she achieved sufficient relaxation that would send no sensation to me.

“Got any more of those funny jokes Brad?” she asked.

“Yes, I came across a printed page of them during our clean-up, the kids at school thought they were howlers,” I was led further into her trap.

“Tell me one?” Mary asked.

“Ah, Confucius jokes were very popular in those days,” I began. “What about Confucius say, ‘Woman aviator flying upside down must surely have crack-up.”

We both giggled particularly as she was a woman aviator. ‘Like taking candy from a kid’ Mary giggled to herself as well.

“Or, Confucius say couple who fuck in graveyard fucking-near-dead,” More giggles. I was really enjoying this now with my attention drawn to amusing Mary my attention was beginning to fade from thinking of our bet. As she giggled Mary had tickled my little inert nipple and kissed the other so as to keep her lips well away from mine and her eyes well away from mine as well. She knew she already had the head of my penis within the Gate. It only needed a little more time for her to relax a little more before she would pounce. She knew she was slippery and receptive. I was really getting into it now.

“What about ‘Confucius say couple who fuck on hillside not on the level’.” still we both giggled. ‘Won’t be long now,’ Mary was thinking to herself.

“Or, ‘Confusion say unwise man gives wife grand piano for birthday. Wise man gives her upright organ.” Mary was laughing loudly now.

“The ‘Did you hear the one about’ jokes were also popular with the kids too,” I managed to say between my laughter.

“Such as darling?” Mary asked innocently.

“Did you hear the one about the parson who thought it looked nice out, so he left it out,” more giggles, I was almost helpless.

“Did you hear the one about the girl who chased the parson around the church and caught him by the organ?”

That’s it Mary thought.

“And I’ve got you by yours Adonis,” Mary cried happily. Mary now sent a string of contractions up and down my trapped organ clearly proving her win. Bringing her head up and claiming my lips, inserting her tongue through generating more in and out sensations through my body and denying me any chance to speak. She then commenced hip movements to allow me to join in the fun. I found that when my concentration returned to my groin, I was far more excited and erect than I was before Mary made her wager. It was only a few short thrusts before

Mary had to break from my lips as we rose into a crashing orgasm together.

“I love you so Adonis,” Mary almost sobbed with joy.

“You little vixen Aphrodite,” I smiled back at her. “You got me again didn’t you; you knew I had no chance before you made the bet?”

“Of course I did, darling.” It’s the only way to gamble: only back certainties,” Mary replied.

“And now I must thrill you within the next four hours or face a lay-day tomorrow,” I added.

“That’s the confidence I have in you Adonis, I had to make sure you would be keen to go the distance,” Mary said. “Here endeth the second lesson.”

“Are there many lessons in this course darling?”

“Yes, and the curriculum is still to be completed,” Mary dropped back into her professorial mode.

“Then I will re-enrol for as long as you’re my lecturer, tutor and counsellor,” I vowed.

“Sounds fine by me lover, but for now we must eat, do some serious packing and allow you to pay your dues before the midnight bell.

While all this talking had been going on we had soaped and rinsed each other’s bodies. We dried ourselves, and each other, put on wraps and set to work. We decided that a division of labour was required. Mary started selecting and laying out the clothes we would be taking while I chose some finger food from the freezer and put it in the oven to warm.

I found the food trolley, loaded it with the food, coffee and still unfinished champagne and collected our flutes, and trundled the lot into our bedroom. We toasted each other with the last of the wine as we packed. Mary asked how much we could take and I replied, "As much as she wanted; if we didn't have enough cases we would use cardboard boxes for the remainder. I reminded her just how big Bravo Mike Charlie's luggage bay was and that it was impossible for us to come anywhere near maximum weight. She chose well but still carefully. She knew it was silly carting anything around the world that she probably wouldn't wear. Besides a girl must have some excuse to go shopping.

The cases and cartons therefore were minimised, but I could see that it was going to be two trips to the airport in the XK. I stacked our cases by the front door, ready for the morning, as Mary packed. It was eleven o'clock when the last carton was stacked, and the bed was free. I quietly turned back the bedclothes, dimmed the lights, took Mary gently in my arms and placed her ever so lightly on the bed. I sat on the bed beside her. I had no intention of hurrying to meet the deadline, this was not going to be a sprint to the line but the bedding of a young maiden about to be wooed and seduced by her most admiring beau. My first movement was to let free her upswept hair from where it had remained since arriving home and teasing it out over the pillows and sheet somewhat like it had been in the spa on Tuesday night. I turned to join Mary on the bed and slid my right hand around her shoulders so that I could raise her slightly to meet my lips with delicately soft and long caresses. Mary felt my hand through the back of her wrap and would expect her wrap would soon be coming off and thrown aside. That was not my plan. Just as she had teased me, I was about to do the same for her, not that any thought of payback was in my mind but simply to ensure I thrilled her before midnight. I brought my left hand gently down her right breast, still over the fabric, and barely paused over her right nipple. I undid the sash holding her wrap and moved the wrap back. Not hurriedly, but almost hesitantly revealing a little more than half of her right breast with its firm nipple protruding. Instead of letting my hand rest on any of the delights that it had found it continued down the outside of her right thigh until I found the limit of my reach at her knee. I felt how delicate her kneecap was and passed across to her left knee and gave that a gentle hand caress too. Mary felt the thrill of my hand coming up her left thigh, this time of necessity on her inner thigh as I was lying to her left.

I continued to kiss Mary's lips with a little more firmness and the hint of the tip of my tongue reaching out to touch her lips softly.

"You're not taking me to where I was on Tuesday night are you Adonis?" Mary quietly asked. "I want to recall every second of this hour."

"No Aphrodite, I wouldn't dare. We both want to remember this special occasion," I answered with a sincerity that couldn't be denied. Emboldened now I loosened the sash at her waist and still lacking the confidence to just throw it back to reveal her nakedness I gently let it drop halfway. Mary watched as I eased the wrap from her right shoulder and fully off the right side of her body. I was not playing the seducer but the timid new lover, afraid to rush things and scare away this lovely creature that I found in my arms.

My soft, slow and tentative exploration of her body was my way of seeking her permission to be bolder; I considered her so fragile that she might break in my rough hands. Had I felt any resistance in this slow progress I would have frozen, and held her close with further kisses, until what I thought was a red light turned again to green. I was loath to take my lips from hers to gain greater reach down her thigh in fear that she might rebuke me but there had been no resistance. I ventured to bring my hand up over her ribs and cup her breast and now confident enough to take my lips from hers and take that little prominence of her nipple into my mouth to suck and tickle.

I was delighted to feel her writhe a little and push up against me. I could hear almost silent gasps coming from her now as I continued my embrace of her breast. I could feel her hand reach for my waist and take away the strap from my gown and with more urgency than I had offered push my wrap from me. She raised my face to claim my lips again and began pushing her groin against my erection as it had gained full strength. I had gained all permissions, all clearances to invade all and every part of her territory. To accept her surrender and plant my flagpole right there in its centre which she was gently holding apart awaiting this act, granting me ownership, accepting me as master of her fate.

We responded to each other's desire to give not only possession of our bodies but also possession of our souls. Mary, having now fully comprehended my purpose refrained from further demonstrations of her remarkable capabilities: one of which she had very ably demonstrated only four hours ago, and allowed me the privilege to deliver the thrill that she had won in my own way. We fell into a smooth rhythm with our pubes coming together and pulling apart. All the time we were kissing, and Mary clung to me while my hands explored her breasts, back and thighs. This time when my left hand reached down through her little curls her legs were wide apart; my fingers found her clitoris to tease her and Mary went into a wild orgasm. She reached a peak she rarely achieved and vocalised loudly with those sounds of joy easily mistaken as cries of pain or anguish. My mind flashed back to my childhood when as a small boy I had heard these same sounds coming from this very room. I thought my beloved father was bashing my more beloved mother to death. The next morning to my parents surprise they saw the young Brad come racing from his room, bash into his father's thigh with both firsts and yell 'Don't hurt my mummy. Don't hurt my mummy.' Both his parents became stressed and came down to his height to console him, but seeing his beautiful mother showing no hurt at all, but for the worry he had now brought her, the young Brad had broken away and run tearfully back to his own room. As I had grown into adolescence, I came to understand these passions and when I sometimes overheard these cries, having now entered puberty, I would masturbate keeping to the perceived beat with my father's penis and my mother's sighs. Were the seeds of this night sown so many years ago? Bruce had soon regained my trust and over the years a great bond and camaraderie had developed between the three of us. Now, reliving these moments in my mind I felt my ejaculation build to the point of no return and burst forth into Mary where its sudden arrival into her most sensitive and waiting vagina brought her immediately to another climax echoing those sounds that I had heard so long ago. We clung to each other desperately as our joint climax slowly faded.

"I really thought he was killing you, I was shattered," I said, clearly at the point of sobbing.

"Adonis darling what are you doing to me?" Mary asked.

"I saw everything this time in a perfectly clear, beautifully coloured, three-dimensional replay. I was seeing Bruce and me on our wedding night. After we had rather shyly got into bed. This shy seventeen-year-old with what appeared to me was a much more mature and worldly-wise man were faced with the task of coming together for the very first time. I soon realised that my husband was just as shy and uncertain as myself. He made tentative attempts to arouse me until finally he managed to take off my negligee and could no longer resist the urges flooding in to him to fondle my breasts and to suckle and tongue tickle my immature nipples. His fingers were ready to arouse me as I shyly opened my legs as wide as possible and hold my, as he called it, 'Gates to Paradise' wide. I had started my wedding night burdened down with old wives' tales: that all men were beasts. I thought I might be saving myself pain by making his entry as easy as possible. Bruce was now seeing clearly what he had no ability to perceive in our few hasty groping and fondling sessions in his car. The great tenderness that he had used to explore my body had excited me so much that the secretions in my vagina welcomed my husband's hard horn and we quickly reached our first orgasm together.

"Darling, I didn't go looking for this memory as you slowly brought your hand down outside the fold of my wrap, I wanted to throw it off, wrap my legs around you and suck you in as you know I can. But when you reached my groin and carried on down my thigh, still receiving your most delicate kisses I was that seventeen-year-old bride again. From that moment I was reliving Bruce and my first joining. I'll swear you were conceived that night. You were that defining punctuation mark when Bruce's most vital sperm reached my first marriage blest egg and bound Bruce and I together tighter than any vows might do professing until death do us part. We were so ignorant of the process that we didn't even consider the stage of my menstrual cycle. Some people were shy about talking about such things even though the sexual revolution was well advanced by then and women could attempt to do anything and challenge the men. But when you acknowledged that instance of hate against Bruce thinking that he was killing me I went again into that uncontrolled orgasm that you have just felt. darling, did we conceive a devil or a saint? You are revealing things to me: me a scientist and a full-blown professor in genetics. I should be simply helping you come to grips with your lust and then calmly going about my other duties. I shouldn't be head over heels in love with you, as I was with Bruce, but I am. I shouldn't be prepared to walk out on what the ANU have put before me, so as to be with you: no matter the cost, no questions asked, but I am. I shouldn't be having mystical experiences in your arms, but I am and could never deny it."

"Darling, I daren't say or promise anything unless I know for sure that I will be able to fulfil any promise and deliver on any duty. How can I be the devil's child if I was conceived by Bruce and you and delivered at great cost? For the same reason, we shouldn't talk sainthood. Our heads may be in the clouds, but our feet must remain rooted to the earth. I'm sure we can build on what you have already done and what Bruce has left to us. If I can be convinced I have found my starting point for my life's work in the next twelve months, I will be a very happy man. I must be my own man. To follow blindly yours or Bruce's path, or anybody else for that matter, no matter how much I might admire them would be fatal for me. Then I may well become a devil. I'd rather never go to university if it meant there was any chance of me losing my own identity. I don't know for sure what it is, but I do know that it exists for anyone to find; there are not many in this world who find it. Bruce and you did, and I want to as well. Don't ever fear that I will leave your side. That morning when that sobbing girl asked for comfort it was if I heard Bruce saying, "You must look after her now Brad, without any limit." I feel him with us always. His spirit or energy is probably with us right now; guiding me to bring you to that beautiful explanation of my conception. I didn't do that on purpose. I started out only hoping to maintain my honour and not lose tomorrow's dose of Docs medicine."

"Hug me a little longer Adonis," Mary asked, "There's still a few minutes on the clock before we must tackle the day which has every chance of being our most demanding yet."

We hugged and woke about six to tackle this momentous day.

Saturday 8 December 2012 – 0600 hrs

I packed the XK with the first load to take to the plane while Mary prepared our breakfast. I told Mary to leave her long gowns for any formal evening occasions flat as I would hang those in the limited hanging space on board; she believed we would be living out of the cases and cartons for the rest of our needs. We were parting again for the day: Mary to keep her hairdresser's appointment at ten and me to pack Bravo Mike Charlie and ensure that everything possible was ready for our getaway. Mary wanted to leave the house spic and span and write any last-minute notes for Chris and Jo. She wanted to take a stroll around her now happy garden and then have time to put her feet up and do some relaxation exercises before getting ready for our last duty — attending the dinner in her honour. I would be home by five and make sure Mary hadn't drifted off to sleep. I would shave, shower and dress in my old bedroom as I had done on that first night together and then call for my date at six to take her to the dinner.

I left as soon as possible after breakfast. I delivered my first carload of cases and cartons and stacked them near the cabin steps. I had packed the cases and cartons, so their contents would go together in the cupboards, drawers and wardrobes. The packing was done quickly, and I returned to collect my second load. I packed the refrigerator and freezer and put everything away in its assigned space. I carefully prepared Mary's lab with everything ready for use. I tested every new piece of equipment and arranged the desktops and the galley. I moved through the cabin examining every surface, testing every door and drawer that they would self-close and be secure in turbulence. I tested every new appliance ensuring they were working to specification.

On my second trip I collected our two Lalique flutes from the crystal cabinet. The rest of the crystal I had purchased new and it had already been positioned in their individual felt lined holes in the mini-crystal cabinet. There were four each of, whiskies, clarets, champagne flutes and beer mugs. Apart from the Lalique all the other glassware was Waterford with a modern pattern that had immediately impressed me. I knew that I couldn't take that many items from the crystal cabinet at home for even though there were only a few more hours to pass before we left: I felt sure Mary would notice. I had bought a four-place Wedgewood Cornucopia setting and there was a four-place cutlery setting in their moulded to shape drawer with covers that came down when the drawer shut to stop the cutlery shuffling around, being damaged or causing damage, as we flew.

I had chosen four of everything because our dining table catered for four. I had no plans to be hosting guests in this way, but if it happened, I wanted to be prepared. Any other hospitality we might like, or be expected, to provide would be done in an appropriate restaurant or hotel. As a reminder of that special night I had collected a similar stem of orchids as a centrepiece for the table. To make sure that the orchids remained in place during our take-off and climb. I fixed the stem to the vase with two-way tape and the vase to the table in the same way. The vase would hold in place and the tape would be removed later without damaging the table. The only thing I had left to do, before signing off my checklist, was to complete the networking of our notebooks with Mary's lab notebook.

I sat again to study the scene. I was satisfied that not a cent had been wasted. The value of the finished job was far greater that the cost of its component parts. The colour scheme and coordination provided by the joinery shop's designers made the whole area attractive. Although compact it did not look small, each area looked appropriate to its purpose, the galley, Mary's lab, the workstations, the dining area with table retracted turned into an intimate area for talking and reading. Everything I was viewing was as neat and functional as the equally beautiful flight deck now behind my back. Most of all, with the divan lowered, and the privacy screen pulled across, that area became the lady's boudoir. Lights could be dimmed as desired and adjusted to tint the cabin walls. It was indeed a magic carpet ready to fly Aphrodite and Adonis away.

I pulled across the temporary curtain that I had arranged to block any view of the cabin from Mary as she entered. I planned to withhold this view of our magic carpet until we levelled out at thirty-thousand feet.

I arrived home at five o'clock. Mary was in the shower, "I'll be ready at six o'clock darling," she called.

As I shaved, I was careful not to cause one of those pesky little cuts that could bleed for a long time and be red and prominent for a long time after. With fifty minutes still available I decided on a half-hour of solitary relaxation in the spa would be better than a five-minute shower and fifteen minutes of waiting and working up a nervous sweat. I soaked and relaxed and on leaving I drained the spa and cleaned it. Having briefed Chris and Rick on the cleaning, filters and chemical balance of the spa yesterday I left it to them to refill and test to their own satisfaction. I had a grin to myself as I thought of some of things that Mary and I had done right here. I dressed calmly and confidently in the dinner suit that now felt more comfortable to me, 'Was it only three weeks ago?' I asked myself.

The last thing I did was to collect a small bottle with a drop plunger in its screw-top lid. The chemist had given it to me, assuring me that it was a natural product highly effective for controlling tears. Two drops under the tongue had helped Mary and me throughout the day of Bruce's memorial. When its effects wore off in the evening Mary had broken down into those frightening sobs leaving me feeling helpless until she asked me to hold her and let her cry in my arms. 'But that was long ago,' I thought as I dropped the bottle into my pocket; just to make sure that we had a little support if our night became weepy due to totally opposite but equally powerful emotions. A feeling of great expectation took hold of me as I gave a confident knock on our bedroom door.

Chapter 6

Surprise! Surprise!

Saturday 8 December 2012 – 1800 hrs

"You don't have to knock on your own bedroom door darling, do you?"

"Of course not," I grinned, "I just wanted to see you emerge as you did three weeks ago. You look just as beautiful and exciting as you did then."

I studied her for a full half minute. Mary presented herself with her usual elegance and dignity. Her new gown was based on the Cheong Sam with its customary high collar at the neck, bare arms and a split. The split in this case was only to her knee to allow Mary to walk without flashing any thigh. The cut too did not hug her figure as much as usual to ensure that she could move and sit comfortably but despite these modifications, that Mary thought the occasion demanded, her figure could not be totally hidden. The colour of the dress was light fawn that complemented her honey blonde waves that had been carefully swept up for this evening, exposing her neck and shoulder line. Over the dress was a fine black lace with a pattern of black roses appearing as blooms on a stem. Her overdress covered her otherwise bare arms. Mary carried an evening stole that was supported by her elbows and looped around her back with the ends hanging just above her knees. In her left hand she carried a matching evening bag. She wore no jewellery except for simple gold clip-on earrings and her gold wedding ring. She was all and everything that the most discerning company could expect of a beautiful woman so recently widowed.

"You look nice too Brad," Mary was first to speak.

"But you look exquisite darling," I found my voice at last. "Was I staring?"

Saturday 8 December 2012 – 1830 hrs

We drove into the hotel's carpark and an attendant was waiting to guide us into a space being held for us next to the lift to the third floor.

Most guests it appeared were arriving at the drive through reception entrance, but the guest of honour was being kept away from outsiders' view and was to be accompanied directly from the carpark. I noticed a few celebrities turning in at this entrance. 'My God,' I thought as I saw a black limo with a crown in the position of the number plate.

"I wonder where the GG's going. Could it be the same place as we are?"

"I think we'd better have a couple of drops of this darling?" I spoke quietly. "They worked pretty well before and while the emotions tonight will be the opposite they can still be just as devastating."

Mary answered by opening her mouth and I placed two drops under her tongue. We had been asked to arrive around six-thirty. We had been told the program would allow time for some mingling before proceedings commenced at seven when guests would be asked to take their seats for dinner. The dinner will take the Degustation form with five small courses. Guests could choose from a list of five delicate dishes for each course. There was a card at each setting for the staff to collect before the first course. The strategy for the dinner was to allow diners time to chat and talk between small courses and the few essential speeches to be made while diners were not eating. Having collected all orders before the first course the kitchen would be able to serve all tables as each course came around, the last table being served within four minutes of the first.

After the first course the Pro-Chancellor would welcome guests. The Chancellor would be making several announcements during his speech and of course will be confirming Associate Professor Clifford's progression to Professor. All this seemed innocuous to Mary and me. We wondered what other Uni business was coming up to make this so ceremonial.

Usually moving from associate to full professor status was more noticed in the pay packet and possibly a little more respect around the campus from students and staff.

It was never as formal as the annual awarding of degrees. The Vice had sounded me out about incorporating an address from someone on the ANU Council delivering a tribute to Bruce, but I had felt that it would put a further strain on my mother. Anyone who really knew Bruce had already been involved in his memorial. The Vice seemed relieved at my response and suggested that it might be wise if I made the response on Mary's behalf to the speeches that the Chancellor and he will be making. I had felt a little daunted by this prospect but trusting in the thought that the Vice believed I could do it for Mary, better than she could do it for herself, without Bruce at her side, I undertook the task and promised to do a thorough preparation.

"I know that you will do it well Brad," he had said.

I held the car door open for Mary and taking her hand helped her from her low seat. A member from hotel security guided us to the waiting elevator. He took us to the third floor and pointed us in the direction of the ballroom door. We saw other couples entering, all in evening dress and some wearing their ceremonial academic gowns. Mary and I joined in a few paces behind.

"Looks like a swell do Brad, let's drop in here and mingle," Mary said,

“We might get a good feed here by the look of it, Mary, they wouldn’t notice an extra couple.”

“Not in this clobber Brad?” Mary answered.

We had refrained from any of our usual endearments fearing any of the people around could hear us. Turning into the ballroom, we found ourselves on a red carpet. I thought to myself, ‘Nice touch, I should have got a bit of this stuff to drape on the steps of Bravo Mike Charlie.’ The two drops under my tongue were beginning to relax me and with a quick glance at Mary I could see she showed no a sign of stress. ‘Good start,’ I thought to myself. I felt my confidence shift a little bit south as I looked to see where we were heading, only to see three couples between the Greeting Party and us. The Chancellor and his wife, the Pro-Chancellor and her husband and the Vice-Chancellor and his wife were receiving the guests in turn. The academics were splendidly attired and their spouses equally so in formal dress. The Pro-Chancellor’s husband was even sporting tails. Mary had taken my arm on entering in the manner that everyone expected and now gave my arm a gentle squeeze of encouragement. She wasn’t daunted by the sight.

Since moving from student to the academic staff she was always present at formal occasions in her own robes. Mary knew it would be more daunting for me. The only person in this room anywhere near my age would be the student representative on the University Council and even he was two years into his degree and active in campus student politics. Mary knew from seeing him around that he looked very immature against the man whose arm she held. I consoled myself that at least I would feel comfortable with the Vice and nobody else would have the slightest interest in me while Mary was around. When Mary and I reached the beginning of the line the Chancellor greeted Mary warmly and there were flashlights going off as he expressed his pleasure of her company. The official photographer was delighted with his subject as the venerable old man greeted a beautiful young lady. It would only be photos from this camera that would be released to the media and he knew that one of these shots would certainly make the cut. He didn't bother stopping us for our names as more were now arriving and he mustn't delay the line's progress. Mary introduced me to each member of the greeting party.

'Congratulations Mary on your Professorship' or 'What a lovely gown Dr Clifford' and Mary would respond with, "Please do call me Mary and I'd like you to meet my son Brad."

"That wasn't so bad was it Brad?" Mary asked as we passed out of hearing range.

"No," I admitted, more for Mary's sake than my own confidence. We ran into the arms of our Grands and Greats who were waiting in a group for us to appear in the welcoming line. They hugged and kissed us. The husbands were warned by their wives to be careful not to spoil Mary's makeup as she was bound to be subject of more photos before the night was over.

"What do you think of this lot Brad?" Great Grandpop Clifford asked.

"Bit out of my league, I'm afraid, I'm a fish out of water Pops," I answered.

"Now don't you worry Brad; nobody could look out for Mary's welfare better than you," Nan Franklin said.

"We'd better be making our way to our table," Gran Clifford said, "it's getting towards seven."

"We've scored a table together," Granddad Franklin advised.

Mary and I escorted them to their table; I thought we may have been seated with the family but when I put that question Nan Franklin was quick to point and say:

"Oh no, you're at the head table as befits the Professor."

Pride and satisfaction were literally beaming from the elders; they were so pleased to be celebrating a happy event that no one mentioned Bruce, not that he wasn't in everyone's heart and mind tonight. No one was prepared to say anything that might start a chain reaction of tears reaching to the Guest of Honour. Nothing was to take any of the joy away from Mary's big night. They were right of course that Mary and I would be thinking of Bruce, but they could never realise that their thoughts were in no ways like ours. They would never understand that Mary and I could be so convinced that Bruce was with us always, guiding us, helping us and even down to the revelation that we had experienced only last night in bed. Nobody else would understand so why try to explain.

I ushered Mary quietly to the head table, found our place cards where Mary had been placed with the Chancellor on her right and the Vice-Chancellor on her left. I was placed opposite between the Pro-Chancellor and the highest-ranking dignitary in the land, our country's lady Governor General. As none of our dining partners had yet finished their 'meet and greet' duties I collected my meal order and with Mary we quickly ticked off our five dishes.

"No doubt they're all good darling but I'd sooner share a biscuit and coffee with you at thirty-thousand feet than dining on this feast with the finest in the land,"

"That's a lovely thought lover; so, it's Plan B then," Mary replied.

"It sure is," I was quick to respond. "How long do you think this is going to last?"

"We're starting early, and a lot of these oldies will want to be taking their leave by ten so I'm guessing three hours," Mary said.

"I can manage that," I replied.

"And so can I," Mary agreed. "Have you seen some of the people who are here?"

"I can see a sprinkling of those funny hats that Chancellors wear," I said.

"That means that each of those funny hats represents one other invited university. We don't have that many universities in Australia Brad," Mary replied.

None of the lesser lights of universities was wearing their ceremonial robes although Mary recognised many other professors from her own and other universities. In a way it was a compliment in that rather than having a sea of academic gowns it was left to the Chancellors of universities to represent their campuses and let it be seen how universally important this night was considered.

"Don't look now Mary but that's the PM and Foreign Minister over there and the Leader of the Opposition and representatives of his Front Bench at the next table.

We heard the Master of Ceremonies invite guests to take their seats and to make their selection on their menu cards to help the staff provide them with the timing and flow of the courses that would match the flow of this evening's business.

I waited with Mary until the Vice-Chancellor arrived with his wife and after exchanging greetings again, I returned to my own place. The GG arrived partnered by her son. The Vice-Chancellor introduced Mary and me and the six now present took their seats. The GG broke the ice by quickly asking me what was expected of her regarding her menu card. 'Poor little bugger, fancy having to face this lot at his age, and just out of high school,' I fancied she would be thinking. I showed her my marked card in explanation and added:

"They all look quite delicious ma'am," I hoped I had obtained the right inflection in my voice.

"I'd better put my glasses on then, check what I'll be eating, we girls have got to watch our figure you know Brad, don't we Mary?" Mary smiled her winning smile and heartily agreed with the GG. I knew of course that the GG was an old hand at this sort of thing and was quickly moving to make these two youngsters as comfortable as possible. She was one of the few fully conversant with tonight's proceedings and indeed a little fearful that I might be overwhelmed by the responsibilities now to be thrust upon Mary.

The Chancellor and Pro-Chancellor arrived; the seated men at the table were quick to their feet and after further welcomes and apologies for being last all were seated again and had their menus completed by the time the waiters had reached them.

It was easy conversation now with all relaxing and all most careful to include Mary and me in their talks, without any thought of being condescending, or pressing us with any questions: particular about Bruce. All present, including the GG, had known Bruce, worked with and respected him for many years. Despite his relatively young age, he too was a figure of note on the campus as he shared his knowledge of developing trends in engineering and design. As an adjunct professor, he held at least two seminars of several days a year on campus.

The first tempting course had been delivered; the drinks waiters had hovered offering a selection of wines they had judged most fitting to suit the course. Now, as the last plates were being cleared away, the MC was saying 'Honoured Guests may we have your attention for the

Pro-Chancellor's Address of Welcome'. The Pro-Chancellor rose from her place at our table and elegantly moved to the central microphone. She paused to allow the chatter to fade away and in her clear and educated voice spoke:

"Madam Patron, clearly nodding to the GG seated next to me. Chancellor and members of your Council. I am proud to have the honour to extend your welcome to our most honoured and illustrious guests. None in this room is undistinguished and fortunately, had not more than a few others who were unable to be with us, at short notice, due to prior commitments, we would have been embarrassed. A hall that could cater for and seat in comfort more than four hundred people was not available at such short notice. I especially welcome a number of guests to show to the public, both at home and abroad, the magnitude of the announcements that will be made by the Chancellor this evening.

"I welcome the Chancellors of other Universities. One can easily see that every Australian University is represented. I must point out that Chancellor Flynn from Cambridge on receiving his telephone call on Tuesday morning immediately booked a flight to be with us this evening, as did Chancellor Roujet from the Paris-Sorbonne University, President Hawkes from Harvard and Chancellor Williams from our near neighbour Auckland University. Fortunately, the Chancellors from Bonn, Brussels, Los Angeles, Antwerp, Beijing and Moscow were visiting and attending meetings in Australia and are present."

Madame Pro-Chancellor paused for a moment, took a sip from the glass on the nearby table and having just acknowledged academia without referring to any notes proceeded in the same manner.

"Prime Minister and Ministers accompanying you, The Honourable Leader of the Opposition and representatives of your shadow cabinet, Chief Justice of the High Court of

Australia, Departmental Heads of the Federal Public Service, The Chief of the Australian Defence Forces and your Heads of each service. Dining with these gentlemen I welcome the Chairman of the Joint Chiefs of Staff representing the United States Armed Forces and the US Secretary of State representing the President, Congress, the Senate and Judiciary of the United States and our recently honoured Corporal Jason Wellington VC."

I noticed at this point as the Pro-Chancellor indicated the table where these military representatives sat. How resplendent they appeared in their perfectly turned out dress uniforms, ablaze with rows of campaign ribbons and awards and tassels, sashes and braid. I knew that they would give it all away in return for that crimson ribbon on the chest of the corporal. Tonight, as requested, the ribbon was supporting the rare Victoria Cross. Although the Australian military does not salute inside and bareheaded, had they been wearing their hats they would have willing followed the established custom of saluting the wearer of the VC no matter how much lower in rank the recipient was. Instead, as he joined their table he was warmly welcomed with the firm handshakes of brothers-in-arms, made at ease, and included in all their conversations. 'This must be something pretty big the Chancellor is going to drop,' I thought to myself, I had never heard Bruce or Mary speak of anything like this occurring before. I had kept a quiet watch over Mary, hopefully unnoticed. 'Why anyone would be looking at me, a mere boy in the eyes of this company I thought.' Our eyes had met at times. I knew instantly in those fleeting seconds that my little girl was handling things OK. Mary likewise felt safe and happy under my strong protection. I brought my thoughts back to the present to hear the Pro-Chancellor continue.

"I extend the Chancellor's greetings to the Ambassadors of all the embassies in Australia with whom our country maintains a diplomatic presence."

The Pro-Chancellor continued in this vein acknowledging all the professional societies and associations represented, running through the Law Society, Australian Medical Association, The Australian Society of CPAs, The Chartered Institute of Accountants, Institute of Engineers, The College of Surgeons, the RSL, Legacy and the major charities. She welcomed the Bishops and how the invitation and gone out to all denominations and all ethnic minorities. Understandably, at such short notice many had to decline but all would be looking forward to receiving the press releases and to receive the formal document to be published and distributed world-wide. The Pro-Chancellor closed by saying:

"I have left to the end to acknowledge the table to my right where the representatives of the Clifford and Franklin families are seated. These families have, still do, and will continue into the future to provide the ANU with endowments, gifts, bequests, students of high academic achievement and members of staff in all categories. We trust they will also accept this acknowledgment and represent all those other like-minded people who we had no capacity to invite. Frankly, if we had the ability to invite all we would have been holding this gathering at the Manuka Oval and dining on pies and beer. If I have failed to acknowledge any person, please accept my sincere apologies."

The Pro-Chancellor now left the microphone and returned to her seat with a resounding round of applause. She was greeted with admiring eyes and someone asked, "How did you do that without notes," she graciously replied, "It comes with practice, I do hope that I didn't miss anyone, I've never had so many dignitaries before."

The talk soon started around the table again. I noticed that little was made of the Pro-Chancellor's references to the Chancellor's soon to be released announcement. The rest of our dining companions, being so high in the pecking order at the ANU, would already know and just not think it polite to advise anyone else before the Chancellor spoke. The next two courses with their accompanying wines came and went with the expected table chatter. I thought the Vice was rather quiet tonight. I put it down to the knowledge that the Vice would be proposing a toast to Mary's health after the Chancellor had confirmed her professorship following the next small course.

As the third-round dishes were quickly whisked away the Chancellor rose and went to the microphone.

"Good evening Honoured Guests. For my first most pleasant duty tonight I invite Associate Professor Clifford to join me here."

"Now Brad," the GG whispered. I needed no prompting. I had started to rise as soon as I heard the Chancellor finish the sentence. I moved smoothly to the back of Mary's chair, helped her move it back and extended my left hand to help her rise from her chair. I kept Mary to the left so that this august audience could see her, and I would be barely visible. I delivered Mary in front of the Chancellor as a father might give his daughter away at the altar and moved back into the shadows and retraced my steps. It was almost a classic dance movement. I had been briefed that the Chancellor would return Mary to her chair. I now stood quietly behind her chair waiting for her return. It was almost as if the hall and gone into slow motion.

"Good evening my dear, let me place your new ceremonial robes around your shoulders," the Chancellor began.

He was speaking only to Mary but in this now silent room the slightest whisper was clearly communicated from the nearby microphone. Without expecting Mary to respond he gently placed the robe and tied the tassel at her neck. The official photographer started shooting.

“I’ll leave you to place your new cap, I’m afraid I might be a little clumsy.”

Mary took the cap he offered. The photographer snapped away catching good angles of Mary, her new academic robes, her brilliant complexion enhanced with a smile and most of all he wanted to capture those honey-blonde waves. Her appearance contrasted with her smart but rather subdued dress, the black academic gown trimmed with a new dark but brilliant blue trim he had never seen on ceremonial robes before — neither had any of the dignitaries in the audience and that included Mary. Mary raised the cap to her head realising that it was unlike any mortarboard that she had previously worn. The cap that she was adjusting on her head was similar but much smaller than the Chancellor’s grand headpiece; it was more like a French beret that Mary knew the Mademoiselles of Paris could wear with flair. These thoughts passing rapidly through Mary’s mind brought the smile of the night to her face and the photographer snapped away happily. ‘These pics will be going further afield than the academic and main press,’ he thought, ‘this one could well be gracing the cover of VOGUE’. Once Mary had her cap in place the Chancellor took her right hand turned full on to the audience with Mary naturally turning with him and proudly proclaimed:

Honoured Guests I present to you Professor Mary of the Australian National University.”

There was an immediate standing ovation of long, loud and sincere applause. Mary standing with a little separation from the Chancellor as he held the pose of holding her hand out in the presentation had a beaming smile for all. She had never seen any such presentation in her nearly twenty years at the ANU. She didn’t know what she might say if in fact anything was expected of her. As the applause subsided and the guests took their seats the Chancellor, still holding the same pose, escorted Mary back to her chair. Once there he turned to Mary doffed his floppy headpiece in style and as Mary raised her new cap, he flicked the floppy thing back on his head, and after a small bow turned and returned to his former position. Before sitting I placed the expected chaste kiss on her cheek and whispered, “That wasn’t too bad after all.”

“No,” Mary replied tears of joy and relief not too far away.

“Congratulations Professor Mary,” the Vice said. He had immediately picked up on his Chancellor’s use of Mary instead of the normal Professor Clifford usage in addressing her. Whether the Chancellor had done this deliberately or whether it was a simple slip by an old gentleman he did not know except he liked it. With all the political correctness, and with the never-ending feminist movement’s activities, female academics had insisted on there being no distinction of gender in their awards and titles: they were to be bachelors, masters, doctors, lecturers and professors. Bacheloress or even worse bachelorette for the women would be intolerable and degrading. Along with the demand for equality in this regard the use of surname just automatically went with it as that had been the men’s custom. The Vice too happily planted a kiss on Mary’s other cheek. The others at the table softly added their congratulations as the Chancellor was nearing the microphone to continue. I whispered across the table to the GG whether she minded me remaining where I was rather going back to her side.

“Of course not Brad, if you don’t mind us on this side turning our backs on you to listen to what the Chancellor has to say next.”

They had all smiled and now I happily took the Chancellor’s vacant seat next to Mary and we could turn to each other in comfort. I ached to take Mary in my arms and it was obvious that she was aching too. We had to console ourselves that the best we could do was to hold hands a little below the table line.

"Plan B," Mary said to me and I smiled again.

"Ladies and Gentlemen," the Chancellor commenced. "Having returned Professor Mary safely to her seat I can now explain the reasons for tonight's function and the significance of the ceremonial academic cap and gown she now wears. As some know, the ANU has played a major role in the Human Genome Project and Professor Mary has led the ANU's contribution. Professor Mary will claim little of the success this project has already achieved: that more was due to her peers in other Universities and her staff here. The institutions involved in this work have known for some time that this emerging research should move out from its present hosts, usually a medical faculty, and that the results already achieved and the even greater promise of things to come warranted the creation of a new faculty throughout academia. In consultation with our partnering institutions it had been planned to formalise this arrangement with public announcements in April next. It had been agreed that Professor Mary would occupy the first Chair in this new faculty and the first such faculty would be here.

We had let the then Associate Professor Clifford know that she would be taking over Professor Jack's role when he retired in April: we did not mention the direction her role would then take. We didn't want to create any jitters with still six months to go. Our partners were quick to support Professor Mary as the first Chair appointed but insisted that she also chair the coordinating committee of her peers. Her reputation amongst her peers is so high they would accept no other appointment."

Now the Chancellor took a sip from his glass. There was silence in the room; Mary dared not look too hard at me as she felt many eyes were turning to her. She was squeezing my hand with greater pressure. I was feeling her growing stress.

"Don't worry. It'll be over soon," I whispered.

I hoped but felt there was more to come. The Chancellor continued.

"To jump now to Thursday last week, Professor Mary arranged a meeting with the Vice-Chancellor requesting a year's study leave overseas. This request could not be refused: she was long ago entitled to it. Her only concern was that her lab and research might be diminished in the hands of the new Professor to replace Professor Jack in April. Professor Mary had no concern that she would be passing up her professorship, her only concern was for her work and her students. The Vice-Chancellor was aware of the stress that Professor Mary had been under and alerted the Council to ensure full attendance at that night's scheduled meeting. He immediately rearranged the agenda to ensure that this matter was to be settled before anything else would be considered. He then got to work contacting the Vice-Chancellors of the partnering institutions. With the time zones around the world it was a busy period for the Vice-Chancellor right up to the commencement of our Council meeting. It was obvious to the Council that this professorship must be awarded now. Professor Jack agreed to remain as Professor Emeritus in her absence to ensure her that the research and teaching capability of her department would not be diminished. In these days of instant communications and teleconferencing she could participate in the ANU's activities and management as she wished. Professor Mary was most grateful to hear this news and was happy to be the guest of honour at a little function to announce her professorship this evening." There were some muffled chuckles from around the hall following the Chancellor's last remark.

"Little function," Mary whispered to me. "There are four hundred dignitaries here."

"I'm afraid we couldn't tell Professor Mary how many guests would be attending as of course we didn't know at that time. Professor Mary received news of her immediate advancement to Professor at a meeting with the Vice-Chancellor on Friday morning and was relieved that she could have Professor Jack covering for her and the Council's commitment to her research confirmed and left in greater happiness, having expressed her fears only the day before. I must commend the Vice-Chancellor and his staff in bringing all ends together resulting in this gathering tonight. I must confess to Professor Mary that I insisted that her application for leave be torn up. In her unique academic standing it would be an insult by the ANU to allow her to go swanning through another University's domain without presenting hers and, by definition, the ANU's credentials to the resident Chancellor or President. Naturally, the little matter of leave and other entitlements have been adjusted accordingly. I trust Professor Mary will allocate say ten to fifteen hours a week to Faculty business, but I suspect she will devote far more; just as she would have done if she had been granted a sabbatical. You see Professor Mary, those around you, and your peers around the world, know you far better than you have ever imagined. The thought of some conglomerate gobbling you up, patenting your research and discoveries and only doling them out to a world in need according to the profit they could extoll for their shareholders was too painful to allow. This gathering is an attempt to impress upon you the support that you have: here, and as you will come to realize in all centres around the world."

"I wish he would stop Brad. I would rather be criticised than this," Mary almost sobbed as she squeezed my hand all the harder.

"He's coming to the end now, it won't be long. Just think Plan B," I replied calmly.

“So finally, Professor Mary. Please take your new ceremonial robes with you and wear them at the formal academic functions where your attendance will be required. Let academia see for the first time the colours of the new Faculty of Genetics that very soon will be worn by its graduates and then higher degrees in the very new future.”

“Brad, he’ll be coming back to sit next to me can’t you stay, I can’t squeeze his hand.”

“No, my darling; we mustn’t dare. I will rise and hold the chair back for him. You will thank him for such high praise. Just keep thinking one hour to go to Plan B; it’s a lovely moonlight night out there.” I tried to help her with a mild challenge and pleasures to come if we can hang on for one hour more. I finished with, “I think the moon is full tonight.”

“Then fly me there darling,” Mary begged.

“I’ll do better; I’ll fly you over it,” I replied in earnest.

By the time the Chancellor had reached the head table he had received long applause and many handshakes on his way back. When he arrived, I was dutifully standing at the back of his chair ready to assist the aging academic regain his seat. Being quite an old gentleman, he was clearly stressed and after receiving the congratulations of his dining partners including the congratulations of the GG he was relieved to take his seat.

“Thankyou sincerely Chancellor,” Mary said. “That was so generous.”

“Nothing less than you deserve dear,” the Chancellor replied.

During the Chancellor’s walk back to his chair most of the tables had been served their final selection and now the head table could be served. I was seated opposite Mary and I tried to avoid too much eye contact. I felt that just the opposite was required. The guests were happily eating and drinking. Mary and I only picked at our final selection and only taken a couple of sips from our wine. We each suddenly realized that we were still on the wine that was to complement our first dish. We looked at each other and grinned. We only had to survive the Vice-Chancellor's toast to Mary and we were away. I was waiting for the Vice to get up from his chair so that I could quickly move in and sit at Mary's other side.

The Vice started well: describing how Mary was a high achiever in her student years, as an undergraduate, graduate student, doctoral candidate and her post-doctoral research. I had felt that this was going well, and I felt Mary relax alongside me. She had taken my hand again as I sat but the stress was no longer there. It was too good to be true. The Vice was aging; he had always been a classicist and a romantic. He couldn't hold back his admiration for Mary. He compared her with the trail-blazing Madame Curie who also lost her husband in a tragic road accident, albeit an out of control galloping horse-drawn hansom cab. However, applying Sir Robert Menzies adoration of the young Queen Elizabeth II on her first visit to Australia in 1954 and now addressing it to Mary was becoming unbearable for her.

"I but saw her passing by – And yet I'll love her till I die," he quoted. I quickly realised that it had become too much for the Vice-Chancellor as I saw him break off his speech and, with a hand to his face, headed back to his chair. The Vice hadn't reached the point where he was to propose his toast to Mary, I jumped up from his chair, pulled it back to allow him to collapse into it, his hand still to his eyes and speechless.

"Two drops under his tongue Mary," I said very quietly as I pressed the little bottle into Mary's hand and briskly strode up to the microphone. The Master of Ceremonies hadn't called me forth, like everyone else he was caught by surprise by the Vice-Chancellor's abrupt departure.

"Honoured Guests," I began. The spotlight went from the Vice-Chancellor to me and all eyes followed. "As you have seen the Vice-Chancellor is slightly distressed at this point, so I trust you will permit me to speak on behalf of Professor Mary: as was requested of me by the Vice-Chancellor two days ago. Knowing that it was impossible to brief Professor Mary fully he feared that on top of her recent distress it would be improper to make her respond to such high appointment in front of such an august gathering," I spoke out with, what I thought, a clear calm voice and a confidence beyond my years. There was no noise in the room.

"Having known Professor Mary for a number of years," I commenced. I noted the subdued laughing from the guests who knew that it was a relatively small number of years. "Not as professor, not as a peer, not as a colleague, not as a member of staff nor as a student, but I sincerely hope, as a dutiful son; I would like to express to you what I believe she might say on this occasion.

"I can assure you that Professor Mary would have thanked the Chancellor for his thoughtfulness in easing her into tonight's proceedings gently: having her back in her chair with no need to speak before hearing what lay ahead of her.

"I can assure you that her first reaction would be almost one of dread. Professor Mary can suffer criticism; she would not be damned by faint praise. However, she would be in dread of overpraise. She would be aghast at being put on too high a pedestal from where she might easily trip, fall, and do irreparable damage thereby. I don't think that even in that event she would have been in fear of her own hurt but the hurt she may have caused others by having failed to live up to their high expectations.

"I can assure you that she would have accepted the Vice-Chancellor's comparison of her to Madame Curie only to the extent that she would emulate that most famous lady in wanting any honours bestowed on her to reflect on her colleagues and any monetary awards go to her further research.

"I can assure you also that seeing such a gathering tonight representing the whole spectrum of occupations, vocations and beliefs in our community would give her great heart that the work being done by her team at ANU and, as I now understand, with similar teams around the world was being taken very seriously in high places.

"I know that Professor Mary would soon perceive that much more had gone on over at least the past year, and possibly longer, to bring this new faculty into existence. A number of universities just happening to agree to move their research and the teaching of genetics, out from under the umbrellas that had fostered them, into a full-blown faculty of its own world-wide simply cannot be done in a few months. Governments must be involved, and funding must be established. This gathering only illustrates how high and wide the consultations must have been to bring this about. Professor Mary would have been heartened to see the Prime Minister and representatives of his Cabinet sitting with the Leader of The Opposition and representatives of her Front Bench; clearly indicating that this is a bipartisan commitment that Australia will be supporting long into the future.

"I am sure that Professor Mary would accept the responsibility and I am honoured to readily do so now on her behalf.

"I am sure Professor Mary would express her thanks to not only her peers who elected her to this position of leadership but would have comprehended that it would not have been possible for them to do so without the concurrence of the organisations represented by the honoured guests present and those who have sent their apologies.

"Professor Mary would have instantly recognised that so many diverse organisations trusted her to bring out the secrets of the Genome in a fair and honest way: laying only scientifically established results before all interested parties.

"I know without equivocation that she would have pledged to you that it will be so and again I am confident in doing that on her behalf.

"I think that she would have pleaded for caution. That while early results have produced some startling outcomes and new discoveries in medicine, archaeology, the solving of cases long gone cold and the capture of criminals, and in matching the person to the work to be done, there is so much more to discover. The Genome is so vast and complicated that it will take many years if not lifetimes of dedicated researchers like Professor Mary and her fellow researchers to harvest all its secrets. I am certain Professor Mary's belief in caution is her conviction to only proceed by accepted scientific method: results must be repeatable, and not published until full peer review has taken place. Having been published, academia can build on these new facts and produce new solutions to old problems. Her caution is well illustrated by keeping in mind the admonition of Alexander Pope that she taught me when I was much younger, several years ago, and I quote:

A little learning is a dangerous thing
Drink deep or taste not the Pierian spring;
There shallow draughts intoxicate the brain,
And drinking largely sobers us again.

"I know that Professor Mary subscribes to the charge that 'All men are born equal,' to the extent that all seven billion of us are individual, and only in this sense equal; as were the ninety billion or more members of HOMO SAPIENS who have preceded us. Even now the door is opening to the possibility of producing individual drugs to cure sufferers individually.

"I also learned that we can never go back; none of us can change anything that has passed, however, we can look back and learn and we ought to often, to ensure that we do not continue having to relearn lessons by making the same mistakes again. Second by second, we are rushing ahead in an ever-changing world. The only constant is change: even the speed of light as the only constant is coming under review.

"I can assure you that Professor Mary subscribes to the WISDOM OF SOLOMON in that enigmatic statement that there is nothing new under the sun. She remains humble in the knowledge that all her work is dependent on those who have gone before; that any discovery she and her teams might make using their sophisticated and high-powered equipment would not have been possible without the discovery of the lens. Found artefacts of this now very sophisticated component of microscopes, telescopes, cameras and spectacles reach back over three thousand years. None of these things could exist until some human intelligence started marvelling at some ancient crystal. Our modern instruments could not have been designed and constructed today without that first curiosity of a thinking individual. Over thousands of years other curious intelligences could see other applications and make further refinements. Now, in a relative few years we have manned and unmanned space travel, world-wide communications and transmission of data and video from the outer planets of our solar system, and the Hubble Telescope revealing the marvels of myriad galaxies expanding out over limitless time and space."

"In our family there are many pilots. We are all kept humble by the recognition that no matter how sophisticated designers, engineers and manufacturers of aircraft have become, their efforts depend on one very simple fact recognised by the First Australians. Their boomerangs were the first known application of the aerofoil. It was not until one hundred and twenty years ago that the persistence of people like the Wright Brothers brought the world's attention to the possibility of world-wide air travel for all. In every endeavour, new developments and possibilities are being made known at a faster rate than ever before.

"I think it fair to say that genetics is the youngest of the sciences. The new kid on the block. This is not to discount the contributions to the study of inherited characteristics in humans, other species and plants which go back thousands of years. For most of us we learned about Mendel, and his experiments breeding peas from 1856 to 1865, in high school. Fortunately, high school science now goes much further into this area and I learned that in 1944 Avery, MacLeod and McCarthy showed that DNA holds the gene's information. In 1953 James Watson and Francis Crick showed that DNA's structure was a double helix. Over the next twenty years there was continuous work in laboratories around the world by several Nobel Laureates, and their teams, to unravel the secrets and nature of DNA, chromosomes and genes.

"We jump forward to 1972, just forty years ago. Walter Fiers and his team at the Laboratory of Molecular Biology of the University of Ghent in Belgium were the first to determine the sequence of a gene. I submit to this gathering that the science of genetics was born at that time. Since then developments have been profound and in the living memory of almost all those present tonight. Most significantly: the completion of the Human Genome Project in 2003, only nine years ago, cemented genetics status as a science.

"The Faculty of Genetics that has been instituted tonight comes into being with a proud inheritance from 1972 and a long pre-history of the work done by scholars and thinkers over several thousand years.

"I have been speaking of these things to assure you that from a family perspective, and I am speaking here on behalf of my grandparents and great-grandparents, that you have indeed chosen the right person for the job at hand. We can vouch for her integrity, her humility, her respect for the truth and her dedication to any duty she may undertake. She knows that her Faculty will be standing on the shoulders of all who have gone before and will see to it that all who carry the work forward will know it too.

"There is only one thing that Professor Mary might ask of you. Having recently been exposed to the unwanted attention of the media, including harassing her family in her absence, that those able to suggest to editor's that no mention or speculation be made of unpublished work going on in the labs of this new Faculty. Public and official functions she would understand are newsworthy and that publicity is understood and accepted; but when it comes to the faculty's work then it is a matter of be patient until proven results are published. Don't ask, don't speculate we will come to you. The role of the coordinated faculties of genetics will be to report to the world: not government by government or any other grouping but plainly for all to adjust to whatever truth is revealed."

I looked to the Vice-Chancellor and received a nod and a small movement of his hand asking me to conclude for him. I saw Mary sitting calmly next to the Vice having helped calm him, she now looked perfectly composed herself.

"Ladies and gentlemen," I began again. "I have just received an indication from the Vice-Chancellor asking me to extend his apologies to you and for me to complete the toast which he was about to make.

"I ask you to charge your glasses and rise," I spoke clearly and slightly louder than before. Glasses had been well charged by the drink waiters during my speech and finding a glass placed very close to my hand on the lectern, I raised my own.

"To Professor Mary, First appointment to the Chair of the Faculty of Genetics at the Australian National University Canberra and Coordinator of the Faculty World-Wide."

I thought that would do her justice without going over the top. I had for one horrible fraction of a second thought I was going to say Princess Mary, but all was well. I too now felt relieved. Our last duty in Australia for the next twelve months was ending. The toast 'To Professor Mary' was loudly supported in voice and clapping. The qualifier was dropped as was intended but guests were adding their own as many Good Healths and Congratulations were added. As the cheering stopped following the loud call by the Master of Ceremonies for Three Cheers for the Professor, I turned to regain my seat.

Mary was rising to her feet still capped, gowned, and outstanding in this company as the lights fell upon her. I quickly moved into the shadows to avoid blocking anyone's view as did the Master of Ceremonies who at that moment was about to wish guests a fond farewell and bring the function to a close.

"Honoured Guests," Mary spoke in a clear and composed manner. "I now feel sufficiently composed to speak directly to you and thank Brad for the response he delivered on my behalf.

I can now endorse the pledges he has made for me.

I can now offer my sincere thanks to everyone for selecting me for this position.

I can confirm that I fully understand the gravity and responsibility of this duty; it is not a job, it is my life's work and now it has been expanded greatly.

I thank the Chancellor sincerely for having me seated before these announcements were made. I had no idea that genetics were to have its own faculty was even being considered. And, I thank my friend the Vice-Chancellor for his gracious remarks and for stopping before he expressed any goals which might have been beyond my reach. Thank you again; this is Adieu and not Goodbye."

It was short, it was sweet, and it was sincere. As Mary sat the crowd still on its feet and the small band that had provided background music throughout the dinner broke into FOR SHE'S A JOLLY GOOD FELLOW and as this faded, and the audience sat the Master of Ceremonies again stepped forward. This time the GG was moving out to the microphone; all could hear her saying to the Master of Ceremonies in the gentlest, pleasing manner:

"I'm sorry Master of Ceremonies," the GG began. "I do believe that I have the privilege of the Last Word: if not in my role as Paton of this University then in my other role."

"I rarely pull that one," the GG said mischievously. "It would be most remiss of me though to let this moment pass without extending to you the sincere thanks of the Chancellor and his Council which represents all the institutions on this campus. In my other role, I am delighted to both welcome you and at the same time thank you for your attendance this evening and then farewell you on behalf of the government, the administration and the people of Australia. This has been a most significant occasion to which future generations will point as the beginning of the New World Order. I refer not to the greedy one so feared by conspiracy theorist, not even the one at present envisaged by the futurists but one that is based on the messages we each bring to life in our genetic code. Finally, I must thank Brad. I thought his speech on behalf of Professor Mary so sincere, delightful and perceptive that I must warn him not to let himself become lost to those delightful young ladies he will be introduced to during this forthcoming venture. We want you back here; indeed, I should say we need you back here. Finally, I would ask Brad to escort Professor Mary to make her goodbyes to your family and let us send you off in the traditional way."

I moved from the shadows to assist Mary from her chair and offering my hand in the same manner as before I escorted her to the table occupied by the Grands and the Greats. There were hugs and kisses and handshakes from the men. Mary said to them that there was no way we could have any sensible talk now, and I told them I would arrange a conference call tomorrow afternoon.

After breaking away, we passed by the PM's table. Auld Lang Syne was now starting softly in the background; it would soon get very loud as we neared the door with everyone in the audience singing along. The PM said, "Congratulations Professor Mary, great speech Brad; have you thought of politics as a career."

"No ma'am I replied I really don't think I would fit in."

"Why not play on our team Brad?" the Leader of the Opposition said.

"No thanks sir, same reason," I replied. The US Secretary of State proffered her congratulations.

"Please let me know when you will arrive in Washington, Professor, I know the President wants to meet you and I would like to make that introduction myself."

"I would be honoured," Mary managed as she felt the pressure rising again. In the meantime, our Foreign Minister had come to me. He put an envelope into my inside jacket pocket.

"There are some phone numbers and email addresses you might find helpful. Don't hesitate to call any of our ambassadors if you need any assistance."

"We don't intend to get locked up Minister," I said jokingly: knowing that was the most common report one heard from unruly travellers and drug- runners abroad.

"Go on, get that young lady out of here I'm sure she has had enough of this for one evening," the Foreign Minister gave me a firm pat on the back. "Loved your speech by the way; the young Bob Menzies would have done no better."

With Mary again at my side and only a little way before we reached the run for the door Doc was waiting alone for us. As we approached, he reached out as if to shake us by the hand. He took my right hand in his right hand, Mary's left hand he held from the palm in his left hand and with a delicate movement while looking us in the eye, moving from one to the other pressed my hand down quite firmly on the back of Mary's and held our two hands together between his.

"Congratulations," Doc said sincerely.

Mary kissed him on the cheek. The audience didn't even notice the gesture as I raised Mary's hand back to the way it was before, and we continued our way to the door. There had been waves and congratulations coming from everywhere since we left the Grands and Greats, but none had touched us like Doc's almost silent tribute. The band raised its volume and the crowd now gave Robbie Burns' classic full voice. When we arrived at the door we turned, faced the crowd, but saw nobody, and after waving for a few moments turned and hurried out. A security guard was immediately at our side.

“I’ll escort you to your car sir, ma’am,” He said. We barely heard but hurried along. AULD LANG SYNE faded away and now a loud singing of:

“IT WAS MARY, MARY, LONG BEFORE THE FASHION CHANGED,”

The guard drove the lift to the carpark and guided us directly to the XK.

“Thanks very much mate,” I said as I held the door open for Mary.

“Are you allowed to accept a tip?” I asked, not wishing to offend either way.

“No sir,” was the reply.

“Will you anyway?” I tried again.

“No sir,” was echoed.

“Well thank you very much,” I replied sincerely as I started the engine.

“I’ll see you through the boom gates sir. I wouldn’t like to see you get into any hassle.”

At last we were through the gates and on our way. We had hardly spoken since I rose when The Vice broke down. I was now looking for a quiet spot to park for a few moments. I found one and went to Mary’s door and helped her out.

“Let’s get that ceremonial clobber off you? I can’t give my best girl Professor of all she surveys a big kiss in that gear, let alone in the rather tight XK,” I announced. Mary said nothing but shed her gown and handed it to me to fold up and put it on the small rear seat. Mary turned to me and we instantly wrapped our arms around each other, hugged, and squeezed as if checking we were here and at last free. Mary raised her lips to mine to receive my ardent kisses which I broke occasionally to say ‘Congratulations’, ‘Congratulations darling,’ or ‘Congratulations Professor’. Each time I broke away Mary pulled me back to kiss her again. Finally, after about ten minutes and fearing that half the departing Honourable Guests might pass this way we agreed to drive on, “Plan B?” I said more as a statement than a question.

“Plan B it is Captain,” Mary confirmed. “Remember you promised to fly me over the moon.”

“You know I always keep my promises darling,” I replied.

“That I do, I’m just curious as to how you are going to do it this time,” Mary replied. “Wasn’t Doc sweet,” she added.

“You don’t need to say much to impart a blessing, do you?”

“No, I read it as a blessing too darling,” Mary replied. “In our little kiss and cuddle back there, I forgot to thank you for my speech.”

“No thanks are required, you know that. But if you feel obliged you can bestow your thanks on me later,” I replied

“Thank you darling, I’ll remember that,” Mary said. Our talk continued in this quiet almost drifting manner as we wound-down from the night’s business. We had thought that perhaps one hundred would have been mustered from the local professors and other functionaries in the City of Canberra, not that four hundred representatives of world leaders would be present. We had expected Mary’s promotion was just a fill in to the main event, not that she was the main and only event on the program. The whole bash had been put on just for her.

“I shake whenever I think of it Brad, let’s talk about something else please?” Mary finally said with only ten kilometres to go to our refuge.

"Would you activate our flight plan please darling?" I asked, "It's on the Flight Service App. What's the time by the way?"

"Ten-forty," Mary replied. "Is that important?"

"Only that I have requested start-up for twenty-three hundred. They'll give us a little latitude, but we should be OK," I replied. "Do you mind waiting to change until we're straight and level, we'll need to crank her up as soon as we're on board?"

"Whatever you say Captain, whatever you say. I almost feel like drifting; all the science has been drained out of this little science professor. I wouldn't dare be critical of any of your decisions. I am totally in your hands and I love it."

"Thank you darling, we'll soon be there and putting all of this behind us," I replied. I was feeling a little guilty now as Mary was releasing her stress. I had started the conversation merely to establish a reason to strap her in quickly until we were steady at thirty thousand. I will then release her to view the cabin and get a second big shock for the night. I now wanted this shock to cancel out some of the fears that her new role might have imposed on her. When I started this project, I had no idea that it would be as valuable to her as it obviously will be in her new life.

I was now quite prepared to give away any thoughts of an academic career for me if it meant that I be her pilot, chauffer, bodyguard, escort, confessor, message boy and lover. We rolled into the hangar. I helped Mary out of the car, guided her up the steps and into her seat as co-pilot. I put her headphones on her head, told her that I needed her to back me up on the communications while I did my pre-flight. After taking off, she could happily go to sleep.

I went back down the steps, did my pre-flight inspection, gathered Mary's new robes from the back seat, left my keys in the car so that Greg Howard could look after it during our absence and then turned off the hangar lights. On return I retracted the steps, locked the door, hung Mary's robes and took my seat. I noticed that Mary was very close to sleep.

Chapter 7

Over the Moon

Saturday 8 December 2012 – 2300 hrs

Fly me to the moon
https://www.youtube.com/watch?v=mQR0bXO_yl8
Let me play among those stars
Let me see what spring is like
On a-Jupiter and Mars
In other words, hold my hand
In other words, baby kiss me

"Canberra Ground this is Bravo Mike Charlie," our escape was underway.

"Bravo Mike Charlie, Call Tower on one two fife decimal fife," was the reply.

This was a frequency that I hadn't been given before and it was not listed on the charts. Dutifully, I followed instructions and clicked the second radio to that frequency.

"Tower this is Bravo Mike Charlie on one two fife decimal fife," I reported.

"Good evening Brad this is Pete from your arrival back home ten days ago. Just thought I'd give you a call when I heard BRAVO MIKE CHARLIE was on the move again. It's OK this is a discrete frequency, no records. Doing another runner mate?" Peter sounded very friendly.

"Not this time Pete it has been well planned," I replied.

"Oh, I thought you might be getting out of town fearing the media would be after you again. Or should I say that extremely pretty co-pilot of yours."

"Why?" I asked.

"Because you're all over the late news tonight, or at least she is. You don't come up bad in your dickie suit either. Pretty fine speech you made they were saying."

“Shit Pete I never dreamed they would have it out this quickly,” I replied.

“We’re are you heading mate, so I can give you some cover if needs be?” Pete asked.

We’re flying all night to visit friends south of Darwin. We’ll push off from there late tomorrow afternoon or the next day and check out through Darwin. A couple of pit stops will see us in London in about a week. Our schedule is quite flexible. My co-pilot, also known as Professor Mary, has to don her academic robes from time to time for some posh affairs along the way,” I said.

“When will you be back mate?” Pete asked.

“Twelve months Pete,” I responded.

“Some buggers have all the luck. Give my regards to Professor Mary and bon voyage. Flick back to the other channel and I’ll clear you for take-off, there’s no traffic in the area but we need to put the formal bits on the tape. Good luck mate.”

“Thanks for all your help Pete,” I said as I brought up the regular tower frequency to receive my clearance for an immediate departure and climb to thirty thousand feet on published procedure to Darwin.

I turned onto the active runway, eased the throttle forward and with the landing lights blazing in front of me we were racing along the centreline.

“V1 – Rotate,” Mary’s voice came through my headset, sounding much more alive and ready to go. After clearing Canberra and with Bravo Mike Charlie trimmed for two thousand feet a minute climb I turned to Mary and seeing she was wide-awake said:

"I thought you were sleeping darling, I got a little busy back there talking to Pete right up to the turn onto the runway. He sent his regards by the way."

"I know, but I didn't want to butt in. It's nice to hear compliments when they think no one is listening, you know you are not being flattered or buttered up," Mary replied.

"I know he was envious of me, he would have loved to be in my place. We'll be settled in cruise in fifteen minutes. You will be able to get changed and freshen-up with a level floor then. Don't be too long though I've only got the next hour to fly you over the moon."

"Can you turn the seat belt sign off Captain, I want to come over and kiss you," Mary pleaded.

"Not until we are in cruise and you have changed out of those fancy clothes, co-pilot," I instructed using my authority.

"Permission to leave the bridge, Captain," Mary asked ten minutes later. "We're straight and level now."

"Granted," was all that I said. I didn't even glance at Mary as she rose and left. I was struggling to keep any emotion from showing in my voice or on my face.

"Whew, I've done it," I spoke aloud, but only to myself. **Aphrodite's Diary http://www.futuristic.guru/copy-of-aphrodite-10**

I had hung my dinner jacket behind my seat when I came on board and I now shed my shoes and socks and tucked them behind my chair, out of danger of the rudder pedals. I took off my suit trousers and folded them over Mary's chair; she would hang them up for me when she returned, I thought. Now comfortable in my boxers and shirt I relaxed. The whole aircraft was kept moderately warm by the air-conditioning and I was comfortable, at peace and extremely happy. I had set a playlist running when we came on board and now, I was hearing it for the first time. The sky was clear, and the stars were bright; the full moon was where I had anticipated from the met reports. I smiled as I could see the little LED lights come on and then off, one by one as Mary opened doors, cupboards and drawers. I had the electrician install this repeater in the cockpit as a security measure to alert the pilot to any door coming open in flight and allowing its contents to fly out and possibly do some damage. I was now regretting not having turned the computers on, so I could see the look on Mary's face as she moved through the cabin. The LED for the galley stayed on for quite a while as no doubt Mary was checking out the fridge, freezer, pantry, crockery and china. The LED in the lab stayed on even longer. I could imagine Mary sitting on her lab chair, examining her new equipment, looking in her drawers for accessories and supplies. Coming back down the cabin I saw the wardrobe LEDs light while Mary examined how her clothes had been arranged. A little while without a LED as Mary no doubt was examining our matching workstations and the dining table and chairs. Perhaps she was admiring the orchids, I thought. The LED for the toilet came on and then off followed by the shower LED coming on. She must be enjoying the shower after this evening's stresses. Finally, the shower LED went out. 'Won't be long now to know my fate,' I was thinking to myself. Mary is having another look at her lab I could see as its LED flickered again but this time only for a short period. As my playlist moved on, I could hear 'WHAT A DIFFERENCE A DAY MADE...' just as Mary came back to me. She was dressed now only in her new lab coat with her Mile-High-Club badge clipped to its lapel. She wore her new ceremonial cap jauntily as a French girl would wear her beret and her honey blonde waves were reaching out to her shoulders. At the first sight of her my old fella sprung to attention through the long split in the front of my boxer shorts. I pushed them down quickly and Mary straddled me.

"Adonis, darling this is magnificent," She quickly pinned my Mile-High-Club badge to the collar of my shirt. "Even if they had thrown in a Nobel Prize it wouldn't have matched this."

Aphrodite clung to me desperately, long kisses with a little to-ing and fro-ing of our tongues. There had been no time or need for any foreplay. My left arm had reached behind Mary's back ensuring that her grip on me didn't slip away and my right hand moved up her ribs to cup her left breast. I could feel the Gates to Paradise opening and my old fella went straight home.

We abandoned ourselves to our genitals as the two millionaires came together and only after several seemingly uncontrollable motions, we experienced equally uncontrollable orgasms. Mary knew that we had lost the chance to make this one of Doc's special occasions by denying ourselves earlier in the day, but that didn't mean that she would give up without making this the best double-banger I could hope for.

Now, as we allowed our breathing and heartbeats to regain some normality Mary was applying some small squeezes occasionally to my dick: permitting it to relax but keeping it reminded that it would be required for more duty before the day was done. She knew we still had fifteen minutes before midnight and if she couldn't pull it off by then, so to speak, she thought with a little grin, she would claim Eastern Standard Time and gain an hour when we crossed the Queensland border. She knew that she could even claim Universal Time because that was what it was in every cockpit in the sky at this moment and gain another ten hours. Mary didn't want to do that as she wanted to lock this day away in its own compartment, in the same time zone as it had begun. Mary was still clinging to me but now able to remove her lips for a little while and begin talking again.

"Brad, you know I only went there believing that I was to hear the announcement of my promotion and to receive congratulations from the ANU campus?" Mary began.

"Of course, I do darling. That was my expectation too. Even when you came back with the Chancellor, I had no idea that the reason why so many dignitaries were there had anything to do with you. Surely it was to do with something else," I replied.

"I soon realised that they had me in a position where I couldn't refuse. They had announced that my peers wanted me in the job; the Chancellor had cloaked me in the robes of a new faculty that I didn't even know was going to exist. Officially it didn't exist until the moment he announced it and declared that sitting over there was little Mary Clifford now installed as its first Chair and the coordinator of similar faculties around the globe. They had me trussed and ready for the pot; they had me by the short and curlies."

"No darling, only I can do that," I said. I kissed her more passionately now and Mary responded with more contractions of her vagina stirring my old fella to greater attention.

"Let's be quiet for a moment. I promised to fly you over the moon and I will in just a few moments more," I said. Mary obeyed but still hugged me tightly not letting my erection go away. The auto-pilot had been doing a perfect job of flying Bravo Mike Charlie and I knew that while I was on plan and maintaining the assigned altitude there would be no reports for a while and little likelihood of contact from Flight Service unless to alert us to unexpected traffic or changing weather conditions. I also knew that at least one pair of eyes was watching all traffic in this area.

I could see the bright orb of the full moon on the now calm waters off the coast of Sydney. We had been routed out over the water from Canberra in somewhat of an arc over the sea to avoid climbing through the busy flight path between Sydney-Canberra-Melbourne and to avoid Newcastle where air force jets can be flying around at any hour; we will cross the New South Wales coast at Kempsey on a direct course for Darwin. I lowered the left wing to give Mary a better view.

“There darling, just look down,” I said softly.

“Beautiful isn’t it. It looks as though it was placed there just for us,” Mary said.

We hugged, we kissed, and I felt compelled to fondle both her breasts and tickle both nipples. Mary locked her lips on mine and I couldn’t hold back from making deep and exhilarating plunges into her vagina.

This time we withheld our climax, wanting to make our joy last after my first sudden ejaculation. Soon we could hold back no longer and with the same abandonment as before our orgasms came together. We were spent. As Mary felt my old fella slip away more quietly than before she glanced at the panel clock that I kept on local time to see it showing twenty-three fifty-eight.

“Two minutes to spare,” Mary said. A little smile of satisfaction crossed her face, “You’ve thought of everything Adonis, it’s beautiful.”

It was another fifteen minutes that we held together. Mary at last saying:

“I’ll get you something to eat and drink lover; we’ve hardly eaten all day. I noticed that you didn’t eat much at dinner either and hardly drank anything.”

“Only if you hurry back darling,” I replied.

“I promise, only a little clean-up; all that exertion has undone some of the benefits of the shower and I want to try out my new galley,” Mary added.

“I tried to fit in a spa darling but thought that would be a little over the top,” I added.

“All of this is over the top, it’s magnificent,” Mary was waving her arms about in delight, finally hugging herself for good measure.”

“Would you toss me in a sponge, towel, clean boxers and a sports shirt please,” I called after her.

Mary wasn’t gone long before she was back with my request. Mary was stark naked now as she had stripped off her one piece of clothing to clean-up. She gathered up my clothes from the night before and I stepped out of my slightly stained boxers.

“You can look but don’t touch,” Mary giggled as she would have done in her Water Nymph role. “We don’t want to starve to death before we even leave Australia, do we?” Mary was gone to her galley.

I sponged myself down; I would have my shower sometime before reaching Bob’s airstrip. Now in clean boxers and shirt I sat down and selected a news channel on one of the radios. Bravo Mike Charlie’s communications capability was to airline standard. The news was all about last night’s promotion of Associate Professor Mary Clifford of the ANU to a full professorship. Professor Mary was to be to be the Inaugural Chair of the new Faculty of Genetics at the ANU and the Chair of the coordinating committee establishing faculties of genetics worldwide. It had appeared that the Chancellor had deliberately broken from tradition: instead of presenting Professor Clifford to the assembled dignitaries he presented Professor Mary it seemed he was ensuring that nobody might make any confusion between any other

Professor Clifford in the world and ANU's Professor Clifford. The Vice-Chancellor did the same and it is evident that this is how she will be known. Not only is it distinctive but nobody else would adopt it in fear of falling way short of its owner and look ridiculous thereby. The newsreader continued: "When reports of this event reached the newsroom the immediate question was: Who is this Professor Mary? Searches were made of the ANU news releases over the past four years and found that Professor Mary, as Associate Professor Clifford had been the leader of ANU's research contribution to the world-wide Human Genome Project. With her team, she had been published in scientific journals in recent years and established a strong bond and connection with other universities. Despite the numerous reports that should have drawn their attention to this rising star the realisation now hit the journalist that this was that elegant young lady with two bars on the shoulders of her airline like pilot's shirt while her four-bar wearing captain was none other than her eighteen-year-old son as they orbited Sydney Harbour."

I had pressed the record button when I switched the radio on and now hearing Mary returning, I turned off the sound leaving the rest of the story unfolding. Mary placed a mug of freshly brewed coffee in my cup holder and handed me a Wedgewood entrée plate bearing a thick steak sandwich. She left but was quickly back with her own and sat in her own seat. She looked as delicious as any meal she could put before me. Her wavy hair still down, the small blue bolero knotted under her petite unrestrained breasts; her bare midriff and tight little shorts made her the picture of everyman's dreams.

"Smells delicious darling," I said.

"Get that into you Luv," Mary replied as you might hear at any Aussie barbecue. We both laughed aloud.

"Where do we begin Brad?" Mary asked. "How do we come to grips with last night?"

"I don't know darling I was gobsmacked when the penny dropped, and I realised that all those toffs were there only to see you and to make sure you didn't back out." I was not going to mention the news report until our meal was out of the way and I could hold her on my knee to listen to the replay.

"I swear that I would have taken off the robes, politely handed them to the Chancellor and in a clear voice, hiding my fury, I would have said, "Thank you Chancellor and your Honoured Guests but I do not see this as my role in life."

"That would have left everybody in a mess, wouldn't it?" I said.

"It certainly would but fancy them bushwhacking me in that way. It was almost immoral," Mary almost swore.

"What would your friend the Secretary of State say to her President then? What would all those Ambassadors say in their reports home after their governments having obviously supported you?" I reasoned with her.

"I know, perhaps I'm being silly. I know I had no choice what with all the ANU top brass, not to mention the GG all there. You were my only strength Brad; when you took over proceedings when Don broke down and everyone else was gawking, I felt that with your strength I can do it too. But accepting this for me will change things for us darling."

"Not at all; it will change our itinerary no doubt, but we had left that wide open."

"That's right darling, we'll deal with the other changes as they come along. We will live day-by-day for now: daytight compartments," Mary added much more cheerfully than the way she was feeling deep down.

"We haven't even talked about the refit yet. I want to know how you managed it."

"Well, if you wouldn't mind clearing up the dinner things steward, we can talk about such things for the rest of the night," I replied.

"Oh, so I'm demoted now, now that you've had your way with me," Mary started in her mock disappointment and acting the discarded vamp, "I'm beginning to think you only want me for my body Mr Brad Clifford."

"Out wench," I raised my voice. Mary disappeared holding her hankie to her eyes.

Sunday 9 December 2012 – 0100 hrs

"Come sit on my knee child," I said on her return. Mary dutifully obeyed. I held her to me and we exchanged passionate kisses.

"I'm beginning to like this," Mary said. "How long to Bob's place?"

"Pretty near to four hours depending on the winds," I replied.

"Good, I thought we might have been closer, I want to lay in your arms and talk; so much has happened unexpectedly."

"Just before we talk, I'll replay the late news for you. If you feel like getting upset or emotional just laugh and squeeze me. We're going to rise above all this, keep our dignity, never respond to any media nonsense, and ignore any of their guesses. We must never lower ourselves to their level as we can't fight dirty — promise."

"I promise Captain," Mary said, giving me a big hug to confirm it and turning her head up to kiss me once more.

I flicked on the replay and sat back in my chair. I got Mary comfortable in my lap and felt at peace with the world. I had asked Mary if she needed a wrap or blanket, but she declined saying that 'she had her love to keep her warm'. We spoke little in the next half hour. With her head on my shoulder, her left hand on my chest and her right behind my back I could feel her giggle and chuckle at some of the story being told. Most of this report was true and factual with little conjecture. We realised we were having the last laugh over the Sydney Harbour incident. That she was not just some pretty face in the cockpit with some hunk of a pilot. That even the Secretary of State for the US was there with her country's Chairman of the Joint Chiefs of Staff to honour her. Mary and I laughed aloud as the newsreader admitted that Australia's news reporting was sadly lacking to let the build-up to this monumental occasion go unobserved. They couldn't understand how with so many embassies and dignitaries involved there had not been some leak from someone. The media didn't even know that any important gathering was planned in Canberra for last night.

"We weren't the only ones fooled darling," I said, still laughing.

"What would they have said if they could have seen their sweet little Professor Mary ringing your bells twice between eleven-thirty and midnight?" Mary too was laughing aloud.

"They would never dream that it could be happening," I replied.

"Doc would," Mary said still smiling happily.

“I hope so, I’d hate to disappoint him. I’m sure he would be expecting us to follow doctor’s orders,” I said and we both broke out laughing again.

All the while since entering cruise, the autopilot was flying Bravo Mike Charlie. At the same time, during our talks and glorious double-banger, I had maintained my scan of the panel, had an ear cocked to acknowledge any communication immediately and ready to take manual control in an instant. Ground lost in a hasty withdrawal from the battlefield can be regained later but the loss of our magic carpet and its most precious professor would be irreplaceable. Finally, I switched off the radio.

“We’ll have a look in at the morning TV news at five-thirty central time. It’ll be six o’clock in Sydney then. We’ll see what photos they got hold of,” I said.

Mary wanted to know every detail of how I managed the refit in only ten days. She didn’t give the slightest hint of wanting to know the cost. She knew of course that I now had my own estate and who was she to question me on how I chose to use it. Thoughts such as these always prompted her to squeeze me and reach for my lips as a way of saying, ‘Thank you,’ which she had found herself saying so often that she feared it may be coming too repetitive for me.

At five-thirty, with Mary still nestled on my lap, I reached over and brought up the early TV news on my weather radar screen. There was nothing being reported on the radar as it was such a clear full-moon night.

“We have some surprise news clips for our viewers this morning. An event that was held in Canberra last night …,” the announcer’s descriptions and explanations of the film clips of the evening’s procedures ran for a full forty minutes. The regular news that kicked off the show each morning was pushed aside. During the presentation the announcer would slip in at an appropriate time, ‘This segment is being brought to you by …,'. several of these were inserted for the best and most reliable of the station's advertisers.

With the announcer now off the screen and only providing a voiceover, clips from the function ran for the next thirty minutes. Every feature and speech from the evening was included, from the receiving line until Mary and I waved leaving the hall to the sound of AULD LANG SYNE and FOR IT WAS MARY. There was a final short clip as we disappeared into the lift.

"That was fair darling, don't you think?" Mary asked, now sitting up in my lap so that she could face me again. We had hardly spoken during the segment as we watched the story unfold and listened to the announcer's voiceover.

"Yes, I have no complaint; it will save us a lot of explaining from now on," I replied. "Seeing who were there it will be all around the world by tonight. Professor Mary, I like that: it acknowledges your uniqueness."

"Darling I've told you we are all unique so many times, you even made it a key point in your address," Mary almost complained.

"Of course, I know. I would like to say some are more unique than others and I know that is nonsense too. What I really mean is in academia you are now unique. There will never be any confusion with any other Professor Clifford."

"I don't think we should meet them like this do you?" I asked with one hour to go. "What with me in open fronted boxers and you with those delightful little titties bobbing about," I teased. "You go first darling; when you come back you can hold the fort for me and then I'll take her in."

"I wouldn't like to land her tonight darling," Mary turned to me for a final big hug and kisses before reluctantly leaving the comfort of my lap.

"I'd better let Bob know we're coming," I said. I didn't use the radio although I knew Bob's personal call sign. I used his air to ground mobile instead; following the good advice I had received from Jack on our previous trip. As soon as Bob answered I went into my prepared presentation.

"Bravo Mike Charlie requests clearance to land at Bob's airstrip at zero seven hundred hours. The big one not that tiny thing in your backyard."

"Bravo Mike Charlie, Clear to land, your transport will be waiting. I wouldn't be game to put your bird down in my backyard with a fifty-knot headwind. Thought we might be hearing from you. You two were all over the news last night and breakfast TV this morning. How's Mary?"

"Mary's great mate, we'll tell you all about it on the ground," I replied.

"See you soon mate," Bob said in parting.

"I'll have my shower and when the LED goes out you can start down," I said.

I was back in twenty minutes feeling totally refreshed. I took over from Mary and increased our descent rate. The next approach and landing was as important to me as the one I did in Sydney. I suddenly realised that this was the first time I had flown Bravo Mike Charlie since arriving home ten days ago. I further realised that I had contributed little to this flight since Bravo Mike Charlie had flown herself after I established cruise settings. Expecting Bob would have binoculars on me I flew a conventional circuit as if landing at a busy GA airport, however, here I was ensuring there were no early morning wild life grazing on the strip. I touched down smoothly and ran on the mains until the nose wheel came down gently on the imaginary centreline. I timed my engine shut down so that by the time our bird was approaching Bob and Kay the big prop was windmilling to a stop.

We were straight out of our seats and before opening the door and while out of view through any of the windows we paused to embrace and kiss.

We came down the steps and Bob shook my hand strongly and Kay embraced Mary in a motherly hug. We quickly changed so that Kay could give me a hug and kiss on the cheek and Mary could do the same for Bob.

"C'mon you lot, breakfast will be ready soon," Kay said happy that the Cliffords were with them again.

"Wouldn't you like to see inside?" Mary asked.

"We did that last time, remember?" Bob said also keen to get us home and relaxed.

"Not the way she is now?" Mary said with a little bit of a tease coming in her voice.

"OK," said Kay, "let's see."

Sunday 9 December 2012 – 0700 hrs

"Take Kay through to the back and work forward Mary," I began, "I'll entertain Bob up front for a while."

Mary led Kay up the steps and took her through to the galley. Gasps and words of surprise met Bob and me as we entered.

"Take the seat facing aft Bob," I said easily. "You'll get a better view from there. We'll let the girls do their thing, Mary will love to show another lady her new home for twelve months; she saw it for the first-time last night once we were up and in cruise. I'll give you a good look back there when they finish."

"I'm amazed Brad; never seen anything like it," Bob began. "You only got home ten days ago. There's a year's work in what I can see here. How did you do that in ten days and get the CAA approvals to fly her again."

"As it turned out it wasn't so difficult," I began. "Shortly after we left last time, I told Mary that I couldn't start Uni next year because I just didn't know what line of study I would want to pursue. I announced that I was going to take a gap year and find out through some travelling what really interested me. Well, to cut a long story short, Mary declared that she was going to take a year's sabbatical and come too. She couldn't get out of the country soon enough, what with Bruce's death and the media harassment. Her promised professorship and the ANU could all go to pot. I had found an article about a sheik's Pilatus that had a factory special and I built on that to design this. I was careful to make sure that I only selected equipment and fittings that had already been approved and were available from Pilatus in Sydney. Everything was ready for assembly as soon as we got home, and I had my LayMe and joinery lined up and ready to use as much of their labour force as necessary to get the bird ready for approvals on Friday. We intended leaving on Sunday following what we thought was to be a campus announcement of her promotion on Saturday night. What you have seen on the TV shows us walking in to a grand event and then thinking that Mary's was a convenient side event were shocked to find that she was the sole purpose of the bash and people had come from all over to hear the Chancellor's announcements. As soon as we could we were out of there and invoked our plan B which was to fly out as soon as we got out of the hall last night."

"We I'll be buggered," was all that Bob could say. "And you've flown all night?"

"Yes, beautiful night for flying," I replied.

"What say when the girls have finished you pack an overnight bag and have a couple of days with us to unwind," Bob offered. "You're not on a tight schedule, are you?"

"Not at all, we've got a year. We are planning for Mary to make her first business stop presenting her credentials to the Chancellor of Cambridge University in a week, that's no problem," I replied quite calmly.

"And you're taking Bravo Mike Charlie all the way?" Bob asked a little incredulously.

"Of course, wouldn't you mate, she's a honey," I replied.

"I'd love too, but I haven't the ratings or the guts to pull on such a challenge," Bob replied with growing admiration in his voice.

"It's not so tough really, Mary and I have both got IFR ratings, she's an easy plane to fly single handed, long hops are quite enjoyable and one can have a sleep any time they want, or work or shower or make a meal. Last night was a first flight with the new set-up and everything worked beautifully."

Mary was returning with Kay.

"Bob would like us to stay a night or two and relax a little before we fly away, happy with that Mary?" I asked.

"I'd be delighted Bob, we can have a really good chat this time Kay," Mary replied.

"OK, grab a bag and we'll go and have breakfast, I'm starting to feel a little peckish. We can come back later for a better inspection of this beautiful bird," Bob said as I ushered the ladies down the stairs.

Kay opened the rear door for Mary leaving me to ride in the front with Bob.

"What's your next stop Brad?" Bob asked.

“We’ve got to check out through Darwin but then Singapore. I’d like to have a beer in the Long Bar at Raffles, with the ghost of Somerset Maugham,” I replied.

“Can you leap so far?” Bob was more concerned about my planning than talking about famous writers.

“Oh, I forget to mention that we’ve got an extra two hours in the tanks now,” I added almost casually.

“I can’t get my head around how you got so much done in ten days, let alone getting it approved,” Bob continued.

“Like I said back there,” I began, “I didn’t have to do anything. My work was done by the time we got back to Sydney.

“I can say that if I hadn’t seen it with my own eyes only three weeks ago, I wouldn’t have believed it no matter who told me,” Bob was clearly puzzled and turned to Kay. “If you had told me darling, I would have thought you were pulling my leg.”

“It doesn’t matter how you did it Brad it is simply beautiful and so functional,” Kay was quick to praise. “What did you think Mary when you first saw it?”

“I didn’t know what to think. When we got to the drome Brad hurried me up the steps, made sure that I was strapped in, handed me my headset and told me we needed to start-up immediately to be within his requested clearance. He told me I could get changed when we were in cruise and had a level and safe floor,” Mary began. “Fifteen minutes later I was set free. We’ll you’ve seen what I saw, it was heady stuff to suddenly appear in front of you at thirty thousand feet. The cabin lights were on and dimmed, one of Brad’s playlists was running on the sound system, a stem of orchids on the table, it was beautiful. Well, the curiosity got to me and I inspected everything, I had a galley, a lab, a boudoir with full length mirror; my clothes were hung in a wardrobe, my underwear folded in drawers and my shoes on shoe racks; I thought we were going to be living out of cases and cartons for twelve months. We each had a workstation with our notebooks in place. I don't know how long it took me, but I eventually got around to getting changed. I took off my evening dress and hung it up in the wardrobe. It felt so strange to be doing that in an airplane. It felt stranger still to peel off everything else and step into a warm shower. To be able to take as long as I liked, clean my teeth, go to the toilet and know that there wasn't a queue out there and there hadn't been others who had passed through this bathroom today. It was heaven in heaven."

"I hope you rewarded Brad with a big kiss, Mary?" Kay spoke up.

"I did, I did," Mary replied with a little dab to her eyes.

'We've been sprung,' was my immediate thought, 'this is so like Doc's way of confirming what he already knew. We were pulling up to the veranda now.

"I'm with you Bob, I'm hungry too," I began cheerfully. "Remember too much praise makes us Cliffords nervous. We begin to fear ourselves and anyone who flatters us."

"We're not flattering you Brad, wouldn't think of it. But you can't deny us admiring beauty when we see it. You do that yourself or that bird wouldn't be sitting out there now."

"Thanks Bob, I take your point," I finished the discussion and we went in to eat.

Chapter 8

Sprung

Sunday 9 December 2012 – 0800 hrs

Mary helped Kay serve their typical country breakfast. It didn't matter if they didn't eat much during the day; having set up well they could look forward to a relaxed dinner when each day was done. Over breakfast I told them that I had brought my notebook from the plane to have a conference call with my full set of four grandparents and eight great-grandparents and I wanted to introduce Bob and Kay to them, I announced, obviously proud of our friendship. They were delighted to accept because they would be seeing each other face to face on the screen with all present. The conversation floated around happily and then the table was cleared away and we resumed our seats to talk some more.

"Please don't be alarmed or embarrassed," Bob said as he reached his hand across the table and grasped my arm at the wrist. Kay had reached across and taken Mary's hand reassuringly. There was nothing but pride and understanding that could be read in their faces or eyes.

"Young lovers can't hide their love for each other from old lovers. We knew from the first time we saw you that you loved each other dearly. There were so many signs last time: like when the sing-along got around to **People Will Say We're in Love, https://www.youtube.com/watch?v=VEwVAV3VPw4** we saw the looks and the smiles that you were trying to restrain, and when I SANG WHAT A DIFFERENCE A DAY MADE I knew that Mary didn't just stumble causing you to catch her and glide her into the shadows, or in Darwin the way you were concerned for her. I could see the veins tensing in your hands and arms ready to form a fist and knock down anyone who approached her.

"Seeing you on the tele this morning it was obvious to us the depth of your love, not to mention your little Taj Mahal in the sky; to us that was the same tribute to love as the real one," Bob paused.

"What gave us away so that you tell us all about this now?" Mary asked quietly. Flushed and with another little dab to her eyes, but no disappointment or any sign of shame or remorse.

"Kay spotted that little pin on your lab coat lapel, the coat was rather crumpled, and she knew you wouldn't have been looking down your microscope last night," Bob continued, "and having one of her own she knew how you had expressed your thanks to Brad."

We all laughed and giggled and shared handshakes and kisses.

"We would have liked to let you know sooner but needed to know for sure before we could broach such a delicate subject," Bob began again. "If we had been in error, in the slightest way, we would have lost two delightful friends forever. We only wanted you to know that there is no need for any pretence here. There are no rules, no laws. Mary has only achieved this high honour through the love that she has poured into her work and students. All those bigwigs last night want more of the same and on a grander scale, they would exhaust her, eat her up, then throw her out, and look for another Mary; they wouldn't find one of course. Mary had a constant and true inflow of love from Bruce and that's what places her so high in her calling. It's obvious that you must fill this role now. I'd hate to imagine what might happen if she tried to replace Bruce's love in the arms of any other man. I can only think of two possibilities: you would either flee the scene and never see Mary again or you would kill the three of you."

"That's how Doc explained it to me last week," I replied.

"Who's Doc?" Bob asked.

“He’s my obstetrician,” Mary began; she had now regained her composure and was happy to explain. “He saved Brad and me when Brad was born.”

“Was he the old gentleman you gave that parting kiss to Mary?” Bob asked.

“Yes, that’s Doc,” Mary spoke with pride.

“I knew he must have been special,” Bob said. “I caught that bringing of your hands together.”

“You don’t miss much mate, do you?” I spoke up equally proud of this friend.

“Did you spare a thought for your classmates down there whooping it up at Surfers and thinking they are having fun?” Kay asked me.

“Not for one moment Kay, I didn’t even know it was on and I wouldn’t have gone anyway.”

“Only teasing Brad,” Kay replied with a big smile. “As if you would.”

“I suggest that you two try to catch up on some lost sleep before lunch,” Bob began. “After lunch I will give Brad some lessons in short fields in the Cessna, it seems he is lacking a bit of confidence in that area. I didn’t mention that the gang is coming for a sing-along tonight, so you need the sleep to withstand that. Your room’s ready, there’s a good fan in the ceiling.”

“I’m glad I’ll only have to wash one pair of sheets now,” Kay chuckled. “It’s so annoying when you find people bed-hopping after they think you have gone to sleep and then see one bed rumpled but not really slept in and the other bed mussed up completely.”

We all enjoyed another good laugh and Kay pointed us to our room. Mary and I folded the bedclothes back, stood under the ceiling fan and I stripped down to my boxers and Mary to her bra and panties. We laid down hand-in-hand rather than our usual arms around each other as the day was quickly warming and the humidity was high. We slept soundly for the next two hours. **Aphrodite's Diary http://www.futuristic.guru/copy-of-aphrodite-11**

"I really needed that," I began when I joined Bob on the veranda. "I took the chair opposite him knowing that any sort of tight or embarrassing situation you should always let the other party see your face and eyes.

"Thanks very much for letting us know that we had been sprung, mate."

"Think nothing of it mate," Bob said. "We're only too happy to help. We know how hard it can be, no pun intended of course." We both laughed at his quip.

"You're eighteen going on twenty-six and Mary's thirty-six and nobody would think of her being a day over twenty-six. You look perfectly good together as everyone in the country will have seen by now and if they haven't they will see it again in the news tonight. Nobody hearing your speech or seeing your flying would believe your age if you told them. As for Mary, few would believe that she is the hottest property in academia; seeing her for the first time they would think that she was a top model or actress at least. You don't often get brains and beauty in the one package Brad; someone that you love talking too as well. I know, I was lucky too and I tell her so every day. We're both blest mate; it's the greatest blessing that can be given any man."

"Here come the girls Bob," I said. I automatically rose from my chair as they entered the room. It wasn't expected but it was instinctive for me to do so. I knew that the manners my Grands had taught me as a child were going to serve me well escorting Professor Mary. I had been a little ill at ease in addressing the guests last night, but I had never expected that I would be thrown in at the deep end like that. Next time I will know who should be called 'Your Grace,' or 'Your Honour,' for tonight though first names and mate are the standard and perhaps a 'cobber' here and there is OK too.

Lunch went by with plenty of fun and laughter. With the last barrier broken down there was no need for any attempt to hide. I was free to call Mary 'Darling' and she to call me 'Lover'.

"Don't believe all you see or hear while we're away please," I spoke to them both as one. "we must be seen in public in the way people will expect and can understand. I will be expected to be seen with an attractive young deb or two or three; Mary will be expected to be seen dining with a middle-aged Chancellor or a rising professor in their field, everyone will expect young Brad Clifford to be sowing his wild oats on the continent. There would be something wrong with him if he didn't. We could never hide any truth from you though neither could we from Doc. Don't bother to say otherwise if you hear anyone speaking about us, for or against."

"No way mate," Bob was quick to confirm. "We can keep a straight face as good as anyone; can't we Kay?"

"No one will get one past us," Kay confirmed.

"I still can't quite come to terms with the refit Brad," Bob was back to his previous bewilderment. "If you were planning a camping trip and a love-fest, what's with the lab? I can understand the galley, the shower, the boudoir, but why take your girl's work along as well. That's the last thing most blokes would think of, they'd just want to get her away from all that."

"Sometimes Bob even you can be a bit thick," Kay jumped in saving me the need to reply. "For a start, Brad's not 'most blokes', he knows you can't hold your love by putting her in a cage and just admiring her for your own pleasure, he knows that if anything came up that required her attention at ANU she would have to break away and catch the first flight home. By putting all the other things she loves at her finger tips he knows she will have no need to fly away."

"Of course, you're right of course, in fact now it was almost prophetic that he did so seeing what happened last night," Bob agreed.

"Now you're getting the idea darling," Kay said as she gave him a kiss on the cheek nearest her.

"Which reminds me," Mary said. "We must introduce you to the rellies or they will be worrying why we haven't called."

I collected my notebook from our bedroom. I noticed the sign 'Cliff's Room' hanging above the door

"I take it Bob that the apostrophe indicates a contraction not the possession by some bloke named Cliff," I remarked to Bob.

"You noticed brother," Bob came back. "It's for you and Mary anytime you want to visit whether we're at home or away."

"Hello Mum, we're with some friends of Bruce's and of course ours just south of Darwin. Hello everyone, we can see all of you. How is it from your end?" Mary had rattled off.

"Clear as a bell, dear, so good to hear from you," Gran replied.

Mary took Kay and then Bob in front of the camera and introduced each to the twelve elders of the Clifford/Franklin dynasty. They could all see everyone at the opposite end of the conversation and Bob and Kay joined in too. Naturally, the conversation got around to last night's happenings. The Grands and Greats were bursting with pride at their third-generation in Mary having such honours and responsibilities thrust upon her; they knew she would be a wonderful success and what with their fourth-generation Brad at her side she would never want for protection and support. The older generations of the Clifford/Franklin dynasty would have died happy at that moment had they been called upon. By the time they closed the conversation Mary was clearly spent. She had largely run the show; mostly while standing and being the main topic of conversation. The realisation that she and I were now leaving the country for a year brought with it the realisation that some of the elders we had been chatting with might not be there to welcome us home. I put my arm around her and she rested her head on my chest; I dabbed a few small tears as they appeared and after about five minutes, while Bob and Kay made themselves busy in the kitchen, Mary regained her composure.

"Take this bloke flying Bob," Mary spoke brightly, now fully recovered. "Leave us to enjoy a little girl talk."

"Yes, buzz off you two," Kay was quick to take up the theme.

"We'll be back for afternoon tea," Bob said as we headed out the door. "Brad will be ready to need some ballast in the back seat by then to complete his training."

The girls didn't know whether this was meant as a compliment but felt that being referred to as ballast was not complimentary at all.

"OK Brad," Bob began. "What struck you from your last trip in the Cessna?"

"The main thing was that this little strip had a down grade away from the house and where the one-eight-two was lined up," I replied.

"And?" Bob asked.

"You took off downhill and landed uphill, and afterwards I realised that I hadn't noticed which way the wind was. I doubted that it would have done a one-eighty though, I would have noticed that," I replied.

"You're a good student Brad," Bob quickly gave credit. "You realise that our most important work is done on the ground and not in the air."

"You'd have had a fair bit of time on Cessnas no doubt?" Bob continued.

"Sure, we have one at home, Mary was fully licensed and when Bruce had to be away on business Mary kept her hand in, practised for her instrument rating and gave me plenty of time to practice my flying and navigation before I was old enough to get a licence. She's a very competent pilot. She wouldn't fly last night after the shock she had received except to hold the fort while I showered and dressed before coming in today. The Pilatus holds no fears for her, she loves it."

"OK," Bob agreed. "So why did you refuse to take the keys?"

"I didn't have to think about it really, there were so many things against me taking up your offer. I knew I could do a good short field in our one eight two on a strip this short, but I had only done that in training with an instructor or an examiner alongside, apart from a couple I had done solo just for the fun of it. But the real trap was that although I knew I could do it in the space available it was a different matter doing it on a level airport with thousands of feet in front of you and plenty of room on either side if you mucked up. It's a totally different thing than doing it here having never flown this one eight two, a rough strip with no margin for error, with four on board, including the most important person in my world and not knowing what was in the tanks, I knew I was on a hiding to nothing if I attempted it."

"You know you have already passed this little ratings test," Bob said. "Now I'll tell you how I do it and then we can do a couple of circuits."

"Firstly, I always take off downhill and land uphill just to gain that little bit of extra speed for the take-off and extra braking power on the landing. The wind here is usually very light mornings and evenings when I would usually be doing these short fields. If the wind direction makes it any way dangerous Kay just drives me to the big strip and I take the crop-duster. Or, if I arrive home and conditions are crook, I just call up Kay and she drives over to the strip to pick me up.

No big deal, no heroics, of course I know this bird like the back of my hand and that's very important too. You must hold her on the brakes and develop maximum revs before you release her. By the time you reach that peg over there you must be on the numbers or apply full brakes while you can still stop her. You must keep your eyes on that marker about two hundred feet past your take-off point and forget about the rough edges either side. If you can hold that line you can't go wrong. When you land just imagine you were doing that landing and quick turn off, we saw you do in Canberra, much the same really. When I saw you do that on the tele I knew you could easily do this. The only difference is the way you pull off the power. The stall warning will be at full screech as you touch down on the mains at the slowest possible speed. Brake as much as you can before you bring the nose wheel down but don't wait too long because you'll need more than the rudder to keep her on line. There's another peg over there two hundred feet past the runway at this end," Bob had laid out to me how to do it. "Feel like taking her up now?"

"Sure, let's do it," I said confidently. I went immediately to the oil dipstick cover and lifted it to check the oil. "I've done all of that stuff this morning," Bob called out as he made his way to right seat.

"Sure, but you gave me the keys, didn't you?" I replied.

"Your right of course," Bob conceded, "Do it properly."

I quickly stepped up on each strut in turn, dipped each fuel tank, drained the samples and checked for water, walked around the bird testing the movement of the control surfaces and finally removed the pitot tube cover and jumped into the left seat. I opened the window flap and called 'Clear Prop,' and started the engine. Now, while bringing the engine up to speed I checked the mags and oil pressure; I gave a crisp 'all stations' call to alert any pilot in the vicinity that I was taking off. Now with full power and my feet firmly on the brakes I held her for just a few seconds more to ensure she would hold to maximum revs and then released the brakes. I glued my eyes on Bob's markers and tore down the narrow strip. As soon as I knew that I had the right speed I pulled the nose up quickly to reach for fifty feet as soon as possible where I levelled out to regain the normal climb speed and slope. We hadn't talked about the fifty feet part of a short field but that was a very import part of the exercise too. The pilot was not only required to get off in the minimum distance for the aircraft type but to clear a fifty feet high obstacle as well. I climbed out to one thousand feet and commenced a circuit that would take me back to the other end of the strip so that I could do an inspection of the strip before extending past the end from where I had just lifted off and then circled to come into the same end to land uphill. I set up my approach early, had the speed well back, full flaps down and with the stall warning screaming had the mains on the ground just as the bird wanted to stop flying.

"Pull her up when we get to the top of the hill mate; I'll get out, so you can do one by yourself," Bob said. As soon as the Cessna stopped moving Bob was out the door and went directly away from the prop. I took her back to the starting point and repeated the exercise. This time I brought the Cessna to a full stop, shut down the motor, locked the control column and the brakes and got out.

“Quite a bit of difference with your weight gone from the front Bob, she wants to point much higher on lift off,” I remarked, “she’s very nice and smooth to handle.”

“Let’s go and have that cuppa Mate, we’ll give those girls a bit more cheek, eh,” We were both laughing as we went inside.

After our tea-break we returned with the girls for me to repeat the exercise with four on board. Bob hopped into the back seat with Kay putting the much lighter Mary in the front.

“I reckon we’d be about a hundred pounds under the limit, mate,” Bob advised. I quickly adjusted my mental plan for the extra weight for the first steep ascent because that and the actual touchdown was what it was all about. I performed the routine flawlessly and after congratulations all around, including a handshake from Bob and kisses from Mary and Kay we headed back to the house.

“I’d fly with you anywhere Brad,” Kay announced, “I’d love to stowaway when you go. But I couldn’t leave this old bloke behind could I?”

“Would you like to have a go, Mary?” Bob offered; knowing that it would only take a little ground training pointing out the markers and the touch required, and she would do the job perfectly too.

“Not this trip Bob,” Mary declined quite simply. “I’d love to on another occasion though. I can’t let this bloke get too far ahead of me, can I?” While Bob and I had been flying Kay and Mary had been getting ready for tonight’s sing-along.

The fairy lights were rigged; the long buffet at the side of the veranda was in place with everything but the food to be brought out from the fridge. The hot finger food was ready to be popped into the oven and as customary space was left on the table for the contributions that the wives would be bringing. There were two Eskys packed with ice and stubbies and again more would arrive with the men. The girls went to their bathrooms to freshen-up and Bob and I chose a beer and sat on the veranda.

"Life's pretty sweet mate, isn't it?" Bob said more than asked, knowing an answer was not required.

"Sure is Bob, it's a pity that so many don't see it," I answered.

"How do you mean Brad?" Bob asked.

"Well if you and Kay had got tired of each other and she was no longer that primary school kid and you were now at each other's throats these people wouldn't be coming here tonight: they'd know there was no joy to be had here."

"Your wise beyond your years' mate," Bob replied, "That's why I sing love songs to her every day; I'm sure it helps keep us both young at heart no matter how many years go by."

"Is your career path any clearer now Brad?" Bob asked.

"It certainly is Bob. Mary's new job is going to keep me pretty busy: as she must visit the universities to launch the faculty on their campus. But the big change is the realisation of the plight of many in the outback. I told you last time that I had studied the Wheat Board Scandal and the hardship caused by the Landmark – ANZ buyout, but that was in the classroom. It is a very different matter when you talk to the people who are suffering because of others' greed. It has confirmed my belief that the

Boom/Bust economies are doomed. I just have to find a better system to replace it."

"From what I saw on the Tele, mate, I know you and Mary together will change the world." Bob replied with certainty.

We sipped our beers quietly for a while and soon the cars were arriving.

The first ladies to arrive wanted to hug Mary and ask all about last night: how we had got here so quickly and all sorts of things. Kay was quick to step in.

"Come on girls, give Mary a chance, let's wait until everyone's here so she doesn't have to repeat herself over and over."

They agreed, reluctantly; they knew at the last sing-along that Mary was beautiful, talented and did research at the ANU, but they had no idea that she could be so important. They had all seen the TV of course but were eager to be in her presence and hear it, 'from the Horse's Mouth' so to speak knowing that the old saying was inappropriate to Mary. The men got drinks for their partner and self and the conversation returned to mundane things. The last guests to arrive were Jack and Barbara from Cairns; they had run into some headwind and been slowed by thirty minutes. I was amazed that they flew six hours in their Cessna at such short notice and Bill and Faye had flown four hours from the other side of the country from their property outside Broome. They greeted Mary and me and then found seats and now the keenest of the ladies called out, "Can we start now Kay?"

"Let's hear it for Professor Mary," Bob stepped forward raising his glass and the small party tried their best to match the standing ovation they had heard her receive last night. They toasted her: they sang, 'FOR SHE'S A JOLLY GOOD FELLOW,' and made the usual attempt at, 'WHY WAS SHE BORN SO BEAUTIFUL,' but fading away to nothing when it came to the 'at all' bit, what a loss that would have been. Mary helped save any embarrassment by speaking for all to hear."

"Please don't play FOR IT WAS MARY, Kay," as she quickly realised that would be the next thing on her playlist. "I would have worn my new robes if I had thought I would receiver this welcome," Mary managed a little quip.

"Where are you off to now?" Someone asked.

"Cambridge will be our starting point. We won't know our itinerary until after we get there," Mary was answering each question quite calmly now. She was still standing next to me with her left hand resting on my right shoulder where she had stood for the toast.

"Who are you flying with?" another asked.

"With Brad," Mary answered thinking it a strange question.

"No, I mean which airline," from the same person. Mary was unable to put the right names with the right faces from a month ago, so she didn't try.

"We're taking the Pilatus of course," Mary replied as if anyone wouldn't do what we were about to do.

"By yourselves? Can she do such a trip? Won't it be too slow?" Questions were coming rapid fire now.

"Yes, Yes and No; we've planned on a week to get to London although we could do it in a couple of days if we wanted to," Mary replied.

"It's only got one prop though," another one stated.

"That's OK, it's arguably the best turbine in the world and from thirty thousand feet it's got a long glide and I'd rather be behind a silent prop in this one than managing a working one on one wing and a dead one on the other in a light twin," Mary said.

The pilots on the veranda, and there were quite a few, male and female, all supported her contention with nods and 'That's right,' or 'me too.'

"You should see this little bird now," Bob spoke up, giving Mary a break. "It's a magic carpet. They could fly direct to London only landing every eight hours to fill her tanks and be off again. They've got a flushing toilet, shower, and galley; with fridge, freezer, stove and oven, and a little washing machine under the sink. There's even a lab for Mary with a powerful looking microscope and all the other gear.

"They've got work desks, a dining nook; that folds down for a bed and what could easily be described as a boudoir for Mary. I honestly couldn't believe my eyes," Bob finally stopped for breath.

The party quickly decided that they had to see this magic carpet so that they could believe what they were hearing. They declared a long-weekend and would have a picnic lunch at Bob's strip tomorrow to see for themselves. The time was set for midday. Bob and Kay would bring their outdoor catering stuff. There was bound to be enough tucker and drinks left over from tonight so nobody need do anything. Kay immediately offered Jack and Barbara from Cairns and Bill and Faye from Broome beds for the night and everyone else would return tomorrow.

"Is that all right Brad?" Someone finally thought to ask me.

"Of course it is," I was quick to confirm. "But I must make one stipulation: there can't be any photos."

I explained why photos weren't allowed and promised them a copy of the book. They all acknowledged their agreement.

"I'd like to include some happy snaps of us picnicking with our mates at the strip before we left the country. I want readers to know that Professor Mary is a real person," I finished, "if you won't mind being seen in print?"

There were confirmations of 'Love to be in it Brad,' 'Looking forward to it mate,' and similar.

"Tucker's up," Kay was back on the scene, several of the girls were laying out the food and all realised that it was time to eat.

The conversation became more general now as some sat, and others wandered around with their finger-food, chatting to one another.

"Bob tells me you did some circuits in his backyard today Brad?" Ron asked.

I nodded my head and indicated that I had food in my mouth saving myself from further explanation.

"'Never been game to try that one mate, even in my own Piper."

"What did the Secretary of State say Mary?" I heard someone ask.

"She wants me to let her know when I will be in Washington so that she can introduce me to the President," Mary giggled. "I couldn't believe what I was hearing; I felt as though a curtsy might have been required but realised they didn't go in for that sort of thing in the USA and saved myself from embarrassment."

"I loved your dress Mary; it was so elegant," Another said.

"It will be two dresses as I can wear it without the black overdress," Mary replied. "I know the word is overused but the evening did seem surreal."

“What about the PM Brad, what did she say?”

I answered calmly as if quite unimpressed, “She wanted me to join her team, but I told her that I couldn’t see myself in politics.”

“What about the old gent you planted a kiss on just before you left Mary, I didn’t recognise him.”

“No, you wouldn’t Jack,” Mary had started to put faces with names now, “he’s a very dear old family friend, no doubt I’ll be planting a kiss on your cheek when you get to his age,” Mary finished on a note of levity; no way was a conversation going to develop into that area. Bob and Kay knew but they would never tell anyone else, particularly having noticed how Mary had just handled Jack’s question. Bob stepped in to tell how he and Kay had been introduced to the Cliffords and Franklins that afternoon, how they were so proud of Mary and of course Brad who was the fourth generation of a full set of great-grandparents. Bob could see Kay heading for the piano and everybody getting ready to sing and dance and now was his chance, “Last time I was the only one made to do a solo love-song,” Bob began. “Tonight, everyone is expected to do a love song from the movies, duets will be allowed if you feel you lack the confidence to fly solo,” he added. “Oh, there’s got to be a prize hasn’t there? We’ll make it a competition to determine the viewing order of Bravo Mike Charlie tomorrow.”

“Who’s the judge?” Bill called out.

“Me of course,” Bob was quick to make it clear. “I’m ruling Kay and me ineligible as we’ve already been over her this morning. Besides, I would have won anyway. Brad and Mary must compete but can’t win because they will be hosting the viewing.”

“Come on,” Kay began. “Let’s have a warm up around the piano and a loosen-up on the floor if you like, before we get down to the competition.”

Kay headed for the piano, others were going through the pile of sheet music looking for something that they might handle alone instead of in the anonymity of group singing around the piano,

Kay started the sing-along with a bouncy rendition of DINAH, with a couple of other happy tunes to follow; DON’T SIT UNDER THE APPLE TREE would be her next. Guests were coming forward with their choice of music and handing it to Bob.

Diane Williams chose ALL THE THINGS YOU ARE for herself and handed AINT’CHA COMING OUT TONIGHT to Bob for her husband Geoff.

Ron Wilson handed in BECAUSE YOU’RE MINE for himself and DREAM A LITTLE DREAM OF ME for Joan.

Rex Watson was going to sing I LOVE YOU SAMANTHA to his wife who everyone knew as Sam.

ANSWER ME, BE MY LOVE, BELOVED, THAT OLD BLACK MAGIC, DANCING IN THE DARK, IF YOU WERE THE ONLY GIRL IN THE WORLD, JEZEBEL, JEALOUSY, FALLING IN LOVE WITH LOVE and HEY GOOD LOOKING, were all handed to Bob. Finally, I handed BOB PEOPLE WILL SAY WE’RE IN LOVE, for Mary and me to sing a duet.

Kay had already made up her mind to sing AND THIS IS MY BELOVED to Bob and then he could finish with his signature tune WHAT A DIFFERENCE A DAY MADE, she would then flick on the iPod to play GOOD NIGHT SWEETHEART and take hold of Bob and join the others on the veranda for the last dance.

My selection, being the last, was now on top and confident the Cliff's would get the ball rolling and set a good pace Bob announced:

"From OKLAHOMA — Brad and Mary Clifford will sing PEOPLE WILL SAY WE'RE IN LOVE.

The guests had moved back around the walls to give the singers space to sing and move and dance a little if they felt it would enhance their performance.

For the moment, Mary was Laurey and I was Curly. Curly had just taken Laurey's hand in his and was walking her around the room to the music. With an occasional side-step so that they could look into each other's eyes as the questions were being put:

Laurey
Why do they think up stories that link my name with yours?
Curly:
Why do the neighbours gossip all day behind their doors?
Laurey:
I know a way to prove what they say is quite untrue
Here is the gist,
A practical list of "don'ts" fer you.
Don't throw bouquets at me
Don't please my folks too much
Don't laugh at my jokes too much.
People will say we're in love.
Curly:

Laugh at your jokes-
Laurey:
Don't sigh and gaze at me.
Your sighs are so like mine
Your eyes mustn't glow like mine
People will say we're in love
Don't start collecting things
Give me my rose and my glove.

Sweetheart, they're suspecting things
People will say we're in love.
Curly:
Some people claim that you are to blame as much as I
Why do you take the trouble to bake my fav'rite pie?
Grantin' your wish I carved our initials on that tree,
Just keep a slice of all the advice you give so free.
Don't praise my charm too much
Don't look so vain with me
Don't stand in the rain with me
People will say we're in love.
Don't take my arm to much
Don't keep your hand in mine
Your hand feels so grand in mine
People will say we're in love!
Don't dance all night with me
'till the stars fade from above
They'll see it's all right with me
People will say we're in love!

The applause was long and strong.

"There you are folks," Bob was back in his role as MC, "that's a good start. Next, we have Harry Smith trying to seduce Alice with HEY GOOD LOOKING.

"You've been practising for this," Bob said as I escorted Mary from the floor.

"Of Course, we knew we would be coming back and needed to lift our game for this company," I said. "We'll be looking in from the veranda for a few minutes I need a cold one after that.

Bob just punched me on the upper arm. I led Mary out onto the veranda but instead of going to the beer fridge took her to the veranda railing and turned her to me so we could kiss.

"That was better than a cold one darling, wasn't it?" Mary asked looking up into my eyes.

"Of course," I replied, "but I'm even hotter now and I don't want to lose any of my new-found control. What would you like?"

"Cold water would be fine; I don't need any more heating either."

As usual, neither of us had finished one drink for the evening.

"Let's go back," I whispered. "People will say we're in love."

We joined in the fun with cheers, jeers and clapping as each single or partnered performance took place.

Kay rose from the piano after the last performance and taking Bob's hands slowly guided them both around the little floor; all the time looking in his eyes and singing, 'FOR THIS IS MY BELOVED.' Kay had left the sheet music for this song on the piano and someone soon dropped into her place and accompanied her. At the end of her song she gave Bob a big hug and kisses.

"Come on lover, give us your song," Kay said as she returned to the piano and played the first bars of WHAT A DIFFERENCE A DAY MADE.

Bob immediately broke into song.

"It must mean a lot to them too darling," Mary whispered to me. This time we kept our emotions under control, but we silently mouthed the words to each other and I still held her hands.

Everyone drifted onto the veranda as GOOD NIGHT SWEETHEART started playing. They danced cheek to cheek or ladies with their head on their lover's chest. After a little while, with the pecking order settled for tomorrow, they were taking their leave; thanking their hosts and assuring Mary and me that they would see us tomorrow and there was no need for goodbyes tonight.

Kay and Bob, Jack and Barbara, Bill and Faye and Mary and I sank into veranda easy chairs and relaxed.

“Wonderful night thanks,” I said with great sincerity.

“You weren’t testing my theory were you Mary?” Bob asked.

“What theory Bob?” Mary didn’t quite catch on.

“That lovers would know and love you more for it; but those without equal love would never know or believe it if you told them so outright,” Bob said.

“It wasn’t meant to, and we didn’t start out that way, but it felt so good I feared we might be giving a bit too much away,” Mary replied.

“Don’t worry Mary, it was obvious to us too when you called in three weeks ago,” Barbara said.

“It was beautiful Mary and it certainly made everyone else step up and give their best,” Kay added.

“Thank you for all the help and good advice you gave us when we dropped in on you and our time with your other friends will never be forgotten,” I said.

“They’re your friends now Mary and Brad,” Jack added, “you’ll never be forgotten by them either.”

“Brad told our extended family in his speech at his birthday party that it was Bruce’s intention to introduce his family to his outback friends,” Mary told them.

"It was a pleasure mate; we never expected to be seeing you again so soon or to be celebrating anything like this with Mary."

"Time for bed wouldn't you agree?" Barbara broke the reminiscences.

"We'll need to be out there fairly early tomorrow to set up before they arrive; they certainly won't be late," Bob said.

There was no dissent. Mary and I knew that it had now past eleven o'clock and we hadn't followed Doc's prescription once today. On the way to our bedroom I gathered up my notebook. I had placed it where it wouldn't draw any attention and before the singing and dancing began, I had clicked a little icon on the screen that would call the Grands and the Greats, and they could share in the evening's entertainment from their homes in Canberra. When we returned from the veranda we paused to wave and blow kisses. I felt confident my little plan had worked.

Having said goodnight, we went to Cliff's Room and closed the door behind us. We turned the ceiling fan up high and stood under it as we quietly undressed each other. No panic, no rush. After unclipping Mary's Bra and placing it on a chair I delighted in holding her to me while sliding her panties from her hips with my free hand and letting them fall to the floor. Mary was pulling down my boxers and commending my old fella for behaving so well today and tonight and telling him that he had better spring to attention and soon receive his reward.

Hand in hand we went to the en-suite and took a cold shower; it was a typical territorial night with the wet season almost upon us. We bathed each other in the way we most enjoyed. Mary was most careful not to provide any further stimulus to my old fella as neither wanted to respond rapidly to an impending quick orgasm denying us some cuddle time first and take it a bit more leisurely than was possible at thirty thousand feet. We were soon dry and with Mary's ponytail released so her hair could flow we folded back the bedclothes, spread a soft towel over the bottom sheet and collapsed into each other's arms. Before long and after some kissing and stroking and my right hand on Mary's left breast I felt her thigh rising up over me and pressing me back she joyfully took her medicine; by midnight we had drifted into sleep in each other's arms.

Monday 10 December 2012 – 0700 hrs

We woke at seven, still naked and with only a sheet over us protecting us from the direct draught of the fan. We showered and dressed. Mary's hair was in that flattering ponytail and now dressed in shorts, shirts, and casual shoes we went to join the others in the kitchen. Kay had just begun serving breakfast.

"Good timing Mate," Bob greeted us. He explained that he would be taking the trailer as they had stackable plastic chairs and several collapsing tables for the picnic. There would be a couple of umbrellas and ground sheets and several Eskys of food and drinks. He also had a quick mounting tent that would come in handy and a porta-loo with its own tent as he didn't want forty people traipsing through Bravo Mike Charlie, running her water supply out and filling her black water canister.

Mary asked Kay and Bob to stay for dinner after the picnic. We would never entertain more than two at a time and she wanted them to be our first guests, if they were prepared to be guinea pigs for her cooking in the new galley. Bob and Kay were happy to accept.

By eight-thirty breakfast was done. The girls set about cleaning up and then gathering last night's leftovers of food and drinks; as predicted, there was ample with the addition of only a little more salad. Bob, Jack, Bill and I loaded the trailer. Bob had everything needed to cater for forty in the open air. I could see that this wasn't the first time that they had continued a party like this. By nine o'clock we were rolling out the gate heading for the strip.

By ten o'clock the picnic site was set up with only the trim to attend to. Mary and I changed from shorts into jeans, changed our casual shoes for boots and collected our Akubras; we were going to give the public what we wanted them to see.

"Mary, don't forget to take that badge off your lab coat; there'll be plenty here who have one of those," Kay called out.

"Whoops, thanks Kay, I had forgotten," Mary called back.

By eleven o'clock we had each done a final inspection, looking for anything that the others had missed, and a few minutes later we heard the first Cessna in the circuit. More cars and planes followed and by eleven-thirty all were present. Mary and I took the winning pair from last night before on board. All the women wanted to see and admire Mary's evening gown. The guests to a man, and woman, spoke little, except to ask the odd question. They were taking it all in with their eyes and the running description they were receiving; hardly anyone noticed the soft music in the background. By one-thirty the last couple had been through. Bob and Kay had been collecting each couple as they left the plane and made sure they had a drink and a seat. When Mary and I appeared with the last pair the guests insisted that Mary don her robes and do a parade up and down the entry steps. The food was laid out and we all tucked in. They were quiet at first but having been fed, the questions started again. Can it really fly eight hours non-stop? At five hundred kilometres an hour? At thirty thousand feet? What's your itinerary?

"At this point we're planning on having a drink in the Long Bar at Raffles tomorrow night, with the ghosts of Ernest Hemingway and Somerset Maugham," I began, everybody knew where Raffles was, "we want to see as much of this world's greatness while we have the chance."

"Agra and the Taj Mahal are only eight hours away from Singapore in this bird," Ron, an ex-Qantas captain, said. "The Taj is the grandest gesture to love ever conceived. It might put you in a good frame of mind for the whole year."

"Please send us some happy snaps," Faye asked, "nothing like that sad picture of Diana sitting alone and hopelessly lost."

"I promise they will be happy snaps," I acknowledged. "Expect them in your inbox on Friday."

"You could make Rome from there in a day too," Joan quickly added. "I'd love you to throw a coin in the Trevi Fountain for Max and me."

That suggestion brought forth 'Me too please' from the ladies speaking for themselves and their partners. Everyone was happy; people were going to their pockets and purses to produce their coins.

"Thanks Ron, and everybody," I said, "that takes care of week one very nicely. Expect your Trevi Fountain pics by Sunday night; we'll send you anything we think might interest you from time to time. I'll get some envelopes for your coins."

I went back to the plane, took a pack of business sized envelopes from my desk drawer and a marking pen. I distributed the envelopes and asked that they write their names and email addresses on the envelope, put their coins in and seal them. I didn't want to get anyone's coins nixed up.

My last job before the party broke up was to get some group photos. Typical picnic shots of people talking in groups; sometimes with a glass or stubby in their hand

and finally a couple of shots of everyone together. I had been taking these shots with my camera mounted on a tripod and with an electronic shutter release. It was now approaching four o'clock and with distance and daylight to consider the picnic had to come to an end. We broke up with many hugs, kisses and handshakes. If they could have sung, they would have but they had to leave. After the last car had driven off and the last small plane lifted off Kay, Mary, Bob and I sank back on our folding chairs.

"Let's have a cold one Bob," I began. "I haven't had a beer all day."

We laughed as we realised how full the day had been and how quickly it had passed. After we finally had a full beer down Bob and I packed the trailer while Mary and Kay went to prepare our meal. We had agreed that another late night wasn't desirable as they still had to drive home and unpack. Mary and I too were going to take-off early for our trip into Darwin and then on to Singapore. I didn't want to make my first approach into a foreign international airport in the dark. When Bob and I joined the girls, Kay was standing with one arm around Mary's shoulders.

"Everything OK?" Bob asked.

"Of course, it is darling, just a little girl talk."

Kay went back to the galley with Mary to finish their preparation. It was a slow-cooked rabbit stew with mashed potato; a good country meal that all would enjoy. The stock pot had been simmering since the last guest had left the plane earlier in the day. I turned on the early TV news and sat back.

"It's on again girls," Bob called as Mary's smile lit up the screen. There was more of the same with a few new clips.

"It was expected that Professor Mary and Brad Clifford were going to leave on their tour on Sunday," the announcer began. "But now it turns out that nobody has seen them since Saturday night. They were not booked on any flights out today and nobody appears to have their itinerary. The question tonight is, "Have they pulled another vanishing trick?"

"Wouldn't they love to know?" Mary said, "Plenty do but nobody will tell this time. Let's turn this off and enjoy the music and talk."

"If you would take that seat Kay," I said, indicating one window seat. "Bob can take the opposite so that Kay can look into 'her beloved's eyes' as she did last night. I'll just get the wine."

Mary was delivering our meals as I returned with the bottle of Dom Perignon. I popped the cork and started pouring. Mary had now taken her seat at the table.

"This bottle is with Bruce's compliments," I explained. "He would be delighted to see it being drunk tonight."

"To Bruce," was the somewhat sombre toast. "Come on I'm sure he would be touched but he would be saying, 'Get on with it; life is for the living'," I reminded them.

We enjoyed our food and talk was brisk and cheery.

"I saw a lovely pair of Lalique flutes in the cupboard Mary, obviously, you wanted the matching set used but they were striking," Kay was excited.

Mary told the story of how I had bought them for our special dinner party, knowing that she could reveal these things to other lovers and they would understand.

"All these electrics, Brad; they won't run you short for start-up tomorrow, will they?" Bob asked.

"No mate, it's a totally separate system. It has a low weight battery pack; the system is twelve volts and if we run short, we can take the two-point-five kilowatt Yamaha out from under there and run it from a cable away from the plane," I quickly explained.

"Silly question, I should have known you would have thought of everything," Bob admonished himself.

We sat and talked and laughed until eight o'clock. Kay wanted to help Mary clean-up after the meal, but Mary wouldn't hear of it; Bob and Kay still had to drive home while Mary and I had nowhere to go before dawn. We walked with them to the car.

"Remember to sing her love songs everyday Brad," Bob shouted from his window.

Mary and I stood arms around each other and waved as they drove away.

"It's only us now darling," I whispered. I recognised the enormity of our task and the fact that we were alone. I was desperate to assure Mary that while we might be alone we would never be lonely while we had each other. It was a poignant scene as Mary lifted her head and pressed her lips to mine. **Aphrodite's Diary http://www.futuristic.guru/copy-of-aphrodite-12**

"Come on lover," Mary said as she broke away. "Let's get cleaned up so we can get down and dirty," Mary giggled, lifting our spirits knowing that she hadn't followed Doc's orders yet today and this was to be our last day on Australian soil for quite some time.

By nine o'clock, we had washed up, squared everything away in the galley, replaced every item of crystal, crockery and cutlery into their individual slots and mouldings and secured the cupboard doors ready for departure. I let down the divan and pulled out the bedding. I retracted the dining table and loosened the separating curtain effectively making two compartments. Mary saw her boudoir appearing before her eyes. When I was finished, I held my arm around Mary at the entrance to the galley and lab.

“It’s lovely thanks Brad, a real lady’s boudoir,” Mary turned and kissed me again. We were both becoming excited as we imagined ourselves locked together in this little love nest.

“Can I go first?” Mary said, knowing that there wasn’t space for us to shower together.

“Don’t be long darling,” I replied. “I wouldn’t want to start without you,” I teased.

“As if,” Mary dared me.

I sat back in one of the chairs and reviewed my day. I couldn’t think of anything I had missed or any offence I may have given, or any hurt I may have caused. I had phoned Pete, my mate in the Canberra Tower and asked him if he could do anything to smooth our way through Darwin. ‘Leave it to me mate; I’ll get them to clear you to the military side of the drome. They’ll have Customs and the fuel truck waiting if you can give me your ETA.’ I had told Pete seven o’clock; that would give us plenty of time to reach Singapore before dark, if we didn’t waste too much time in Darwin.

“Where are you landing next Brad?” Pete asked and was completely unfazed when I said Singapore.

“What cruise do you want mate?”

“Thirty thousand if I can get it?” I replied.

“OK, I’ll see what I can do, it should be fine; I’ve done it for others before and we always reciprocate with requests coming in the other direction. I’ll call back in about an hour.”

I had felt heartened with Pete's co-operation, man-to-man with no perhaps or maybes. Pete did of course ring back and confirmed that all had been arranged. We only had to arrive in Darwin at our nominated ETA to be leaving the country as quickly as possible. If it meant we must cut our sleeping time a little it didn't matter at all as we could take it in turns to have a nap in the eight hours, it would take to reach Singapore. I came back from my reverie as Mary walked past with a towel around her and a shower cap still on her hair, "Your turn lover," she said as she walked past without giving me even a peck on my head.

"Don't be too long or I might have to start without you," Mary returned my earlier tease, with a cheeky glance as she disappeared behind the loose curtain and with a small but ineffectual tug, she indicated that she might close it all together.

I needed no prompting. I shaved, showered and dressed in my light and short dressing gown and was ready to seek Mary. I turned off the forward cabin lights as I passed and entered her boudoir.

"Come to me lover," Mary said holding her arms apart enabling me to see her breasts as her movements let the opening of her almost sheer, elegant yet sexy negligee fall apart. Mary was supported by two pillows at her back; the sight was enchanting, with the lights dimmed further than how I had left them, a scent that Mary had lightly sprayed was in the air and on the sheets, the dividing curtain providing an intimacy to this area that would not have been possible without it. Beethoven's MOONLIGHT SONATA was playing softly on the sound system as I took the one step necessary to allow Mary to pull away the sash on my gown. I quickly shed my gown and sunk onto the bed afraid that I might go weak at the knees. I reached for her and held her tight. Mary responded with passionate kisses and not a word was spoken until we had joined, and our first climax had passed.

“My boudoir is the nicest part of my surprise Adonis,” Mary said giving my old fella a squeeze and imparting a lingering kiss to my lips.

“As befits beautiful Aphrodite, my love,” I replied with our passion rising again.

It wasn’t long before my old fella was once more knocking on the Gates to Paradise and Mary throwing her legs apart for me to roll onto her and bring her to another great climax.

Tuesday 11 December 2012 – 0500 hrs

The alarm sounded at five o’clock and I was on my feet as soon as it rang. We had decided to do only what was essential this morning for our appearance and comfort and make sure the cabin displayed its modern office and laboratory appearance ready for work. We were in the air by six-thirty and by six-fifty on final to land in Darwin. We taxied down the long Darwin strip with clearance to take the left exit to the military side of the drome. As we left the runway a Ute with FOLLOW ME displayed on a board across the tray moved in front of us and we were led to a fuelling point. As we stepped down a Customs car pulled up alongside and a friendly man in suit trousers and open necked business shirt got out.

“Good morning Professor, Brad; your mate Pete in Canberra gave us a call and asked us to look after you. The name’s Reginald but I prefer Reg. What can I do for you?” Reg accomplished all this in one breath.

“We just want to fly off the Island Reg, never done it before,” I said light heartedly.

“Where’re you heading mate?” Reg asked.

“London: but Singapore tonight,” I replied.

"You look after your refuelling Brad, the Professor can show me around; I've got to check for stowaways, somebody could be doing a runner, you know. I can check your passports too," Reg waved me away, quite happy to be left in Mary's hands if only for the fifteen minutes that this was going to take. I checked with the refueller and explained the loading of the long-distance tanks; I was pointed to the dumps for grey and black water disposal and where to top up our fresh water. While the fuel was being pumped, I went to the Flight Service office only fifty metres away and got the latest briefings for our route. I asked for a briefing on what to expect from controllers along the way explaining that this was my first international flight. The middle-aged briefing officer was only too pleased to help and particularly so as I was so open about my position and had the good sense to seek him out. After ten minutes, I thanked him sincerely and with the latest Mets in hand I headed back to the Pilatus. The refueller had finished his pumping and was writing out his delivery docket for me to sign and enter my fuel card number. I checked the fuel-load and tanks, filled the fresh water tank and checked that all caps, covers and doors were fully secured. I did my regular walk around and went back to the cabin. Mary had made a coffee for Reg while they were waiting and now poured one for me.

"No stowaways found Brad, and Reg reckons were pretty fair representations of our passport mug-shots, so we can go and see the world," Mary said as she handed me my coffee.

"Mary showed me her lab Brad, I've never seen anything like it before," Reg said.

I gave Reg a warm smile. I instinctively knew that Mary would have insisted that any person approaching her with honesty would be put at ease and told to drop the Professor business. I also knew that Reg like any male would sign or stamp any document that might assist her on her way. To be held in high regard by this lady in the future was all anybody would be seeking. We drank our coffee slowly not wanting to convey any hint to our guest, for that is what Reg had now become, that having our documents signed and stamped we were anxious to take to the air and happily leave Australia for a while. At last, Reg drained his now very cool coffee and handed Mary his cup and saucer. He thanked her, wished us 'Happy Landings,' and took his leave. It was as if Mary and I had done him a favour or service and not the other way around. As soon as Reg had gone Mary whisked the coffee cups and saucers away and quickly washed up, wiped them and put them away. By the time she slipped into the co-pilot's chair and put her headset on I had powered-up and contacted the controller.

"Bravo Mike Charlie Clear to taxi please accept FOLLOW ME guidance for your runway entry point," Mary heard the controller say.

"Bravo Mike Charlie," I acknowledged.

"Bravo Mike Charlie Clear to take-off. Climb to two thousand on runway heading. Call International operator on one two three decimal four at two thousand for onward clearance goodbye and bon voyage," the operator reeled off.

"Bravo Mike Charlie two thousand on runway heading thank you for your assistance," I acknowledged.

Mary had jotted two thousand and one two three point four in figures on the palm of her left hand; she hadn't had time to gather her knee pad.

"V1 - Rotate Captain darling," Mary called joyfully.

We had flown on in silence until I called International. I immediately received our clearances to climb to the cruise level of thirty thousand that I had requested. Now settled in cruise and up to eight hours of straight and level in front of us I could relax and take a good look at Mary once more. It was a delight just to look at her smiling face.

Chapter 9

Adonis Accepts

Tuesday 11 December 2012 – 1245 hrs

"Will you have the first sleep Adonis?" Mary asked.

"I'd love to darling," I replied. A sudden weariness had overcome me after having kept my surprise for Mary secret for three weeks now. I made my way to the divan and lowered it. It only took a few minutes after taking off my shoes that I was fast asleep. I slept soundly for three hours and when I returned to Mary, I took coffee and freshly toasted cheese sandwiches. After we ate Mary cleared away our mugs and plates and I took over the controls.

"Mind if I flatten your creases darling?" Mary asked. I just pulled her a little closer.

This time we were dressed in slacks and shirts. Mary had slipped off her bra so she could feel my hand on her breast through the fabric of her top: she knew it would reach there before long. There was no thought of Mile-High badges this morning though; we were still in the afterglow of our last night in Australia.

"Where are we darling?" Mary asked.

"Halfway between Darwin and Singapore," I replied.

"Then we've passed the point of no return?"

"Yes, some minutes ago," I replied. "Is that important?"

"Yes darling, but it's more symbolical than important. It's further to go back now than go on. I'm taking you out into the world darling: giving you to the world would be more like it.

"I don't understand, Mary."

I saw in her eyes and by the tone of her voice that she was very serious and choosing her words carefully.

"Darling, you remember I said your acceptance of my new job will change things for us?" Mary began.

"Yes, I said we can easily change our itinerary."

"It's more than that darling, much more."

"I don't understand Mary; I haven't changed; I still love you the same as before your appointment: you're still the same Mary."

"I love you the same too darling, more than before if that is possible," Mary looked me in the eyes as she spoke and then hugged and kissed me. "But I'm not the same Mary. Just listen please and I'll try to explain," Mary added when I was about to answer.

"When you accepted my new job for me, we passed the point of no return. You sealed my fate and at the same time sealed yours. You really are Adonis, darling; when I woke-up in your arms I was your lover Aphrodite. I thought I could keep you to myself; you could have your gap year and I my sabbatical. We would be Adonis and Aphrodite for twelve months, but now we can't."

"Surely we don't have to tell your committee that I'm Adonis?" I said.

"There's one factor that will compel me to tell them Adonis's identity. When Project Adonis was initiated the three women needed to be Adonis's goddesses were sought. One was in England and only the professor-elect at Cambridge can access her details. The same applies to the girl in Australia; I am the only person who can match her record identifier with her personal details. When I was at the ANU on Thursday saying goodbye, the leader of my team told me that the third girl was identified last week in India; only the professor-elect at Delhi University can identify her."

"Mary, I'm confused, what does this mean?"

"It means darling that now Adonis's three goddesses have been found the Coordinating Committee will want to implement Project Adonis immediately. I will have to give them your name."

"What about us Mary?" I asked.

"Us, darling?" Mary replied and pushed her head against my shoulder. "It's been all about me from the moment I crept into your bed. You've done everything for me: when we woke so spectacularly, I called you Adonis. I told you I was dreaming of Adonis and I was Aphrodite being ravished by her lover, but I wasn't dreaming. I'd known you were Adonis for four years and in this most desperate moment of my life you were materialising to save me. I was instantly Adonis's mythological lover Aphrodite. You comforted me and brought me back to life. You've been my most attentive lover: you've taken me into a world where we can't recall what happened, you've let me see our auras, you took me back to the moment you were conceived, and you spoke for me. If you had asked me what I wanted to say about chairing the Coordinating Committee I would have said 'No!' Now you have given up your gap year to look after me on stodgy university business and you've provided this wonderful magic carpet for me to do it in."

"You've made a man of me Mary, I was just a boy until you returned my love on my birthday," I said and hugged her to me.

"I was powerless not to Brad. It was Adonis breaking out. Everything you did and said from that moment was the new version of you. It was what Bruce's friends in the Outback recognised in you; our families knew you had changed at your birthday party, particularly Jan. It would have been what the people you had working on the refit responded to and it was plain for everyone to see when you made my acceptance speech. Any woman you pay attention to is immediately overcome with desire as I was."

"I don't want to desert you Mary."

"You won't be deserting me Brad. We've got to go on to open the other universities. Remember Brad, I can't give you babies and you're the last of the Clifford/Franklin line. I want you to add another generation; I want to be a grandmother and Bruce a grandfather. Can you love me enough to do that for me even if we only have these last seven days together?"

"How could I not love you Aphrodite. This is not the end darling is it?" I asked.

"Not unless you choose to put us into a spiral dive Adonis. We'd have three minutes in a spin before we hit the water. We'd go out with a bang darling," Mary said, "if they found us, we'd be locked together in death."

"I couldn't do that to you, no matter what," I said.

"I couldn't do it to you either Adonis. There was a time during that horrible night when I thought the only way out was for me to kill both of us. Bruce was gone, and I didn't want to go on. Then I came to you for comfort and woke up in the arms of Adonis. I'm sure your goddesses will grant us some time together."

"Is this what I was born to do Mary?" I said, more calmly.

"It is your birthright Adonis and only you can pass it on to the world."

"There's no university course for my profession. I will have to feel my way."

We grinned and hugged, dissipating our tension, as we realised there would be a good deal of 'feeling my way' impregnating one hundred girls a year.

"You do have the right touch for the job darling," Mary said.

"But the Faculty will need to help reduce the indiscriminate population growth we have come to accept," I said.

"I know, darling; other than China, governments have ignored the problem. Everyone says we need more young people to support the aging population as life expectancy is increasing too. Many governments are responding to pressure groups that see a growing population as more customers and more profits; others see more soldiers. The Faculty is working on proposals to curb the growth. We will shortly prove that the world's woes have been bred into the race and therefore they can be bred out again. Project Adonis will set the standard darling. You could say the Faculty will be working on the problem from top down while you will be tackling the problem from the bottom up."

Again, we grinned and hugged as we realised Mary's reference to my task being from the 'bottom-up' was an apt description for my role.

"We have seven day-tight compartments left before we reach Cambridge Adonis," Mary said.

"We'll make the most of them Aphrodite," I promised.

We shared a lingering kiss with my hand having come up under Mary's blouse to fondle her bare breasts.

"Can you tell me who the Australian girl is Aphrodite?" I asked.

"I shouldn't before the committee meets but you deserve to know. It's Jan, darling."

I didn't speak for quite a while. I was stunned and delighted by what Aphrodite told me. I held her tighter.

"Are you pleased darling?"

"Of course I am. She's a delightful girl. I've always liked her, you could say loved her, but we are cousins."

"That's all been taken care of darling. Your genomes have been studied by each university and all agree you will be a perfect match and make beautiful babies. I'll make us some lunch darling and when we get to Raffles, we'll have the afternoon to ourselves," Mary said quietly. **Aphrodite's Diary http://www.futuristic.guru/copy-of-aphrodite-13**

"What will your world be like in twenty-fifty Adonis?" Mary asked after we had finished our lunch and she had made herself comfortable in my lap again.

"Is it up to me Aphrodite?" I asked.

"Remember, I said that everyone of child-bearing age will be your descendant by then. They will be carrying your genes and implementing your goals and desires so it's important for you to know what you want for the world before you father your first child," Mary said. "Think of it as what do you want for your children, grandchildren great grandchildren and beyond."

"My children must be fed, no matter what their age, no matter what they work at, no matter how far down the generations they are."

"That's a good start Adonis," Mary said and gave me a hug.

"My children must be clothed and housed, and it will be recognised that they each have different needs and requirements. The best health care must be available to them always and they must know from the time they are born that they are loved and wanted. As they grow, they must understand that they are needed here, and their unique abilities must be recognised and encouraged."

It was becoming easier for me now as thoughts from my own happy childhood came back.

“As children they must be allowed to play and learn from it, and as they grow participate in sports. They’ll learn to look after themselves and not expect to be waited on. They’ll claim no special privileges by birth or being a celebrity. They’ll receive the best in education and have their questions answered when they ask them. Before twenty-thirty all knowledge will be available to everyone instantly and education, along with every other activity will be unrecognisable with what we have today.”

“And when your children grow-up Adonis, what then?” Mary asked.

“When they turn eighteen Aphrodite, and it might be younger by then, they are children no longer. I will no longer instruct my children. If they ask questions of me or seek my advice, I will give it freely as I believed it to be true, but I would make sure they knew they were under no obligation to act upon what I said. My children will treat their children in the same way, and respect and care for their parents.”

“As you have cared for me darling Adonis?” Mary asked and hugged me again.

“Of course Aphrodite, but if Bruce had been here it wouldn’t have been needed.”

“What sort of world will we be living in Adonis?” Mary asked.

“For a start there will be no countries or sovereign states by twenty-fifty. There will be one world government and every citizen of the world will register their personal vote on every question of importance. There will be no such thing as political parties, no lobbyists, no advisors, no press secretaries or campaign offices.

“Following on from this there will be no wars, no munitions industry, and no terrorism. In business and industry, the only advertising that will be tolerated will be statements of fact that must be substantiated. Nobody will be able to claim their product ‘may do this, or that …’, their claims must be subject to the same scrutiny as pronouncements from the Faculty of Genetics will be. Of course, newspapers and trashy magazines will have disappeared well before twenty-thirty as any real news is becoming instantly available around the world electronically. There will be no more lies and posturing by parochial politicians, truth will be the yardstick. Factory work has been diminishing for years already, as robots and mechanisation has been introduced. By twenty-thirty this trend will be complete as will the computerisation of all record keeping and communications.”

“Many people will be out of work Adonis: armed forces, politicians and bureaucrats, advertising, newspapers, factory and office workers, the flow on will be world-wide depression.”

“That’s the excuse that has always been given for doing nothing, Aphrodite. There’s no shortage of work to be done, only a new appreciation of what is important. To me the street-sweeper or the person who cleanse public toilets is more important than the so-called ‘shock-jocks’ who pour out wild accusations and ill-considered opinions on radio — and be highly paid for it. For a start, we must heal the world. For hundreds of years we’ve abused our home; now we must clean the rivers and the oceans, replant the forests and bring life back into the deserts. We must clean the air we breathe. It will take an army of workers to do these things. Then there is the need to care for all the people suffering from the maladies that the twentieth and earlier centuries have imposed on them. And, remember, one-third of the people are living in poverty; these people must be re-housed, fed and taught skills to make them useful in the new workforce.”

"Can it be done, Adonis?" Mary asked.

"It's not a question of 'Can?' Aphrodite, it is a question of 'Must?' and the answer is 'Yes'. It must be done before we blow-up our planet or poison our water, soil and air any further."

"What about the question 'How?' Adonis," Mary continued. "There's never enough money now to meet the demands put on governments."

"*Bucky* had the right idea: he said that 'all that was required to make everyone on earth a multi-billionaire was a new accounting' and I believe he was correct."

"Who is Bucky, darling?"

"*Bucky* is the name his friends call him, Aphrodite. His full name is R. Buckminster Fuller. The R is for Richard. He died in 1983, just 11 days short of his 88th birthday. He was one of the most remarkable men of the 20th Century. Bruce first told me about him when he explained to me the geodesic dome. I'm surprised he hadn't discussed him with you."

"Not that I can remember, darling. I might easily have been engrossed in my own problems at the time," Mary replied. "How was he exceptional?"

"He was exceptional in many ways. At 31 years of age he considered himself a misfit and a failure. He had been expelled from Harvard twice and by now he had a wife and a new baby to support, having lost his first child through illness five years earlier. He resolved to make an experiment of himself to show what one person might do, starting from nothing, to advance the course of all mankind. He began by recording every event and transaction in his life: including every letter, agreement and shopping docket. Good, bad or indifferent, he recorded everything without judgement. He called this his Chronofile and he was what he called Guinea Pig B: a faithful history of what an unknown, moneyless person might do on behalf of all humanity.

"He didn't consider himself special in any way, but he put aside his fear and worked, as an individual, for the betterment of all. Over the years he became an outstanding architect, designer and inventor and wrote 30 books on his discoveries, thoughts and reasoning. He was recognised for the Geodesic Dome and he contributed much to the advancement of science and design. He was invited to lecture at universities in many countries. He was awarded many patents and honorary doctorates, received awards from professional and prestigious societies. He was awarded the Presidential Medal of Freedom. Late in life he declared he and his work were the property of all humanity."

"Just like you have declared for the Faculty and me, darling Adonis," Mary said.

"Yes, darling Aphrodite. You remember the morning I woke early and went for a run?"

"Yes, darling, I will never forget it. It was our last morning before we returned home."

"I was very excited because, for the first time, I could see clearly my role in life. I hadn't thought that impregnating one-hundred beautiful girls a year was my career, it was just something that I was happy to do for you, but when I realised the only way to make this world a suitable place for my children to live was to implement the new accounting that Bucky spoke about. He believed that *Utopia* was still available to us if we dedicate our work to the good of all mankind.

"While much of *Bucky's* work is evident in the world today, particularly his principle of ephemeralisation where more and more is achieved with less pounds of material, less ergs of energy and less hours of labour, his concept that we should all be living as multi-billionaires has not developed at all. He only seems to have left one clue as to how this will come about. One line in *Spaceship Earth* declares that it only requires a new accounting to bring this Utopia into existence."

"And you want to establish this new accounting Adonis?"

"Yes Aphrodite, when we visit California, I will find some time to search the R. Buckminster Fuller Collection at Stanford University. I might find something in **Bucky's** massive Chronofile to help me.

"I know now we, like *Bucky,* are both working for the good of all mankind. It has never been the money or fame. It's time I got our clearance into Singapore, Mary."

Suddenly, we were called back into the world of today and after a final hug and kiss Mary returned to her chair and donned her headset. Our landing was uneventful, and we refuelled immediately ready for a quick getaway tomorrow. There was no need for a customs inspection as we were only transiting overnight. A customs official came on board to check our passports and confirm our booking at **Raffles http://www.futuristic.guru/raffles**for the night. He had a cursory look in our overnight bags and placed seals on our door. **http://www.raffles.com/singapore/**

Tuesday 11 December 2012 – 1400 hrs

We registered at Raffles reception and were shown to our room. The desk clerk barely looked at our passports; he'd seen Mary on the news and with scant regard to me paid his and his establishments welcome to the Professor.

"See, I told you it would be useful," I teased Mary on the way to our room.

I had armed myself with a number of US five-dollar notes for tipping porters, door openers and similar and now pressed one into the porter's hand. As I closed the door, I slipped the 'Do Not Disturb' sign over the knob. Mary had already shed her clothes and was heading for the en-suite when I returned.

We were surprised to see a nice spa in the bathroom. I ran the water and shaved while Mary did a few odds and ends including choosing the perfumes and the bath salts she sprinkled into the water. She turned the piped music to low and turned on the central fan to keep the air moving. We slipped into the spa together and lay quietly with our arms around each other.

"I should have told you sooner darling," Mary began, "but I didn't want to spoil Saturday night after finding your surprise in Bravo Mike Charlie. To mention it on Sunday or Monday with Bob and Kay would have been wrong too. I thought it would have spoilt our last night in Australia, so I chose to wait until we reached the point of no return today. Are you angry with me?"

"Of course not: how could Adonis be angry with Aphrodite?"

Mary hugged me tightly and slid her body up onto me to claim a long kiss.

"I was going on my gap year to find my future path and four hours out from Darwin I find I'm already on it. Like you, I would never have selected the role for myself but being confronted with it I could only accept it or put us into that spiral dive into the Java Sea."

"You see how special you are Adonis," Mary said.

"I'm sure it won't change me Aphrodite," I replied and kissed her.

"Would you wash my hair please darling?" Mary asked. "Don't put me to sleep though."

"I'd love to and you're not going to sleep just yet, Aphrodite," I said bringing her around to me so that I could give her a nice long kiss and let her feel how hard I was thinking about our talk in the sky.

I massaged Mary's neck and every part of her body to her fingertips and her toes. I eased away the cramps of the long flight and I could see Mary reviving. I had noticed Mary putting Doc's balm on the side of the spa and I now turned Mary into a position where I could apply it for her. After all, sitting in my lap for all that time could easily produce the need for a little aftercare. Without a word Mary assisted me by getting into a position that made it easy for me to bring my fingers into play and then gently into her vagina with Mary moving her pelvis to ensure her vaginal walls got their fair share.

"My back please darling," I asked and handed her the sponge.

"Can I do your front now?" Mary asked.

"No lover you might excite me too much," I answered having already begun to scrub myself briskly. Although Mary was a light weight, sitting in the one position on my lap tended to reduce my circulation and that's not good when you're up in the clouds. Mary watched with a smile as I finished my scrub and turned my attention to the touchy bits.

"Can I do that for you then darling?" Mary had asked jokingly.

"That would be worse before I get you on that nice big bed in there and then you can have your way with me," I answered.

We were both laughing and refreshed when we got out of the spa. I dried Mary with the soft towels: wrapping her up in them and rubbing her all over. I undid the ponytail I had created and spread her hair to use the blow dryer. I handed Mary her hairbrush, leaving her to brush it out the way she might want it and dried myself. I loved to see her breasts move up and down as she raised and lowered her arm with the brushing motion. It was a sight that any man would respond to and now I felt my old fella responding very well indeed. I effortlessly lifted Mary into my arms and carried her to the bed. I lay down beside her, wrapped my arms about her, and smothered her with kisses. We both noticed the music change to WHAT A DIFFERENCE A DAY MADE and broke off our kisses to laugh.

My old fella was trying to breach the Gates to Paradise and Aphrodite quickly adjusted herself to surrender, acknowledging she was powerless to resist Adonis but didn't want to anyway. "I give up," "I give in," she was whispering in my ear and all the time grinding up against me. "It's a special occasion day darling."

"Rotate Captain darling," Mary called much louder.

Without missing a beat, I rolled from where I was forcing Mary down into the bed, onto my back bringing Mary on top of me. Mary had clung to me and clung even tighter with a good contraction onto my old fella to make sure I didn't lose any ground.

"Why didn't you do that last time to my command Captain?" Mary teased.

"A little close to the ground don't you think co-pilot darling," I replied.

"What about at thirty thousand, would she roll like that?" Mary asked.

"I expect so, but I would never do it unless it was an extreme emergency," I replied.

"Why are you talking about flying Adonis? You know I only gave that command, so I could get on top and fuck you," Mary said.

"You're in command Captain Aphrodite; you've got the driving seat," I handed over control to Mary and she turned around to face my toes. She brought her mouth down onto my tool, licked, sucked, and took my head into her mouth to make him wet and slippery with her saliva.

Her position meant her pussy opened up above my lips and I immediately went to work with kissing and licking her labia and clit and giving caresses to her inner thighs with my fingertips. On Saturday afternoon before we got ready for my party, she told me she wanted to give me a blow-job and taste me as I had tasted her. Now she was going about her business with purpose and I was intent on giving her an orgasm with my tongue and lips. When I tickled the opening to her vagina with my tongue, she tried to suck it in and then I replaced my tongue with my fingers and she sucked them in to her vagina while she sucked my dick with her mouth. I drove her wild with my kisses to her clitoris and her labia and she took me in deep. Her silky-smooth lips and soft fingers were bringing me rapidly to a climax and I had to struggle not to bounce around and do her some injury, she knew I was coming but she wouldn't stop. I let go with a full ejaculation and she took it without gagging, except for the dribbles that ran down her chin and my shaft, lubricating her hand. I didn't pause, my hands by now were running up over her belly and catching her breasts. Mary went orgasmic. She turned around and collapsed on me giving me an open-mouthed kiss to share my semen. She reached back and guided my horn into her to stop him from collapsing and I clung to her while her orgasm faded away.

"You taste divine darling Adonis. I'll have that to remember you by when we are apart." We drifted off wrapped in each other's arms for the next hour.

"Wake up Adonis; I'll buy you that beer in Maugham's bar," Mary whispered in my ear.

"Is that where we are Aphrodite — Singapore?" I asked.

"That's right Adonis. You tore me away from Australia and brought me screaming here in your magic chariot and ravished me," Mary teased.

"I don't recall you complaining Aphrodite," I replied as I came out of the fog.

"I'm not complaining, but we must see more of this famous place than the lobby and our bedroom."

"I forgot to tell you darling, this is the Somerset Maugham Suite. It is the suite he occupied on his last visit to Raffles in 1960.

"If we don't find his ghost in the Long Bar maybe his ghost will find us as we sleep tonight," Mary suggested and giggled.

We got-up, freshened-up, dressed-up and headed for the bar like any two young honeymooners.

The Long Bar took us by surprise, it was one of the best equipped bars one could imagine; typically, a bar but also with comfortable chairs and tables spread around and situated adjacent to the billiard room. We found a table near the window and I changed my plan to have a beer with the ghost of Somerset Maugham and ordered, more appropriately, two SINGAPORE SLINGS instead. Later, I took photos of Mary with a glass in her hand and she took photos of me. The obliging waiter photographed us together. We posed to accommodate the ideas of different people who would be receiving them. For Doc, Bob and

Kay we didn't hold back: we could have been newlyweds on our honeymoon. For the Grands and Greats, we were more conservative but still able to let our affection for each other show. We wanted to let The Vice see we were thinking of him and visiting the bar of famous authors. We composed our messages and attached the photos. One by one I hit the send button. I was very careful to attach the right photo to the correct note and the right address. Mary added a kiss to each message. We knew that our emails would be landing in an inbox well before we even left the bar for dinner.

As seven approached, we wandered off hand-in-hand to see what the chef had prepared for us.

"There's no doubt darling that Doc's prescription works wonders; I've never felt better in my life," I declared.

"Me too darling, I feel like skipping in to dinner like a little girl," Mary added.

"Have I told you lately … "I started.

"Of course, you have darling only two hours ago on our bed remember?"

"Yes, it's coming back to me now; I thought I might have been dreaming," I said.

"You couldn't possibly have been having a wet-one darling after what I've been doing to you," Mary was again teasing. "I would be most hurt to have failed you that badly," Mary had a big smile and her eyes were bright.

"I love it when you talk dirty, darling," I had the last word as we entered the dining room.

Mary squeezed my hand as the Maître d' greeted us and showed us to our table. As was only to be expected the meal was exquisite: tonight, we chose fish and a clear white wine for entrée and a prime filet mignon with a merlot for our main, we shared a cheese board instead of any sweet dessert and had black coffees. Tonight, we savoured and enjoyed our meal. It was only three nights back that we had sat through a very high standard five plate Degustation featuring Australia's finest foods and chefs for one of the most honoured gatherings ever hosted in Canberra. We had passed that night picking at our food and not even finishing one of the wines that were offered. However, tonight everything had changed. We had planned to run away and have a year to ourselves. Last Saturday night had changed our lives forever and today we had accepted our new roles and were now running towards them. As we left the dining room we felt as though we were walking on air. It was only a little past nine o'clock so hand-in-hand we strolled the public areas and marvelled at the fine masonry. On the way back to our room we called at the desk and I paid our account. Before we took to our bed, to confirm that this was truly a special occasion, we wandered out onto the balcony through high French doors. A gentle breeze refreshed us as we looked out over Singapore and the sea.

"It's hard to imagine the fall of Singapore in nineteen forty-two," I said.

"Darling you know we can only look back to learn," Mary began quietly, "we can't change anything. It is pointless to bring any animosity against the present Japanese people. We can only bring our abilities forward to make a better world."

"I know darling," I replied, "wars are so futile; there must be a better way."

"You are the better way Adonis," Mary said so very sincerely.

I held her close to me and we kissed in the moonlight. Going back inside, I turned back the bed, turned on the music and turned down the lights. I gently undressed her, placing her clothes on a side table. Mary stood with me removing my shirt and undid my belt.

"I've got to go to the bathroom darling," she whispered. "Don't start without me." The lilt was back in her voice, she skipped across the room with her breasts giving a little jiggle.

"As if I would lover," I called back. I finished undressing and passed Mary on my way to the bathroom. We smiled and touched hands in passing. My joy in the day had returned and I soon joined Mary in bed. Actually, we were lying naked on top of the bed as the fan gathered up the fresh breeze from the Singapore Strait and blew it down on us. We lay wrapped in each other's arms for a little while; there was no need to rush. We had released the emotions from Mary's confession earlier in the afternoon and now all we wanted was to confirm to each other our acceptance with kisses and the feel of our naked bodies pressing together. We knew of course our pressing would become more demanding and eventually more urgent and Aphrodite would slide her right thigh up over Adonis and invite her tormentor to ravish her again. For now, we even talked a little of the day's events, confirming again we must follow the paths that had been assigned us. I wondered what my three goddesses would be like and Mary assured me that I would know as soon as she met with her committee in six days' time. She said I would have no trouble loving them and they would be enchanted by me. Almost without realising it my sword was sheathed again in Aphrodite's quiver and we were enjoying long and gentle rhythmic plunges and withdrawals trying to prolong the bliss of our closeness until little moans and sighs escaped Aphrodite and Adonis delivered his second gift of semen for the day. By midnight, we were asleep.

Wednesday 12 December 2012 – 0700 hrs

"What does today's compartment hold for us darling?" Mary asked as she sat up and stretched in the early morning sunlight.

"Oh, what about we just pop over to Agra and admire the Taj Mahal?" I replied casually.

Mary was up out of bed, still naked from last night and again skipped across the floor to the bathroom. Again, I admired her firm small breasts doing their own little jiggle and Mary's tight but rounded bottom that would always deny her age.

It didn't take long before we were back at the airport doing our pre-flight inspection of Bravo Mike Charlie.

"Your turn to be Captain," my voice was quite definite. "Delhi International will be busier than Canberra but the procedures will be the same. We have about eight hours in the air today, but we gain two and a half hours on the clock. We'll be able to drive to Agra to see the Taj Mahal in the afternoon sun. We'll stay overnight and take a guided tour tomorrow."

Yesterday while Mary was flying, I had left her and gone to my desk on the excuse that I was going to start organising the photos we had gathered while visiting Bob and Kay. I had called the Vice-Chancellor on Skype and we had a face-to-face chat. I asked whether he could arrange a Chancellor-to-Chancellor request with the Chancellor of the University of Delhi for a permit for us to land and overnight at Agra Airport, it being an India Air Force facility. Professor Mary would love to see the Taj Mahal as she would be passing nearby on her way to Cambridge. "How could I refuse Brad after what you and Mary did for me on Saturday night, you filled the gap beautifully and I had no time to thank you before you took her away."

"It was our pleasure sir, I can assure you," I replied.

"Please call me Don. I know you will understand when the formals are required," Don replied.

"Thanks Don I consider that a privilege," I acknowledged.

"You know their Chancellor was with us on Saturday night?" Don continued.

"No, but I thought he may have been considering the number of Chancellor headpieces I could see; I knew they represented many more Unis than we have in Australia," I replied.

"Did you know he is the Vice-President of India?" Don continued.

"Yes Don, I discovered that from Wikipedia before I called," I replied.

"The Chancellor would love to do it," Don continued. "He may kick it upstairs to the GG if he feels that protocol demands it but there'll be no trouble there; they'd be fighting over who was going to help you two."

"Call me at the same time tomorrow Brad, but I'm sure it will be all right."

"Thanks again Don and till tomorrow," I ended the conversation.

Today I did the same saying I was going to organise the photos from last night. I will admit my white lies later, but I loved to spring enjoyable surprises for Mary.

I was back at the computer as the minute clicked over at the bottom of the screen. I clicked on Skye and Don's number.

"All set Brad," Don was pleased to say. "The Chancellor sent my request immediately; he's a personal friend of his opposite number and wasn't going to hand it over to the GG."

"That's great Don," I said. "Mary will get one big surprise when we don't have to go into the International at Delhi and then drive to Agra. She'll be flying that leg."

"I got your photos Brad thanks, they are really great. I passed them around the people who care. They won't end up in the press or on YouTube. The media hasn't woken up to how you got away and nobody's telling. They wouldn't believe you were flying by yourselves. Flying around Sydney Harbour was one thing, but this would really leave them scratching their head. Love and best wishes to Mary Brad. Give her a kiss from me. Goodbye for now," Don closed the line before I could respond; perhaps he was getting a bit emotional again.

We had departed Singapore at seven-thirty and it was now ten-thirty. We hadn't eaten so before I returned to Mary, I prepared a late breakfast.

"Cereal and fruit for starters, darling," I said presenting a knee tray for Mary. "The coffee is percolating and what would you like on your toast?"

"This look's nice; I was starting to think that we had missed something. Marmalade will be fine thanks; we did stoke up well last night."

"I'll be back soon; weather's great isn't it," I added not expecting a reply but kissing her hair as I left. I came back with coffee and toast for us both.

"When we have finished this I'll relieve you for a rest," I began.

"That would be nice," Mary began. "You really wore me out yesterday you know, and I will have to take my medicine tonight as well," I laughed as I realised what had started out as a mock rebuke ended up as a promise. I would have loved to tell her that Don sent his love and best wishes but that would have to wait.

"I'd say that you have three hours at your disposal Mary," I began. "I've lowered the divan for you; I'll give you a call in time for a shower and getting dressed for your arrival. You never know, the press could be there to get a photo of Professor Mary."

Mary grimaced at that one, but she got the point.

"I'll keep her nice and steady for you," I continued. "I'll fly her from here to get some right seat practice; I'll leave your seat so that you won't have to adjust it when you come back," I was letting her know that her first approach to a foreign International was going to happen.

"Good night darling," Mary said as she left and kissed me on the lips. "This little birdie is going to night, night."

"GOOD NIGHT SWEETHEART I'LL BE WATCHING O'ER YOU … I started singing into the intercom as Mary went through the cabin to the divan. She kicked off her shoes and curled up on the bed; the last few days had been long and intense with only minimum sleep at night.

I found the next two hours to be a peaceful relaxation too. I didn't go to sleep of course, although I believed that if I had I would have woken later down the track and still been on course. It had happened more than once before by two pilot crews with plenty of international flying time in their log books and a full load of passengers on board. My thoughts had turned to my own academic career and if and when it might start. Could it be that spreading my genes around the world would really change HOMO SAPIENS, I wondered? Could it be an army of little Brads working together could achieve what no individual leader has ever been able to achieve.

I was suddenly aware that for all the breadth of Saturday's guest list there was one group who were under-represented. There was no representation of the Big Money families of the world

"Ah Ha, is that what's been troubling me?" I asked myself aloud.

"Coffee, lover," Mary announced as she arrived back in the cockpit. Mary was now wearing crisp pale blue slacks a matching short sleeved cotton top which outlined the shape of her breasts but without making any emphasis, her hair was held with a bright but small scarf supporting her ponytail. I took my leave for a toilet break and a quick freshen up. I was satisfied that my present rig would do as nobody would be looking at me too closely and provided, I didn't spill any coffee I was OK. I had noticed that Mary had placed our lightweight bomber jackets on the chair nearest the cabin door; we would certainly look the part of the competent young aviators we were.

"Bravo Mike Charlie this is India Central," I heard as I slipped on my headset.

"Bravo Mike Charlie" I heard Mary respond.

"I have a diversion for you indicate when ready to copy," Mary now glanced at me and saw me hold up my kneepad to show I was backing her up.

"Bravo Mike Charlie ready," Mary replied with no hint of nervousness that she felt receiving a diversion just as she was ready to ask Central for her descent clearance.

"Bravo Mike Charlie turn right to zero three zero in three minutes commence descent to two thousand feet call air force controller at **Agra http://www.futuristic.guru/agra** airport on one four fife decimal fife at two thousand for landing instructions. Reason congestion in Delhi International Control Zone."

Mary looked at me to see me nod indicating that I had the clearance down.

"India Control this is Bravo Mike Charlie heading zero three zero in three descending to two thousand Agra Air Force Controller on one four fife decimal fife at two thousand," Mary confirmed clearly and crisply as if she was doing this full-time instead of a new professor so recently appointed higher than her wildest dreams.

"Bravo Mike Charlie," India Central replied.

I was looking at Mary with the admiration that I had seen in my mind. She was not looking so cool from this side of the conversation with a high flush to her cheeks but also a glow of satisfaction. In the three minutes to her turn Mary had quickly tuned Agra's approach point on the panel's navigation screen and set her descent rate accordingly. She had come this far, and she was going to produce nothing less than her best knowing that some pretty sharp jet fighter pilots could be around. She had no need to advise Central of her turn to the new course. Eyes would be watching the radar panels and knowing what she was doing. She had twenty minutes to run and now dared to look at me. She knew I could see her flush; she knew I could see the satisfaction she felt.

"Was that good enough Captain did I pass?" Mary asked.

"You slayed them darling," I was quick to respond. I imagined the controller turning to his nearest team member and with admiration say, 'Cool chick this one, that was so calm and spot on; she wouldn't be expecting that diversion.' His mate would reply with something like, 'Bravo Mike Charlie, isn't that Professor Mary's call sign, I saw her on TV the other night; she wasn't looking too cool then but she's gorgeous.'

The twenty minutes passed very quickly, and I now watched and listened as Mary threw a curve ball of her own.

“Air Force Agra this is Bravo Mike Charlie.”

“Bravo Mike Charlie welcome, you are expected please confirm ready to receive landing details,”

“Bravo Mike Charlie request clearance to do an orbit of the Taj Mahal first,” Mary replied.

“Bravo Mike Charlie Affirmative I suggest you do a left orbit down river this will give you the best view in this light from your cockpit windows. maintain clearance of Taj Mahal restricted area. No known traffic in the area for sixty minutes.

“Bravo Mike Charlie fifteen minutes will do and thank you sir,” Mary replied.

“A pleasure ma’am,” was the response.

We did two good circuits of the Taj Mahal complex and visited some of the other grand structures in the area. Neither Mary nor I had realised the size of the Taj or the number of magnificent structures surrounding it. When her fifteen minutes were up, she keyed the mike.

“Bravo Mike Charlie requests landing clearance with Delta.”

“Bravo Mike Charlie join downwind for zero six report short final.”

Mary and I both knew that not only eyes would be upon us, but tower radios were often monitored in airport clubs, other pilots’ cars or smartphones.

Mary flew a faultless circuit and then:

“Bravo Mike Charlie short final,” Mary announced.

“Bravo Mike Charlie clear to land FOLLOW ME will lead you to your parking bay.”

“Bravo Mike Charlie,” was all Mary was required to say and although she would have liked to thank the controller it was not expected and would take up a few precious seconds as she entered the most critical part of our eight-hour flight. No time to look at me; Mary put in a little crab to counter for the crosswind and then greased Bravo Mike Charlie on, touching down first with the right wheel and a slightly lower right wing and without any bounce she lowered the left and straightening on the centreline. Mary slowed the plane smoothly to come up behind FOLLOW ME to her park.

“Beautiful darling, beautiful,” I declared. “that will get the hangar talk going.”

Immediately we were back to business and closed Bravo Mike Charlie down for the night. I opened the door and lowered the steps to allow Mary to go first. At the bottom of the steps she was met with a very smart salute.

Chapter 10

Agra

Wednesday 12 December 2012 – 1600 hrs

"Welcome Professor Mary, it's a pleasure to have your company," said a very smart and handsome Group Captain.

"Thank you, Group Captain, this is most flattering, for us to be welcomed in this way seeing we are just passing through," Mary said.

"Oh no, Professor you're with us for tonight and tomorrow night, you'll have our best guide to this beautiful area and probably a fighter escort out on Friday morning," he said. "Call me Geoff by the way."

"Thank you, Geoff, I don't understand, but please call me Mary and this is Brad."

"Hello Brad," Geoff jumped in. "I'm sorry but I did recognise you of course. Let's get in the car, I'll explain as we drive over to the Mess; it's too sticky out here."

After holding the back door open for Mary and me Geoff got in with the driver and turned to watch as Mary found her voice.

"What have you been up to Brad?" Mary asked, "I know you must be behind this."

"Oh, I just had a little talk with Don on Skype yesterday; he insisted I call him Don. He thought it a great idea that he asks the Chancellor to have a chat to the Chancellor at Delhi to see if he could get us diverted here to Geoff. He didn't like the idea of us getting tied up with Customs and all that at the International and having to drive a couple of hundred kilometres each way to see these marvels. Don was confident it would be OK but thought the Chancellor might have to kick it upstairs to the GG since the Chancellor of Delhi's day job is Vice-President of India. He told me this morning that the Chancellor wouldn't hear of letting this become some sort of diplomatic affair and that as the Chancellor of Delhi was an old mate, and his guest in Canberra for your bash last Saturday, there would be no trouble at all. As you know, you got the diversion as soon as we entered India's air space," I was done.

"It's all right Geoff. You can close your jaw now. Brad likes to pull these little surprises on me," Mary explained.

"Your lips are sealed Flight," Geoff said as he recovered his composure.

Flight was a middle-aged Flight Sergeant not far from retirement.

"Not a word Sir," Flight confirmed.

"Or I'll find someone else to show our charming guests the wonders of Agra," Geoff finished with a wink to the back seat. Geoff told us later that Flight knew more about the area and its history than many of those born here. He had been on the base for twenty-three years and all his spare time was spent studying the monuments. He also confirmed that Flight was one of the most trusted people on the base of any rank.

"Frankly Brad, I can't imagine how you managed that one," Geoff remarked.

"I can," Mary said. "I'm sure you know what a PC-12 is supposed to look like inside. Ours was standard too. Two weeks ago, I thought it was going into the shop for its hundred-hourly after our little trip in Australia. Brad wouldn't let me see the interior until we were in cruise after we did our runner from the dinner. I won't try to explain it; we'll show it to you tomorrow."

We pulled up at the officers' mess and Geoff ushered us in. He showed us to comfortable chairs and asked what we would like to drink. "A cold beer please," we both said.

"Before this place starts to fill up let's make some arrangements for your stay," Geoff began. "Of course, you will dine with us in the mess tonight. Wednesday nights are quite casual and there is always some homemade entertainment afterwards. You'll probably be asked, or challenged, to sing; just be prepared," Geoff finished with a grin. "We have single quarters available upstairs. As you know, Flight is booked to be at your call all day tomorrow and I must confirm that you couldn't be in better hands. He's far better than any of the professional guides around here. Dinner again in the mess tomorrow night unless you would like to go into the city: there are plenty of good hotels and restaurants as you would expect in a city of this importance. We'll have you all gassed up for Friday morning departure. Anything you would like done on the PC-12 our chaps can handle for you; they are all Pilatus company trained and approved and no doubt you know we have a few PC-9s ourselves. Anything else you think we may be of assistance with just say the word."

"That sounds marvellous Geoff," Mary began. "We're most happy to put ourselves in your hands and Flight's. We'd much rather dine in your company tomorrow night than in the city. We don't require your accommodation though as we are kitted out to sleep on board and all our gear is there, as you will see tomorrow."

"Fine Mary, just a couple of other things; its hats off in here of course which means its first names all around, I know you will be quite happy with that. I won't get a chance to personally introduce you to everyone but I'm sure they will introduce themselves at the first opportunity. There are quite a few girls in the mess since they do much more in the service now than answering switchboards and typing letters; they'll be interested in both of you I'm sure. Which brings me to warn Mary to look out for some of the fighter pilots; they might want to get a bit personal after they get a few beers on board. The squadron leaders are the worst," Geoff said, again winking as he noticed one hang up his hat and walk close to us.

“Once a reasonable number have come in, I will ask the vice chairman of the mess to give you a brief introduction: something like, ‘I'd like to introduce Mary and Brad, a couple of good friends who have just dropped in from Australia. You might have noticed their Pilatus out there, they'll be with us until Friday morning, they're on their way to London.’ That should save you from answering the same sort of question over and over. I'm not the Vice-Chairman of the Mess; I'll introduce you to him when he arrives,” Geoff was finished.

Mary and I thought it sounded like a very long clearance from the tower, but we took it all in with nods and smiles.

“Here's Vice now,” Geoff began. “He was about to say, ‘who's that distinguished looking gent with him’ but only, ‘Oh God’, came out.

“Not God Geoff,” Vice had heard him; “only the Vice-President of India,” Vice, as many called him, quickly moved passed his little joke and performed the correct introductions precisely.

“Professor Mary, may I introduce the Vice-President of India the Honourable Dr Hamid Singh and as you would know the Chancellor of your sister University of Delhi,” Vice had spoken with the clarity and certainty of a Regimental Sergeant Major but in a volume suitable for the confined space of the Mess.

“I'm delighted to meet you Chancellor, I'm afraid there wasn't much time for introductions on Saturday night.”

“Please call me Hamid, particularly in here, we wouldn't want to upset Vice would we Mary?”

“Not at all Hamid,” Mary accepted the privilege.

"How do you do Brad, I couldn't help but admire your speech, particularly the way you stepped in for Don. No doubt it was a bit daunting in front of all those dignitaries.

"Thank you, sir."

"There are no sirs in here Brad, Hamid goes for you too," Hamid quickly acknowledged. "You showed we were all equal, not in the way that Jefferson meant but in the only way the statement makes sense."

"Is it correct Mary that you had no idea that you were the main course and not just some little entrée?" Hamid turned his attention to Mary.

"I'm afraid it is Hamid," Mary began with a chuckle. "I'm supposed to be so smart and I didn't even know a new faculty was being discussed; it's a wonder they didn't dump me right there and then."

"You're being too modest my dear; it only demonstrated how engrossed you are in your work. I'm sure Don believes you are destined for great things too," Hamid continued. "I've known him far too long to believe it was just an old man becoming a little over emotional. He knows you better than anybody: probably better than yourself in some things.

"Thank you, Hamid, Don has always supported me and had faith in my work," Mary replied.

"I'd love to stay and chat, but I have a car waiting," Hamid began to get ready to leave. "I was just leaving the government offices where I had business today when I got the call that you had arrived. I'm so glad that I could get an almost private conference before we get to meet again in Delhi."

"I'm sure we will get an opportunity again when those dates are set Hamid," Mary said.

"And thank you Hamid for arranging our diversion to Agra," I managed to say.

"It was a pleasure Brad and I'm sure Mary and you will be delighted with what you see here," Hamid replied.

Hamid took his leave and our little group was silent for a few moments absorbing such an unexpected visitor.

"Mary may I now introduce the Vice-President of our mess committee," Geoff began, 'somewhat lower than God and Vice-President/Chancellors but still a good bloke really; Squadron Leader Phil Wallace, but you are welcome to call him Vice."

"Hello Vice, I'm very pleased to meet you," Mary gave him a big smile and shook his hand.

"I'm not going through all that again Brad, this fellow here is Vice."

"Pleased to meet you Vice," I was quick with my outstretched hand and gave Vice a good outback handshake.

As the mess was now filling with members milling around the bar and talking, Geoff asked Vice to welcome Mary and me. As soon as Vice finished and while the applause was still being heard Vice extended his arm to Mary and invited her to accompany him to the dining room. Seeing Vice's gallantry, the rest of the Mess chose partners and joined the parade, although many males were left to accompany one another I was picked up by a charming young lieutenant who grabbed my arm before any of the other girls could do so.

"I'm Rosemary, Brad, everyone calls me Rose," Rose was quick to begin.

"I'm pleased to meet you Rose," I sounded even a little shy at having been taken hold around my left bicep so quickly and firmly.

"Sorry if I startled you but I had to move quickly before one of the other girls got to you," Rose was so cheerful and open. "I admire your flying Brad."

"That wasn't me it was Mary," I quickly explained.

"No not that although everything about it was professional," Rose began. "We'd been listening in on the tower repeater in the workshop since the moment she made contact. The boys were betting on whether it was a bird flying the bird or she might just have been doing the radio duties. There was some cheering when you rolled to a halt and we could see it was Mary in the left seat."

"I didn't see anyone around until Geoff greeted us," I still seemed confused.

"Of course not, we had you in sight with binoculars all around the circuit," Rose supplied.

"Well Mary will be surprised when I tell her," I said.

"She's probably been told already," Rose continued. "You don't think that when we heard Bravo Mike Charlie being diverted here it was just because of congestion at Delhi International; they would have just put you into a holding pattern along with everyone else. This sort of thing never happens; we knew someone of importance was on board and wanted to see if the pilot was up to his job. Just the same as if it had been Air Force One; I pity that bloke: he's got to be perfect on every approach because there are always cameras on him. The papers would be printing 'Pilot gives President a shakeup,' or something similar," Rose paused.

"I know what you mean," I began. "We've attracted a little unsought publicity ourselves."

"That's what I was saying Brad, I admire your flying," Rose was quick to respond.

"Rose, are we going around in circles here?" I asked with a big grin.

"No dummy, I mean in Sydney Harbour," Rose sounded a little exasperated that I could have been so slow picking up her meaning.

"Oh that, how did you know about that in Agra India?" I asked.

"Brad, you're pulling my leg," Rose replied. "Everybody knows: it was on the TV here, on YouTube, in the newspapers and magazines, on the cover of FLYING with a big article inside. Where have you been?"

"Well for a start: after the harbour orbit we flew on to Cairns where we found out our orbit of the harbour had become a media event and quickly took refuge with some friends in the Outback until the fuss blew over."

"Where's the Outback, Brad?" Rose asked.

"Oh, anywhere really except cities and large towns. We sometimes call it the Bush or the Scrub; some people say it's any place 'Beyond the Black Stump'.

"Sorry to interrupt again, but where is the Black Stump?"

"It's mostly a figure of speech meaning any place further west of it is remote or dessert or simply far away. A couple of towns lay claim to once having a burnt-out tree stump that was the original black-stump of legend. Most of the grazing properties out there are measured in square kilometres rather than hectares or acres," I answered. "We changed our plans and spent the next ten days visiting my father's other outback mates. We kept out of sight of the media; we had a great time and made a lot of new friends. We arrived back just in time for my delayed birthday party and then last Saturday night Mary became Professor Mary."

"And now four days later little me is on the arm of a great aviator being taken to dinner in the Officers' Mess at Agra."

"I've no claims to be a great aviator Rose," I was quick to deny her.

"You can't fool me; I teach these young blokes. It wasn't only Sydney Harbour: I saw your approach in Canberra when you returned, I judged that the controller had given you preference over all the other aircraft lined up for departure. That had the potential for a very messy landing if you missed it. I could see the point where I knew your eyes were glued. I knew you were flying her with hands and feet instinctively," Rose was quick to defend her judgment. "These blokes can throw a F18 around up high but get them down low and slow where it needs finesse and they're not so sharp."

We had reached our chairs as Vice proposed the toast to the Queen, a tradition still honoured in most Officers' Mess. Rose and I paused for the toast and sat together with only little greetings to acknowledge our dining partners.

"You said you flew Singapore to Agra, where did you refuel?" Rose recalled that this fact was mentioned in passing.

"Nowhere," I remarked quite naturally.

"You're pulling my leg again," Rose chided me, "PC-12s only have about three thousand kilometres range."

"Not this one Rose we can easily do four," I replied. "After you saw the hangar door close when we returned to Canberra she didn't come out until late Saturday night:

except for Airworthiness approval. She's a totally different PC-12 than any other in the world now," I explained.

"Could I see it Brad, before you leave?" Rose almost pleaded.

"Of course, Rose," I replied trying not to be too keen to show off my pride and joy. "Geoff is coming at eight o'clock before Flight takes us away to visit the Taj Mahal. Is eight- fifteen OK?"

"I'll be knocking on the door," Rose replied, and we laughed.

We chatted away all through dinner; occasionally we joined in the general conversation or paused to watch the amateur performers who provided the evening's entertainment.

Vice rose to his feet and struck a small gong calling for attention:

"I've just had a signal from an old Qantas captain friend, now retired to a station south of Darwin. It states, and I quote, 'Make Mary and Brad sing for their supper. They did PEOPLE WILL SAY WE'RE IN LOVE as their contribution at our sing-along on Sunday night. Don't tell them that I dobbed them in though'."

The applause was deafening, Mary glanced up to see me as Rose brought me forward.

"We can't squib it Mary," I said as Rose handed me over. "It would be as bad as bouncing Bravo Mike Charlie on landing."

Several tables and chairs were quickly pushed back, and the pianist started the lead in. I sashayed Mary onto the floor and as we went through our respective stanzas and joined together in the chorus, we had lifted from the good performance from Sunday night to a very good performance tonight. When we finished the applause was again deafening and now, we heard cries of More, More and Encore.

Mary sat down as soon as the number finished and didn't feel like facing the crowd again, duty had been done. She leaned towards Vice, "Tell them that I would like Rose to sub for me," Mary said.

Vice was quickly to his feet, "Mary thanks you for your applause and points out that she has done her duty as she did not eat a very large supper. Mary has asked Rose to sub for her to ensure that Brad fully pays for his appetite."

Again, loud applause as the pianist started again. The audience was most appreciative, for Rose too had a beauty all her own. She was admired and respected on the Base; she had never had an affair with any of them although not for the lack of offers. She was an instructor in flight and aerial manoeuvres and would never consider getting involved in any of the ground-based kind. She was Eurasian in that combination of breeding where an elegant and successful British businessman produces a baby with an exceptionally beautiful Hindu lady. On the floor with me she was a little taller than Mary and just that little bit more girlish. I enjoyed singing Curly's words while looking into Laurey's eyes and the feel of her body against mine when we came together for a few steps was exciting. Soon the moment had passed, and Rose and I sat with the Vice, Geoff and Mary as some seats had become vacant at their table.

"Thank you, Mary and Brad, for rising to the challenge, it put the seal on the evening. Thank you too Rose," Vice said.

"And we are to throw his coins in the Trevi on Saturday too," Mary joked.

"I feel like telling him that we were running short and spent them," I joked too.

"I don't know how he found out that we would be here tonight; I only spoke to the Vice-Chancellor in Canberra. He knew we were going to take in the Taj Mahal on our way to London, in fact he suggested it, but it was the Chancellors that got us in here instead of Delhi International." I felt that was quite enough explanation for tonight. The Mess was emptying now, and un-needed lights were being turned off.

"May we walk you home, Mary?" Vice asked.

"That would be nice; it's a lovely night and not far. No sense getting a car out," Mary replied.

"We'll see Rose home safely after we deliver you," Geoff added.

As soon as we got outside Vice offered his right arm to Mary and his left to Rose. Geoff obligingly offered his left arm to Mary and she took it without hesitation. Rose was glancing back waiting for me, quickly took my right arm, and gave it a good squeeze. We were a happy group walking down the middle of the main road between the Officers' Mess and Bravo Mike Charlie.

"You don't mind if I bring Vice in the morning do you Mary?" Geoff asked.

"Of course not, I'll be delighted to show you through," Mary was happy that they were interested and keen to show off my gift.

"I've invited Rose too," I advised. "Thought it was the least I could do after ear-bashing her all night about how this PC-12 was like no other. Rose will arrive about eight fifteen to let you have a good look around first. Five on board at once would be a bit of a crowd."

Again, Rose delivered a squeeze to my arm, indicating how pleased she was not to have to make any explanation to her senior officers why she was present. She knew of course that it was she who had done most of the ear-bashing and drawing forth answers to her many questions. She also knew there were many more questions she would love to ask and enjoy a little more leg-pulling to boot. For now, she was happy to hold on. We broke formation at Bravo Mike Charlie's steps. Rose delivered a kiss to my cheek and Mary did the same for her two escorts. Mary and I paused at the top of the steps and watched Rose in the middle holding an arm of each of her superiors.

"Eleven o'clock and you haven't taken your medicine yet darling," I reminded Mary. Not that she needed reminding, but it was reassuring to let her know I cared.

We showered, not together, for that would have really taken up too much of the available floor space, and it was only fifteen minutes before we were on the pulled down divan. I placed my arms gently around Mary and allowed her a few minutes to relax.

"It was a lovely night darling," Mary said at last. "I was beginning to feel jealous of that girl paying you so much attention and you were lapping it all up," Mary teased. "Now do you see the effect you have on women Adonis? You hardly looked at me until our names were called and then Rose almost dragged you forward and waited to pounce on you as soon as I sat down."

"Oh Aphrodite, that's not fair," I said. "What with egging on two much older men all night; do all girls go for men in uniform?" I continued without waiting for an answer. "And what about the Vice-President going out of his way to pay court to you? I must say though you handled it beautifully."

By this time my old fella was at stiff attention as would satisfy any parade ground Regimental Sergeant Major and Mary was delighted now to put her teasing aside. She quickly performed her thigh up my side movement that always outflanked me and left my old fella unable to save itself from being captured and me to feel it being swallowed up through the Gates to Paradise. Mary performed her exercise routine quietly.

"Now do you see how girls are attracted to Adonis darling? Could you bring yourself to fuck Rose to improve the gene pool?" Mary asked.

"Of course, I could she's a very beautiful lady, so bright and intelligent, I'm sure I would thoroughly enjoy the experience," I declared with honesty and sincerity, "but there is a lot of difference my darling between could I and would I, isn't there?"

"I know darling," Mary began, "but you've never fucked another girl. You might be so fixated on me you can't get it up for anyone else."

"Let me really thank you for another great surprise Adonis," Mary said, quickly changing the subject.

"You'd better not spring too many surprises on me or I might think up a few of my own," Mary added and at the same time delivered a thrill through my groin that reverberated all over me. I was intent on prolonging the night just a little longer. I clasped her tight to restrict her movements and massaged her back with my fingertips. It thrilled her in a way she could not understand and had her sighing Oh Adonis, Oh Adonis, repeatedly. She was certain that I could bring her to a climax with my fingers on her back alone. She worked on my shaft with the muscles in her vaginal wall until I could hold it back no longer and she made me release us both from our helpless state.

"We'll get up early and prepare for our guests darling," Mary whispered. "Hold me a little longer please."

I replied with a little hug and whispered, "Good night sweetheart," We drifted off in each other's arms as was becoming our custom.

Thursday 13 December 2012 – 0600 hrs

The day dawned bright and cheery, Mary and I were out of bed at six o'clock: we were happy to have two hours to prepare. I shaved while Mary showered and when I was dressed for the day Mary had bacon and eggs ready to serve. We had time to enjoy sitting in our dining room to start the day. We tried to select yesterday's memories to take forward: there were so many that we couldn't find any that we didn't want so we kept the lot. We were confident that today's compartment would be just as memorable. By seven-fifteen we were doing the washing up and stowing each piece in its exclusive spot. We turned the bed back into a divan after consigned its linen, and the clothes that we had worn since leaving Bob's, into laundry bags for collection. We tidied our desks, went over every inch of the cockpit to ensure all knobs, switches and circuit breakers were in the correct shut down positions, even to what channels were pre-set on the radios. These guests were no casual lookers: they were experts and would notice the slightest out of place item. Mary replaced her orchid on the table and all was done.

"No mile-high badges on view darling?" I asked. Mary went running to the lab, retrieved her badge and mine and hid them in the bottom of the small handbag she was using for the day.

"Thanks darling, that was close. I never thought I'd get caught that way again." We laughed at our narrow escape. What people might think was one thing but to rub their nose in it was unthinkable. We did a careful walk around Bravo Mike Charlie's exterior and finding nothing out of place returned and gave the interior a good spray of air freshener. Bravo Mike Charlie looked the same as when Mary first saw it at thirty thousand feet five days ago. We relaxed, and I placed a kiss on Mary's forehead. At eight o'clock Geoff's car stopped at the steps.

"Good Morning Geoff, Vice," I greeted them warmly, "Mary will show you through. I'll have a yarn with Flight until Rose turns up."

Geoff and Vice went up the steps to be welcomed by Mary with her customary big smile and self-assurance. I received a rundown from Flight on what his plans were for the day. He would return Group and the Squadron Leader to their offices and be back for Mary and me at nine. He told me that he would be collecting a picnic hamper from the Mess so that we need not lose any time hunting for food amongst the tourists. Flight would have us back by six. By the time Flight had given me all his messages I noticed a VeeDub coming towards us. This would be Rose, I thought, and she is five minutes early. I was pleased that she was early as it would give me more time to talk to her before Geoff and Vice left the cabin. I was sure that they wouldn't be early leaving. When Rose stopped a short way from Flight's car, I excused myself and went to greet her.

"Good morning Rose, mind if I have a seat?" I said as I opened the passenger side door.

"Of course not, Brad, I was just about to offer," Rose gave me a big smile. "I hoped I would be here before Group got finished and I hoped you'd be waiting for me."

"That's a compliment," I answered, smiling too.

"Would you come with me for dinner in town tonight please Brad?" Rose asked catching me by surprise. "I had such a good time talking to you last night but went home feeling that there was so much more to talk about. I'm sure the Mess would not leave us to ourselves. Geoff will take good care of Mary for you for a few hours."

"I'd love to Rose; I'm honestly flattered that you'd want me too. What's the drill?" I asked.

"Have you got a reasonable business suit on board, nothing too dark or formal; I want to take you to a very nice restaurant that has a dance floor and band. I enjoyed dancing with you too, or didn't you notice?" Rose asked.

"I noticed Rose and I enjoyed it very much also," I confirmed. "I'm sure I will enjoy it better tonight without the Mess looking on."

"You know that it was Mary who pushed me in to dancing with you: not me pushing in. I only pushed in to grab your arm in the first place and I apologised for that. Of course, I would do it again if necessary. There are few men of quality who come by here and I haven't noticed any paying much attention to Flight Lieutenant Rosemary Sastri."

"More fool them Rose, they don't know what they are missing," I replied sincerely. "What time?"

"I'll pick you up at seven and have you back here at eleven; I know you are flying out at seven in the morning for Rome. It's a long haul and I wouldn't keep a pilot up late before that trip: quite a few intersecting airways in that area." Rose replied with the same certainty as pilots do when they are knowledgeable about the topic being discussed or following standard communications. "Not that I would mind keeping you all night Brad," Rose concluded.

"That's another compliment Rose," I replied. "Be careful that you don't burden me with a debt I can't repay."

“That’s OK Brad,” Rose began but stopped. “Here comes Group and Vice. Time for you and me now?” It was eight thirty, Geoff and Vice had taken fifteen minutes longer than expected.

“Good morning Group, Squadron Leader; may I call on you after I’ve had a look and confirm tomorrow’s arrangements,” Rose asked.

“Certainly Lieutenant, prepare yourself for a surprise,” Group said.

All was formal now in front of Flight. Mary had come down to wave away Geoff and Vice.

“Good Morning Mary, did you enjoy the Mess last night?” Rose asked.

“Hello Rose, of course I did it was great fun, much like the parties we’ve been treated to in country Australia. I can’t get over a certain retired Qantas pilot though,” Mary finished with a laugh.

“I’m glad he did,” Rose was quick in support. “Otherwise we wouldn’t have heard you and Brad singing.”

“You did very well yourself Rose,” Mary returned the compliment. “Let’s get cracking before Flight gets back.”

“Mary will lead the way Rose; I’ll answer any questions on the technical bits,” I said.

“Would you mind if I stole Brad away for a few hours this evening, I’d like to show him some of the city at night? I’ll have him back by eleven for your early start tomorrow,” Rose asked as we entered the cabin.

“No need to ask me Rose, I’m sure he has already said yes,” Mary said with a great big smile. “If he hasn’t, I’ll put him over my knee and spank him.”

Mary was sincerely pleased. She knew she mustn't let me implant on her permanently: it wouldn't be fair to me and it wouldn't be fair to her or our forebears; she wanted grandchildren — lots of them.

I sat back in the rear-facing chair at the other end of the cabin and watched. Rose wanted to see everything, she had seen plenty of airliner galleys but never one like this in a relatively small aircraft; it even had a running-water sink and a washing machine under it, backup generator and everything in its assigned place. Rose marvelled at Mary's lab and although it was out of her league, she could see that it was serviceable and complete, and Mary was clearly excited about using it; she hadn't yet because the first time she saw it was about eleven o'clock on Saturday night. She was fascinated by the amount of wardrobe space, complete with full size mirror and drawers and slots to suit different articles and shoe racks. At the sight of the pull-down divan with its bedside cupboards and reading lamps Rose could easily imagine the divan extended with the beautiful linen it would surely have. I imagined what it would be like to have Rose in my arms on the divan. Mary showed Rose her new academic robes and Rose asked to see the gown Mary had worn; it was equally chic with or without the black overdress. She had been so impressed seeing Mary receive her robes and escorted back to her chair by the Chancellor and she had been totally wrapt by my speech. They worked up through the mundane office arrangement and smiling at me moved on to the toilet and shower. Finally, they had finished, and Rose sat in the seat opposite me and Mary sat beside her. The orchid spray was midway between the three of us, the centre point of a triangle.

"Mary it's beautiful, there can't be another Pilatus like it anywhere in the world," Rose began. "Brad can tell me about the technical stuff tonight, but before Flight gets back and takes you away, I did hear right that she went into the shop last Wednesday week as a standard Pilatus and came out last Friday night just like this and certified with all the new mods," Rose asked incredulously.

"I swear it's true Rose, I thought it was going in for its hundred-hourly and didn't know any different until about eleven o'clock on Saturday night," Mary stated.

"Honestly Mary, I wouldn't have believed it had I not heard it from you," Rose replied. "If I heard it from a man I would have laughed and thought he was just out to chat me up. And it now has a range over four thousand Ks, eight hours in the air?"

"That's how we got here from Singapore," Mary confirmed. "It's in our logs and in all the IFR records."

"Thanks very much Mary," Rose said. Mary walked Rose to the door and gave her a big hug shoulder to shoulder.

"Until tonight Brad," Rose called. She looked back with a smile on her face and waved as she skipped down the steps and back to her VeeDub.

I turned the interior lights off at the master switch, retracted the steps and locked the door.

Thursday 13 December 2012 – 0930 hrs

Flight was waiting for us. He held the door back for us to enter and shut it behind us.

"Without speaking out of school sir, Group and the Squadron Leader were amazed by what they saw," Flight was quick to acknowledge.

"Please call us Brad and Mary Flight; we're just a couple of air tourists blown off course a little," I put Flight at ease.

"I'm Roger at home Brad," Flight immediately provided.

"I bet you get Roger Roger quite a bit?" Mary asked.

"Not so much now Mary, it's worn a bit thin around here. Some new pilots coming in can't help it though."

"I'm sure Mary would like to see our masterpiece first. It will take us all morning to do it any sort of justice. Folks are always coming back whenever they can for another look," Roger was obviously smitten and could go back and walk about the Taj Mahal at any opportunity. "I swear you can feel the love that built that structure."

"It was absolutely stunning from one thousand last night Roger. Brad got lots of shots from a starboard cabin window as we went around. I had no idea that the grounds and minor buildings on the sight were so extensive. We got the best of the afternoon light but haven't had a chance to properly review the photos yet."

"I meant to ask you whether you would like to view our PC-12 seeing Group was so impressed?" Mary added.

"I'd love to Mary," Roger was quick to accept. "I'm instructed to have you back by six as Group will be escorting you to the Mess at seven fifteen."

"So, we'll have time then, that's good," Mary said sincerely.

Roger glided the big car into a parking space and directed us to the electric bus that would take us to the complex. Everything possible was now being done to protect this magnificent structure from modern pollutants. I paid the entrance fees for the three of us and was about to stuff the rest of my five-dollar notes into the nearby donation box but, fearing that I might be seen as showing off, resolved to see that a new recipient was added to the Clifford Company's anonymous donations list. I had my camera slung around my neck, a sturdy but compact retractable tripod in one hand and held Mary's with the other. I much preferred mounting the camera on a tripod for our shots rather than handing it to strangers and asking them to take our photos. We first visited the reflection pool to take the typical happy snaps that tourists always do. I mounted the camera on the tripod and with an electronic shutter release I posed with Mary in various happy laughing or smiling poses; in some we would be holding hands, in others both waving independently and, in some Mary was hanging onto my arm. Roger stood back obviously happy with our performance. I came back to the camera and added a filter to the lens.

"I'm trying to suggest an early evening shot," I said to Roger. "Don't be embarrassed mate, it's a special request."

Mary heard this of course and was ready for me when I stepped up beside her. I now put my right hand around Mary's back. I gently pulled her closer and she rose up on her toes and lifted her face to me to be kissed; my left hand was just under Mary's right breast but clearly indicating that the next frame would see her breast covered. It was the classical pose of lovers. I had taken my shot, but the moment lasted just a little longer. Mary and I went back to Roger's side and gathered up my camera gear.

"Truly lovely folks," Roger said. "Now that you've got your postcards can I take that gear back and lock it up in the car. I'm sure you won't want to waste your time clicking and adjusting with what you will see today. You've got your aerials from yesterday and I've got copies of my collection on a USB stick for you. I know you won't get anything as good with all these tourists about."

"Thanks Roger," I said. "They do get in the way if you're not using them."

"Just go over to the garden walk; we'll stroll around the garden first before we approach the tomb, I won't be long," Roger spoke almost reverently. Roger was into his mid-forties and would be retiring soon. In his years studying the Taj Mahal he was quite used to seeing young lovers and honeymooners of all ages affected by this site and Mary and I were no different even if we were mother and son. He'd seen my reaction when Rose drove up this morning and instantly registered that there was certainly a connection building between Rose and me.

"Take us around Roger," Mary said happily, as she took Roger's left arm and my right ready to be escorted as a happy group.

Roger was beaming with pride to have Professor Mary on his arm. He'd love to tell the boys in the Sergeants' Mess tonight, but he wouldn't. Why give away your precious moments for others to tease or jeer at; he could imagine his fellows saying 'You wish' or 'Pull the other one old man'- it would be his secret. He now regretted his haste in getting rid of my camera: he would have loved to have a shot of Mary on his arm to take home to his wife. His wife, also a Mary, would want to know as much as possible about Professor Mary seeing that only a month ago, she was unknown. As we came to a minaret, Roger pointed out its special significance and the meaning of the fantastic ornamentations and scrollwork. He walked us around the outside of the building: again, explaining the style and meaning of what we were seeing. He was able to quote in English the Arabic quotations from that long-ago period of three hundred and sixty years. He quoted many of the verses from the Qur'an with ease as we walked through the passageways until finally, we reached the tomb. He had deliberately taken the long way around to ensure that his guests appreciated the thought and care Shah Jahan had taken in the creation of this monument to his third wife. He explained how in 1631 Mumtaz Mahal had died in childbirth delivering their fourteenth child.

"Brad and I would have gone that way too Roger if it hadn't been for the skill of an eminent modern surgeon," Mary felt free to confess.

For some time, Mary and I had been holding a hankie in our hands and occasionally would dab a building tear away. When we entered the tomb, Roger left us to inspect quietly this magnificent room. When we re-joined him, he explained that the Shah and his beloved were actually entombed on the floor below, on their right sides facing Mecca. He quoted Shah Jahan's own words describing this monument:

Should guilty seek asylum here,
Like one pardoned, he becomes free from sin.
Should a sinner make his way to this mansion,
All his past sins are to be washed away.
The sight of this mansion creates sorrowing sighs;
And the sun and the moon shed tears from their eyes.
In this world this edifice has been made;
To display thereby the creator's glory.

"Roger it is so beautiful; can we go now please," Mary pleaded.

Roger was quick to realise that the Shah's words were affecting us far more than he had thought, and he had got a bit carried away with his love of this place. Mary was clearly distressed with her hankie now wiping tears away and I was fighting to hold my tears back in fear that it would only make Mary's distress worse. Roger quickly took the central position and taking Mary's arm in his right hand and mine in his left walked us out of the tomb and back to the fresh air of the garden walk.

"I'll go and get the car Brad," Roger said. "I'll wait for you at the entrance gate, no need to hurry."

Roger though did hurry away. He was chastising himself for being insensitive to the emotions that were building in Mary and me since our happy snaps earlier. I turned Mary to me and held her tight while she released her sobs. We remained that way for several minutes oblivious to other tourists taking in the sights.

"I'm OK now darling. It wasn't just beautiful it was shatteringly so. Nothing of what I have seen of this place on TV, in paintings or the Internet does it justice and Roger: quoting the Shah's description was too much for me. I am glad I was here with you. I'm sure you need to be in love to really feel the power here."

"I know darling," I began. "I was only able to hold my own tears back because I was afraid of stressing you further. Roger of course wouldn't think of mentioning this to anyone else; he would feel proud of having assisted us."

"I'm OK now; lunch will do us good," Mary replied.

I took her hand and we walked more purposely towards the gate with heads up and smiles on our faces again. Roger was waiting for us.

"Thanks Roger, I'm feeling good again now," Mary offered. "The beauty of the tomb brought me undone I'm afraid."

"No need to apologise for that Mary," Roger replied. "Sometimes when I translate an old quote or understand a floor design or the meaning of the precious and semi-precious stone patterns, I feel a bit weepy myself and I don't care who knows it. I've got a nice quiet and cool spot by the river for lunch."

When we parked, Roger was quick to pull out three folding chairs and a folding table from the boot of the car. He brought out the hamper and a wine bottle carrier; he had a tablecloth on the table and put a savoury plate in front of each chair. He took platters of cold cuts, small sandwiches and salads each in a lettuce leaf and placed them on the table and finally three wine glasses.

"Finger food today; when the cook realised who I was driving he took much more care than usual and grudgingly said he had put some in for me too," Roger said still trying to cheer Mary up a little more. "He's jealous of course."

“Looks great I’m hungry now,” Mary replied and was the first to fill her plate.

Roger poured the wine, “The cook selected the Moselle as he thought I would make the wrong choice and spoil his preparation.”

After lunch we paused to discuss what we had seen.

“It would be impossible to recreate today with all our technology, cranes and everything else,” I marvelled. “Not just the money, although that would be prohibitive, but where could you find the artisans to do such work, they don’t exist anymore. I’m afraid that mankind’s glory days are all behind us and it’s all downhill from now.”

“Not if the Faculty has its way,” Mary began. “The Genome Project has revealed that we can stop the rot and reverse the flow. We saw how the other disciplines are for it now on Saturday night. There’s a new energy in the air and hopefully the expectations won’t be too great too soon.”

“I think the big wigs got Brad’s message Saturday night,” Roger spoke up. “That was a bold speech in front of that lot Brad.”

“Someone had to say it Roger and I knew Mary wouldn’t say it for herself; she had just been completed sandbagged. Mary was almost in shock when I had to get up but the Vice-Chancellor in need of her help pulled her around,” I explained simply as fact and not modesty.

“Well the thirty minutes that worldwide TV gave it was the best show of the whole night; what with all those dignitaries and Mary centre stage; more than a billion people must have seen it and then there were the repeats,” Roger explained. “Who’s Professor Mary?” Roger continued with a grin. “Nobody had ever heard of you Mary, until Brad’s orbit in Sydney Harbour of course, but to then pop up two weeks later in that company, well the mind just boggles. You're the two most recognizable people on the planet; except perhaps for the Queen and the President of the USA."

"It was only Saturday night Roger," Mary began; a couple of days and it'll all be forgotten."

"Haven't you seen any TV or read any newspapers?" Roger asked with surprise clearly showing.

"We saw that thirty-minute segment on Sunday morning while we were up there," Mary began pointing to the sky, "Sunday night and Monday night we spent with friends outside Darwin; that's where our ex-Qantas mate and others helped plan our route to London. Tuesday night we spent at Raffles, last night in the Mess and tonight we are here. Tomorrow and Saturday nights we'll be in Rome; we have an appointment with the Trevi Fountain on behalf of our friends. We'll fly to Cambridge on Sunday morning. My new job really starts on Monday when I pay my respects to the Chancellor."

"Then you haven't seen or heard any of the media since Sunday morning?" Roger asked.

"No, we've been too busy enjoying friends' company like last night and flying; we've had twenty-five hours in the air since Saturday," Mary said, and I confirmed with a nod.

"It hasn't stopped," Roger began again. "There was a lot of speculation on where you went after you left the party on Saturday night but that stopped on Tuesday when the ANU Vice-Chancellor simply announced that you were en-route to London. You got through Singapore without being spotted but there's a big photo of our Vice-President chatting with Professor Mary while passing through Delhi. Of course, there was no mention of Agra or the Officers' Mess, that sort of thing is definitely off-limits. The Vice-President's aide took the photo in the Mess, but it came out looking like it was a transit lounge in Delhi."

Mary looked at me to see me looking at her; we were so surprised to hear what Roger was saying that we had no idea what to say. We laughed and laughed, and Roger laughed with us. Mary was almost back to tears again but tears of a very different kind. All the morning's emotion had evaporated with our laughing and our picnic lunch. Finally, Roger produced a plastic container of water and towels for us to wash our sticky hands. I helped Roger pack everything back into the boot including our bag of rubbish and after checking our picnic site we were off looking forward to viewing the lesser but equally important outer buildings. We studied the Great Gate, the mosque, the mausoleums of the Shah's two other wives and that of Multan's favourite servant. By the time we were finished it was after five o'clock and again we walked back to the car with Mary holding Roger and me by the arm. When we commenced our visit, our faces showed excited expectation. Now we showed happy satisfaction.

Roger pulled up alongside Bravo Mike Charlie at five thirty.

"Let me show you around Roger; nothing like what you have shown us I'm afraid," Mary said.

I lowered the stairs and Mary led the way. As usual, I took the rear facing dining chair and watched as Mary showed Roger the plane's features. Mary showed him her new robes as a matter of interest.

"I'm sure my Mary would love to see the gown you wore the other night," Roger said.

"Here it is," Mary began, "I had to bring it with us as I still had it on when we did our runner. Can I get Brad to email a photo of it to you?"

"Yes, please Mary will be delighted," Roger replied.

"Me in it or just the dress?" Mary couldn't help herself.

"Both please Mary; I'll decide whether I give her one or both," Roger carried on the joke.

Roger eventually got back towards the cockpit and sat across from me.

"Of course, we wouldn't want to compare her with Taj Mahal but for its purpose it is so perfect and complete," Roger said. "Rose will tell me the engineering details I'm sure."

"We'll be back before long, perhaps you would like to go for a spin," I suggested, "no doubt you've still got your licence."

"Too right, I'd give up driving before I gave up flying, I don't get to do much now as I'm mainly looking after Group and his important guests, but I keep up to date."

"Good mate, we'll keep you posted," I said.

Roger was on his feet, "Must go and let you good folks get ready for your dates."

"This will always be one of our special days thanks to you Roger," Mary said as he was leaving.

"My pleasure entirely I've never had guests who appreciated what they were seeing like you did," Roger disappeared down the steps.

Thursday 13 December 2012 – 1900 hrs

"It truly is a special occasion Brad. It's a pity they will be here so soon to pick us up darling," Mary said.

"I'll be back before midnight Aphrodite, don't start without me," I said.

"Take this with you Brad; I've got a distinct feeling you'll need it," Mary said and pressed a condom in its sealed packet into my hand. “It’s a collection condom darling: they’re made specifically for the collection of semen for analysis. Afterwards tie a knot in it and bring it back to me. You will be the first subject for my lab. There’s a littler tube of Doc’s balm for Rose too.”

“I don’t plan to,” I began but Mary put a finger to my lips.

“Darling, I know what Rose wants and it will be good for you too. Only ever having had sex with me isn’t a great recommendation for Adonis is it?”

I answered her with a lingering kiss and promises of more to come before the night was over.

As expected, Rose was first to arrive. I saw the lights of her VeeDub coming towards us and had the door open to welcome her. She negotiated the steps quickly and easily in her high heels and I found the girl coming towards me hardly resembled the one we had shown through Bravo Mike Charlie only this morning. Now out of uniform and dressed in an evening frock which came just below her knees and with a top supported by one shoulder strap. It wasn’t the length of the skirt that caught my eye but its fullness. Although there was little breeze its soft fabric moulding to her body and fell between her thighs as she walked. I had only seen her hair restrained under her pilot’s cap but now it was unrestrained and swept to one side.

“Do you recognise this young lady Mary?” I asked as I took Rose’s hand and ushered her through the door.

“I don’t know Brad,” Mary said, “Is it that young pilot that you paid so much attention to in the Mess last night?”

“I think it might be,” I continued the tease. “Scrubs up pretty-well doesn’t she?”

“You didn’t come up too bad either Brad,” Rose now got into the act, “and you Mary look as charming and elegant as I've seen you since I met you four or five days ago on TV."

"Thanks Rose but you should see me in my work clothes," Mary replied. "Of course, you two could join Geoff and me in the Mess or the four of us could go out on the town."

"Please Mary, can't I have some time alone with Brad for just a few hours," Rose said with a clear note of panic in her voice. "I promise to bring back unharmed — scout's honour."

"She's only teasing Rose; let's go before Geoff gets here," I consoled her.

"Remember Mary it's not only the young ones that you have to watch out for in there, but Geoff's all right he's all gentleman," Rose called as we left. Rose and I were driving away and passed Geoff as he arrived. With a big beep from the little VeeDub, and with the distinctive growl of its exhaust, we were gone.

"How did you go with Flight at the Taj Mahal today?" Rose was quick to start the conversation.

"He's a marvel Rose, he looked after us in the best possible way; his knowledge is encyclopaedic, the whole site is exquisite, the tomb is beyond description and when Roger quoted Shah Jahan's description of the building it was almost too much for Mary and I was struggling to hold back from crying like a baby too," I replied. "I don't think I told you but when I was born, they nearly lost Mary and me too. It was only the presence of an expert surgeon that saved us: that's the reason I'm an only child." I didn't know why I was telling an acquaintance of twenty-four hours all this, but it felt right, and it felt better to get it off my chest. Rose reached across and squeezed my hand, a manoeuvre not too difficult in the close quarters of a VW.

“Brad, I know too that your father died only four weeks ago,” Rose spoke softly, “please go on if it would help but there must be no more doom or gloom when we get out of the car; we’ve only got a few hours and we are going to make the most of them.”

“You’re so right but that place sure gets to you,” I replied. “You look so different in civvies Rose; it wasn’t all a jest back there,” I quickly changed the subject.

“It does a girl good to get all frocked up occasionally; it’s so easy to live in uniform or overalls on the base,” Rose said.

“Do you live there all the time?” I asked.

“I have a unit in Delhi; I try to get home most weekends.”

“What about husbands, lovers or other boyfriends, big brothers?” I began. “Sorry for prying but it would be fun to know. I wouldn’t want to get king hit for dancing with you.”

“Your safe Brad, not a husband, lover, boyfriend or big brother in sight and never has been,” Rose explained.

“Now you’re pulling my leg.”

Without answering, Rose drove into a parking space at the restaurant she had chosen. I was quickly out and at Rose’s door, fearing that she might try to do the same for me. I held the door back and held out my hand to help her out. Again, the light fabric fell down between her thighs, ‘it’s marvellous how such little things can excite a bloke,’ I thought. Once out of the car Rose kept my hand in hers as we walked in.

The Maître d’ greeted us and looked at me, “Name Sir?”

“Clifford,” I answered without hesitation. As we were being directed to our table I glanced at Rose.

“Wouldn’t want them to think that I had to pay for blokes to take me out Brad, would you?” Rose began.

“Of course not, just a sensible bit of flight planning Lieutenant,” I said and gave her hand a gentle squeeze.

We reached our table and before we sat, I led her out onto the dance floor where only two other couples were dancing. We moved onto the floor to the soft tones of a six-piece band playing **Begin the Beguine**. **http://www.futuristic.guru/begin-the-beguine**

I effortlessly took Rose in my arms and raised her right hand to dancing height. I saw her smile and her face slightly flush as I held her to me with my right hand in the small of her back as we danced away.

“I’m so pleased you did that Brad,” Rose said softly, “I would have hated having to eat a three-course meal before you got around to asking me to dance.”

“Anyone in the company of a beautiful woman would certainly use the excuse of dancing to hold her in his arms: even for a little while,” I replied softly.

“You’re very kind Brad,” Rose spoke softly and pulled me a little closer.

“I’m with you once more under the stars,
And down by the shore an orchestra’s playing”

I started singing softly catching up with the band. Rose had let her head come forward to rest against my cheek and we glided around the floor to this somewhat haunting melody. At times I caught a glimpse of us in one of the wall mirrors, the skirt that I had admired as she got out of the car now flaring out as we made our turns. Anyone seeing us would think that we had been dancing together for years instead of this being the first time, apart from our performance last night, but that didn’t really count.

“Do you know where our table is Rose?” I asked, “I really wasn’t paying a great deal of attention,”

“Inattention is very bad in a pilot Brad,” Rose teased.

“I didn’t mean it that way: my attention was elsewhere,” I replied and again she squeezed my hand showing she knew where my attention was and delighted that someone was taking notice of her. Rose spoke truthfully when she said there were no men in her life, except of course at the base where none would ever interest her romantically. I naturally held Rose’s chair for her and as soon as I was seated the waiter was at my elbow with the wine list.

“By the glass please Brad,” Rose suggested. “I couldn’t help you drink a bottle even if it was the best vintage ever grown.”

“That goes for me too Rose, I’m flying tomorrow remember?” I replied.

“I know but I’ve been trying to forget,” Rose replied. “I’d get you blind drunk if I thought that would keep you here, but Mary would just tie you to the divan and fly you away from me anyway.”

“Two house whites please,” I addressed the drink waiter.

The food waiter moved in as soon as our wine order was taken. He read the Chef’s Recommendations and handed the large a la carte menu to each us. We barely glanced at the large menu before selecting an entrée and main course that the chef had recommended. We knew that we only had a few hours to ourselves and we both wanted to spend some time without others watching us.

Our entrée arrived and as we ate, I was telling Rose that I didn’t expect such a European style restaurant and music here. Rose was delighted that her choice suited me so well. There would be plenty of time to introduce me to some of the other cultures if I came back again. For tonight, she only wanted me to have eyes for her. Rose didn't even follow-up on the specifics of Bravo Mike Charlie although as an aviation expert she wanted to know and understand the details. Our entrée plates were removed just as the band started its next bracket. I was out of my seat and helping Rose from her chair.

"Come on Rose, let's not waste last night's practice run," I began, "it will be much better on a smooth floor and with a band."

Why do they think up stories that link my name with yours?
Why do the neighbours gossip all day behind their doors?

We sang the song and danced as though we had just stepped out of OKLAHOMA. No other diners joined us on the floor. The band knew that Rose and I were providing an unexpected floorshow for them and the other diners were admiring our performance. Rose and I were word perfect and the band played the full version of the song. We not only sang well but our dance steps and eye contact did all that could be expected of practised actors, but we weren't acting.

As the number ended there was prolonged applause; other dancers were coming onto the floor and I escorted Rose back to our table; we were a little bemused and embarrassed that we had taken over the floor and nobody had joined us.

"PEOPLE WILL SAY has been on my mind all day Brad. I had to look up the lyrics when I finished work," Rose said when I complimented her on her performance. The drink waiter hovered but seeing our glasses still more than half-full moved quietly away. Our main course was placed in front of us and we talked of simple things while we ate. I apologised for having drawn so much attention to us. I was sure I had seen a camera flash and who knows where photos could end up these days.

"I don't mind being seen with you Brad no matter where the photos might appear," Rose said proudly. "It would let the mob at the base know that I'm not a spent force wouldn't it?"

"Yes, and if they got back to Australia people would be happy that I was sowing my wild oats as they expected," I laughed, and Rose laughed with me.

"Do you want to sow some wild oats with me Brad?" Rose asked somewhat shyly.

"I should say your place or mine, but your place is two hours away and mine is too public," I replied.

"You don't want dessert I hope?" Rose asked.

"No Rose let's go for a drive," I was quick to agree. "I'll go and pay."

"I'll join you at the door," Rose said. "I'll visit the little girl's room."

We rose together and parted; I slipped one of my fives under my plate and another under the almost empty wine glass, not so much for the service but for bringing our orders quickly and keeping out of our way.

We met at the door. Rose was refreshed and radiant. She took my hand and we walked back to the VW in silence. I waited while Rose unlocked her door so that I could hold it open and help her sit. Now at my own door I peeled off my suit coat and put it onto the back seat. After sitting down and while Rose started the VW and backed out, I removed my tie and tossed it behind me onto my jacket.

"Oh, that's better, I was getting a little warm in there," I stated.

Rose drove to a little park on a small hill looking down on the Taj Mahal.

"We'll be safe here Brad, we'd see a car approaching for five minutes or more," Rose spoke quickly.

I went around to Rose's side, opened her door and helped her to her feet. Rose turned to me and I wrapped my left arm around her and placed my hand in the small of her back. My right hand went to her right buttock and I pulled her close and kissed her. Rose responded passionately. My right hand came up to her breast and I applied a little pressure there. Rose responded by unclipping a catch that was hidden in the shoulder strap of her dress. The front fell loose making it easy for me to expose her breasts.

"Are you sure about this Rose?" I asked honestly, as I brought my hand up to her left breast.

"Brad, I'm a twenty-five-year-old virgin please help me?" Rose almost pleaded.

"I can't offer you anything Rose, I'm flying out tomorrow and we might never see each other again," I warned her.

By this time my hand was fully on her body, cupping her breast and touching her nipple. Rose could feel my rising erection through our clothes and pushed herself against it.

"Oh, don't stop Brad, please don't stop," Rose was pleading now but didn't dare fumble for my zipper.

"I must wear a condom darling, I'll explain later even if I have to send you a letter," I told her.

"I'd love to have your baby Brad, I was head over heels in love with you when I saw and heard you on the tele," Rose admitted. "There's a box in the console Brad; I bought them four years ago when I thought I might get lucky some night, they're all still there."

"Past their use by date Rose, I'll use mine," I stated.

“You came prepared too?” Rose was excited by this.

“I didn’t set out to, but Mary insisted: she knows us better than we do ourselves,” I told her, and Rose giggled.

“Let’s see if we can get more comfortable. I brought a couple of rugs and even a pillow in the hope that I could seduce you.”

I went to the front of the car and Rose popped the lid from the button on the dashboard; out tumbled a couple of picnic rugs and a pillow. I spread one rug on the ground and placed the pillow. The other rug I had ready to pull over us for although the night was mild a chill was starting to form as the evening progressed. I took off my shoes, socks trousers and boxers and tossed my still wrapped condom down near the pillow. I was about to strip off my shirt when Rose came up behind me. She had taken off her good dress and folded it over her car seat. Her shoes and bra went too, and she now turned and pressed her bare breasts against my chest. Rose was already unable to withhold little sighs of delight as she ran her hands over my biceps and chest as if assessing my strength. Our flat stomachs were pressed together, and I had a full hard-on coming up between her thighs. She parted her legs a little and squeezed me with her thighs. Mary’s thought that I might not be able to get it up for another girl was quickly dispelled.

“Will it fit darling?” Rose asked in some doubt fearing that she might be in danger.

“I’m sure it will Rose,” I assured her. ‘The condom’s lubricated and you will produce a little moisture too.”

“Have you had many girls Brad?” Rose asked.

“You’re the first Rose, I promise,” I said knowing that technically my answer was true as I would hardly classify Mary as a girl, but I had become more experienced and proficient in four weeks than most men do in a lifetime. I knew I would thrill her and cause her no harm.

I started to move down to the rug encouraging Rose to lie beside me. With Rose on her back I gently caressed each breast and teased each nipple with my lips and tongue. I kept coming back to plant gently kisses on her lips and apply a little tongue pressure where her lips closed. We kissed and cuddled and felt each other all over. I was most sincere when I stroked her hair and looked her in the eyes when I told her I thought her beautiful. I was equally sincere when I told her I must leave tomorrow and could promise her nothing. With my left arm around her shoulders I was running my right hand up and down inside her thigh and Rose was becoming more excited as I ran my fingers through her pubic hair and applied some pressure to her Mount of Venus. I didn't rush and while Rose clung to me around my chest with both arms and we kissed my right hand paused on her pussy. With two fingers I encouraged her lips to part so that I could spread the secretions from her vagina around her lips and further excite her clitoris. Little signs of 'Oh' from Rose punctuated our kisses.

"I think I'm ready darling," Rose whispered as she stretched her legs apart.

I found my condom and opened its pack.

"Would you like to roll it on for me darling?" I asked.

Rose sat up and took the rolled-up condom from my hand. I now lay on my back with my old fella pointing to the stars. Rose pressed a little kiss on the one-eyed beast and giggled as she felt a dribble of slippery stuff on its tip.

"You're sure it will fit?" Rose asked again.

I eased Rose onto me so that I wouldn't be pushing her into the grass. In this position it was easy for Rose to spread her legs wide and for my horn to align with her vagina. With extreme gentleness I rocked my penis up and down between her lips and with kisses to her mouth and massaging her breast I knew Rose was waiting and expecting the deeper plunges to come. Rose's hands had taken over when I took mine from her nipples and when I felt the entrance to her vagina relaxing, I placed my left hand in the small of her back and slid my right hand between us to impart gentle tickles to her clitoris. With a little extra push, I felt my old fella opening up Rose's vagina, stretching its walls for the first time in her twenty-five years. With a gasp of pain and joy Rose felt strongly these new sensations. She found that she could make the pace and I would respond to every motion. I kissed her deeply whenever her breathing permitted and kept my hands stimulating her skin: back, neck, sides, thighs and if one of Rose's fingers came near my mouth I kissed and sucked that too. I took her to the brink several times, holding my ejaculation to let Rose feel the joy my horn was producing as it glided in and out on the secretions from her cervix. My old fella throbbed with each spurt of semen and Rose went wild with an orgasm that she never thought was possible.

"Brad, Brad, Brad," she cried in delight and collapsed on my chest gasping and shuddering. My movements slowed to ease her down from the unexpected heights she had reached. I pulled the rug up over us and we clung together for the next hour. At last my old fella shrunk and slid from her.

"You were pulling my leg again Brad when you said you had no other girls," Rose spoke with her head still lying on my chest. "Surely all men don't have their first fuck this way and their girls so happy and satisfied while they are being stretched for the first time?"

"It is true darling," I assured her. "But it is too long a story to tell you tonight. I won't keep you waiting until I come back, we can have some long talks on Skype if you would like to know it all,"

“I’ve got a card to give you with my phone, and other details,” Rose explained. “I was hoping you would want it. I’d better take you back. I don’t know what time it is, but it must be getting late.”

Rose wiped up with a sponge from her evening bag.

“Mary said that you might like to insert a little of this and smooth it around,” I said. “It’s a balm she uses to keep her pussy strong and flexible.

“I’m so happy I waited for you Brad,” Rose said and hugged me again. “I’ve no more questions until we can talk for an hour or two,” she added.

We packed up, dressed and were on our way. It was now eleven o’clock, but it was only a few minutes back to the drome. Along the way Rose told me that Mary would have all the information for our departure and that she would be my wingman on my port wing; I had better be flying and blow her a kiss when they broke away. She would indicate they were going home with a salute with ten seconds to go. Rose didn’t believe I would see her as she would be in full kit including helmet as was required to fly an F18. We shared a final kiss in the confines of the VW and then Rose was off to her quarters.

I went straight up the steps and opened the door, I dropped my coat and tie on a dining chair and went to the curtain to see Mary in a skimpy see-through nightie and lying back against two pillows. I caught a glance at the cabin clock to see it reading eleven-fifteen.

“I was just about to call out the guard to look for you lover,” Mary chided me.

“Give me ten minutes to freshen up darling and I’ll be right with you,” I replied.

I quickly shaved, showered; and with hair combed, fresh aftershave and now in my light dressing grown I slid into bed beside Mary. I reached for her and she was quickly in my arms and wrapping her arms about me.

“I thought I might have had to take my medicine alone darling,” Mary said as she reached up to receive a genuine passionate kiss.

“Rose and I fucked, darling,” I just provided the information, not as a guilty admission, not asking for forgiveness but wishing to tell her without being asked.

“I’m so happy for you darling and for Rose too,” Mary was genuinely pleased to hear the news. “You know I want grandchildren for Bruce and me and to put another Great up there for our forebears.”

“But only with a girl who has her gene map examined by your team,” I spoke indicating that this was my point of concern about my actions.

“Shhh darling we’ll have plenty of time to talk tomorrow,” Mary said.

While we had been talking Mary had been quietly running her hand up and down my inner thigh and occasionally giving my old fella a little tweak.

“I’ve got another collection condom here for you Adonis, I’ll test them both tomorrow morning,” Mary said.

Now having brought me back to another full erection she rolled the condom on to my horn and then slid over me and impaled herself on it.

“Fuck me now Adonis; I need to do my exercises.”

We had made it before the clock moved to midnight; and held each other close while we talked for a few minutes more. Finally, I rolled the condom from my shaft, knotted it tightly and wrapped it in tissue for Mary to test tomorrow.

"This was truly a special occasion day; what with all we saw and heard and felt at the Taj Mahal. It is surely man's greatest tribute of his love for a woman," I spoke softly.

"You've created my Taj Mahal right here Adonis and everyone who sees it sees your love for me, as Bob and Kay did, and I'm still alive to enjoy it."

"But we didn't take advantage of Doc's prescription."

"You have Adonis and that's fine by me," Mary began. "I could have danced the encore with you last night, but I pushed Rose into your arms instead. You owe me a special day, but we'll wait for a day when we have no commitments. I'll fuck you awake on your Morning Glory and you can fuck me to sleep that night. All day long we can eat and drink and play and sing and dance it will be beautiful."

"Don't forget our Day-tight Compartments Aphrodite," I spoke softly with no rebuke.

"I've got the details for tomorrow darling, I suggest that we get up at five o'clock and get busy. We can take turns to sleep during the twelve hours to Rome."

Mary was asleep; I adjusted my alarm and turned out the lights. Tonight, I slept with two women in my dreams.

Friday 14 December 2012 – 0500 hrs

My alarm went off at five in the morning; I shut it off immediately as I wanted Mary to have another thirty minutes while I showered and dressed. By five-thirty I had my clothes from the night before secured in the wardrobe and drawers or in the laundry bag. I had cereals and fruit on the table, coffee was starting to percolate, and bread was ready to toast as soon as Mary woke. The smell of coffee brought Mary around.

“Smells lovely darling can I have ten minutes to get cleaned up; don’t go too far darling I need you to give me some tender attention after the banging you gave me last night,” Of course everything after ‘cleaned up’ was more of our game playing.

While waiting for Mary to call for me I made the bed and folded it back into its divan position and secured it for the flight. By five forty-five, Mary and I faced each other across the dining table for breakfast. Mary told me the main points of her night in the Mess with details to come in flight. Our departure time was seven o’clock local and Mary suggested that we have the bird ready for flight and then study the route as our last task. Mary said that in our absence Bravo Mike Charlie was refuelled, sumps drained, and fresh water loaded. She had been washed and polished from tip to tail, the base’s best engineer had done a thorough inspection of her outsides and found everything in order. I couldn’t see this work when I came back last night as there were no external lights to show it. I went and did my usually thorough pre-flight for even though I would find nothing amiss I knew there would be eyes watching to see if I did so. I would never take a plane aloft under any circumstances without satisfying myself that all was well. Mary in the meantime washed, wiped-up and stowed our breakfast dishes in their allotted places and secured all cupboards and equipment. By six-thirty we were back at the dining table and Mary produced the package that she had received from Geoff last night. We found that we were to be escorted out of Agra via the Old Fort on climb to twenty-nine thousand five-hundred which was a reserved altitude for Indian Air Force traffic. We would be accompanied to Surat where we would set course over the Arabian Sea and Gulf of Oman to Riyadh in Saudi Arabia. We would be expected, and refuelling arrangements had been booked. Our escort would depart at Surat and return to base. Flight Lieutenant Rose Sastri would be on our port wing and Group Captain Geoff Johnstone would be flying starboard. Bravo Mike Charlie was assigned the military call sign of Pilatus Alpha

Uniform, with the AU to represent Australia. This entitled Bravo Mike Charlie to invoke Air Force priority and privileges anywhere in the world simply by contacting Agra Air Force Base by any of the methods listed. To facilitate the use of these privileges Brad Clifford had been accorded an honorary commission with the nominal rank of Squadron Leader and Professor Mary the nominal rank of Flight Lieutenant. The Group Captain was sure that these provisions would be of assistance in smoothing our passage to London and in the world travel that was before us. These provisions were approved by the Vice-President and were supported by a copy of the approval document. Finally, there were two envelopes containing coins. One had the note 'Toss these for me please Mary' and signed Geoff; the other read 'Toss these for me please Brad' and signed Rose.

To say that Mary and I were staggered by these developments would be an understatement of the first order. We immediately recognised the immense importance these privileges would confer on our work and us. The press would no longer be able to get anywhere near us. While reporting under the call sign of Alpha Uniform military controllers would be in charge of our flights. Although no ownership of our bird was required, and no salaries would accrue with our rank, once our privileges were invoked, we were on charter to the India Air Force. Mary and I were astonished. We took our seats in the cockpit with five minutes to go. With two minutes to go I entered my new role.

"Agra Tower, Pilatus Alpha Uniform Ready."

"Alpha Uniform, Clear to start-up and FOLLOW ME to runway zero six Report at holding point your escort will fall in behind you."

"Alpha Uniform clear to taxi," I acknowledge with no sign of the nerves I was feeling.

"Don't they know that I have never flown in formation?" I said. I had one quick glance at Mary and received a smile as her only answer. I calmed to concentrate on the job at hand. I knew there were many eyes upon me. With my lover of last night, a vastly more proficient flyer than myself, about to come up close under my left wing and the Base Commander, our host for the past two days who had now performed incredible services on our behalf, coming up under my right wing, I was once more 'on a hiding to nothing' and knew it. I made the decision and turned the autopilot to stand by. I would fly this lady by hand, at least until I was turned loose at Surat. Reaching the holding point and seeing FOLLOW ME pull away to the taxiway and the driver waving farewell, I keyed the mike:

"Alpha Uniform Ready," I said crisply with no sign of nerves.

"Alpha Uniform clear for take-off make left turn to three two zero abeam Old Fort clear to climb to flight level two niner fife published procedure to Surat call Air Force International on one two niner decimal six for onward clearance approaching Surat."

On hearing the clear to take off I immediately released the brakes and made a slow turning roll onto the centreline while acknowledging the rest of my clearance.

"Alpha Uniform left to three two zero abeam Old Fort climb two niner fife published procedure to Surat onward clearance from one two niner decimal six."

"Alpha Uniform farewell and clear skies sir."

"Thankyou tower we have had a most enjoyable visit."

While the communications had proceeded, I had smoothly brought the bird up to full power and stuck like glue to the centreline, knowing that out of sight two F18s were powering up behind us.

“V1 - Rotate,” I heard Mary call. I eased Alpha Uniform up into two thousand feet a minute climb holding heading and climb right on the numbers so as not to upset my escorts. Coming up to Old Fort I performed a smooth climbing turn onto our new heading without any communications to our escort as I knew they had heard my clearance and it was their responsibility to keep station on Alpha Uniform. On reaching my assigned altitude, I again levelled the plane and stuck religiously to altitude, heading and speed.

“Alpha Uniform call one two six decimal niner now.”

“Alpha Uniform” I acknowledged the call and recognised it was Rose.

I keyed the frequency on my second com.

“Alpha Uniform,” I declared my presence on the frequency.

“Nice flying Brad, thanks for the best night of my life,” Rose began.

“This isn’t going out for the whole Base to hear Rose?” I sounded concerned not only for myself but for the four of us.

“No way lover, this is my discrete frequency not even Mary or Geoff can hear us. I’ll be back from the Mess by eight o’clock local which I think is about six o’clock in Rome can you call me any time after that. Don’t panic if you can’t, just drop me an SMS or an email so that I don’t cry myself to sleep. Take a glance out of your window. I could tickle you in a number of delicate spots from here.”

“My God, Rose I’ve never done this before, I’ve always been taught to keep separation not dance cheek to cheek,” I said seeing Rose so close to my wing tip.

“I’d never done that before last night either lover, but it’s fun isn’t it being so close? You haven’t forgotten, have you?”

“I’ll never forget Rose, you know that. We’ve got some serious talking to do just as soon as possible. I’d better concentrate on this job now as Surat will be coming up in ten. Until tonight darling.”

“Looking forward to it Brad,” Rose replied. “Thank you ever so much for making a woman of me.”

“You don’t look like my girl from last night, but it doesn’t matter; I know what’s under the helmet and the uniform and I love it. Until later,” I closed our chat.

Looking across at Mary I could see that she was talking to Geoff.

“Air Force International this is Pilatus Alpha Uniform,” I called on the radio.

“Alpha Uniform go ahead.”

“Alpha Uniform Surat in three at two niner fife request onward clearance to Riyadh.”

“Alpha Uniform turn to two seven fife at Surat maintain altitude, heading and speed maintain listening watch this frequency report one hundred miles south of Riyadh for descent instructions.”

“Alpha Uniform two seven fife Surat maintain altitude heading and speed report one hundred miles south of Riyadh,” I reeled off.

“Alpha Uniform Escort departing in ten seconds have a good flight Squadron Leader and your crew and do come back,” Geoff bid us farewell.

"Thank you sincerely Group, and we will see you again soon."

I quickly turned to my window to see Rose salute me and I hoped she could see me blow her the promised kiss.

Aphrodite's Diary http://www.futuristic.guru/copy-of-aphrodite-14

Chapter 11

To Cambridge

Friday 14 December 2012 – 0830 hrs

At Surat I rolled onto my new course and set my new flight details on the autopilot. I could now look at Mary.

"I'll get you a coffee darling; you must need it after that departure."

I sat back and relaxed. It had been a stressful ninety minutes since rolling out at Agra. Not just the flying, but the thought of having Rose so close to my left wing-tip and Geoff so close to my right had been really daunting. They must have known how little experience I had, and I had told Rose when she came up alongside that I had never flown in formation and here I was in our mini-airliner with two highly sophisticated war birds in close formation. The Pilatus's planned speed was five hundred kilometres an hour to make Riyadh safely with our fuel load. Our escorts could zip along at nearly four times that speed. What they couldn't do though was to fly from Agra to Riyadh without stopping for fuel. Our new heading took us out over the Arabian Sea. We were on a direct track to **Riyadh http://www.futuristic.guru/riyahd-rome** in Saudi Arabia. **https://en.wikipedia.org/wiki/Riyadh** We will overfly Oman and UAE, but we knew that clearances had been arranged by Geoff's staff in Agra.

"That must have been a bit hairy for you darling," Mary began as she returned with the coffee. "Did I see you turn the auto-pilot off?" Mary sounded quite surprised.

"Yes, I wasn't going to have four lives and I don't know how many millions of dollars' worth of hardware in the hands of a machine. It was just another occasion of being on a hiding to nothing, and if our lives were to be on my head then they would be in my hands too."

"No wonder they made you a Squadron Leader darling and me a Flight Lieutenant," Mary said. "I'm happy to be in your hands; I know what you can do with them.

Particularly after last night darling; you must be all shagged-out," Mary teased, and we laughed some more. "Just give me ten minutes to process your specimens from last night and then you'd better have the first sleep. I'll keep watch. We've still got five hours to go to Riyadh."

With my coffee mug empty, I waited for Mary to return and then gave her a big kiss and left for the divan. I let the divan down into its bed position; kicked off my shoes and within two minutes of trying to review the past two days' activities, I was sound asleep. It was nearly three hours later that I came back to the cockpit to hear Mary acknowledging our clearance over Oman."

"Can I get you some lunch darling or do you want to sleep first?" I asked.

"I'll take the sleep thanks Brad," Mary began. "We can eat while we refuel and talk all afternoon."

"You're relieved Lieutenant," I adopted my Air Force role.

"Thanks Captain," Mary replied as she rose from her chair.

I had been standing during our conversation and before Mary could leave for the cabin, I held her close with my left arm around her and my right hand on her breast.

"Do you want to talk this afternoon Adonis, or do you want me to pin on my Mile-High badge. You have never fucked a flight lieutenant before. Oops, I shouldn't have said that should I, I'd forgotten that the beautiful girl you were with last night was even in the air force."

"I think we should save it for Rome and have a good talk this afternoon," I gave her a light pat on her backside and released her to go and sleep.

I now had a chance for quiet consideration of last night. I hadn't set out to fuck with Rose but with Mary slipping the condom in my pocket I knew she was comfortable with the idea, even wanting it to happen. I couldn't quite come to grips with it though as I knew how deep our love was for each other; surely, she must consider that I was cheating, but her response to me when I came home was more of congratulation than anything else. And Rose, I had only met her twenty-four hours earlier, and although she had really thrown herself at me then, I knew she was the only girl in the room who I would have approached to dine with me. Her pleading for me to end her virginity couldn't be ignored and I felt proud of being her first lover. Mary wanted grandchildren as badly as she wanted me, perhaps even more so, but I knew that there would need to be gene matching by the Faculty before I could go in that direction, not only for mine and Mary's sake but for Rose's too. The last thing that I would want is to know that the clinic showed up a better match for Rose than me. I did love her and believed that it was more than desperation that attracted her to me. We certainly had a lot to talk about this afternoon. I had of course been keeping up my scans of the instruments, noting our progress along our track and keeping abreast of the weather and our fuel burn. It wasn't long before I had my descent and approach instruction to the Saudi Air Force base near Riyadh and just as I was about to call Mary, she entered the cabin with fresh coffee and took her seat. I quickly brought her up to date and the fact that we had thirty minutes to go surprised her.

"That was a wonderful sleep darling thank you," Mary began. "I'll be ready for anything after lunch and we're sky high again; your choice?" she giggled.

I laughed too. The past four weeks had produced experiences that I had never dreamed of but some considerations beyond day-tight compartments must be looked at since Mary told me I was Adonis and Rose had come into our lives.

The now familiar FOLLOW ME vehicle arrived, and I dutifully fell in behind. Great system I thought: particularly as it relieves the pilot from the chance of misadventure while taxiing on a strange airport, more so after a long flight over unfamiliar terrain. After we shutdown I lowered the steps for Mary to precede me. I took my small satchel of passports and important documents ensuring our arrangements for Riyadh were confirmed and went down to meet the fuel truck that was already pulling up alongside. There was a wave received and acknowledged from the FOLLOW ME driver. A staff car pulled up at the same time as the truck driver was running out his hose. The Base Adjutant stepped out of his car. He snapped a smart salute to Mary and addressed me.

"Good Morning Sir, welcome to Riyadh. My name in English is James; I'm sure that would be most convenient," the Adjutant provided.

"Thank you very much James. My name is Brad Clifford, and may I present Professor Mary Clifford."

"I'm delighted to meet you Professor Mary. I can assure you that we have kept up to date with your most recent appointment and your progress to accept our hospitality. I see you have brought your documents with you; I suggest that we go to the Mess to get out of the sun. Give your fuel keys to Raal, Brad. He will attend to your needs and I can offer you lunch while we complete the documentation. No need to lock up Brad, nobody would dream of entering uninvited."

"Thanks James I'll just tell Raal where the long-range tanks are."

Mary was in the cool of the car when I came back, and James was waiting to close the door behind me and join his driver up front.

“There is a cold buffet for lunch Professor; do you mind helping yourself and something for Brad while we attend to these formalities. I must stamp your passports and tick a few other boxes,” James advised us.

“Please call me Mary, James” Mary replied.

“Thanks Mary, Geoff tells me your PC-12 is rather special inside; he gave me a call after he’d set you free this morning. Oh, he said: tell Brad that Rose said she’d fly in tight formation with him anytime.”

I laughed, and Mary laughed along with me to cover the possible embarrassment that I might show. James laughed too not really understanding what we were laughing about.

“I told her that I had never flown in formation when their F18s came close to our wingtips. It was a bit scary,” I explained.

“It certainly can be,” James replied I don’t get to do a lot of flying these days, but I was never very comfortable with it.”

“We had them alongside from take-off, through the climb and all the way to Surat,” Mary backed me up.

“All done folks,” James advised. “I know that you will want to get underway for your next long hop to Rome. The Italian Air Force will take over midway across the Mediterranean.”

“Thank you for your hospitality James. Would you like to have a look over our bird while Brad does his pre-flight?” Mary offered.

“I’d love to Mary; Geoff says it’s unique.”

While I signed for the fuel and provided my charge card Mary ushered James on board. As others who had seen this interior before him, he was similarly impressed.

"The bed is usually up as a divan in the daytime, it gives us more floor space, but I had a couple of hours sleep before we arrived and might catch up with a bit more before we reach Rome," Mary explained.

"It's marvellous Mary, you've thought of everything," James said.

"No James, I didn't know anything about it until we were straight and level at thirty thousand last Saturday night. It's all Brad's design," Mary explained.

"I'd love to stay and talk with you both, but I mustn't be the cause of you having to make a night approach to Rome. I know you would do it but it's far better to see a new International in the daylight."

I was back in time to shake James' hand and thank him again for accepting us. We climbed out and were on track for Cairo. Although it was one-thirty local time and we had seven hours to run, it would only be five-thirty local when we approached Rome: giving us daylight right down to the runway.

"We've been blessed and protected on this trip Mary," I began. "It's not even a week yet since we did our runner."

"What did you want to talk about lover?" Mary asked.

"Why were you so keen for Rose and me to fuck last night?" I asked. "You've always insisted that couples should be mutually compatible in their genes. Do you know something about Rose that I don't?"

"No darling I could only see what you were seeing right from those first moments in the Mess. I could have danced the encore, but I pushed Rose forward to see how you moved together. I think you make a lovely couple," Mary was sincere.

"Rose told me she was a twenty-five-year-old virgin that would love to carry my child," I began, "without being vain about it she said that no man had interested her until she saw me speak on Saturday night. When she heard Bravo Mike Charlie being diverted to Agra, she thought her prayers had been answered: no wonder she pounced on me in the Mess. Of course, I was flattered and enjoyed her company immensely."

"Who was the Pilatus Captain that had me diverted to Agra; to give me a surprise?" Mary asked.

"Me of course," I admitted.

"Never mind darling, look at all the good things that have come out of your little plot. The night in the Mess, your first lover, a glorious day at the Taj Mahal with Roger, and now we hold honorary commissions in the Indian Air Force, Bravo Mike Charlie has an extra and most important call sign; just that could make all the difference in our coming travels. Nobody will know that Alpha Uniform is Bravo Mike Charlie in uniform. I don't know darling whether it was you wanting to make my experience of the Taj Mahal better or Rose calling for you over time and space. I'm happy with either. You do love her, don't you?"

"Of course, I do; she's a beautiful person. I can't understand why she is not married with two or three children by now. It doesn't mean that I love you any the less Mary. When you gave me that condom, I knew I had your blessing. There was only a cuddle and a few kisses before I told her that I could promise her nothing: that your database might contain a man who would provide her with a more compatible partner and better father for her children. Finally, I was happy to help her rid herself of her virginity if I wore a condom and then we would get your help to see if I was the best match for her genetically," I spoke gently and without stopping until I had made my statement.

"I could ask for nothing more Brad? You must have done a fine job of remedying her virginity problem: that's what she was referring to with her tight formation message. The only reason she hasn't married or even had a lover before now is that she is so discerning. At least now she will know that someone she loves loves her too. I'll brief my opposite number in Delhi to be ready to help her and give her all the information she can to assist her. I'll give you her contact details for you to pass onto Rose when you call her tonight,"

"What about my compatibility for Rose?" I asked.

"That's no problem Brad; you're perfect for Rose," Mary said.

"How do you know?" I asked.

"I told you, Adonis will produce better babies for any woman than any other man in the world. Now I'll get us coffee," this time Mary bent down to kiss my hair.

"While I was waiting for the percolator, I wrote down my opposite number's details for Rose to contact," Mary said when she returned.

"Rose should be home by now, Agra's four and a half hours ahead of us so I'll give her a call and give her the details,"

"Go ahead Captain, but don't leave me to make the approach to Rome please," Mary said.

"Rose, you're home," I spoke with relief in my voice.

"Yes, I've just got in. I'm a little puffed from hurrying in case I missed you after I nominated the time. Did you enjoy your send-off darling?"

"A little hair-raising, I told you I had never done it before," I answered.

"Then I'm pleased to have relieved you of your virginity after you relieved me of mine last night," Rose replied. "It was delicious darling."

"I thought you must have enjoyed it when the Saudi Air Base Adjutant passed on your tight-formation remark. He didn't get it, but Mary and I did of course."

"So, Mary knows what we were up to," Rose asked.

"Of course, darling I told you Mary gave me the condom. If you've a pen handy I'll give you the details for Mary's opposite number at Delhi. She will give you every help to find out if I'm the one worthy to father your children or whether there is someone better they can put you in touch with; either way you'll get what you want if you desire to be a mother?"

"Let it be you please darling," Rose asked, "I've never wanted anything else so badly."

I dictated the name and details for the professor at Delhi University for Rose to contact.

"I'm already registered with the Delhi University Brad," Rose began. "The university canvassed all air force personnel for DNA samples three months ago and most of us at Agra complied."

"Mary will be meeting the professor from Delhi when we get to Cambridge Rose; I think the best thing to do is leave it to Mary to arrange," I told her.

“Yes, please Brad: only you can be the father of my baby. I don’t want anybody else darling, good night,” Rose said as she hurriedly broke off our conversation.

I had visions of Rose sobbing far away and alone in Agra.

“Feel better now darling?” Mary asked.

“Yes, I gave Rose the details, but she’s already provided her DNA to the university along with most of the people on the base. We’re leaving it for you to talk to the professor from Delhi when we get to Cambridge. Rose assures me she is happy, but I think she brought the call to a close quickly to have a good cry.”

“Are you starting to see what affect you have on women Adonis: it’s not just me,” Mary said. “Let’s stay on board tonight darling, I want to cook you a proper meal and use our fine China. We could get out the flutes. You could send our happy snaps from the Taj to all the people waiting for them.

“And then we can go to bed early for a change; none of this rushing to get it in before midnight. I haven’t had time to tell you about my night out in the Mess. My date was pretty swish too; you didn’t see him,” Mary said.

“To a lady he’d look pretty dashing in his uniform too I guess?” I replied. “Isn’t he getting on a bit though?”

“Not at all he’s only forty-eight and very distinguished; he could sweep a girl of her feet,” Mary replied with some passion. I won’t mind if you’ll be thinking of Rose darling,” Mary offered.

“Do you want to be thinking of Geoff, Mary?” I teased her.

“Not at all; he could never do for me what you do,” Mary answered.

"Tomorrow Brad we can have a day off. With no early departure to make we can lie in. Start the day with a bang; phone the folks back home. It will take us quite a while to throw all the coins we've been collecting. We could have lunch out and an early night," Mary said.

"Sounds delicious, Mary. I'm going to take the camcorder tomorrow and send them video clips of their coins going into the air rather than trying to get stills," I replied.

"They'll love that darling," Mary assured me.

"Darling, in the time we have available before your goddesses descend on you, I'd like to declare every day a special occasion," Mary began after a short pause.

"You mean we will fuck twice a day from now on?"

"In the interest of science darling and preparing for your future: I want you to use a collection condom and I'll test your semen volume and sperm count," Mary replied.

"It's not as good as going bare-back darling," I said.

"I know darling; it's not as nice for me either: not feeling you come inside me and go all squishy. But it will give us a lot of information about your ability to father children. Besides, you've given me everything in the lab to do these tests professionally," Mary added and gave me one of her most disarming and enchanting smiles.

"They are all special occasion days now Mary and I'm always happy to play my part: so long as when we fuck you are still Aphrodite and not a stuffy university professor."

"I can't be anything but Aphrodite when I'm in your arms Adonis: no matter if we have clothes, condoms or anything else."

"How did my samples from yesterday turn out?" I asked.

“Volume wise terrific: particularly as there was less than two hours between Rose and me; the sperm motility values are measured over time and I’ll be assessing them again when we reach Rome.”

“Back to work Lieutenant; here comes out descent for Rome,” I said. It was all business again.

We were given clearances for the descent and approach to Centocelle Military Airport. We were both feeling more comfortable with international flying seeing it was not yet a week since our first flight. Since being adopted by the India Air Force everything had become so much easier. This time at fifty nautical miles from **Rome http://www.futuristic.guru/rome** a Eurofighter Typhoon loomed up near my wingtip and the pilot welcomed us to Rome. He introduced himself as Major Romero and said they liked to give first time visitors to their airport a lead-in as the approach can be a little tricky. He explained that he would stay downwind of Alpha Uniform and once I had captured the glide path he would land after us so we didn’t get any of his jet wash. I thanked him for his consideration and now I only had to do another greaser to show that we were worth it and at the same time probably capable of getting there unaided.

“You wouldn’t get that at a commercial airport darling,” Mary said through her mike.

“If Rose was calling us to Agra it wasn’t just for her needs,” I replied.

Our approach and landing were performed by the book and seeing Alpha Uniform joining up with FOLLOW ME Major Romero bid us adieu. As soon as we had parked a staff car brought the Base Adjutant to our door and this time instead of going to his office or the Officers’ Mess, we invited him on board. When we were offered the hospitality of the base we politely declined as we had been in the air for forty hours in the last six days and now craved sleep and a quiet time before flying on to England on Sunday morning. For now, the one duty we had in Rome was to throw many coins into the Trevi Fountain. The Adjutant was most impressed that we would come this way to visit their famous fountain and in addition to stamping our passports and filling in his log he gave us temporary visas for tomorrow to carry along with our passports. He arranged our refuelling and said a car and driver would be at our disposal tomorrow morning. He admired Alpha Uniform's fit-out and we showed him through in detail and answered all his questions. After he left, I attended to the refuelling and Mary spent some time in her lab examining slides of my sperm. When I returned, she sat me at the microscope to view slides from my two specimens. Mary showed me how the size, shape and characteristics of the head and tail of my sperm were so ideally formed and explained how the volume of semen, and the sperm count of each specimen, were such that each ejaculation could easily have resulted in a pregnancy, had an ovum presented itself during the life-time of my sperm.

"You chose an excellent microscope darling," Mary said and clicked the screen on her notebook computer. "This is the enlargement of what you were viewing, and it's all being recorded so I can measure the life of your sperm. Would you like to see a human egg cell?"

I nodded, and Mary selected another file on the notebook and immediately a round colourful egg almost filled the screen. Surrounding the egg were thousands of male sperm all trying to penetrate the cell and in the following frames one, and only one, sperm had succeeded in breaking through.

"That was my specimen from yesterday morning darling and your sperm from the night before. I would have been pregnant now if I had a uterus where my fertilised egg could implant."

I swivelled the lab chair around and took Mary down onto my lap.

"Can dinner wait a while Aphrodite?" I asked and kissed her.

"Of course, it can Adonis," Mary replied and started undoing my shirt.

Not wanting to risk the lab chair to any stresses we stood up to quickly undress. I closed the cabin door while Mary unwrapped a collection condom. I made a great show of presenting my hard-on for her to cover and then took her down onto the divan where we clung together for some kisses and cuddles before Mary opened her legs. It had been an early start and a long flight, but we were both wide awake and refreshed. Whether it was the sight of Mary's egg being fertilized by my sperm that had refreshed and excited us we didn't know but we both confessed afterwards to having felt as randy as hell.

"Biology was never as good as this Professor Aphrodite," I said acknowledging Mary's desire to study my sperm production as a scientist, but also that she was still Adonis's lover Aphrodite.

With passionate kisses while holding her in my right arm, my left hand found those areas of her back that excited her the most. I made every effort to fill my condom with semen for her to study while Mary, with contractions of her vagina milked me for the last drop. This time we didn't wait for my old fella to go slack in case we lost some of the condom's contents in the process. I rolled it off carefully, knotted it and wrapped it in tissue.

"Just as well we scientists don't have to collect all our specimens this way Adonis," Mary said with a big smile coming over her face and her eyes bright.

"It would be a mile-long queue outside your lab door Professor Aphrodite," I told her and took her in my arms to kiss.

"I'll get dinner darling," Mary said.

While Mary prepared our meal, I turned my computer on and saw there was an email waiting for me from Rose:

Hi Brad – Have a look at the attachments I hope you like them:

The Alpha Uniform shots are from Vice in our camera ship which also accompanied us to Surat.

Roger gave me the one of you three at the Taj Mahal. A friend of his saw you coming but didn't let you know he had taken any photos.

You were right lover there was a camera at the restaurant and it was aimed at us, I think it's very nice – hope you do too.

Love Rose

The first photo in the attachment was a very good shot of Mary in the middle holding onto Roger and me. The second and third photos were of Rose and me dancing and singing to each other; they were beautifully clear photos that captured that instant in our dance but also the expression in our eyes. The next five photos were of Alpha Uniform in various stages of our flight. They showed us lifting off with the F18s slightly behind and further apart. The three of us climbing out and turning at the Old Fort in a banked climb with the three planes working as one. The next shot showed us in straight and level flight with the escorts in tight formation guarding Alpha Uniform. The break away at Surat was spectacular as each F18 peeled off on opposite banked turns and finally Alpha Uniform leaving the coast of India alone and facing the vast expanse of the Arabian Sea.

I immediately hit the 'Reply' button.

Dear Rose – Thank you so much for the photos. I think they are terrific; particularly the two of us. The Alpha Uniform series is great for the story of Bravo Mike Charlie on this trip. Please thank Roger, Vice and Geoff for the Alpha Uniform series and the photographer from the restaurant if he ever turns up. If he is looking for payment, ask him to give you his account details and I will be happy to pay him.

Love to you Rose until I can come back.

I clicked 'Send'.

I took the time to download the photos from the Taj Mahal and make my selection of which photo to send to the people on my mailing list. The one of Mary and me kissing was reserved for Doc, Bob and Kay the others were sorted for family, Don, other members of Mary's staff and the rest of Bruce's friends in the outback who had looked after us. I thought of sending one or two to the Australian news agencies but that would be unwise and challenging. With each email I planned to attach a couple of shots of the Taj Mahal. I selected the best I had taken from the air and one or two from Roger's collection. With my sorting done and only waiting for Mary to see what I had selected and help me compose the accompanying notes there was nothing more to be done before dinner. I had got myself a cold beer when I returned from my work outside and now had another good drink from my crystal beer mug; drinking from the bottle or can was all right on a camping trip but not if there was a glass of any description about. On Bravo Mike Charlie all glassware was crystal. For the first time this trip I got the electronic keyboard from my desk cupboard. All members of the Clifford family and the Franklins could dance, sing a bit and play a musical instrument at various levels of competency. Mary and I were right at home in the outback as that was the way we had been brought up. For me it had been the piano. At

Bob and Kay's I hadn't taken a spell at the keyboard as there had always been others willing to slide onto the seat. For a moment I was Gene Kelly and Mary was the young Debbie Reynolds as they sung from SINGING IN THE RAIN:

At this point Mary emerged from the bathroom, "Where did you get that? I didn't pack it for you," I asked.

Mary was wearing an elegant pale blue sari that had a raised and very delicate pattern over its surface. She had also emphasised her eye makeup to enhance that beguiling look Bollywood actresses are noted for.

"Rose left it with Geoff for me last night," Mary said, "I think that she was a little too shy to give it to me when she called for you."

"Considering her job bossing those young pilots around and having spent so much time in workshops with engineers she is very shy, quiet and retiring. She hadn't seen a man with a hard-on until last night and was concerned that it wouldn't fit in," I thought it no harm telling Mary this: I just wanted her to understand Rose better. I would never tell another soul.

"I know darling, I know you would have taken it very gently; Rose is very special, and I would love her to carry my grandchild," Mary sealed it with a big kiss and I found her soft breast through the folds of her sari. "Now have your shower while I get our dinner ready,"

I shaved, showered, and was ready for dinner as Mary was dishing-up.

I poured our wine and we sat and toasted each other. Mary slipped out of her seat and came back with the soup and chunky herb bread. We now had time to talk. "I've had an email from Rose with some happy snaps for us," I began. I went on to tell Mary what they showed and that we would look at them after dinner and send off our Taj

Mahal photos. Some of the new pics could also be included.

As we ate, we considered the route we would take to visit the other twelve university cities for their Faculty opening. In the coming months we will be visiting Paris, Ghent, Moscow, Ankara, Beijing, Tokyo, Delhi, Kuala Lumpur, Abuja, Los Angeles, Mexico City, Brasilia and then to Washington DC to meet the President. We wouldn't know the sequence in which the faculties will be opened until we reach Cambridge, but we took the time to consider the weather conditions we might expect as we travelled. We were particularly aware of the benefit being adopted by the Indian Air Force was going to be.

By the time we had finished dinner it was nine-thirty. We decided to get our photos off to our family and friends before ten o'clock, so we could get to bed early for a change. Besides, we had agreed this morning that until my goddesses arrived every day would be a special occasion and wearing a condom wasn't so bad after all.

Mary agreed that my selection of photographs matched the recipients. We included the one of Mary, Roger and me arm-in-arm at the Taj Mahal but decided to hold the Alpha Uniform photos for the book I would publish at the end of the trip. Mary persuaded me that the photos of Rose and me dancing should be provided, through an intermediary, to the social editor of the Canberra Times to show that Brad Clifford wasn't wasting any time in getting to know the ladies. Mary shared the job of putting the appropriate comments to the emails and sending them off at her computer. Today's work was done at ten o'clock and we could go to bed.

Although winter was closing in at our destination it was still a mild night in Rome. We laid on top of the sheets with the blankets pulled back, the lights dimmed and soft music playing. I started to undo my sari wrapped lover. It's just like Christmas I told Mary or when she enrolled me in the Mile-High-Club out over the Gulf of Carpentaria: Mary had gift wrapped herself on that occasion too. Finally, with Mary unwrapped but with the sari pulled up over her back she slid my boxer shorts off my hips and I kicked them out of bed. My sports shirt went too, and we came together in a warm embrace.

"Another lovely day thanks Adonis," Mary said. "We were in the air for fourteen hours and then with time on the ground before we left, our time in Riyadh and now with little under two hours to go until midnight we've had a twenty-eight hour and thirty-minute day."

"That's the beauty of flying west Aphrodite," I replied. "It's going to be different going home."

"Home is where the heart is Adonis," Mary said. "Is your heart here with me or in Agra with Rose?"

"There is no point in me pining for Rose if I might never see her again Aphrodite," I said. "We've agreed to live in day-tight compartments."

"What happened to Rose, Adonis, was the same thing that happened to me when I woke in your arms. Now do you understand what I have been saying? Last Saturday night you broke out. You stepped out of the shadows and in thirty minutes showed yourself to be a man of distinction. darling you held that hall full of dignitaries in the palm of your hand: not just the women but the men too. Just think back over the past six days; the men in the outback accepted you as a mate before your birthday party but that was mainly on their friendship with Bruce, they would expect to do as much as they could to help. Last Sunday and Monday though it was a completely different matter they knew what you had done for me, they also knew what you were doing to me or I should say we were doing together. They were proud of the fact that you could short field Bob's Cessna and marvelled at what you had done to Bravo Mike Charlie. Rose grabbed you in the Mess because she was the smartest, most intelligent girl there. She was a shy twenty-five-year-old virgin as you said but she had the good sense not to waste her time on any man who failed to meet her ideals."

"I'm feeling weak Mary," I began. "Are all girls going to throw themselves at me?"

"No darling only the most suitable girls for you would dare; what we have seen with this instant passion between you and Rose is a sudden realisation that here was someone you're truly compatible with; it was a relief for both of you wasn't it?" Mary asked.

"Of course, but she's not you Mary," I answered.

"But she can give you children and help you change the world," Mary said.

"But I'm still only one man and even if I impregnate one hundred girls a year it's going to take a long time to make a profound effect on this world," I replied.

"You're the mathematician Brad," Mary began. "But you're forgetting basic geometric progression. You're dwelling on the one hundred girls you need to fuck but forgetting the one hundred babies they will produce. In eighteen years' time you are going to have fifty sons a year joining you: each impregnating one or two hundred girls a year. Each year another fifty sons will be joining your army and after eighteen years ten thousand grandsons will join your ranks each year. darling, within fifty years you will be the most recent common ancestor of every person of child bearing age and every child born thereafter. You will be the new Y-chromosomal Adam."

"My God," was all I could say when I realised how narrow my focus had become.

While she had been talking Mary had undone the collection condom and she now claimed my lips again and reached her hands down between us to roll the condom onto my now hard horn.

"Let's fuck Adonis," Mary said.

Saturday 15 December 2012 – 0700 hrs

I woke on this Saturday morning in a vastly different state and on a different continent than the one from only one week before. Mary didn't even know about this boudoir then until near midnight when she donned her lab coat and pinned on her badge.

"Roll back darling," I heard Mary say. Mary was pushing me onto my back with her left hand and holding onto my Morning Glory with her right. I fell onto my back as Mary rolled the condom on and straddled me.

"I promised I would fuck you awake today, and you promised to fuck me to sleep tonight, Adonis, and I always keep my promises," Mary was Aphrodite again claiming her lover's lips, denying him any chance to reply.

I responded by answering with kisses and helped support Mary by cupping her breasts in my hands, with my elbows on the bed and taking some of her weight Mary could plunge on me the harder. It didn't take long before Mary was rolling us back on our sides and pulling her lips away from mine and her head back a little so that she could look me in the eye said:

"Are you awake now Adonis?"

"I certainly am and ready to go: almost," I replied.

"So, I kept my promise then?" Mary asked.

"Of course, and I'll keep mine tonight," I answered her and received a big hug. "But you won't go to sleep before I finish keeping my promise, will you?"

"No but you will be judged on how quickly I go to sleep afterwards," darling.

"Today's our first day to ourselves, a real special occasion," Mary added.

While Mary prepared breakfast, I listed the names of the people for whom we will throw coins.

"We didn't get to talk more about this fatal charm I'm supposed to have for women darling," I said. "We got carried away before we finished that topic. I asked you about others coming to me like Rose and you replied only the very special ones and others wouldn't dare."

"That's right Brad; unless you gave them the slightest encouragement and then they would be all over you. Age, colour, caste, creed, social status, marital status; none of these things would matter to them," Mary explained.

"Rose could be Adonis's goddess in India?" I asked.

"She could be darling. One girl between eighteen and twenty-eight years old in a country of 1.2 billion people is a long-shot, but possible," Mary said. "I hope so darling; I really like her. If Darwin had seen what I saw when you two were together he would have claimed that was proof of natural selection and the survival of the species."

"When will we know who these girls are?" I asked a little sheepishly.

"When we get to Cambridge darling, all the professors will be there to reveal the girl from their area and I'll be there to reveal Adonis to them. We must do it properly darling. I don't want my first act as chairperson to ride roughshod over them," Mary said. "Can't I have you to myself for just three more nights Adonis?"

"Of course, Aphrodite, I only wanted you in the first place. Being Adonis and having three goddesses wasn't my idea. Do I have to father children with the three girls if they show up?" I asked.

"It won't be a hardship I promise you. You'll fall for them as completely as you have for Rose and just as you can love Rose and me too: even to the extent of fucking us both on the one night. You did enjoy it and find satisfaction with both of us, didn't you?"

"Of course, you know I did," I was feeling a little sad at the thought of Mary being disappointed.

"I know," Mary consoled me and stretched her hand over the table to take mine and squeeze it. "I was just trying to convince you that you we're doing nothing wrong. You'll find that these girls will be seeking different satisfactions from you and you will be giving them that. They won't mind sharing: they'll probably become the best of friends knowing that when you are not with them you will be with someone they trust," Mary said. "We should be heading to the Trevi Fountain. Can we talk more about this when we get back so that we can really make this our special day?"

"Of course, we can, we've got from here to Cambridge before your new duties take over. While you're getting ready, I'll go over to the Adjutant's office and sort out our departure time for tomorrow and our driver for this morning."

I visited the Adjutant and told him that we would like to be taking off as near to eight o'clock as convenient. The Adjutant assured me that eight o'clock local time would be satisfactory, and we would be sent-off on a direct route for Calais. Once we entered UK airspace we would be directed to RAF Wyton where we are expected and would be based while in the UK.

I asked the Adjutant if he knew of a professional photographer I might engage for an hour or two at the Trevi Fountain only to be told that our driver today would be Lieutenant Raoul whose other job on the base was official photographer. "Please keep him with you as long as you need him," the Adjutant said.

Lieutenant Raoul turned out to be as obliging and knowledgeable as Roger had been in Agra. On arriving at the fountain, he explained to me that he would do a ten-second pan of the area applying his own voice-over saying, he suggested:

Today at the Trevi Fountain in Rome
With
Professor Mary and Brad Clifford

He would leave a ten second break between this introduction and the first coins thrown to allow Mary and me time to take the position he had for us in front of the Fountain. We would have the same break between each throw, so we could swap or change our pose. When we copied each clip to email, we could add the intro to each. Mary went first with me at her side:

Mum and Dad here go your coins
Make your wishes
We're having a wonderful time and will talk again soon

We moved through our list. Mary had worn a bright print frock for this occasion and I a sports shirt to add more colour to our videos. I had anticipated I would be able to buy fifty new Euros at a money changer for the coins we were going to throw for friends. Included in this list were our dining partners from Saturday night including, the Chancellor, Pro-Chancellor, Don the Vice-Chancellor of course, the Governor General, Doc, our house-sitters: Chris, Jo, Rick and Carol, our cousin Jan and the friends who had looked after us on our run from the media but were not present at Bob and Kay's. Finally, at one o'clock we had finished. Lieutenant Raoul had become engrossed in this morning's shoot and knowing that his charges only had today available to them, offered to drive us around the major sites for the rest of the day. Mary and I were happy to accept provided Lieutenant Raoul accompanied us to a light lunch first. The afternoon passed quickly as we were taken to the Forum, the Vatican. St Peter's Cathedral, the Colosseum and Palatine Hill, the Pantheon, the Piazza Navona and the Stadium. Each site was approached so that I could get out and take my photographs from the best possible position for the available light. It was eight o'clock when we arrived back to Alpha Uniform and as Raoul had expressed interest in Alpha Uniform, we invited him aboard.

"I'll get us a snack," Mary said after Raoul departed.

I started both computers and downloaded the day's video and stills. With the number of coins we had thrown there was quite a bit we had to do before we went to bed. In my mind was the fact that Cliffords never made promises they couldn't keep, and nothing would keep me from delivering on mine tonight, besides every day was a special occasion day now. By the time Mary was back with our snack I was well into joining the intro with the throwing sequence and copying each segment to a new file in the name of the recipient. It was agreed that Mary would do a short note to each, attach our video-clip and click the send button. With Mary proceeding faster than me it was only one minute after I had finished my editing that Mary had the last email on its way.

"Well, that feels good," Mary said. "I'm sure there will be some happy faces around tomorrow."

"You first darling," Mary smiled indicating the bathroom.

"You always go first," I replied.

"Yes, but that is only your good manners putting the lady first," Mary replied. "Tonight's my treat so you can be waiting in bed for me instead of the other way around,"

Mary ended the discussion and I headed for the bathroom kicking of my casual shoes as I went. I was quite proficient in the limited space that our bathroom offered and had soon shaved. Mary could hear the shower running and as she tidied our workspace, selected a playlist and started singing along with the first number — WHAT A DIFFERENCE A DAY MADE ...

When I reappeared wearing nothing, but a smile Mary was waiting to enter the bathroom stark naked as well. She only accepted a brief passing kiss before she entered.

"Don't start without me darling," she called.

Mary's boudoir was softly lit and there was a delicate perfume in the air. Mary hadn't been wasting her time while I was showering. I had nothing to do but wait and listen to the music. It was all emotive of course as I had a penchant for the old love songs. I lay back on the pillows and let my thoughts drift to Mary. My old fella came up hot and strong as it had done in Doc's surgery. I took the opportunity to roll on the collection condom and resolved to fill it again for Mary tonight; after all, today it had been fourteen hours between encounters, yesterday had been five hours and the day before between Rose and Mary only two hours. The whole project of Mary validating my potency was becoming a fascinating exercise since I saw a swarm of my little swimmers attacking Mary's vastly bigger egg. I marvelled at how my sperm was still living on outside my body, seeking an ovum to impregnate. I saw the lights go out in the rest of the cabin and then saw Mary peeping around our privacy curtain. She glided into the boudoir and in the very limited space did a very nice dance suggestive of the 'Dance of the Seven Veils' until at last seeing me lying there dressed only in my condom she came near enough for me to pull away her final veil and clutch her to me. "Let's not talk any more about serious things darling," Mary pleaded. "We've got three hours for that on our way to Cambridge."

I answered her simply by kissing her continuously and massaging any stresses I could find in her neck, shoulders, arms and back. Of course, I didn't deny her breasts and inner thighs although I didn't expect to find stresses there. After about fifteen minutes of my attentions and the soft music playing in the background Mary could easily have drifted off to sleep if it were not for her knees opening wide as if involuntarily to ensure that she wouldn't be denied. We had entered that mystical place where time and space drifted away. I had kept one arm holding her to me, my left hand on her right breast and long and gentle kisses on her lips, while keeping a slow rhythmic pulsation in her vagina; tonight, she felt no need to help me in any way. Was I showing her how gently I had taken away Rose's virginity: if so Mary was delighted to understand how Rose, so desperate to have me for a lover but knowing so little of what to do, found herself in the embrace of the one man who could so gently raise her to these new sensations and delights. With these thoughts in her mind Mary found herself in a sustained orgasm unlike any she could remember. It lacked any of the extreme passion and feelings that so often accompanied her climax, no vocalising, not even extremely heavy breathing and panting but a beautiful fulfilling orgasm none the less as I too climaxed and she felt my semen fill the end of the condom. For a moment she regretted the professor who was using Adonis and Aphrodite for her investigations; she would have much preferred to have that burst of semen lubricating the walls of her vagina. Nothing had been spoken as words were not required. After a few minutes, Mary felt me slip out of her. I was supported by our two pillows and in a half sitting position. I had moved so that Mary's left hip was supported on the bed, her legs with knees together now were raised across me and over my other side, her head lay on my chest and still with my right arm supporting her back with my left hand I deftly removed my condom and knotted it with without spilling a drop. I returned my left hand to gently stroke her wavy hair and the last thing that she was conscious of was me singing so quietly:

Lullaby and good night,
With roses bedight,
With lilies o'er spread
Is baby's wee bed.
Lay thee down now and rest,
May thy slumber be blessed.

Sunday 16 December 2012 – 1400 hrs

"**RAF Wyton http://www.futuristic.guru/raf-wyton** this is Pilatus Alpha Uniform," Mary heard me saying as she came back from testing last night's samples.

"Alpha Uniform this is RAF Wyton Go Ahead please."

"Alpha Uniform mid-Channel en-route Cambridge," I answered.

"Alpha Uniform call for clearance at Harwich"

"Alpha Uniform," I acknowledged.

"It won't be long now Aphrodite," I said when I received our landing instructions at Harwich. From the ATIS I knew that I had a 20-knot crosswind from 40 degrees to contend with and had Alpha Uniform crabbing into the wind early in my approach. The right wheel touched down at the instant I brought her nose onto the centreline and the left wheel followed before her nose wheel settled to run out truly and roll up to the FOLLOW ME vehicle. We were led to the hangar that had been provided for us then with a wave the driver pulled away.

Mary and I had each packed an overnight bag for our first night at the hotel. Mary took a smart suit and I a casual suit, shirts and a couple of ties. I too would be introduced to the Chancellor tomorrow and I didn't want to let Mary down with my appearance. After all, Mary made a very smart impression whatever she was wearing.

Within two minutes, the Customs car pulled up to check Alpha Uniform for contraband and validate our passports. A man and woman stepped out: a captain and a lieutenant. I met them at the steps and ushered them on board to do their inspection. They had never seen another aircraft of its size so thoroughly fitted out. Mary happily made all her drawers, cupboards and wardrobes available to them and took no offence at the woman's need to rummage through her underwear or anything else. Mary was more cautious with the lab as the equipment was valuable and fragile in the wrong hands. However, there was nothing to concern the customs people. I had placed our open overnight bags on the table for inspection and shown the male officer the workings of the toilet and shower. The inspection was complete. They asked us to complete our entry cards and then stamped our passports. We were told that now we had been cleared into England we could fly anywhere in the British Isles and the EU as a local flight with no further customs entries required. All of this was good news.

"Group Captain Page asked me to extend his apologies Brad," Captain Williams told me. "He's off the base for a couple of days; he said he will phone you to make a time to meet with you and Professor Mary when he returns."

"I do hope you have a rewarding time in England Professor Mary," Captain Williams said. "Can we offer you a lift into Cambridge?"

"Thank you, my next question was going to be, 'Where do we get a taxi?' We're booked in at the Menzies tonight."

"That will be no trouble at all we were going in to Cambridge after checking you in."

We had chosen Menzies for this first night more on its name association with Australia and the ANU than anything else; except that it was close to the university;

we will make other arrangements when our future commitments are known.

We had booked a two-bedroom suite, for propriety's sake. We hung our clothes in the wardrobe for tomorrow's meeting with the Chancellor and left everything else until we had a light lunch at the buffet in the dining room. I had brought my notebook computer with me, as it wasn't certain when we would get back to the Pilatus, and I would be checking to see whether there were any responses to our emails. We made our selection from the buffet and found a table in the quietest part of the dining room.

"We made it darling," I was first to speak, "Half-way around the world in six days with parties and great times all the way."

"I had no doubt whatsoever that you would deliver me safely, Brad, even if I had to take a little punishment along the way," Mary teased me.

"I didn't hear you complain darling, I would have stopped immediately if I ever thought I would hurt or disappoint you," I assured her.

"I wasn't complaining darling and I hate to make comparisons even between one moment and the next; but last night was exquisite," Mary said. "I hope you got some sleep too. I woke up to see you still watching over me, I had been sleeping like a baby."

"There's a nice big spa up there and a Do Not Disturb for the door knob," I suggested.

"FOLLOW ME," was all that Mary said.

Undressing each other and stepping into the spa brought some real-world normality back into our lives. I had no need to keep my head down as I moved about the cabin and a spa offers so much more than a shower can ever do.

“Would you like to wash my hair darling?” Mary asked, “But don’t put me to sleep please I don’t want to miss a minute.”

I was sitting with my back to the side of the spa and Mary in my lap with her back to my chest. I had been holding her breasts from behind and now released her so that I could free her hair from its pony tail and spread it out. I turned her around bringing her up to lay on me so that I could kiss her and at the same time run the shampoo through her hair with my fingers.

“He does get in the way sometimes,” Mary remarked as my old fella started demanding more of the space between us. “I’d like to put him where he fits best but that would be better after our spa wouldn’t it?”

“Yes darling, I want to concentrate on one job at a time for you,” I replied.

“I’ll just hold him between my thighs then, so we can stay closer together,” Mary said and we laughed again. “Without having my lab handy there’s no point in collecting your semen Brad. But we can still make these days special occasions darling.”

Now safely delivered to England and a new life opening-up from tomorrow it was as if we were saying goodbye to the past. We went slow to ensure we took all our good memories with us and from coming together on the bed for our first kiss until finally releasing all our emotions in a cry of delight an hour had passed.

“What say we stay here and order room service for tonight?” Mary suggested. “I don’t want to get dressed and mix with other people.”

"That's great by me darling, will you order?" I asked. "Would you like a cold drink from the mini-bar?"

"I'll join you in a cold beer darling," Mary replied. "Let's put a wrap on for a while; we could even watch the TV news for a change. Have you seen whether we have any emails yet?"

"I'll log on now Mary," I replied. "Yes, there are replies from almost all of them. You'll have to read them yourself there are so many."

I skimmed through the list; opening and reading those I was most interest in. The academics I hardly knew. Rose's answer after the expected thank you read: 'Bet you can't guess what I wished for Brad?' I immediately answered, 'Bet I can.' I then came to my cousin Jan. 'Who was that lovely girl you were dancing with Brad? She made me feel so jealous.' The photo of Rose and me dancing to PEOPLE WILL SAY WE'RE IN LOVE was added as an attachment to Jan's email; it had been scanned from Sunday's Canberra Times with the caption 'Brad Clifford not wasting any time meeting the local lasses on his world trip.' I left it to Mary to open the replies that interested her, and I made no special mention of Rose or Jan's responses. I knew that Mary would look at them too.

Mary accepted the room service trolley from the waiter at the door and handed him one of my five-dollar notes. She brought the trolley to the easy chair where I was sitting and pulled up a chair for herself. She handed me one plate of the lobster salad and took the other for herself and after sitting we toasted each other with our beer and ate our salad.

"Many emails darling?" Mary asked between mouthfuls.

"Nearly everyone has replied," I said, "I didn't open them all but the photo of me dancing with Rose was in this morning's Canberra Times with a caption that said something like Brad Clifford not wasting any time."

"Well that's true isn't it," Mary chided me. "Twenty-four hours and you were ripping each other's clothes off."

"We didn't rip any clothes darling," I replied. "I was most careful about that."

"Don't worry darling it will be good publicity for you," Mary began. "I told you everyone would be expecting you to sow your wild oats on this trip. Now when you get home everyone will be satisfied."

Mary went to the bathroom and I put our dinner trolley outside the door; after my trip to the bathroom we turned off the TV and main lights and headed back to bed. It was only nine o'clock, but the past week had been very intense; but If we didn't fall asleep quickly it didn't matter. Mary's appointment wasn't until eleven o'clock on Monday, so we had plenty of time in the morning to do anything that might be required. Mary would have a look at our emails then. We didn't go straight to sleep. I was holding Mary in my arms and kissing her in between more questions.

"Where will these girls be?" I asked.

"The professors from each of the universities will provide our list of prospects Brad and they'll brief the girls we select on what is required."

"Would that mean that I might be impregnating a Russian in Moscow, a Spanish girl in Madrid, a black girl in Nigeria, a Chinese girl in Beijing, a Japanese in Tokyo and a Brazilian girl in Brasilia?" I asked.

"Would that be so terrible darling," Mary replied. "I noticed that you didn't mention the Indian girl in Delhi."

"I didn't mention the English girl or the Australian girl either darling," I replied.

"Brad, as I said before," Mary began again, "they will all be beautiful, all very different, all very intelligent, all very suited to carry your child, all will know exactly where they stand with you and the Faculty and all will know that you can't provide any fatherly support to their child, but the Faculty will. They will all part in the knowledge that they are carrying a child who one day will play a major role in world affairs."

"Not quite in yet darling, I'm only holding you in my thighs," Mary whispered. My answer was simple. I pulled her closer to me and kissed her passionately, as Mary's thigh came up my fingers were opening the Gates to Paradise for my swollen head to enter.

"I'm so relieved darling. You have no idea how important this is going to be for the world," Mary explained. "There will be generations of clear-thinking men and women coming," Mary managed to whisper these things before being overcome by her desire to please me with everything she could give me. She wanted to go to sleep tonight not in the delicate way that she had done the night before but totally exhausted, utterly fucked.

"Shoosh darling, I said I'd do anything for you and I meant it. I'll keep my promise."

There was no time for talk now for I sealed her lips with kisses, only breaking away when her breathing became distressed and then Mary would seek my lips again. I fondled her breasts, teased her nipples, ran my hands up and down her back. At other times my hands stroked her inner thighs and occasional I slipped a finger in to tickle her clit. All the time Mary was following Doc's prescription and showing me how well she could excel by holding my old fella tight so that I couldn't move, but by her sending rippling sensations up and down my shaft I felt that I was providing the motion. She would release me and with legs wrapped around me encourage long thrust from me. We had never had any interest in anal sex and very little oral sex for that matter. Our bodies always wanted to feel the other front-on and enjoy kisses to lips, brow, neck and breasts. My horn always wanted to go home into the sheath Mary had for it.

"I'm done Adonis," Mary whispered at last.

"Brace yourself Aphrodite," I replied, and our orgasms were stronger than any we had experienced.

There was nothing left unsaid, nothing that needed to be discussed with any fear of upsetting the other and perhaps damaging our most unusual and exquisite relationship. We both knew that tomorrow would be the beginning of a new life for each of us but as we had promised to live in day-tight compartments we gave our tomorrows no thought.

"You told me that I had no need to change in any way for my new job Brad and now I'm telling you the same. You have plenty of love to satisfy all of us," Mary whispered her last words for the day. "You'll have no need to build a Taj Mahal to declare your love for a departed wife. Your goddesses' children will declare that."

Monday 17 December 2012 – 1100 hrs

I held the door to the Chancellor's outer office open for Mary to precede me.

"Good morning Professor Mary. It's so good to see you here; I'll let the Chancellor know you've arrived," the Chancellor's secretary greeted Mary.

"This way Professor Mary the Chancellor will see you now," the secretary put down her phone and ushered Mary to the door.

"Professor Mary I'm truly delighted to welcome you to Cambridge," The Chancellor began. "I've followed your work for years and I'm most happy you have accepted this post," the Chancellor said as he ushered Mary into his office.

I took a seat in a comfortable visitor's chair and picked up a copy of this year's Cambridge University Review. I had only scanned the opening pages when the Chancellor came out of his office.

"Come in Brad, I didn't realise you were waiting," the Chancellor welcomed me with his hand outstretched.

"How do you do sir?" I greeted the Chancellor as the door closed behind him.

"I was just telling Mary that my name is John and I would prefer you to use that on these informal occasions," John advised.

"Thank you very much John," I replied. "Might I ask if you have a relationship to the late Reverend?" I knew the Chancellor would know to whom I was referring.

"Unfortunately, no, my parents admired him greatly as I do," the Chancellor began. "I'm sure there is no need for me to tell you how important his work was to Australia and the world."

"No John, his is one of the special lives that inspire me. Do you know that the RFDS now operates the fourth largest fleet of aircraft in Australia and half the fleet are Pilatus PC-12s as ours is?" I offered.

"It confirms again what one man can achieve doesn't it?" John said not expecting an answer. "And you and Mary have flown alone from Australia?" John continued.

"It's not the challenge that the early aviators were faced with John. Brad had her refitted when he thought that I was just going with him on his GAP year to get away for a while," Mary spoke with obvious pride. "We can stay aloft for eight hours at 500 kilometres an hour, we've got a complete galley, bathroom, workspaces and I've even got a lab," Mary told him.

"I'd like to see her; I used to fly myself, nothing like yours of course, mine was a Cessna 172."

"I'll be available any time to show you over John," I offered, "I've always got my phone with me, but our other details are on the card including Bravo Mike Charlie's ground to air phone. We must add another call sign now as we've been granted military status by the India Air Force as Pilatus Alpha Uniform. We were assigned Alpha Uniform as AU is the international abbreviation for Australia. We flew military routes under the military commands of India, Saudi Arabia, Italy and the UK since we left Agra. It has been a great benefit; we disappear from the commercial airwaves, we get military processing of all customs requirements, we don't go near an international terminal where photographers and reporters hang about asking stupid questions and we have top class security. It is going to be of immense value as we go on to open the other twelve universities on the list."

"How did you manage that Brad?" John asked.

"I don't really know," I began. "It all started when I asked the Chancellor at the ANU if he would ask his opposite number in Delhi to get us permission to divert to India Air Force's strip at Agra. I knew Mary wanted to see the Taj Mahal and I didn't like the thought of driving between Delhi International and Agra. I didn't know until I Googled 'University of Delhi' that the Chancellor's other job was Vice-President of India, and maybe the fact that a certain Base Commander was rather taken with our Professor Mary, we ended up with honorary commissions in the Indian Air Force and the ability to convert Bravo Mike Charlie into a military aircraft under the protection of

NATO at any time we please. I'm sure a similar courtesy will be forthcoming when we head to the USA."

"Mary, Brad, you two people amaze me," John began. "I promise not to be amazed in the future. Now, Rod Senden will be here any minute to take you to lunch; you know him of course Mary from all your collaboration over the years."

"We've never met though John," Mary said. "When we began there was no such thing as Skype conferencing. None of our group of fourteen really knows each other."

"Well, all that will change from now on. The other professors-elect will join you for a discussion after lunch. They will be attending tomorrow night, and all will be together for your conference in Paris on January third," John said. "Here's Rod now."

"Come in Rod," John called. "You know Professor Mary of course; she's just been telling me that you've never met?"

"That's true John, Hello Mary," Rod managed and taking her hand placed a soft kiss on her cheek. "It's great to meet you face to face at last, so much better than those flat images of you in your lab coat and glasses on Skype."

"You don't scrub up too badly yourself Rod," Mary began with a laugh. "I'd like you to meet Brad: my pilot, my bodyguard, my escort, my only confidant and I usually fail to mention my son as he gives my age away."

We all laughed, and John ushered us out. "I'll see you tomorrow night in our glad rags," he called after us.

We had lunch in a small restaurant on the campus that had few patrons as most of the university had wound down as Christmas was so near. The lunch passed quickly as Rod wanted to know as much as possible of our exploits in just a little over a week. Rod was amazed that Mary had no idea of what had been happening over the past year.

“I don’ know what I might have said if Brad hadn’t said it for me. I could well have tossed off the robe and run sobbing out of the hall,” Mary said. “By the time Brad had finished I realised that I had better put a brave face on it and surrender sweetly.”

Rod wanted to know about our flight from Australia and was most impressed with our acquisition of military status and honorary commissions.

“What rank are you Mary?” Rod asked, “does it outrank Professor.”

“I’m an honorary Flight Lieutenant and Brad a Squadron Leader,” Mary answered. This time Mary got in first. “I think a pretty Flight Lieutenant Instructor might have had something to do with that,” Mary said giving me a wink at the same time.

“Was that the girl Brad was dancing with?” Rod asked. “More than pretty I would have said.”

“How did you know about that?” Mary was first to ask.

“There was a very nice picture in the Sunday Sun yesterday,” Rod answered.

Mary and I could do nothing but laugh.

“Have you anything planned for this afternoon Brad?” Rod asked. “I think you would be pretty bored listening to us talking genetics all afternoon.”

“I would have excused myself Rod,” I answered him. “I’ve got things to do with the plane this afternoon and emails and research to do on the Internet,” If you give me a call when you’re about to finish, I’ll come and pick up Mary.”

"Good Brad, walk back to the office with us so that you'll know where to come."

After leaving Mary with Rod, I walked to the taxi rank that I had seen on the way to Rod's office. I hadn't gone far when a very attractive girl was approaching and heading in the opposite direction. She was tall; it wasn't hard to realise there was a lithe body with long legs hiding under the winter clothing. She had auburn hair peeping out from her beret and her face showed her typical 'English beauty' complexion. For an instant, our eyes met, and I had a fleeting feeling that I had seen a shy recognition in her eyes. However, I had never seen her before and hurried on to the taxi rank. I resisted the urge I felt to look back and appreciate her rear view as she walked away for the fear that she might have taken another look to confirm whether she had recognised me.

It didn't take long for the taxi to get me back to the airport and I peeled off my suit and hung it in the wardrobe and pulled on overalls. The fuel truck that I had ordered on arrival started filling Alpha Uniform's tanks. The hangar was well equipped with the appropriate drains, plenty of bench space and shadow boards of the most regularly used tools. There was a supply of oils and a generator for the air compressor to inflate tires and a battery charger. I had the bird ready for flight within two hours.

I packed away my overalls and decided to shower here in readiness for whatever the evening might bring. Rather than use the on-board facilities which were now drained, cleaned and replenished with fresh water. I used the bathroom that was provided in the hangar. I dressed in sports trousers, round-neck shirt that would be covered by my polo necked jumper and I took a blazer that I could put on over the top if needed. I looked passable as a well off young Englishman. I spent the remainder of the afternoon answering emails including those I thought might be more appropriate for Mary to answer by saying that she was already working with colleagues at Cambridge University.

'Rod is driving me back to the Hotel' read an SMS from Mary instead of the expected call to collect her from Rod's office. Mary and I arrived at the hotel at the same time, meeting in the lobby.

"You look smart sir," Mary said. "You could pass for a suave and successful Englishman; so long as you don't call all the men you meet 'mate'."

I laughed at her flattery and joke. Her first day on the job must have gone well.

"Have you been drinking?" I asked and was obviously surprised.

"I had one beer with Rod after work," Mary replied, "we thought a celebratory toast shouldn't be drunk in tea or water." **Aphrodites Diary http://www.futuristic.guru/copy-of-aphrodite-15**

"What about you?" Mary asked.

"Bravo Mike Charlie or Alpha Uniform is ready to fly away again. Tanks full, drains flushed, perishables discarded, cupboards restacked, dirty clothes at the laundry to be picked up tomorrow and emails answered. I took the liberty to reply on your behalf to some of the people I don't know; I told them that we had arrived in Cambridge after a great trip and you were already at work but would be getting in touch soon," I reported.

"I could do that first thing in the morning and we could have a Skype call to the Grands and Greats," Mary suggested. "No good calling now, they would think that some disaster had happened, it's four in the morning in Canberra. Rod is taking us to dinner tonight with his daughter; they'll be calling for us at seven."

Mary was shedding her clothes and hanging her suit in the wardrobe as she talked.

“I’ll do in this won’t I Mary?” I asked, “I showered at the drome after I’d cleaned up Bravo Mike Charlie.”

“You’ll do fine darling. It’ll be quite informal,” Mary called back.

I took off my jacket and polo necked jumper and went to the bathroom to shave, I hadn’t thought it necessary back at the drome but in this light and going out socially with new people I felt that I’d better present well.

“We should be back here by eleven, darling,” Mary said as she stepped out of the shower and saw me admiring her.

Monday 17 December 2012 – 1900 hrs

At seven o’clock we went to the lounge in the lobby just as Rod pulled up at the front door in his BMW. He opened the front door for Mary and ushered me into the rear seat alongside Kate.

“This is Brad, Kate,” he said.

“It was you Brad, I thought it was,” Kate was the first to speak.

“You were the girl on the path today,” I sounded pleased.

Rod quickly remembered that in his excitement he had failed to introduce Kate to Mary.

“I’m so sorry Mary. I’d like you to meet my daughter Kate,” Rod corrected himself. “Kate this is Professor Mary.”

“Please call me Mary, Kate; I’m sure we’ll be great friends,” Mary immediately put her at ease.

“Thanks Mary I’d love that: but I must say I’m delighted to meet you after seeing you on TV; you looked so calm and gracious," Kate stopped afraid that she might sound gushy.

"I wasn't feeling it Kate, I was shaking in my shoes once I realised what was going on," Mary told her.

"You didn't come up too bad either Brad," Kate shifted her focus. "Really put your mother right in it though, didn't you?"

"Yes, I did and I'm proud of it," I responded, and Kate reached over and squeezed my hand to indicate her words were meant in admiration and not criticism.

As Rod cruised out of the hotel, he caught Mary's eye and gave her a knowing wink.

At the restaurant, there was no valet parking, so we parked and walked back to the entrance. Mary had immediately taken hold of Rod's arm and Kate was quite happy to take mine. We were shown to a table alongside the dance floor. Mary removed her lambs-wool lined winter jacket and Kate her heavy, high-necked cardigan. They now looked more womanly, but I knew that they were both hiding more under their winter clothes. Seeing Kate in this light she was hardly recognisable as the girl I had seen on the pathway. Her beret had mostly covered her rich auburn curls and her scarf hid the profile of her face that I could see was beautiful and with those big blue eyes clearly intelligent. I wanted the band to start playing so I could ask her to dance. My thoughts brought the band back to the little stage and the trumpet player who doubled as a soloist started singing: 'I'LL SEE YOU IN MY DREAMS…'

"Shall we dance Kate?" I offered.

Kate answered by rising from her chair just as the waiter was arriving to take our orders.

"Will you order for me too Mary?" I asked not wanting to stop and study a menu.

"Me too Dad," Kate spoke up as she couldn't wait to get started. Dancing the old-fashioned way was the one place you could be held closely by a man with impunity and no commitment and she was keen to find out what it would be like being held closely by me.

"I've told her to call me Rod when we are out like this. I'd much rather be seen escorting a beautiful young lady than merely a father providing company for his daughter," Rod said to Mary, "it would do wonders for my ego," he added with a chuckle.

"And hers too Rod to be seen on the arm of a distinguished gentleman," Mary said.

"It's OK tonight though Mary, with you as my date there'll be a few envious eyes coming my way."

"Was I right or was I right?" Mary asked with a giggle.

"You're right Mary," Rod confirmed. "Anyone who is in love or has loved can see it all over their faces."

Entrée came and went; Kate and I came and went, and two old friends brought their personal lives up to date. Kate and I arrived back at the table as the main course was served.

"Kate tells me that she is enrolling in genetics next year Rod," I stated, "She won't be a teacher's pet, will she?"

"No, I won't even have her for any lectures," Rod began. "What do you plan to tackle after your gap year Brad?"

"My plans for a gap year have changed somewhat with Mary's appointment," I answered, "I'm committed to be involved in the management of our family business and I'm drawn towards economics. But I don't want to study the accepted economic, monetary and political theory because I believe it is fundamentally flawed. The thought came to me at the ANU presentation for Mary that for all of the high-powered representation from around the world there was one group conspicuous by its absence. They are the one group which could do the most damage to the Faculty's declaration of solving the riddles of the Genome by scientific method and then placing the results freely on the table for all to see and use."

"And that group Brad?" Rod asked as the girls watched silently.

"Big money Rod, I don't mean the billionaires you read about in Forbes Rich List but the trillionaires you never hear about. They buy governments, start wars, stop wars and control most of big banking and production. Through their nominee companies they have already patented many products based on the genomic information that they have uncovered in their own laboratories or bought on the cheap from the universities. These are the people that will carry out an undeclared war on the faculty," I concluded.

"I agree Brad the corporates have been my biggest worry too," Rod began, "but I saw it more in the light that they are hiring our best graduates by offering them more than we could ever afford and then patenting their work for the company and controlling its release to the public. You've taken it further here. It's war you envisage?"

"Yes Rod, there is a core of families who control everything. They wield their power surreptitiously through their nominee companies where the true owners remain unknown and they corrupt many leaders of governments, industry and the professions to do their bidding. In many cases, the corrupted don't even know they have been corrupted: they just think it is good business to screw their customers because they are rewarded with big bonuses when their company's shares go up. I'm sorry ladies, it's not really the right time or place to be discussing these things."

"What else takes you attention Brad?"

"If I said love songs," I began, "you really think I was a crackpot and not let me dance with your daughter, so I'll say philosophy."

They laughed at my easy manner of bringing their attention back from the most serious observation that I had put in front of them. An observation that the others hadn't seen because they were too close and too engrossed in their work to appreciate that the real power in the world wasn't going to lose its domination without a fight. With our main course finished the band moved into, "PEOPLE WILL SAY WE'RE IN LOVE.

"Come on Mary let's show Rod and Kate how we do this one," I said while assisting Mary from her chair. We did a round of the floor and before the band replayed the number, I returned Mary to the table and took Kate onto the floor as I had done with Rose in Agra.

The band's next number was WHAT A DIFFERENCE A DAY MADE, and Mary and Rod joined us on the floor. I could hear Rod singing softly to Mary as they danced slowly around the floor. When the music ended, we returned to the table and picked up our coats. I left some more of my five-dollar notes on the table and paid the account while Rod went to bring the car to the door.

"Will you come shopping with me tomorrow Kate; I need something suitable for tomorrow night?" Mary asked.

"I'd love too, what time?"

"Would ten o'clock suit you?"

"That would do fine, what will we do with Brad?" Kate asked Mary instead of asking me directly.

"Do you play golf Brad?" Rod asked. "I feel like playing hooky tomorrow. I won't be missed unless I don't turn up tomorrow night."

"A little, I don't get much time to practice though," I replied.

"What if I pick you up at eight o'clock, the frost will be off the fairways by then. We'll match you up with a good hire set in the pro shop and then have you back here by three in the afternoon.

Rod pulled into the front of the hotel and Mary gave him a kiss on the cheek.

"Thank you Rod that was a lovely evening," Mary said.

"And thank you Kate you're a delight to dance with," I said. Kate had move closed to me on the ride home and was now positioned to deliver a genuine, but not too long kiss on my lips.

"I'm looking forward to tomorrow night Brad," Kate said as I got out and she moved to the front seat with her father. They drove away with a wave and Mary and I walked hand-in-hand to our room. It was eleven-thirty. We took off our clothes and tumbled into bed.

"Time for you medicine professor," I informed Mary.

"What's stopping you doctor," Mary teased me. "It wouldn't be a certain long-legged English beauty, would it?"

By now my old fella was resting between Mary's thighs.

"Not at all darling though I wouldn't complain she's really a lovely girl," I replied.

"And she worships the ground you walk on darling," Mary added.

I was holding Mary quite tightly and as she paused for breath, I kissed her lovingly.

"The other professors were at the University for a meeting this afternoon darling," Mary began. "We opened the file on Adonis's goddesses."

"And?" I asked.

"Kate, Jan and Rose, darling," Mary said. "See what you're getting in return for making rash promises?"

"The heads of the other twelve genetics faculties are here for tonight and the rest of the week so a conference has been set up for us for the next three days. There's so much to talk about and so many decisions to be made that we won't have much time for you and Kate, but you'll look after her Brad, won't you?"

"Of course I will darling, you know that, particularly after what you have just told me," I confirmed eagerly. "How could I refuse even if I wanted to which I don't. You were right though. If I had met these goddesses one at a time I would have been totally confused. If I hadn't woken up as Adonis, I would have got up the courage to pursue Jan by now and if I ever happened to meet Rose and Kate I would have been in a turmoil of love and lust."

"Don't go getting her pregnant Brad, at least not yet," Mary warned, "I want to bring your three goddesses here for a good talk with their virtual mother-in-law and I want to get Doc to advise them about their own bodies and how to get the best out of their pregnancies."

"There's none better than you to help them darling," I said. "Rose's knowledge about her own self down there was very naïve and I don't expect the other two will be much better informed."

"When we get the girls here, I'll suggest they do some planning to space their pregnancies for the next few years; it would be most unfair on you if the three of them were all due to deliver in the one month," Mary said.

"But you are the only girl in my arms right now Aphrodite," I said and claimed her lips again. I couldn't keep my hands still as they wanted to feel, stroke and massage her all over. I could feel her back arching, pushing our pubes together and pushing me deeper and all the time she was doing her contraction exercises on my horn. We knew that we couldn't keep this up long, but Mary waited until I was on the point of losing control and I waited for Mary. We collapsed into a heap of 'Ohs', Gasps and Sighs.

"You wouldn't kill him Adonis, would you?" Mary at last asked.

"Whatever do you mean?" I asked in return.

"You said if you found me in another man's arms you would kill him," Mary said.

"I meant it then Aphrodite, but I don't now. So much has happened in a month and besides Adonis is incapable of murder, isn't he?" I said.

"Of course he is darling, I knew that then, but I couldn't argue with you."

"Is it Rod's arms I might find you in?" I asked.

"Could be Adonis, but nothing is going to change between us except you're going to have three gorgeous women craving your love and another hundred waiting for you to father their babies next year. I'll only claim a little of your time as we visit the other universities."

"I'll always have time and love for you Aphrodite no matter which way you want to claim it?" I said.

"Goodnight Adonis," Mary reached up and gave me a final kiss.

Unlike Mary, I was a little while getting to sleep, seeing that I had gone from being an eighteen-year-old virgin, a little over a month ago, to now being a skilled lover thanks to my mother's mentoring. To now having three outstanding women presented to me for my support, comfort and pleasure was almost beyond my comprehension. But sleep did come, and I woke at seven o'clock refreshed. **Aphrodite'sDiary http://www.futuristic.guru/copy-of-aphrodite-16**

Tuesday 18 December 2012 – 0800 hrs

I was waiting as Rod rolled up to the hotel lobby. I had woken Mary just before leaving so that she would be ready for her new daughter-in-law when she arrived at ten.

On the way to the golf course Rod and I talked of inconsequential things, mainly about last night. When we got out of the car, we had a short walk to the pro-shop.

"Well, what did you think of my little girl Brad?" Rod asked.

"She's beautiful and delightful company Rod, you must be very proud of her," I was quick to respond.

"Did Mary tell you what we've learned from our database about you, Kate, your cousin Jan and Rose, Brad?" Rod asked.

"Yes Rod, last night after we got back to the hotel, it's a bit daunting isn't it?" I replied.

"You accepted of course?" Rod asked.

"With some trepidation, Rod, particularly with the other duties I must perform around the world." Rod appreciated my sincerity.

"You'll still be a very young man in ten years' time and have three goddesses providing you with a family to look after," Rod said.

"You're happy getting one-third of a man for Kate Rod?" I asked.

"One third of you Brad would be far better than one hundred per cent of most men I see on the database. Kate would rather settle for none I'm sure," Rod said with conviction. "I've done everything for her Brad, her mother died when she was six and she has never had any other man in her life. I don't want her to be fixated on me, I can't give her babies and you can clearly see she's all woman. I couldn't have been happier to see the way she was with you last night."

"Thanks Rod. I understand what you've done and appreciate it," I said.

"Mary's a very smart lady Brad, as if I need to tell you that. We opened the files yesterday and we could have told Kate before the dinner last night, but Mary suggested that we see how you two took to each other naturally rather than being thrown together by a computer. It worked, Kate's over the moon so we want you to tell her when the moment is right," Rod finished.

"Of course, Rod, after your Faculty is instituted tonight might be a good time," I confirmed.

I selected clubs and we played a leisurely nine holes. Golf wasn't really the aim of this get-together and we both realised that the moment the invitation had been extended last night. It was a good chance to just have a yarn about all that was happening and particularly Rod's hopes for the faculty. He expanded my knowledge of the scope of the genome; how human genes are present in rats and how microbes and viruses play a yet to be understood role in the great scheme of things. We discussed how commercial interests would only pick at the genome for discoveries that could show a quick profit and make no effort to understand the full picture. The same thing happened with nuclear energy. Sure, cheap power has been generated providing greater profits for the investors, but nobody can assess at what cost. The investors were only concerned at getting the greatest profit now and happy to leave the problem, and cost, of waste disposal to future generations to solve. The investors in the original mines in England, and elsewhere, were long gone when the sink holes caused by bad mining practices started opening-up. It has always been the same: everyone is taught to exploit the next lower rung on the ladder and in every downturn, it is the one with little who loses the most. We talked away as we came together to walk down the fairway after separating to play our own ball. After nine holes Rod was one over the card and I was two over.

"You said you didn't play much Brad. Two over is pretty good. I only beat you by one and I play in the Saturday comp here every week," Rod said admiring my card. "Let's have something to eat before we head back. I doubt if the girls will be back by two-thirty."

Over lunch Rod wanted to talk about the threats the new Faculty will face from big business.

"They won't come openly Rod. They have already given their approval to the world's governments for the Faculty to be instituted. Most likely their minions will come offering endowments or funding for specific research. They will always be appealing and not in the form of a bribe, but there will be strings attached."

"How can we protect ourselves, Brad?"

"Fortunately, all the world has heard my claim that the Faculty will be observing scientific method in its pronouncements and its results will be laid before all parties. Thankfully, Mary stood up and endorsed all I claimed for her. Otherwise, lobbyists will be telling governments that I was just a young bloke who got ahead of himself, making claims he didn't understand.

"What do you suggest we do?"

"Mary told me last night you were to have meetings with the other professors-elect this week. If you as deputy-chair made your first address in support of Mary's claims for her role, and asked all your committee members to endorse it, I think you will strengthen the foundations of the Faculty immensely."

"I will Brad. I was wondering how we could get our first meeting off to a good start. We have a long list of general tasks and responsibilities to coordinate but your suggestion goes to our core principals. Any other suggestions?"

"Only in relation to my undertaking to impregnate one-hundred girls a year. Mary tells me they will be carefully selected and be highly desirable people. She has told me there are millions of girls who would be eligible. I think a major selection criterion should be the girl's family. From what Mary has said my children will be exceptional, so it will be important to put them into families where they can do the most good. We will be fighting the undeclared war of the elite with an undeclared war of our own."

"You've certainly given me plenty to work with Brad. I'd better take you back and get myself ready to face the music tonight."

Tuesday 18 December 2012 – 1915 hrs

"Have a good game with Rod darling?" Mary greeted me as she entered our apartment.

"Great actually, we only did nine holes and I managed to keep within one stroke of Rod. I was pretty pleased with that," I replied. "How was the shopping?"

"We had a great time together. Kate is a lovely girl."

"Would you like a tea or coffee? We've got time, Rod won't be picking me up until six thirty and Kate's going to collect you at seven fifteen," Mary said.

"We've got time?" I turned it into a question.

"Not for that darling. I've got to be Professor Mary tonight remember."

I took her in my arms and kissed her passionately, "Will I see you later?"

"Of course, not darling. You'll be with Kate and I don't go in for threesomes."

"What about you taking your medicine?" I was concerned.

"I plan to borrow Rod's rod for that darling, you don't mind, do you?"

"It's not the end for us darling is it?" I was feeling distressed even though I was gaining three beautiful young girls in return.

"Of course not, we've got days of being together in our travels, this year alone. I know you'll find some time for me without depriving any of your goddesses or taking you away from your other duties, just remember that we are about to change the world and might have to forgo some pleasures from time to time. Besides your running around the world each year will be over in ten years and you will have more time for your family."

Mary was gone to bathe and dress.

"Zip me up please darling," Mary asked when she returned. "When will you tell Kate, darling?"

"After the opening tonight will be the best time. That looks very enticing Mary," I said having zipped up the back. I turned her to me and saw that she had her makeup done; I planted a gentle kiss on her forehead.

"Just as well you will be wearing your ceremonials on stage darling. Nobody would be paying any attention to the Chancellor and Rod otherwise. Did you have fun with Kate this morning?"

"We had a great time and I'm looking to having more great times in the future, we're leaving it to you to tell her she's entitled to a third of you," Mary giggled. "That looks like Rod pulling up downstairs I'd better go and get ready. Good luck for tonight."

I was stripped off and shaving when Rod arrived, so I missed seeing Rod pick up Mary's overnight bag, her fleecy jacket and ceremonials. Mary had put on her light raincoat covering most of her gown and the scarf over her hair. They called 'See you later Brad,' as they walked out the door.

I didn't waste time, nor did I rush. I made a point of giving myself a clean shave and showered carefully. I dressed with equal care and was ready except for donning my dinner jacket. I went through the unit making sure that everything was tidy; particularly the bathroom for I knew that Kate would be unimpressed if there was any trace of neglect. The staff had left ample towels and I had cleaned out the shower myself before I left it. The bed was as the staff had left it this morning as I hadn't taken Mary there today. Crisp white sheets would welcome Kate if it came to that. Finally, I pulled on my jacket checked my tie and cuffs in the mirror, picked up my wallet and room key and headed for the lobby with four minutes to go to seven-fifteen.

Kate pulled up at the door at seven-fifteen and I was quickly in beside her.

“Good evening sweet lady,” I said picking up her left hand and kissing it. “I should have been calling for you of course.”

“But I’ve got the car and now I can take you anywhere I please,” Kate laughed.

“We’d better give our parents their due first don’t you think?” I chided her.

“Yes, I guess so,” Kate replied with a sigh, “let’s go there for a start.

Kate drove into her reserved park at the university and we walked from there to the theatre under cover. Kate kept her raincoat over her dress and the scarf over her head; she knew that she could hand them in quickly at the cloakroom on our way to the after-party ticket holder’s entrance. Two hundred special guests were seated on the small upstairs balcony while the two thousand other guests representing all the faculties throughout the EU and many from further afield were seated on the lower level. As before all facets of the public service, military and the professions were present. The gallery and after-party were reserved for the Chancellors of Universities and their special guests; holders of high political and other offices and of course Bad Clifford, son of Professor Mary; and Kate Senden, daughter of Professor Senden. Amongst this illustrious company Kate and I stood out by our youth, something that all others on this balcony would love to have a bit more of.

Having handed her raincoat and scarf in at the cloak room Kate gave her head a quick shake to bring her hair into place as the hairdresser had set it and a little shake of her hips to make her ballerina display as designed. She now lifted her stole to cover her shoulders and bare back, down over her upper arms to her elbows and then fade into the rest of her gown. She took my arm with one gloved hand and held her evening purse in the other.

"You look stunning Kate, absolutely gorgeous," I complimented her with great sincerity.

"Mary said I had to keep my head up and shoulders back, as if I wore this type of thing every day," Kate said and imparted a little squeeze to my arm, "she insisted on buying it for me and helped me a whole lot."

"She asked my help to find something that would excite Dad and so I asked her to help me find something that would excite you Brad," Kate admitted.

"And you succeeded Kate, not that you hadn't done that last night," I said.

"I'm not being too pushy Brad, am I?" Kate said. "I've had no experience with this sort of thing."

"Of course, not Kate," I answered, "but don't excite me too much, not here anyway."

I lightened the conversation and put my hand over hers where it rested on my arm. "Here we go," I said as we reached the head of the receiving line.

"Good evening Chancellor," I said and shook the Chancellor's hand.

"Good evening Brad, you look lovely tonight Kate," the Chancellor offered.

"Thankyou Chancellor we had to do our best for our parents," Kate replied calmly.

The Chancellor turned to his wife:

"May I present Professor Senden's little girl Kate and Professor Mary's son Brad, they make a charming couple don't they my dear?"

"Good evening Kate, Brad, I bet you'd rather be out dancing though," Lady Flynn said.

"I won't deny that Lady Flynn, but we couldn't miss this either," I responded.

"I'm so glad you spoke up for Mary as you did in Canberra Brad. She never gives herself enough credit," Lady Flynn added.

"I'll pass on your concern Lady Flynn, good evening."

Kate and I were greeted by the other dignitaries in the line and after moving out into the foyer started the spot the celebrity game. I felt a welcoming pat on my shoulder and turned with Kate to face the gentleman claiming me.

"Good evening Brad would you do me the honour of introducing me to your charming partner?"

"Certainly sir," I replied.

"Kate, may I introduce the Chancellor of the University of Delhi Doctor Hamid Singh. Doctor Singh's day job is Vice-President of India."

"Chancellor may I present Kate Senden, daughter of Professor Rod Senden who as you know will be awarded the Chair of the Faculty of Genetics tonight."

"I am honoured to meet you my dear, you both do your parents great honour," the Vice-President replied.

"Thank you, Chancellor, I too am honoured," Kate replied confidently and smiled.

"I take it you have a particular line of study Kate?" The Vice-President continued the discussion.

"I've just completed my Masters: in microbiology and will be joining the Genetics Faculty next year to research for my doctorate. As you know the scope in genetics is so wide that my degree can be built on, particularly in the area of partner suitability," Kate provided.

"Yes, I hold the new Faculty as the most important area of study and research for the future of our world," The vice-president concluded. "We'll need to take our seats soon, so I'll say goodnight."

"Goodnight Chancellor," Kate and I said in unison.

"Let's go in Brad," Kate said. "Who else do you know around here Brad?"

"Not as many as those that know me," I replied with a laugh. "Everyone will know you too now that you have a famous father."

The usher took us to our seats that were on the aisle of the central block and only the second row back from the front row of the balcony. We had a perfect view and as the official party moved onto the stage to take their seats, we could see each member clearly. The people on the stage were seated in two groups. To the left one group comprised the Chancellor, Pro-Chancellor and Vice-Chancellor of Cambridge and immediately behind them the six other members of the Cambridge University Council. To the right were fourteen chairs for the professors of the new Faculty of Genetics. Mary led this brigade onto the stage and took the nearest seat to the Council followed by Rod and the remaining heads of the present departments. By this time all the guests had taken their seats. The MC for the evening stepped forward.

"My Lords, Ladies and Gentlemen may I have your attention for the Pro-Chancellor to offer his address of welcome."

The evening proceeded in much the same way as that in Canberra ten days ago.

Rod duly received his new robes and returned to sit next to Mary, doubling the representation of those entitled to wear this distinctive new colour. The Chancellor gave his speech in honour of Rod's appointment but this time it lacked the drama of Mary's night because everyone knew what was coming. Again, it was stressed that Rod had been the choice of his peers and received world wide support from all areas of society represented by their delegates tonight. The Chancellor pointed out that the professors to be awarded to the Chair of the other twelve co-operating universities were with them tonight but couldn't be jointly appointed until similar gatherings as this were held on their own campus.

Rod made a fine speech of acceptance and for the support he had received. Professor Mary introduced the other twelve professors and advised that they had been elected and approved to take the Chair at their respective universities and all current work will continue pending the opening of the Faculty on their campus. She pointed out that the committee would be meeting in Cambridge during the remainder of the week to determine dates for the opening of the remaining faculties and would be deciding on the distribution of the work between the co-operating universities. Finally, Mary restated the Committee's already announced policy that only irrefutable results would be published, and all results would be put in the public domain.

The evening ended at ten o'clock. The downstairs guests quietly moved out of the hall and the balcony guests moved out through the entrance door into the foyer which had now been expanded to allow the guests to mingle and select finger food and drinks from the waiters hovering in their midst.

"I'd like to take you dancing Kate Senden," I whispered in her ear.

"I'd like to go with you Brad Clifford," Kate answered, and again giving my bicep a squeeze and a feel. "We'd better find Mary and Rod first and then we can go."

"Hello Brad," It was the familiar voice of Don. "Thanks for the photos and the coins in the fountain my wife was delighted to receive them."

"Kate, I'd like you to meet Vice-Chancellor Champion from the ANU and Mary's and my very good friend. Kate is Professor Senden's daughter Don," I said.

"I don't know how it is that these professors of genetics have such fine children; I'm very pleased to meet you Kate."

"Mary did fine without you tonight Brad," Don added.

"Yes, she knew what was coming tonight. Your people really sandbagged her last time, didn't they?" I scolded him.

"It was a bit callous of us but when she came in that Monday morning wanting to get away for a year and quite prepared to throw her professorship out the window the Council felt it had no alternative but to act fast. Thank heavens you were there Brad and thank you again for helping me out."

"There's no thanks needed Don." Don offered his hand and I shook it firmly.

"Here they come now," Don said.

Rod and Mary had taken off their robes and caps and Mary now shone in her new gown and hairstyle. She was holding Rod's arm the same way as Kate was holding mine and she immediately kissed Don on the cheek and introduced him to Rod.

“I’m representing the ANU tonight; the Chancellor couldn’t make it,” Don explained.

“Brad introduced me to the Vice-President of India Rod,” Kate was quite excited as she told her father. “It seemed as if they were old friends.”

“We are, he dropped into the Officers’ Mess in Agra to pay his respects to Professor Mary,” I explained. “Thanks for your assistance with that little diversion for us Don, I’ll tell you about it sometime when we have a couple of hours free.”

“I’m sorry Rod,” I continued, “I’m late with the congratulations, but congratulations,” I shook Rod’s hand vigorously and Kate gave him a big kiss on the cheek.

“Do you folks mind if I take Kate dancing now?” I asked.

“Not at all Brad,” Rod spoke up.

“I wouldn’t be hanging around with the oldies if I had a pretty girl on my arm Brad,” Don said enthusiastically.

Aphrodite’sDiary.

http://www.futuristic.guru/copy-of-aphrodite-17

Chapter 12

Goddess Kate

Tuesday 18 December 2012 – 2200 hrs

We walked back to Kate's car with my arm around her waist and her head resting on my shoulder. At the car I took her in my arms and we kissed.

"Do you really want to go dancing Brad?" Kate asked.

"Of course I do, but it doesn't have to be tonight," I gave her a hug.

"Your place or mine?" I asked.

"Yours please, I've never been taken to a man's hotel room for a one-night-stand," Kate again teased.

"This is no one-night-stand young lady," I admonished her, "You don't know what you're getting yourself into."

"You'll tell me then?" Kate asked.

"Before morning, I swear," I answered her.

"Will you drive, please?" Kate whispered.

I helped her into the passenger seat and slid back the driver's seat so that I could get in. I didn't attempt to adjust her seat belt to me but hurried away for the short drive to the Menzies. On arriving I collected her bag and casual jacket from the car, helped her out and after locking it, we moved quickly to the lift and up to my room. Kate hadn't spoken a word and I feared that she had gone to sleep and that she was only walking because I was still holding her around the waist. As soon as we were inside the room though Kate turned to me, gave me urgent kisses, and pressed her body hard up against mine. My hand was stroking her bare back and finding the top clasp to her zipper, I slowly pull it down.

"Would you like to get out of this?" I asked.

"Yes please, it's too good to get it all crushed up," Kate whispered. "I wouldn't want to disappoint Mary. She looked beautiful tonight as usual Brad, you must be very proud of her."

"Yes, I am Kate. You looked very beautiful too and I'm very proud to be seen with you as well. I'm a very fortunate man."

I had her zip down now to the start of her rounded bottom and gave it a gentle squeeze.

"I'll step out of the dress Brad," Kate said, "You won't find much under it except me."

Kate stepped out of her gown and handed it to me to hang. I hung my jacket too and while I was undoing my shirt, I turned back to Kate to see her framed in the window and bathed in the moonlight. Her breasts were now free as the cups of the built-in support were part of the dress. She wore a tiny G string and high heels. I undressed quickly and hung my suit. I had been looking back at her standing in the moonlight, she had her head up, shoulders back and her pert breasts took on a delightful appearance with their nipples silhouetted, and she knew it. There was no false modesty of drooping her shoulders forward and covering her pubic hair with her hands and after I had dropped my shorts, she slipped her G string off and tossed it on a chair. Now, with her hands and arms apart she waited and when I went back to her, she closed her arms around me and kissed me passionately. When we stopped kissing, I sang to her:

Moonlight becomes you, it goes with your hair
You certainly know the right thing to wear
Moonlight becomes you, I'm thrilled at the sight
And I could get so romantic tonight
You're all dressed up to go dreaming
Now don't tell me I'm wrong

"I'd give you a PhD in love songs Brad," Kate said as we wrapped our arms around each other and kissed.

My old fella was well aroused and pushing against her thighs.

"Standing up, sitting down, lying down or in the spa; your choice Kate?"

"Let's start by lying down on the bed darling and then see what happens as the night goes on," Kate suggested.

I picked her up in my arms and carried her to the bed.

"I've been aching for you for ten days and thought it could never happen and now your almost on top of me and hard so please fuck me Brad," Kate almost pleaded. She pulled me down onto her; kissed me with long tongue kisses and spread her legs to guide my old fella in.

I made every effort to give her the thrill she was so desperately seeking. She wasn't disappointed as I massaged her breasts, teased her nipples and kissed and sucked them. I stroked her back and thighs, I teased her long wavy hair out over the pillows and ran my fingers through the tight curly auburn ones on her pussy. With cries of Oh Brad, Oh Brad, Yes, Yes, Yes! she burst out in a climax the like of which she didn't know existed. Before her orgasm ended, she found that she had given me the release that I too had urgently needed since I saw her take off her coat and scarf much earlier in the night. I was pounding her as my semen burst forth into the depths of her vagina.

"I never knew it could be like that," she managed to whisper.

I held her tight and kissed her forehead and hair as everything else was out of reach.

Wednesday 19 December 2012 – 0400 hrs

"I think I'd like that spa now Brad," Kate said and woke me from my drowsing reverie. It was four o'clock in the morning and pitch black.

"I'll go and run it for you darling," I said and eased her head from my chest and onto my pillow.

I turned on a playlist of soft love songs and after watching the spa fill, I went back for Kate who had just put her legs over the side of the bed. I picked her up in my arms and she placed her arms around my neck and kissed me.

"Are you going to carry me around like this all the time, darling?"

"Wouldn't mind, but the neighbours might complain," we laughed.

"Drop me at the loo door please Brad."

I dropped perfume into the spa from the collection on a tray, unwrapped the scented bath soap and gathered a soft sponge. I adjusted the volume of the music to suit the bathroom and finally poured two champagnes from the mini-bar. When Kate came back to me, she gathered up her long hair and pinned it under one of the shower caps provided by the hotel.

"I'd wash it for you if you would like?" I offered. "I'm quite good at it."

"Of course you would be darling, but, I only had it set this morning."

I handed Kate a glass.

"What's the toast darling?" Kate asked.

“To you of course, Kate Senden,” I said as I raised my glass and drank.

“To you Brad Clifford,” Kate replied and started to cry.

I put my glass down, took Kate’s from her and put it down with mine on the floor.

“Whatever is the matter Kate I thought you were having so much fun?”

“I was, and I am, but I’ve been enrolled in the Faculty’s find the perfect genetic match program for two years as I couldn’t find a man, and none had taken an interest in me. I’m content to be a single mum and never see the man again.”

“Why is that a problem?” I asked.

“Because just before we left the party Dad whispered to me that he had found my match and I thought that now that I’ve found you this would just be a one-night-stand before my match comes knocking on my door and knocking me up,” Kate managed to get spoken amidst her tears.

I was holding her close to me in the warm water and catching her tears in the soft dry sponge.

“Darling if he is your perfect match, he will be perfect for you too, don’t you see?”

“I guess so darling, don’t let it spoil our night together,” Kate sobbed.

“Did Rod tell you who your perfect match is?” I asked.

“No, that’s all he said when I congratulated him.”

"I can tell you who he is Kate, but it comes with a catch," I began. "Have you heard about the Faculty's Project Adonis?"

"I only heard Dad mention it on the phone one day; he was probably talking to Mary about it and I don't like eavesdropping."

"I'll tell you what I know," I reassured her.

"The professors who participated in the Human Genome Project constructed a theoretical gene map of the man who should become the next Most Recent Common Ancestor by the male line. This baseline man they dubbed Adonis and hence Project Adonis. From Adonis's genes they determined that to have a happy Adonis they would need not one perfect woman but three. Adonis's goddesses would each satisfy a part of Adonis's make up. Most men have a narrow or specialised view of life and can be happy following one line of work or profession for their whole working life. Adonis was a generalist who could excel at many things. Women are just not made that way and they were never meant to be. Being who he was Adonis could never become a party member or church member or be any other joiner or follower. The Faculty planned to carry out this operation as a secret research project to enhance the world's gene pool that is currently in a very sad and sorry state, particularly on the male side. Adonis is to produce a family of his own with his three goddesses, say four children each. Adonis is also required to father one hundred children a year with women the Faculty chooses from around the world. The Faculty is certain that his three goddesses would, by their very nature of being an Adonis goddess, be free of any jealousy and would quickly form a strong bond of sisterhood."

As I spoke, I had been gently soothing Kate, soaping and sponging the parts of her body I could reach. Although sexy, I didn't want to stimulate her further until I had got everything out and laid it before her. It was up to Kate if she wanted to be my goddess.

“Who are the lucky girls Brad? Mary must have told you if she’s told you this much,”

“The professors opened the files at yesterday’s meeting; there’s Rose, the girl I was dancing with in Agra, there’s Mary’s cousin Jan in Canberra and shy little Kate Senden in Cambridge if she can be persuaded to be a goddess,” I declared.

“And who is Adonis Brad?”

“You’re looking at him darling; if you’re prepared to take a third share.”

“I’d take one-tenth or even one hundredth would give me four nights a year with you, I’d rather have one night a year with you than every night with anyone else. Give me a big kiss please; I’m the happiest girl in the world,” Kate said with tears now streaming down her face and laughing between her sobs.

I lifted her on to me and kissed her passionately. We broke apart and Kate lent back so I could see the joy on her face and in her eyes, and she could see the pleasure and delight in mine.

“So, this is what Dad meant and I got it all wrong,” Kate said. “I do hope Dad and Mary are finding as much joy tonight, he must be relieved to have got free of his scared little girl.

I poured the rest of our bubbly into our glasses and gave Kate hers.

“To my little Goddess,” I proposed.

“To my Adonis,” Kate replied with a giggle. “Come on Brad, finish me off so we can go back to bed.”

I turned her around to face me and with her feet now in my hands started soaping, massaging and sponging as I had done for Mary. Kate soon caught on to where this was going and as I inched forward with my sponging, she inched towards me. When her Gates to Paradise were at my fingertips, I picked up the tube of Mary's balm that I had placed on the spa and without knowing what I was going to do Kate opened her Gates to Paradise for me with her fingers. I gently massaged her outer lips with the salve.

"Oh, that feels so good Brad," Kate spoke softly.

I applied just a little more to my finger and eased it into her vagina and very gently spread it over its walls.

"Oh, that feels better still darling; what is it?" Kate asked.

"It's Mary's special balm that her obstetrician formulated for her after her reconstruction," I said simply.

"What happened?" Kate asked.

"Mary nearly died delivering me, and me along with her, it was only the skill of her Doc that saved us. Had it not been for him there wouldn't have been a Professor Mary or Adonis," I said as I brought Kate back to lay on me while I kissed her.

"Then I owe Doc a big thank you, don't I?" Kate acknowledged.

"Everyone does darling, not only the conspirators in Project Adonis, but soon the world at large, and they will never know they're in his debt."

We kissed again with more fervour and I soaped and sponged myself while Kate watched. When I got to the Family Jewels, I soaped the sponge and handed it to her.

"There you are darling I trust you not to hurt me where the pain can be excruciating," I said, showing I had as much faith in her as she had in me.

We left the tub, dried and dusted ourselves.

"It's only six and sunrise isn't until eight o'clock; would you like some breakfast now and talk a little more before we go back to bed and hope some sun shines through. We don't have to rush anything now; I've got you all to myself until your other lovers arrive and want a piece of you," Kate said with her tears now gone and a happy smile on her face. "Just ask for two English Breakfasts darling. That will set us up for the day and won't take them long to prepare. I'll put something on to keep the chill off."

When we came back together, I took Kate's hand and sat her on my knee. Kate was wearing a hotel supplied gown over a baby-doll negligee. I put an arm around her and kissed her, my free hand rested on her now covered thighs.

"I brought this nightie to wear to bed last night darling but once you touched me, I didn't want you to stop," Kate said and smiled at me. "You don't need to go on paying for the hotel darling we could go to my place for the next few days, I've got two bedrooms," Kate said.

"What do we want two bedrooms for; you're not going to put me out are you?"

"Of course, not silly; just in case Mary wants to stay but I think she will be happy with Rod for the next few days, don't you?"

"I don't think that Rod would have any thought of putting her out," I answered with a laugh.

Wednesday 19 December 2012 – 1100 hrs

"What would you like to do later? Go for a flight in Bravo Mike Charlie?"

"That would be fun; I've never felt freer than I do right now with your arms around me. Where will we go?"

"We could be in Moscow in eight hours, or go to Paris for lunch, or go and throw some more coins in the Trevi Fountain and be back before tea or we could go around England and Scotland in four hours?"

"That will do; let's go around England," Kate decided.

There was a knock at the door and I went to receive our breakfast trolley. Kate was up and arranged our breakfast on the table. Our bacon and eggs were sitting above small lamps keeping them warm and the coffee was percolating.

"I'm really going to enjoy this darling; I haven't felt much like eating for the last couple of days. I was acting like a silly school girl infatuated by a rock star," Kate had been smoothing her long auburn hair back over her shoulder as she spoke, and I was happy to watch and admire. Before I sat, I flicked on the early news report.

We both had a good appetite now that our stresses had gone, and it wasn't long before Kate removed our empty cereal bowls and glasses and laid my bacon and eggs with sausage, tomato and toast before me. She poured our coffee and joined me at the table. We were half way through our bacon and eggs when the announcer started describing the events that had happened at Cambridge University last night. The first clips were of the receiving line and the longest part of that was when the Chancellor welcomed Kate and me and introduced us to his wife. The camera was still on us as we walked away, "Oooh I remember doing that," Kate giggled as the camera picked up that moment when she had pressed her right breast against my arm as she was squeezing my bicep. The camera stayed with us and showed the Vice-President of India clapping me on the shoulder and his obvious friendly manner as I introduced him to Kate. The announcer had been explaining to his listeners who the people were and named our illustrious parents. The commentary then went on to the robing of Rod, Rod's acceptance speech, the Chancellor's remarks, Mary's update on the work the Faculty would be doing and then Professor Stephen Hawking; likening the understanding of the human genome to the understanding of the universe. The segment finished showing shots of the after-party and again most of this was devoted to Kate and me. They showed us talking with the Vice-Chancellor of the ANU and then Professor Mary, looking ravishing in her new gown now that she had shed her ceremonial robes and on the arm of Professor Senden who had just been installed as the inaugural chair of the Faculty of Genetics at Cambridge.

"Well you stole the show darling," I said proudly.

"Brad don't be blind, Mary looked absolutely ravishing after she got rid of her robes and cap and she looked pretty good in those too as she made her speech. Her robes flapped about just right to hint at the gown being kept covered," Kate was quick to support Mary.

"Of course she did, but she only had a little part after she got rid of her robes while the camera was following you soon after we arrived," I claimed. "If you've had enough, I'll put the trolley out and hang up the Do Not Disturb."

"I'm finished darling."

I replaced the dishes on the trolley, slipped a five under the coffee percolator and wheeled the trolley out the door. The Do Not Disturb was still in place from last night. I visited the bathroom, turned out the lights so that the sunrise might be seen and returned to our bed. Kate was sitting up in bed in the dark waiting for me.

I slipped in beside her and found her still wearing her dressing gown. I kissed her, undid the tie at her waist, and slipped my hand under the fold to find her negligee blocking my way. With Kate clinging to my lips and offering no resistance, but no help either, I slipped her gown from each shoulder and let it drop behind her. My hand went under her negligee between her knees and I brought my hand up between her thighs, over her mound and up across her stomach to her breasts. The negligee came along with my hand until it felt the resistance from where Kate was sitting on it. She now assisted by raising her bottom the slightest amount, so the negligee came free and went up her back. I applied both hands to her breasts and then lifted the negligee over her head and let it fall away.

"It's been so nice Brad, last night, the spa, making me a goddess, the way you just peeled me I've never been happier," Kate poured out her heart to me, "you will come and stay with me for a while?"

"Of course, darling, I couldn't be happier either. We are going to be recognised wherever we go, that can be a problem," I told her.

"We'll worry about that when it happens darling. Remember, you said daytight compartments. Let me see if I can do something for you now."

Kate pushed me down on my back and straddled me. There wasn't the same urgent passion of last night but now it was a beauty of a different sort: two people had opened their souls to each other to find a welcome waiting. We knew there was no need to rush anything in our lives as a long and happy future awaited us, and children who would be enjoyed and honoured and who would bring honour upon us. I could feel Kate tiring, so I rolled her with me onto our sides. I slipped my free hand between her thighs and stimulated her clitoris. It only took a few minutes as the daylight filled the room before we enjoyed a full-bodied orgasm together. I held Kate close wanting her to feel how my old fella would shrink and slip from her hold without our doing anything. I told her it was now spent but it wouldn't be long before it was looking for her delights and wanting to thrill her again. Kate held me, kissed me, pulled back, looked me in the eye, and said:

"Thank you, Adonis, I feel like a woman at last."

"You're not only a woman darling but a goddess and it won't be long before you have a beautiful baby replacing me at your nipples." Adonis replied.

"For now, Adonis, I'm thrilled to suckle you."

The clock showed nine when we decided to get up. I phoned reception and asked them to make up my bill as I would be vacating at ten o'clock. There was a message on my phone from Mary asking me to bring her things from the hotel to Rod's house tonight and for us to join them for dinner. Mary added that she had sent messages to her staff at ANU to notify Jan and Rose that their perfect match had been located and was in London. They were asked to join her there on twenty-seventh of December. This date was chosen to allow Rose and Jan to spend Christmas with their families. Mary had also phoned Doc. She said that Doc had agreed to come to the committee meeting in Paris on January 3rd. She would give me the details later.

I simply replied GREAT, we'll see you tonight.

I reached for my phone; I should tell Rose: I would have done it last night, but things got out of hand, or in hand, very quickly and then it was too late. I thought that now she knew that the Faculty had found her genetic mate she should know urgently that it was to be me.

"Rose, it's Brad, how are you?"

"I should be happy darling but I'm not," Rose began, almost sobbing.

"The Faculty advised me yesterday that they had found my perfect match and I'm booked to fly to London on the twenty-sixth to meet him," Rose poured out.

"Isn't it what you wanted Rose?" I asked.

"Yes, but I wanted it with you darling," Rose was quite distraught.

"Rose, it is me. I'm sorry we had to do this over the phone instead of you being in my arms, but I had to let you know as soon as I heard. There is a catch though. I'm part of Mary's faculty's project to improve the human gene pool. I'm to have three girls to share my life and we can't marry of course."

"I don't care Brad. Tell me about it when I'm in your arms. Do I have to wait until next Thursday until I come to you?"

"How soon can you come Rose?" I asked.

"I could pinch an F18 and be there in a couple of hours so long as I didn't get shot down along the way," Rose joked. "But seriously I could get a direct flight from Delhi to London on Sunday morning if that will be all right? My family will understand when I tell them I can't be there for the holidays."

"Leave it to me darling. I'll have your original ticket cancelled and make your new booking on something that will get you to Heathrow by early afternoon. I'll be there in Alpha Uniform to pick you up," I said.

"That will be heaven darling. Is Kate one of your girls too darling?" Rose was quick to pick up the connection.

"Yes darling, I'm sure you'll like her," I said.

"If Mary and you like her, I'm sure I will too; you both have impeccable taste and know a good thing when you see one don't you?" Rose praised them and herself by association.

"Who's the third girl, darling? Rose asked.

"Her name's Jan and she's Mary's cousin. Jan arrives on Thursday afternoon," I said. "She's delectable too darling. We've never been kissing cousins, so I might find things a little bit strange at first," I told her.

"Don't worry Brad, Kate and I'll give you some time to get acquainted I'm sure," Rose replied. "You've made me the happiest girl in the world Brad; I'll go and have a little cry now if you don't mind, we'll talk soon."

Kate appeared from the bathroom in pale blue slacks and body-hugging top. Her curls hung down from her shoulders again and she now did present herself as a secure and confident woman.

"You've got me to yourself for four days and nights darling, I'll tell you all about it on our way to the drome; for now, I've got to take everything of ours to your car."

"Wait for me Brad I can carry some of the things," Kate said as she picked up her overnight bag and followed me.

We went to Kate's flat on the way to the drome and left Kate's overnight bag and our clothes from last night. Kate carefully hung her new gown. She wanted to wear it again soon and go dancing with me. On the way to the drome Kate opened the Cambridge Gazette that had been delivered with our breakfast, but we hadn't bothered to read. I was doing the driving and Kate was happy to sit back and be chauffeured.

“Oh Oh,” Kate began, “I think we’re going to be easily recognised darling; and my lovely new gown is going to stand out like a beacon,” Kate almost cried.

“What’s the matter?” I asked plainly concerned.

“If you thought we got more than our share of publicity on the news just wait until you see this,” Kate said. “Don’t look now, let’s wait until we get to the drome.”

Near the airport entrance I spotted a pilot’s shop and pulled up to get a set of British Isles Low Level Charts.

“Have a look at this darling,” Kate said as she handed me the newspaper.

“Oh my God,” I said as I leafed through the several pages that reported the Cambridge University event. “I don’t know what to say right now darling, we’ll talk about it when we’re aloft.”

At least a one-quarter of the photos showed Kate and me, some of course included other dignitaries like the Vice-President of India, The Chancellor and his wife in the welcoming line and the Vice-Chancellor of the ANU, Don. About one sixth of the pictures showed Mary and Rod and all the other dignitaries amongst the two thousand downstairs and the two hundred upstairs had to make do with the rest.

It was the same with the editorial and text, ‘Kate Senden this...’ and ‘Brad Clifford that...’ Word has it that this charming daughter of Professor Senden has fallen for this tanned Aussie son of Professor Mary.’

“At least that bit’s right darling,” Kate said. “Wouldn’t they love to know how hard and what if we told them I only get a third; that’d shock them wouldn’t it?”

That made Kate laugh, and we laughed aloud together.

“I’ll go and get the charts,” I said and got out to go to the shop.

“Could I have a set of VFR Charts for the British Isles please,” I asked, not really looking at the attendant as my eyes were going around the items on display,

“I’d better have a copy of FLYING too,” I said as I saw the photo from Sydney Harbour and continued my scan.

“And a Mile-High-Club badge, no make it three of those please. That’s the lot thanks.”

“Going to take her up and give her one eh Brad?” The attendant remarked.

“Do I know you?” I asked with a somewhat puzzled look coming to my face.

“No, I just recognised you from the newspaper; yours and the little lady’s photos are all over the TV and papers this morning.”

“I didn’t think I had ever seen or heard of you before because any person who knew me, and I don’t care how big or tough they are or think they are, would never dare make such a remark about any lady in my presence, let alone about the lady you have just insulted with your grubby little mouth.”

I reached over the counter, took hold of the attendant by the wrist, and effortlessly pulled him over the counter and down to his knees in front of me.

“Have you any idea what I could do to you now with just one punch, one kick or one flick of my wrist?” I said in an equally calm tone of voice.

“I guess that you could fuckin’ near kill me,” the poor frightened young man said.

"Not fuckin' near mate; fuckin' dead, do you get my point mate?"

"Yes, Brad I'm sorry,"

"I didn't ask you to call me Brad; I don't know your name or who you are, and I don't want to know. Just remember that we Aussies have two ways of saying 'mate:' one way is between men who respect each other, and the other way is the way you have just heard, so don't be a smart arse with Aussies if you know what's good for you. Now take my credit card so that I can pay for my goods. You can then go out and softly tap on the passenger side window of that Ford Focus and when Miss Senden lowers the window you will calmly say, 'I'm sorry Miss Senden I made a disparaging remark about you. Please accept my apology and I'll never make such remarks about a girl or lady again,' Have you got that?"

"Yes Mr Clifford," the frightened attendant said.

"Then let me hear it," I told him; still maintaining a firm but frightening evenness in my voice. The poor fellow got the words out. He completed my purchase and almost ran out to the car. As expected, Kate wound down her window and heard his apology.

"I'll accept your apology of course but I don't understand why you are making it?" Kate replied.

"Because Mr Clifford said so Miss," he said and ran back into the store. On leaving the pilot shop I noticed a photo of Mary in the window of the newsagent next door. The photographer from her big night in Canberra had captured the perfect pose. He knew it was right for VOGUE and there it was on the front cover of the latest edition. I went in, purchased a copy, and noticed that several other local and London newspapers were carrying similar stories of last night's events. I didn't bother buying them. Instead, I hurried back to the car and gave Kate the copy of

VOGUE. We headed off to the hangar to get up into the sky and away from this nonsense.

“This picture of Mary is gorgeous Brad,” Kate announced proudly. “The photographer captured her charm perfectly,” Kate spoke as a happy daughter of a beautiful mother rather than what might have been expected of a one-third stakeholder in a virtual mother-in-law. “What was the problem with that chap back there coming out to me like that?”

“I took exception to his attitude to women in general and you in particular, darling; I didn’t hurt him although I think his pride is suffering,” I said. “Let’s forget it and go and enjoy ourselves,” I explained.

We parked the Ford in the free space inside the hangar. I unlocked the door and lowered the steps for Kate to enter Alpha Uniform.

“Brad this is beautiful. Mary said that you did this in ten days and didn’t let her see it until you were on your way here.”

“That’s really not right, I didn’t do anything, the engineers and joiners and their crews did all the work, I only designed it and accessed the parts and I started that while we were visiting friends in the outback. Come and I’ll show you around; your job today will be to make coffee and get us a sandwich for lunch. We’ll be aloft for four hours.” I took her by the hand and described the features as we passed:

“This is how you make coffee darling,” I showed her. “This is how you use the stove/oven darling,” I showed her.

“How do you lower the divan darling?” Kate asked. I showed her.

"Then come and give an admiring goddess a little kiss," Kate asked and again I showed her. We kissed and lay together for some moments.

"I truly can't get over this it's fantastic, we could happily live on board," Kate was clearly amazed. "Mary's lab is better than some I use at the university."

"Where would we put our babies darling?" I asked. "Babies were the furthest thing from my mind when this was created," another long and passionate kiss followed.

"Come on let me show you your country. We'll go clockwise so that you can get a good view of the coastline from the right-hand seat. I'll get the camera out of the cupboard and you can snap away at anything that takes your fancy."

Kate was right behind me, now anxious to get going and put her passion on hold for a few hours. She walked with me as I did my pre-flight inspection. I made my call to the tower requesting clearance and advised that I was making a clockwise circuit of England and Scotland outside controlled airspace and below ten thousand feet with two persons on board and a return ETA of four in the afternoon. It felt strange to me that here in Cambridge. Universal Time was Local time and all aircraft flying and planning anywhere in the world considered now, midday on Wednesday nineteenth December was their time too. While waiting for my clearance I taxied Alpha Uniform out of the hangar and locked the door behind us. We got our clearance, taxied to the active runway, and were soon airborne. Kate found that we could talk quite comfortably using the headsets and that if the controllers wanted to talk to me, they simply overrode any cabin talk. We headed southeast back to Harwich from where Alpha Uniform approached only three days ago. We had been cleared out of controlled airspace at fifteen hundred feet and I held that height to the coast. Kate was already snapping away at the towns we were overflying having never seen them from this angle before. At Harwich, I brought the plane down to five hundred feet over the water and locked the altitude hold as I intended to give Kate the best view of the coastline and the towns and villages. We were heading south west now smoothing out the rugged coastline so that we could complete our trip before dark. Had we gone into every waterway and river estuary we would need two days to complete the trip. We swung east to round Margate and back south towards Dover.

"That's the Dover to Calais Ferry out there to the left," I told Kate and pointed to the ship.

"It's as if we're surfing the waves Brad," Kate called to me. "We'll have plenty to show Mary and Rod tonight darling."

She clicked away at the White Cliffs as we turned south-westerly to pass Folkestone.

"Not a real lot to see for a while Kate; like to try your hand with the coffee pot?"

"Aye, aye Captain," Kate called as she left to try her hand in the galley.

"I only made us toasted cheese sandwiches, I'm not very hungry after that breakfast and Rod will have a good feed for us tonight. How's the coffee darling, to your taste?" Kate was pleased to be able to contribute and was really getting to like low-level flying. Alpha Uniform cast a perfect shadow on the water and she photographed that for her record. We went on past Hastings, Eastbourne, Brighton and approaching the Isle of Wight I told Kate we would change seats so that she could get some good shots of Cowes and the coast as we flew down the Solent. When we changed back again, I kept hold of her hand and sat her down in my lap. With one eye on the instruments I held her close for a moment and kissed her firmly,

“Back to your seat co-pilot,” I must keep my wits about me at this height. I applied a little squeeze to her bottom as she got up.

“I’d rather be getting our photos right now darling, but you’re on a promise for tonight,” Kate laughed as she sat down again and started clicking away.

There were channel ferries and all types of shipping passing under us or within our sight.

“I’ll bet they’re watching us too darling,” Kate called.

We were passing out of The Channel and could see Penzance. I rolled into a gentle left turn to take us further south to round Land’s End and then head north for Milford Haven. I planned to track the coast of Wales through St George’s Channel into the Irish Sea. I would leave Ireland for another day as I wanted to have a good look at Dublin and Galway as future departure or returning points on our crossings to the east coast of North America.

“Can you reach the US from here darling?” Kate asked.

“Yes, and we can go coast to coast over there in one hop of eight hours as well.”

“Can this little goddess do that with you one day Brad?” Kate asked.

“You certainly can and will Kate,” I confirmed.

We flew around the Isle of Man and then out to fly around Scotland. We were surprised to see the extent and ruggedness of Scotland’s west coast and its many islands. We flew along the north coast past John O’Groats but bypassed the further-north small islands to ensure we would be back in Cambridge before dark.

We swung out over the North Sea and I climbed to six thousand feet. With the autopilot engaged I invited Kate to sit on my lap. It only took one long and passionate kiss with my hand going down between Kate's thighs to excite her.

"Here Adonis?" Kate asked.

"Here Goddess Kate: the gods and goddesses must have done it in the clouds."

Kate quickly undid her slacks, stepped out of them and threw them onto the co-pilot's seat. I, having planned for this, pushed my trousers down around my ankles. I wasn't wearing boxers leaving my old fella free to jump to attention. I pulled Kate's panties from her hips and she peeled off her jumper and reached behind her to unclip her bra. By the time she straddled me I had my shirt off, wrapped her bare body in my bare arms, and claimed her lips again. Kate's arousal was instant, no further foreplay was needed, as she guided my horn straight into her hole and rode it. Her orgasm made her squeeze her eyes closed but it didn't stop her milking the last drop of my semen. Kate clung to me with her head on my chest, I gathered my shirt from where I dropped it and pulled it over Kate's back to keep her warn. The aftershocks of her orgasm slowed and ceased.

"I'd better go to the bathroom darling," Kate whispered after my erection collapsed and she was released. "Can I try the shower?"

"Of course, I'll hold the floor steady for you."

I had brought a sponge, towel and my unused boxers with me and dressed again. When Kate returned and before we buckled up again, I held her to me and slipped the Mile-High-Club badge into her jumper.

"What's this for darling?" Kate asked.

“Let’s say it’s your first aviation rating Kate,” I said. “It shows that you have performed a highly satisfactory fuck while more than a mile high in the air.”

“It was more than highly satisfactory for me darling. Was it for you too?”

“It was more than for me too, but they only provide the one badge,” I replied.

We took our seats and put on our safety harnesses. I brought Alpha Uniform down to five hundred feet again to let Kate continue getting her photos of Scotland. Kate was still interested in what she was seeing but her heart was still up there at six thousand feet. It wasn’t even twenty-four hours since she went to my hotel room and only a little over twelve hours since I revealed myself as Adonis and claimed her as one of my three goddesses — now she had entered another new dimension: six thousand feet up in the sky.

We were flying south now passing close to Aberdeen and then Dundee. I climbed to fifteen hundred feet to pass overland closer to Edinburgh, crossed the coast again at Scarborough and descended to five hundred feet for the run down the east coast. At Harwich, it was back to fifteen hundred to fly over land and obtain my clearance to RAF Wyton. I was touching down into the setting sun at three fifty-five. I rolled into the hangar and closed-down. Kate removed her headset and now came and sat in my lap without any request from me. She put her arms around my neck and we enjoyed a long kiss.

“That was lovely thanks Brad. I’ve lived here all my life and I never knew it would be anything like what we’ve seen today, or what we did at six thousand feet.”

This time Kate drove as I didn’t know the way to Rod’s house.

“Hello Kate, you looked lovely last night, your dress suited you perfectly.”

“Thank you, Mrs Williams. This is Brad Clifford he’ll be staying with me for a few days so don’t be concerned if you see a strange man about the place,” Kate made light of introducing me.

“I wouldn’t call him strange dear, I thought you were most gallant last night Brad,” Mrs Williams said and offered her hand. “The photos in the papers were charming.”

“Thank you, Mrs Williams, I did my best to show Kate off,” I shook her hand but was tempted to kiss it to show her I could really be gallant.

Kate opened her door and we took our things inside. I went back to the car for another load and by the time I returned Kate had the kettle on for a cup of coffee before we went to Rod’s house. As soon as I had placed my load on the bed Kate was in my arms for a kiss.

“It’s OK I’ve got two bedrooms,” Kate said with a giggle.

“How thick are the walls darling?” I asked.

“We can always turn the music up,” Kate replied.

The music would have to wait though as we wanted to be at Rod’s as early as possible. We assumed the conference would be breaking up by five o’clock. At five fifteen, we arrived at Rod’s home in a well-off suburb mid-way between the city-centre and the university. It was comfortable, classy and substantial without any sign of ostentation. There was a circular drive at the front that allowed cars to drive in the entry gate and out the exit gate without needing to reverse. Seeing Rod’s BMW in the garage Kate pulled up at the front door. She opened the door with her key and called out, ‘Anyone home’.

Mary and Rod emerged from the lounge room to welcome us. Mary kissed us both and Rod shook my hand firmly and kissed his daughter.

“Come into the lounge and tell us what you’ve been doing today,” Rod directed us. “We’ve just got in and were about to have a drink. We can get the things out of the car later Brad.”

“You’re looking happy darling,” Mary remarked as she looked at Kate. “Don’t you think Rod?”

“I see my shy little girl as a confident and happy woman now Mary,” Rod said. “No doubt Brad told you all about the Adonis Project?”

“Yes, Rod he did: not only told me but showed me of course.”

“And you’re happy about it darling?”

“Of course, I told Mary yesterday that I would be thrilled to have one-hundredth share of Brad. I don’t think I would be capable of managing more than one-third.”

“And all of the others?”

“That too Rod.”

“No need to ask you Brad,” Rod began. “It was your call and you wouldn’t be here now if you had called it any other way. Congratulations and I’m very proud to have you as a son-in-law albeit a virtual one. Mary and I will be looking forward to becoming proud grandparents. No laws can take that away from us. Sit down while I get the drinks.” Rod took our orders and we settled for Johnny Walker Red. “Good choice for a cold night,” Rod said as he went to pour them.

“What did you think of the TV and newspapers today Kate?” Mary asked.

"Embarrassed because there was so much of Brad and me when there were all those famous people there," Kate began. "And my beautiful dress will be recognised wherever I wear it and people will instantly know Brad and me by it."

"Did you go dancing when you left?" Mary asked.

"We intended to but when we got to the car park and Brad kissed me for the first time we decided to go straight to his hotel instead," Kate told Mary without the slightest embarrassment.

"I'm so happy for you and Brad, Kate," Mary pressed her hand as she said it.

"Here's some more publicity for you Mary," I said and handed Mary the copy of VOGUE.

"It's certainly upmarket on most of the other photos that have been published isn't it?" Mary said without a lot of enthusiasm.

"It's perfectly beautiful Mary it epitomises brains and beauty," Rod said as he placed our drinks. "What else has Adonis and his goddess been up to today?"

"Oh, we flew around the island at five hundred feet above the waves and I took lots of photos of what we saw," Kate replied.

"Which island Kate?" Rod asked, a little unsure of what she meant.

"England, Wales and Scotland," Kate replied. "We didn't have time to do Ireland.

"The Pilatus is absolutely fabulous Mary; and you were just going to go camping in it before the Faculty came up?"

"Yes, Brad thought I might be called back to work if I couldn't do anything necessary on the run," Mary told her.

"How did your conference go today?" I asked.

"Great," Rod now took over. "We told them that Adonis's goddesses had accepted their role. We've organised flights for Rose and Jan that will have them arriving on the twenty-seventh. Project Adonis has been activated and the full committee is delighted that the project has not only commenced but also in the choice of the participants. Rose is the only one who hasn't family connections with Mary or me but the furthest thing from their mind is any suggestion of nepotism. They know how important we consider this project to be and they have access to the data to do any checks themselves if they wish.

"As you know, Mary is sure that Doc is the best person to talk to you and the girls on all things to do with getting babies. He has found that most men and women are ignorant or badly informed on these most important aspects of life and no such ignorance can affect our project. The committee believes that Doc will not only help the goddesses but be able to advise it on other matters as well.

"The next thing settled was the timing for the opening of the other faculties. Unfortunately, Brad, we couldn't get them to follow your itinerary as steps were already in place to open the other universities. The order from here in is Sorbonne-Paris University in Paris on Friday, January 4th. A committee meeting is planned for the day before, so they can meet Adonis and his goddesses. The members of the committee are remaining in Europe until then. Some will only be able to participate in the remaining openings by tele-conferencing and the full committee will meet again in Canberra in January 2014.

The White House would like Mary's introduction to the President by the Secretary of State to be held on

Wednesday, 16 January. We can then get on with the other openings. The dates are:

The University of California Los Angeles on Wednesday 23 January;

University of Mexico on Monday, 4 February;

National University of Brasilia on Monday, 11 February;

University of Tokyo is opening on Thursday, 7 March;

Peking University on Monday, 18 March;

Delhi University on Monday, 1 April;

Ankara University on Monday, 15 April;

Moscow State University on Monday, 22 April;

Ghent University on Thursday, 25 April;

University of Abuja on Monday, 27 May;

University of Malaya on Monday, 10 June;

Mary and Brad will be back in Canberra on Monday, 17 June.

How does that sound Brad? Your schedule has been mucked up quite a bit I'm afraid," Rod concluded.

"The schedule part Rod is no problem at all," I began. "Essentially it's my itinerary running in reverse. We go to the USA before we do the rest of Europe, that's fine. I like the idea of getting these universities all formalised in five months too because that will give us all more time to be in one place and Adonis's goddesses must always be a high priority and claim on his time. I really like it Rod."

"Me too Rod," Mary confirmed. "Like Brad said, it gets this part over with and we can get down to our work proper."

Kate had been naming each university on a map displayed on Rod's computer.

"You'll be going around the world in the next six months; can your goddesses come too, or some of the time, we might even be able to help," Kate asked excitedly. **Faculties of Genetics http://www.futuristic.guru/faculty-city**

"Of course, darling but we'll have to wait until Rose and Jan get here next week so that you can plan your pregnancies together, nobody else will interfere in those decisions, not even Brad," Mary added

"We can tell the committee tomorrow that the dates cause no problems for your flying then Brad?"

"No problems Rod," I replied. "The only thing that concerns me a bit is the publicity I've been getting for the last month. I thought that I'd need to spend some time with these girls to have them happy with me but now I mustn't be seen in public with any of them."

"That came up today too Brad," Mary said. "The others all know that they must now protect you and the girls from any sort of press. The only females you can be seen with are me or one of the goddesses. You've already been seen with us and everyone knows or thinks they know what the connection is. In the rest of the openings there won't be any need for you to be at the formal function."

"The other thing that concerns me a bit is the race thing," I said. "I've never thought myself racist, but I never thought of me having children with Asian, African or South American girls either."

"Each faculty will be selecting girls to benefit the most from your genes Brad. They will all be compatible and attractive to you; you won't mind doing what you have to do, and they will be delighted to have your child," Rod reassured me. "Now that the dates for the various faculty openings are know their staff will be seeking girls who will be ovulating at that time. They will be so keen to be impregnated, if you meet the girl on a Monday morning, she will leave you with a smile on her face that afternoon. Nothing else matters."

"That clears up everything we need for tomorrow Brad," Mary said. "By the way, the committee liked the idea of us flying under the protection of the military as it gives us much more privacy not having to go through international airports."

"My mother invited us to spend Christmas with them in Glasgow," Rod told us. "Kate's maternal grandparents will be there too plus a few aunts, uncles and cousins. Being a geneticist Mary, by looking at Kate and her grandmother you'll see her mother and where she gets her good looks from."

"When do we go Rod," I asked.

"The conference will finish on Friday night," Rod began, "If we got away fairly early on Saturday morning we could be there by mid-afternoon."

"Or if we left mid-morning on Saturday we'd be there for lunch in Alpha Uniform, it's only an hour's flight," I offered.

"Let's do that please," Kate was keen for more. "There's a ball on the Saturday night before Christmas so we could go to that and I can wear my dress again."

"Yes please," Mary agreed. "I love to dance too."

"I'd love to go for a flight in your plane Brad; Mary tells me it's a magic carpet," Rod accepted too. "We've talked so long I suggest we go to the little pub on the corner to eat rather that preparing anything now," Rod added.

By ten o'clock we had eaten, talked some more about all sorts of things and Kate and I made ready to leave. Rod went with Kate to collect something she wanted from the spare room and Mary and I were alone for the first time since getting ready for the function the day before.

"Are you happy Aphrodite?" I asked Mary, deliberately using her boudoir name.

"I'm very happy Adonis," Mary answered. "Yes, I did take my medicine last might and I will tonight too, and it was very nice as well. Poor Rod, it's been sixteen years since his wife died. However, don't forget me while you're dallying with your goddesses; there'll be times on our travels when we will need each other. It's easy to see that you thrilled Kate Brad, she's really radiant."

We said goodnight and were back to Kate's unit by ten-thirty.

With only a small lamp burning and music playing I took Kate in my arms and sat down in a lounge chair. She clung to me with arms around my neck and kissed me for a long time. It was as if she had been starved of kisses all her life; there was just so much a doting father could do for a blossoming teenager and young woman and passionate kissing hadn't been in his curriculum. She wanted to make up for those lost years.

"Was it only today that we flew around the coast darling?" Kate began.

"Was it only last night that we kissed for the first time and then rushed back to the pub to fuck for the first time darling?"

"Was it only this morning that we had that lovely spa, had breakfast at six and went back to bed to fuck again while the sun came up?"

"Was it only this afternoon that we went a mile high in the sky to fuck again?

"Yes, darling it has all happened in the last twenty-four hours. There's a song about that. Would you like me to sing it to you?"

"Yes, please darling," Kate answered.

With Kate still on my lap and resting her head on my chest I softly sang,"

What a difference a day made, twenty-four little hours
Brought the sun and the flowers where there used to be rain
My yesterday was blue dear
Today I'm a part of you dear
My lonely nights are through dear
Since you said you were mine
Oh, what a difference a day made

Kate snuggled closer. I started to undress her, and she responded by lifting an arm, so I could remove her cardigan, turning her chest slightly towards me so I could undo the buttons on her blouse and arching her back a little, so I could undo the clip at the back of her bra. She raised her head from my chest as I removed her bra so that I could kiss her nipples and at the same time undo her skirt. With my left arm around her back I lifted her a little, so I could slip her skirt down and then ease her pantyhose down the same way. I gathered her curls and brought them around over her left breast. I took hold of the rug that was folded on the chair to my right and pulled it over her, so she wouldn't get cold. She turned her head to me and we kissed passionately. I was able to reach to her knee and began massaging her inner thigh. Kate's left leg slipped from my knee so that with her toes on the floor her knees came well apart inviting my fingers to enter after feeling up her thigh. My lips moved from her nipple to her lips, my left hand kept stimulating her left breast and my right moved from her knee all the way up to tickling her clitoris and then going back to her knee to start all over again. At the end of each movement she was making little thrusts against my fingers and I could feel her dampness.

“Oh Brad, Brad: I’m coming, I’m coming, I can’t stop, and I can’t help it,” Kate cried.

I responded by kissing her harder and slipping my tongue in and out between her lips to match the motion that Kate was generating in her groin. At last the throbbing stopped and I lifted her left leg back into my lap and tucked her up in the rug. We clung together without speaking for a good twenty minutes. I had slowed my hand movements until now I was just cupping her breasts and I planted a series of gentle little kisses on her brow and on her lips.

“I’m sorry Brad; that was mean of me. I should have waited until we got into bed,” Kate said sincerely, “but once you started feeling my thigh like that I was out of control,” she kissed and hugged me the more, “I don’t have a spa, but I do have a big bath, I’m sure we would both fit. Come on I’ll pay some attention to you.”

With that Kate got up off my lap, wrapped the rug around her and went to run the bath. I started a new playlist and soon the bath was run and hot. We stepped in and hugged, standing as we became accustomed to the heat of the bath. Kate’s nipples were still prominent, and her curls tumbled down over her chest.

“He’s all soft and droopy darling,” Kate said as she took hold of my old fella.

“He’ll soon answer to your touch darling don’t worry.”

“What do you call him darling? Penis sounds so silly and medical, not friendly at all and I feel he’s a good friend of mine already.”

"Cock, Dick, Joystick, Snake, Baby Maker, Pork Snork, Sausage, Banana, Jolly Roger, Middle Leg, Short Leg, Chick Sticker, Roger, Love Stick, Horn. Crack Splitter, Fuck Stick, Dong, Old Baldy, there's no end to them really, I've always found 'old fella' as pretty friendly. Then of course there's the erect penis which is a term only doctors and medical books would use along with erection. Mostly a bloke would be referred to as having a hard-on, or a boner, or a fat, or a stiffy, cracking a fat, or ready for action. Of course, when you refer to penis and testicles as a unit then it becomes the Bat and Balls, Family Jewels, Love Bunch, Big Jim and the Twins,

Kate was laughing away at some of the silly euphemisms.

"Come on old fella, get a hard-on; I want you to come out and play," Kate teased. By now we had sunk down into the water and Kate was lying alongside me with her right hand holding on to my old fella.

"Surely a Master of Microbiology has heard all these and more, I dare say you could earn a PhD in researching euphemisms and common language," I said.

"What about girls' parts Brad?" Kate asked, ignoring my remarks about her degrees. "What do boys call our bits?"

"If we start here," I said, bringing my left hand across and onto Kate's right breast. "The most common expression taking breasts and nipples as one is tits or titties; hence Bristol Cities or shortened again to Bristols, Bra Buddies, Knockers, Boobs, Bouncers, Bumpers, Baby Pillows, Bazookas, Cup Cakes, Ear Muffs, Fun Bags, Swingers, Brace & Bits, Wobblers, there are far too many to think of now. They describe all shapes and sizes, from Bee Stings to Boulders, and tell a lot about the person who uses them; some are decidedly offensive when some lout in a car yells out at an unknown girl in the street 'Show us yer tits luv'. I really take offence at that and if I could get my hands on the slob, I'd teach him a few manners in a very short time."

"Like you did for me today at the drome darling?" Kate asked and reached up to kiss me. "Or was it yesterday I have no idea what the time is."

"Something like that darling but don't let's talk about that I don't like getting angry," I said. I turned the hot water tap on with my foot and went back to answering her question. Many have become everyday expressions that you'll hear newsreaders say like Boobs and what with all the rage for breast implants the TV is full of these expressions. Of course, women have always used their busts to attract and arouse men; whether they flash them about with deep cleavages or cover them up, wear bras or don't, flatten their chests or pump them up they're always playing the game.

"What is this thing called; love?" Kate asked and giving a fair rendition of the first line of the song but with the emphasis moved slightly as she moved my hand from her breast to her groin and giving me a big kiss at the same time.

"Well that opens up a very fertile area for the prudish and the comedians and the wags of all kind. Australians all know about the Map of Tassie where the pubic hair represents Australia's smallest state below the mainland, of course there's less use of the term now as girls shave off most or all their pubes for the sake of fashion. The old favourites of course are all alive and well. Like; pussy, fanny, snatch, mound," I paused slightly as my fingers moved down between Kate's thighs.

"And, what's this thing called: love?" Kate was now applying more pressure to my hand as she spread her knees apart and ran my finger up and down her crack.

"Well what we can see from the outside with the legs apart is officially the vulva, but men never use that term and Cunt is the best understood and Crack, Slit. Slot and Twat get some usage too" Kate was giggling now and increasing her hand movements on my old fella while I was doing my best to remain calm. "Men generally use the terms to represent the whole structure including the vagina and cervix and clitoris. Most don't understand the workings of these except for the fact that Playboy stories frequently use the abbreviation Clit. Most blokes that you hear in pubs and locker rooms think foreplay a complete waste of time; they have no understanding of the girl's needs, their interest is for themselves and you hear things like 'Whip it in, whip it out and Wipe it."

"Thanks for the lesson darling," Kate said kissing me again. "Bring your hand up out of my cunt darling and cuddle me please."

With our lips locked together and my free hand stroking her hair Kate increased her movements up and down my shaft. She could feel my excitement growing as I parted my legs to let my balls fall free.

"You'll have me shooting my bolt if you're not careful darling."

"Would you mind Brad?"

"Don't you want him in your front passage darling?"

"I've felt him in there three times now and it was beautiful and when you shot your bolt it really made me squirm, but I didn't see it. I couldn't see what you were giving me."

"Your wish is my command darling; just some nice even ups and downs as if you were sitting on me and doing the hide the sausage with your pussy. She could tell by the noises I was making that she had got her rhythm right and bent down to see my balls bobbing up and down. She kissed the head of my horn and tentatively opened her lips and gave it a little suck before letting it go again. She put her head back on my chest to watch my old fella as I reacted to her efforts and with some hip movements that she recognised from last night I shot off and my semen went up over my stomach and had she been closer I would have shot her in the left eye. She kept up her stoking until the last spasm passed and my old fella gave up its last drop. I rolled to her and wrapped both arms around her.

"Thank you darling," Kate began, "no wonder it felt so good last night with that hitting me so firmly. Can I keep holding your cock until it goes soft?"

"Of course, darling, it might take a while with you hanging on though."

"We've got plenty of time Brad, at least for the next few days. But I won't mind sharing I promise. Just now though I want to make up for lost time and understand what the other girls were talking about. I know you wouldn't be like other men Brad, you would never put your needs in front of those of your girl and now you're going to have three of us to satisfy."

"I'll just keep you all bare foot and pregnant," I said, "that'll calm you down."

"You can teach me some more later darling but next time we'll get into bed first." Kate said. My old fella had shrunk away, and Kate giggled as he slipped out of her hand.

"Thanks for the hand job darling," I said.

"You too lover boy. You saw how delightful mine was," Kate replied.

We got out of the bath, dried ourselves and went to bed. We didn't even look at a clock but wrapped our arms around each other and were soon sleeping peacefully.

Thursday 20 December 2012 – 0630 hrs

Kate woke first from the pressure she could feel growing between us and was looking down at my erection growing to full strength again. She knew that she hadn't done anything to excite it and I was still asleep.' I woke to see her staring at in surprise.

"I didn't do anything darling," Kate said.

"It's all right darling, men often wake up with a horn: it's a Morning Glory, or Morning Wood. Sometimes it's just Piss-Proud."

"It looks like a bonus to me darling," Kate said as she slid a leg over me and sat up for me to massage her breasts and she bent down to be kissed.

"Good morning darling; do you want me to get your breakfast or do you want to fuck me first."

"What if I said breakfast darling," I teased her.

"I'd say that you can't wake me up with your rod coming to attention and waving it around in front of me and still expect me to go and cook."

"I'd like you to grill my sausage darling," I said. I kissed her passionately, teased her nipples and then eased her into position. With my fingers and kisses I soon had Kate lining up my sausage for grilling.

"All the better for knowing what was going on in there darling," Kate hugged me while she waited for my sausage to cool. She had grilled the fat out of it, but it wasn't yet ready to slip away.

"What would you like to do today?" I asked.

"I could start showing you around Cambridge darling," Kate offered.

"And I'd like to take you dancing tonight," I said, "so if you're a good little housewife you can get off me and get my breakfast and then we'll go shopping to find a nice dress for you to wear."

"But I've got the lovely dress that Mary bought for me, Brad," Kate protested.

"You're going to take that to Scotland you said," I reminded her, "besides everyone knows it now and if we do happen to end up in the papers again they'll be saying 'Poor Kate's only got one dress'. That would never do for a goddess would it?"

"No, I keep forgetting I'm a goddess now; keep on reminding me please darling."

Kate let my wrinkled sausage flop out onto my belly and was gone to the bathroom.

"I'll get breakfast under way darling," Kate announced as she left the bathroom ready to face the day.

I was out of bed and into the bathroom to shave and shower, anxious not to waste a minute of our time together but taking enough time to allow Kate to prepare breakfast for us without any help or suggestions from me. I presented myself in the kitchen dressed for a cold winter's day in polo-necked jumper and slacks and solid shoes.

"Mmm, smells good darling," I said as I came up behind Kate and gave her a little kiss to the back of her neck.

Kate placed a plate of bacon and eggs with a sausage, fried tomato and hash browns in front of me and put her plate opposite. She was straight back with a plate of buttered toast and a pot of percolated coffee which she put between us.

"Dig in," Kate commanded.

"It looks lovely darling; we won't need much lunch, will we?"

"That's the idea darling; if you start the day well stoked in this wintery weather, you'll end the day much happier and no fatter," Kate declared.

"Where's the best dance in town tonight Kate?" I asked.

"Oh, the best dance will be the Arts Faculty Ball. I didn't reply to my invitation though because I didn't have a partner."

"Surely you could phone someone to say you'll be there after all?" I asked.

"It's formal so you would have to wear your dinner suit," Kate warned me.

"So, we'll have my suit dry cleaned and dress shirt laundered while we shop for your dress," I replied.

"OK darling, I'd love to show you off," Kate said.

"I'll be showing you off darling, you'll be the centre of attention tonight."

"Not amongst some of the snooty young ladies I've gone to school and university with darling; I nearly said bitches, but I knew you would disapprove, they always looked down on Professor Senden's mousy little bookworm."

"Was Rose excited to be joining our little triumvirate, darling?" Kate was excited too.

"Well, if you call wanting to pinch an F18 and be here this afternoon excited, you could say she was," I replied. "she'll be here Sunday afternoon which means that we'll need to adjust our arrangements for Christmas with your Gran a little."

"Fire away Adonis, your wish will be my command," Kate said gaily.

"If we go to Scotland on Saturday morning, as I suggested last night, and I take you to the ball and stay with you until mid-morning Sunday, I could fly back to meet Rose on Sunday afternoon. We could then come back for you, Mary and Rod next Wednesday afternoon or Thursday morning before Jan arrives that afternoon."

"That sounds great lover. It must be hard for you to work out how to keep three gorgeous women satisfied; you'd better get one of us pregnant pretty soon just to reduce your work load a little," Kate teased. "Let it be Rose though, if she hadn't spotted you Jan and I would still be waiting and not knowing what we were missing. Besides, by Christmas Eve I should be back to my fertile days: I'd have to put the shutters up, or you'd have to wear an overcoat inside, put the nose bag on the stallion, as it were. What do you think of those euphemisms?"

"I think you had better watch out or I'll have you back on the bed ready to teach you some more and then you'd miss out on the lovely gown I was going to buy you today."

"Your turn Brad," Kate called as she threw me the car keys.

Our first stop was the dry cleaner where I was told my suit and shirt would be ready at four-thirty. Kate had decided to start the search for her new gown at the same boutique where she and Mary had found their dresses for Tuesday evening.

Thursday 20 December 2012 – 1100 hrs

"So pleased to see you again so soon Miss Senden," The shop assistant greeted Kate. "And this must be Mr Clifford," she said as she turned and offered her hand to me.

"Please call me Kate and I'm sure Mr Clifford would much prefer to be called Brad."

"I'd be grateful if you would call me Joan dear. I didn't realise it was Professor Mary you were with on Tuesday; I knew she was too young to be your mother, so I thought she must have been a friend or older sister."

"No, I only met her the night before, she's a colleague of my father and she was helping me choose a gown for Tuesday night's function," Kate satisfied her curiosity without mentioning that Professor Mary was my mother.

"What can I help you with today Kate?" Joan got her thoughts back into commercial mode of making the next sale that could well be her best sale of the day.

"Unfortunately, Tuesday's gown got so much publicity that I can't wear it where we're going tonight because some of the other ladies will just say poor Kate has only got one dress, so I'm in need of another gown."

"Well I was delighted to see you and Professor Mary in the papers and in the TV reports: you were the best dressed ladies in the theatre, and I was so proud to have had some input in your selections. What sort of function is tonight Kate?" Joan asked,

"It's the Arts Faculty Annual Ball, it's formal and the girls always try to outdo each other."

"Any ideas Brad?" Joan asked just to bring me into the conversation and stop me from becoming bored and wanting to hurry Kate away.

"I think that Tuesday's gown was stunning, and the off-shoulder style certainly suits Kate, what with her long auburn hair and delicate shoulders, but this time a fuller length might be better for a formal ball and a lighter background, even white with a bright highlight might do the trick," I spoke confidently without the slightest hint of embarrassment. "If you have a matching length evening coat that would be a good idea for these cold nights and long white gloves would complete the picture. Oh, and it must be comfortable for dancing."

"How perceptive Brad, you're not in the trade are you?" Joan asked.

"No, I'm a pilot," I replied with a laugh.

"Why don't you go for a walk for half an hour Brad while Kate tries on a few things before she shows you any of them?" Joan suggested and led Kate to the change room.

I was quite happy to stroll along the main street of Cambridge. There was no rush. Now that the itinerary for our main travels for the year was set there was going to be plenty of time to get a better picture of life in the England of today and the England of the past. In all the countries I had read about it was the same. It was always the Golden Rule – *he who has the gold makes the rules*. I knew that this was unacceptable in the twenty-first century and was never even justified in the past. The educated and uneducated alike thought it just had to be. I knew that changing people's beliefs was one of the hardest tasks anyone could hope to perform. In most cases when it had been achieved it had been one rotten belief being exchanged for a worse one. I was certain too that the world's trillionaires would fight by every dirty means in the book to maintain the status quo where they were the real beneficiaries of everyone's labour. I knew that waiting twenty or thirty years for my progeny to take control was going to be too long. While the Establishment might make their plans for fifty years into the future, I couldn't believe they had any faith in their forecasts. Surely, they knew that the world of twenty-sixty was going to be nothing like the world of today. I knew that I had to find the trigger to bring down the world's economic masters. I had no idea yet what it might be but knew that if I could perceive the problem there must be the means available for me to solve it. I saw Project Adonis as a war and one that must be won if the Faculty was going to achieve its high and rightful goals. I took heart in one thing: this was the Electronic Age; Social Media had arrived with worldwide instant communications and nothing could be kept hidden for long. How could some lowly young private release hundreds of thousand secret documents to the world and at the same time the very top of that man's chain of command, his general, was sending thousands of erotic messages to his secret lover. If it had been the other way around it would have been more believable. Such thoughts kept me very busy as I wandered back to the boutique.

"Brad's back Kate, come and see what he thinks of your outfit," Joan called to Kate.

Kate stepped out from the change room. Her gown was only visible as a splash of white where the front of the red evening coat parted. She had brushed her hair to the left and it now fell over her shoulder. She was wearing new white shoes that the boutique had purchased to suit the gown. She did a small turn to show how it fell at the back. Kate removed the coat and handed it to Joan. The real effect of her outfit was now displayed. It was strapless and self-supporting. The bodice hugged her figure to show her tiny waist, the skirt fell to her toes, and while it produced a nice curve around her bottom and hips it was full enough to give her room to move and dance comfortably. The left side of the bodice had a very elegant tapestry spray of wild flowers in delicate but bright autumn tints and this pattern was repeated down the left side of her skirt. The white gloves, to just below her elbows, completed the picture. She looked elegant and confident and gave me the most beautiful smile.

"I think the outfit complements Kate's beauty, don't you Joan?"

"We tried several Brad but his is the one Kate feels most comfortable in and I think it suits her perfectly."

"Well you certainly did a good job last time and this one will be noticed too," I said. I took Kate's hand and turned towards the full-length mirror with her.

"Of course, I'll be scrubbed up a bit and wearing a dinner suit," I said to Joan.

"You'll make a splendid couple," Joan replied. "I'll watch the newspapers for the next couple of days."

"We're not looking for any more publicity Joan," I replied.

"This one darling?" I asked Kate.

"Yes please darling, it's beautiful," Kate replied

"We'll take it thanks Joan," I said. "How do you think an orchid would go on the right side of the coat near Kate's shoulder Joan?"

"That would be nice Brad, even a small spray of Lily of the Valley would look elegant and add a little more white to the front view before Kate takes her coat off."

While Kate changed, I paid for the clothes and shoes and asked Joan to mind them until we were on our way home; if she would leave the dress and coat on hangers with plastic bags over them for protection, we will lay the clothes on the back seat when we arrive with the car.

"I'm walking on air darling Adonis," Kate said as she clung to my arm. "They are so beautiful darling, I would never have thought of an evening coat as well. It could be worn as a dress too."

"As befitting a goddess, darling," I said.

We walked along the street to look for the restaurant where Mary and Kate had lunch two days ago.

"Let's go in here Kate," I said at the door of a jewellery store. "I think I've seen something to suit."

I spoke to the store manager and he produced from the window an eighteen-carat gold necklace supporting a gold Love Knot pendant; it was an exquisite but delicate piece of jewellery. In the display box with the pendant was a matching pair of clip-on Love Knot earrings.

"Would the lady care to try the necklace for length?" The manager asked. "We can adjust the length to where you wish the Love Knot to fall."

He removed the necklace from its case and handed it to me to drape around Kate's neck. To my eye, the pendant sat exactly where it should once Kate was wearing her new gown.

"How does that look to you darling?" I asked.

Kate managed a smile and a quick nod of her head. She was afraid to speak, at least with the manager so near. In fact, she was scared that she might break into tears the necklace was so beautiful and said so much. The manager tilted the price tag towards me and I acknowledged that I had seen it with a quick nod of my head.

"Have you two more sets?" I began. "No sorry make that three?"

"Not already made up sir, but our jewellers could have them ready by tomorrow afternoon if that is satisfactory." The manager was bristling with pride that he had just made one of his best sales of the year.

"I'll pay for the others now if you don't mind," I said offering my credit card.

The manager crossed his fingers behind his back as he swiped my card and waited for me to enter my PIN. He breathed again when he saw the word 'Approved' appear on the display.

"I made a price adjustment for the other three sir, I've never had such an obliging customer before," the manager thanked me.

"I'd appreciate it if you forgot the name on my credit card. I dislike any sort of publicity," I said.

"Of course not sir; it's nobody's business but ours."

I took Kate's arm and led her out the door. We walked past two more shops on the way to the restaurant. Before the third shop was a narrow lane and Kate pulled me into the lane and flung her arms around my neck.

"Oh Brad they're exquisite," Kate said and kissed me passionately.

"I was just doing my Christmas shopping darling," I replied. "Would you like yours to wear to the ball tonight?"

"What a silly question, darling you know I would, that's why you bought it. It's perfect to complement that lovely gown," Kate giggled.

"Come on, let's go and have coffee and something to eat before someone snaps us on their phone and we end up in the papers before the ball," I said.

We ordered tea and sandwiches then sat and talked.

"That's better darling I was getting quite emotional back there. For a moment I thought I was going to burst out crying; especially when you added another set for Mary."

"What's the theme for the ball darling?" I asked.

"Music from the Big Band Era with a bit of Old Time thrown in, there's quite a deal of nostalgia for the good things from those days," Kate explained.

"That's perfect darling, just the sort of music I like. I was afraid I might have to Rage or something; that would have been awful as I wouldn't be able to hold you close and dance cheek to cheek," I told her.

It was time to go and collect Kate's gown. Passing an ATM, I realised that I had no local currency and that some could be needed for tonight and tomorrow; I withdrew a thousand from the machine forgetting for the moment that I was dealing in pounds instead of dollars. We collected my dinner suit on the way to the car and then drove to the boutique to collect Kate's gown, coat, shoes, and gloves. On the way home, I spotted a florist and stopped to buy Kate a delicate spray of Lily of the Valley, deferring to Joan's good taste and judgment of what would best suit her outfit. Home at last we took our clothes inside. It was five o'clock. Kate took my hand and led me to the bedroom where she kicked off her shoes and pulled me down onto the bed with her.

"Shall we fuck so that I can thank you properly now Brad, or shall we wait until after the ball," Kate asked sincerely.

"If I accept your thanks now darling, we might not even get to the ball," I replied with equal sincerity.

"That's what I hoped you'd say darling; it won't matter then if we fuck until the sun comes up and I couldn't miss the ball after the trouble you have gone to for me," Kate told me. "But we've got to get undressed to have a shower, haven't we?"

Kate reached across me with her right hand to take hold of the bottom of my polo necked jumper and grabbed the other side with her left hand.

"Come on, skin the rabbit," Kate said as I raised my arms to let her remove my jumper. I was undoing the buttons on Kate's winter cardigan as she was undoing the buttons on my shirt. With our buttons undone but with our backs and arms still covered it only took me an instant to unclip her bra and raise the cups to free her breasts; her nipples were showing the excitement of the day's shopping so without any further stimulation we pressed our bare chests together and kissed.

"This is so comforting Brad," Kate whispered.

"Where will we eat darling?" I asked.

"What about where we ate with Rod and Mary; that was nice and cheerful," Kate said.

"If I book for eight o'clock. I doubt if the ball will be in full swing before ten," I said.

I undid Kate's skirt and slid it down her hips.

"You can't have a shower with that on darling," I whispered.

Kate was undoing my belt and then zipper and reached her hand in, "I'll just free Willie for you darling," Kate said as she pulled my old fella out from the restriction of my trousers to poke into her thigh.

She gave me a big kiss and raised her leg and then brought it down on my old fella to trap him between her thighs. "Tell him it's just a sniff now darling but he can fuck me all night after the ball," Kate teased me. "Just as well Rose and Jan will be here soon, or I'd be worn out before my time."

Kate got up, peeled off the rest of her clothes and ran to the bathroom. I phoned the restaurant and booked a table for eight o'clock. I took off my clothes, hung them, and followed Kate to shave while she showered. She made a stunning sight behind the steam coated shower door as her hand on the sponge moved over her body up, down, around and under. I was ready to step in as Kate stepped out. By the time I was out of the shower Kate had left for the bedroom to dress. I dried myself slowly not wishing to get in Kate's way as she did her makeup and dressed. Now dressed except for clipping on my bow tie and fixing my studs and cuff links I went to get them from the bedroom.

"Zip me up please darling?" Kate asked as she turned her back towards me.

"Pleased to oblige darling," I said, and I meant it as the bodice began to cling to her as I zipped. Kate adjusted her breasts inside the built-in cups and now faced me and smiled.

"I haven't put on my lipstick yet darling," Kate said inviting me to kiss her.

"That's good because I would have messed it up," I replied, "Does it get monotonous when I keep on saying your beautiful?"

"Not at all darling, I want to be beautiful for you, forever."

We kissed again, and I held her to me for some time.

"Can I put my lipstick on now darling?"

"Reluctantly yes," I replied, "I'll put on my tie and studs and be ready to go. I'll get a taxi for ten minutes, OK?"

In just a few moments Kate stepped into the lounge room. She was now wearing her high heel shoes and holding the red coat open so that I could see the effect and fall of her dress. The Lily of the Valley spray was clipped high on the right of her coat and her hair fell in waves to the left. Joan had inserted a permanent clip into the coat that allowed a corsage or brooch to be worn without the need for pins to break the fabric. Her white gloves and small evening bag which at the moment was held by a gold chain over her left wrist completed the picture

"I haven't had time to gift wrap your Christmas present or to buy a card," I said as I handed Kate the necklace case. "But I would like you to wear it tonight."

"Thanks darling, that's another thing for me to thank you for afterwards," Kate said. "Would you do-up the clasp for me?" Kate asked and passed an end in each hand back to me.

"I won't be a moment," Kate said as she went to see her jewellery in the mirror.

There was a beep from a car horn and Kate and I went down to our taxi.

At the restaurant we were shown to the same table as we had three nights ago with Mary and Rod and although the small group was playing dance tunes we stayed, and this time carefully read the menu. When the drink waiter arrived, we only ordered a glass of house white each and asked for iced water as well. There would be a bar at the ball, but we would not drink much in any event. We had met at this table only three nights ago and we slowly went over the events that had transpired since. We went to our own beds that night although we would have happily gone off together if we could. Now we were together again content to talk softly about these things and hold hands on the table. Our fish entrée arrived, and we ate without haste for now we could relax and savour these pleasures. Kate hadn't felt the need to remove her coat for although the room was heated there was a draught as the doors came open as other diners arrived.

"It was natural selection at work darling. Mary had seen it at work between Rose and me and she and Rod already knew that I was Adonis and you were a goddess. Mary was convinced that her assessment of Rose was correct, and she wanted to see if we would make the same connection without the aid of her computer. We did and then her judgment was vindicated when Rose became the third."

"But what about Jan darling did you have the hots for her too?" Kate asked.

"Not really, over the last three years Jan was the only relative in my age range who I really got on with, but the age difference is pretty drastic between a fifteen-year-old boy and an eighteen-year-old girl who is already in her second year of university. I was big for my age and we were good dancing partners, but our contact was limited to extended family gatherings and we were cousins after all. I only got to dance with her once at my eighteenth birthday party and I had a distinct feeling that Jan liked being held tightly as we danced. I hadn't seen her since her twenty-first birthday two months earlier and haven't seen her since. I felt compelled to throw some coins in the Trevi Fountain for her although she hadn't asked or wouldn't even know that we would be going there. I don't know what to expect when she arrives and finds out her best matching genes will come from me."

"I'm sure she will be delighted darling, just like Rose and me," Kate reassured me.

"Hello Kate, going to the Arts Ball?"

"Hello Kay, Barry," Kate began, and I was immediately on my feet. "I'd like you to meet Brad Clifford. Brad this is Kay and Barry Jamieson. Kay and I have done microbiology together and Barry is a structural engineer in the City."

"Pleased to meet you Kay, Barry," I said with a genuine smile and warm handshakes. "Please sit down and join us. Or are you meeting someone else?"

"Are you sure we're not butting in? Were on our own too," Kay replied. "We're meeting two other couples at the Ball but we've two extra seats at our table your welcome to join us there. The Williams were going to meet us here and go on to the ball with us, but they had to cancel this afternoon, they have a sick baby."

"That would be great Kay; I wasn't going this year until Brad turned up on Monday," Kate said.

"What do you do Brad?" Barry asked.

"I'm Professor Mary's pilot," I gave my standard reply.

The waiter appeared to take the new arrivals' orders.

"Hold our mains please until our friends catch up," I asked.

"It's all right Brad, you can tell Kay and Barry you're also her son. They're old friends of my family. I bet they saw the Canberra TV reports and magazine articles," Kate declared proudly.

"I'd die to look like Professor Mary when our boy is Brad's age," Kay added.

"That's why I never call her Mum and only call her Mary or Professor Mary as the surroundings require," I laughed.

"You should see them dancing and singing PEOPLE WILL SAY WE'RE IN LOVE. You wouldn't believe they could be mother and son," Kate continued.

"We practised the act for a friend's party in the outback, everyone had to perform, and we all love to sing and dance. Some couples came over fifty kilometres on country roads just for a good night out with good friends and one couple flew 1200 kilometres," I completed the story.

“I loved your dress from Tuesday night Kate,” Kay began. “It looked great in the photos. “Are you wearing it tonight under your coat?”

“No, I would have but it got so much publicity from Tuesday that if I wore it tonight certain girl friends of ours would be saying ‘Poor Kate Senden’s only got one dress.”

“You’re right of course and I know the ones you mean,” Kay was quick to support her. “I’ll bet they’ll be jealous seeing you dance with Brad, I’ll watch,” Kay added mischievously.

“Makes you glad you’re a bloke Barry,” I said. Barry agreed as their entrée arrived.

Kate and I kept our conversation mainly to ourselves while Kay and Barry ate. I told Kate about the talk I had with Group Captain Geoff Johnstone in Agra regarding our continued use of military air routes and protection.”

“And you’ll be flying all that way in your own plane Brad?” Kay asked.

“Yes Kay, it’s set up for it. We can cross the North Atlantic in one hop and go coast to coast in the USA in one hop too. We’re both fully qualified so one can sleep while the other flies,” I said. I went on to tell them how we had been taken under the wing of the India Air Force and flew to England as a military aircraft. I told them how helpful it was with customs and maintenance and what great friends you make along the way. By now, our main course was before us and I was glad I could stop talking; I was afraid I had been doing too much. As soon as we had finished eating Kate came to my rescue.

“How are the twins Kay?” Kate asked.

“They’re three next week Kate; of course, Barry spoils them terribly,” Kay replied.

“That’s the trouble with having girls Brad; they wind you around their little finger,” Barry said now getting into the conversation. “They bat their eyes at you and you can’t say no.”

“Do you think it will be twins this time Kay?” Kate was clearly interested.

“My gyno believes there is every chance of another pair, but we won’t know until the scans in ten days’ time,” Kay answered.

“Better be boys eh Brad? Otherwise I’m going to be outnumbered five to one,” Barry lamented.

“Come on Barry don’t tell me you don’t get a lot of love in return from the three you have already, besides these days girls can do anything they want to even become PMs and the US is bound to have a woman president before long,” Kate told him.

“And about time too?” Kay declared.

“Speaking of time,” Barry said. “It’s about time we headed for the ball.”

“Come on Kate it’ll be a lot less crowded here,” Kay rose and took Kate’s arm as she stood.

“Marvellous how girls can’t take a pee alone Brad, isn’t it?”

We both laughed at this observation that had been observed by men for ever.

“I’ll bet Kay wants to quiz Kate about you Brad,” Barry explained how his wife’s mind worked. “You know, what are his intentions? Is he good in bed? When are you getting married? Or aren’t you going to bother about that? So many girls these days want to have their daughters as bridesmaids.”

"I don't think she'll get much out of Kate," I said with a good laugh.

I wasn't far wrong as Kate told me in bed how Kay had quizzed her:

"What a gorgeous gown Kate?" Kay began. "Is it new?" Of course it was, anyone could see that, but being a woman she had to ask.

"Yes," I answered simply and without any elaboration but knowing the next question would be 'Where did you get it, I haven't seen anything like that around here' or 'How much? You can't get much from your research work.' Or, 'Did daddy buy it for you?' wanting me to say 'No, Brad did.' But none of these questions came as Kay had spotted my necklace and earrings.

"What a lovely necklace Kate, a gift?" Kay began her new probe.

"Yes as a matter of fact, an early Christmas present," I confirmed. "Here comes the biggie I thought."

"A Love Knot too: from Brad?" Kay went straight for the jugular.

"Yes," I answered trying to keep my emotions from revealing too much.

"Are you going to marry him darling?" Kay asked me, unable to not show her enthusiasm.

"Kay I only met him on Monday night," I told her.

"That doesn't matter Kate, we know we can get what we want," Kay continued.

"Is he good in bed darling; he looks as though he would be but some of these hunks are gay you know."

"Kay you know I wouldn't answer that," I replied without any sign of annoyance at the grilling I was receiving. I adjusted my coat and checked my hair.

"Come on Kay, I want to go dancing with that hunk; feel his arms around me and have him hold me close. That's the best of the Big Band Era; a dance is as good as a cuddle."

"It had really been fun darling. I couldn't tell her you weren't gay as that would have only confirmed that you were good in bed," Kate completed her story.

Kay and Kate were both laughing and in high spirits when they came back to Barry and me.

"Good timing girls, we've paid the bill and that would be our taxi coming up to the door," Barry told them. It was a mini-bus and the girls had plenty of room to enter and sit without crushing their clothes and then it was away to the ball. As soon as we entered the main ballroom Kay got a big wave from a table off to our right. It was from one of the girlfriends Kay and Barry had booked with.

"We picked up this stray couple at the restaurant on our way and as they were dressed appropriately, we shanghaied them to fill our two empty seats,'" Kay began. "You all know Kate of course so Brad, this is Joanna, call her Jo, Jo's boyfriend Franklin, call him Frank, this is Rebecca, call her Becky and this is Becky's husband William but don't call him Willie call him Bill. Kate can fill you in with everybody's surnames, qualifications, jobs, bank balances and all that other stuff later as I want to get the intro over before the band starts playing again. Brad is Brad Clifford who claims he is Professor Mary's pilot, but we have it on good authority that he's also her son, bodyguard and escort."

There were the customary welcomes and please have a seat, and so glad you could join us. They had never seen

Kate looking as radiant as she did tonight, nor so elegantly turned-out. The photos of her on my arm from Tuesday night were outstanding but that was on her father's appointment. However, tonight she was just going out to a ball. Nobody passed any special compliment for fear of causing any embarrassment, but Bill couldn't help saying 'I can't believe Professor Mary could have a son your age Brad.' I only replied, 'Beauty ages well mate,' and the talk moved on to other things until the band, which was a ten-piece orchestra with instruments from the era commenced again. There wasn't a guitar in sight. The leader, clarinet in hand announced:

"Ladies and gentlemen take your partners for a bracket of jazz from the Great Glenn Miller"

He played the orchestra in with AMERICAN PATROL. BUGLE CALL RAG and INDIAN SUMMER followed. With the first notes I was on my feet asking Kate to dance.

"Excuse us please," I addressed the table at large. "I've been looking forward to this."

Kate slipped out of her evening coat leaving it draped over the back of her chair and walked out onto the floor with me. With one small step that took her into my arms we glided away.

"I bet you're getting the once over right now darling," I told her. "You do look radiant you know."

"I feel it darling thanks to you," Kate replied.

"Thanks were for later, remember?" I chuckled.

"I remember, and you will too after I get through thanking you," Kate replied.

We managed to keep talking these things and more without missing a beat and with quick steps, spins, turns and pivots glided around the hall. When the Glenn Miller bracket came to STAIRWAY TO THE STARS the band leader took the clarinet from his lips and did the vocal in a fine tenor voice. I held her close through this quiet number and sung along softly so that only Kate could hear. The band leader couldn't hear me, of course, but after many years in his trade he knew he was seeing the outstanding lovers of this night. He knew when such a couple danced to his music, they inspired the others present to get up and do likewise. This was going to be a great ball. Kate and I kept responding to the changes of beat so typical of Glenn Miller. At times we would be swinging our hips and shoulders away; at others I would spin Kate out to arm's length and then bring her back with pirouettes under my raised arm which then dropped to the small of her back as we waltzed or quickstepped away. Other tunes required short skipping steps with swings and pivots. The bracket finished with the MISSOURI WALTZ and we waltzed back to our seats.

"Thanks darling, that was fun," Kate smiled up at me. It was meant for me alone, but Kay was right alongside and all ears. I pushed her chair in for her and lifted the top of her coat to drape over her shoulders.

"I got you a beer mate, fourex out of the fridge OK?" Barry asked.

"Great Barry thanks; beer out of the tap's a bit warm for me I'm afraid," I replied.

"I got you a Pimm's Kate, Kay likes them," Barry continued and then placed the other drinks from his tray around the table.

"Thanks Barry; it looks good, I've never tried one before," Kate said.

Becky and Bill had also been dancing and now came back to the table after talking with friends along the way.

We talked around the table until the bandleader moved forward again.

“Mind if I take your lady for a spin around the floor Brad? Kay’s not up to it tonight,” Barry asked.

“You’d better ask the lady not me; I’ll mind Kay for you.”

Kate was on her feet without pushing Barry to ask her to dance realising that few people observed the etiquette these days. Barry was happy that if he couldn’t dance with Kay tonight, he would get at least one dance with the best looking and best dressed girl in the whole ballroom.

“Kate looks stunning tonight Brad,” Kay began.

“I’m sure she always would Kay,” I replied without any attempt at being gallant.

“Oh no,” Kay was quick to say. “Usually she avoids these functions and makes some excuse. She’s always been shy of boys. This is the first time I’ve seen her open up and be relaxed. I think it must be you Brad.”

“I’d like to think so Kay, but I only met her on Monday and we were compulsory partners for Tuesday night,” I replied.

“What happened Wednesday night Brad?” Kay chuckled and winked at me.

“Anyone can see that she only has eyes for you Brad, and that’s the same sort of answer she gave me back at the restaurant, ‘I only met him on Monday night’,” Kay replied.

“You’re a matchmaker Kay; you just want to get all young people married off because you and Barry are happy and want others to be happy too. Besides, I’m flying Mary around the world for the next six months or more and I’m supposed to be starting a degree course and help run the family business back home. I'm much too busy to think about marriage."

"Then I'll just say that Kate will be and pretty soon too. I've seen it before, when these shy retiring girls get the hots for someone it's straight up the aisle before you can say Jack Robinson."

I laughed with her.

"Come with me Faye," we heard a demanding voice behind us.

"No Robert, let me go please," Faye's distress came to me.

"Hello Robert fancy running in to you tonight," I said. I had stood as soon as I heard the anguish in the girl's voice and gripped the man's right elbow; squeezing it in such a way that Robert lost his grip on Faye's hand.

"Sit down Faye while Robert and I go over here and have a chat for old time's sake," I said. Robert didn't dare say a word or offer any resistance as he was only just bearing the pain in his elbow and arm. Faye dutifully sat in the chair that I had vacated next to Kay and I marched Robert to the nearest door on my side of the floor. After passing through I walked him out of sight and up against the wall. Robert was at least my height, older and very solidly built.

"What am I going to do with you Robert? Throw you down those stairs and say that you had too much to drink and slipped. On the other hand, I could apply a little more pressure right here and you would never have any use of your right hand and elbow again. Robert, I can do anything I want with you right now and there is nothing that you can do about it. Do you understand? Just nod your head if it pains you to speak." Robert nodded his head grimacing at the pain. "Of course, I could just leave you in the same degree of pain as you are feeling now, and you would never find a pain killer and never find another girl to hassle as you've just done to Faye," I said.

"You are going to leave this building, you are going to find some transport and get to hell out of Cambridge tonight and never come back, and if Faye happens to run into you by chance at any time in the future you will get out of her way and keep away. You can send for your belongings in Cambridge when you get to wherever you are going. Is that understood?" Robert nodded.

"I'm releasing my grip and I'll bring the circulation back," I released my grip and massaged his elbow for a moment.

"I can't get any money to leave until tomorrow," Robert almost wept.

I took out my wallet and gave Robert two hundred pounds.

"That should get you far enough out of my sight and remember you'd better not let me see you again or I might get really upset."

"Thanks, whoever you are, I'm going," Robert said and took off down the stairs.

I took a moment to straighten my jacket and take a few deep breaths. I hoped the colour had drained from my face before I walked confidently back to the table.

Kate and Barry were back from their dance and all eyes turned to me.

"Where's your friend Brad?" Barry asked.

"No friend of mine Barry, I've never seen him before," I replied and then bending down near Faye said:

"He's gone Faye and he won't be coming back. Would you like us to see you home?"

"No thanks Brad, if I may call you Brad, I'm with friends over there and Robert turned up and started giving me a hard time."

The music was starting, and people were moving onto the floor again.

"Come on Faye I'll take you back to your friends," I said as I helped her to her feet.

"Won't be a moment Kate," I said.

On the way back to Faye's table I took a business card out of my pocket and told Faye that if she ever had any trouble with Robert or even sighted him around Cambridge to call me, any time, any day. Please promise me?"

"Thanks so much Brad," Faye said and kissed me on the cheek.

Back at the table and seated next to Kate all eyes were on me again. I felt no need to make explanations, but it was too much for Kay.

"Brad that poor girl was scared out of her wits," Kay began. "Did you know them?"

"Never saw them before in my life Kay," I replied honestly.

"Then why did you claim him as a friend?" Kay asked.

"Only to break his grip on Faye and get him out of here without a disturbance," I answered.

"Then he won't be back?" Kay persisted.

"I hardly think you'll ever see him around Cambridge again," I answered.

“Come on Sir Galahad come and dance with me,” Kate said as she stood to take me away from Kay’s questioning.

“I might have to keep you out on the floor for the rest of the night to save you from Kay’s interrogation,” Kate laughed and hugged me. “It was a pretty smooth move you pulled back there darling, Kay tells me. I only saw you marching him out as we were coming back to the table.”

“The poor girl wasn’t even here with him. He turned up and started making a pest of himself,” I was still annoyed.

“The chap at the pilot shop got off lightly then?” Kate said,

“He got what he deserved but this one’s lucky to get off as lightly as he did. I hope that running him out of town doesn’t send him off to do the same or worse to some other girl,” I said.

“I think he’ll have got the message, he looked dead scared what I saw of him. Don’t let it spoil our night please.”

“From OKLAHOMA ladies and gentlemen: PEOPLE WILL SAY WE’RE IN LOVE,” the band leader called.

Oblivious to all the three hundred other people Kate slipped into Laurey’s part and I became Curly. We sashayed around the hall singing our separate parts to each other pausing at times to make our response and at others incorporating a quick spin or pivot with my foot coming between Kate’s and all the time gazing into each other’s eyes. We didn’t even notice that we had no other dancers near us and when the music finished, we were embarrassed to find that we had been dancing in a space in the middle of the hall and all the other dancers had given us this space for our performance and had kept dancing around us as they watched.

There was applause for our performance and as we turned to retreat the band leader was at our side pinning a roving mike to my lapel.

“That was a lovely performance,” he said as he pushed his own hand-held mike towards me and nodded:

“Brad,” I had no alternative to say, other than being rude.

“And your charming partner?” He held the mike towards Kate and nodded.

“Kate.”

“Folks I’m sure Brad and Kate will do the routine again for us if we ask them properly.”

The expected applause broke out and the band leader turned to the band giving them the beat and joined them on the stage with his clarinet. I led Kate into the centre of the floor and now as we sung the words came clearly to all parts of the hall.

Laurey:
Why do they think up stories that link my name with yours?
Curly:
Why do the neighbours gossip all day behind their doors?
Laurey:
I know a way to prove what they say is quite untrue
Here is the gist,
A practical list of "don'ts" fer you.
Don't throw bouquets at me
Don't please my folks to much
Don't laugh at my jokes too much.
People will say we're in love.

We sang the song through and when we finished there was loud applause. Kate and I gave little bows and a wave as we went to leave the floor. The bandleader called, "Thanks Brad and Kate, do you know the proposal scene?"

"We haven't practised that one Mate," I answered.

"Sounds like you're from Aussie Brad? What part?"

"Canberra," I called as I ushered Kate into the relative darkness of our table.

"Well you two, we didn't expect you to be the floorshow," Kay teased, and they all clapped us until we sat. Kate and I sat back in our chairs, looked at each other and laughed.

"We didn't either Kay I can assure you, I've had enough publicity to last me a lifetime and now Kate is caught up in it," I said.

Through the evening the band played brackets from Artie Shaw, Benny Goodman, Glenn Miller, Harry James and Tommy Dorsey all the greats were represented.

"Time for some 'Old Time' Folks," the bandleader called. "Take your partners for the PRIDE OF ERIN," It seemed that twice through the most popular tune for each dance was the bandleader's aim and then he would call the next step as the band made their change in beat. "THE MILITARY TWO STEP," he called next followed by "A TANGOETTE PLEASE," and then "THE GYPSY TAP" and then "THE PARMA WALTZ". It was obvious that many of the dancers were keeping an eye on Kate and me as we moved into each new step. "THE LAMBETH WALK DON'T FORGET THE OI" and then "BALLING THE JACK" and now something to really test the ladies in those lovely slinky ball gowns – THE POLKA MAZURKA. Even Kate in her gown was going to struggle with this one but by holding the skirt higher using both hands and with me supporting her arms we were able to see the bracket through. Many dancers had of course left the floor as they passed the level of their competence but had stood around watching those who persisted. The bandleader brought the medley to a halt announcing, “Now back on the floor everyone for a PROGRESSIVE BARN DANCE to finish off.”

The bandleader started the dance by singing as the band played ALONG THE ROAD TO GUNDAGAI

There's a track winding back to an old-fashioned shack
Along the road to Gundagai
Where the blue gums are growing and the
Murrumbidgee's flowing
Beneath that sunny sky
Where my daddy and mother are waiting for me
And the pals of my childhood once more I will see
Then no more will I roam when I'm heading right for home
Along the road to Gundagai

After I passed Kate on at the first change of partners, I greeted each new partner with a big smile and cheery good evening; they invariably congratulated me on the floor show and I was told to give their love to Kate. Everyone seemed to enjoy the progressive as it gave them the opportunity for a few moments with someone else and a few simple steps to move to. The bandleader came back to sing WHERE THE DOG SITS ON THE TUCKER BOX for the final tune in the set:

My Mabel waits for me underneath the bright blue sky.
Where the dog sits on the tucker box five mile from
Gundagai
I meet her ev’ry day and I know she’s dinky di.
Where the dog sits on the tucker box five miles from
Gundagai.
I think she’s bonzer and she reckons I’m good o.
She’s such a trimmer that I’ve entered her for the local
show.
And my Mabel waits for me underneath the bright blue
sky.
Where the dog sits on the tucker box five miles from
Gundagai

“Thank you, ladies and gentlemen, after a short rest I’ll be calling you back to the floor for the final bracket of the evening,” the bandleader announced.

I accompanied my final partner back to her chair, thanked her and said goodnight.

“Thank you Brad it was a pleasure if all too brief,” the lady said with a smile. Kate was waiting for me where her partner had left her without seeing her to her table. She took my arm and gave it a squeeze while pressing her breast against it.

“It’s been lovely thanks Brad, even if Kay persists in giving us the third degree,” Kate said.

“Ssh, thanks come later remember,” I said

“It’s one o’clock, just as well they’re winding down or I mightn’t keep awake to deliver my thanks properly,” Kate teased.

“You two look happy,” Kay began.

“Yes, it’s been a great night,” Kate replied.

“Is there a place called ‘Gundagai’ Brad?” Barry asked.

“Yes Barry, the Dog on the Tucker Box monument exists too. It’s a tribute to the pioneers. The town of Gundagai is east of the Hume Highway on the New South Wales side. As for Mabel, I believe she was the songwriter’s cow which waited for him every day to be milked and the show he was going to enter her in would be the local annual agricultural show.’”

Kay rose to go to the toilet and the other girls went to keep her company.

Frank and Bill moved up to take empty chairs and so that we could hear and be heard.

"Kate looks absolutely gorgeous tonight Brad," Frank began. "We've always liked her, but she's always shied away way from these occasions."

"We've never been able to set her up with a partner no matter how much we've tried," Bill added. "Tonight, she's the belle of the ball."

"What have you done to her Brad or is it the bronzed Aussie lifesaver thing taking over?" Barry added.

"You blokes are bigger matchmakers than Kay," I said and laughed.

"And that's saying something," Barry agreed.

"What happened with that bloke that was giving Faye a hard time?" Frank now asked.

"I just persuaded him that it would be a good time to get out of Cambridge and never come back," I said.

"He didn't look the type who'd go easily Brad," Frank continued.

"They all go easily Frank if you get them in the right place," I answered. "I felt like throwing the bastard down that flight of stairs but fortunately I kept a hold on myself."

"Nice piece of work mate, only this table noticed what was going on. The bastard could have wrecked the night for everyone," Bill added.

The girls arrived as the band took up their positions on the stage and I rose and took Kate in my arms as the first bars of THIS GUY'S IN LOVE WITH YOU came from the bandleader's clarinet. It was soft and low, and we glided around the floor cheek to cheek. We were pressed together and enjoying every second of this last bracket. WHAT ARE YOU DOING THE REST OF YOUR LIFE? Then MISTY followed, all played by the bandleader in the true Acker Bilk style. As the band moved on to DANCING IN THE DARK the hall lights were progressively dimmed, and the bandleader put down his clarinet and crooned the solo. Kate raised her head for a gentle kiss and then snuggled back down on my shoulder. The perfume in her hair wafted under my nose. Finally, GOODNIGHT SWEETHEART was being played by the band and sung by the bandleader. The ball was drawing to its traditional close. Nearly everyone in the hall was now on the floor and partners were dancing close as the last bars were played.

The lights came up again as the bandleader bid everyone a 'fond adieu and a safe journey home'. The dancers seemed to drift off the floor and an air of satisfaction and exhilaration seemed to fill the hall although most were tired and ready for bed. Kate and I were keen for bed too only we did not intend to go to sleep for quite a while. Back at the table the other couples were getting to their feet. It turned out that Jo and Frank had their car and were going Kay and Barry's way and Becky and Bill would take Kate and me home. Everyone agreed it had been a great night and that we should watch for tomorrow's paper as Kate and I were sure to be featured. We agreed to go out for dinner sometime soon but didn't set a date due to my commitments. Finally, we were underway in opposite directions. There wasn't much talk on the short trip to Kate's.

"Can we drop you somewhere Brad?" Bill asked the stupid question. Becky would have kicked him had it not been for the central console.

"I'll be right thanks mate, Goodnight," I managed to say without laughing. I patted the roof of the car to send it on its way.

I turned to Kate to find she was laughing.

"They prod and pry and then ask stupid questions like that," Kate said and took my hand. "Let's get inside darling."

Once inside I helped Kate out of her evening coat and found a hanger for it. I unclipped the Lily of the Valley spray so that it wouldn't stain her coat and handed it to her.

"You look too good to undress darling, but I'll force myself. I'll just get a gown for you first," I said as I went to her bedroom and selected a warm winter dressing gown that would reach to her toes.

"What do you want to do now Brad?" Kate asked, "We've been cheek to cheek and belly to belly all night I don't want any solo performances tonight darling. I'm hot to trot."

"Me too darling it's just that I feel a bit sweaty and a nice warm shower together would freshen us up," I said.

"I'd love that too darling, do you want anything to eat or drink?"

"Not a thing before breakfast darling," I replied, "only you."

"Undo me quick please Brad?" Kate said as she turned for me to unzip her.

I eased her out of her gown and found a hangar for that too.

"My wardrobe never looked so good darling," Kate said as she held me, now naked except for her panties.

I slid my fingers down each side of her hips taking her panties with them and she stepped out and allowed me to wrap her in her dressing gown.

She had taken off her shoes as we entered and all that she had on now were her necklace and earrings with their love knots.

I had hung my jacket as we entered. Kate undid the studs in my shirt while I removed my cuff links and undid my belt. Kate unzipped my trousers and slipped her hand inside.

"Someone else is hot to trot too darling," Kate said and hugged me with her free arm and kissed me passionately.

"I'll go to the loo while you're getting out of you shoes and trousers darling," Kate hurried off.

I stripped myself, hung up my trousers and put our dirty clothes into the laundry basket. I turned up the air conditioning and adjusted the shower. Kate returned for a quick skin to skin hug and gathered her hair into her shower cap and stepped into the shower. I lathered the soap in my hands and massaged her all over and she did the same for me.

"You've really got a stiffy tonight darling," Kate said admiring my hard-on.

"And you're about to get it darling," I told her "I've been holding you in my arms and rubbing against you as we danced remember."

I was bringing the sponge up her inner thighs now and as I had one arm around her waist Kate squatted a little.

"Give my pussy a wash please darling," Kate asked, and little oohs of delight passed her lips as I gently sponged around her lips and clitoris and while still holding her my lips met hers.

"I think we ought to be lying down for this Brad," Kate whispered. "We wouldn't want to slip and fall in here."

We stepped out of the shower and vigorously dried ourselves and each other's back and after turning off the lights went hand in hand to Kate's bed. I had clicked on the collection of Acker Bill tunes and STRANGER ON THE SHORE was playing. I pulled back the bedclothes and we lay and hugged and kissed.

"What does it mean for a man to be going down on a woman Brad," Kate asked. "Becky was saying it was good fun,"

"It means taking my kisses down from your lips and planting them in your pussy darling," I explained.

"Is it nice Brad?" Kate asked.

"I don't know darling I haven't got a pussy, have I?" I replied.

"I didn't mean that. I meant is it nice for you?" Kate said.

"Yes Kate, but I'm not very experienced, Mary and I only did it a couple of times that way," I said honestly.

"Can we try it now darling," Kate asked.

"Of course, if you wish but I mightn't be any good at it," I warned.

I was kissing her firmly on her lips and massaging her breasts and then broke my lips away and started kissing her down between her breasts, abdomen, navel and stomach. I reluctantly took my hands from her breasts so that I could continue going down to snuggle my face into her little curls and by this time Kate was spreading her legs wide and reaching her hands down to open-up for me. My tongue went straight to her clitoris and excited her madly.

"Brad please stop," Kate almost cried out loudly.

I was quick to stop and come back to her side and put an arm around her,

“What’s the matter, did I hurt you darling?” I asked quite concerned by her sudden cry.

“Not at all darling it was terribly exciting, but I wasn’t doing anything for you. It was going to be another solo performance for me, but I’m supposed to be the one doing the thanking,” Kate said, “Remember? How can we do it together?”

“You want to lick and suck my old fella at the same time?” I asked.

“Yes, please darling,” Kate kissed me and held me tight.

“Well that’s a sixty-nine, a soixante-neuf” as the French would say,” I replied. “You need to lay on me facing my feet with your bottom up in the air so that I can lick your pussy and you can suck and lick my cock,” I explained. “You saw what you’ll get in your mouth last night darling.”

“That’s all right Brad it can’t be poisonous, can it.” Kate was keen to try.

“No darling people have been doing it this way for thousands of years,” I explained; “Going this way is a good method of birth control during the lady’s fertile days.”

Kate was soon astride me and I wriggled her into a position where I could reach all around her inner lips with my tongue and gently feel up and down her thighs with my hands. Kate let her long curls fall down over my balls and tickle my thighs and then parting her locks she took hold of my erect shaft and slipped its head into her mouth. She licked around my head and sucked while gently stroking what was left outside. I didn’t find her quite as accessible as when I went down on her but by continuing my hand up her thigh to her now wide-open pussy, I could slip my middle finger into her vagina while I tickled her clit with the tip of my tongue. I could feel her muscles relaxing and knew that it wouldn't be long before she'd want my horn in there. Kate was highly excited, and she came with giant spasms but still managed to suck on my horn. I had no chance to hold back my semen as it blew off into Kate's mouth and then with her saliva, I could feel it trickling down my shaft and around my balls, and Kate using it as lubricant to keep massaging me. She kept hold of my head until she sucked the last drop out and then let it slip and flop between my legs.

Kate slipped off me and turned to lie on top of me and plant a sticky kiss on my lips.

"Thank you Brad for the necklace and earrings, they're truly beautiful," Kate began. "In the powder room Kay spotted the Love Knot and said 'What's he like in bed. Kate? No one would have said that to me a week ago darling," she kissed me again.

"Bit messy darling, I felt myself dribbling on you as I came, what say we have another shower before I thank you for my beautiful evening coat," Kate asked. "We might need to change the sheets too!" Kate giggled as she pulled me up by the hand.

With our faces washed and teeth cleaned, we stepped into the warm shower and I took her in my arms again and kissed her.

"You looked gorgeous tonight darling and it wasn't the clothes," I said. "You looked the happiest girl in the room and I'm sure I was the happiest boy. I felt like asking the bandleader to PLAY IF YOU WERE THE ONLY GIRL IN THE WORLD but then we would have made us do PEOPLE WILL SAY, again."

"Did you see the flashlights darling?" Kate asked.

"No, I didn't notice," I said, "I was looking at you;

"They were there darling; expect to see us in the newspapers again tomorrow, I mean today," Kate replied.

"I brought in a tube of Mary's balm if you'd like me to smooth a little in. You might find it helps if you insist on thanking me for your coat. You know I didn't expect thanks darling," I said.

"I know that but you're going to get well and truly thanked whether you like it or not," Kate replied. "You can't go around liberating twenty-two-year old's and not expect to take the consequences."

I held her again as Kate lowered herself on to my finger that was now carrying the dob of balm, "That was almost enough to bring me again darling. Let's get back to bed."

I pulled the covers over us, wrapped her in my arms and we kissed. Kate was wide open and with her long legs wrapped around me she pulled me in.

"Thank you darling for my lovely coat," Kate whispered as she surrendered each centimetre along her vagina to my advancing, throbbing horn. My knob touched her cervix and I immediately ejaculated. I had held her close to me with my right arm behind her back and kept kissing her passionately while my left hand had been gently massaging her breasts and teasing each nipple in turn. Sensing Kate's orgasm building in response to mine I forced my left hand down between our pubes to tickle her clitoris and she broke into a full-body orgasm shaking all over and clinging to me desperately.

"Thank you darling for my lovely coat," Kate whispered.

We clung together, not speaking, not sleeping but seemingly in a joint dream of a perfect world to come and our role in it. As time drifted so did Kate's right leg from on top of me and I raised myself to get her left leg from under my side. We were now face to face with my right arm still around her and as I slipped from between her legs, I was still planting gentle kisses on her lips. We lay together for an hour or so. I was drifting but then felt Kate get up from my right arm and pressed my left shoulder back towards the bed. Her hand reached for my cock and she whispered to me.

“You must be tired darling, do nothing, I’m going to thank you for my beautiful dress.”

She kneaded my old fella into being half-hard, still weak but soft and floppy no longer. She ran her lips and tongue across my belly and through my hairs. She kissed my knob and gave it a quick suck as she continued working my shaft into a full hard-on and then sat up and straddled me. Sitting on me, she rubbed her wet pussy against my horn and still sitting erect wobbled her tits at me keeping them away from my reach and her lips away from mine.

“Thank you for my beautiful dress darling,” Kate said and blew me a kiss.

She was now moving her hips backwards and forwards massaging my shaft between her lips but not introducing its head into her vagina. She performed this movement several times more with the semen and juices from our previous climax lubricating us both and several times more she expressed her thanks. She could feel my horn coming to full stretch, so she leant forward taking her weight on her hands by my side and brought her lips down on mine; the Love Knot on her necklace bobbed in front of me and now she allowed me to grasp her breasts. As she made her move she released my horn allowing it to spring up pointing directly into the opening of her vagina and with her next push took him prisoner.

“Thank you for my beautiful dress darling,” Kate repeated as she worked her little bottom up and down but also allowed me to help us both along with my hands.

"Thank you for a beautiful evening darling," I answered her thanks with mine. Without dismounting Kate stretched her legs out behind her to lay full length on top of me and I pulled the blankets up around her shoulders and held her in place with both arms around her and we drifted off to sleep. It was bright sunlight when we woke and looked at the clock to see it was already eleven.

Friday 21 December 2012 – 1100 hrs

"Good morning darling," I whispered softly as Kate's eyes opened.

"I didn't thank you for my gloves and shoes darling, will you take that in kisses. I feel all shagged out for now?" Kate asked.

"No but they can be the interest you pay until you honour your debts in full," I teased her and brought her fully awake by sharing kisses with her.

"I've got a few things to do today; I'm expecting a call from the base commander at RAF Wyton," I said as we got out of bed.

"Why's that Brad?" Kate asked.

"I need to have a talk with him about our plans and future travel," I said.

"We've got to do some washing today too by the look of this lot," Kate told me as she stripped the bed. "We've been saving on nighties and pyjamas though," she added.

"I'll shave while you set the washer going and when you shower, I can help you with a bit more of Mary's balm," I offered. "You did get a bit of a work out last night for a shy, sheltered twenty-two-year-old I seem to remember."

"I loved every minute of it darling, but Rose and Jan had better get here soon to help me carry the load of your passion," Kate called back as she ran off to her laundry still naked and giggling.

I checked my messages and, sure enough, there was one from RAF Wyton:

Please call Group Captain Victor Page on 020 7645 6442 after 1300.

'As soon as I shave and shower.' I told myself. I glanced down at my other messages and missed calls there were at least twelve.

I had shaved when Kate came to join me in the shower. She was still wearing her necklace from last night; everything else was now put away or in the wash.

"I've got a long list of messages on my phone darling," Kate began. "I only looked at two and they're congratulations from last night, we're in the papers it seems."

"I've got a message to ring the RAF Base at Wyton, so we'll check the messages out as soon as we finish here," I said.

"I've put some baked beans on for brekkie or is it brunch now, will that do?" Kate asked.

"Fine by me darling," I replied. "We'll probably be dining in the Officers' Mess tonight."

After brunch, I rang Group Captain Page.

"Brad Clifford here Group Captain I'm returning your call," I introduced myself.

"Hello Brad, I've been expecting your call. Everything has been arranged to house you here while you're in England," Group Captain Victor Page replied.

“That’s great news Group Captain we found it of immense benefit coming from Agra,” I replied.

“Call me Vic by the way you don’t have to salute me you know; unless you’re wearing your India Air Force Squadron Leader uniform of course,” Vic replied jovially.

“Thanks Vic; I don’t collect the uniform until my next visit to Agra,” I explained.

“Could you call in at say three this afternoon,” Vic continued. “We can get you all squared away and brief you on our Standard Ops before dark.”

“That would be great thanks Vic. I’ll be there at three,” I confirmed.

“Would you be my guest for dinner in the Officers’ Mess tonight Brad?” Vic asked.

“I’ll have a lady friend driving me Vic,” Aided.

“Tell the little lady it’s quite informal; no need to get togged up like last night,” Vic added.

“Were you there last night Vic?” I asked.

“No way Brad, I was just going by the photos in the paper,” Vic replied. “Haven’t you seen them Brad?”

“No, I slept in after the ball and I’ve been rather busy since,” I replied.

“I think you had better go and get the papers Brad. I’ll see you at three; goodbye,” Vic rang off.

I found Kate making her bed and sat her down to tell her of my talk with Vic, including our invitation for dinner and that it was casual dress. I told her about Vic’s remarks about the photos in the papers and that I was now going out to get them.

I returned with the morning papers and put them on the dining table. I found Kate packing her things for the trip to visit her grandparents and took her to sit at the dining table to view the papers. I remained standing at her side.

"Oh my God," Kate cried as she picked up the Cambridge Times. One quarter of the front page was a full colour photo of Kate and me. It was indeed a beautiful picture with me looking down into Kate's eyes and Kate gazing into mine. We were obviously singing and smiling, and the photo was taken at the instant where Kate was returning to my arms from a spin. The caption read 'Aussie visitor Brad Clifford and local lass Kate Senden steal the show at the Arts Faculty Ball Last Night – full story page 5.'

"It is a lovely picture Kate," I said as I bent down to kiss her. "Look at the way your hair falls out from the spin and your dress flairs at the bottom to show your shoes and ankles and the way you wear your dress so confidently with no straps. Even your necklace and earrings shine."

"You don't look too bad either lover," Kate replied. "There were plenty of girls there last night who would have loved to be in my place and that was just at the ball let alone afterwards," Kate squeezed my hand. "Let's see what they have to say on page five."

Page five had more pictures from the ball but only one other of Kate and me as we danced to Balling the Jack. I took Kate into my arms to dance and sang along:

First you put your two knees close up tight
Then you sway them to the left, then you sway them to the right
Step around the floor kind of nice and light
Then you twist around and twist around with all your might,
Stretch your loving arms straight out into space,
Then you do the Eagle Rock with style and grace.

Swing your foot way 'round then bring it back.
Now that's what I call Ballin' the Jack.

The photographer had captured us in the 'loving arms stretched out into space' movement, holding each other's hands out wide, bringing our heads together check-to-cheek and with happy expressions on our face.

The reporter had interviewed the bandleader who said that Kate and I were the outstanding dancers at the ball.

"Smart informal tonight, is it?" Kate asked for confirmation, "a nice pants suit would be OK?"

"Yes, it's informal and I'm sure a pants suit would be most acceptable," I replied.

Friday 21 December 2012 – 1500 hrs

Kate dropped me off at RAF Wyton at three o'clock and went on to do some shopping for Christmas in Scotland. I was directed to Group Captain Page's office and was admitted immediately. We now introduced ourselves in person having only previously spoken on the telephone following Geoff Johnstone's negotiations from Agra.

"How about showing me over Alpha Uniform before we get down to business Brad?" Vic began. "Geoff tells me I must see it to believe it."

"Of course Vic, it has caused some interest although it was never intended to do so," I replied.

"Have you got time for the Cook's tour?" I asked.

"We'll make time Brad; this is a must see," Vic continued. "I hope you've seen the Cambridge Times by now Brad,"

"Yes, a beautiful photo of Kate don't you think Vic?"

“It certainly is Brad. A couple of girls in the office said that they were at school and Uni with Kate and could hardly believe that it was she. They were full of admiration for her,” Vic added.

“You’ll meet her tonight Vic. She’s coming back about five,” I told him.

I took Vic through every component of the fit-out and explained the electrics, the plumbing, the communications with worldwide tele-conferencing, the networking of the computers with the ability to display on one of the cockpit panels. I showed him the galley and Mary’s lab of course and explained that Alpha Uniform could do Galway to Halifax comfortably and could even cross Galway to New York with a favourable wind and clear sky.

“Geoff told me to see over Alpha Uniform because I wouldn’t believe it if you just told me about it; and he was right,” Vic said. “And you did all this in ten days”

I gave Vic my standard explanation about having only done the planning and others had done all the work.

“Well if you won’t take any credit for the work you must certainly take credit for the design and planning Brad,” Vic persisted.

“I won’t say that it was nothing, but you must realise that my father was a leading engineer and lecturer and Mary as you know is now a renowned geneticist and both of them, and several others in my extended family, are pilots so organising ability and the attention to detail come pretty naturally to me. I’m proud of the finished job of course but the Clifford and Franklin clans don’t go in for much bragging,” I told him. “Not to mention our mates in the Aussie outback. They see right through pride and any attempt to show off. I think that’s why I’m sensitive about the publicity we’ve been attracting. In Mary’s case, it’s not so bad because it publicises the Faculty and that is going to be helpful to its charter, and in Kate's case it's brought a shy little shrinking violet out of the shadows; but in my case I've done nothing yet. I'm barely out of high school and not a degree in sight."

Vic nodded indicating he understood my concern and I continued.

"That's the reason why coming under Air Force protection from Agra has been so important. We've avoided international airports and their photographers and news hounds. We've had on-base customs clearances, we've been invited into Officers' Messes and enjoyed good company."

"I heard you ushered a troublemaker out last night Brad?" Vic made a question of his remark.

"How did you hear that Vic, at least that didn't get into the papers," I said with some relief. "It was just that a half-drunk blow-in was giving a girl from another table a hard time and I managed to persuade him that he ought to get out of town pretty bloody quick or I might get angry."

"My secretary was in the same party as Faye, the girl you assisted. I was told he was a pretty big bugger, you claimed him as a friend and walked him out and he went like a lamb," Vic persisted.

"He was in too much pain not to Vic. I hope I never get really angry," I told him.

"I've brought our known schedule along for the next six months Vic," I closed the subject that was becoming a bit personal now and could lead anywhere. There will be side trips of course; I want to visit Pilatus and show them how Alpha Uniform has come up; they sourced much of the equipment for the refit very quickly for me back home."

"Seeing that Professor Mary is invited to Washington you could've just picked up the phone and rung the Sec of

State's office to get open skies anywhere the US has aircraft," Vic advised, "and that's damned near everywhere."

"I know Vic, but Mary and I would much rather be invited by blokes like Geoff and you than have someone higher up the tree or some bureaucrat sending you signals saying 'Professor Mary will be arriving on your base and to accord her all courtesy,' it doesn't get the relationship off to a good start at all. You're almost obliged to not be yourself as we would not be your guests but only another duty."

"Thanks for that Brad. You're very perceptive because that's the way it works and obviously, you don't want to be treated as celebrities," Vic replied. "I'll set it up with my opposite number at RAF Lakenheath. He'll set you up throughout the US system. The White House and CIA will get a shock that some things get done better without their involvement. Lakenheath is the biggest US base in England."

"I see you're off to Scotland tomorrow," Vic continued. "I can put you up at Prestwick, they're thirty miles south-east of Glasgow, but there are other bases."

"Prestwick will be fine Vic. I'm taking Mary, Kate and her father, Professor Rod Senden up to her grandmother's place for Christmas; they live a little south of Glasgow, so Prestwick will be very convenient. I'll be coming back on Sunday as I've promised to pick up one of Geoff's officers from Agra on Sunday afternoon. I'll land at Denham Aerodrome and take a taxi in to pick her up from Heathrow. Her name's Flight Lieutenant Rose Sastri and I'm appointed her guide for a couple of days. She flies F18s herself, so I'll probably take her for a trip in Alpha Uniform, while she's here."

"I'll give you a list of our Mess functions for Christmas and the New Year Brad; you could bring her along here to escape any unwanted attention. We'd like to have the Professors along too whenever it's convenient. We're having our own mini-ball in the Mess on New Year's Eve; see if you can all come," Vic said.

"We'll have another one with us by then Vic. Mary's cousin Jan will be paying her a visit for the New Year."

"All the better Brad, you'll have a surplus of girls, so your party will be very popular," Vic said. "There's always a surplus of young officers wanting to dance. I guess we'd better go over to my office, so I can brief you on our Standard Ops and anything else you might need to know."

In Vic's office, we went through the procedures for the base and I was given access to the base's restricted web site. Vic explained that hourly bulletins were posted giving officers the latest weather information for the whole of UK Air Force area of interest which included all of Europe, North Atlantic, Northern Africa and the Mediterranean Sea. All new appointments and aircraft movements were posted here, and Vic informed me that something like 'Squadron Leader Brad Clifford would be based with Pilatus Alpha Uniform at RAF Wyton until further advised' would go up at about six o'clock tonight."

"Using the rank wouldn't be considered a bit unearned Vic, would it?" I asked.

"Of course not Brad," Vic was quick to reassure me "Your airmanship is unquestioned; even bringing Alpha Uniform in the other day in that crosswind was noted and passed on to me. Your current duty requires no lesser position; we couldn't have Professor Mary being flow around by a young pilot officer, and I have no doubt that a squadron of pilots would be happy to fly with you. I saw the whole exercise where you were escorted out of Agra and down to Surat. Your wingmen never had to duck or weave once on the whole trip even in that climbing turn over the Red Fort."

“That was Rose on my port wing and Geoff on my starboard,” I told him.

“I thought it might have been they’re two of the best pilots in the whole India Air Force,” Vic informed me. “You flew the whole section by hand, didn’t you Brad?”

“Yes,” I answered.

“Why was that Brad?” Vic asked. “You could certainly have used the auto after you were straight and level.”

“It was a very scary position for me; I could have killed all four of us and wasted umpteen millions worth of good aircraft, so I chose to trust my instincts rather than a machine which had been programmed by someone in Switzerland. I knew that I had been programmed by some pretty good pilots over the last four generations.”

“You made the right decision mate and that’s why we have been sitting here having this little chat,” Vic concluded.

“Miss Senden is here to meet Mr Clifford Sir,” a young lady’s voice came over the intercom.

“Ask her to come in please Julie,” Vic replied.

Vic and I were on our feet as Kate walked through the door. Her new-found confidence was plain to see. Her head was up, shoulders back, a happy smile on her face which was flushed from the cold weather outside. Kate was wearing a light fawn slack suit, the top was belted at the waist enhancing her figure, the neckline was in a short V that allowed just a glimpse of flesh, and she wore her Love Knot necklace on the outside. The colour of her outfit complemented her natural hair colour. I knew that Kate had spent some of her time today visiting Joan at the boutique because I was sure that the picture she was painting tonight did not come out of her old wardrobe.

“Kate, may I present Group Captain Victor Page,” I said proudly. “And Vic this is Professor Senden’s little girl Kate.”

“I’m very pleased to meet you Kate and may I say more pleasing than admiring you dancing on the front page of today’s newspaper.”

“Careful Vic or you’ll have me blushing like a schoolgirl,” Kate replied with a laugh.

“Please take a seat Kate while we wrap up these last few details,” Vic said.

Kate took the spare seat next to me and gave my hand a squeeze as she did so.

“When will you need to refuel Brad?” Vic asked.

“Tomorrow morning about nine if that would be convenient?” I replied. “I’ll give you my card details now so that any charges I run up can be processed straight away, including any Mess bills for me and my guests Vic,” I added. “Don’t let anyone say that any of us were guests of the Mess. If you expect me to be accorded my rank, then I require acknowledging all of its responsibilities.”

“It’s OK Brad I knew you would say that,” Vic grinned at me. “Let’s go and have a ‘sundowner’. Isn’t that what you Aussies call it,”

“Especially in the outback Vic,” I said. “In the city they got tangled up with the old naval saying of the sun being over the yard arm and too many now can’t distinguish between the sun going up over it or coming down.”

Vic ushered us into the bar of the Mess. It was warm and cosy like the classical English pub so often depicted in movies, there was a small fire burning in a grate in one corner even though the whole Mess was heated to a comfortable temperature. We took a table to one side and

Vic caught the eye of another officer and I heard him say 'Bill would you ask the Chief to come over for a minute when he's free.' I followed him and saw him catch the chief steward's eye and beckon him to our table.

"Can I help you sir," the Chief asked.

"Yes Chief, would you open a mess account in the name of Brad Clifford. He's a Squadron Leader elsewhere but as he will be visiting often, he insists on paying his own way rather than risk becoming an unwanted guest."

"Certainly sir," Chief replied.

"Welcome Squadron Leader, Miss Senden, let me know if we can be of assistance," The Chief said as he went back to the bar.

"I'll get the first round Brad," Vic was rising to his feet. "What will you have Kate?"

"I'd like a Pimm's please Vic," Kate replied as if this was her favourite tipple, not that she had tasted one for the first-time last night."

"A cold beer thanks Vic," I added without the need to be asked.

"He only called the Chief over to the table so that he wouldn't take me to the bar and leave you alone Kate," I explained the subtle compliment that good manners give, "otherwise he would have just introduced me to the Chief at the bar."

"He is every inch a gentleman darling," Kate replied.

"Have a nice day shopping Kate?" I asked with a straight face.

"How did you know I'd been shopping," Kate asked clearly surprised.

"Tell me, is that very smart and appropriate outfit new or did you just happen to have it hanging in your wardrobe waiting for an invitation to a RAF Officers' Mess?"

I asked.

"You'd know if I lied, wouldn't you?" Kate laughed.

"Of course, and I suppose it cost you something like half of what you earn in a month at the Uni?"

"More darling but it was worth it if you like it," Kate giggled.

"I like it, but my goddesses are going to have their own card to pay for all their requirements, without any need to ask for money or accounting for it. When we get home, I'll give you the cash for today's shopping and anything you might need while you're in Scotland. On Monday, I'll go to the bank and get your cards organised. You'll have no need to worry about the limit on your card because there won't be one. You'll never get a call to say you've over spent and never have the indignity of hearing a shop assistant say your purchase was declined. Is that understood darling?"

"If Adonis says so," Kate replied meekly.

"Adonis says so and says you've made a very elegant and appropriate choice for tonight and you look ravishing," I replied.

"Then Adonis had better ravish his little Goddess before the night is over, hadn't he?"

"He intends to darling, now here comes Vic with our drinks."

Vic returned and placed our drinks on the table and placed a second Pimm's in front of the one vacant space.

“Good here’s Miriam now,” Vic announced.

We were joined at the table by a very smart woman in a fashionable business suit.

“Darling I’d like you to meet Kate Senden and Brad Clifford; I’m sure you’ve seen today’s TIMES,” Vic announced. “Kate, Brad this is my wife Miriam.”

The conversation as was to be expected revolved around last night’s event and today’s newspaper coverage and then moved on to a discussion of Miriam’s career. This was led of course by her admiring husband Vic who was obviously proud to be married to one of the leading paediatric surgeons in the country. The Pages were interested to learn what they could about Mary’s work and Miriam was convinced that the growing body of information coming from the study of genetics, linking diseases and body structure problems, was in time going to solve many of the problems facing clinicians today. By now the bar was filling rapidly and Vic took us to the dining room. Tonight, there was no rush by a female officer to grab my arm. Everyone had seen the newspapers this week where Kate had obviously staked her claim and was here tonight to protect it. Dinner passed with good humour and plenty of interesting conversation and over coffee some members were calling on others to give them a song, or recite, or play an instrument or tell a story. Kate and I looked at each other.

I said, “I guess it won’t be long now Miriam?” and laughed.

“No, I think you and Kate should expect to be called on in the next ten minutes. After all we don’t get many front-page celebrities here,” Miriam laughed too.

The dance floor was big enough for eight couples to dance at the one time and adequate for our PEOPLE

WILL SAY number. The Chairman of the Mess stood up an announced:

"Ladies and Gentlemen, in case you haven't noticed we have guests tonight who starred at the Arts Faculty Ball last night and who are just waiting to be asked to do their number again tonight."

There was the expected loud applause led by Vic and Miriam. I rose to my feet and offered Kate my hand. Kate of course had left her hat and heavy cardigan at the door and was now a picture of grace and beauty as I led her onto the floor.

"Mr Chairman if I might mention I became a messmate tonight and accordingly I would like to introduce my guest Kate Senden."

A pianist had slipped onto the piano seat and was playing an OKLAHOMA background introduction waiting for us to start.

"Thanks, Brad, for the correction and welcome to RAF Wyton. Now Laurey and Curly will charm us I'm sure."

The pianist moved smoothly into our number and we sang and moved around the floor with the greatest of ease. Our singing and dancing was becoming more polished and convincing with each performance and our eye contact and contentment being in each other's arms in public, with an acceptable excuse, was plain for any lover to see. The pianist took us through the song before calling 'All in folks' and breaking into other melodies. Several couples came onto the floor for the foxtrot that followed and soon I felt a tap on my shoulder.

"Your tapped messmate, we can't do that to a guest," the young officer laughed as he stole Kate away.

"That's the price of acceptance Brad," Miriam said to me "They do that to each other all the time."

"Will you dance with me Miriam?" I asked.

"I thought you'd never ask Brad," Miriam smiled and got up. "I must say you and Kate dance so well together, have you been dancing partners long?" Miriam asked as we glided around the limited dance floor.

"I met Kate on Monday night actually," I began, "her father and Mary have collaborated on their work for many years but had not met until we got to Cambridge on Monday. He invited Mary and me to dinner and brought Kate along as a dinner partner for me. We spent most of the night dancing as we didn't have a great deal of interest in the subjects they were discussing."

The bracket came to an end and we resumed our seats. There were fresh drinks waiting on the table and Kate had just been delivered to her seat too.

"I hope you put them on my tab Vic," I said.

"Yes Brad, I knew you'd be displeased if I didn't and the last thing in the world, I would want to do would be to anger you without cause," Vic said and we both laughed.

"What does that mean Vic?" Miriam asked her husband.

"Just a little joke between Brad and me darling," Vic replied.

"Brad tells me you only met on Monday night Kate," Miriam said. "I can't believe you can dance like that with so little practice."

"Don't worry darling," Vic cut in. "There's another thing you won't believe about Brad unless you see it with your own eyes. Wait until you see his plane. Brad's flying up to Scotland tomorrow afternoon with Mary, Kate and her father and I'm coming over at two to meet them, I'm sure Brad wouldn't mind showing you Alpha Uniform then if you can come."

"Is that OK Brad, it must be worth seeing if Vic says so," Miriam asked.

"Of course, Miriam, and I'm sure Mary and Rod would like to meet you too," I replied.

"Do you mind if we call it a night folks, the staff are getting into their shutdown checklist," Vic said.

"Would one o'clock tomorrow afternoon be OK for you and Miriam, Vic?" I asked as we left.

"That will be fine Brad, Good night Kate," Vic said, and Miriam called 'Goodnight' too.

Kate and I walked to her car where she had left it in front of Vic's office. We each had an arm around the other's waist and gave each other gentle squeezes as we walked.

"They're very nice people Brad," Kate remarked.

"They're the same sort of people we met at other bases on our way here. At their level in the service they possibly carry more responsibility than any other. They're close enough to the action to be personally involved in the life of those around them and can see the result of their decisions at first hand. Further up the tree people become numbers and statistics, acceptable losses, collateral damage and all those other euphemisms they use instead of admitting they stuffed up. Anyway, there'll be no more civil aviation control of our flights, no more civil customs or international airports. RAF Wyton will be our home in England and anywhere we fly it will be under the protection of the military."

"What about when you go to America," Kate asked.

"That will be all set up through Vic's mate at the US Air Force base at RAF Lakenheath.

"Would you drive please darling?" Kate gave me her keys. "I'll just sit back and think about what we're going to do when we get home. Why do you think we dance so well together darling?"

"Because Adonis's goddesses would always dance well with him, wouldn't they?" I answered her.

"Of course they would darling, both standing up and lying down," Kate answered with a giggle.

We were quiet while driving home.

"You're not going to sleep on me darling?" I asked.

"No Adonis I was just thing about it?" Kate murmured.

"About what darling?" I asked.

"How you're going to ravish me when you get me home darling," Kate replied.

"You won't have long to wait darling, just around the next corner," I replied.

We parked and were soon inside. We tossed our jackets onto the lounge along with Kate's hat. Kate went first to the bathroom while I turned up the heating and selected some good horizontal dance music on my smartphone. By the time I had visited the bathroom Kate was in the bedroom waiting for me to remove her bra and panties and I arrived with only my boxer shorts still to shed. I held Kate in my arms while I kissed her and unclipped her bra. I pressed her nipples against me as I slipped her panties to the floor. I pulled two pillows down the bed so that I could lower her with pillows at her back for support and with one hand at her back I pushed her down onto the bed with my kisses. This time I would go down on her as she had asked last night. As I lowered her to the bed, she had no option but to place one foot either side of mine, and her legs came apart as I lowered her. I continued my kisses with my hands on her breasts and then slowly worked my lips down her body until finally I was kneeling on the floor and parting her lips with my tongue. Kate responded by stretching her legs and I kissed her all around her lips and the entrance to her vagina. I kissed her clitoris and pushed my lips down to cover it and tickle with my tongue. Kate brought her left leg up over my right shoulder and pulled me further into her and I responded by increasing the pace of my tongue licking her clit. I looked up over her curly mound to see Kate lying with her back arched over the pillows and her hands on her breasts massaging them firmly and pulling her nipples out. Kate was nearing a climax and I again increased my efforts to please and thrill her. While my tongue worked her clitoris two fingers slipped into her vagina, my forehead pushed down on her curly mound against the bouncing movements her lower body was trying to make and then she broke into an orgasm squeezing my head out from between her legs as they involuntarily closed. Kate's hands left her breasts to pull me up to her by my hair until she could claim my lips and darted her tongue in and out as she felt the last pangs of her climax. I pushed her into the middle of the bed. She wrapped her legs around me and my now roaring horn went straight home into her vagina. It was wet and slippery from her first orgasm. Kate clung to me with arms and legs as I drove my horn in and out while my hands had now taken over breast duties. Our long hard kisses with Kate's tongue matching my plunges into her soon had me coming with a ripple running down my stomach muscles and quivering against her. Kate's second orgasm was stronger and longer and more uncontrollable than the first and finally we collapsed on my side as I held Kate so as not to bring my weight fully down on her. It was at least five minutes before we spoke.

"This little goddess is well and truly ravished thank you Adonis, she's well and truly; fucked, screwed, rooted, shagged, ploughed, gouged, bored, boned and whatever else you like to call it and she couldn't be more pleased or happier. Her gates will always be open for you Adonis."

"You are precious to me little Goddess Kate and always will be and I want you to have my babies."

We hugged gently, kissed gently, and fell asleep.

Saturday 22 December 2012 – 0600 hrs

I was up early and packed for my one night in Glasgow before returning tomorrow to meet Rose at Heathrow. I had decided not to take Rose to the hotel in Cambridge or to Kate's flat but to take her to a top-quality London Hotel where we were more likely to go unnoticed. The last thing I wanted now was more publicity. I studied the London Hotels on the Internet and selected One Aldwyck as it looked elegant and was central. I booked a Deluxe Room for Sunday, Monday and Tuesday nights.

Kate came out of the bedroom at eight o'clock and straight into my arms.

"I'll miss you after tonight darling," Kate began. "Tell Rose that you've worn me out and now it's her turn. Was it good for you too darling?"

"It gets better all the time darling so we've a lot to look forward to; seventy years at least," I said.

"You won't want me then darling I'll be old and wrinkly," Kate teased me.

"I will want you then and you won't be old and wrinkly," I admonished her. "But that is a long way away and we live in Daytight Compartments remember?"

"It takes a bit of getting used to, but I will," Kate promised.

"I'll get you some breakfast while you load the car; that's my case for Scotland by the door," Kate told me.

"Coffee and toast will be fine darling," I called as she went to the kitchen. "I've got the fuel truck coming at nine o'clock."

I loaded the car and got Mary on the phone. We made plans to call for Rod and her at noon. I told her how the Base Commander and his wife wanted to meet them before we left for Scotland and we were invited to the New Year's Eve party in the Mess. We could talk about all the other details during the flight and in Scotland.

After another long kiss, I left Kate and drove to RAF Wyton. I arrived at eight fifty and opened the hangar ready for the fuel truck. On my way to the drome I stopped at a newsagency and bought gift cards and wrapping paper and now while I had a few moments before the refueller arrived I wrote on the cards for Mary, Rose and Jan and wrapped their Love Knot necklaces. Kate hadn't taken hers off since I put it on her, so I wrote on her card and if she wished she could put hers back in its box for Christmas Day. I would give Mary hers before I left on Sunday morning; Rose would get hers on Christmas morning and Jan when she arrived on the twenty-seventh. I refuelled and did a thorough pre-flight right down to the air in the tires and had the interior spic and span for Miriam's inspection. I locked the hangar and was back to Kate's unit by eleven-thirty.

"Your early darling," Kate greeted me. "I'm nearly ready so we've got time for a little cuddle."

I took hold of her hand and sat down in the lounge chair and placed her in my lap.

"No fingers up my thighs darling; you know what happened last time," Kate giggled.

Kate had her right arm around my back and I had my left arm around her shoulders cuddling her to me with her head on my shoulder and lips offered up to be kissed. As I kissed her, she reached for my right hand and pressed it to her breast.

"Don't move it too much darling," Kate whispered, "You've made a wanton of me in just four nights."

We cuddled and kissed for the next fifteen minutes, saying very little and kissing the other each time a conversation was going to continue.

"I'd better finish getting ready darling," Kate said at last.

I released her and watched as she took off her house coat and donned a new trouser suit, this time in lemon; which again complimented her crowning glory.

"I've got eight hundred here Kate; does that cover yesterday's shopping?"

"More than darling, I didn't spend that much," Kate replied.

"Will you have enough for pocket money in Scotland. "

"Plenty darling and I can always tap Rod for a loan," Kate reassured me.

"OK let's go," I replied.

During the trip to the drome with Mary and Rod the first topic of conversation naturally was the Arts Faculty Ball. We had only very brief talks during the week and now Mary was eager to hear more. She was thrilled with our front-page photo and thought the best possible advertisement for young love one could ever find. The Committee was delighted when they realised that they were seeing Adonis and one of his goddesses so clearly in love, so elegant, and they were hard pressed to believe that Kate and I had only met on Monday night. Rod of course was immensely proud of his little girl and now saw her as a confident, talented and beautiful woman.

"You look different darling?" Rod told her.

"Of course, Rod, Brad has made a woman of me," Kate said unabashed.

"Well you did a very fine job of it Brad," Rod complimented me, and he meant it sincerely.

"I loved your dress and coat Kate," Mary got a chance to speak. "Did you get it at the same place?"

"Yes, Brad told Joan what he thought would suit me and she did the rest. He's got good taste, hasn't he?" Kate replied.

"Of course, he chose you, didn't he? It didn't take the computer to tell him who his goddesses were."

"It's not really polite to be talked about like this," I remarked.

"Don't worry Brad we're all proud of you," Rod consoled me.

At five minutes to one we pulled up at the hangar and I clicked the remote to open the doors. We drove in just as Vic was pulling in behind us. I completed the introductions.

"Let me show you through Miriam," Mary was quick to offer.

"Yes please Mary," Miriam was as quick to reply. "Vic told me that I won't believe it unless I see it with my own eyes."

Kate went along with the girls knowing that she could sit out of the way and leave the men to talk. Vic wanted to know more about the work of the Genetics Faculty and of course Rod was the right man to explain it. He quickly understood the need for matching the right man with the right woman: particularly the savings that would be made by having fewer divorces, domestic disputes and violence. He wanted to know whether current technology could determine whether an applicant was capable of becoming a fighter pilot and Rod answered 'Yes' very convincingly; 'if the required abilities and character attributes were properly specified'. Vic understood that bad attitudes could be bred out of a line of inheritance but what about correcting bad attitudes among the living members of that line. Rod explained that these things were before them and within their reach. In the future, prescriptions will match the genetic needs of a patient and mass medication and vaccination will be a thing of the past. Rod also spoke of the emerging realisation that the criminal was not only acting out his own personal antisocial problems but those of ancestors for several generations and no punishment yet devised has been able to correct this problem; in fact, everything to date has only aggravated it. Even the death penalty has only embedded more hatred into the descendants of the executed and has never served to deter others from committing the same crime. There is much to be done he told Vic but at last it is underway. We have been working as small almost isolated departments for many years since the completion of the Human Genome Project but now as an integrated Faculty comprising fourteen major universities, we have a chance.

"Of course, none of this would be happening if it hadn't been for Mary's leadership over the past ten years," Rod explained. "Her insights have inspired the team, the universities and the various governments to make this happen."

"But I heard that Mary didn't know anything about this until it was dumped in her lap two weeks ago," Vic said.

"That's right. The ANU was going to tell her all about it in the New Year and the start date was set for April. But after Bruce was killed, she asked for a year's sabbatical so they had to act fast."

"I saw the TV report of course," Vic replied. "Your speech Brad gave her no way out. It was obvious that Mary didn't realise that the whole night was for her."

"Thank heavens he did Vic," Rod replied. "We would really have had egg on our face if Mary had run out in tears."

"And you just happened to have Bravo Mike Charlie ready to fly her out of town that night?" Vic replied.

"That's right Vic," I said. "I told you, we were going on a world trip."

"And now you're half way around the world escorting a beautiful and famous woman and taking pretty girls dancing," Vic was almost exasperated.

"Good onya mate," Vic said as he slapped me on the shoulder. "Isn't that what Aussies say?"

"Something like that mate," I laughed with him.

"Anything I can do for you while you're away?" Vic asked.

"If someone from your office could ask Heathrow VIP arrivals to collect Rose from her flight and usher her through their security?" I asked. 'That would be a big help. I don't want to get snapped with another pretty woman just yet."

"What a problem to have Vic?" Rod laughed with them.

"I've written her flight details and her seat number on this card. I'll wait at the VIP gate for her," I said.

"Something like please assist Flight Lieutenant Sastri as she's on exchange duty with RAF Wyton?" Vic asked.

“Don’t worry I’ll do it myself Brad. There’ll be a car at Prestwick that you can use for tonight.”

The ladies came down the steps and joined us.

“It’s beautiful Brad,” Miriam began. “Vic was right; I wouldn’t have believed it if I hadn’t seen it for myself.”

“We better let them go Miriam,” Vic said taking Miriam’s arm.

“You will come to the New Year’s party?” Miriam asked. “Bring Rose.”

“We’d love to Miriam,” Mary replied, “My cousin Jan will be visiting by then.”

“Bring her too of course; single girls are in short supply in the Mess,” Miriam called back as I went to make a final inspection of Alpha Uniform’s tanks.

We were soon airborne and reached our cruising altitude of six thousand feet in just three minutes. There was no point in going higher as the trip was only one hour and there were no mountains along our track. We were all seeing the country we were flying over for the first time. The day had started with snow showers but now the clouds had lifted, and weak sunlight was giving shape to the land and towns below. No sooner had we landed and received directions to the parking area an officer from the Base Commander’s staff arrived to welcome us and the promised courtesy car followed. I took the driver’s seat and we headed for Glasgow. Rod phoned his mother as soon as we were underway and told her we would be there in fifteen minutes.

Gran was first to the door to meet us. Her husband Wallace Senden was close behind. I guessed they were both around sixty-three years old and very fit with no surplus fat on their frames

"You do look so well dear," Gran addressed Kate. "Come in everyone."

Gran ushered us into the large sitting room and Rod did the formal introductions.

"So, this is the young man who's swept our little girl off her feet," Gran said as she took my hand and at the same time bestowed a kiss on my cheek. "You looked splendid dancing together Brad."

"Thanks Gran. Kate's so easy to dance with," I replied. "I bet you do a pretty fine waltz too. Will you save a dance for me tonight?"

"I'd be delighted Brad; tonight's the highlight of the year around here," Gran replied.

"And Professor Mary, we've heard so much about you over the years and at last you're here," Gran was clearly excited.

Pop Senden was coming along behind to shake our hands and add his welcome but clearly Gran was the one running the show.

"You're the first to arrive so I'll show you your rooms and we can have a cup of tea and a chat."

"You and Mary are in here Rod and Kate and Brad over there," Gran said opening the doors to our rooms as she went. "I assumed that's the way you would want it?" Gran said, quite up to date with the ways of the world.

"Of course Mum, thanks," Rod replied.

After we had unpacked our cases and Kate and I took five minutes for a kiss and cuddle on the soft old-fashioned mattress. We tested the springs for squeaks before we gathered again in the living room. Gran and Pop wanted to know all about the happenings of the last month before the rest of their guests arrived and a more concise version offered. Gran wanted all the details.

“Mind if I take Brad to show him your garden Gran?” Kate asked politely, knowing that she and I would be a large part of the conversation and we would rather not be present.

“Of course not darling,” Gran was happy to oblige. “I’ll call you when your other grandparents arrive.”

Kate took my hand and led me out through the long veranda on the western side of the house. It was an old house, at least one hundred years old, but so solid and well-constructed that it was good for another hundred years. There were twelve bedrooms and at times during its history they had all been occupied by the one family; but now only her grandparents and Rod’s younger brother and his wife lived here. Tonight, and until after Christmas, the rooms will be full, and the house will fill with laughter, music and singing again.

“I’d love to be staying the whole time with you darling,” I began.

“I know, and I would be pregnant before we got back to Cambridge and that would never do,” Kate told me. “Rose must be first to conceive darling and then we can work out how to space our pregnancies from there. We can’t all be delivering babies in the same month or you’d be worn ragged.”

We strolled around the large garden hand-in-hand. Behind the tool-shed, we stopped for a kiss and cuddle, and then continued into the orchard. The trees had lost their autumn colour and the dead leaves, still showing orange and gold, were on the ground. The garden and orchard covered five acres and we had been strolling for fifty minutes when Kate’s phone rang.

"The Francis family have arrived Kate," I could hear Rod say.

"We'll be right back Dad," Kate said. "I don't need to flatter his ego in front of the family Brad. I'm sure he would much rather I be seen as his grown-up daughter; especially with the catch she's made."

We both laughed and turned to take a direct path back to the house.

The Francis party had arrived in two cars. There was Kate's grandmother Nan, her grandfather Pa, her mother's sister Katherine and Uncle Jonathon, their son Roger, who was Kate's age, and his girlfriend Sue and their nine-month-old baby Annie. Kate's cousin Jack and his wife Katherine were there with their four-year-old son Charlie. Katherine was eight months pregnant again and expecting a daughter. By the time Kate and I arrived back at the house the rest of the Senden family had arrived. Rod's younger brother Horace and his wife Alana had arrived home from work and Rod's sister Anne, her husband Harry and their children Jack who was eight and Curt who was six. There was Rod's uncle Graham Senden and his wife Joanna who were both a couple of year's younger than Pop Senden and their son Oscar and his wife June who were Rod and Mary's age. All Pop and Gran Senden's house guests had arrived and the ladies were anxious to talk to Mary and Kate about the dresses they had seen them wearing in the newspaper photos and all about Mary's work.

"Come on you blokes, time I bought you a beer," Pop Senden announced and led the men out into the typically large kitchen. "The girls can look after themselves for a while, there's some giggle juice in the decanters on the buffet."

"Well what have you been doing with yourself Rod?" his father asked to get the conversation started.

“You’ve seen most of it in the papers except Mary and I’ve spent the past week talking with a lot of professors,” Rod replied.

“The papers have been mostly full of Brad and Kate dancing, I reckon,” Pop continued. While he’d been talking Pop had been getting out several bottles of his home brew from a cupboard in the pantry and Rod’s brother was getting out the beer glasses.

“I suppose this is pretty potent stuff Pop,” I asked. “I’ve got to be able to dance tonight.”

“Don’t worry Brad. We’ll all be dancing tonight. After a couple of these your feet won’t be touching the ground,” Pop replied.

The talk soon broke up into several different topics. Some wanted to know about the flight from Australia, others wanted to know why we had landed at an air force base and others wanted to know more about Rod and Mary’s work. They all knew of course that Rod had been working in genetics for years but didn’t realise that it had such significance until two weeks ago when the Faculty was announced and then this week when Rod was awarded the Chair at Cambridge. And as for Mary they had no concept that a woman who appeared on this month’s cover of VOGUE, (so their wives had told them) could be the leading light of genetics research.

I had gone slowly with the home brew and rather than emptying my glass, along with the others, only had it topped up as the talk progressed. Having to do a lot of the explaining I didn’t appear to be dragging my feet. At last it was time to be getting ready for the ball. I went to our room to find Kate dressed in her frock from Tuesday night and waiting for me to zip her up. She looked splendid in her ballerina length gown with her Love Knot pendant resting on her bare chest above the hint of cleavage and her earrings shining in the light.

“Have a good chin wag?” I asked.

“Yes, great, I explained to Gran that you must go back to London tomorrow for work,” Kate said, “She immediately said that we should come back for a real holiday when the whole family isn’t around. She’d love to show us around this part of Scotland.”

“I’d better get ready,” I replied. “Where’s the nearest bathroom darling?”

“I think the one opposite is free. Take possession quickly,” Kate answered.

“You look as delicious as ever Kate,” I complimented her, “did they give you a hard time in the living-room?”

“Not really darling; they were quiet after I told them you were great in bed and that when you went down on me, I lost all control and then was really stuffed,” Kate couldn’t say anymore because she was laughing loudly.

“The home brew didn’t get to you Brad,” Kate said with obvious relief.

“No way, I wasn’t going to let home brew spoil a good night with you darling,” I said. “I didn’t empty my glass once.”

Kate and I were last to arrive in the living room. Charlie and Katherine were staying home baby sitting and looking after the young ones, as she would only have been sitting around at the ball.

I managed to get the first dance with Kate but after that there was a procession of grandfathers, father, uncles and cousins lining up to dance with her and I made a good fellow of myself by dancing with their partners.

“Here’s your dance Brad,” Gran called as the orchestra broke into a Viennese waltz and this time, I was the first onto the floor leading Kate’s grandmother.

Gran danced the old waltz effortless, and when I reversed, she wasn’t concerned.

“I’ve had many years to practice Brad,” Gran said when I complimented her.

“I would have done better if I had a partner like you Brad, Kate is a very lucky girl,” Gran said. “She told me you have to go back to London tomorrow?”

“Yes, I’m afraid so, but duty calls,” I replied.

“Then you must come back with Kate for a proper holiday when you can,” Gran invited me. “I’d love to show you around our little part of Scotland.”

“And we could show you and Pop parts of Scotland that you can’t see by road,” I offered.

“Kate told me you flew around the coast at five hundred feet on Wednesday; that must have been thrilling?” Gran said.

“Yes, it was, and we’ll do it again when we come to visit,” I said, “We can’t promise when because I’ve got to fly Mary around the other universities before the end of May.”

“At least the weather will be warmer then Brad,” Gran replied.

The waltz ended, and I escorted Gran to our table. As the ball was ending, I claimed Kate for the last dance.

“You were so popular darling I couldn’t get a dance all night,” I tried to be stern.

"It wouldn't have been so a month ago darling," Kate replied, "anyway, I'm all yours now until breakfast time; do what you will with me."

"The walls are pretty thin darling," I said.

"Then we must see what it's like to do it quietly," Kate smiled up at me and gave me a quick kiss.

Once we arrived home, everyone was ready for bed. Kate and I were two of the first. We wanted memories of tonight to last her until after I had collected Rose, and then Jan, and we could all be together in Cambridge. Although I thrilled her, three times before daybreak, she stifled all her usual vocalising and only a few giggles might have been heard outside our door.

Sunday 23 December 2012 – 0630 hrs

Gran was running an on-demand mixed grill as the guests appeared in the kitchen. She was aided by the older children cooking toast and serving cereal for their elders. Kate and I ate together, and I started making my farewells as the others appeared. Rod and Mary had eaten earlier and gone for a walk. Returning to our bedroom I gathered my things to put in the car. I wore the business suit trousers from the night before and carried my suit coat and tie. I wore a white business shirt and I would present myself at VIP Heathrow as a squadron leader from the India Air Force in civvies. I paraded before Kate who approved my appearance and then wrapped her arms around me to give me the kind of parting kiss that would have been inappropriate in front of the assembled guests and their children. We went looking for Mary and Rod and found them in the garden as they returned from their walk.

"Time to go folks," I said.

"Yes, go and get another goddess for us Brad," Rod replied.

"Something to open on Christmas Day Mary," I said as I pressed the package into her hand.

"You shouldn't have Brad. We haven't had time to think about Christmas let alone buy presents," Mary replied.

"Us too, I only bought four gifts, sorry Rod," I said. "I wouldn't know where to start or stop after what has happened in the last few weeks."

"I've still got my laptop with me Brad," Mary began. "Tomorrow I'll send everyone we've met a Christmas message and a thank-you where appropriate. Now kiss Kate goodbye and go and get Rose."

I shook Rod's hand, received a good kiss on the lips from Mary and turned to give **Goddess Kate http://www.futuristic.guru/goddess-kate** a big hug and a kiss,"

"I'll bring Rose with me when I come back for you on Thursday morning," I said, "I'll keep in touch."

After returning the courtesy vehicle to our hosts at RAF Prestwick, and thanking them for their hospitality, I took off for London. In the air and alone I could relax. I loved to be with Kate and Mary above anything else, but all the relatives and friends' interest and expectations did exert an emotional pressure. I knew that my time with my goddesses would always be exciting; Kate had been amazingly exciting for me as she found her own sexuality and blossomed in my arms. I had no doubt that the time I was about to spend with Rose would be exhilarating too, considering what had transpired with her during our fleeting visit to Agra. I had no idea what might happen when Jan arrived next Thursday and decided to put any speculation out of my mind and trust the computer science that had identified her as a goddess. It wasn't long before I had my landing clearance to Denham Aerodrome; from here it was only about a ten-mile taxi ride to the busy Heathrow International where Rose would be landing in an hour. On the way to Heathrow I receive an SMS from Vic, 'VIPHeathrow expect Sqdr/Ldr Clifford to call for F/Lt Sastri, have your card ready,' meaning my India Air Force ID Card.

Chapter 13

Goddess Rose

Sunday 23 December 2012 – 1200 hrs

When I entered the Heathrow precinct, I phoned VIP Arrivals and told them I was there to collect F/Lt Sastri. I was told my taxi could wait in the carpark at VIP Arrivals and that her flight had just landed. I sent an SMS to Rose saying 'Handshakes Only on Arrival' then I went inside, introduced myself at the desk, took a seat and read a newspaper until Rose appeared. I was taken aback at first for I hardly recognised her. Before my eyes was a high-class Hindu lady in an exquisite sari of pink, silver, and trimmed in green. I was immediately on my feet and extending my hand.

"Good after noon Lieutenant Sastri, I hope you had a pleasant trip," I managed to say, loud enough for everyone within earshot to hear.

"Very pleasant sir I was looked after well," Rose replied. "Of course, I would have been here in a third of the time if I'd been flying my F18."

"Let me take your bag Lieutenant," I said as I ushered her out of VIP with a nod of thanks to the girl on reception. I thought the sooner I had Rose safely in the taxi the better and the less likely we would overplay our little charade. I had expected her to arrive in slacks, a bomber jacket and a pilots' baseball-type cap on her head and had been taken by surprise by her stunning, never to be forgotten, appearance. Without a further word being spoken I ushered her into the waiting taxi for the drive into the city. I now had the chance to hold Rose's hand, put my arm around her back and give her a welcoming kiss.

"You didn't seem pleased to see me Brad?" Rose sounded quite hurt.

"I'm delighted to see you Rose but thank heavens I organized a VIP arrival for you or we would have been all over tomorrow's papers. You look absolutely stunning, they wouldn't have believed that Lieutenant business for a minute; they would have assumed you were a Bollywood star," I spoke with conviction and Rose's spirits rose with mine. She clung to my hand for the rest of the drive into London until our taxi came to a stop at One Aldwych. We registered and collected our room key and by the time we reached the room a porter had delivered our bags from the taxi and I gave him one of my fives as we passed.

"This is beautiful darling," Rose said as she ran through the suite.

When she came back from her inspection, I caught her in my arms and kissed her properly.

"I've ached for this darling from the first time I saw you," Rose said as she came up for air, "I didn't dare dream it would happen like this. Let's talk lying down please Brad."

I hung up the 'Do not Disturb' took off my coat and shoes and then lifted Rose in my arms and carried her into the bedroom. The air conditioning was warm and soft music was playing on the intercom. I lowered Rose to the bed and slipped in beside her. While holding her to me and kissing her I unwrapped her from her sari leaving her in her bodice and soft sheer long pants. I felt her breasts through the bodice realising that there was no support holding her in her firm upright stance, I ran my hand down over her belly and mound and realised there were no panties or obstacle below these sheer garments. Rose was now unbuttoning my shirt then loosening my belt while my hand went down the inside of her pants and she spread her legs to let my fingers run up and down her crack.

"No condom this time please Brad," Rose almost implored me, "I want to feel you in there. Feel you come; you couldn't imagine what it has been like."

"No darling we're finished with condoms," I said.

Rose giggled as she pulled my trousers over my hips. My old fella sprung up and she grabbed it and kissed it. We shed the rest of our clothes and Rose fell back on the bed and pulled me onto her.

"This one won't take long darling," Rose warned me as she wrapped her legs around my thighs and pulled me in.

I was pushing Rose down into the luxury of this soft king-sized bed, massaging her breasts and playing with her nipples and all the while kissing her and being kissed in return. It was only about two minutes from entry that I was coming and bringing Rose to a thrilling orgasm. Rose was clinging to me so tightly that I could feel her finger nails in my back.

"Hello Goddess Rose," I said as soon as we had calmed a little.

"Hello darling Adonis," Rose answered me and kissed me again. "Wow that was good. It's as if you're shaking this rigid engineer loose and free."

"That's a nice thought darling," I began. "Look forward to some more freeing up later."

"What will we do while I'm waiting darling?" Rose asked.

"It's now three o'clock on Sunday afternoon," I began. We were still lying in each other's arms while we discussed our itinerary, "I've booked this room for tonight, Monday night, which is Christmas Eve and Tuesday night which is of course Christmas Day. I thought we could take Alpha Uniform for a flight on Wednesday. I'd like to fly around Ireland as we will be departing from there to go to the US. We could have a look around, overnight at a pub, or on-board Alpha Uniform and then pop over to RAF Prestwick to pick up Mary, Kate and Rod on Thursday morning. Thursday afternoon I've got to be back at Heathrow to pick up Jan."

“Then you will have your three goddesses together darling,” Rose said without any trace of jealousy. “I’m looking forward to meeting them darling. I’ll love to have two more sisters and they must be very nice people for you to fuck them darling.”

“I haven’t fucked Jan yet Rose,” I replied. “It feels strange that she’s the third seeing as I’ve known her all my life and she’s a cousin.”

“You’ll manage darling,” Rose replied with a giggle and a hug. “I’m sure Jan will see to that just as Kate and I have.”

“Come on Rose we’ll try that nice big spa bath and then think about what you would like to do for dinner,” I began as we untangled ourselves. “We could have our dinner served here in our own dining room or go and eat in the dining room downstairs. There won’t be any photographers allowed in this establishment and it would be most improper if one guest took photos of another.”

I shampooed Rose’s raven black hair as I had done for Mary and massaged the tensions from her neck and shoulders. I soaped, massaged and sponged her all over and Rose relaxed.

“That’s lovely Brad. More just there please darling. I didn’t know I was so tense,” Rose murmured. I had resisted paying too much attention to her breasts and groin deciding to measure my assault on her over the time we had together rather than shag ourselves silly in our first twenty-four hours together, tempting as it was to us both.

Rose came up onto her knees and after rubbing her nipples over the hair on my chest on her way to implanting a big kiss on my lips she started by washing my hair and then the rest of my body. Finally, we lay in each other’s arms in the warm bubbling water. My old fella was half-rigid, but we were content for Rose to hold it between her thighs as we kissed. We decided to go to the hotel dining room for dinner and Rose would wear something more casual so as not to draw attention to us by wearing her high-class sari. She would keep that to wear on the right occasion with me and sometimes when we were alone. Our hotel offered many features and we strolled around them on our way to the dining room. There was a day-spa, gym and fabulous indoor pool to see and we instantly decided to buy bathers tomorrow so that we could try out the pool.

We paused in the bar for one drink before going in to the dining room and struck up a conversation with a young honeymooning couple from Chicago. I found it refreshing to be able to sit and chat with another young couple who, like Rose and me, only had eyes for each other and wouldn't recognise me or know anything about my activities. We talked about what we were going to do over the next three days and our plans for the future. Rose and I were happy to adopt the role of willing and interested listeners for the most part, because nobody would understand our plans. Let alone the fact that Rose was a serving office in the India Air Force and flew F18s. We went in to dinner together and carried on our conversation during the meal. The American couple told us of a show they had seen the night before just around the corner at the Lyceum Theatre. We felt there would be a good chance for getting tickets for tomorrow night as it was Christmas Eve and most people have other things to do. We talked of the places we wanted to see and how many of them were in easy walking distance of our hotel in Covent Garden. The Embankment, Waterloo Bridge, The Mall, Buckingham Palace and James Park weren't very far away. So many sites in London had inspired love songs over the years: even street names and parks were steeped in nostalgia. I would like to see if there were any nightingales in Berkeley Square. And to visit Lambeth for the sake of the old song from GUYS AND DOLLS and the fun the dance brings out in the dancers. The evening with the newlyweds was special because it was so ordinary: much like how any two honeymooning couples might act together. When asked whether Rose and I were honeymooners too I declared we were even though it was obvious that Rose wasn't wearing any rings on her fingers. I didn't tell them I had just left the girl with whom I had been honeymooning for the previous five days that morning nor that I had another honeymoon coming up on Thursday. I surprised them telling my belief that the Allies prevailed in the Second World War because our troops fought to protect their wives, girlfriends and mothers against aggressors who were driven by rhetoric, personality cults and rabid nationalism. Allied servicemen and women went to war with photos of their loved ones in their pocket or kit and if they had none of their own, they had a photo of Betty Grable and those famous legs. The Allies carried the songs of the Andrews Sisters and Vera Lynne in their hearts while the aggressors marched to the music of the gods of war.

At ten o'clock, we were keen to break up and go to our own rooms to carry on today's honeymooning in private.

I took Rose in my arms to sit in a big lounge chair and listen to the music before we went to bed. There was nothing we wanted to eat or drink; Rose couldn't even be tempted by the hand-made chocolates that the housekeeping staff had left on our pillows. With her head on my shoulder we decided that tomorrow we would go for a stroll of the immediate area and along the Embankment. I had to make a call at the London branch of my bank to arrange for the cards for my three goddesses but apart from that we were free of any other commitment. We would have liked to visit the British Museum, but it was to be closed for the twenty-fourth to twenty-sixth, so we would miss it this time. While we had been talking, I had slipped my hand under Rose's pants-suit top and unclipped her bra.

"I'll just keep you warm," I whispered in Rose's ear as I gently massage each breast in turn and lightly touched her nipples as I moved to and fro and quietly undressed her.

“I think we could do this better lying down darling?” Rose suggested.

I stood up with Rose still in my arms.

“Don’t give yourself a hernia darling, that would never do; what would your other goddesses say of me if I took you back damaged?”

“You’re as light as a feather, darling,” I replied.

To prove my point, I put her down and quickly stripped. I picked her up again with my hands under her arms, lifting her feet from the floor. Her arms went around my neck and her legs came over my hips to cling to me. I brought my hands down to hold her buttocks and could feel my knob contact her clitoris. Rose felt it too, got in synch with my movements and worked my old fella into her vagina. For two pilots this was a new angle of attack akin to some aerobatic manoeuvre performed for the first time. Rose was giggling. She quickly put aside any fear of falling and kissed me passionately. With Rose clinging to me with arms around my neck and legs around my back, my hands were free to move all around her. She was bouncing up and down on my tool and quickly climaxed.

“You’re so strong darling Adonis,” Rose said as I carried her to the bed. She was still impaled, and we went down onto the bed locked together. I maintained slow and smooth strokes with my old fella while keeping my arms around her and giving her loving kisses. Now supported by the bed Rose stroked my face and neck with her hands and continued using her feet to pull me into her and then release me.

“I never dreamt it could be like this darling Adonis,” Rose said as she thrilled to the sensations flowing over her.

"Yes Adonis, Yes, Yes, Shoot me down Adonis!" Rose cried out as her second orgasm rocked her.

Monday 24 December 2012 – 0700 hrs

It was a great day for Rose and me. We had a leisurely breakfast in our room. On the way to the bank we bought a bikini for Rose and trunks for me as we were intent on trying the fabulous pool at One Aldwych; we'd never heard of underwater music before. We paused at the box office for the Lyceum to find that a customer had just returned two good tickets as he was now unable to attend.

"Do we have to waste time on going to the bank today darling; won't your card do, and I've got some money with me?" Rose asked.

"We must darling. I want my goddesses to have a card of their own and if we don't do it today it will be next week before we get back," I replied.

"What's our card for darling?" Rose asked.

"To pay for anything you need or want darling: clothes, travel, housing, your car, anything at all," I told her.

"I have my Lieutenant's pay darling; I live on the base most weeks and only go home for weekends. I don't spend much," Rose replied. "I don't need to be a kept woman."

"Whatever gave you that idea?" I laughed. "You'd be my wife, but the law won't allow a man to marry three girls at a time. They even come down hard on a bloke who marries two," I had stopped walking and turned Rose to face me. We both laughed, and I held her to me and kissed her.

"What about when the babies come along?" I said when we started walking again, "everything will be different then. I don't think the air force will let you up there in their F18s when you're eight months pregnant will they?"

"When do we start darling?" Rose asked, ignoring the money question as soon as I mentioned babies.

"Start what?" I asked, as if I didn't know exactly what Rose meant.

"Having a baby, silly; a girl's not getting any younger?" Rose replied.

"By the feel of you last night darling you might have already started," I told her.

"How do you know?" Rose asked.

"I don't know of course but I just sensed it," I began. "Mary was hoping the three of you would plan out your pregnancies once you could all get together. That's one of the reasons for meeting here this week. Apparently, Adonis has been known for four years and two of the three goddesses for the last two years. They couldn't activate their project until you were found.

"I found you darling, remember," Rose stated. "I pounced on you and wouldn't let you go all night. I wanted to take you back to the single girls' barracks, but I couldn't do that with the boss walking us back to your plane, could I?"

"I don't think we would have got away with that," I laughed with her.

"And don't forget that I had to ask you out for dinner and dancing, didn't I?" Rose continued. "And I had to ask you to fuck me. Didn't I?" Rose was enjoying teasing her great lover.

"Yes, darling you are so right, I wanted to do all the things you had to do but I couldn't offer you anything," I apologised, "you found me and if you want my first child that would be fine with me. When Mary saw us two hit it off in the Mess at Agra, she knew we were meant for each other. That's why she had you take over the dance for her. She wanted to see you in my arms and see how we looked at each other. They'd already spent several million dollars analysing the gene maps of over a billion people for the Adonis Project."

"I don't think Kate and Jan will mind too much darling, I'm three years older than Kate. They could each have four babies by the time they're thirty, but I can't," Rose answered. "We could go back to the hotel and try some more darling?"

"First things first Rose," I said. "We've got to get the money set up first. What would you have to live on when your pay stops? Besides I want to buy you a nice warm coat for this cold weather; it looks like it's about to snow."

"Sorry Brad, I've only been thinking of you and your babies," Rose began. "We've got to be a little practical if we're going to be parents by September, don't we? How many children do you want darling?"

"I think twelve would be good, don't you?" I asked.

"Not from me darling," Rose was concerned. "I'd be old and worn out."

"Of course not Rose," I replied, "Four each should be OK, shouldn't it?"

"That would be fine by me darling," Rose replied, "I hope the other girls are as clucky as I am."

"Mr Clifford to see Mr Williams," I announced to the receptionist.

"Good morning Mr Clifford, good morning Miss," Mr Williams addressed us. "Please come into my office."

"This is Flight Lieutenant Sastri, Mr Williams, please call me Brad."

"Thanks Brad, mine's Frank. I've had confirmation of your account from Canberra, so I just need to see your passport and have a signature for our records and we can get this done in a few minutes," Frank said. "Now what is it you require?"

"I want to open a new account in your bank in my name. I want three cards to operate the account. I don't want any limit on them. I want to pay the balance in full each month by automatic transfer to this account from my Canberra account or earlier if you feel the balance on this account is larger than you would like. I don't want reward points or any other gimmicks or services. Of course, the cards must be usable globally. I don't want any statements printed and posted as I'll download statements on my computer."

"All that will be fine Brad," Frank said. "What about names for the cards?"

"I'd like 'Clifford Engineering' on one, 'Clifford Research' and 'Clifford Music' for the others. Just PINs no signatures," I told him.

"If you would like to come back in thirty minutes, I'll have the cards ready for you or I could have them delivered to your hotel this afternoon."

"I'll come back Frank, we'll be shopping around the area this morning," I said.

"Thanks for your business Brad. I wish every customer who comes in here knew what they wanted," Frank added as he ushered us out the door.

"Come on Rose let's find a store where we can get some warmer clothes for you, we can't have our mummy to-be getting chilled," I said.

"Do you really think I'm pregnant Brad?" Rose asked with a big smile for me.

"If you aren't now you will be before Thursday when we pick up the others," I said.

"Is that a threat or a promise darling?" Rose asked excitedly.

"Both darling," I said as we entered a boutique with winter outfits displayed in the windows and on models inside. There were hats, coats, boots, muffs and scarves and winter woollen suits and slack suits; there were smart winter blouses, skirts, and a wide display of cardigans.

"Good morning miss," I said as an elegantly dressed you lady approached us from behind the counter. 'This young lady has just flown in from India and needs an English winter wardrobe. It looks as if she might find everything here for the next month or two?"

"I'm sure we can help. Would you like to come with me Miss?" the assistant said.

"Please call me Rose," Rose replied.

"I'm Jessie, Rose; where do we start?" Jessie began.

"Everything Jessie, Rose will need some variety for the next couple of months," I called after them.

I made myself comfortable in an easy chair and picked up a copy of THE TIMES that had been placed on the side table for men to read while waiting for their lady. After thirty minutes Jessie ushered Rose out as in a fashion parade. She wore a very smart tailored suit with a bright lemon blouse; she wore long boots with a reasonable heel, gloves, a long scarf that wrapped around her neck and fell to her waist front and back; and a jaunty woollen cap. With her height, trim figure and long back she looked every inch a model.

"That suits you darling," I aid.

"It's lovely and warm and cosy, will I keep it?" Rose asked.

"Of course, darling, that's what we're here for," I replied.

"Jessie's got three more outfits lined up and that's without the coat," Rose sounded concerned that she might be overdoing it.

"You can't be wearing the same thing all the time darling; tell her you will need an evening gown too," I added. "I'll go and collect the cards from the bank while you're making your next change."

It only took me five minutes back to the bank, five minutes to sign for the cards and five minutes to be back at the boutique, Rose now came out of the change room in a pants and jumper suit and substantial shoes suitable for the winter. This outfit with the other accessories would suit any informal occasion, indoors or out. I handed Rose the 'Clifford Engineering' card and told her to pay with that: her PIN was seven five six five and that no one would think she was a kept woman if she was paying for her clothes herself. Rose grinned and punched me on the shoulder.

"I don't mind being your kept woman darling," Rose smiled at me.

All the clothes Jessie had found for her suited her admirably. They were brightly coloured and complemented her black hair and slightly darker skin typical of Eurasian ladies. They were all in winter fabrics of wool and cashmere and most items would mix and match to extend her wardrobe further.

"I hope I don't grow out of the skirts and trousers before spring Brad?" Rose told me.

"You won't be stretching things for a few months darling," I replied

Rose paid for her purchases and wore the overcoat and cap. Jessie said she would pack the rest of the clothes in boxes with tissue paper to protect them from creasing and I arranged to have her parcels delivered to One Aldwych. It was now one thirty; the morning had flown by while Rose chose her clothes. She clung to my arm as we took a short walk to a coffee shop for a light lunch.

"I've never had so many clothes darling and never any so well made," Rose began, excited with her morning's shopping. "We won't get much sightseeing done today though; we must go for our swim in the pool."

Alter lunch we strolled around Covent Garden and were amazed at the scope and history of the place. It seemed that we were being insolent in only granting these shops, theatres and buildings an hour of our time. We consoled ourselves that One Aldwych, the bank the boutique and The Lyceum Theatre were all in Covent Garden and although we were spending our three days here, we will have hardly touched the surface of this ancient part of London.

"I'm sure that it will soon be confirmed that our first child will have been conceived at Covent Garden darling," I told Rose.

"I could hug you to death Adonis," Rose told me as we stood at the window watching the snow which just started to fall.

"Then you would miss all the fun Rose," I told her. "Let's go and try that nice warm pool downstairs knowing that it's cold outside."

"I'll need a little trim down below Brad," Rose said with a giggle, "I've never had a bikini so brief before. Reckon you can help me with that without getting too randy. I wouldn't want you going swimming with a hard-on; they've probably got security cameras down there."

"If you slip out of your panties, I'll show you just how much self-control I can exert," I asserted.

Rose stood and took off her slack suit pants and then stepped out of her panties.

"You'd better try your bikini bottoms on, so we can see what we have to deal with darling," I said, and Rose obliged.

"Hmm, there are a few unruly ones there," I said. "What would you like short back and sides?"

"Be serious darling," Rose replied, "You blokes can get around with hairy chests and backs, hairy bellies and bulging Speedos and nobody cares, but if a girl has one stray curl peeping out everybody's eyes go to her crotch. It's very embarrassing."

"I'm sorry Rose," I said. "I didn't want to tease you. I can give you a little trim with comb and scissors that will be fine for now and you'll have two sisters and a virtual mother in-law for this sort of help when we get to Cambridge."

Rose went to her beauty case in the bathroom and got a wide toothed comb and small scissors. She lay on the bed and parted her legs to let me get at the hairs that were most likely to embarrass. Not wanting to try any plucking or shaving or any of the other tortures girls put themselves through I did some fine trimming and shortening of her pubic hairs until I had as near a match to Kate and Mary's groins as I could remember.

"How does that feel darling," I asked her.

"Great darling," Rose replied as she felt around what would be the edges of her bikini for any strays. "How do you feel darling," Rose continued as she reached for my groin and was disappointed to find I hadn't become aroused as I trimmed her pussy.

"Oh, I thought that would have stirred you a bit darling," Rose said.

"Not when I'm concentrating on the job in hand," I replied. "But if you want to see him come up just undo my zipper and kiss me."

I lay back on the bed and Rose unzipped my fly. She put her hand in onto my soft cock and started kissing my lips. It was only a few seconds before she felt the swelling in her hand and had to pull my now stiff dicky out from the restraint of my trousers.

"Are we going swimming or what?" I asked.

"Or what darling?" Rose replied as she undid my trousers and pulled them down under me. She undid my shirt, shed her own top and bra, and kissed me more passionately until she felt me fully hard in her hand. She now mounted me, guided my head directly into her vagina, and pressed down.

"Having you trim my pussy has made me randy Adonis; so, in case your sperm missed their target earlier we'd better give them another chance," Rose whispered between kisses.

I pulled my feet up the bed to raise my knees and push my groin up to meet her as she pushed down. Rose was still excited with her day's shopping and my belief that she had probably conceived already that it wasn't long before she was making those sounds of distress which were in truth the sounds of exquisite delight. After about thirty minutes we parted to visit the bathroom and put on our bathers, Rose did a little parade in front of the bedroom mirror, sitting, standing parting her legs and even a high kick, not a pubic hair to be seen. We donned our house gowns and scuffs, picked up our towels and took the guest lift to the pool. I dived straight in and turned to watch Rose walk to the edge of the pool and dive in to come up alongside me.

“Did you hear the music darling?” I asked.

“Marvellous isn’t it,” Rose replied. We laid back and floated listening to the music coming up around us.

“I’ll race you up and back darling,” Rose said.

“What’s the prize?” I asked.

“I could say, beat me and you can fuck me,” Rose whispered in my ear. But that would be too soon, so I’ll pay our hotel bill if you win or you can pay it if I win. That fair darling?”

“That’s fair Rose,” I said. “But we’ll have to get out and start from the blocks.”

Rose swam straight to the steps and out of the pool and I tagged along behind.

“Ready, set, go,” I said.

Rose was away from the blocks in a flash and streaking up the pool with a polished freestyle stroke, she performed a smooth tumble turn at the other end and passed me going the other way at least three lengths from the wall. She was back to our starting point standing up and shaking the water out of her hair when I came in six lengths behind her.

Rose was laughing loudly when I stood beside her.

“You thought I’d be a push-over didn’t you Mr Clifford?” she taunted, “a kiss for the winner please, darling?”

I held her and kissed her, too bad if Security was watching.

"That was fast darling," I said sincerely. "Where did you learn to swim like that?"

"Sorry darling, I should have told you I swam for India at the Commonwealth Games six years ago," Rose admitted. "I didn't swim competitively after that because of my work and studies but I've trained regularly as my fitness routine. I can do better in a swimming cap and racing suit. Bikini and flowing hair takes heaps off your time."

"Don't tell any of my mates in Australia that a mother-to-be beat me over forty metres, will you?" I asked.

"No, it will be our little secret," Rose said still with a chuckle and a big smile on her face. "Have we got time to eat before the show?"

"So long as we go now and don't take too long dressing," I said. "We can go out the rear door of the hotel and only have to cross one street to get to the Lyceum. We could have our main course now and a late supper after the show."

"That sounds great: swimming always gives me an appetite," Rose replied.

We returned to our room, showered, I shaved while Rose dried her hair and we dressed for the show. It was a little after seven when we entered the dining room. We selected an entrée and main course and talked. I found it easy to talk to my goddesses and knew it would be so with Jan when she arrived. Tonight, while we waited for our meal, we talked about the effect her pregnancy would have on her career. I had mentioned it before, but Rose had ignored the subject as she was more interested in getting pregnant first rather that what effect it would have afterwards.

"I can leave the service at any time as I've fulfilled all my obligations," Rose replied. "I don't want to just sit around at home waiting for baby though Brad. I always want to be doing something; there are lots of things one can do to keep the mind and body active isn't there?"

"There certainly is darling," I replied. "You could be a director of Clifford Engineering for instance. You'd still get to fly; you could do a lot of your work from home while the babies are small and then we'd have many years working together afterwards."

"Do you think I could darling?" Rose asked.

"Of course you could," I replied. "It wouldn't be the hands-on engineering of a LayMe, but your civil engineering degree would be invaluable. You could be my alternate director immediately. That's what I had in mind when I asked for your card to be named Clifford Engineering."

"I'd love to do it," Rose replied, "I'm sick of breaking my finger nails and skinning my knuckles Brad."

We had finished our main course and stood to leave.

"What are they performing tonight darling?" Rose asked.

"OKLAHOMA," I replied.

"That should be fun we can see how Curly and Laurey do it," Rose said. "We'd better get a move on."

Rose slipped her hand around my arm and held me tight. Her head was touching my shoulder and remained there until the interval between the first and second acts. We went to the lobby for a cold drink and toilet break. Rose was a picture of happy contentment.

Happy with Laurey and Curly's performance of PEOPLE WILL SAY, Rose and I walked back to the hotel. We hung our coats to ensure they dried and ordered our late supper. Rather than anything sweet I chose a cheese sandwich and black coffee and Rose chose the sweeter Petit Four with her coffee. As our Daytight Compartment was ending we couldn't think of one moment that we would want to cast away and not be able to look back on in the years to come.

Tuesday 25 December 2012 – 0700 hrs

Rose woke with my arm around her and her head on my shoulder. She quickly closed her eyes again and lay there to savour the feel of our naked bodies against each other. "So, it wasn't a dream," she whispered.

"Merry Christmas Goddess Rose."

"Merry Christmas to you too Adonis," Rose replied and lifted her head from my shoulder to give me a long and loving kiss.

"I've a little gift for you darling," I said as I lifted the gift-wrapped necklace from my bedside table and handed it to Rose to unwrap.

"It's beautiful darling, a Love Knot: and matching earrings too," Rose said with obvious delight. "I'll never take it off. Please don't give me any more jewellery; would you do up the clip please?"

"It's not the only one in the world darling," I explained.

"I hope you bought three of these darling?" Rose asked.

"Four actually, I bought one for Mary as well," I said.

"I haven't bought you a present darling."

"You are your present to me Rose," I said. Without changing our position we managed twenty minutes of kissing, fondling and thrusting before we climaxed together. Our waking experience set the mood for the day.

We had booked a Skype talk with Mary, Kate and Rod for nine-thirty and then we would add the Clifford and Franklin Grands and Greats into the conversation. We decided that Kate and Rose would stay out of the conversation with the elders as these relationships couldn't be discussed from thirteen thousand kilometres away.

"Have you anyone you would like to call up on Christmas Day Rose?" I asked.

"None who we can call on Skype Brad," Rose began. "Other than Mum and Dad I've only two sisters and their families left in my line. My grandparents and extended family were wiped out in the war between Pakistan and India years ago; I'll give the girls a call during the morning."

This Daytight Compartment was to be memories of our getting to know each other. We never once spoke of what might lie before us, or even the few days we had experienced together in Agra and since arriving in London; this day, like other honeymooners, was spent revealing to each other things about our early years: growing up in our families, our schooling and our likes and dislikes.

"Please don't be offended by me asking Brad," Rose began. "But that night in Agra when I said that I was fed up with being a twenty-five-year-old virgin, and almost demanded that you do something about it, you said that you had never been with a girl either. But you were so kind and gentle with me and at the same time so passionate that it didn't seem right?"

"It wasn't really a lie darling, until three weeks before I hadn't even touched a girl. But since the morning after

Bruce's memorial service I'd been sharing Mary's bed. She came to me for comfort in the early hours and she was on the point of total collapse; even suicide was in her thoughts, even taking me with her, she was so distraught. I calmed her, and she went to sleep in my arms. The next morning, I work as Adonis and Mary was Adonis's lover Aphrodite. We were inseparable until you claimed me. Mary isn't really a girl, is she?"

"Shh darling, you must always look after her too, your goddesses will understand. Rod will help but you will always be her Adonis as she will always be Adonis's Aphrodite."

"I demand a re-match," I said as I thought of the defeat Rose had handed me in the pool. "Only it will be a handicap race like the Melbourne Cup; I should get three seconds start at least."

"You can have five seconds if you like darling," Rose offered. "We'll go just as soon as we make the Skype call."

We dressed to make the call to Mary, Kate and Rod. Mary was first to come into camera range.

"Hello Rose," Mary began. "It's so good to see you again. Is Adonis treating you well Rose?"

"Marvellously well thanks Mary; it's good to see you too. Nice pendant Mary: I've got one as well," Rose said as she lifted her Love Knot from under her round-neck jumper."

"Rose, this is Kate," Mary said as she moved over to allow Kate to be seen fully on the screen.

"Hello Rose, I'm so pleased to see you've arrived OK. I've got one too," Kate displayed her Love Knot. "It will be great to have a sister at last."

After a deal of chatter between Mary, Rose and Kate, Rod put his head between Mary and Kate.

"I'm Rod Rose," Rod said. "I think they've forgotten I'm here."

"Hello Rod, Brad has told me a lot about you but I'm looking forward to meeting you on Thursday," Rose replied. "Is it snowing in Glasgow? It is here."

"It has stopped now but it snowed all night. The youngsters are out making a snowman," Rod said.

Everyone was surprised to know Rose and I were going swimming on such a day and I told them that Rose had beaten me in the pool the day before and she was going to give me a start today. We also spoke of seeing Oklahoma. At the end of the conversation Rose went to get ready for our swim and left me at one end of the conversation and Mary at the other to make connection with the Clifford and Franklin elders. Again, we talked for quite a while for although it was only seventeen days since being with them much had happened in the meantime. Mary introduced her colleague from Cambridge University and his daughter Kate and told them that Brad and she were guests of Kate's grandmother for Christmas. I was coming to them this morning from London as I was there on business and wouldn't be back until Thursday. Finally, with greetings to be passed on to the rest of our extended families our call was over.

I undressed again to don my bathers and looked for Rose. She was not to be seen except for what looked to be a large Christmas Bon-Bon on our bed. It was Rose's brightly coloured sari, but no part of Rose was visible. A large card was resting against it that read: 'Merry Christmas Adonis'.

I began to undo my gift. It wasn't easy considering the way Indian women can wrap themselves in the several yards of fabric that make up a sari and Rose wasn't making it any easier than necessary. I finally peeled back the layer to reveal Rose in her brief bikini and with a big smile on her face. She held up her arms for me to come down between them to kiss her.

"Do you want to go for a swim first darling or second?" Rose asked.

"I think it had better be second darling," I said.

I pulled down my bathers, stepped out of them and laid down besides Rose on top of her open sari. Rose flipped the loose folds from her side up over us to keep us just a little bit warmer than what the room heater was providing. I undid the tie on the left side of her bikini and the front panel flopped down to reveal her neatly trimmed black curls. I couldn't see her hair beneath the sari, but I certainly appreciated it as I ran my fingers through it and around. I paused to undo the tie of her bikini bra and it fell loose and Rose tossed it from between us.

"What are you doing darling?" I asked as I felt Rose's hand rubbing up and down my shaft.

"I'm just giving you five seconds start, darling," Rose giggled and kissed me.

"I don't need a start here Rose," I claimed. "I can beat you off scratch."

"Ready, set, go," Rose called.

It was a funny sort of race. To be stimulated our self we had to stimulate the other even more. Finally, when Rose slipped her hand down between her thighs to give herself a little more help the feel of her fingers against my horn were so intense for me that I was the first to climax and brought on Rose's orgasm almost but not quite instantly.

“You win darling,” Rose conceded. “It would have been a photo-finish don’t you think?”

“I’d say I won by a short half head,” I claimed.

“Or by a touch in swimming terms,” Rose said. “I shouldn’t have tried to touch myself; it did more for you than it did for me.”

I laughed, and Rose’s giggles were felt right down to my old fella causing it to pause in its retreat in case it was required for further duty. After a while we did make it to the pool. We splashed about and swam leisurely laps side-by-side. We didn’t feel like racing or competing against each other. We sank below the water in an embrace listening to the music and we floated around. It was cosy and warm, and we knew the snow was still falling outside. Before we returned to our room, I took photos of the pool area to show the others when we went for them on Thursday morning. We showered again and had a light lunch in the hotel dining room. There was to be a traditional Christmas Dinner in the hotel tonight, so we confirmed our booking for seven-thirty. After lunch the snow had finished falling and the sun had come through. Rose rugged up in her new slacks, polo-neck jumper, coat, scarf, gloves and hat and we went for our walk along the Embankment. We walked across Waterloo Bridge and then took a taxi, telling the driver we wanted to see the old Lambeth. Having asked the driver to wait Rose and I got out and walked a little way to see the remains of the Lambeth of the nineteen thirties that had inspired the dance. The people of this area had very little and while the world was building to the Second World War, they inspired the musical ME AND MY GIRL and raised the spirits of many as the boys went off to fight and their girls stayed home to work and pray.

“The pleasures of the poor darling are few and simple, it has been said,” I managed to say.

“They’re great pleasures though Brad; they make babies for a start,” Rose said and squeezed my arm.

“There has always been ‘the poor’ Brad even the Christian Bible acknowledges that.” Rose tried to raise my spirits.

“Just because Mark wrote: ‘Ye have the poor with you always’. And Mathew wrote, ‘For unto everyone that hath shall be given, and they shall have abundance: but from him that hath not shall be taken away even that which he hath’,” I quoted with ease. “That doesn’t make it right Rose. These quotes tell me that they got it wrong. They conflict with other statements from their own gospels and out of character with the character of the Jesus they are trying to paint. These are statements of apologists for the establishment just like the exploiters of today: they easily justify their grossly overvalued earnings and at the same time sack thousands of workers and send their jobs to cheap labour countries: so that their organisations can earn more money again next year and pay them higher bonuses still.”

“And you will fix it Brad?” Rose asked.

“With our children: yes, the world economy is closer to collapse than people realise,” I declared.

“Then you will be successful darling,” Rose declared her faith in my statement. “But we can’t do anything today darling by getting too far outside this Daytight Compartment, can we?”

“You’re quite right darling, it’s time we were heading back,” I said.

We arrived back at One Aldwych at six o’clock and dressed for dinner. The evening was smart casual, making my grey business suit quite appropriate, and I managed to convince Rose to wear her sari and present herself as the sophisticated Eurasian lady that she truly was. We were a distinguished couple when we entered the bar at seven for a drink before dinner. The honeymooning couple from Sunday night was there and claimed us when we entered. The conversation turned to what we had been doing commencing from where we left off on Sunday. Of course, we had each failed to do all of what we had expected due to the amount of time we had spent in our rooms at the hotel and this produced the expected giggles from the girls and winks from the new husband and me. The girls had each been shopping and the bride asked Rose where she had bought her beautiful sari. Rose explained that the one she was wearing had been a gift from her parents in Delhi on her twenty-first birthday and she only wore it on special occasions. Rose added that I considered it to be Christmas every time she wore it as I will be unwrapping her to take it off. The bride giggled and said it was a lovely thought. Rose told her casually that it was only obtainable in India and in Agra to be specific, 'You know dear, where the Taj Mahal is," Rose added for effect and for my amusement. The honeymooners admitted that they had heard of the Taj Mahal but weren't they building a new one in Dubai, four times larger than the old one in India and going to have apartments, bridal shops and cater for weddings, the bride announced. They'll probably have a casino too darling. The new husband proclaimed; perhaps they should have waited and had their wedding there. Rose caught my eye to see a faint, but sad smile cross my face. I said nothing. I knew that no matter what I said it would not be understood. I changed the subject of our conversation from the past to the future and asked what they planned for the rest of their time in the UK. It was now time to move into the dining room and found that we had been placed at the one table. Tonight, the tables had been arranged to provide a reasonably sized dance floor and a four-piece band was playing background music from the far corner of the room. The dining room produced a warm and welcoming glow and we took our seats and continued our talking from where we left off in the bar. It transpired that the honeymooners were going to visit Scotland the next day and then fly directly to Paris. They asked me what Rose and I would be doing, and I explained that we were flying over to Ireland; we intended to do a low-level circuit and stay over at a typical Irish pub before going on to Glasgow on Thursday.

"You fly yourself?" the new husband asked me.

"Yes, I do, but on this trip, Rose will do most of the flying as she is a hot shot pilot-instructor on those F18 fighter jets that your country makes," I replied.

They looked at Rose with amazement clearly showing on their faces. They would have had no trouble believing that Rose was a famous Bollywood actress, but faced with the truth it was beyond their comprehension.

"Oh, Brad's a squadron-leader I'm only a flight-lieutenant," Rose said.

"Rose is also a Licensed Aircraft Maintenance Engineer: a L.A.M.E, we pronounce it LayMe, rather good don't you think," I said, not to be outdone, "she can pull airplanes to pieces, fix them and put them back together again."

The new bride looked at Rose's fingers and clearly didn't believe what I was saying.

"They're pulling our legs darling," the new husband told his wife and we all laughed. The dancing was subdued foxtrots and shuffles around the floor cheek to cheek and the food was of the highest order. After the main course Father Christmas appeared with a small personally named gift for everyone in the dining room: there were pens, watches, brooches and clips all with the One Aldwych emblem engraved.

Approaching midnight, the newlyweds departed, and Rose and I returned to our room. We gathered our belongings, laid out our clothes for tomorrow and packed our cases for an early departure. We booked an early breakfast and went to bed.

"It's been a lovely three days darling," Rose told me when she cuddled up in my arms.

"We've still got tomorrow darling," I said. "I meant it when I said you'd be flying; they thought we were joking." We laughed as we remembered the looks on the faces of our dining partners.

"I'll fly out and you can do the low-level orbit of Ireland; is that OK?" I asked. I wanted to be in the left seat when we flew out over the Irish Sea where I planned to pin on Rose her new rating: membership of the Mile-High-Club.

"Whatever you say darling, I'll bet it will be smooth to fly," Rose whispered.

I was now massaging her back, shoulders, neck and kissing her brow.

"That's so smooth too darling," Rose said and fell to sleep in my arms.

Wednesday 26 December 2012 – 0630 hrs

At six-thirty I was up, shaved, showered and dressed. I was ready to receive our breakfast and wake Rose to serve her breakfast in bed. By seven-fifteen we had finished our breakfast and while Rose showered and dressed, I took our cases and Rose's clothes boxes to the door ready for the porter to take them to our taxi. At eight o'clock we were checking out of the hotel and I made a booking for Thursday, Friday and Saturday nights as I planned to bring Jan here after she arrived at Heathrow at midday on Thursday.

Although it had been snowing the night before there had now been enough traffic to clear the roads and we made it to Denham in thirty minutes. Forty-five minutes later we overflew Liverpool and headed out over the Irish Sea. We were flying at six thousand feet, on autopilot and no turbulence in the crisp air.

"You need another rating Rose before I can let you take control of Alpha Uniform," I said sounding serious.

"I've got all the ratings possible Brad," Rose replied.

"Come over here and I'll show you, darling,"

Rose unbuckled and when she stood alongside me, I gently pulled her down onto my lap and kissed her.

"This is the rating Rose," I said and held up the Mile-High-Club badge I had for her, "so if you just slip out of those pants, I can induct you into the club."

"I'll be right back Captain," Rose giggled.

I saw the LED for the bathroom go on and shortly after off and then the wardrobe, where she hung her clothes, open and shut. When she returned, she had not only shed her pants but everything else as well except for her Love Knot necklace. Rose had draped her new woolly cardigan over her shoulders leaving her arms free and breasts bare so that no clothing would get in our way. I, in the meantime, had pushed my trousers down around my ankles and had slipped out of my shirt; as I had pre-planned the operation, I had brought a towel to sit on in case of any drips and dribbles. I had set the cabin stereo playing some good themed music and waited. As Rose came back to the cockpit my old fella rose to salute her. Rose took up her position on me with a knee either side, brought her bare breasts down on my chest, and kissed me passionately. We were cruising out over the Irish Sea with little to be seen outside and our attention centred on giving each other joy. Rose could see my eyes leave hers every so often and scan the instrument panel while at the same time guiding my joystick into her.

"You're a great pilot darling, is this what they call a 'Flying Fuck'?" Rose asked.

"I guess that will do darling," I replied.

"We'd better not endorse our logbooks: 'Rated for the safe performance of a Flying Fuck at altitudes greater than one mile', had we?" Rose giggled again this time her giggling and jiggling brought her to a quick and unexpected orgasm that was even more enjoyable due to its spontaneity. With a little more effort and tongue kissing she felt me spurt another burst of semen at her cervix,

"I must be pregnant now darling even if I wasn't before," Rose whispered in my ear. "It doesn't mean that we need stop trying though," Rose was thinking of the one more night she had alone with me before I must go and collect another goddess.

"It's time you resumed the controls Lieutenant, procedure complete," I said.

Rose got up and left to go to the bathroom and dress. When she returned, I went and did the same. When I came back it was with a toasted ham and tomato sandwich and fresh coffee for us. Over the Isle of Man Rose began a descent to five hundred feet, off the coast abeam Belfast, and continued north before commencing a turn to track around the island. We flew south down the west coast and climbed to circuit height to have a look at Galway airport which would be our jumping off point when we went to the US. We had a good look at Tralee where I sang a couple of verses of ROSE OF TRALEE to my Goddess Rose. We went on over Killarney and Cork and then north up the east coast past Dublin until we completed our trip off Belfast. We got our clearance to land at RAF Aldergrove where we would park for the night. Tomorrow morning would be a short run of half an hour up the Firth of Clyde to RAF Prestwick to collect

Mary, Kate and Rod. We were due to meet them at nine o'clock.

After landing we visited the Base Commander's office to introduce ourselves. The base had of course been advised of our visit from RAF Wyton and we gave our hosts details of our forward movements. We would be arriving at RAF Prestwick at nine in the morning to pick up passengers and be back to RAF Wyton by ten-thirty. As Pilatus Alpha Uniform was self-contained, we would sleep on board and had adequate fuel for our mission. Like every other air force base in the world unseen spectators had heard or seen the pilot's approach and landing performance and hearing a young lady in command were all the more interested. We were immediately invited to the Officers' Mess for afternoon tea. It took only a few minutes to see Rose completely at home with fellow officers for me to give away my plans for an Irish pub-crawl. It was so refreshing for me not to be seen as some sort of freak or the centre of attention as all were smitten by Rose's sultry beauty. The officers were delighted to have a guest who knew and understood their problems and interests. The relative merits of the F18 and Eurofighter Typhoon came under discussion and when my opinion was asked, I could only say that my experience with these craft was having been escorted by them and I leant towards the F18 due its pilot rather than the airworthiness of the aircraft. The officers got my meaning and we all laughed. I of course realised that most would love to fly in tight formation with Rose. For a change, few in the Mess had heard of or understood much about the Faculties of Genetics. It was a very pleasant and casual period of pre-dinner drinks where the talk went from flying, to sport, to politics and back to flying again with no animosity shown for any dissenting opinions. A fine Irish winter menu was served in the dining room. Irish Stew was popular as were salmon, cod, oysters and mussels. Chicken, mutton and pork dishes were available and a wide choice of vegetables with plenty of potatoes both mashed with lashings of butter and baked. For dessert there was mainly fresh fruit and cheese selections and most diners had a pint of Guinness on the table.

After dinner, the entertainment came from several tenors and baritones singing classical Irish favourites, even going back to some made famous by Bing Crosby including ROSE OF TRALEE, DANNY BOY and GALWAY BAY. Rose and I were invited to participate. We switched from our PEOPLE WILL SAY performance to do a very good Lambeth Walk and in doing so got a number of other diners on to the floor to join us. Being a dance that didn't necessarily require equal partners we managed to make a lot of noise with plenty of 'OIs'.

By ten o'clock the Mess was clearing, and Rose and I hurried back to the warmth of the Pilatus.

I filled the percolator for a final cup of coffee as we prepared for bed. With the divan lowered, the privacy curtain down, the lights dimmed and soft music playing it really was a lady's boudoir where the lady could wait for her lover. Rose was first to go to the bathroom and when she came back was wrapped in a warm dressing gown. Without removing the gown, she slid her legs between the sheets and sat with her back supported by pillows and her hands clasped around her coffee mug for warmth. We drank our coffee and talked about the evening in the Mess.

"I seemed to hog the conversation darling," Rose said almost as an apology.

"It was lovely Rose to see you as the centre of attention. You were only being polite in answering their questions. I was happy to bask in your glory darling," I said sincerely and leaned across to kiss her.

We finished our coffee and I went to the bathroom. I felt exhilarated with the evening as I had no need to be cautious and was never flattered by our companions. I felt that I had been on some other occasions. I decided to have a shave in case Rose would like one for the road, as it were. I donned pyjamas tonight for the first time since Rose had arrived and pulled on my robe. I left the bathroom, turned off the rest of the cabin lights, and went to the boudoir. Rose was still sitting where she had been when I left but now the thick gown had gone, and she was a picture in a sexy silk negligee that she had purchased in Delhi before she left to meet me but hadn't had time to put it on for any of our other tight formations. The lights, further dimmed by Rose, were sufficient to shine off the silk that covered her breasts and her protruding nipples cast a shadow, I peeled off my gown and tossed it aside.

"A little overdressed aren't you darling?" Rose asked.

I took off my pyjama top and threw it on top of my gown and slipped into bed beside her. I put my arm around Rose, pulled her down from her sitting position to lie beside me, and began kissing her and receiving her kisses in return. The negligee had rucked up around her waist as I had pulled her down to me, but I ignored her now bare groin to slip my fingers between the deeply plunging neckline of her negligee to take hold of her right breast and tease its nipple erect. We kissed almost as desperately as two ardent lovers coming together after a long separation. Rose knowing that my hard-on was trapped behind my pyjamas and her pussy was bare and ready struggled to push my pants out of the way. Finally, I relented and taking my hand from her breast eased my pyjamas down from my hips. We both lent a foot to pushing them all the way to the bottom of the bed. I pulled the bedclothes up over Rose's back and shoulders and returned my hand to her breast. We had managed to continue our kissing throughout these manoeuvres.

"I'm going to miss you darling having had so much of you in a few days after all my frigid years," Rose told me when our lips finally parted.

"Don't worry darling I'll always be near at hand," I replied.

"I'm not complaining Brad. I'll be more than happy with my share. If I had you all to myself, I would be having a baby every year. I would be pregnant or nursing a baby and you would become frustrated, fat and lazy or go looking for it somewhere else. I know we are all going to be happy."

By now, Rose had parted her thighs to let my old fella lay between and then she clamped down on him and started rocking gently. I kissed her and held her tight with my right arm around her back and with my left hand massaged her spine and neck until she finally relented and opened her legs wide and then guided my now swollen head into her very damp and slippery vagina. I caught her raised right leg in my hand and pulled her half on top of me so that we were both supporting some weight, but both could still exert pressure on the other's groin. We were in rapture with each other and I whispered, "Not too fast, let's make this last," such was our delight. We prolonged the inevitable for a full thirty minutes as we kissed and clung together with our arms and Rose exerting pressure to keep my old fella inside her.

"Here we go darling," I whispered as I finally lost control and Rose immediately responded with her throbbing orgasm as my semen rushed into her.

"If I'm not pregnant now Adonis it won't have been for the want of trying darling," Rose told me. "Thank you for giving me the honour to carry your first child Adonis."

"You found me darling, so it had to be you didn't it," I replied. "Adonis would never have been activated if you hadn't come forward and Mary was there to see."

We clung together until I slipped from her and as her negligee wasn't bought for sleeping Rose slipped it up over her head and went to sleep wearing only her Love Knot.

Thursday 27 December 2012 – 0600 hrs

"Wow," I heard Rose say, "is that bacon and eggs darling?"

"I thought that might wake you Rose," I replied.

"I won't be long," Rose said as she hurried through to the bathroom.

I judged that this would be a good time to put on the toast. I did so and laid the table for our breakfast. I flicked up the aviation weather on my laptop and then switched to the local news channel to get abreast of what was happening in our vicinity. As I buttered the toast and put it on the table with several spreads Rose emerged dressed for the day ahead. She wore her polo-neck jumper, warm slacks and winter shoes. I motioned her to the table, dished up the bacon, eggs, and fried tomato and placed it before her. I got my own from the galley and joined her. Today was the day that Rose would meet her new sister and I would go on to collect my third goddess. I didn't know whether I was feeling apprehensive, exhilarated or just plain scared. I decided that apprehensive was the best fit and resolved to do everything to help Jan take this step into a world that she would never have thought existed.

When we looked at each other we smiled and could barely stop breaking into outright laughter at the joy we had experienced last night. Rose felt satisfied and fulfilled and now ready to face the future she would share as **Goddess Rose**. **http://www.futuristic.guru/goddess-rose** We ate, cleaned up, assigned last night's sheets to the laundry bag and remade the bed with fresh linen before folding it into its divan position. By eight-fifteen, we were doing the pre-flight inspection together. Rose was pilot in command this morning and by eight-thirty we were on our way; cleared to RAF Prestwick at the circuit height of one thousand feet. Once airborne it was only going to be fifteen minutes before we would be entering the Prestwick circuit.

After landing, we taxied to the transiting aircraft parking bay and shut down the engine to give our passengers safe entry. I lowered the steps and we welcomed Mary, Kate and Rod aboard. I secured their luggage in front of the divan. Mary did the introductions in the flesh now instead of on Skype and Rose and Kate embraced as sisters. Mary joined Kate and Rose at the dining table and Rod joined me in the cockpit. The turnaround had barely taken ten minutes and the girls were already deep in conversation with the sounds of laughter and giggles coming through to the cockpit. I had little time to talk to Kate except to give her a big hug and kiss and hand her the Clifford Research card and telling her to use it pay for all her requirements.

"You know you're on a hiding to nothing in all of this Brad, you know you're totally outnumbered and out voted until each girl has a couple of sons in their teens and ready to support their father," Rod began. "I know, Brad and I only had one little girl winding me around her little finger?"

"I appreciate your concern Rod but who could refuse them?" I answered him. The hour flight to RAF Wyton soon passed. I was finding it strange that you could traverse a country full of history and many millions of people in the less time than it takes to fly from Sydney to Melbourne. After landing, we taxied Alpha Uniform into its hangar. We loaded Rose's luggage and new clothes and Kate's case from her Glasgow trip into her car and Rod and Mary put theirs into Rod's car.

Starting with Mary I kissed each of the girls' goodbye.

"Until you come back darling," they each whispered to me. I turned to shake Rod's hand briskly and then boarded Alpha Uniform for my return flight to Denham Aerodrome.

"Give Jan my love," Mary called as I closed the door behind me.

Chapter 14

Goddess Jan

Thursday 27 December 2012 – 1200 hrs

I arrived at Heathrow just as Jan's flight was landing. As before, I hired a taxi at Denham and put my travel bag and suit carrier in the boot. I had brought a business suit and my dinner suit as I intended to take Jan to a formal dinner or function as part of her introduction to being a goddess. I planned to take her shopping for an evening gown and have her pampered at a beauty parlour and we would dance. I realised that dancing with Jan at her twenty-first birthday party and my own eighteenth had left an impression on me far greater than I realised at the time. In fact, at my eighteenth I recalled I was becoming aroused as I spun her around in a pivot, but, in those now seemingly far off days I only had thoughts and feelings for Mary. I went to collect Jan at the customs exit. Jan appeared towing her suitcase behind her and with her carryon bag slung over her shoulder. She was looking around expecting to find the person who was to meet her and showing a degree of distress. I went quickly to her side and took her case.

"Brad, I didn't expect to see you, I thought Mary was going to meet me?" Jan asked.

"She's been held up Jan and asked me to come for you and take you back to Cambridge," I assured her.

"I can't go tonight Brad, something awful has happened. The soloist for tonight's London Symphony Orchestra's recital dropped dead on Tuesday night. Their conductor has done some of our performances in Australia and has asked me to fill in. Somehow, they knew that I was coming to London this week. I only got the SMS this morning as we reboarded in Dubai," Jan managed to declare all in one breath.

"That's a tall order Jan, what do you have to play?" I asked.

“**Sibelius’s Violin Concerto**,”**http://www.futuristic.guru/sibelius** Jan replied, “and I haven’t even brought my violin, let alone appropriate clothing.”

“Surely they can supply you with a decent fiddle?” I asked.

“Yes, they will, but I’ll need to do a lot of practice this afternoon to get used to it; they become such a personal instrument at this level Brad. The orchestra is rehearsing from two-thirty to four o’clock; I could put in an hour or so with the borrowed fiddle and a metronome beforehand to get up to speed. I’ve got to do it and I’d hate to stuff it up.”

I sat her down at the nearest seat in the lobby and took control.

“Where are you playing tonight Jan?”

“The Barbican, wherever that is?” Jan replied.

“Here’s what we will do,” I said. “I’ll take everything you don’t need for this afternoon and book you into a nice hotel I know not far from the theatre. You’d be about the same size as Mary. I know of a boutique where they will have something suitable for your performance tonight. When we leave here, I’ll drive you to the rehearsal and then I’ll pick you up at four and take you to the hotel so that you can get some rest before you go on. What time must you be at the theatre?”

“Seven-Thirty Brad,” Jan replied, “the concert will be over at ten o’clock.”

“Do you want to have dinner before or after the concert Jan?” I asked.

“It had better be after, I think,” Jan replied.

“OK, can you see any problems Jan?” I asked.

"Not a one Brad, thank heavens you're here."

"Don't worry about anything in the world beyond the performance for tonight and after your rehearsal you must relax," I said. "now let's get cracking."

"I moved the travel bag from Jan's shoulder to mine, took her free hand and led her out to where my taxi was waiting. I asked her how the family was getting on and what sort of Christmas everyone had and how the Cliffords looking after our house were faring. Everything at home seemed to be going well and Jan's spirits were lifting as she felt that abler hands than her own were putting her affairs in order and protecting her. I left her at the theatre, went on to One Aldwych, and collected my key. I placed our cases in her room, which was already our room for the next three nights, and then went to the boutique to see Jessie.

"Hello Brad," Jessie greeted me. "Can I show you something else for your lovely lady?"

"Not his time Jessie," I replied. "I'm looking for something outstanding for another lovely lady. She learnt this morning on her flight here that she was expected to perform as soloist with the London Symphony Orchestra tonight. She hasn't brought her violin or packed for any such event. She was only coming here on a family visit."

"Is it Jan Franklin Brad?" Jessie asked.

"Yes, do you know her?"

"I competed in the Paganini Competition in Genoa in September when Jan was the winner. She was by far the best violinist they had seen for many years," Jessie told me, "this will be her debut performance Brad. She must be shaking in her shoes: not having her own violin and playing Sibelius to boot. It is more demanding than even Paganini."

“She’s practising right now and will be rehearsing with the orchestra from two o’clock. I’m really looking for something that when she sees herself in it she’ll put her shoulders back, stand up to her full height and walk out onto the stage without a doubt in the world. It will have bare arms, not show any cleavage, be figure hugging but not restrict her walk in any way and it will probably shimmer or sparkle in the spot light.”

“I’ve got just the thing Brad; I haven’t got a model here who can wear it but I’m about the same height as Jan. I could slip in on for you to see,” Jessie offered.

I agreed, and Jessie was back in five minutes dressed in a crimson gown with a full bodice top with a simple scooped neckline that would be sufficient for Jan to wear the Love Knot necklace I planned to give her before the performance. Jessie walked across an imaginary stage with her arms placed as if holding an imaginary violin. After shaking hands with the conductor and first violin she brought her violin to her shoulder. Jessie then lowered her imaginary violin and performed a bow from the waist to her imaginary audience, now on their feet and giving her a standing ovation.

“That’s it exactly Jessie, now we’ll need an evening coat for her to wear over it on her way to and from the theatre and the right shoes for her to wear on stage. I think the coat should have a rather large rolled collar and be fuller than the dress,” I said. “And a light, silky soft scarf would be nice and short white gloves, oh, and matching evening bag.”

Jessie modelled the coat and scarf and then went and changed. She returned with the evening bag and gloves in her hand.

“I don’t suppose you know her shoe size Brad?”

“Can I look over your range please Jessie?”

"How did you do that?" Jessie asked when I made my selection.

"I danced with her at my birthday party four weeks ago."

"I don't understand, but never mind," Jessie replied.

"Wrap them up please Jessie, I'll take them with me now," I said as I produced the Clifford Music card. "You're a good sales lady Jessie," I added.

"It's easy Brad when you have customers with taste and know what they want," Jessie returned the compliment.

While I had been waiting, I sent a message to Mary, Rose and Kate saying,

'Jan is guest soloist with London Symphony Orchestra tonight at eight o'clock on Channel Four – Please Record, Love Brad.'

"No doubt you are going to the concert tonight Jessie?" I asked.

"Yes Brad. I'm first violin in the Beethoven String Quartet. We're playing the first movement of Beethoven's 6th Symphony before Intermission. We had our rehearsal last night, so I was free today to work here. I'm so glad I did and could be of help.

Back at the hotel I hung Jan's evening dress on a hanger on the outside of one wardrobe door and her coat on another. I placed her shoes, scarf, gloves and handbag on the bed alongside her case and travel bag. I had arranged with the housekeeper for me to dress in the vacant next suite and use the bathroom there. I was back at the theatre at three-thirty and slipped into a back-row seat unseen. I listened to the last half-hour of the rehearsal and knew that Jan had nothing to fear tonight except fear itself. When they finished the conductor and orchestra gave her a genuine clap of approval.

“That’s all for now ladies and gentlemen. Thank you very much for your work this afternoon. I’m sure tonight’s performance will enhance the orchestra’s reputation. A special thanks to you Jan for stepping in at such short notice, as usual your performance was impeccable. For those who didn’t know, Jan only received a text message when she reboarded her flight in Dubai this morning,” The conductor finished and there was another round of applause for Jan. The members of the orchestra went to the dressing rooms to put their instruments away until tonight and I followed a few paces behind.

“How did that go Jan?” I asked as I followed her into the dressing room.

“OK, I think,” Jan replied.

“I know what ‘impeccable’ means Jan. The conductor and orchestra seemed very happy with your playing,” I said encouragingly.

“You were here Brad?” Jan asked.

“Only for the last half-hour; you sounded great,” I said. “come on I’ll take you to the pub and you can put your feet up for an hour before you have to get dressed.”

It only took a few minutes for the taxi ride to the hotel. I ushered her into the room and she saw her gown and coat hanging on the wardrobe.

“Are they for me to wear tonight Brad?” Jan asked with a look of total surprise on her face, “they’re beautiful,” Jan lifted the dress down and held it against her. “The length’s perfect I’d better try it on to make sure I can move my arms properly.” She ran off into the bathroom to change and soon returned with the gown on.

“Zip me up please Brad?” Jan asked. I did as I was asked and went and got her evening shoes.

"You'd better try these on too, we can't have you hobbling out onto the stage or tripping over," I said giving Jan the shoes and then holding one hand while she slipped them onto her feet.

Jan studied herself in the mirror and moved her arms about as if she were playing her violin. She practised the typical flourish that violinists often use at the end of their solo. After the last stroke of the bow they lift it briskly from the strings in a small flourish. The left hand usually carries the violin away from the body to allow a small bow from the waist.

"Do these things go back in the morning Brad?" Jan asked, "I could never afford them."

"Of course not Jan, they are all yours here and now," I replied.

"Thank you so much Brad, you and Mary have always been so good to me," Jan said and flung her arms around my neck and gave me something a little more than a familial kiss.

"Now come on," I said. "You have to get some rest before the performance."

Jan went back to the bathroom to change and brought the dress back to hang on the door again. I took Jan's hand and led her to the bed and made her lie down, legs out straight and feet raised on pillows. I covered her feet and sat on the chair beside the bed.

"I didn't try on the evening coat Brad," Jan said.

"Don't worry, it will fit and look very smart on you," I answered.

"Why are you doing all this for me Brad?" Jan asked.

"Because you are you Jan; that's all, now no more questions. I'll wake you at six o'clock, so you can get dressed," I said.

I sat quietly on the chair beside the bed and watched Jan's eyes move from the dress to the evening coat and back again. A happy smile had spread over her face and after a little while she drifted off to sleep. I took time to review my day: I had planned to collect Jan from her flight and bring her straight to this room and lay my cards on the table. I'd tell her that I was the person Mary had selected for her. It wasn't going to be a one-night-stand to hopefully get her pregnant and a member of the sole-parent-working-mother of the only-child-fraternity. Instead she was to be one of Adonis's three goddesses to have as many children as she desired and share him with two others for the rest of our lives. My plans had amounted to nothing. I had met a beautiful young lady for sure but one who had that morning been thrown in to something that she felt she was unable to do justice and could embarrass herself and many others by trying. I hoped that my efforts so far had built her confidence so that she could deliver what was expected of her and I knew that the performance was well within her repertoire under normal conditions. I hoped too that my care for her today would help her understand her role as one of Adonis's goddesses where her slightest wish would be my command. I must now wait until after the concert to break all this news to Jan since I knew instantly that had I mentioned it when she arrived at Heathrow it would have only made her position worse.

"Jan," I spoke quietly as I took her hand and patted it. "Jan it's six o'clock, time to wake up."

"You're still here Brad that was sweet thanks. I might have overslept and been a no-show and that would have been worse still," Jan told me.

"No more doubts or worries please. You've nothing to fear," I began. "You'll find everything you might need in the bathroom, so you have a little over an hour. I'll be back to collect you at seven-fifteen and we're less than five minutes away."

Jan got up from the bed and waved to me as I went to the door and she went to the bathroom.

At seven-fifteen, I knocked on her door and it was opened by a radiant Jan. She had showered and washed her hair and now highlights shone as she moved. She wore minimum makeup but having performed in her Australian orchestra knew that a certain amount of makeup was necessary to avoid looking washed out under the lights and on TV.

"Just in time to do up my zipper again Brad," Jan giggled as she presented the sight of her now bare back about to be hidden with the closure of the zip. "How do I look?" she said as she stepped back into the room and then turned to face me.

"Absolutely beautiful Jan and I'm not trying to flatter you," I said with all honesty. "Here's a little Christmas present for you Jan. I think it might go well with your dress.

"Brad it's beautiful, a Love Knot, do you think that much of me? Will you do it up for me please?" she asked as she reached the ends back behind her.

I did as she asked and refrained from answering her first question. Jan went to the mirror and clipped her earrings in place.

"I'd give you a big kiss Brad if it wasn't for this theatrical makeup," Jan said. "I wouldn't want to mess you up; you look so smart in a dinner suit."

"I can wait Jan," I replied intimating that I expected a big kiss later.

I took her coat down from its hanger and held it open for her to put her arms into the sleeves. I arranged the fold of the collar and placed her scarf around her neck. I handed Jan her gloves and she put them on. I held out my hand for her to parade in front of the full-length mirror.

"Now let me take the virtuoso to her performance," I said. I had booked a taxi for seven-twenty and when we went down to the lobby the taxi had just arrived. We pulled up at the stage door and I held the door open with one hand and assisted Jan out with the other. I noticed a couple of flashes as Jan looked up to me and smiled and then we walked in to find her dressing room. Jan retrieved her violin and after hanging her coat in the wardrobe and taking off her scarf and gloves started tuning it. I walked her to where the orchestra was assembling and after being introduced handed her over to the conductor.

"You look lovely this evening my dear," the old and respected conductor said. "Thank you Brad we'll look after her now, the usher has a seat reserved for you."

With a soft good luck kiss to Jan's cheek I went to find the usher and my seat.

The usher told me that there would be a short after-party following the performance and asked me to join the orchestra backstage. He showed me to one of the best seats in the house: front and centre, directly in front of where the soloist would stand but far enough back that she would not be distracted by my presence.

I could see the theatre filling rapidly: its capacity was two thousand and tonight was a sell-out. At eight o'clock the theatre lights dimmed, and the orchestra took their places on the stage. They waited standing and applauded as the conductor came to the podium.

The evening commenced with a selection of three Beethoven Overtures: PROMETHEUS, CORIOLAN and

EGMONT. The orchestra performed these works flawlessly as they were using these simpler works to loosen up and work into the major event for the evening. A short break between each number allowed the audience to applaud, the strings to fine tune as the theatre warmed and for the brass to clear the condensation from their instruments.

Prior to the intermission, the orchestra lights went out and the Beethoven String Quartet took their places in the centre of the stage. The members of the quartet were all girls and it was obvious from the opening bars that Jessie must have been a serious contender in the Paganini Competition. The PASTORAL is one on my favourite compositions and hearing it played by a string quartet instead of the full orchestra was a new and remarkable experience for me.

The intermission followed but I saw no point in leaving my seat as I didn't expect there would be anyone present who I knew.

"Ladies and gentlemen," the conductor began: after the orchestra had reassembled and the audience had quieted. "You will have observed the insert in tonight's program announcing the sudden death of Herr Otto Fisk, our renowned soloist listed for tonight's concert. On Tuesday evening I contacted my friends at the Australian National Orchestra to request their first violin, Miss Jan Franklin, to substitute. As Miss Franklin was already en-route to London the concert manager accepted on her behalf. Miss Franklin is this year's winner of the prestigious Paganini Competition and I am sure you will agree with me that we could not have found a more capable person to bring you this outstanding work for the violin."

The conductor held out his hand as Jan walked smartly onto the stage. She took his hand to be presented to the audience and be met with a welcoming round of applause. Jan beamed a smile at the audience and stepped back to accept the hand of the first violin before taking her position in the conductor's view, ready to take her lead from his baton. There was a spotlight on Jan for the performance; her every movement and facial expression could be clearly seen and would be even more obvious to the TV audience. I smiled to myself; her gown sparkled and was set off by her wavy brunette hair. The Love Knot at her neck twinkled as the light caught it and she appeared relaxed and perfectly at home with her surroundings. Her eyes were now focussed on the conductor as she waited for his baton's upstroke and then she led the orchestra into this difficult concerto that demanded a virtuoso to do it justice. Jan opened the performance flawlessly and continued that way throughout. The conductor had told her he liked to see the Sibelius played joyously and with vigour and she followed his instructions and the subtle signals he was passing from the podium effortlessly. The orchestra behind her had lifted their performance far higher than what had been shown in the three overtures. Much of the arrangement had the soloist introducing and featuring parts of the score and the orchestra responding. It was a thrilling performance by a master conductor, a powerful and skilled orchestra and a brilliant young soloist. As the Finale ended and Jan gave a bow the audience was on its feet, cheering and clapping as Jan left the stage. The applause continued waiting for the expected return of the star of the evening and the conductor went to the wings to lead Jan back onto the stage. If she looked relaxed and in control on her first appearance, she now showed that she was pleased and proud of her performance and had done credit to all who had been involved in her journey. She bowed again and waved, and the lights shone on her gown and every now and then on the Love Knot at her neck. A young girl rushed onto the stage and after handing Jan a bouquet gave a little curtsy and ran back to the wings. Jan bowed again and left the stage. There were calls of 'More' and 'Encore'. Jan returned, and the conductor whispered to her. He tapped his baton on the lectern and the audience fell silent as Jan brought her violin back to her chin. I quietly left through a side door and made my way into the wings where Jan had come and gone. There wasn't a sound to be heard as the audience immediately recognised Paganini's difficult **Caprice 24 . http://www.futuristic.guru/caprice-24** As the last notes drifted away Jan bowed again, and this time ran from the stage; straight into my waiting arms where I was standing in the wings.

The orchestra too had been standing and clapping along with their conductor and he now turned to the audience to thank them and trust they had enjoyed the evening's entertainment. More applause followed and now he tapped the podium with his baton and the orchestra took their seats and played the audience from the theatre with a soft rendition of **Beethoven's Moonlight Sonata.http://www.futuristic.guru/moonlight-sonata** You were brilliant darling," I said. "There I've claimed the kiss you promised me," I hadn't meant to use the endearment before I told her all that was afoot; it just slipped out in my excitement.

"Here's another darling for all that you have done for me today," Jan still held me and this time it was a passionate kiss we held.

"I'd better escort you to the after-party; they will be looking for their brilliant soloist," I took her by the hand and we went backstage to where the orchestra had assembled. The conductor was quickly at our side.

"We're so proud of Jan's performance tonight; I can't remember when we've had a better audience response to a soloist and I've never heard our orchestra rise to such heights before," The conductor said and shook my hand again.

"Where would you like me to put the violin sir?" I asked.

"Please call me Jonathon, but the violin is not to be returned; it's for Jan to keep as a memento of this evening. It's not a Strad dear but I suspect you might have one of those at home?" Jonathon said.

"Thank you, Jonathon, I'll treasure it and I don't have a Strad," Jan replied.

"You will one day Jan I'm sure," Jonathon said. "I suppose you must want to get away, it must have been a long day for you and no doubt a nervous one?"

"Yes, on both counts," Jan admitted.

"Gather around people if you wouldn't' mind," Jonathon called to his players.

"Jan has had a long day and as you know a very demanding one and must take her leave," Jonathon announced. There was applause from the orchestra and Jessica came forward to give Jan a hug.

"Jessica was a big help to me Jan choosing your dress," I said.

"Brad didn't need much help Jan, he told me exactly what he wanted for you. Congratulations. I knew you would nail the SIBELIUS after the way you won the PAGANINI."

"It's a relief that it is over Jessica. I can't believe I have soloed with the London Symphony Orchestra. Nothing could have been further from my dreams or goals in life," Jan said.

"Get used to it Jan, you are going to be in demand around the world now. Nobody has ever played like that here before. Good luck."

Jessica kissed us both on the cheek and was gone.

I ushered Jan out to her dressing room to put on her evening coat. We went out the stage door to a cab that was waiting: the driver knowing that there would be several needed as the party broke up.

“What would you like to do for dinner Jan; there are all sorts of places open in London?” I asked.

“I don’t think I could eat anything much at all Brad, I’m too excited to be hungry,” Jan began. “But you haven’t eaten. Could we go back to my room and have some room service.”

“Suits me fine Jan. I want to talk to you about some things that would be hard to talk about in a restaurant,” I said as I gave the driver our address.

We pulled up at One Aldwych and I helped Jan out while carrying her gift violin in its case under my arm. There was a flash from a camera as a freelance news-cameraman recognised that people arriving at One Aldwych, dressed so well and carrying a violin might probably have some news value. As soon as we entered Jan’s room, I sat her in one arm chair and sat opposite her in the other.

“If tonight’s event has come about by chance Jan, what was it you came to London for?” I asked.

“Must you ask Brad, I feel a bit silly and embarrassed about it at the moment,” Jan began. “I really should talk to Mary about it,” Jan paused, and she was obviously thinking about what I had asked.

“Brad you’ve been so good to me I do owe you an explanation, I’m sure Mary won’t mind; it is only my own embarrassment that I’m afraid of,” Jan said.

“It’s been a good day for facing your demons Jan, I won’t laugh whatever you say,” I replied.

"I've been on Mary's database for some years and although I asked her to find a suitable match for me none had come up and neither had I found anybody or have anybody pay the slightest interest in me. Last month I told her that if there was nobody with whom I could make a permanent commitment was there a man who could get me pregnant so that I could have another soul in my life. I have felt so alone as my friends grew up around me and got married or gone off on high-level careers. I would be happy to be a single mum," Jan told me. "A little over a week ago Mary emailed me that she had found a solution for me, but it was complicated, and could I come to London to talk about it, Mary of course arranged my fare and here I am."

"I think I can tell you what Mary would have told you Jan," I replied. I reached forward so that our foreheads nearly touched and picked up her hands in mine.

"Four years ago, Mary identified one male specimen whose gene map was considered ideal by all her collaborators. Since then all gene samples for men have been matched against this base specimen to whom they gave the name Adonis," I began. "They determined that Adonis's characteristics were such that any woman would be compatible with him and produce better children than she would have with any other partner. The committee's goal was then that Adonis should impregnate as many women as possible around the globe to bring about an improvement in the world gene pool. They knew that Adonis would not be interested in becoming a worldwide stud with no home life of his own, so they set out to find a bride for Adonis. It was soon obvious that Adonis's interests and capabilities were so wide that no one woman would hold him for long as she could only satisfy a third of him and he would soon find that he was more unsatisfied than satisfied."

Jan's face was showing signs of incredulity at my narrative.

“Is this really true Brad?” Jan asked.

“Yes, Jan it’s the honest truth,” I said. “Now to cut a long story short; the committee needed to identify three women who between them would satisfy Adonis’s every need. They called these women Adonis’s goddesses. Two years ago, they had identified two of them and it wasn’t until ten days ago that the third goddess was identified.”

“Who are the goddesses Brad?” Jan asked hardly daring to think she may be one.

The two identified two years ago Jan are Rod Senden’s daughter Kate and you Jan. The Goddess identified ten days ago is Rose Sastri who I was dancing with in Agra.”

“Dare I ask who Adonis is Brad, or will I guess?” Jan asked as she stood up and took off her evening coat. “It’s you Brad?”

I nodded my head and Jan sat down in my lap. She wrapped her arms around my neck and kissed me more passionately than before. I returned her kisses and she was trembling with desire.

“But were cousins darling,” Jan said with a note of distress coming in her voice.

“Cousins darling yes, and it has all been checked out and verified by thirteen other professors of genetics. There is no risk involved to any of our children.”

“Do you really want your skinny little cousin for a goddess darling?” Jan asked.

“Of course I do, but the question really is do you want to share me with two other girls?” I replied.

“I’d share you with ten or even a hundred if that what was required darling,” Jan answered. “Will you unzip me please Brad?”

We stood, and I peeled off my dinner jacket and then unzipped the back of Jan's gown. Jan stepped out and handed it to me to hang up on the cupboard again.

"Are you hungry darling?" Jan asked.

"Not for food darling," I said as I held her close and unclipped her bra.

"It feels funny getting stripped by my cousin, Brad," Jan began, "but it would have been funny getting stripped by anyone I guess."

I held her close as I peeled her bra away from her firm little breasts and felt Jan let a brief 'OOoooo' escape from her lips before pressing her lips to mine and dropping her hands to my belt and opening it, and then sliding my zipper down and very tentatively feeling inside for my now roaring horn. We moved towards the bed and sat to allow me to remove my shoes and socks and get out of my trousers and shorts. I slipped Jan's panties down and ran my hand up her thigh and gently placed a finger to part the hairs between her legs. We stood to pull back the bedding and climb inside and with only a dim back light we clung together and kissed,

"I don't know what to say darling?" Jan whispered to me and giggled.

"What's the matter Jan?" I asked.

"I don't know what to do either?" Jan giggled again.

"With your sense of timing, rhythm and beat you will have no trouble at all," I said. As we had been talking, I had been massaging her breasts and easing out the stiffness from around her neck and shoulder where she held her violin.

"You really stunned them tonight darling, they didn't expect that performance and from where I sat I could see the orchestra rising to follow you. The audience was ecstatic," I told her.

"I couldn't have done it without you darling. What would I have looked like if I had turned up in the clothes that I had in my case? They would have laughed at me," Jan said.

"Nobody will laugh at you again darling," I said as I kissed her again and moved my hand down amongst her brown curls and she found her legs spreading automatically. She welcomed my probing fingers and pressed herself against them. I gently tickled her clitoris while I pressed more passionate kisses to her lips. She could feel the mounting dampness in her vagina and was wondering whether she could manage my horn without crying in discomfort; she quickly dismissed the thought for any brief discomfort now would soon be forgotten in the years of pleasure now opening before her. She had used a vibrator once to break her hymen and of course had experimented with her fingers but had found little pleasure in these solitary pursuits. She had seen herself as a wallflower and dreaded the thought of becoming an embittered old maid like some she had come across in orchestras. Jan wanted more than just music in her life.

Jan was now adding her movements to mine and she could feel my old fella creeping deeper within her. My fingers were teasing her nipples, she could feel the thrill right down to her toes, I kissed her the more, and now she responded by slipping her tongue in and out to match my thrusts into her. I moved my left hand down between us and tickled her clitoris as her excitement grew and our breathing became heavy. I discharged inside, and Jan squirmed and bumped and cried out as she broke into her first orgasm.

"I've always loved my cousin, darling," Jan began. "When we had that one dance at your birthday party, I could feel you getting hard and I thought that I might hear from you soon to ask me to go out with you. But within a week there you were making your speech to the world and then you were gone."

"My birthday party was less than one-month back Jan," I reminded her.

"Yes, but it felt like a year to me," Jan replied. "When you made that speech, I became quite wet down there and felt like writhing around on the floor and then I saw the photos of you dancing with Mary and then Rose and Kate and I was terribly jealous of these beautifully turned out ladies. And today you meet me out of the blue and I'm one of your beautifully turned out ladies and I've been squirming under you. Thank you, Adonis," Jan was exhausted and asleep in my arms.

Friday 28 December 2012 – 0700 hrs

Jan woke at seven in the morning and looked up at me.

"I wondered where I was darling waking in a man's arms and only wearing my necklace," Jan said.

"Good morning Goddess we fucked last night remember?" I asked.

"I remember, you took all my troubles and worries away yesterday and last night, all my Christmases had come at once," Jan replied. "I'm hungry now Brad, we didn't eat last night, did we?"

"No darling we satisfied another hunger though," I said. "I used to fancy you Jan when I was fifteen but didn't dare say anything because you were all grown up and eighteen."

"I had a crush on you too Brad, even at fifteen you looked at least eighteen and you were taller than I was and fun to dance with even then," Jan admitted. "And now I'm going to have your babies after all, or at least some of them," she giggled. "I won't be jealous whatever you do darling, I promise," Jan said, and we kissed.

"I'll order breakfast and then we could have a nice long soak in the spa and work out what we want to do today," I said. I reached for the house phone and called room service for two English breakfasts and the main papers.

"Fifteen minutes darling," I said as Jan returned from the bathroom. "I can cuddle you for ten minutes more and then we can have our breakfast before the spa."

"I'm walking on air darling, this time yesterday I got the message that I was required to solo for the London Symphony and now look at me," Jan said as she sat next to me on the bed with her hotel-supplied gown wrapped around her. She leant back into my arms for the promised kisses and cuddles and then came the knock at the door. I hopped out of bed and pulled my gown on to collect our breakfast trolley. We were hungry and took to the bacon and eggs, sausage and tomato eagerly.

"Marvellous how much better it tastes when you're hungry darling," Jan said. "I'd never eat a hot breakfast like this at home.

"Have a look at this darling," I said as I folded the DAILY EXPRESS and passed it to her.

One picture showed Jan looking up at me as I assisted her from the cab at the theatre. The next photo showed me helping her from the cab at the hotel. The article made reference to the young man from down under escorting the star soloist to her performance last night with the London Symphony Orchestra and then to her hotel afterwards. The journalist was unable to ascertain whether this new man about town merely escorted her to her door or stayed for breakfast.

"They are good photos darling," Jan remarked. "Shall we ring up and tell them you're still here and will be here tomorrow as well. I feel like telling someone; what about Mary?"

"I hardly think that's necessary," I replied. "She'd be most disappointed in both of us if I hadn't stayed."

"Now this is better," I said as I handed her THE GUARDIAN. The cover had a small head and shoulders and most of her violin in the photo with the caption. 'Glamorous young Aussie Soloist wins Hearts at London Symphony Concert last night' — Story pages 4 and 5. Jan turned to page four to see a two-page spread of last night's concert. There was a good-sized picture of Jan during her performance. This was supported by slightly smaller photos of the conductor introducing her to the audience, receiving her first standing ovation, receiving the conductor and the orchestra's congratulation, a touching shot of the little girl presenting her bouquet another shot of her playing the encore and another standing ovation showing Jan walking from the stage and waving. The articles accompanying the photos were generous and surprisingly accurate. One pointed out that Jan had only been advised on the morning of the concert that her services were required, she hadn't come prepared for any performances as she was only visiting her cousin who is now known to be Professor Mary and knowing this it was easy to see a very close family likeness between the two cousins. Another article described Jan's gown for her performance and even mentioned that her only jewellery was the Love Knot pendant and earrings. The article described how elegant she looked for her performance and her appearance arriving and leaving in her fashionable evening coat. I was only shown in this photo spread in the shot where we were leaving, and I had her gift violin under my arm. The article described how Jan had at first been provided the violin for the performance as she hadn't brought her own with her and later how she had been presented with the violin by the conductor as a token of the orchestra's appreciation of her work and willingness to step in at a moment's notice.

"That's better darling, don't you think?" I asked.

"It comes close to flattery darling," Jan replied.

"Not at all, it's all true. I was there too; I saw it all better than you. It was a marvellous night and I don't only mean at the theatre," I confirmed. "We'll take these papers back with us but no doubt the Cambridge papers will have much the same. You'll probably be on the evening news in Australia tonight."

"I hadn't thought that might be possible," Jan said with some alarm.

We had finished our breakfast, so I wheeled the trolley out of the room and hung up the DO NOT DISTURB.

I returned to the bathroom and shaved while the spa was running, and Jan was soon at my side. Jan sprinkled bath salts under the water tap to create immediate bubbles and dropped some perfume into the water. When the water was up to its level I turned on the jets and we stepped in. It was wonderfully warm and invigorating as we sunk under the water and Jan perched herself on my knees.

She was in a great position to be kissed and to kiss in return and her breasts pressed into my ribs when I wrapped my arm around her. We resisted the urge to engage in heavy petting or foreplay as we had the whole day before us and tomorrow morning and Sunday morning as well until we left for Cambridge. I thought to ask Jan what clothes she had brought with her to learn that Mary had told her they would go shopping for winter clothes when she arrived so travel light. Her Australian winter wardrobe would not be much use here anyway. I told her that as soon as we were dressed, we would pay a visit to my friend Jessie and see what she could provide for her.

"There's something you don't know about me Brad?" Jan teased.

"And what's that?" I asked.

"I got my Private Pilot's Licence before Christmas and a rating for variable speed prop. I've been flying a Cessna 182," Jan told me.

"That's great Jan, what prompted you to learn to fly?" I asked.

"Mary mainly, she's always been my role model and you and Bruce and several of the other family members are pilots," Jan said. "I thought if they can do it so can I."

"Well, we'll only have to get you a turbine rating and you'll be able to fly the Pilatus," I said.

"Could I darling?" Jan asked clearly excited by the prospect of flying such a marvellous bird. "Will you teach me?"

"We can do better than that," I began. "Rose is a flying instructor in the India Air Force; she'll do a better job of training you than I could."

"What does Kate do darling?" Jan asked.

"Kate has a Master of Microbiology degree and will be studying and doing research in the Faculty of Genetics in the New Year," I told her.

"Haven't you got an interesting lot of goddesses darling," Jan said giving me a squeeze. "I'm looking forward to meeting my new sisters.

While we had been talking, I had soaped and sponged Jan all over and myself as well and now told her that I had some of Mary's special balm that Doc had prepared for her to use after her reconstruction and it would make her feel more comfortable after last night's escapade. Jan had heard stories from her mother about how Mary had taken a beating in delivering me and nearly died but that was a long time ago and her memory was rusty. I said I'd leave it to Mary or Doc to explain the details, but I had a tube with me for her to use after our first fuck.

"What do I do Brad?" Jan asked.

"It will be better if we stand and I'll support you and you can squat a little and open up for me to rub the balm in and smooth it around," I explained.

"Sounds like fun darling," Jan said and stood up in the spa.

I stood alongside her and squeezed a liberal amount of balm onto the index and middle fingers of my right hand. I put my left arm around her waist and kissed her while Jan lowered herself and held open her Gates to Paradise with her fingers; allowing me to gently massage her outer area and then carefully insert my middle finger into her vagina and massage its walls.

"Oooh, that felt so nice and soothing, I must have been a little raw from the pounding you gave me last night darling," Jan said. "But I'm ready again when you are."

"Let's wait until you get the effect of my little massage," I said. "We'll get dry and go shopping for some winter clothes for you," I said.

It wasn't long before we were dressed and ready to go. I gave her the card which read Clifford Music and told her to use it to pay for her purchases at the boutique and for any expenses she might have in the future. I explained to her that there was no credit limit on the card and that it would be replenished whenever necessary; just keep your receipts in case you need them for tax or warranty claims.

"You're just handing me an open cheque Brad?" Jan said in a tone that suggested disbelief.

"Of course darling, you're a goddess, why should I do anything less. If I did you would not be a goddess would you?"

"We're certainly lucky little goddesses darling," Jan said as she hugged me tightly to her and kissed me.

Jan had on the heaviest clothes she had brought with her and coming from Australia's summer into a London white Christmas they were nowhere near heavy enough. I wrapped her in my bomber jacket which did a marvellous job keeping out the breeze although it looked a little strange seeing that where it fitted to my waist it now gathered in under Jan's backside. It only took us a few minutes to reach the comfort of Jessie's boutique.

"Jessie, we were hoping you would be back at work today. I didn't get a chance to tell you how I liked the Pastoral played by a string quartet, it adds a new dimension to it in my memory. Now I want you to do for Jan what you did for Rose on Monday."

"Jan, you looked stunning in the outfit Brad chose for you last night," Have you seen yourself of TV. I watched the concert right through it was fascinating."

"Thanks Jessie we haven't seen it yet, but friends have recorded it for us," Jan replied. "You do have lovely clothes here."

"Come with me Jan. Let's see what we can find for you. Warm but bright and colourful is what we are looking for," Jessie said as she took her hand and led her away.

"How long are you here for Jan?" Jessie asked.

"Until the end of January with a trip to Paris for a week," Jan replied.

After fifteen minutes and like a replay of shopping with Rose on Monday Jan paraded before me in the various outfits she had chosen.

“I’ll be the best dressed girl in Canberra next winter Brad, you know how cold Canberra can get,” Jan said on one occasion.

Finally, with her purchases complete we decided to have most of Jan’s clothes sent on to Kate’s unit, but we kept a slack suit, overcoat, hat, boots and gloves and scarf to wear in London. Jan used her card to pay for her purchases.

“Will you be bringing any more charming young ladies to me to outfit Bad?” Jessie asked with a giggle.

“No more Jessie but we are bound to be back sometime in the future for spring and summer clothes and we may bring a sister along then.”

I gave Jessie the delivery instructions including the phone number for the courier to ring before delivery. Jessie thanked us again and we left with Jan now protected from the weather in her new overcoat, hat, scarf, boots and gloves. Jan’s slack suit and shoes and my bomber jacket I carried in a shopping bag supplied by Jessie. We took the shopping bag to the hotel lobby with a word to the concierge that we would collect them on our return and headed out to walk up The Mall to Buckingham Palace. We ate afternoon tea in a small café on our way back to the hotel and as we were passing the Novello Theatre we bought tickets on the spur of the moment to see MAMMA MIA performed tonight. Our hotel was next door bar one to the theatre. On entering the hotel, we collected our parcels from earlier and booked for an early dinner at six o’clock which gave us two hours before show time. It was now three-thirty and on entering our room we took off our coats and shoes, pulled the bedspread over us and had two hours in each other’s arms. The stresses, strains and surprises of the last day and night had evaporated, and we were two people enjoying the simplest of all joys in taking pleasure in our closeness. We kissed quietly and gently and fell asleep.

We woke at five-thirty and with no need for dinner suits and evening gowns and stage makeup we were dressed in warm clothes for our walk of only forty metres to the theatre. We entered the dining room at six o'clock and unlike my dinner with Rose earlier in the week we were not joined by any other diners but had a table to ourselves and were happy to eat alone. To date our opportunities to talk alone had been limited to the time I told Jan about Adonis and our pillow talk had been very limited too as our lips had been so often pressed together. Every so often Jan would giggle and say, "You're my cousin Brad; it's hard to imagine this is happening." At other times we would discuss what would be the ideal family size and what did Jan want to do with her career.

"I hope you will never give up your music Jan you play so marvellously, and you will always go on to play better and more inspiringly to your audience. For me I think that the family business interests and the Faculty work will keep me busy for quite some time," I said

"As for my music Brad, I'm very lucky because I can play through my pregnancies; even in our symphony orchestras there are always pregnant women at various stages of their pregnancy. I can practice at home and play to our babies; even before they are born, they hear the music.

"Time, we left for the theatre," I said and rose to hold back Jan's chair for her.

We had both seen MAMMA MIA THE MOVIE with Meryl Streep in the lead. It was a fun show with the Abba music sung with gusto. Now sitting in the theatre and having the players live on stage we were in a completely different paradigm. The actors weren't helped by the camera's view of the Greek Isles, the jetty, the yacht, the path to the motel, the various rooms. The audience was limited to seeing the few sets that could be accommodated on stage. The success of the evening now depended on the relationship that could be established in only two hours between the players on the stage and each patron individually: every member of the audience was going to see and understand the presentation differently. For the actors too: there were no second or third takes, no film editors, no voice overs; they had to do it once and do it right and if they made a slight variation from night to night their partners on the stage had to accommodate them. The night then was dynamic for everyone, actors and patrons alike. It was their unique experience. Unlike the canned entertainment that was put out to the world to be watched on a flat screen, be it in a cinema or on a television set. If the cinema wasn't barren enough, then the television was the last place to be part of the experience that they were sharing with the cast. Seen live in the theatre there was no opportunity to pause or rewind, there were no incessant advertisements to break up the flow of the presentation; the audience had to participate mentally and not sit back and stuff themselves with chocolates or drink.

I saw a parallel or synchronicity with this theatrical performance of which I was a part and the duty facing me on behalf of the Faculty. I had instinctively ruled out the distribution of my semen for artificial insemination and I could now liken that to the distribution of canned film that had been created by teams of writers, actors, and editors and canned music created in the studio with sound mixers and synthesisers and distributed by other disinterest parties. My semen wasn't to be taken by hand into a sterile container without thought as to where it was going. It wasn't to be handled by clerks, nurses and technicians to impregnate an artificially taken egg and doctors to dispassionately implant it into an unstimulated uterus of an unknown woman when all it took was two participants;

the actor on the stage and the member of the audience. The actor must deliver his performance with the conviction and sincerity that will thrill the audience as they accept it and leave both parties fulfilled by the act.

The actors too would create the same magic with members of the next night's audience and no member of any audience would be jealous of the actors' gift to others nor would the actor feel any guilt of having delivered night after night and never expecting to see the same faces before him again.

Jan had done the same thing last night. The live, vibrant and beautiful young lady that the audience saw was there with them in the here and now. Every man in the audience was in love with her while she was on the stage and every woman admired her and would like to emulate her or have a daughter like her. If she had stumbled, missed her notes, or got off beat all two thousand of the audience would know, their heart may have gone out to her but there would have been no consummation of the performance for them. They wouldn't have gone home fulfilled. As it had turned out the audience would remember Jan for years to come and some would one day tell their children of the night they saw Jan Franklin and the London Symphony Orchestra perform *Sibelius* with *Paganin*i for an encore. I now knew that in my work for the Faculty I would have to be an artiste.

We walked the few metres back to the hotel hand in hand and with our own thoughts. Jan could see herself playing along with the singers, enjoying the performance with them, and picking up the audiences almost imperceptible little movements of shoulders, hands and heads as the actors sung the words of the songs. The audience like the performers were immersed in the production; they could see in their minds the Greek Isles and the motel and feel the emotions of the young bride-to-be as she sought her father from amongst her mother's three former lovers. I was wondering how I was going to deliver this vastly different form of love to unknown numbers of no doubt very attractive women that the Faculty would provide and keep it totally separate from the love I now felt for my three goddesses and Adonis's mother. As Brad, it would not be possible but as Adonis I knew it was inevitable and essential.

When Jan and I pulled the bedclothes over us and reached for each other it was if we were enacting some beautiful opus from one of the great masters. I had turned the piped music off and there was little noise to be heard beyond our breathing and sighs.

"What do you hear darling?" I asked.

"MOONLIGHT SONATA darling," Jan replied without giving my question any conscious thought.

"So do I darling, it is one of my favourite pieces," I told her.

We would soon realise as we spent more time in bed in each other's arms that the one asking the question was not confirming that we were hearing the same music simply to please the other. We took to writing our answer down and found we always agreed. We determined that the vigour and passion that we brought to our coupling was reflecting the mood of the music we were hearing. We decided that we were singing from the same song-sheet in key and always on the right beat.

Saturday 29 December 2012 – 0900 hrs

"Come on darling, remember I offered to take you for a flight in the Pilatus at my birthday party?" I greeted her.

"Of course, and then you told me I would have to wait a year," Jan replied.

"Not any more, let's do it today. You could even have your first lesson. Apart from being bigger than the Cessna it's really only the engine that is different: except for the wheels going up and down."

At nine o'clock we arrived at Denham and Jan had her first viewing of Alpha Uniform. Like everyone else, Jan was amazed at what she saw; she would have been quite happy to lower the divan and spend the morning there. I had other plans: we were going to Rome for Jan to throw some coins into the Trevi Fountain.

I settled Jan in the captain's seat for the outbound flight; I would fly from the right-hand seat. Jan's experience to date would all have been from the left seat with her instructor in the right-hand seat. The instruments and displays were identical but there was a different perspective to the runway centreline and controls that you reached for with your right hand are now operated with your left. I pointed out the instruments she would need to scan and told her the speed at which she was to call 'V1-Rotate'. After that she was to watch what I was doing and listen to my tower and airways communications.

"It's English everywhere in the air darling and the words are the same as at home," I said.

I received my clearance and then we were speeding along the runway."

"V1 – Rotate" Jan called clearly as the numbers came up.

I got our climb established.

"Hold the control column Jan and put your feet on the rudder pedals," I began. "Hold the little bit of right rudder I've got for the crosswind and keep the climb going. We'll be levelling-out at thirty thousand."

"I've never been above ten thousand in the Cessna, Brad," Jan said excitedly as we shot past twenty-five thousand on the altimeter.

Jan held the rate of climb constant: easing the power back slowly as the Pilatus reached thinner air. Approaching thirty thousand I saw her lowering the nose to hit our assigned level without me telling her.

"In five minutes Jan we turn right to one seven four," I said.

Jan again banked into our new heading without gaining or losing anything on the altimeter.

"OK, turn on the auto-pilot and have a rest," I said. "You've done very well."

"I'm supposed to know where we are as well, but I don't," Jan admitted.

"That's all right; it's a big jump up from the 182, isn't it?" I said.

"It certainly is but it's beautifully smooth like a good violin," Jan replied.

"We are over the English Channel Jan, that's the coast of France ahead, we'll cross halfway between Calais to our left and Le Havre to our right."

Jan was fascinated by what she was seeing from thirty thousand feet and from the moving map display on the panel as she zoomed in to see more detail.

When I received my approach instructions from Centocelle Military Airport; It didn't register that we were now in Italy.

"Where are we darling?" Jan asked.

"In Rome Jan, it's time for lunch. My co-pilots usually make me coffee on flights of more than one hour," I added.

"I'm sorry darling, but I don't have a rating to operate your galley," Jan said.

"We'll get you some ratings on our return flight Jan," I promised her.

I called into the Adjutant's Office but neither the adjutant nor Lieutenant Raoul was on duty. We chatted with the duty officer for a few moments who must have thought us a little strange flying from London to Rome for lunch and to throw a few coins in the Trevi Fountain. However, after having a look at Jan and seeing the happy smile on her face and the way she hugged my arm to her breast he thought I was smart rather than strange. We took a taxi to the city and direct to the Trevi Fountain.

Jan and I turned our backs to the fountain and tossed our coins high over our shoulders.

"The wish I made when I played the video you sent me has come true darling," Jan said and clung to me and kissed me in front of all the tourists milling around.

"What was it Jan?" I asked.

"That it was me being here throwing a coin with you Brad," Jan said and kissed me again.

"I hope this one comes true for you too Jan," I replied.

We strolled off arm-in-arm along with other lovers who had been making their wishes. We found a small restaurant and without rushing ate an authentic Italian spaghetti dish. We had no schedule to keep or flights to catch; Alpha Uniform would be waiting for us. It was nearing three in the afternoon when we arrived back at the Pilatus.

"The first rating for you to earn this afternoon Jan is the percolator, stove, oven, refrigerator and washing-up department. This includes knowing where to find everything and how to secure it for flight," I began.

Jan grinned at me but took her instruction seriously along with a congratulatory kiss when she showed her proficiency with each task. It was three-thirty when we climbed out of Centocelle and with an estimated flight time of three hours thirty minutes we would be arriving at Denham in the dark.

"This will be a new experience for me Brad," Jan remarked as she had only been in the cabin of commercial jets on any previous night flights.

I grinned to myself as I thought seeing the sunset through the cockpit windows wouldn't be the only new experience Jan would have this evening as she undertook the examination for the other new rating I had in mind for her. By three forty-five we were straight and level and Jan left to exercise her new coffee making rating. When she returned, she sat in my lap to watch the shadows lengthening while our coffee cooled. After we finished our coffee Jan displayed her proficiency in her new rating by taking our coffee mugs to wash and wipe and return them to their individual holes in the china cupboard.

"It's marvellous how everything has a slot or hole of its own darling," Jan said when she returned and sat in my lap to watch the last rays of the sun and see bright stars suddenly come to light in the dark sky.

"You're ready for your next rating darling," I said.

"What's this one darling?" Jan asked in all innocence.

"It's the Mile-High Rating," I said. "You've got to find a hole to secure my old fella in."

"There are no spare holes in the cupboard darling," Jan replied as she quickly caught on to what was required.

"Will the one between my legs do?" she said and held my kiss for quite a while.

"I think that would do very nicely Jan,"

"Then I'll just go and get it ready Captain," Jan said and left me.

I quickly made my own preparations. I took off all my clothes, folded them and put them on the co-pilot's seat. I placed the towel from behind my chair over the seat and made myself comfortable; I was becoming proficient in awarding this rating now, for not only had Mary inducted me thoroughly and given me a couple of flight reviews since, I had also inducted Kate and Rose into the club in the last ten days. I sat back in my chair and made my final preparation; I let my mind review the ratings I had awarded so far, and my old fella came up to be a strong and hard horn: something I considered my applicant was entitled to expect.

Jan returned wearing her Love Knot necklace and nothing else. Only the orange and green glow from the instrument panel moulded the smooth shape of her body as she silently straddled me and claimed my lips. The full moon rose over our starboard wing and the light shone in revealing the smile of satisfaction on Jan's face as she worked her little bottom driving my old fella into the only hole on board made for it. I helped her along with kisses and my hands as I massaged her back, breasts and thighs. I didn't consider I was coaching the candidate; she had her rating won as soon as our pubic hairs came together ensuring my old fella had a safe fit. Now I was judging how much turbulence he could take before he broke and slipped from her hold. The moon rose higher and had we taken our eyes from each other we would have seen bright stars against the dark sky. I saw Jan's eyes squeeze tight as she began the strongest and loudest orgasm she had yet experienced. At thirty thousand there was no need to consider guests in adjoining rooms, or staff passing in the hall and she let it all go: including an uncontrolled squirt into my groin which flowed over my balls onto the towel beneath me. My old fella responded with a strong ejaculation of its own and we clung together for ten minutes until my old fella decided that its allotted safe hole was only any good when he was proud and strong, but it had better just hang around with me at other times.

"Did I pass darling?" Jan asked.

"With flying colours Jan, I can't endorse your log book but I have a membership badge for you. There's nowhere to pin it just now though."

"What were we playing Jan?" I asked. "I wrote my selection down while you were dressing."

"Tchaikovsky's 6th First Movement darling," Jan replied.

"Will you accept **This is a story of a starry night**?"**https://www.youtube.com/watch?v=clkqi7lkvBk** I said.

"That's close enough for me Adonis; we really are in tune aren't we," Jan replied.

"It's a pity so many people turn up their nose at classical music; particularly when so much pop is drawn from the great themes. How would you get someone interested in classical violin works, Jan?"

"I'd suggest they Google **La Campanella.https://www.youtube.com/watch?v=YAAKOXR44Q4** It's available on YouTube with a very good rendition by Sayaka Shoji. It's the third movement from Niccolo Paganini's Violin Concerto No. 2. Paganini was an outstanding performer as well as being a composer and his works test all others who play them. He is reputed to have big hands with double-jointed fingers; making it difficult for us girls to match him. Have I got time for a shower before we come back to earth?"

"You have an hour at your disposal darling, just throw me out a damp sponge please."

Thirty minutes later I was dressed, and Jan returned to sit in my lap and cuddle.

"Did I stain your seat darling?" Jan asked.

"No Jan, my towel caught our dribbles. The seat is genuine leather and wipes clean."

"That's a relief Brad; I'd hate to mark her in any way," Jan replied and hugged me. "It was delicious darling. Did I earn my rating?"

"In the first three minutes Jan. Here's your badge," I said and slipped the Mile-High-Club badge into the collar of her cardigan. "Reluctantly you must take your own seat now. I've got work to do."

I received my descent clearance to come in over Portsmouth on track for Denham and thirty minutes later Jan was on the edge of her seat as Alpha Uniform came down the glideslope with it lights blazing and not moving from my touchdown target at the five hundred feet markers. She watched silently as I let her wheels touch gently and run out along the centreline, braking smoothly.

Tomorrow we only had a ten-minute flight to RAF Wyton and had no need to refuel even though we had been to Rome and back. Jan too found it difficult to understand how so many people, with different national loyalties, can live in such close proximity. We knew, of course, how troubled these relationships had been for all recorded history.

When we returned to our room at One Aldwych, I took Jan into my arms to hold her close.

"We're early enough for dinner in one of the restaurants Jan and there's also a dinner dance in the ballroom," I offered.

"Could we have room service Brad? It's been a lovely day and I'd like it to continue for a little while with just the two of us."

Sunday 30 December 2012 – 0800 hrs

When Sunday morning arrived, we had a leisurely breakfast and took our time bathing in the spa. Afterwards, I picked Jan up in my arms and took her back to bed.

"We're not expected until two o'clock darling," I told her.

"It would be a shame to waste it Brad," Jan said and gave me a big kiss.

"Did I say anything to hurt you at my birthday darling?" I asked.

"No darling, why?" Jan replied.

"Mary thought I did when she saw you dabbing your eyes as you went to the ladies' room."

"It was the thought of you going away for a year Brad: not anything you said; you've never said a word or done anything to hurt me. The only hurt I have ever suffered was not having you in my bed. I'd always hoped, but when you said you were going away for a year, I thought all hope had gone. Then there were the photos of you and Rose and you and Kate. I was devastated and jealous. When I got Mary's message, I was happy to agree just to get you out of my mind."

I pulled her over to straddle me and kissed her deeply while I stroked her hair. She raised her bottom and with her right hand brought my horn up to her vagina and pushed herself down and my old fella in.

“Oh Brad,” she said.

When she looked at me tears were running down her cheeks. She laughed between her sobs as I soothed her with soft words encouraging her to let it all go in tears or laughter or in the orgasm that wasn’t far away. I kissed her continuously, stroked her hair and then worked my hands up her back; then I brought my hands around her thighs for my fingers to work her inner thighs like a pianist as she rode my horn. It couldn’t last much longer and when I let go and my semen splashed her cervix Jan instantly shuddered with delight. Tears were still streaming down her cheeks and for an instant I thought that she was in pain, but they were tears of joy and relief as she let go all those years of wishing for what was now happening: so suddenly and unexpectedly. When she collapsed on my chest, I rolled her over onto her back and now on my knees kept up my now gentle thrusting in and out; still kissing her and holding her to me with my arms around her shoulders.

“Have we died and gone to heaven darling,” Jan asked after I ejaculated again, and she rode out her second orgasm for the morning.

“No darling we’re here for a long time yet,” I replied.

We clung together for another half hour; mostly kissing but with me sending tingles through Jan’s body just with the gentlest pressure of my fingertips on her spine. When Jan broke away to get ready to leave, she picked up her violin and still naked played Aker Bilk’s **Harem**. **http://www.futuristic.guru/harem**

“Come on darling, take **Goddess Jan** **http://www.futuristic.guru/goddess-jan** to your harem,”

Jan said and then skipped away to the bathroom to shower.

The great Glenn Miller hit (c1942) THIS IS THE STORY OF A STARRY NIGHT is derived from Pyotr Tchaikovsky's theme 5:50 minutes into his 1893 composed - ***Symphony No 6***

Chapter 15

Harem

Sunday 30 December 2012 – 1400 hrs

When we arrived at RAF Wyton, around two o'clock, our mini-honeymoon was over. Since arriving in Cambridge on the sixteenth I had several days alone bonding with each goddess in turn. Now we would have to learn to live together, a daunting prospect in any relationship after the first flush of love or lust subsides but in a relationship of four the permutations are much greater. Now we would be going to combine as one unit. The girls were quite happy to share my time and ability to thrill them and now they would have a new relationship as sisters. In some ways, I would become the loner. There were many things about our unusual relationship that I must leave to my goddesses. I wouldn't even know which goddess was going to share my bed until she slipped in beside me.

I had told Mary that I would bring Jan from RAF Wyton to Kate's unit by taxi rather than bring everyone to meet us at the airport. When we arrived, I led Jan into Kate's lounge room and Mary, after giving her cousin a kiss and hug, made the introductions. Kate and Rose came forward to give Jan a hug. While Jan and I had been in London, Kate and Rose had some time to do some bonding of their own and wanted to include Jan as soon as possible. The girls shared the three-seater lounge with Jan in the middle and Rose and Kate each holding a hand. Rod told us he had booked for dinner at the Chinese restaurant on the corner of the street, so we would have more time to talk.

"Rose and I have done some serious thinking over the last three days and we think Jan will agree. We don't want to have three homes with Brad running around visiting each of us in turn; we want to have one home where we raise our children knowing their half-siblings," Kate got the discussion started.

"Where will you be based Kate?" Rod asked.

“We think it must be in Canberra Dad,” Kate began. “It would be much easier for Rose and me to transfer there than Jan and Brad coming here or to India.”

“We think our children need to be born Aussies and there are Brad’s Grands and Greats and the Clifford company, all in Canberra; and Mary too when she’s at home,” Rose added.

“When can you leave the air force Rose?” Mary asked.

“My term is complete; I can leave at any time. After the meeting with the committee in Paris I’ll fly back to Agra and resign my commission,” Rose answered.

“And I’ll join Mary at the ANU if she’ll have me,” Kate said with a big smile at Mary.

“What do you think Jan?” Kate asked.

“I think it’s a wonderful idea; we’d rarely see our sisters if we had three separate homes,” Jan replied.

“Nobody has asked Brad,” Rod spoke up.

“Whatever my goddesses want is what I want too,” I replied.

“You’re a brave man Brad. They’ll gang up on you, so you had better have many sons to support you,” Rod said.

“I’m delighted girls and you’ll be welcome at the ANU Kate,” Mary added. “Rod will miss you of course, but it’s easier to keep in touch now and we will be travelling a lot.”

“Shall we go and eat?” Rod asked.

“I’d like to tell you some news before we go,” Rose began, “I think I’m pregnant. It’s too early to know, so no congratulations please, but I'm late and I've always been regular."

"We'll keep our fingers crossed Rose," Kate said. "We want you to be first."

"I have a little bit of news too, but not so important," Jan began. "I had a message this morning inviting me to solo with the Paris Symphony Orchestra on Friday 11 January, and an afternoon concert with the National Youth Orchestra the next day; will we still be in Paris for those dates?"

"Mary doesn't meet the President until the sixteenth, so we can leave for Washington on the Sunday," I was quick to say.

We spent a social ninety minutes in the restaurant with the conversation revolving around Mary's and my trip from Australia to London and the girls mini-honeymoons with me.

"Where did you get that Jan?" Kate asked with her eyes going to the Mile-High Club badge still showing from the collar of her cardigan.

Everyone laughed, and Jan blushed when she realised it was still there from when I gave it to her.

"I got mine over the Irish Sea," Rose said quickly to dispel Jan's embarrassment.

"I got mine over the North Sea," Kate added.

"I got mine over the Mediterranean Sea: the sun had just set, and the stars were coming out and it was beautiful," Jan replied happily.

They told Jan how they had liked her performance and her stage presence.

“Did you bring your gown and coat from Canberra?” Kate asked.

“No, I didn’t even know I was playing until that morning,” Jan told them. “I had no suitable clothes with me and didn’t bring my violin. I was pretty much a wreck when Brad met me at the airport, but he got me to the rehearsal and then went shopping for my clothes. He made me sleep before the performance and built up my confidence. Before we left for the theatre, he gave me my Christmas present and when I walked out on the stage my only thought was that I couldn’t let him down.”

“You didn’t know you were a goddess then Jan?” Rose asked.

“Brad didn’t tell me about being a goddess until after we got back to the hotel,” Jan told them. “He was worried that I had enough shocks for one day and held it back until I got the performance out of the way. Just as well as I would never have gone to the theatre at all.”

“You played like a goddess Jan, that was an inspiring performance,” Rose said, and Kate agreed.

We walked quickly back to Kate’s unit and Mary and Rod left without going inside. As soon as we entered the lounge room, we shared a joint hug and I kissed each goddess in turn. It was only nine o’clock, but we decided to get ready for bed. We thought we would bundle together for a while for some cuddles in bed and later Rose and Kate would take the bed in the spare room leaving Jan to spend the night with me. Rose and Kate had agreed that they had each had a four-night mini-honeymoon while Jan’s had been only three, therefore tonight should be Jan’s. After tonight they would simply take it in turns as to who spent the night with me and she would be queen for the day. Kisses and cuddle times would be taken as and when they presented themselves, as now. They would know when it would be proper for me and my queen-for-the-day to have some privacy, although privacy wasn't so much of a concern as the need for space for one to stretch her legs and even roll about. We took to the bathroom, which was never designed for four bodies at once, and although it steamed-up quickly, making it difficult for me to shave, we managed with two girls in the shower and one in the bath while I shaved. When it came to drying ourselves there was not enough room for eight arms and four towels to be working at once so we spread out into the lounge room. There was a bouquet of smells as deodorants, powders and perfumes were applied. I was first into bed and a noticeable stepping-up of tempo as the girls competed to see who would get the first cuddle. Jan hung back knowing that she would be there in the morning. Rose slackened her pace letting Kate skip through in front of her as she hadn't felt my arms around her for eight days now.

"I've missed you darling," Rose and Jan heard Kate say between kisses.

Kate had got into the bed on the right-hand side and I was turned towards her, holding her in my arms. Rose and Jan entered from the left and while Rose waited for me to turn towards her, she put her arms around Jan and kissed her.

"I'm so glad were all together Jan," Rose said sincerely.

"I was so jealous when I saw photos of you and Kate dancing with Brad, but I'm not now. I know Brad needs the three of us and we need each other too," Jan said.

After a little while Kate left for the spare room and I turned to Rose.

"I had a feeling you conceived that first night in London Goddess Rose," I said.

"It's too early to be sure darling; I'm only two days over. It might be just my rhythm getting messed up with all this unexpected love and sex," Rose replied. "In another four weeks we should be sure. Goodnight darling," Rose added and left to join Kate.

She's so much like Mary I thought as she rubbed her inner thigh against me and wriggled over on top of me. My free hand left her breast and went down between us to part her hairs and open her Gates to Paradise. Jan was quite damp, and I teased her and made gently little thrusting movements at the opening to her vagina as I said, 'Open the door for daddy darling,' and Jan responded with similar movements of her tongue between her lips and whispered, 'mummy's ready darling'.

As my old fella made gentle movements within her so recently opened vagina, I played delightful melodies on her body; running my fingers up and down her spine and massaging her neck and shoulders. When she rose up on me, with our genitals locked together, I imparted gentle kisses and licks to her nipples and then claimed her lips again as my fingers reached low to run up her thighs. Jan couldn't hold in her sounds of delight as I continued to thrill her and withhold her climax, she felt like begging me to bring her to an orgasm but at the same time wanted to hold me back for more of what she was already feeling and experiencing. Jan had no way of knowing then after only three days coupling with me that each occasion would be different to any previous time that we had come together, and each time would be ecstatic. Sometimes it would be the full orchestra in a four-movement production and at others an overture to better delights to come later in the day. On other occasions, it would be an elegant and beautiful piano or violin concerto as it had been when we played Beethoven's Moonlight together. Tonight, as the fourth movement came to an end with and outpouring of semen from me and delightful cries of joy from Jan we collapsed into a soft and delicate motions of a fifth movement that could easily have been called 'afterglow'. We had no idea how long we clung together as Jan only roused as my old fella shrunk and slipped from her now gentle hold.

"The Pastoral Symphony darling; that's what I heard and felt tonight," Jan said.

"I suppose the fifth movement gave it away Jan?" I said.

Monday 31 December 2012 0900 hrs

"Good morning Goddess," I greeted Jan with my regular kiss and hug and slipped my hand under the top of her housecoat to squeeze her left breast.

"Good morning Adonis," Jan replied. "Your good mornings are as good as your good nights,"

"Good Morning Goddess," I greeted Kate and Rose in the same way.

We sat to eat our English breakfast that Kate was so fond of preparing and started talking about a possible performance for the party at RAF Wyton.

"The University Players did Mikado this year," Kate began. "I thought we might borrow the costumes for *Three Little Maids from School* and do that."

"We'd have floor length kimonos to put on over our other clothes, matching black wigs and brightly painted parasols to twirl; the words are simple, and we can all giggle," Kate added.

"Did you and Rose giggle last night Kate?" I asked.

"Yes, a couple of times Brad, it must have been lovely for you and Jan," Kate answered truthfully and sincerely.

The girls agreed that they could manage *Three Little Maids from School* and Kate phoned a friend in the Players' group and arranged to borrow the costumes. She arranged to collect them at ten o'clock and they would rehearse during the day.

"Well that lets me off the hook this time," I said.

"You could do the piano accompaniment I," Jan said. "I know you play well."

"That was a family secret Jan," I began. "Kate and Rose didn't know I could play at all."

They pressed me into playing the piano for them and that I was to be back at five o'clock for a full-dress rehearsal. They knew that Mary and I would be working in the office on the plane selecting the girls who I would impregnate while we were in Paris. Mary would be examining the girls' histories, charts and gene maps and I wanted to know the social and political backgrounds of their families. Although I was to take no part in their upbringing, I still felt a responsibility for the children's wellbeing. I would still be their father even though I may never see them.

"Will you drive please Brad?" Mary asked as she threw me the keys to Rod's BMW. "You know the way to the drome."

I had my ID card ready when we arrived at the gate at RAF Wyton. We were waived through with a salute and went directly to the Base Commander's office and asked for Group Captain Page.

"Come in Brad," Vic said as he emerged from his office to greet us.

"Come in and sit down," Vic invited us.

"We just called in to say we're on the base and will be working in the office on board this afternoon," I told him.

"Fine Brad," Vic replied. "You are coming back tonight? You said there'd be two blokes and four girls so there's a table for six reserved up-front for your party."

"Yes Vic, they're all looking forward to spending New Year's Eve here. Will we be expected to perform again?"

"Only if you want to Brad but I expect you'll be heckled if you don't after last time," Vic laughed.

"The girls are cooking up something today, but we'll leave our professors as part of the audience," I replied.

"The Mess is open if you would like lunch Mary," Vice offered.

"Thanks Vic but there's food on board," Mary said. "We'll be going light until dinner."

We drove up to the hangar and I opened the door with the remote and closed it behind us. I plugged in the remote power cable to the hangar power and we went on board. I turned on the lights and heating and soon the relatively small space was comfortably warm. Mary had gone to the galley to heat up frozen meals for us and percolated coffee. I set up our notebook computers so that we could view the individual profiles and data from our own desks. We sat at the dining table and ate our lunch.

"We have fifteen candidates for you on this visit darling," Mary began. "How many do you think you can handle."

"It sounds so clinical and scientific Mary," I replied. "I don't want to become some sort of fucking machine."

"I'm sorry darling," Mary replied. "Come with me."

Mary rose from the table and took my hand making me get up and follow her. When she got to the divan she hit the 'Down' button and then sat; took off her shoes and moved over to the centre of the bed.

"Come here please Brad?" Mary asked as she held up her right hand towards me.

Unable to refuse I kicked off my shoes, took off my jacket and joined her on the bed.

"That was so indelicate Adonis," Mary began. "I'm truly sorry; I was in my Chair of the Co-ordinating Committee role instead of being Aphrodite. I wanted to get that part of the afternoon over quickly in the hope you would want me like this."

I had wrapped my arms about her as she talked and now kissed her gently but at the same time urgently. Her hand went to my belt buckle and undid it and quickly unzipped my fly. She released my old fella from prison and held him as I undid her blouse and unclipped her bra,

"You keep on being perceptive darling," Mary said as she tossed aside her blouse and bra; freeing her upper body of all but her Love Knot necklace.

I pushed my trousers and boxers down and over my feet so that I was stripped bare and then Mary was all over me.

"I thought you might not want me at all now that you had three beautiful goddesses at your beck and call darling," Mary said, and I felt a shudder of relief pass through her.

"But I'm at your beck and call Aphrodite," I said. "I'm sure my goddesses understand that too."

As we talked Mary had been rubbing her right hand over my chest while holding my old fella in her left. I had been massaging her back with my right hand and teasing her nipples with my left. Sentences were punctuated with long passionate kisses.

"And now you are going to be a daddy Adonis," Mary said. "Congratulations,"

"And you are going to be a granny Aphrodite," I replied. "Isn't that what you wanted to be?"

"It certainly is darling, and Bruce would be very proud of you," Mary replied.

Mary's right thigh was rubbing up my leg now and arching over me. I rolled toward her and she guided my stiff horn between her hairs into the entrance of her vagina. She made one of her inward moving contractions followed by another and another and I was sucked deeper into her a centimetre at a time.

"Are you happy with Rod darling?" I asked. "Not that it's any of my business."

"Yes, it is Brad, and it's sweet that you care. Rod's a fine gentleman and good for me and it allows both of us to be free of our baby's fixation. But it will never by like it is with you Adonis. Only you and I and Bruce can ever share this. I'm Mary with Rod but I'm Aphrodite when I'm with you."

While Mary had been speaking, I had taken her right nipple between my lips and tickled it vigorously.

"Oh, Adonis that was delicious,' Mary said as a quick orgasm flowed through her and I came too,

"That's for Goddess Rose thank you Aphrodite," I said without pausing my thrusts into her. "She is so bright and intelligent. I want her to take an interest in Clifford Holdings once she leaves the air force."

I rose up on my elbows a little so that I could look deeply into her smiling eyes and to let me work both nipples with my fingers and my old fella made occasional rubbings against her clitoris. Mary started writhing under me again pushing herself against me as if I had more to give but was somehow holding it back. We broke into another orgasm.

"That's for Goddess Kate thank you Aphrodite," I said. "She's so outgoing and sensual that every time I look at her, I get a hard-on. She has been waiting to burst out for years and now she has."

I now rolled onto my back and Mary followed in my arms. My old fella didn't miss a beat in the manoeuvre and I now slipped a finger between her curls to tickle her clit. All the while I was kissing her, and she was slipping her tongue in and out keeping the beat. Again, we rose to a climax and this time I held nothing back. Mary couldn't hold back her cry of delight and tears ran down her cheeks.

"That's for Goddess Jan Aphrodite," I said. "Sometimes when we fuck it's as if it is you in my arms; she is so like you and exquisitely sensitive. We hear the same music when we do this."

Mary hugged me and cried. Everything that had happened in her life was worth it and she knew the best was still to come. It was an hour later when we woke. Mary was still lying on top of me with my arms around her. She recalled sometime in the last sixty minutes my old fella shrinking and slipping out of her. She had tried to keep hold of him but with her exhaustion and the excess of our combined fluid in her vagina it slipped out and flopped into my groin.

"We've had a couple of double-bungers darling, but we've never had a triple-bunger before," Mary whispered when she saw my eyes open. She bent down and kissed me with the tips of her nipples just touching the hair on my chest causing her to say 'Oooh' and I felt a little shudder go through her body.

"We're not going to get much work done today Aphrodite," I said as I looked at the bedside clock and saw that it was three-thirty. "I'll boil the kettle while we get cleaned up and then we can talk about it over coffees."

Mary slipped off me and went to the bathroom. I filled the percolator and followed her. We washed our faces and sticky bits to make ourselves presentable and dressed. Over coffee, we decided that for my first campaign on behalf of the Faculty would be with six girls, spending one day each with them in a hotel room booked by the Paris Sorbonne University. We had eighteen girls put forward from the Paris faculty. All had met the selection criteria of gene compatibility: no prior unprotected sex and in perfect health and physical condition. Either they must have a husband in waiting, whose genetic makeup ensured that he would be a good role model for a child and protective of its mother, or the girl's own extended family ready to fulfil that role. Everyone involved must be ready to cooperate with the Faculty's aims. "We must eliminate two-thirds of the candidates, Mary."

"What a pity darling," Mary said after her first overview of the candidates. "They are all beautiful and intelligent; they could all be Miss Universe Finalists,"

"There's only one of me Mary and Paris is only our first stop," I said. "We need to apply some more criteria. Firstly, we must know that each girl is at her highest point of fertility for the day of her appointment. Let's take one from Ghent, one from Lyon, one from Paris, one from Zurich, one from Frankfurt and one from Rotterdam. That makes six but at least most of the Sorbonne's area of influence is covered. We can take in the other countries next time around.

"That brings us down to fourteen darling," Mary said reluctantly.

"Our main criteria must be to place a child into a family where it will be able to have the greatest effect on society," I continued. "For example, if we can infiltrate the families who exert the most control over the world's wealth then we will have allies on the inside when we bring about our new world order. We must find families who have had dynastic control of countries no matter what political persuasion they proclaim and families with great industrial power. The corrupters and the corrupted must be our targets. If it gets down to a choice between two girls in any one city, then we must accept the younger."

"You are approaching this as a general darling," Mary said.

"Yes darling, it's war."

"You are going to wage war with your dick and your semen."

"That's right Aphrodite," I told her. "Adonis must make these girls willing collaborators in just one day."

"From their family background darling there are only six in the list who qualify," Mary said.

"That makes the selection easy then Mary," I said. "In this first year or two we must use all our powers to fight greed and corruption. There already exists a lot of love and forbearing out there that is kept hidden because people can't afford to fight for themselves. It is being expressed as rage by both men and women and the more they rage the more they are suppressed and then the more their children rage."

"Do you want to see who qualify for Paris darling?" Mary asked.

"No thanks Mary," I said. "I can't get my emotions involved any wider than they are now. I must meet these girls on the day and probably never see them again."

Mary came to my side of the table and sat in my lap.

"I know you will do it Adonis," Mary said as she hugged me. "Even if I had more children it wouldn't have helped. Only you can do it."

"Come on Aphrodite," I said after sharing a lingering kiss with her. "I'm due to rehearse with my goddesses in fifteen minutes."

"What are you going to do?" Mary asked.

"Kate has borrowed the costumes from the University Players and they're going to do Three Little Maids from School, I told her.

"That's wonderful Brad, what are you doing?" Mary asked.

"I'm doing the accompaniment on the piano and I might just do *I've Got a Little List* as an intro," I answered. "You and Rod won't be called on."

"Thanks darling," Mary answered. "I've done my best performance for today don't you think?"

"Yes, you have Aphrodite and thank you," I said. "A happy New Year darling."

I gave her a New Year's kiss of the kind I would not be able to give her in the Mess at midnight. I arrived at Kate's unit ten minutes before five as the girls were donning their costumes for our rehearsal. After receiving welcome home kisses from my goddesses, I collected the sheet music and went to the piano.

I did a slow practice run by myself and then declared I was ready and would give a four-bar introduction before they entered from the hall. They had moved the dining room furniture back against the wall during their earlier practice and had about the same space available to them as they expected they would have in the Mess. I played the intro and Kate led the trio into the room, dancing and singing and twirling their parasols. At each opportune moment they gave the audience naive but cheeky looks over their shoulders with flutters of their false eye lashes and then modestly hiding their faces for a moment behind their twirling parasols.

"I'm sure that will get you much applause tonight goddesses," I said as I stood and clapped.

The Goddesses lifted their wig from their head, undid the tie of their kimono and slipped it off their shoulders. They were wearing the evening gowns that I had bought them and now looked anything but three little maids from school. They were three very elegant young ladies who would receive many admiring glances in the Mess tonight.

"Come on Brad," Kate said. "You need to wear your dinner suit tonight. We've laid out your clothes on your bed."

I left them packing their costumes and doing their final preparations and went to shave and shower. It wasn't very long before I returned to the dining room looking every inch the suave young gentleman accustomed to escorting a charming lady or three.

"Ready girls," I announced. "You look charming tonight, Rose, Jan, Kate" I added as they entered the dining room.

I took the case containing their costumes and we left for the car.

As we entered the Officers' Mess we were greeted by Vic and Miriam. They had placed themselves near the entrance to greet the wives and girlfriends, and now sometime husbands and boyfriends, of new officers who were visiting the Mess for the first time.

I introduced Rose: Flight Lieutenant Sastri from Agra and Jan Franklin, Mary's cousin: to Miriam and Vic.

"Hello Rose," Vic said as he greeted her. "Geoff speaks very highly of you. He sent me the video of you and Geoff escorting Professor Mary and Brad out of India."

"I'm pleased to meet you Jan," Vic greeted her. "We loved your performance on Thursday night."

"Thank you, Vic," Jan replied.

"You must be a proud man tonight Brad, escorting three charming young ladies?" Miriam teased me.

"Proud and honoured Miriam, I can assure you," I replied, "although I might be struggling to get a dancing partner with the number of unattached officers here."

"Perhaps if you would join Vic and me at our table they might be better behaved under the glare of the master. The professors too of course; I see them coming in now."

Vic and Miriam had met Mary and Rod when we left for Scotland and now welcomed them as friends. A three-course meal was catered by a local company and a four-piece group had been playing soft background music since we arrived The Mess had been extended tonight by the removal of partitions making the floor bigger for the dancers. I took their orders for drinks and went to the bar. When I returned, I found that my three charming ladies had been pressed to dance with unaccompanied bachelors and Miriam too had been whisked away. Mary remained and as Vic and Rod were engrossed in their discussion about local golf courses, I soon had Mary on her feet to dance with me. Her face lit up in a big smile as I held her close to me and we glided away.

"I thought I might not have the chance to dance with you Brad seeing that you had three beautiful girls to dance with already," Mary said.

"You see; I turn my back for two minutes to get them drinks and they're off with other blokes," I said in jest.

"Last time you wore that dress Mary I became bold enough to slip my fingers through that slit in the front onto your bare breast," I reminded her. "Do you remember?"

“Of course I do darling,” Mary replied. “The memory is still there, and the feel of your fingers is too. It was a special night darling.”

“It could have been just you and me Mary,” I said.

“I know darling,” Mary replied. “We could have been happy beyond belief but knowing what I knew about you the guilt would have got to me in time and you would have hated me, and by then it would have been too late. Your life would have been wasted. Cheer up, a new year and new life is starting for all of us.”

“We had our happy new year this afternoon darling,” I said.

“Yes, and we’ll be leaving for our trip around the world in two weeks,” Mary said. “We’ll find some time to be together darling. Now you had better dance with the girls,”

At the end of the bracket I took Mary back to our table and waited for Kate, Rose and Jan to return. They each introduced their dance partner and then we sat as the next course arrived. During the evening I got to dance with each of the girls and Miriam as well. Miriam loved to dance but for the most part Vic preferred to sit and talk. When I was dancing the remaining goddesses didn’t have to sit around as wallflowers or dance together as there was always a keen young pilot officer waiting to glide them around the hall. They all wanted to dance with Rose of course as they had never danced with a flight-lieutenant instructor who was also a glamorous young lady; it would be something to tell their friends about. We had decided that the best time for their little act would be later in the evening after sweets had been served and one or two other performers had taken the stage to soften up the audience. I had found a small dressing room for the girls and put their costumes there in readiness.

The meal had concluded and there had been a soloist singing Christmas carols then another dance bracket. A ventriloquist was the next item and he kept the audience amused with some clean and not so clean dialogue between his three dolls. After the next dance bracket, the MC announced that Brad Clifford and guests would do a short selection from the Mikado. I was seen in a spotlight walking towards the piano and once I seated myself I turned to the audience.

"I've got a little list," I declared in a good baritone and at the same time playing the accompaniment myself. With one hand I pulled about a third of a roll of toilet paper from my suit pocket, held it up to the audience and holding it at one end let the roll fall and spread out on the floor. At this point the four-piece group joined in as I had pre-arranged. The girls quietly slipped away from the table and went to their dressing room by a side door. I moved straight into my performance naming all the people in my view that wouldn't be missed should a perpetrator needed to be found. There were politicians of all parties, lobbyists, corrupters and the corrupted. There were all those people given to exaggerate the efficacy of their pills and potions; there were used car salesmen that wound back the clock and rebirthed wrecks over different IDs. There were advertisers whose claims could never be supported and spin doctors, crooked jockeys and trainers. There were bookmakers who only accepted bets on horse that couldn't win because their connections didn't want them to and financial advisers who only advised clients to take their principal's products. There were bankers who insisted that they were entitled to more profit each year so that their bonuses would be secure and miners who raped the land were on the list. Bosses who demanded ten hours a day's work for eight hours a day's pay were on the list with the pimps and drug pushers who lived off the earnings of prostitutes. The list was extensive and after each group I stood and with my hands invited the audience to sing the chorus with me. I brought my song to an end by emphasising the final chorus and slowing the music.

The spotlight went from me as I sat at the piano to play the opening bars of *Three Little Maids from School*. The girls took their cue and with the band accompanying them danced onto the stage with mincing steps in little black slippers pointing out from their kimonos. In addition to their afternoon rehearsal they had applied white powder to their faces and painted cupid-bow lips; they now looked to be the typical three little maids played by many artists over many years. Their diction was clear and high, and their giggles were delightful, they easily managed their coy looks at the audience and their assumed shyness behind their parasols and showed that their intent was to be swept away to marriage by a handsome suitor. When they finished their routine, they bowed to the audience. The applause was so loud that the band started the number from the beginning and to calls of 'More' the girls departed. The calls continued so the girls circled down the hall to enter by the door again and repeat the performance. This time when they finished they danced off the stage into the wings and straight back to their dressing room. I joined them as they slipped off their kimonos and wigs and changed the slippers from the costumes for their own high-heels. I waited for them while they washed off the white powder and extra lipstick and after repairing their normal makeup, we made our way back to our table. The lights had been dimmed a little now and the band was playing the next bracket. We regained our seats with little attention and Mary, Miriam, Rod and Vic were full of praise for their performance. They had taken everyone by surprise. Many of those present had seen Kate and me dancing to *People Will Say…* but they had just seen a performance of *Three Little Maids* equal to any that could be seen in the West End. Vic had fresh drinks for us, so we paused a while before venturing back to the dance floor. It was only a few minutes before the band started playing out the old year with Auld Lange Syne. Our party of eight stood, linked arms and joined in with all the others on the floor. Everyone sang and kept their eyes on the large clock above the band. As the second hand came around to ten- to-go the crowd began the countdown and on the stroke of midnight partners turned to each other to embrace and kiss. My three goddesses enjoyed a group hug with me; Jan and then Kate kissed me and as I was turning to kiss Rose I felt her being pulled from me.

"Come on Rose. One for me," I heard one of her dance partners from earlier in the evening say.

"Let go please, no!" Rose replied.

"The lady said 'NO' sir," I said as I held Rose to me with my right hand and applied a vice like grip to the offender's right elbow with my left. I gave the young pilot a withering look with cold steely eyes.

"Now say 'I'm sorry Rose' or you'll never be able to sign your name let alone fly a plane."

"I'm truly sorry Rose please accept my apologies and to you too Brad. It was stupid of me."

Rose kissed him on the cheek and I released my grip.

"No hard feelings mate," I said and sent him on his way with a pat on the back.

"You can't really blame a bloke for trying Rose," I said. "Happy New Year darling."

I now gave Rose the kiss that was rudely interrupted.

"I suppose I should be flattered darling," Rose whispered.

Rose and I joined the others. I kissed Mary and Miriam and shook hands with Vic and Rod and Rose kissed them all. The party wound down and it wasn't long before we were heading home.

Tuesday 1 January 2013 – 0100 hrs

"I'd like to make a suggestion, goddesses," I said after we had taken a seat in the living room, "on occasions like this it should be up to you alone to decide who sleeps with me. I will just go to bed and I'll be thrilled by whoever comes to join me."

"That's a nice thought darling," Kate began. "You go to bed and we'll decide."

Ten minutes later the bedroom door opened and with the dim light being reflected from the hallway, the three little maids giggled and danced into the room. Naked now, with no twirling parasol to hide behind and not the slightest sign of modesty or shyness, they sang:

One little maid is the pregnant, Rosie
Two little maids in attendance come
Three little maids is the total sum
Three little maids from school

"But I only have one dick, goddesses," I said when they each jumped on my bed.

"Of course, darling," Rose replied. "It's Kate's night tonight. We're her hand maidens. Or your hand maidens might be better."

Kate climbed up from the bottom of the bed to lay over me and Rose took my right side and Jan my left.

I quickly had a stiff dickie as Kate rubbed over it with her breasts then her belly to place it between her thighs. Rose and Jan each took a hand and guided it down to their groin, fingers up. They released my hand once they knew it understood what was expected of it and lowered themselves onto their sides. I stretched my legs up between Kate's thighs to open her wider and to let my balls hang free and Rose and Jan each ran a hand up and down Kate's inner thighs as I would have done had my hands been free to do so. By turning my head to one side I could join my lips with Jan and then turning to the other I could kiss Rose. From time to time Kate brought her face down on mine to be kissed. The two girls not being kissed were releasing soft Ooohs of satisfaction and when Kate lent forward to put a nipple in my mouth all three were moaning. Kate and Jan's hand that wasn't stroking Rose's thigh was massaging their own breasts and moving between nipples to tease and squeeze them.

"Happy New Year goddesses, I love you truly," I said.

My declaration provoked an immediate response in Kate and she pounded me, claimed my lips to herself, and gave me long tongue kisses. Rose and Jan stroked her thighs in unison so that their hands met around my horn as Kate withdrew and then came down again to squeeze them. Kate climaxed, and I did too. Rose and Jan now clung to my thigh with their hand pulling themselves closer to me and burying their faces into my shoulders and kissing my bare skin.

With Kate's orgasm fading and Rose and Jan in a heightened state from being part of our pleasure, Kate lifted her head from me to allow me to kiss Rose and Jan in turn. I worked my fingers into them so that I was stimulating their clitoris and at the same time slipping two fingers a little way in and out of their vagina. Their orgasm came immediately and intensely. In a little while I brought my hands up to wrap my arms around Rose and Jan with Kate lying on top of me. She pulled the bedclothes up over us, our panting, sighs and giggles slowly faded away, and we drifted into sleep. It was a very special New Year.

After the sun's rays finally reached our bedroom one by one the girls slipped away to the bathroom and to dress. When I emerged thirty minutes later, it was to the smell of Kate's English breakfast being prepared in the kitchen. I quickly showered and pulled on warm slacks and a thick polo necked jumper and joined my goddes: kitchen. I greeted each of my goddesses with a hug.

"You look charming this morning darlings," I greet "Happy New Year,"

"Yes darling," they replied, again in unison. I tho myself that when my three goddesses were togethe thought and acted as one. I was conscious of their u personalities when each was alone with me but tog now, and in the early hours of this morning, they fused into the one perfect partner for Adonis. I could s in their eyes when they looked at me or spoke to m was their twenty-first century reincarnation of mythological Adonis.

"You look worried darling?" Rose was first to speak. Ka and Jan moved closer and they each had a look (concern on their face.

"No, not worried just a little concerned that I might not be up to the task I have set for myself," I replied.

Our ETA at Vélizy–Villacoublay, French Air Force Base, was planned for one o'clock in the afternoon.

"It sounds like Rod's car now," Kate announced.

We got up from the table and prepared to greet Mary and Rod.

"Happy New Year again everyone," Rod announced as he came through the door.

There was a round of hugs and kisses with a firm handshake between Rod and me. We collected the rest of the luggage that I hadn't yet taken to the plane and loaded some in Rod's and the rest in Kate's cars. The girls and I rode with Kate and Rod and Mary followed. When we got to RAF Wyton Miriam and Vic were there to see us off. They immediately talked about the New Year's Eve party and how the Little Maids act had been appreciated. While we talked, I had excused myself to do the pre-flight of Alpha Uniform and Miriam and the girls had drifted away a little to answer Miriam's questions about their coming move to Australia.

"Time for start-up ladies," I called as I returned to Vic and Rod.

"Thanks again for all your help Vic," I said as we shook hands.

"Clear skies, mate," Vic replied and turned to shake Rod's hand.

Miriam and Vic positioned themselves at the steps to kiss each of the girls as they boarded and as I was last to board Miriam kissed me and gave me a big hug.

"I'd be stowing away on board if it wasn't for this old bloke Brad," Miriam said as she gave her husband a loving look.

I waved and pulled up the steps. As we rolled out of the hangar I looked back to where Miriam and Vic were standing. They had an arm around each other's waist and waved with their free hand

Rod was sitting up front with me and the girls were sitting at the dining table in the cabin. Mary was just one of the girls, and just as excited by the prospect of their first visit to Paris for although Kate had lived so close, with Cambridge being far closer to Paris than Melbourne is to Sydney, she had never had a good enough reason to make the trip. Jan was wearing the same cardigan that she wore when she arrived on Sunday afternoon and her Mile-High Club badge was still pinned in the collar. Kate and Rose got out their badges too to show solidarity and have a giggle. When they gathered again at the table Mary was wearing her badge.

"I got mine over the Tasman Sea from Adonis's father girls," Mary announced proudly.

Mary made coffee and brought Rod's and mine to the cockpit and returned to take up her talk with the girls.

The girls showed Mary the calendar they had prepared for the year ahead. How it planned for the opening of the remaining faculties and Adonis's work to be done along the way. By 17 June all the Faculties would have opened and been visited, and we would go home to Canberra to organise renovations to our house to make room for the goddesses and the babies to come. The calendar showed that the time between faculty openings wouldn't be sufficient for me to fulfil my commitments to the Faculty for the year by mid-June, so I had planned another trip while the house was being renovated. We had fallen into the habit of referring to my undertaking to the Faculty to impregnate one hundred girls a year as Adonis's day-job and accepted that situation as being a natural thing for a mythical god to do. The gods having sex with mortals was a recurring them in mythology as Homo sapiens evolved and developed. When each of them found themselves in my arms, or in my bed, they felt they were truly goddesses and I was Adonis and they were living the mythology where gods freely had many lovers and no demarcation was made between wives, sisters, mothers and daughters. The goddesses looked upon Mary not as a mother-in-law but a loving older sister who was Aphrodite, Adonis's mother and first lover, and who had now found them as suitable brides for her beloved son.

"I think Kate you must take over the responsibility for assessing the girls for Adonis to impregnate. I'm sure the Faculty will keep me too busy to do justice to the task. I don't want to see someone outside our group doing this and your degree will be most valuable. Brad and I made the selections for Paris yesterday and while we are in Paris, I will teach you how to do the genetic appraisal," Mary said.

"Brad told me yesterday that he wanted me to manage his portfolio, as he so delicately put it. I think he was a little shocked when I said I would be the best little procuress possible," Kate replied.

The calendar also showed that I had left my nights and weekends free to be with my goddesses and we would use this time in doing whatever they desired. This was to be family time and while we might need to fly from one university to the next using up some of this time at present, it would be most important in years to come when we had children to raise.

In the cockpit, Rod and I were discussing more mundane matters of world affairs. The trip passed quickly, and it wasn't long before the French controller broke in:

"Pilatus Alpha Uniform good morning."

We both heard on our headsets.

"Here comes my changeover to the French Rod," I said and transferred my attention to the controller and my instructions to Vélizy–Villacoublay Air Force Base.

I took down my clearance and radio frequencies and established Alpha Uniform on her new course

"We could talk some more this afternoon Rod after we pick up Doc," I said. "I'm going to shut-up now Rod, I've never been here before."

I reached up and clicked on the 'Fasten Seat Belts' light and settled back to concentrate on my approach and landing. As usual, Alpha Uniform settled gently on the runway and straddled the centre line. I rolled out until I picked up the FOLLOW ME so typical of air force bases that we had visited. It wasn't long before we were parked and powered down and I clicked off the seat belt sign. An officer from the Base Commander's office arrived to welcome us and sight our passports. The mini-bus we had booked arrived and we headed to our hotel. We had booked one room for Rod and Mary and a two-bedroom suite for me and the girls. Our hotel was only ten kilometres from Vélizy–Villacoublay and only two kilometres from the Sorbonne so it was only thirty minutes from getting into our cab that we were checked in and being shown our rooms. We met in the cafeteria for a light lunch before the girls left to go shopping and Rod and I took a taxi to Paris-Orly to meet Doc.

ABOUT THE AUTHORS

Douglas E. M. Young & Betty M. Young

Betty was born in Hobart, Tasmania, on 3 September 1932. She passed on from this life on 14 May 1988.

Doug was born in Hobart, Tasmania, on 9 April 1935. He is still with us and will be for many years to come, as he and Betty relate the adventures of *Adonis & Aphrodite* as they make known to us what life will be like in the next *Millennium.*

Betty and Doug were born into the *Great Depression* and entered primary school in the early years of the *Second World War.* Betty attended Ogilvie High School and Doug, Hobart High School. They both left school for work at the end of fourth-year, as a university qualification was self-funded in those days and neither wanted to become financial burdens on their parents.

Doug likes to tell the story of their meeting: on a cold winter's-night in 1952. "I saw Betty across a crowded ballroom, the band was playing *Some Enchanted Evening* from *South Pacific.* Like in the song, I went to her side and claimed her. With work, accountancy studies and National Service it was the nineteenth of March 1955 before we could marry."

With babies in 1956,1957 and 1960 Betty soon became a full-time homemaker. Doug completed his accountancy studies in 1958 and over the next fourteen years gained a wide experience in commercial practice and industry in general. In 1972 he was appointed *head-of-department – Business Studies* at the Devonport College of *TAFE.*

"The job seemed to have been waiting for me," Doug said. "It gave me the opportunity to develop business simulations and games to bring active vocational training into office-work. Remarkably, it is only now, forty-nine years later, that the technology exists to take this remarkable facility to the world. Initially, our son set up a printery to produce the simulations and Betty joined in to typeset for him. Along the way I took up the suggestion to write an accounting package, and training simulations, for the early desk-top computers. I got stuck in the computer software business for quite a few years."

"I can't see any connection here, Doug, as to where *Adonis and Aphrodite* came from."

"In 2003, following a health concern I handed over my computer clients to my grandson. When I recovered, I was pestered by an old friend to develop one last package for him. As a working name I called it *This is It.* In 2009, after another medical event, I retired for the second time. This time when I recovered, I found I could no long write software or present what I had to a prospect. I turned to writing fiction."

"But where did you get *Adonis and Aphrodite?"*

"I really don't know, other than having been led to them on the web as I explored ancient fables."

"Did Betty approve of your theme?"

"Again, I don't know. In one of my earlier attempts at fiction she made suggestions that I followed and then apologised for having influenced me. She decided to wait until I had a finished a manuscript before commenting in future. I'd say that before she passed, she might not have approved, but since she has, she has told me, *everyone loves them*."

"You still talk to Betty, Doug?"

"Yes, since the day she passed. She knew that she was going. I had a stroke a year ago and she had been afraid I might go first, she didn't want that to happen. Betty believed my writing was important and I must continue. The big smile she gave me and the little hankie she put in my hand as they wheeled her into the examination room told me, *she knew she had won."*

"So now at eight-three you are going to continue to write?"

"Yes, a clairvoyant told me forty-five years ago that I would be starting a new career when most other people were retired or given-up. I believe I can describe myself as an author now, Betty believes I am, and I can only be beaten if I give-up."

"I wish you the best of luck with you endeavours, Doug."

"I'd be happier if you wished me *good health,"* I said.

49713822R00405

Made in the USA
Columbia, SC
26 January 2019